BROKEN BY MAGIC

DRAGON GATE, BOOK 3

LINDSAY BUROKER

Copyright © 2021 by Lindsay Buroker

All rights reserved.

No part of this book may be reproduced in any form or by any electronic or mechanical means, including information storage and retrieval systems, without written permission from the author, except for the use of brief quotations in a book review.

ACKNOWLEDGMENTS

Thank you, good reader, for following along with my epic fantasy series. I suspect you've been waiting for some fun dragons to show up (not only those crusty predatorial dragons), so I hope you'll enjoy meeting the hatchling.

Before you jump in, please let me thank my editor, Shelley Holloway, and my beta readers, Sarah Engelke and Cindy Wilkinson, for sticking with me for these *long* manuscripts. Also, thanks to Jeff Brown for the cover art and map for this series.

Now, I hope you enjoy the new adventure...

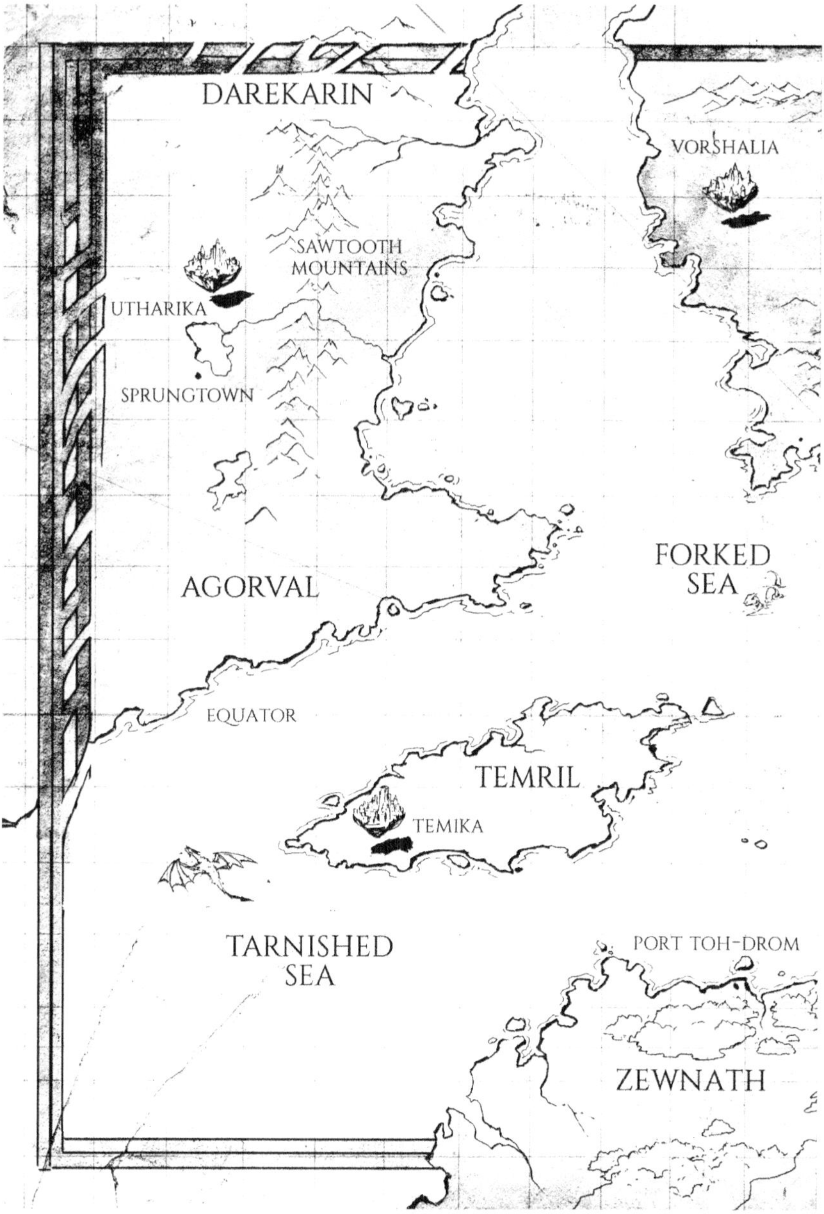
DAREKARIN
VORSHALIA
SAWTOOTH MOUNTAINS
UTHARIKA
SPRUNGTOWN
FORKED SEA
AGORVAL
EQUATOR
TEMRIL
TEMIKA
TARNISHED SEA
PORT TOH-DROM
ZEWNATH

TORVIL

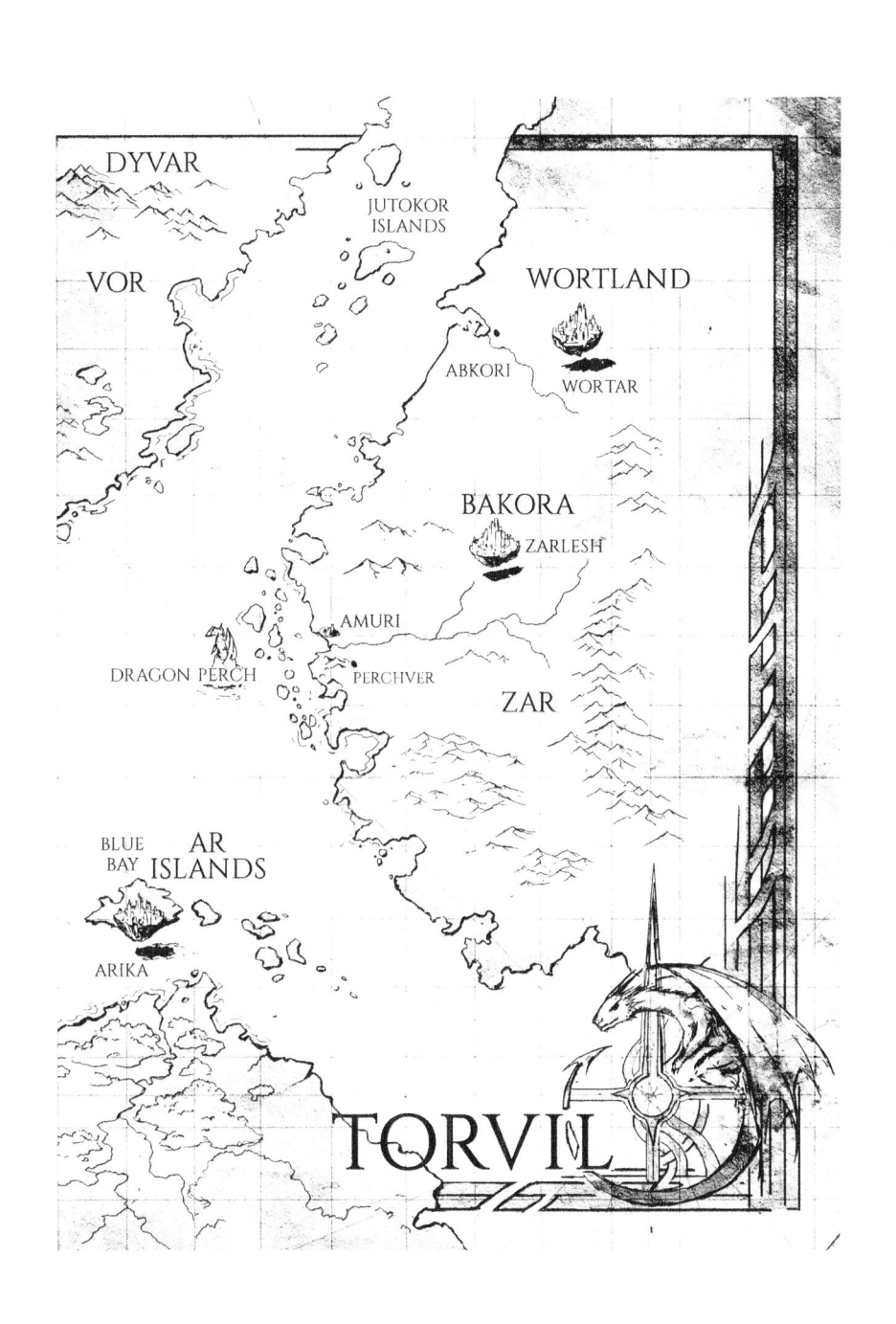

- DYVAR
- JUTOKOR ISLANDS
- VOR
- WORTLAND
  - ABKORI
  - WORTAR
- BAKORA
  - ZARLESH
  - AMURI
- DRAGON PERCH
  - PERCHVER
- ZAR
- AR ISLANDS
  - BLUE BAY
  - ARIKA

1

Jakstor Freedar frowned as his charge ignored the plate of fish, curassow, and pokran meat he'd finagled from the yacht's kitchen. Instead, the dragon hatchling prowled around the bed, burrowing under the blankets and tackling the already ravaged pillow, determined to transfer the stuffing from the inside to the outside.

It had been three days since the hatchling emerged from his egg, amid a disgusting mess of shell, amniotic fluid, and whatever those sparkly magical dots had been. The dragon hadn't eaten since.

"Babies are supposed to be hungry all the time." Jak waved a piece of red meat in front of the creature's snout. "Especially *big* babies."

The hatchling wasn't as large as Jak had expected, given the size and heft of the egg he had carried back through the portal. He'd come out about the size of the parrots squawking in the jungle trees outside his porthole. He had scales instead of feathers, rich blue scales that were neither the mottled brown and gray of the dragon that had tried to kill their party on the other world, nor the iridescent blue of the frolicking dragons that the portal had shown Jak in visions.

Would this hatchling grow into a friendly dragon, such as those who had long ago worked with humans when they'd visited Torvil? Or would he turn into an evil dragon that killed others of his kind and slew humans for sport—and dinner?

The scaly snout sniffed at the meat as slitted yellow eyes peered up at Jak. At a glance, they looked like the alien reptilian eyes of a snake or lizard, but there was a curiosity and expressiveness in them more akin to a human's. And intelligence, Jak thought, for he'd caught the hatchling watching him while he worked on his latest map, peering both at his writing utensils and what he was creating.

At first, Jak thought the hatchling might somehow recognize the world he'd been drawing—after all, it was the frozen snow-and-ice-covered realm where they'd found the egg, locked up in a glacier with dozens of others. Then he'd eaten a charcoal stick and used his tail to flick a pencil across the cabin. It was possible he'd only been considering what on the desk would be the most fun to destroy.

"Do you want me to chew it first? Mother wolves do that for their pups." Jak tossed the gamey pokran in his mouth to soften it. "Actually, they chew the meat, *swallow* it, and regurgitate it when they get back to their dens, but that's not within my repertoire." He drew out the macerated pokran meat and offered it again. "I also think vomitus may be forbidden on a fancy flying yacht owned by a wizard king. Given how readily they punish the servants, I would rather not take chances."

Jak eyed the open door that led into the parlor of the suite that he and his mother had been given and used his burgeoning magical senses to make sure there weren't any crewmen nearby to hear and judge him. Hypothetically, he was a guest here, and King Uthari hadn't punished him or his mother, but they also didn't have the freedom to leave or even wander about the ship without an escort. Just that morning, guards had come in to take his mother down to one of the tents set up around the portal so she could do some research. Jak didn't know what sort of research yet, nor did he know if she would return to the yacht.

The hatchling took the meat from his hand, and hope stirred in Jak. Since the creature had hatched, he'd been worried that he didn't have the means to care for it. He'd tried milk, even though Mother had assured him that reptiles did not nurse their young, as well as various kinds of meat. He'd even tried slices of fruit and bamboo in case dragons had a vegetarian streak the history books hadn't warned them about. Nothing interested his charge.

The hatchling shook his head on his long neck and released the macerated meat. It flew across the cabin, hit the porthole, and stuck to the glass.

The creature jumped up and down, little wings flapping—thus far, they lacked the power to let him fly—and emitted squawky noises that sounded like a temper tantrum.

"It's not my fault you don't like anything here." Jak rubbed his face. Maybe dragons could only eat meat from their homeland. "I'm sorry I didn't think to carve steaks out of those ugly bat creatures that attacked us on... whatever that world is called. We don't even know."

Though a knock didn't sound at the door, Jak sensed someone powerful entering the suite. He stood and turned, hoping for Malek, but General Tonovan was the one to appear in the doorway.

Jak's gut twisted with revulsion. Not only had the odious general leered at Jak's mother and made sexual comments about her, but he'd been in the process of raping Rookie Tezi when Malek had distracted him so she'd been able to escape—by springing over the railing of a mageship to what she had believed would be her death.

Though Jak wanted to strangle Tonovan, he radiated almost as much power as Malek. Jak had no doubt that the general could flick a finger and kill him. He kept his face—and his thoughts—blank as Tonovan glowered at him, a gesture more menacing than ever now that he had only one eye.

"Professor Freedar isn't here? How disappointing. I know how she enjoys chatting with me." Tonovan's lips twisted into something between a smirk and a sneer, like one of the melodramatic villains in an Egarath the Eternal play. Davroloth the Dark, perhaps.

"Yes," Jak said, "she pines at night when you're not here to entertain her with lewd innuendos."

"I'd entertain her with a lot more than that if I weren't busy." Tonovan waved toward the porthole and the mageships outside, a dozen belonging to King Uthari and a dozen more that had been sent by other kingdoms. They also hoped to use the newly operational ancient portal to travel to other worlds.

Jak clenched his jaw and kept from responding, not wanting the man to have a reason to stay. Why had he come, anyway? And why did he want to harass Mother? She was in her early forties, and from what Jak had heard, Tonovan preferred to molest women even younger than Jak.

"Because it irritates Malek." Tonovan smirked again, though there was no humor in his remaining eye. "And she's not bad looking for an older woman. Still firm and soft in all the right places." He groped suggestively in the air.

Raw rage flared in Jak, and he balled his fists and envisioned himself springing across the cabin and throttling Tonovan. He should have been trying to guard his thoughts from the mind-reading general, but he was too furious to concentrate on that.

"Go ahead, boy. I don't know why Uthari and Malek want to let you live, but Uthari wouldn't punish me for defending myself against a reckless wild one." Tonovan's eye narrowed. "I'd enjoy killing you, for the same reason I'd enjoy screwing your mother."

Jak couldn't control his rage. He snarled and leaped at the general. Even as he tried to wrap his hands around Tonovan's neck, he sensed a magical barrier pop up between them. Jak willed a mountain to fall on it, a fierce wind to tear it away.

Thus far, he'd had some luck performing magical feats, using nothing but sheer willpower, but not this time. Not against this experienced and powerful wizard.

He smashed face-first into the barrier and bounced away. A crushing weight slammed onto him from above, and Tonovan's power drove him to the deck. It was as if a mountain had landed on him, and he couldn't budge. Invisible fingers wrapped around his throat, cutting off his air.

Idiot, Jak told himself. *You stupid idiot.*

Tonovan chuckled as he applied more force around Jak's throat. He hadn't budged, not so much as lifting a finger, and used only his magic. "To kill you, or not to kill you? It was *clear* I was only defending myself, wasn't it? There's even a witness, assuming one can read the mind of a scrawny dragon hatchling."

Jak couldn't move, couldn't suck in air to reply, nor to replenish his lungs. They ached in his chest, already longing for oxygen.

The hatchling jumped up and down on the bed, wings flapping. Whether he was complaining about this assault or that his food was unacceptable, Jak didn't know, but the realization that he might not live to find out terrified him.

Again, he tried to draw upon his own power—everyone kept saying he had great potential, so it ought to be good for *something*. He envisioned himself within a ring of mountains—the Impact Mountains once formed by an asteroid strike in Northern Agorval—with their tall peaks separating him from Tonovan, driving the general back, forcing him away.

It didn't work. Not against this foe.

Malek? Jak thought telepathically, trying to pinpoint-deliver the message so Tonovan wouldn't hear him. *I did something stupid, and if you're on the yacht, I could use some help.*

The hatchling leaped down from the bed and half walked and half hopped past Jak toward Tonovan.

"This is the mighty dragon, eh?" Tonovan drawled, eyeing him even as he kept Jak pinned, maintaining enough pressure around his throat to prevent him from breathing. "It doesn't look like much. How funny to think that primitive people turned a dragon into a god. Shylezar the Great. What a farce. Terrene humans are easily manipulated simpletons."

Jak's rapid heartbeat pounded against his eardrums, and darkness crept into his vision. He would pass out and die at this man's feet, and the bastard wouldn't care one iota.

"Let him go," came a voice from the parlor.

The pressure around Jak's throat and the weight pinning him to the deck disappeared in an instant. He gasped in air and rolled away from Tonovan as the general turned to face Malek.

Even though he didn't lower his barrier—if anything, Jak sensed Tonovan strengthening it at Malek's approach—the hatchling somehow hopped through it.

From his position gasping on the deck, Jak had a perfect view of the creature springing in and biting Tonovan on the back of the calf. Tiny sharp teeth gnashed through the red material of his uniform trousers.

Tonovan yelped and kicked the hatchling away.

Swearing, Jak lunged to his feet as his charge flew across the cabin. The hatchling smashed against a wall, then bounced onto the bed.

Jak almost blacked out, his body still struggling to recover from the lack of oxygen, but he scrambled onto the bed, terrified the little dragon's bones might have broken. He was just a baby and who knew how fragile. Jak swept in and gathered the hatchling in his arms, cradling him to his chest. Dazed, the creature only gurgled slightly.

"What are you doing in here?" Malek asked from the doorway, glaring at Tonovan, though he glanced at Jak and the hatchling.

"I came to see what popped out of that egg." Tonovan lifted his leg and rubbed his calf, but he didn't comment on the attack—or the fact that the hatchling had somehow slipped through his barrier as if it didn't exist. "Your teenage prodigy attacked me, so naturally, I had to defend myself."

Jak's neck throbbed, as if real hands had been wrapped around it, and he wondered if he would have bruises later. He was more concerned about the hatchling and wished he knew how to tell if any of his bones were broken or if he was only dazed.

"Which of the women he cares about did you threaten to rape?" Malek asked coolly.

Tonovan smirked and put his leg down. Alas, he wasn't limping. "His mother, but I wouldn't need to use force on her. She would enjoy wrapping her mouth around my fat—"

Tonovan jerked back, as if he'd been slapped.

Malek hadn't moved, but his dark eyes were as hard as obsidian, and Jak had sensed the attack, a mental jab that could strike even through a mage's barrier. Sadly, Malek didn't follow it up with another attack or try to kill Tonovan. Jak would have gladly helped, even if all he could do was shout at the general and distract him.

"You sure you want to threaten me, Malek?" Tonovan said with ice in his voice. "When you're recovering from near-death wounds and aren't at your strongest?"

"I'll duel you any time you wish." Malek pointed upward, as if to suggest they should challenge each other on the open deck of the yacht. "And I've recovered nicely from my wounds. They won't impede me."

"I'm so happy to hear that." Tonovan didn't move toward the

corridor or give any indication that he would accept the challenge. "Uthari would be so saddened by your loss. He wouldn't have anyone left who's as eager to kiss his ass."

"You've seen the hatchling. Get out." Magical power laced Malek's voice, and when he stepped aside to clear the way to the exit, Tonovan lurched forward, taking two steps before clenching his jaw and visibly stopping himself.

But it was only for a moment. He glared back at Jak—and the hatchling—then strode toward the exit.

"See to it that you get your trousers mended," Malek added. "Something has frayed them."

Not responding, Tonovan walked out, slamming the door behind him like a petulant child.

Jak slumped against the wall, his body aching after the encounter. The hatchling chirped in his arms, then nibbled on the cuff of his sleeve.

"I *know* you're hungry," Jak whispered. "Just tell me what you like."

Malek stepped into the bedroom, wearing his usual tan trousers, beige shirt, and brown jacket, his main-gauche and basket-hilted longsword in their scabbards on his weapons belt. "Are you all right?"

"Yes. I'm sorry you had to come, but thank you. I made an unwise decision." Jak grimaced and rubbed his neck.

"Tonovan likes to goad his enemies into doing that." Malek pointed at the hatchling. "Is *it* all right?"

"I think so."

The hatchling had recovered from being stunned and was trying to climb up Jak's arm to his shoulder.

"Hopefully, he's tough. He's so magical, even as a baby, I think he'd have to be." Jak had been able to sense the magic of the dragon eggs when they'd been encased in ice, and the hatchling's aura was even more noticeable now. "But he hasn't eaten anything since he hatched. I'm worried that the food on our world doesn't agree with him."

Jak pointed at the plate of delicacies, then at the piece still stuck to the porthole glass. A couple of flies had arrived in the cabin and were buzzing around it. Jak made a note to clean the macerated meat off the glass. If there were rules about vomiting on yachts, there were probably rules about leaving half-chewed pieces of pokran sticking to things.

"You still need to work on guarding your thoughts around mages," Malek observed.

"Sorry. I wasn't trying."

"Your mental barrier should become habitual, something you keep up during all of your waking hours. So that enemies don't know if they're successfully goading you to anger and nearby allies aren't afflicted with imagery of you regurgitating food to your hatchling."

"I didn't *do* that. I was just thinking about it. Wolves do it, and dragons are predators, so..." Jak shrugged, a little embarrassed, but if Malek poked into his mind, he couldn't truly be offended by what he found. It had to be better than what was in Tonovan's mind.

"No doubt about that." Malek stepped closer, peering at Jak's charge. Since he'd been recovering from his wounds, he hadn't been by to see the hatchling yet, and he had to be curious. It sounded like the word had gotten out. *Everybody* might be curious.

Jak could handle visitors, as long as they weren't vile like Tonovan, but he worried someone would want to take the dragon to raise and turn into a trained killer. Uthari had said Jak could watch over the hatchling, providing Jak and his mother obeyed Uthari and did all that he wished, but he wasn't the only powerful mage here. And then there were the druids in the jungle. What if one of them sneaked aboard and kidnapped the hatchling while Jak slept?

"Are you sure it's a he?" Malek asked. "It doesn't look like it has recognizable sex organs."

"Mother thinks so, but she admitted it would be hard to know for sure unless we had a female for comparison. Apparently, there isn't a lot of surviving information on how to sex baby dragons."

"I'll hazard a guess that there was *never* a lot of information on that."

"Possibly true. She's going by how one tells on lizards."

Malek arched his eyebrows. "And how is that?"

"Males are more swollen at the base of their tails than females, and they have a pair of enlarged scales near their cloaca." Jak, not certain how familiar Malek was with lizards, lifted the hatchling so he could see the underbelly. The dragon's tail whipped back and forth in the air, and he tried to spring to the porthole. In case he had developed a new interest in the meat now that it had aired out, Jak lifted him to the ledge. "Apparently, there are behavioral clues too. The males tend to be more aggressive. This one likes to throw temper tantrums and destroy the pillow."

"And it bit Tonovan." Malek's voice and face were never that expressive, but he smiled with faint approval.

"Through his barrier."

"I noticed that. I'm not sure if Tonovan just wasn't paying much attention to what was behind him or if it truly sauntered through as if it weren't there."

"*I* was behind him." Jak touched his chest. "He should have been paying attention."

"He doesn't see you as a threat."

"I wish I could say that was a grievous mistake and he'll one day rue that failure, but I was licking the deck at his feet two minutes ago." Jak sighed.

"Give it time. You're only starting to develop your power. I had to endure ten years of zidarr training before Uthari deemed me fully ready to receive the mantle and go on missions for him."

Talons scraped as the hatchling hung from the porthole ledge. His head darted all around the meat, but he didn't remove it. He seemed to be tracking the flies.

"So, in ten years, I'll be able to defend myself against Tonovan?"

"Maybe fewer. Learning to defend oneself is a simpler matter than learning to attack someone else through *their* defenses."

"So, only five until I can keep him from crushing my windpipe?"

"Maybe three. Have you named him?" Malek nodded toward the hatchling whose tail was swishing back and forth against the wall.

"No. I wasn't sure if that was presumptuous. Right now, he's a little runt, but when he's powerful and intelligent and speaks the language of the dragons, the dragons who had the wherewithal to build those portals and other great artifacts, he might not appreciate having been named by a human." Admittedly, Jak didn't know if the hatchling would be able to develop fully without the influence of his own kind. It wasn't as if humans learned how to speak in a vacuum. Would Jak be able to one day find adult dragons—*good and kindly* adult dragons—to give him to? And what about all the eggs that were still frozen back in that glacier?

"Give him a mighty name that acknowledges his nobleness, and maybe he won't object."

One of the flies landed on the glass, and the hatchling froze like a dog on point.

"I'm not sure how long this little fellow will survive if I can't figure out what he'll eat. We may have to go back to his world and get some meat there." Jak grimaced at the idea of returning to that frozen wasteland. Even though he loved the idea of exploring and mapping new places, he shuddered as he remembered all of the bones—the *human* bones—that had littered the dragon's lair, and how their team had almost been lured to their deaths.

"Dragons lived here for a time and presumably traveled to all the worlds linked by the portals. One would think they could subsist on meat from places other than their homeland."

The fly buzzed away from the porthole. The hatchling blurred into motion, surging up and snapping his jaws before it could escape. He caught the fly, wings flapping for stability as he kept himself from falling off the ledge, and chomped it down.

"Or *insects* from places other than their homeland," Malek said dryly.

"They eat bugs? Noble, magnificent dragons eat bugs?" Jak pushed a hand through his hair. "That isn't what I was expecting."

The hatchling shook his tail and shifted his focus to the other fly.

"Perhaps Fly Slayer should be his name," Malek said.

"That doesn't sound mighty or noble."

"Maybe he'll one day graduate to crickets."

Jak eyed Malek, still a little startled when the great and powerful zidarr showed glimpses of humor. When Jak had first met Malek—first been *kidnapped* by Malek—he'd only been able to think of him as King Uthari's loyal, and extremely deadly, henchman. Neither his position nor deadliness had changed, but since he'd saved Jak's life more than once and had started helping him learn to use his magic, Jak no longer feared him.

Maybe that was unwise, since Malek had always been clear that his loyalty was to his king—and Jak longed for nothing more than to dethrone all the wizard kings ruling over terrene humans—but he couldn't help how he felt. And he appreciated these quiet moments when Malek seemed more like a mentor than an enemy.

The remaining fly buzzed away from the porthole, and the hatchling stretched for it again, catching it and devouring it in a gulp. This time, he lost his balance and slipped off the ledge.

Jak caught him. The hatchling scrambled up his arm, talons digging through the material of his sleeve, and perched on his shoulder. He peered around the cabin, tail swishing as he looked for more prey.

"Insects are high in protein," Malek said. "Maybe they're a staple food on the world where dragons evolved."

"But they're so little. And dragons are so *large*."

"Yes." Malek touched his side where dragon fangs the size of swords had pierced him less than a week earlier. "I remember. There are large insects in some parts of the world, and there could be even larger ones where dragons come from."

"True. I think he's still hungry."

"If he hasn't eaten since he hatched, that's understandable."

"Do you think the mage crew would find it odd if I wandered around the yacht hunting for insects?" Jak would prefer to go down into the jungle and poke around under logs. Would the dragon like grubs? But he doubted Uthari's guards would let him leave.

"Perhaps—" Malek eyed him thoughtfully, "—this is an opportunity for a lesson."

"A magic lesson?"

"Yes."

"One that will help me defend myself against powerful bastards?"

"All lessons that help you develop and refine your skills are useful."

"That sounded like a no." Jak tried not to feel disappointed. He would gladly learn any skill that Malek was willing to teach him.

"It won't specifically help unless you want to pelt Tonovan with crickets."

"I wouldn't be opposed to that."

Malek rested a hand on his shoulder. "Come. Bring the shikari."

The hatchling peeped as they headed for the door.

"Yeah, that's you," Jak told him. "You've impressed Lord Malek with your extreme hunting prowess."

The hatchling chewed on Jak's collar. Well, that wasn't any worse than the pillow.

∽

Tezi Tigan sat cross-legged on the dirt floor of one of the tents that Thorn Company had been given, charging magelock rifles in a portable filler for her comrades. It was a mindless task, but she didn't resent it, since it gave her an excuse to stay out of sight instead of going out on the patrols in the jungle that the others were being assigned.

Thorn Company wasn't the only mercenary unit in the area, and tensions were high. By now, everyone had heard about Tezi's dragon-steel battle-axe, and she'd caught numerous speculative glances in her direction. In *its* direction.

The tent flap stirred, and Lieutenant Sasko and Captain Ferroki walked in.

Tezi rose to salute, then grabbed their freshly charged weapons for them.

"Thank you, Tezi," the captain said.

Sasko accepted hers and sat on a crate of rations, the closest thing the tent had to furnishings. "You figure out how you're going to carry a rifle *and* a giant battle-axe on your back yet, Rookie?"

"The axe isn't that heavy, ma'am."

"That's good. I was afraid the weight would crumple your scrawny legs."

"My legs are fit and firm, ma'am." Tezi was used to razzing from her squad leader, Sergeant Tinder, but the lieutenant always got in her fair shots too.

"She helped kill a dragon, I hear." Ferroki sat on a sack of potatoes. "Perhaps you shouldn't tease her anymore."

"Tinder said she was useless against the dragon, that they all were, and that Lord Malek killed it. I will definitely not tease him."

"Wise," Ferroki murmured.

Tezi wished she could say she *hadn't* been useless, but none of the magelock rifles had perturbed the dragon. It hadn't even *noticed* them, as far as she'd been able to tell. Jadora's explosives had at least distracted it, though that had likely been more because of the noise than their power. Only Malek's magical sword had pierced the dragon's armored hide. Presumably, the battle-axe would also have such an ability, but Tezi hadn't discovered it until *after* the battle.

Too bad. She wished she could have landed at least one serious blow on the dragon. She hadn't been so terrified that she'd frozen and been too stunned to react—as they'd been creeping into its lair, she'd feared that might happen—but it hadn't mattered. In the end, she'd not only almost gotten herself killed, but Malek had been bitten because he'd leaped on the dragon's tail to keep it from reaching her. She hated that she'd been useless, and she hated even more that she owed a zidarr her life.

It still surprised her that Malek had bothered to save her. Did he even know her name? She wasn't sure.

"Are these charged?" Sasko pointed at the other rifles Tezi had done.

"Yes, ma'am."

"I'll give them back to their owners. There could be trouble out there any time." Sasko scooped up the weapons and left.

"It's true that I didn't do much on that mission, ma'am," Tezi admitted when she was alone with the captain. "I *tried*. I hit the dragon several times with magelock charges, but they did nothing."

"No matter how brave the mouse, she cannot defeat the lion," the captain murmured, likely quoting from one of her fables.

"How does a mouse survive in a world run by lions?" Tezi asked.

"By treading carefully and carrying a big thorn." The captain pantomimed shoving a thorn in a lion's paw, then pointed at the axe and smiled.

"I don't deserve this weapon, ma'am. I scrounged it from a dead man. All that remained of him were a few charred bones and a blackened suit of armor, but he must have once won it bravely in some battle. It doesn't seem right that I lucked into it because he died."

"If he's dead, he's not coming back for it. And even if he had a rightful heir, I don't know how you would find the person and return it."

"Nobody was alive there. Nobody human."

"Then it's yours."

"Are you sure, ma'am? Maybe you should wield it. Or... Lord Malek was the one to kill the dragon. If he wanted it—"

"*He* has enough. Two lesser-dragon-steel weapons. Few in the world have such blades, even among the zidarr."

But dragon steel was even better than *lesser* dragon steel. Admittedly, Tezi didn't know how or why, but everyone had been quick to point that out.

So far, all she knew about the axe was that it was surprisingly lightweight, seemingly indestructible, and that it had pierced the hide of that giant worm when few other attacks had. Also, it was warm to her touch, and even though she was as sense-dead as any terrene human, she could *feel* the magic that it radiated. As with the portal, its magic was so great that anyone could detect it.

"I've never trained with an axe," Tezi admitted.

In truth, she didn't *want* to give up the weapon. Given how stacked the odds were against her, with every powerful mage she encountered wanting to kill her because she'd killed two of their kind in the past, she could use an advantage. The mages she'd taken down had been vile people who'd tormented others, but that didn't seem to matter. All mages believed it was a crime deserving of death if a terrene human killed one of their kind, no matter how loathsome the person had been.

"No?" Captain Ferroki stood and grabbed her rifle and a short sword. "Let's practice then."

"Me and you, ma'am?" It was silly, but Tezi had never sparred with the captain. Sergeant Tinder usually led weapons practice for the company and paired up the troops. The fact that Ferroki cared and wanted to help Tezi touched her.

"Me and you, Rookie." Ferroki smiled and headed for the flap. "I don't know what calamity is going to strike us next, but I fear we'll both need the practice."

As they headed off to find a quiet spot, Tezi eyed the portal looming beside the pool, its magic keeping it standing upright. As far as she knew, it was still active, and more monstrous creatures could fly through it at any time.

If dragon-steel weapons were one of the few things that could harm them, she had better do more than practice. She had better *master* the battle-axe.

2

Jak followed Malek to the railing of the yacht with the hatchling on his shoulder. Shikari.

He'd thought the word a silly name at first, given that his charge had only managed to capture flies thus far, but as the hatchling grew into an adult dragon, he would learn to hunt down large and dangerous game.

"The trees are full of insects." Malek extended a hand toward the jungle canopy below the yacht, branches shivering as a breeze whispered through, the air promising it would rain later.

On the other mageships in the area, crewmen gazed curiously over at them, either because it was always worth noting what a zidarr was up to, or because of the dragon hatchling riding on Jak's shoulder.

"I would guess the whole jungle is full of insects." When Jak paid attention, he could make out their buzzes and chirps in the background. At night, the noise was more noticeable, but it existed during the day too, punctuated by howls and hoots from monkeys and squawks from birds. He didn't know what was responsible for the screeches he often heard in the distance, and he didn't want to find out. "The mosquitoes have found and sampled me often."

"Now you have a mosquito hunter."

The hatchling peeped.

"You sound like a baby chicken when you do that," Jak told him. "It's not at *all* ferocious."

The tail dangling down his back swished up to flick at his hair.

"Since he's too young to fly, you'll have to catch insects for him." Malek extended his hand toward the trees, a reminder that this was to be a magic lesson.

"Do you want me to muddle through figuring out how to do that on my own? Or are you going to give me a tip first?" Jak remembered when Malek had shared his thoughts back on the frozen world, some kind of mind link that had allowed Jak to see and sense how he was creating a barrier. It had made it much easier to grasp the tactic than when people simply explained a magical act, leaving it to him to figure out a methodology that worked for him. "Our hatchling is hungry, so the sooner I can provide food for him, the better."

Malek rested a hand on Jak's free shoulder, then looked toward the leaves ten feet below. Again using a mind link, he shared what he was doing as he produced strands of magic, the thin tendrils forming from power that flowed out of his body. In seconds, he wove them together into an invisible net that was tangible to Jak's senses. Though Malek performed the act quickly and easily, it looked complicated.

The net descended between the trees, and with a fresh nudge of magic, Malek created a breeze that swept through the leaves. It blew in with just enough power to knock insects from their perches in the trees. They tumbled into the net and stuck, as if it were a spider's web instead of something crafted purely from magic.

Malek drew up the net, wrapped it around the tiny winged

prizes stuck to it, and dropped the wad on the deck behind them. The hatchling watched, hopping up and down on Jak's shoulder.

"Does he prefer live prey?" Malek asked. "Or should I kill them?"

"We haven't had that discussion yet. I'm waiting for him to learn Dhoran."

Shikari sprang off Jak's shoulder, startling him, since the hatchling couldn't fly yet. Jak lunged after him, afraid he would hurt himself jumping from such a height, but Shikari landed without trouble in the middle of the net.

The insects were batting against the woven strands, trying to escape their imprisonment. Jak thought Shikari might get trapped as well, his talons sticking to the magical web, but he hopped about without trouble, snout descending to pluck up bugs.

"It's interesting that the magic doesn't affect him," Malek said. "Though perhaps not surprising. The dragon I fought was very resistant to my attacks. I did land a few blows with magic—especially when I targeted its eye—but my sword was more effective."

Shikari chomped down the fifteen or twenty bugs the magical net had caught, then looked expectantly up at them, his tail swishing on the deck. He crouched and pounced on Jak's boot.

"Are you sure that's a dragon and not a cat?" Malek let his net dissolve, the magic fading until there was no trace of the strands.

"Reasonably sure. He is somewhat... kittenish."

"It's hard to imagine him growing into something like the one we battled."

"I'm hoping he won't, at least not in the humans-are-delicious-so-I-am-luring-them-to-my-lair-to-eat kind of way. His scales are blue like the good dragons." Jak didn't mention the lack of an iridescent overlay. Maybe that would come later.

"The good dragons?" Malek raised his eyebrows.

"In my dreams—ah, the visions the portal has shared with me —there are iridescent-blue dragons that play in the pool and frolic with each other. There are also brown-and-gray mottled dragons, like the one we faced, that are evil. Or at least mean and not playful. They kill the blue dragons as well as people."

"Hm. I'd wondered if this one would grow into a threat to us."

"Hopefully not to *us*. If we treat him well. They're as smart as we are—smarter, probably."

Shikari chewed off the end of Jak's bootlace and spat it out.

"Clearly," Malek said.

"I'm sure you weren't doing anything that advanced when you were three days old. My experience with babies is that the highlight of their early months is when they discover their toes." Jak admittedly didn't have *much* experience with babies, other than occasionally visiting his married cousin who lived with his little daughter on the outskirts of the city, but he doubted zidarr spent much time around them either.

"We'll leave to explore another world in the morning," Malek said. "I've recovered sufficiently, and King Uthari is insistent that we don't delay. Will you take the hatchling along or leave him here with someone?"

"I can't leave him." Alarm surged through Jak at the thought. "He needs me. I'll make a sling so I can carry him."

Jak had brought the hatchling into this world, so he felt responsible for him. Not only that, but he still worried that one of the ambitious mages would get ahold of Shikari—why did Rivlen's face come to mind?—and try to shape him into some loyal minion, a future servant.

"He might be a hindrance," Malek said. "Or be killed if we end up in battle."

"I'll take care of him. I know I can. And he won't be any trouble."

Shikari, having rejected the bootlace, looked expectantly up at Jak again.

"I think he wants more insects," Jak said, hoping to change the subject.

Maybe if Jak showed up at the portal with Shikari in a sling, Malek would simply accept that he was coming along.

"Yes. And you'll provide them." Malek pointed at the trees. "The net is intricate, as far as magic goes, and it may be beyond your skills at this time. You can either try it or come up with your own solution."

It *had* looked intricate. As much as Jak would have preferred to show off his vast abilities by perfectly making a magical net on his first try, he doubted he could. Even having watched and sensed how Malek had done it, it was a daunting task that he would prefer to first practice in private, especially since a number of mages on their ship and on others were watching. They probably cared more about the dragon than Jak's magic lessons, but if he failed utterly in front of them, he would feel like a fool.

Maybe Jak could eschew the net and simply create the same kind of wind that Malek had. If he struck the insects hard enough, it might stun them, and he could sweep them onto the deck of the yacht. Shikari could use his killer instincts to pounce on them and devour them before they regained consciousness.

Thus far, he'd had most success performing magic when he could relate what he wanted to do with a cartographical feature on one of his maps. Mountains for defense. Rivers for funneling some of his power into other people to use. And a geyser to levitate someone upward into the sky.

He envisioned the kind of harsh hurricane winds that drove storms off the sea and to shore, battering the beaches hard enough to erode land and reshape the coastline. He willed such a blast of wind to gust through the treetops, knocking free any insects loitering on leaves and funneling them up to land on the yacht's deck.

But *wind* was a dubious cartographical feature, even if it

shaped the terrain of the world over time, and his power seemed to sniff disdainfully at this notion. Long seconds passed as he concentrated, sweat pricking at his armpits, and nothing happened beyond the natural breezes whispering through the trees.

Though Malek didn't say anything, he watched Jak. That made Jak feel self-conscious, and heat rose to his cheeks. He wanted Malek to believe he was worth teaching, that this wasn't a waste of his time. Maybe the other mages around had sensed that Jak was trying to do something—trying ineffectually to do something—for many of them had paused to watch too.

If Jak couldn't even catch flies, would Uthari realize he was useless and forbid Malek to teach him? Or decide that it wasn't worth letting a *wild one* like Jak live?

Feeling like a clock was ticking toward a deadline, Jak gave up on the wind. He'd used water imagery effectively before. Frustrated, he envisioned storm waves crashing to the shore. *They* shaped coastlines far more quickly and dramatically than *wind* did.

Snapping and rustling rose up from below as a wall of water—no, of the magical force that Jak was creating by envisioning water—rushed through the treetops. The tops of trunks snapped off, branches tore free, and thousands of leaves flew into the air.

Realizing he'd used too much force—and nothing like the finesse of Malek's net—Jak released his concentration. But the wave of magic kept rolling along. Like a real wave, it couldn't be stopped until it crashed to the shore. In this case, it crashed to Uthari's yacht, bearing a deluge of leaves and broken branches and tree trunks on it. The wave slammed into the ship, making the entire vessel quake as it dumped most of the debris onto the deck.

"What in all the caves in the slavemasters' Hell was that?" the yacht's captain bellowed, rushing out on deck with other officers on his heels.

"Are we under attack?"

"What the—" They stopped and gaped at the knee-deep layer of foliage, branches, and treetops blanketing the deck.

Jak buried his face in his hand, wishing he could disappear. If his cheeks had been warm before, they flamed like a sun now.

"Hm," Malek said.

Uthari strode out, frowning around at the mess before his gaze settled on Jak. The officers might have been confused, but he seemed to know exactly what had happened.

"We're not under attack," Uthari told the captain. "At least not by *enemy* fire."

"Yes, Your Majesty." The captain glared at Jak. He was one of many doing so.

Only the hatchling appeared pleased by this mistake. He hopped among the debris, poking his snout under leaves. A cricket that the magic had indeed stunned tried to hop away, but he caught it and chomped it down.

"What is going on, Malek?" Uthari walked up to them, branches crunching underfoot.

Jak lowered his hand, wondering if Uthari would punish him. And if so, would Malek stand by and watch? Numerous things that he'd said within Jak's hearing implied Malek believed a zidarr who didn't perform adequately *deserved* to be punished. Would he feel the same about a young pupil?

"Feeding time," Malek said.

Did he sound amused?

Jak couldn't tell, but he hoped so. Unfortunately, *Uthari* didn't look amused, not in the least.

Shikari's tail swished as he searched for more insects.

"It eats leaves?" Uthari asked.

"Insects. Jak is experimenting with ways to retrieve them."

Uthari looked at the mounds of jungle debris layering his deck. "A *net* wouldn't have sufficed?"

"The net looked daunting," Jak muttered.

Uthari frowned at him. "The net looked daunting, *Your Majesty*. If you're going to make a mess of someone's personal yacht, the least you can do is address him respectfully afterward."

"Yes, Your Majesty."

"And clean it up." Uthari turned a frank look on Malek. "I trust you can teach him to do that without overly *daunting* him."

"Possibly." Malek *did* look amused. His eyes were glinting.

Uthari squinted suspiciously at him, then shook his head and stalked away.

"Worse than the water-tank incident," Uthari muttered, then called over his shoulder, "Don't think I've forgotten that, Malek."

"I was sure you hadn't, Your Majesty," Malek called after him.

Shikari found a clump of leaves afflicted with foliage-munching worms and proceeded to devour them while ripping the foliage to shreds.

"Water-tank incident?" Jak asked.

"During the first year of my training," Malek said, "I knocked a water tank off the roof and flooded the castle courtyard."

"Oh?" Jak allowed himself to feel hope that such incidents might be common among mages in training and that he wasn't a total dolt. "What were you trying to do?"

"Catch a butterfly."

"Really?"

Malek nodded. "Raw power comes first and finesse later, though you have to work for it. Some mages never get past using their power like a bludgeon. They don't make it far and usually get killed in battle early on by someone more subtle."

"Ah. I likely should have tried the net then."

"Likely." Malek smiled slightly, then waved to the mess. "Let's separate the insects from the debris and toss everything that isn't supposed to go down a dragon's gullet over the side. I'll show you, and you try emulating me this time. You can be creative later, ideally when you're alone without anyone around who might be injured."

"Funny."

"Yes. Zidarr are known for their wit."

"I don't think that's true."

"No? Distressing."

Jak grinned and nodded that he was ready to learn and try to do exactly what Malek did.

As they worked together, Malek proved a surprisingly patient teacher. It reminded Jak of when his father had taught him about excavations and stratigraphy and how one did not, contrary to Jak's original belief, simply dig holes to search for artifacts.

A pang of nostalgia came over him, along with the realization that he appreciated having someone to teach him again. It wasn't as if he needed another father, or that anyone could replace the father he'd lost—he would never want that—but having a mentor was... nice.

But, as they used magic to sweep the debris off the deck, Jak reminded himself that Malek wanted him to swear loyalty and use his power to help Uthari. That had to be the only reason he was teaching Jak, not out of the goodness of his heart. As all the stories assured him, zidarr no more had hearts than they had wit.

Still, Jak couldn't help but think that everything would be much easier if he went along with Malek's desires. He hated the idea of becoming some wizard ruler's loyal minion, but if he did, could he make sure his mother and grandfather were safe? If so, that would be worth a lot. Maybe even his freedom.

On the other hand, if Jak learned from Malek only to later turn on him and Uthari, they would try to kill him. To kill him *and* his family. Even if all Jak did was try to escape them, would they forgive him for that? For learning the secrets of mage powers and running back to the world of terrene humans?

He worried that neither Uthari nor Malek would allow that.

"Interesting," Jadora murmured, turning the knob on the microscope. "*Extremely* interesting."

She was in one of the many tents that had been erected around the waterfall-fed pool by both Uthari's people and mages from the other fleets. Uthari had sent her down that morning, promising she would like what she found, which had included the microscope and all manner of laboratory equipment he must have brought along, hoping his team would find the longevity-inducing plant he sought.

During the last few days, she'd been hard at work translating the stories in the centuries-old tome the druids had lent her, and it was a worthwhile project, but *this* was her passion. She was examining some of the specimens she'd amassed during her journey, plant samples collected from all over, including the tunnels underneath Uthari's sky city, the druid monuments in the jungle, and beside the pool here—the spot where the magical dragon portal had chosen to have itself placed. The plants she'd gathered here had particularly intrigued her, and she was glad for the chance to examine them under a microscope, but she wouldn't admit it to Uthari or any of his people.

Even though she wasn't bound by shackles, Jadora and Jak were his prisoners. Even worse, Uthari now also held her father prisoner on his yacht. To ensure her *compliance*.

"Is she talking about the green smudge on the rectangle of glass?" Sergeant Tinder asked from the entrance to the tent.

"I believe so," Captain Ferroki said.

They were Jadora's two guards today. She didn't quite understand how the Thorn Company mercenaries had come to be working for King Uthari, when less than a week ago, they'd been employed *against* him by another alliance, but from what she'd heard, it had to do with their previous employers being killed and them being given an ultimatum. Work for Uthari or be abandoned in the jungle, a thousand miles from the coast and civilization.

They weren't the only mercenaries that Uthari had gathered that way—numerous tattooed roamers strode the decks of several ships in his fleet—and Jadora had no doubt he would throw them away as cannon fodder should fighting break out again. Since the battle with the worm, the various fleets had been holding an uneasy truce, but she had little doubt that every commander longed to claim the portal—and whatever wonders the other worlds might hold—for their masters. Further, some of the other fleets had brought mercenaries of their own, who were also camped in the area, and tensions were high whenever the different groups of soldiers crossed paths.

"Is that typical for scientists?" Tinder asked.

"I believe it is," Ferroki said. "We each have our own passions. To the anteater, ants are interesting."

"Huh. The things *I* find interesting are combat bonuses, exotic foods, and new toys for the bedroom."

"That's because you're typical for a *mercenary*."

"Am I, Captain? I always thought my knowledge of explosives and love for constructing, throwing, and precisely placing them made me unique."

"All mercenaries enjoy those things. You just excel at them."

"Thank you for noticing, Captain." Tinder opened the tent flap, peeked out, and frowned. "You know what else I excel at? Keeping rowdy soldiers in line." She stalked out and started yelling at people who were apparently lounging on the flat rock alongside the pool and swimming in the water instead of taking their duties seriously.

Jadora's current guards were chatty.

She opened a fresh journal that had been waiting on the table when she arrived and drew what were the most unique chloroplasts, if that was indeed what she was looking at, that she'd seen.

Maybe later, she would ask Jak to peer into the microscope and do more accurate drawings. She didn't have his deft touch with a pencil.

Outside, a tremendous splash sounded, followed by a man yelling for Tinder to get naked and join him. The last Jadora had seen, off-shift soldiers were climbing the cliff to the top of the waterfall, jumping into the river, and letting it carry them over the edge to plummet into the cool, deep pool.

Given the humidity that made sweat bead on her forehead, even here in the shade of the tent, she couldn't blame the soldiers, but she had a feeling some of the stern mage crewmen would come down from their ships and put an end to anything that might be considered fun. Since another deadly predator might fly through the portal at any time, someone out there should be standing guard assiduously, ready for that possibility.

"I hope we aren't distracting you from your work, Professor," Ferroki said quietly. "Especially since I assume your work is at King Uthari's behest. I don't wish to draw his ire."

"It's fine. I was just thinking of collecting another specimen. It's possible this plant represents a mutation." Jadora didn't think that was true, unless each of the plants in that patch was mutated, but she wanted to rule it out. She opened the flap, intending to walk to the portal for another sample, but one of the roamers was sprawled naked atop the green patch of plants, his hands behind his head, his bronze skin drying in the sun. "Perhaps I'll wait."

If the portal activated, and another giant man-eating worm flew out, he would be its first meal.

Ferroki looked out beside her. "What do you need?"

"Another sample from under that large fellow."

"Tinder." Ferroki waved to get her sergeant's attention and pointed at the greenery. "Collect a plant from under that roamer for the professor."

Tinder eyed the drowsing roamer. "From *under* him?"

Jadora shook her head. "Roamer-adjacent is fine."

Tinder ambled over, eyed the fronds of the plant, and pulled out a dagger to cut off some of the foliage. The roamer opened his eyes, said something in a sultry tone, and fondled her calf. She stepped on his wrist, pointed her dagger at his genitals, and replied in a clipped tone. He chuckled and released her.

"At least our combined forces are getting along," Ferroki said as Tinder walked away.

In Jadora's academic world back at Sprungtown University, she wouldn't have considered that *getting along*.

"And nobody has tried to kill our rookie for that axe yet," Ferroki murmured, her gaze toward an open area where Tezi was sparring with two other female mercenaries. "I've been concerned about that. It's garnered a lot of interest from mercenaries *and* mages."

"Not surprising. Even weapons made from *lesser* dragon steel are rare and coveted." Jadora thought of the blades Malek wielded. He'd admitted that he'd won them in battle against dangerous foes. "Their inherent magic gives them abilities beyond simple steel weapons, and dragon steel has even more power and magical properties. There are a handful of dragon-steel relics in museums and private collections around the world—and even a few monuments left in remote locations around Torvil—but neither smiths nor mages have ever learned how to smelt either material. The hottest heat we can make isn't effective, nor is any kind of magic. The material is impervious to it."

"So I've heard. One wonders how the tools were originally made."

"The hypothesis is that dragons have the power to manipulate the magical alloy. Our methods of dating artifacts suggest that all the dragon steel and lesser dragon steel on Torvil comes from the time period they were known to be visitors to our world. It's likely they made the weapons for the humans that befriended them—or served them. It was all more than ten thousand years ago, so the records are fuzzy on which it was. Perhaps some of both."

"It seems like it would be wise to befriend a dragon if at all possible."

Jadora shivered, remembering the brown-and-gray mottled dragon that had almost killed Malek. It had almost killed *all* of them. "I don't think it's always possible."

Tinder delivered the plant sample.

"Thank you, Sergeant." Jadora accepted it. "That was brave of you."

"Nah, that one's all right." Tinder pointed her thumb toward the lounging roamer. "He was flirting with Sasko earlier and accepted her *no* when she gave it. They don't always. I was a little surprised Sasko said no, to be honest. He's all muscled and sexy, if you're into that type. Which she is." Tinder smirked. "She may be pining for the mage engineer that we lost last week."

"Lieutenant Vinjo?" Ferroki asked. "She was avoiding him, not pining, when last they spoke. I believe Colonel *Sorath* is the one who misses him. A talented engineer willing to make magical gadgets for terrene humans shouldn't be cast aside lightly."

Jadora took the plant back to her worktable and cut a piece off the frond to make another slide.

"Maybe he'll show up so neither of them needs to pine," Tinder said. "It sounded like he effectively sabotaged Uthari's ships, and Vinjo was with a zidarr, so they should still be alive out there."

Jadora well remembered that sabotage and the subsequent crash. That she and her son were out here in the middle of a bunch of enemies who would prefer to kill each other rather than work together toward a common goal did not make her feel good about their future prospects.

As she placed the new slide under the microscope, she

thought of her father. Uthari had permitted her to speak with him but only a couple of times and briefly.

"Same chloroplasts," she murmured, taking a couple of notes. "Captain, do you have any troops who would be willing to escort me around the area? I'd like to see if there are any other plants here that are unfamiliar to me."

"*All* of the plants here are unfamiliar to me," Tinder muttered.

"But not to me. This is my field." Jadora waved at the microscope and herbalism and chemistry books Uthari had thought to stock along with the laboratory equipment. "Or it was before I took up my late husband's archaeology work to find the portal."

Something she already regretted. She feared it might have been better for mankind if the ancient artifact had remained buried on that volcanic island.

"I don't believe this plant is native to Torvil." Jadora pointed at it. "It's clearly been able to thrive and reproduce here, but the cellular structure is so different from typical that I suspect it has extraterrestrial origins. There are things in the cell that I don't even recognize. I can pick out a nucleus, plastids, and chloroplasts, of course, but even those are subtly different from anything I've seen before."

"Extraterrestrial?" Tinder's brows rose. "Is that as weird as it sounds?"

"Not... necessarily. We believe the portal insisted on being placed in the same spot it was thousands of years ago when it was used by dragons—and possibly, given the human bones and armor and axe we found elsewhere, humans. It's not surprising that those travelers might have brought back seeds that fell near the portal and took root. It is fascinating, however, and might give me insight into the flora we'll find out there. That could help me with turning the Jitaruvak, if we're able to find it, into the longevity-enhancing compound that Uthari wants."

The quicker she could do what Uthari wished with that plant, the sooner she could get her father back to safety. She hoped. Dare she believe that Uthari would keep his word about that? She'd come to trust Malek—whether that was wise or not—but only to be honest and do what he said. Not to balk at his king's orders or stop injustices Uthari might perpetrate.

"Just what we want," Tinder muttered. "Mages who live longer."

A woman's yell and the bang of a rock—or of a weapon striking?—sounded outside. Ferroki and Tinder rushed out of the tent.

Jadora, certain they were more qualified to handle trouble than she, intended to stay with her microscope, but it was hard to ignore the raised voices and the thumps of fists striking flesh.

"If you want a fight," a woman growled, "we'll give it to you."

"Not a fight, Surly. A little friendly tussle behind the trees there. Enjoyable for all."

"She said she's *not* interested." That was Tezi.

Jadora grimaced, feeling more attachment to the young woman than the others, since they'd spent time together and Tezi had confessed to what a hard life she'd led.

"You know what *I'm* interested in?" a man asked. "Besides your tits? That axe."

"Yeah," another man said. "I'm real interested in that too. Did you see when Lord Malek threw it? We'd been fighting that monster for an hour and barely dented it, and that axe slid right in and *killed* it."

"She found the weapon," Ferroki said, her voice calming, "so it's rightfully hers. Perhaps, if you speak with your commanders, you might be placed on one of the teams that goes exploring through the portal, and you will have an opportunity to find one of your own."

"Any weapons like that are sure to have owners," the man replied. "How'd she even get it? By robbing from someone? You can't tell me your pretty little girl mercenary beat a man in a fair fight."

"Its previous owner was eaten by a dragon," Tezi said coolly. "He didn't need it any longer."

"You *found* it? Then you've no more right to it than anyone else."

Someone grunted, a thud sounded, and noises of scuffling followed.

Jadora looked around the laboratory, seeking inspiration. Something she could concoct to stop a fight without permanently harming anyone—though she wouldn't mind withering up the testicles of some of the idiots out there. But it would take more than noxious smoke to do that.

Fortunately, she'd taken an inventory of ingredients earlier, so she knew what the tent laboratory contained. A little ferroot and some screaming yaryar... Yes, that would do.

As the sounds of fighting escalated, Jadora donned goggles to protect her eyes and pulled her shirt over her nose and mouth. It wasn't ideal, but she didn't have time to hunt for better protection. She mixed the chemicals, carefully pouring them into a beaker, and green smoke wafted from the top. She covered it, the fumes from the concoction burning her palm, and ran to the tent flap.

Outside, several of the Thorn Company women stood back to back with Tezi. She was gritting her teeth and brandishing the axe as men surrounded them, some darting in and trying to snatch it from her.

Tezi didn't look like she wanted to use the weapon on them, and Ferroki, Tinder, and the others gripped magelock pistols but hadn't yet fired. The tense set of their faces suggested they might soon. So far, the men from the other unit were acting more like playground bullies than true enemies with deadly intent, but as Jadora watched, the brawl escalated.

One man caught the haft of Tezi's axe. She kicked him in the shin as she jerked it away. Tinder snarled and shot the man in the shoulder. The rest of the men drew their weapons.

Though Jadora lamented that her concoction would affect allies as well as enemies, she ran and hurled the beaker into their midst. The liquid inside spilled out, hitting the ground as well as people's clothing as it spattered. It would burn their skin a little, but the smoky green fumes would irritate their eyes and mucous membranes far more.

Some of the people closest to the beaker started coughing and cursing right away, while others wrestled and threw punches for several more seconds as the smoke spread.

"Knock it off," a male voice called from the trees. Colonel Sorath.

He came running into the clearing with several Thorn Company women he must have been on patrol with, and they charged toward the group. But the fight was already breaking up as mercenaries reeled away from each other—and the smoking beaker on the ground. They coughed and clawed at their eyes as they ran off into the trees. Several jumped, fully clothed, into the pool.

Sorath's charge slowed, his nose wrinkling as he came within range of the fumes. He halted as he reached Ferroki's side. A moment earlier, she'd been fighting, but now she bent over, gripping her knees with snot streaming from her nose.

Jadora winced, again wishing she could have attacked their enemies without hitting her allies, but it had to be better than being shot.

Sorath patted Ferroki on the back and led her away from the fumes. He noticed Jadora and must have guessed what happened —the beaker in the dirt wasn't exactly something a mercenary would have tossed. He gave her a salute, then pulled out a kerchief for Ferroki.

"That's one way to end a brawl," a familiar dry voice commented from behind Jadora.

Startled, she jumped, even though she recognized the speaker right away.

Malek stood beside the tent, his oval skyboard tucked under his arm, suggesting he'd just come down from one of the ships. Jadora hadn't seen him since the night they'd returned through the portal, when he'd barely been able to walk, due to the grievous punctures the dragon had left in his abdomen. Her relief at seeing him fit and hale made her take a step, wanting to hug him, but she halted before reaching for him.

Uthari's words echoed in her mind. *I would trust Malek with my life and my kingdom, but women always tend to complicate matters of loyalty between men. If I deem it necessary, I will remove the complication. Don't assume your value to me is infinite.*

Even if she wanted Malek to be well and appreciated how often he'd helped her, Jadora dared not show that appreciation with a physical display. Or anything that suggested romantic interest.

Besides, she *wasn't* romantically interested in Malek. He was better than the other zidarr and most of the mages she'd met, but he was still... what he was.

Malek smiled faintly—and maybe a little sadly—doubtless reading her thoughts. That sadness made her regret thinking them, but it didn't change anything.

"Are you unhurt?" Malek looked her up and down briefly before eyeing the mercenaries, the portal, and their surroundings, as if scanning everything intently for danger or sign of anything amiss. "I heard the commotion from the ship."

The ship. Uthari's yacht hovering a couple hundred feet above them, the mages up there able to look down on their mercenary minions without having to interact with them. The same as they looked down upon their terrene human subjects from their sky cities.

"I'm fine," Jadora said. "Per Uthari's suggestion, I'm familiarizing myself with his laboratory, so I'll be ready when we find the Jitaruvak and can begin synthesizing something pharmacologically suitable for his needs. The sooner I do that and he releases my father, the better."

"Yes." Malek's tone was neutral, not sympathetic, not willing to admit that Uthari was an ass for using an old man to get what he wanted.

Jadora didn't think he approved, but as long as he allowed it, did it make a difference? To be a part of their world and the crimes they committed—to support the king by working for him—was as bad as being one of the rulers subjugating her people.

Another reason they could never be… anything.

"Your fingernails are green," he noted.

Jadora had been scraping off the epidermis of a plant earlier to make a compound. She hadn't realized she'd gotten chlorophyll under her nails but couldn't pretend to be surprised.

"I'm sure they're not the only part," she murmured.

His gaze drifted up to her forehead. "No," he agreed, the smile returning.

Had she rubbed it on her face? Wonderful.

"I came to inform you that we'll leave in the morning," Malek said. "Uthari is aware of the tensions down here—the climate is equally tense among the mages. He's received communications from almost all of the kings and queens, and they've all sent or are sending more troops, more mageships. He wants us to find his plant and more dragon-steel weapons before they arrive en masse and he's no longer able to control the portal. Right now, he only can because he has the key, but if someone manages to take it from him…"

"He wants us to find the plant *and* dragon-steel weapons?" Jadora didn't miss that Uthari's desires had expanded.

"He is contemplating taking Tezi's axe for himself."

"Oh, good. Another bully."

Malek's eyes narrowed slightly. She didn't care. She refused to mince words about what a bastard Uthari was—about what a bastard *all* of the powerful mages were—just because Malek was one and lived in their world. Maybe it was stupid, but she'd come to believe he wouldn't use his power to punish her for speaking freely.

"No," he agreed softly, "but others will. Please don't goad anyone powerful. I have let it be known that you and Jak are under my protection—" Malek turned a cool gaze toward several drenched male mercenaries who were muttering and pointing at Jadora, perhaps having figured out who'd been responsible for the fumes, "—but I can't watch over you every hour of the day. Also, there are some who hate me and would hurt you simply to spite me. Others hate Uthari and would hurt you for the same reason."

"I know." If she'd believed he would protect her because he liked her and valued her as a person, Jadora might have been flattered, but he was doing it for the same reason he'd kidnapped her. Because she had value to Uthari, and Uthari wanted her alive. For now.

Malek opened his mouth, as if he might say something—some protest to that line of thinking?—but he closed it again. With his next words, he changed the subject.

"I let King Uthari know I would not approve of him taking the axe. Since Rookie Tezi found it, it is rightfully hers. But even I must admit that it will cause trouble and be a target as long as it's in the hands of someone the others do not fear. If Uthari claimed it, few would dare plot against him to take it."

"*She* can use it." Jadora pointed to where Tezi, Tinder, and several others knelt by the pool, splashing water onto their faces to wash away the chemical residue. "To help her unit and protect herself from goons. Uthari would mount it on the wall above his toilet, the same as that other dragon-steel artifact he has."

Malek snorted. "Surely, an axe would go above the fireplace, not in the lavatory."

"You know what I mean."

"Yes, but I'm not wrong about the rest. I'll wager that skirmish started because of the axe?" Malek raised his eyebrows. He must not have seen the genesis.

"I believe it started because the women didn't want to *tussle* behind a tree with the men. The axe came into it later."

His eyebrows drew back down as he mouthed, "Tussle," and looked toward the nearest tree. A moment passed before his brows lifted with enlightenment. "Ah."

Either people didn't use a lot of euphemisms for sex around the zidarr—maybe they were too terrified of them and their fearsome reputations to speak freely in their presence—or he wasn't the most experienced in such matters.

That would surprise her, since he was handsome, and there were plenty of daring women who were more attracted than deterred by *fearsome*, but he'd mentioned that romantic entanglements were forbidden for zidarr. What punishment, she wondered, did they receive if they let themselves develop feelings for a woman? And who handled the punishment of some of the most powerful mages in the world?

"The kings themselves," Malek said quietly. Then, clearly not wishing to dwell on the subject, he repeated, "We will leave in the morning. If you provide a list of necessities you may need—such as skirmish-ending chemicals—I'll do my best to see that they're provided."

"Thank you," she murmured.

Her mind, less willing to change subjects, envisioned Malek on his knees before Uthari, crying out in pain as the old man delivered some vile punishment to someone who'd been nothing but loyal to him. She shivered, gazing at his chest and wondering why Malek remained so steadfast.

"Have you finished translating the druid tome and garnered any clues as to which of the worlds might hold the Jitaruvak?" Malek asked, not commenting on her thoughts.

"I've translated more stories but not all of them. As I said before, that's the work of at least two weeks, maybe more. But each of the tales, and each of the accompanying runes that matches a rune on the portal, has been one of warning. Every tale—every historical event—has spoken of a specific deadly creature that came through when a passageway to another world was opened, either by the druids or by the creatures on the other end that wanted to come here. Unless you want to give me more time, my only suggestion is that we choose destinations that *aren't* listed in the tome."

"Uthari insists we not delay further. You said there are nineteen symbols in the tome?"

"Technically, twenty, but there's no story recorded under the twentieth."

"Leaving twelve others not mentioned."

"Eleven. One of the ones not mentioned is our world, and we already know what's here."

"Of course." Malek nodded. "Were any of the deadly creatures that came through the portal in the tales that the druids recorded dragons?"

"Yes. They're the stars—the antagonists—in six of the stories."

"We believe the Jitaruvak came from the same home world as the dragons. Perhaps that means we *should* choose one of those worlds to visit."

"Do you truly want to face more dragons like the one that almost killed us all?"

"If we must," Malek said grimly. "This time, I will bring

another talented mage with us. That way, we'll have a better chance of dealing with a dragon or other powerful predator."

"Not Tonovan." Jadora couldn't keep from jerking her gaze up to his, fear flashing through her.

"No. I've requested Captain Rivlen. She wishes opportunities to prove herself to Uthari, and she is powerful and capable."

Jadora couldn't quite hide a grimace, not when Rivlen was the one who'd been instructing Jak on how to use his magic while Jadora had been with the druids. Had it been out of the goodness of her heart, Jadora wouldn't have objected, but Jak believed Rivlen wanted to use him to further her own goals.

Jadora missed the days when the only thing her son had been precocious about had been math, maps, and finding his way out of the woods without getting lost.

"Jak will come, as well," Malek said. "He wishes to do so—and to bring the hatchling—and I assume that you also prefer he be with you."

When the alternative was him staying here among all these power-hungry mages? "Yes."

"Is there anyone else you wish to go with us? Who might have some value on our expedition?"

She almost said her father, for the same reason she wanted Jak along—because it was safer away from these people than with them—but she stopped herself as the memory of the dragon battle stampeded into her mind. Maybe she was a fool for even wanting to take Jak, though he wouldn't forgive her if she forbade him from visiting and exploring other worlds, however dangerous. Besides, he had some penchant for communicating with the portals. Not only had the one here protected him numerous times, but the one on the world they'd visited had picked him out as the person to share the location of those eggs with. He could be invaluable on their journeys.

"I know you'd likely prefer scholars," Malek said into her long silence, "and I regret that I can't supply you with many of those. Uthari has also said we may not take Colonel Sorath."

"You would want him? Doesn't he want to kill you?"

"Many want to kill me. He has a strategic mind and could be useful when we run into trouble."

When, not if. Jadora agreed with the sentiment.

"But Uthari wants him here," Malek said. "That was his sole reason for hiring the female mercenaries."

"Colonel Sorath is not a female mercenary." As far as Jadora knew, he'd been swept up along with Thorn Company but wasn't a part of their unit.

"No, but he cares about them."

It only took her a moment to parse that. "The same way I care about my father? And I cared about Darv?" She shook her head bleakly, lamenting the loss of her old colleague and that she hadn't even had an opportunity to send a letter back to the university to explain what had happened to him.

"To ensure compliance, yes." Malek said the words matter-of-factly but not, she thought, without any sympathy.

She wished that made it less awful, but it didn't.

Dusk was falling, and monkeys hooted in the distance. The call of the cicadas started up, or maybe it was only in Malek's long silence that she noticed what had been there all along.

"Tezi," Jadora said.

"You want to bring her along? She didn't do anything useful against the dragon."

"*None* of the rest of us did anything useful. It was impervious to my explosives and the mercenaries' magelock rifles."

"Jak funneled his power into me when I needed it."

"Yes, but none of the mercenaries can do that. I assumed you wanted me to choose from among them, not mages from Uthari's crew."

"The older and more experienced mercenaries are capable

enough fighters, and I thought you might want someone along as an assistant." He nodded toward the laboratory tent.

"I'm sure Tezi can hold pipettes and test tubes for me if need be. And if she and the axe are with us, they can't be a point of contention here."

"Ah, I see."

"If they'll part with her, Dr. Fret too. You can heal people, for which I'm grateful—" Jadora remembered kneeling at his side in their cabin as he used magic to repair that horrible spear wound that Jak had received, "—but you're also the strongest warrior and most likely to be targeted by enemies. If you're unconscious..."

He nodded. "Yes, I understand."

"And we might as well ask for Sergeant Tinder too. She doesn't mind collecting roamer-adjacent plants for me."

His brow creased again, much as it had when she'd mentioned *tussling*.

"And she can build explosives. She probably has some chemistry knowledge beyond knowing what goes into black powder."

"She's the one who wanted to leave me dying from blood loss on an alien world while the rest of you fled," Malek said.

He didn't sound bitter or aggrieved. Thus far, he hadn't been disgruntled when his prisoners tried to escape. He always seemed willing to accept that his enemies would act in their own interest.

"Not everyone loves a zidarr," Jadora said.

"Not *anyone* does," he said, the faint smile returning.

It was probably a joke—though she wondered if he ever lamented how true it was—but she couldn't keep from replying seriously. "I hope Uthari does, given how faithful you are to him."

Malek only inclined his head to her and stepped back. "Tinder, Tezi, and Fret. I will inform Captain Ferroki of your choices. Pack what you need, and don't forget to give me a list. We'll leave at dawn."

3

Rain pattered against the great leaves and dripped onto Colonel Sorath's head, catching in his thick, wiry hair and making it heavy with moisture. Earlier, a macaw had landed on it, investigating the possibility of making a nest, no doubt.

Maybe it was time to go back to shaving his head. He'd kept it that way for his whole mercenary career, only letting his hair grow when he'd gone incognito as the scribe Vorzaz. That name and identity were useless now.

"Do we really expect enemies to approach on foot?" Lieutenant Sasko asked, her straight black hair back in a bun, her brown Thorn Company uniform as wet and stained as Sorath's mishmash of clothing, clothing that had been selected for the desert climate of Perchver, not this humid jungle. "When we're a thousand miles from anywhere and there are fifty million mage ships hovering over the area?"

"At last count," Sorath said, "it was twenty-nine."

"Might as well be fifty million."

The two other Thorn Company mercenaries on the patrol with them mumbled and nodded agreement. They gazed wistfully toward the distant camp, a few lights visible through the trees. Twilight had fallen, making it hard to see on the crude trails they'd hacked through the undergrowth, so Sorath didn't blame them, but an attack was more likely to come during the night than the day.

"Any threat will probably come from within or above the camp," Sorath said, "from the mages and mercenaries who want to take control of the portal from Uthari, but it's also possible the druids will attempt to acquire it again."

Sorath had attended meetings with Uthari, Malek, General Tonovan, and the rest of Uthari's high-ranking officers, so he'd learned what had happened to them during the time Sorath and Thorn Company had been in King Zaruk's employ.

"You mean the mages and mercenaries we were working *for* last week?" Sasko eyed her comrades. She'd already made it clear, numerous times, that the side switching didn't sit well with her.

Sorath didn't like it either, but after capturing the company, Uthari hadn't given them a choice. The captain they'd been working for was dead, and whether they wanted it or not, Thorn Company had a new employer. Surviving as a mercenary meant being flexible, but it did anger Sorath that he was now working for one of the men who'd been responsible for the destruction of his old unit, the deaths of more than a hundred men who'd served him faithfully for years.

"We're still alive. Sometimes, that's the best you can hope for. That and a future that's sunnier than the past." Sorath looked toward the sky, though he couldn't see the gray rainclouds through the dense tree canopy. "Or the present."

"No kidding," Sasko said. "I'd like to hope that something horrible comes through that portal and eats all the mages here, but that would mean we'd be eaten too."

"Likely so." Sorath didn't know what to hope for.

When he'd first met Professor Freedar and her son Jak, they'd spoken about using the portal to find allies to bring back—*dragon allies*—to battle the wizard rulers and overthrow them and their tyrannical governments, but now, Jadora and Jak seemed to be working for Uthari without complaint.

Sorath couldn't blame them—like Thorn Company, they hadn't been given a choice—but he couldn't help but wish someone was still planning an uprising. Someone with the power and resources to make it a reality.

Who that might be, he didn't know. He could lead armies, but completely mundane armies could never beat the millions of mages in the world. And even if dragons were out there and could be lured back to Torvil, why would they side with terrene humans against people who were magical like themselves?

Lost in his musings, Sorath didn't detect anyone nearby until invisible power wrapped around him, halting him in his tracks. Curses came from behind him as the Thorn Company women were also halted.

Sorath tried to lift his pickaxe arm to defend himself, but he couldn't budge it. He gritted his teeth, glowering at a shadow that moved between the trees.

Expecting druids, Sorath twitched in surprise when two familiar figures stepped into view. Lieutenant Vinjo and the black-clad zidarr, Night Wrath, who carried a mace and short sword, the latter glowing white and illuminating his hard, cold face.

"Well, well," Night Wrath said. "We've found the traitor, Colonel Sorath."

Vinjo's expression was more weary than cold or hard. With grease and dirt stains on his wet uniform, tools sticking out of his pockets, and a toolbox in hand instead of a weapon, Vinjo appeared very little like his brother. They both bore skyboards strapped to their backs, but the magical devices couldn't have brought them all this way without being recharged.

Sorath found he could move his mouth enough to spit out, "I've betrayed no one."

"You betrayed *us*." Night Wrath thumped a fist against his chest, glanced at Vinjo, and also pointed over his shoulder. To indicate more comrades in the jungle? Or perhaps the ship that had been wrecked hundreds of miles away, Zaruk's *Skimmer*. Its crew had been left to die when Thorn Company had been plucked up by Uthari's troops.

"We were taken prisoner." Sorath tried to inch his hand toward the pocket where he kept pop-bangs, explosives he could throw to distract a mage. He'd used all of his originals, made by a smith back in Perchver, but Jadora had made some replacements for him. They weren't as refined, but they would do. *If* he could reach them.

"You expect us to believe you're *prisoners*? When you're wandering about with all your weapons, clearly on patrol for Uthari?" Night Wrath pointed from Sorath to Sasko and the others. "You were working for Uthari the whole time. Accepting our money while selling us out. How much did he pay you to keep tabs on us? To report our sabotage? To report the *Skimmer*'s position?"

"That's not what happened," Lieutenant Sasko said. "We were as surprised as the crew by the appearance of Uthari's fleet."

"I'll bet," Night Wrath snarled, increasing the pressure that gripped Sorath—that gripped all of them.

Gasps of pain and frustrated snarls came from the women. The pressure mashed down on Sorath's shoulders until his legs gave out and he ended up on his knees in the mud, glaring up at the zidarr. He read his death in Night Wrath's eyes along with his frustration at what he perceived as a betrayal.

"You can read minds. Read mine. You'll see the truth." Sorath willed himself to think about that night, not the explosive he was trying to reach.

"I'll see your lies and how quickly you'll turn on your employers," Night Wrath said, not checking Sorath's thoughts at all.

But Vinjo squinted at Sorath. "No... he's telling the truth, Veejar. They didn't know."

"Don't call me that." Night Wrath thumped Vinjo on the chest, more like a blow than a brotherly pat. "He's *fooling* you."

"I'm not an inept mage." Vinjo glowered at his brother. "I can read the minds of terrene humans."

"Only enough to be fooled by them."

"I'm not fooled. *Look.*" Vinjo flung a hand toward Sorath. "The colonel is all right. He didn't betray us. And that's the lovely Lieutenant Sasko, who admired my assets in the engine room. She also wouldn't betray us. Certainly not me." Though Vinjo was frazzled, with his damp hair dripping water into his eyes, he managed to flash a smile at Sasko.

She groaned, sounding more tormented than touched by his attention.

"You only want to believe Sorath is innocent," Night Wrath said, ignoring the part about Sasko, "because he called some of your junk *clever*."

The pressure didn't go away as the men argued, but Night Wrath was distracted and not paying as much attention. Sorath managed to slip his hand into his pocket and wrap his fingers around one of the explosives.

"It *is* clever," Vinjo said, sounding like they were resuming an argument they'd had before—maybe they'd been sniping at each other during their whole trip. "It would be nice if you would acknowledge that I'm not useless."

"You weren't useful enough to keep Uthari's mages from fixing the ships you sabotaged. If you want people to think you're valuable, you have to do better. And not be a screw-up all the time."

"I did *my* part. Far more than *you* did."

Though he couldn't rise from his knees, Sorath managed to

flick his wrist enough to toss the explosive. It struck the ground in front of Night Wrath and blew. Softly. Either because of the rain or the mud it landed in, it lacked its usual oomph, but it surprised Night Wrath enough that the pressure around Sorath lessened.

He surged to his feet, another explosive already in hand. As Sorath charged the zidarr, he threw it right at him.

Night Wrath already had a barrier up around himself. The explosive struck it and blew up without harming him.

Sorath was aware of the Thorn Company women coming to help—or were they charging toward Vinjo?—but Night Wrath was focused on him, so he dared not look away. Expecting a counter attack, Sorath sprang to the side instead of continuing toward his foe.

A *whoosh* of power blasted through the air where he'd been. Behind him, a tree snapped and toppled, foliage rattling loudly as branches crashed down.

Sorath threw another pop-bang, not at the shielded Night Wrath this time, but at a tree beside him. It exploded, sending branches and chunks from its trunk flying. Though still behind his barrier, the noise and flying debris made Night Wrath glance toward the tree. Sorath tugged out his black-powder pistol and fired as Sasko and one of the women tackled Vinjo. If the lieutenant had gotten a barrier up, he'd lost his concentration and dropped it.

Unfortunately, Night Wrath wasn't as easily distracted. The bullet bounced uselessly off his barrier—and drew his attention again. Night Wrath hefted his mace and short sword and sprang for Sorath.

Sorath traded his pistol for his own short sword, though he deflected the first blow with his pickaxe. Barely. The zidarr's magical weapon shaved off part of the tip, cutting through fine steel as if it were butter.

Cursing, Sorath kicked out to keep the man back. But Night

Wrath was every bit the trained fighter that the zidarr reputation promised. Sorath defended with sword and pickaxe, but he had to give ground as the magical blade swept for him again and again, frustration and hatred burning in the zidarr's eyes. He truly seemed to believe Sorath had betrayed him.

A *thwomp* came from the side, and a blue magelock blast slammed into Night Wrath's barrier. Though it didn't get through, he glanced in that direction. Lights bobbed in the jungle, and mercenaries and mages ran through the trees toward the skirmish.

Night Wrath cursed. "Next time, you *die*, Sorath."

He dropped something that puffed softly when it hit the ground, and a cloud of smoke appeared. Sorath kept his weapons up as he backed away from the haze, expecting a parting attack.

He wasn't wrong, but the blow came as a magical burst of energy instead of a sword slash. It rammed into his chest, sending him flying into the air. His back collided with a tree, and he slid down it, branches battering him from behind. He barely managed to keep his weapons up and land on his feet in a crouch instead of on his ass.

By the time the smoke cleared, Night Wrath was gone.

Red-uniformed mages from Uthari's ships were securing the area, alongside more of the Thorn Company mercenaries.

"One of Zaruk's zidarr was here," a mage called. "Find him!"

As they spread out to search, Sorath walked away from the tree, grimacing at what would turn into a dozen bruises on his back. He'd never bested a zidarr in his life, so he couldn't be surprised that he hadn't managed it, but he was disgusted that he'd been caught by surprise when those two showed up. He shouldn't have been idly musing while out on patrol. He knew better.

"Don't kill me," came a cry from a knot of Thorn Company soldiers. "I'm valuable! The colonel said so!"

Sasko and the rest of their patrol had Vinjo pinned. He lay on his back, her boot on his chest, something in his hand thrust straight up in the air, as if it could shield him.

Worried it might be an explosive—or one of Vinjo's other inventions—Sorath jogged over to the group.

"Lieutenant Sasko?" Vinjo peered blearily up at her, his hair in the mud. "Is that *your* boot on my chest? Crushing my sternum? When I'd envisioned us together, it was more your *chest* that was mashed against mine. And there was rubbing and stroking, enjoyable to all."

"Can I shoot him?" Sasko had a magelock pistol in hand, though she didn't point it at Vinjo, only vaguely toward a fern next to his head.

"Certainly *not*." Vinjo squeezed his hand, and the gizmo he gripped started flashing green light.

"Uh." Sasko removed her boot and backed away from him.

Eyeing it warily, the other mercenaries also scooted away. One of Uthari's mages remained in the area while his colleagues searched for Night Wrath, but he only watched Vinjo with a bland lack of concern.

"Someone disarm him, will you?" the mage said. "King Uthari will want him questioned."

"I refuse to answer questions that will endanger my brother or my people." Vinjo climbed to his feet while keeping the device aloft, the green flashes highlighting branches and vines in nearby trees. "You *cannot* interrogate me."

"Is that a bomb?" Sorath sheathed his sword and stepped closer to Vinjo, worried the mage version of an explosive might do a lot more damage than one of Jadora's pop-bangs.

"It could be." Vinjo, a muddy boot print on his chest, wriggled his eyebrows at Sorath. "What's important is that you *think* it is."

Sorath snorted. That sounded like a no.

"What's it do? Turn you invisible?" Sorath knew Vinjo had a device that did that, and he had indeed called it clever.

"Of course not. The clandestineness creeper doesn't flash. This is a recent invention that I knew would be indispensable. I crafted it while the others were repairing the ship." He lowered his voice to a whisper. "It's a dragon-steel-artifact-locator compass. When I briefly had access to the portal, I ran a magical imprinter tool over it and captured imagery of its essence, which I stored in this device. Now, I could track that portal halfway across the world if necessary."

"Imagery of its essence?" one of the mercenaries asked. "What does *that* mean?"

Sasko sighed. "That I didn't need to take my boot off his chest."

"Confiscate it," came a new voice.

General Tonovan walked out of the trees, a few of his mages trailing him.

Vinjo lifted his head. "I won't give such a valuable and brilliant device to my enemies."

"You will or I'll kill you," Tonovan said coolly. "What did you hope to accomplish by sneaking up on the portal at night?" He eyed the tools sticking out of Vinjo's pockets. "Are you the one who sabotaged our ships' engines? And kept the portal's magic from being activated in battle?"

"I'm just an engineer," Vinjo said.

"Search him," Tonovan told his men. "Take everything he has, and smash it to pieces. Then take him up to my ship for questioning."

"No, no, that's not necessary. Very undesirable, in fact. I'm an engineer, not a warrior. I don't even know anything." Vinjo hopped behind Sorath, as if he might keep Tonovan from capturing him.

Though Sorath didn't want to see the engineer interrogated—and no doubt tortured—he couldn't think of anything he could say or do to protect him. As the grim-faced mages approached, he held out his arms, showing he wouldn't try to deter them.

Surprisingly, Vinjo stuck something in one of Sorath's pockets.

"Don't let them have this," he whispered. "Or this. Or—dear flying dragons—*this*."

No fewer than five objects were slipped into Sorath's pockets.

Sorath almost swatted his hands away, not wanting Tonovan's men to haul him up for interrogation—*another* one—alongside the engineer. But Vinjo's devices tended to be useful. It would be a shame to have them smashed under someone's boot.

The mages reached them and dragged Vinjo away, someone forcing him onto a skyboard. Some of Tonovan's men kept searching for Night Wrath, but Sorath doubted they would find the zidarr. The rest of the mages climbed onto skyboards of their own to escort their prisoner up. Surrounded, Vinjo peered back down at Sorath and Sasko, a pitiful, beleaguered expression on his face.

"What a nice brother he's got," Sasko muttered, "leaving him to be captured."

"Night Wrath probably has plans to skulk around in the woods until he gets a chance to cause mayhem," Sorath said.

"And that required that he sacrifice his brother?"

"Apparently. We'll have to double the patrols."

"Oh, good," Sasko said. "I was afraid my nights would be full of blissful sleep instead of tramping around in the rain, risking being eaten by wild animals."

"At least your nights will be better than his." One of the mercenaries pointed toward Vinjo as he disappeared over the railing of one of the ominous black-hulled mageships.

Sorath expected a snarky retort from Sasko, but she shook her head and muttered, "Poor fellow. I should have let him go."

"If we'd lost both of them," Sorath said, "the mages would have taken out their ire on us."

"I suppose. I am tired of mage ire."

Sorath sighed. So was he.

The double doors to Uthari's suite on the *Serene Waters* opened as Malek approached. He'd been settling in to sleep for the night, wanting to be well-rested before venturing to another world, when Uthari telepathically summoned him.

Malek sensed Tonovan inside and sighed inwardly, not in the mood for his vitriol tonight. He'd minded Tonovan less before Jak and Jadora had come into his life. Per Uthari's orders, his duty was to protect them, but he'd also come to *want* to protect them, whether it was his duty or not. And that Tonovan thought nothing of threatening them—and might even be threatening them on purpose to irk Malek—irritated him.

When Malek had walked into Jak's cabin and found him pinned to the floor and unable to breathe, he'd almost attacked Tonovan on the spot. Especially since Tonovan had appeared to be contemplating more than punishment for Jak. Calculation had lurked in his eyes, as if he were imagining what excuse he could give for *accidentally* killing Jak, as he'd *accidentally* killed Professor Darv. In self-defense, he'd assured Malek when they'd spoken after that incident. As if the seventy-year-old professor had been a true threat to him.

As he stepped into the suite and turned into the office, where Uthari sat behind his desk with a glass of water and Tonovan sat opposite with some amber alcoholic beverage in hand, Malek schooled his features into neutral indifference. He would not let Tonovan get his hackles up tonight.

"Yidar is performing adequately?" Uthari asked Tonovan, continuing a conversation as he waved Malek to the seat beside Tonovan.

Malek opted to stand beside the seat instead of taking it. He clasped his hands behind his back.

"He's being pompous and sanctimonious, which I suppose is

adequate, or at least *expected*, for a zidarr." Tonovan smirked over at Malek, a gesture with a sneer wrapped up in it.

"My concerns," Uthari said dryly, "are about his loyalty and whether he's working to further our kingdom's goals or if he's angling for personal gain. With so many fleets here, commanded by subjects loyal to other rulers, it's likely that someone will attempt to turn him against me. I would be surprised if some of my peers' intelligence gatherers hadn't learned of Yidar's betrayal back in Utharika."

"He doesn't confide in me, Your Majesty," Tonovan said. "All I can say is that he frequently gazes off into the night with a scheming expression on his face. Unlike the pomposity, *that* isn't very zidarr."

"No," Uthari murmured quietly, his face pained for a moment as he gazed into his glass.

Malek suspected that Yidar's betrayal had hurt. To personally select someone for zidarr training, and to handle much of the magical training oneself, and then to have that protege turn against one... It couldn't be easy.

Since zidarr were not allowed to take apprentices themselves, nor have families and sire children, Malek had never experienced what it was like to invest that much time in someone, but he could imagine it. How would he feel if, after years of training, Jak were to turn on him?

Right now, Malek wouldn't blame Jak, who was, despite Uthari giving Malek permission to teach him, still their prisoner. But if Jak agreed to be loyal to them, trained with Malek for years, and *then* turned on him, it would surely sting.

A strange thing to admit. Malek had never thought he would care about others beyond Uthari, his mentor and the closest person he'd ever had to a father. All through his life, he'd been careful not to allow himself to grow attached to people. Why he seemed inclined to allow it now, he didn't know.

"Continue to keep an eye on him for me, General," Uthari said.

"Certainly, Your Majesty."

"Night Wrath has arrived in the area." Uthari looked at Malek. "If you weren't leaving through the portal soon, I would be tempted to send you to find him."

"Was he discovered in the midst of some sabotage?" Malek wasn't surprised that one of Zaruk's zidarr had arrived.

"He's the one who sabotaged our ships back at the river," Tonovan said. "We couldn't capture him, but we *did* capture his brother. I've been questioning him. I'd expected to have to apply a great deal of force, but he crumpled and blabbed everything he knew before I'd barely hurt him. How surprising that he is the brother of a zidarr. Despite being a weak-willed wimp, he was the one who built the devices that Night Wrath attached to our engines."

"And to the portal?" Malek asked.

Tonovan shrugged. "Apparently."

Malek thought of the battle where Jak hadn't been able to coerce the portal into assisting with their enemies as soon as expected. He'd found a magical device concealed on it, something that interrupted its ability to respond to Jak or do anything at all. When Malek had examined it, he hadn't been able to determine how it worked. His crafting background was not extensive, but he could usually detect how magical devices operated.

"Night Wrath has likely taken refuge on one of Zaruk's ships, or a ship of one of Zaruk's allies," Uthari said. "Since he was discovered before he had time to sabotage anything, as far as we can tell, I am not that concerned about him. We are debating if there is any reason to keep the brother alive. His name is Lieutenant Vinjo."

"He doesn't believe his brother will attempt to rescue him, nor that his family will care overmuch if he's killed. An accident could befall him in his cell on my ship." Tonovan drank from his glass, then refilled it from a decanter on a silver tray on the desk. "Normally, in war, we exchange prisoners that we capture, but it doesn't sound like anyone wants him. And I'm annoyed at the damage he did to my ship, even if it's since been repaired. Such brazen arrogance should be punished."

"Your opinion, Malek?" Uthari, always more interested in using people if they had value, than being petty and killing them for no reason, arched his eyebrows.

"My only familiarity with him is from his work," Malek said. "The device he used to nullify the portal is in my quarters on the *Star Flyer*. I can bring it over before I leave tomorrow so you can look at it if you wish. It's possible the engineer is quite good at his craft and may be worth letting live if you can convince him to work for you."

"Nullify the portal?" Uthari lifted his eyebrows.

It wasn't until that moment that Malek realized the ramifications of a device that could do that. He almost smacked himself in the forehead.

"Yes. At least it seemed so. It's possible it wouldn't work to stop a passageway from another world from forming, but we should experiment with it."

Uthari was already nodding as Malek spoke, having twigged to the possibilities right away. Malek felt like a fool for not thinking of it earlier.

"Stop one from forming?" Tonovan's brow furrowed. "What do you mean?"

"It couldn't be placed while we had a team out in another world," Malek told Uthari, ignoring Tonovan, "or they wouldn't be able to return."

"True," Uthari said, "but the rest of the time, if it could prevent unwanted visitors from coming through, that would be a boon."

"Yes."

"And the druids would have no reason to object to our continuing to use the portal."

"One would hope."

Tonovan scowled at them.

"If the device, when placed on the portal," Uthari explained patiently to him, "nullifies its magic, a passageway between worlds would not be able to form, thus ensuring that giant mage-eating worms can't fly through. Should it work."

"Oh," Tonovan said. "Does that mean the engineer can't meet with an accident on my ship?"

"Correct. Keep him safe for now while I think of a way to coerce him to work for us. Perhaps he can build something even more effective and permanent." Uthari tapped his chin. "Perhaps he can build other tools for us."

"His brother might object if he switches sides," Tonovan said, "and try to rescue him. Or kill him."

"Perhaps his brother will have to believe that he's already dead." Uthari waved a hand dismissively. "We shall figure it out. You're dismissed, Tonovan."

"Yes, Your Majesty." Tonovan emptied his glass and set it down as he rose. "I'll leave you to enjoy punishing Malek in private." He smirked wolfishly as he headed for the door. "For teaching a wild one, one who knocked down half the jungle to get his dragon a few bugs."

Malek said nothing as Tonovan approached. He must not have been told that Malek had permission to train Jak. Malek stepped out of his path, hoping the general would leave without one of his tedious parting insults.

"Perhaps while you're here being punished," Tonovan said, "I'll visit your professor. She's all alone in that tent, isn't she? Pining for male companionship, I imagine. Since *you're* not permitted to sate her desires, perhaps I—"

"If you touch her, physically, mentally, or otherwise," Malek said, amazed he kept his voice steady and refrained from throttling the man, "I will kill you."

The statement seemed to surprise Tonovan but only for the briefest moment. "If you do that, I'm sure that would result in *further* punishment. Given our current predicament, the king needs his best troops, and I am *the* best. As valuable as any *zidarr*."

"Malek is not being punished," Uthari said coolly. "He has my permission to train the boy."

Tonovan's surprise was far more thorough this time. "Your Majesty?"

"You heard me. Leave now, and stay away from the professor. I've asked before, and if I have to ask again, there will be ramifications."

"Of course, Your Majesty." Though he appeared shaken, Tonovan recovered and bowed deeply to Uthari. "I did not truly intend to visit her, only to nettle Malek."

"Find another hobby, General," Uthari said.

"Yes, Your Majesty." Tonovan bowed again and walked out.

With a flick of power from Uthari, the door closed firmly behind him.

"You are not easy to goad into losing your temper," Uthari said, "but one day, he will succeed, and you will kill him."

It seemed a statement of fact and not a suggestion. Too bad.

"Would you mind?" Malek did not foresee himself killing Tonovan in cold blood, but every time he suggested a duel to the general, he longed more and more for Tonovan to accept the challenge.

"He is right that it would be inconvenient to lose him right now. This is a perilous situation." Uthari gestured for Malek to come closer to the desk and poured him a glass, not from the alcohol decanter but from the water pitcher. He knew Malek's preferences.

"It is," Malek agreed.

"And he is correct that his power makes him invaluable, but perhaps, you'll find some dragon-steel weapons on your excursion, and I could arm other loyal subjects with them, giving me more troops of nearly equal value."

"You believe a dragon-steel weapon could make a lesser man the equal to a wizard?"

Malek was more curious than offended. He'd seen that the dragon-steel axe could kill a magical creature where lesser weapons had failed, but he hadn't had an opportunity to study one thoroughly. It was hard to believe it could be as versatile as a powerful magic user, but then again, the portal could shoot out lightning stronger even than Uthari's bolts. Perhaps the axe that Tezi had recovered also had such an ability, should the wielder know how to call it out.

"One weapon might not be the equal of one wizard, but perhaps ten, in capable hands, would be."

"You wish me to bring back ten battle-axes? I had better take a cart."

Uthari snorted. "Bring back a hundred if you can. I doubt that more will be found lying around as easily as that one, unless you wander into another dragon's lair."

"I hope to avoid that. I was *looking* for a greenhouse."

"How easily those are mistaken for dragon lairs."

"You'd be surprised." Malek took a sip from the glass, less because he was thirsty and more to hide his embarrassment. He'd sensed he was walking into a trap, and he'd done it anyway. He was fortunate that he'd survived the battle and that Jadora had refused to leave him behind.

"If you find even one more dragon-steel weapon, I would be pleased to have it." Uthari drew a lesser-dragon-steel dagger that he carried now and then. Rarely around the castle when he was back home, but Malek wasn't surprised that he'd brought the blade with him on this journey. "If it is twice as valuable as this weapon, I would be impressed." Uthari lay the dagger on the desk between them. "Since you have similar weapons, I'm sure I don't have to tell you that they have unique capabilities."

"No," Malek agreed, though they'd never spoken of this before.

His weapons occasionally gave him flashes of insight through visions and dreams, but he'd worried Uthari might think him foolish if he mentioned such things. Others hadn't spoken to him of having similar experiences, so he'd wondered if he might be thought crazy—or superstitious or daft—if he brought it up.

"You'll take the professor and her son on the mission with you?" Uthari asked.

"Yes. I assumed you would want me to. Her to recognize the plant and perhaps offer insight into languages and translations, and him..." Malek hesitated. He did not truly need Jak for anything, other than that it would be convenient to take him along if he meant to keep training him, and it was possible that someone with cartography skills might be useful in a foreign land. "She would prefer to stay with him, I know. She's said so. But if you would prefer he stay here, I would not object."

"No." Uthari smiled sadly. "*He* is not the one I have reason to object to."

Malek considered the words before responding, puzzled about what they implied, and feeling dense for not immediately grasping it.

"Do your blades ever give you visions?" Uthari rested his hand on his dagger. "Insights of what might happen in the future?"

"Yes."

"I assumed so. Mine does as well."

Malek's heart pounded as he started to catch the gist. If Uthari's blades gave him flashes of insight, of possible future events that might play out, was it possible he'd seen something that upset him? Something related to Malek?

Malek frowned. What could he possibly do in the future that

would bother Uthari? He had no betrayals in mind, nor could he envision any situation that would force that to change. Maybe Uthari had seen him fail and was disappointed because he believed it would happen.

"Earlier," Uthari said, "when I meditated with my dagger by my side, I received two visions. If they are to be believed, you will once again face a dragon."

"In battle?"

"Yes. It was trying to kill you."

"I hope you didn't see my death." Malek smiled, though the thought naturally disturbed him. If he were to die, he would prefer Uthari not warn him of it, unless in the warning, there was some way to ensure the event did not pass.

"I did not. I saw only the battle, next to an ancient pyramid surrounded by trees not dissimilar to the ones here. At first, I thought it *was* here, but upon reflection, I do not believe the foliage had the same coloring."

"I see. I will keep an eye out for dragons."

"Do. I would find it unacceptable if you were to die and leave me with only Tonovan for company." Uthari's smile seemed genuine.

Malek had no reason to believe it otherwise. "That would be tedious."

"Very much so."

"Do you wish to share the second vision?"

Uthari removed his hand from the dagger, sighed, and sat back in his chair. "In the second, you were engaged in passionate kissing with our professor."

Malek blinked. "That seems far less likely than a dragon battle."

"Indeed. I've never known you to be passionate, Malek. With a woman or otherwise." Uthari smiled again, but his eyes seemed bleak, as if this genuinely concerned him.

Malek did not know what to say. He frowned at the desk in frustration. As he'd reluctantly admitted to himself when he'd been hunting for the druid compound with Jadora, he did feel some attraction to her, but he had no plans to kiss her, passionately or otherwise. For him to form a romantic attachment to a woman would not only go against the Zidarr Code and Uthari's wishes, but it would put *her* at risk. If Uthari believed Malek was developing some loyalty to her, he might order her killed. Or, given the professor's importance to his plans, Uthari might order *Malek* killed.

Malek would like to think he was too valuable for that, but Uthari would be within his rights to execute him, per the Zidarr Code.

"Don't look so glum, my friend," Uthari said. "I cannot condemn you for something I only dreamed and that may or may not come to pass."

"I am as puzzled as I am glum, Your Majesty."

"Puzzled by the idea of you with passion?"

"Puzzled because I know your wishes, and I cannot envision a situation in which I would be so overcome by ardor that I would disobey them. I am not a teenager brimming with lust that cannot be contained."

"Then perhaps she will find the kiss disappointing and push you away." A hint of humor replaced the concern in Uthari's eyes.

"Your Majesty—"

Uthari lifted a hand. "I apologize for teasing you. You are everything I ever could have wished from a zidarr, from an apprentice. It is not right of me to tease you for being all that the Code asks. I should not have brought this up."

Malek wished he hadn't. Now he would fear that this event, like the dragon battle, might come to pass if he didn't cleverly find a way to avoid it. Had this been another woman, he might have thought she planned some manipulation, some seduction of him for nefarious purposes, but he could not imagine Jadora in that role.

"She refused to leave me behind to die when she could have," Malek said, reasoning aloud. "Even though it would have benefited her, for she might have escaped to another world. Because of that, I do not believe she would betray me in any other manner."

"Such as by seducing you?" Uthari asked, as if he'd been reading Malek's mind. Or maybe he also had an easier time envisioning a woman trying to seduce Malek than envisioning Malek lost in passion bestirred by his own desires.

It wasn't that Malek didn't *have* desires, but he'd always been able to sublimate them. He remained perennially wary of anything that threatened to lead him astray from his duty. As the Code said, anything that one longed for intensely should be handled as carefully as a viper, for it too could lead one to his death.

"She will not," Malek said. "I have seen her thoughts and know that they are far more likely to be of plants and runes than men. Even if she did make such an attempt, you know I would not allow it."

"So I assume. Perhaps my vision, like the dragon attack, will not come to pass. Though I daresay you would be far more prepared to handle the latter." Uthari smiled, more friendly than teasing this time.

"My tools are more sufficient for that task."

"Yes. Go forth, Malek. You know what I wish you to find."

Malek set down his glass. "I do."

"I thank you for being willing to take such a great risk on my behalf."

"Do you refer to the possibility of a dragon attack? Or seduction?"

Uthari's eyes crinkled. "Both."

4

Jadora stepped out of her tent in the morning, a magelock pistol on her belt, vials of acid and smoke bombs in a pouch, and the pack that Malek had made for her strapped to her back. He'd admitted that its magic allowed it to hold more items than a volume equation implied it should, but it also seemed lighter than it should have, given all the food, medical supplies, and herbal and chemical components she'd wedged into it. On a whim, she'd even disassembled the microscope to tuck inside.

She shouldn't allow herself to feel gratitude toward him—and certainly not affection—but it was the most useful present she'd ever received. And the fact that he'd enhanced it with his own magic to specifically meet her needs... meant something.

"Yes," she muttered to herself. "It means you better never let Uthari read your mind when you're thinking about Malek."

Not that Uthari would care if *Jadora* had feelings for Malek. The problem would be if Malek developed feelings for her. She had no doubt Malek would always put Uthari above her, but he wasn't as aloof as he'd originally been, which might mean... something.

"Such as that *he* better never let Uthari read his mind either," she grumbled.

As Jadora was about to head to the portal, Tezi jogged up to her. A pack bounced on her back, a canteen hung from her shoulder, and she carried a rifle and the big battle-axe, each of the two heads of the weapon larger than her own.

"Professor." Tezi thrust the battle-axe toward her, hilt-first, fortunately. "I need you to look at something."

"Unless it's a plant, an element, or runes, you're outside of my area of expertise."

"It *is* a rune." Tezi juggled her belongings to point the bottom of the four-foot haft toward her. "I think. At first, I thought they were just scratches, but when Sorath saw this, he thought it might be one of the languages that's on the portal. You can barely see it unless it's in direct sunlight."

"Interesting." Jadora took the weapon, surprised at how light it was, and walked into a sunny spot. She squinted at the weapon's butt, the haft made from the same blue-black dragon steel as the heads. "Huh. It's the chicken-scratch language."

"Ma'am?"

"That's how I've been thinking of it." Jadora trotted to the portal, where Malek, Captain Rivlen, Sergeant Tinder, Dr. Fret, and Jak were already waiting for them, several skyboards in their arms. Jadora wondered who would be in charge of the *Star Flyer* while Rivlen went on this journey with them.

Jak stood next to Malek, the hatchling in a sling across his chest. He was waving his hat in the air, as if explaining something to Malek—or practicing some magic?—and it occurred to Jadora that theirs was another relationship that might disturb Uthari. Would the king object if Jak grew attached to Malek but not to *him*? The mages had to consider someone with magic more of a threat than someone without. Even if Malek grew to like Jadora, it wasn't as if she could ever threaten Uthari. He could blink at her and kill her with a thought.

"Are you ready?" Malek looked at the axe in her hands and arched his eyebrows.

"One moment." Jadora pushed thoughts of death-by-king from her mind—a part of her was thankful they were leaving the world and all of these mages again—and squinted at the runes and constellations engraved on the inside of the portal. "There it is. It's not the same symbol—or word—but that does look like the same language."

Since she was looking upward, movement atop the cliff where the waterfall tumbled over the edge caught her eye. A huge spotted jaguar crouched up there, looking down on the portal and the camp.

She swore and nearly dropped the axe.

Malek followed her gaze and spotted the great golden-eyed cat. "It won't attack with so many people around."

"No, I would assume not. It just startled me." Jadora shifted her focus back to the rune.

"That's Toddles," Tinder said. "He was here this morning too. We named him."

"The jaguar?" Malek said.

"Yes. He seems to find us fascinating."

Malek gazed up at the cat again, considering it for a longer moment.

"I don't sense anything magical about it," Jak said, then looked to Malek and Rivlen for confirmation.

"It's just a cat." Rivlen scoffed. "Toddles."

As Malek watched it, the jaguar spun away and disappeared into the brush. "I also did not sense magic from it, but it's possible a druid could be watching us through the eyes of the animals here."

"Is that bad?" Dr. Fret glanced at Tinder. "That sounds bad. I heard the druids object to the portal."

"They do," Rivlen said. "They attacked us when we were bringing it here."

"Does that mean Thorn Company could be in trouble while we're gone?" Fret asked.

"Thorn Company was *already* in trouble," Tinder grumbled.

"It's unlikely the druids will attack with so many mages and zidarr here," Malek said, "but I will inform King Uthari of the possibility that our camp is being watched."

Jadora pulled one of her new notebooks out of her backpack and made a copy of the rune before handing the axe back to Tezi.

"Do you know what it means?" she asked.

"No idea," Jadora said. "That language isn't from our world, and as far as I know, there are no books or resources covering the languages of other worlds. Until I saw those bones around the dragon's lair, I would have assumed that humans only lived here on Torvil, but... whatever we find in our explorations could alter everything we know about our humanity's past."

"Is that rune in the druid book?" Malek pointed at the chicken-scratch symbol on the portal.

"Yes." Jadora grimaced.

"As a header for one of the stories you've translated?"

"Yes. According to the tale, dragons came through from that world, dragons that preyed upon people and ravaged a druid settlement."

"If dragons came from there, the Jitaruvak might be there," Malek said. "And if that axe also came from that world, there might be more dragon-steel weapons there."

"It sounds like there are more dragons who want to eat us there," Tinder said. "How about we visit a different world? One full of bunnies and coconuts."

"Coconuts?" Tezi asked her.

"Fried coconut cakes are delicious. My mother made them when I was growing up."

"Unless you can think of a reason not to go," Malek said, looking at Jadora and ignoring the mercenaries, "I believe that should be our next destination to investigate."

Fret lifted a finger. "*I* can think of a reason not to go. The dragons that like to eat people."

"We'll do our best to avoid dragons this time," Malek said, though he glanced at Jak's hatchling, who was napping in his sling with his tail hanging over the side. "Let's hope having a young one along doesn't draw them."

"I think the possibility of fresh *meat* is what draws them," Tinder said.

Malek looked at her. He didn't scowl, but Jadora had the sense that he doubted she was worth bringing along.

Fret elbowed Tinder and whispered something.

"I think the possibility of fresh meat is what draws them, *my lord*," Tinder said, though Jadora had never seen Malek insist on honorifics.

Malek said nothing, only stepping toward the portal as he drew the medallion from his pocket. Uthari must have given it to him for the journey.

Jak scowled, also noticing it.

Days earlier, Uthari had taken it from him, an open theft. Jadora didn't know where her husband had originally found it, but he had, and after Jak had carried it in his hat's headband for five years, it didn't seem right for someone else to have it.

Once Malek inserted it in the matching hole on the portal, he gazed into the center. He must have applied some magic, for the chicken-scratch rune lit up, glowing blue in the morning sun. A moment later, blackness appeared in the center of the portal, with pinpricks of light simulating stars. They swirled about before arranging themselves in the constellation next to the chicken-scratch symbol, a handful of stars in an arrangement reminiscent of a pudgy dog.

Jadora eyed the portal nervously, hoping no hungry dragons would be waiting for them when they stepped out on the other side. Her last experience hadn't given her hope that further explorations would go well.

"You are still under my protection," Malek said quietly, reading her thoughts, or maybe only the worried expression on her face.

"I appreciate that." Jadora would have felt more bolstered by his words if she didn't know first-hand how difficult dragons were to kill.

"I will go through first, and you may wait so that I have time to deal with any threats before you arrive." Malek removed the medallion and returned it to his pocket, one he could button securely. "But do not wait long. Once the key is removed, the portal will close within minutes."

"*I* will not cower back here while you risk yourself, my lord." Rivlen stepped up beside him, her hands resting on her weapons and a stern no-nonsense expression on her elegant face.

"I'll go first too." Jak hopped up to Malek's other side. Perhaps wakened by the magic, the hatchling climbed out of his sling to perch on Jak's shoulder. "Then I'll have more time for mapping," Jak added.

"I have no problem cowering," Tinder muttered. "I don't even know why we're going along."

Malek looked toward the cliff where the jaguar had been. It hadn't returned. Hopefully, that was a good omen.

He strode through with Jak and Rivlen at his sides.

"I'm sorry, Sergeant Tinder," Jadora said. "I requested that Tezi come, in the hope that fewer people would be after her axe if she wasn't back here in camp, and Dr. Fret because of her medical expertise, and you…"

"Because of my wit?"

"Your expertise with explosives. I thought it might be useful."

"Of *course* it's useful." Tinder wrinkled her nose. "But next time, I can send a diagram along on how to make grenades, maybe a box of some of my custom blends."

"You'd stay here while I went without you?" Fret asked.

"No. But you could also send a diagram along. About how to sew up mangled intestines and such."

"There are entire books that cover surgery."

"Jadora likes books." Tinder pointed at her. "She's a scholar."

"I'm less fond of mangled intestines," Jadora murmured, then headed for the portal, afraid to wait too long. Without the key, they couldn't reactivate it.

Hoping the others would follow, and wouldn't resent her for choosing them, Jadora stepped through the portal.

On the deck of the *King's Courage,* Yidar faced off against three opponents, capable sword fighters from among the crew, and they gave him a decent workout. It kept his reflexes and muscles honed and his mind off the portal below. The portal that Malek had just led another team through so that he could explore, find resources for Uthari, and gain honor for himself.

Yidar's mouth twisted. Why Malek alone was being sent on these missions, he didn't know, but Uthari should have chosen him. Or at least sent him along. If there were dragons to battle, Yidar could be invaluable.

But, as he'd decided earlier, he would have to make his own fate instead of waiting to be chosen by a king who couldn't see his true worth.

Distracted by his thoughts, Yidar almost missed a practice blade stabbing toward his groin. Growling, he deflected the blow, then unleashed his sword and dagger on his foe, driving the man back until he tripped over his own feet and pitched to the deck.

The two other men tried to flank Yidar, but he sprang ten feet, eluding their slashes, and spun in the air to come down facing them. He was on the verge of leaping in to take them down when a young lieutenant ran up to the sparring match. He came to attention, waiting to be acknowledged. It was the lieutenant who worked in navigation and answered the dome-jir when communications came in.

Normally, Yidar would have made him continue waiting, but he wondered if Uthari had sent a message. Maybe he'd had second thoughts about not using Yidar to his fullest and wanted him to lead a team through the portal.

As he waved for his practice partners to pause and faced the lieutenant, Yidar realized that couldn't have happened. As far as he had heard, there was only one known key to operate the portal, and the group had taken it with them when they left. The week before, Yidar had been speculating that more keys might have survived the centuries, and that they might be on this continent somewhere, but until he could find one, he couldn't travel to other worlds.

None of the crews that had arrived on mageships representing other kingdoms could either. Something that had caused a lot of dissent. None of those fleet leaders had contacted Yidar, but he'd seen numerous representatives fly over to Uthari's *Serene Waters* to argue that their people should be allowed on future exploration teams.

"What is it, Lieutenant?" Yidar asked.

"I have received a message, my lord." The man lowered his voice. "It contains sensitive material. I believe I should relay it to you in private."

Yidar attempted to skim the lieutenant's thoughts, but he had his guard up and gave away nothing. "Very well."

He led the officer to his cabin and closed the door. Fully expecting this to be a missive from Uthari, he didn't think anything of the request until they were alone. The lieutenant licked his lips and wiped sweat from his brow.

In this tropical heat, sweat wasn't uncommon—Yidar grabbed a towel to wipe his own brow—but if the lieutenant had been sitting in navigation, it seemed strange. Was he nervous for some reason?

"Speak," Yidar commanded, adding a hint of compulsion.

The young lieutenant might have been able to hide his thoughts, but he didn't have the power and experience to resist a zidarr.

"Yes, my lord," he blurted. "It was from a druid."

"Oh?"

Not long ago, Yidar had been contemplating contacting the druids. They'd made it clear when they attacked the *Star Flyer* that they wanted the portal—or at least didn't want it to be set up and activated in their land. Given that a deadly creature had emerged from it the first night, their motivations were understandable. Since then, nothing as bad as that giant worm had arrived, but a couple of lesser magical creatures had flown out a couple of days earlier. The mages guarding the portal had worked together to slay them before it could be determined if they were threats, but they'd had sharp claws and beaks, so it seemed likely.

Since Yidar cared more about carving out a kingdom in this world for himself than exploring others, he would be willing to help the druids with their goal—if they would be willing to help *him*. The druids weren't aligned with any kings or zidarr. Indeed, they'd been invaded often enough in the past that they *hated* the magic users in the rest of the world. If Yidar could establish an alliance with them, they could be the powerful allies he needed to fulfill his ambitions. There would be no need to travel through the portal into the unknown, seeking dragons or whatever else Uthari and Malek hoped to find out there.

"Yes, my lord. It didn't come over the dome-jir. Last night, when I was on duty alone in navigation, a druid reached out to me telepathically from the jungle. I sensed that she was by the waterfall." The lieutenant pointed toward the top of the cliff where the river tumbled into the pool below. "She was with a jaguar. Some of the mercenaries have mentioned seeing it previously, and there's been speculation that it's a druid's animal companion or is otherwise controlled by a druid."

"What did she say?" Yidar didn't care about the druid's pet, only the druid. "And why did she pick *you* to speak with?"

How strange that a druid would choose such an insignificant mage to reach out to.

"I believe because I was one of the few officers awake, my lord. And stationed in navigation, so perhaps privy to important information on the ship's movements." The lieutenant licked his lips again. "That's what she wanted, my lord. Information."

"She tried to read your mind?"

"At first, I believe so. I sensed a tickle, as if someone powerful was attempting to scrape through my thoughts." The lieutenant pointed to the side of his head. "But just because I'm young doesn't mean that I'm weak." He lifted his chin. "She got nothing from me, my lord."

"Until she bribed you?"

"Yes. I mean, *no*." His eyes flew open at his mistake. "She *tried*, my lord. She offered to pay me a large sum of money in the local currency or give me magical baubles or gems. She seemed open to a number of things. She even implied that she might offer a sexual encounter." A hint of intrigue and interest entered his eyes as he whispered this last. Excited by the idea of a green-haired woman, was he? "Whatever she offered wouldn't have mattered. I would never betray the king, my captain, or you, my lord."

Yidar almost laughed since *he* was thinking of betraying the king. It also amused him that it had taken this lieutenant eight hours to report this bribe. Had he truly been affronted by it, wouldn't he have knocked on Yidar's door in the middle of the night to report the conversation? When the druid was still close and Yidar and others might have hunted her down?

"Of course not," Yidar said. "You are a loyal officer of the fleet and sworn to serve the king."

"Yes." The lieutenant exhaled audible relief at being believed. "I played along for a while, curious what she would tell me, and what I could pass along to you. She wants someone to report to her on the goings on here. She wanted to know who went through the portal, where they went, and also to know if all of these ships would remain here indefinitely. That last made me wonder if the druids are considering attacking us, my lord. That would, of course, be suicidal. I don't care how many druids are in this forsaken jungle. They'd be no match for so many mages."

Yidar was less certain about that. On the journey to this pool, what might have been only a handful of druids had given the *Star Flyer* a hard time. If that was a sign of how strong druids had grown in the centuries since a kingdom fleet last attempted to invade Zewnath, they could indeed pose a threat. Especially if there were hundreds of them roaming around in the jungle.

He smiled and salivated at the thought of gaining that many allies.

The lieutenant, perhaps uncertain how to read his expression, kept talking. "As I said, my lord, I played along and led her to believe I might be tempted. I gave her a couple of pieces of information that are widely known and would not threaten our security in any way. I said that Lord Malek had gone out to seek dragons."

Yidar didn't think dragons were what Uthari sought and snorted at the idea of this *widely known* information being shared.

False information. The druids should have sought out a more connected informant.

"Did she give you anything for this information?" Yidar thought about pointing out that the lieutenant shouldn't have spoken to the druid at all. He should have reported the communication immediately and nothing else. Yidar had already figured out that the lieutenant had been tempted by the druid, perhaps contemplating all day if he could get away with being a spy for them. Likely, he was only reporting now because he'd decided he would be caught and get in trouble if he went forward with it.

"Nothing yet, my lord, except a way to communicate directly with her whenever I wish." He dug an oval green stone out of his pocket. It emanated faint magic, but it was so slight that Yidar hadn't thought anything of it. Many of the crew had magical tools and jewelry designed to assist them in battle. "Before she left, she floated this over to me. She said to communicate with her using it whenever I have more information and that she would meet me in the jungle and reward me for passing it along to her."

Yidar took the device from him. "You were right to give this to me. I will tell Uthari and see what he wants to do. Likely, he will send *me* to meet with this druid, to track her down and slay her for her presumptions."

Disappointment flashed in the lieutenant's eyes. No doubt, he'd been envisioning himself meeting the exotic woman for a tryst in the jungle. But he covered up his feelings and nodded.

"Yes, my lord. We must ensure that the druids are not a threat to the fleet or the kingdom."

"Exactly so." Yidar waved him toward the door. "Dismissed."

The lieutenant hesitated, as if he'd expected some reward from Yidar for belatedly reporting what he should have immediately reported. Yidar shooed the man out.

Once he was alone, he regarded the small communications device. With his magic, he easily discerned how it worked, and when he closed his eyes and envisioned a matching oval in the jungle, he sensed it three or four miles away. He couldn't sense the druid owner, but he was sure she was there. Perhaps *many* druids were there. The potential allies Yidar wanted.

He smiled. Tonight, when the crew—and Uthari—slept, Yidar would communicate with the druid woman and find out if she was someone he could work with, someone who could be lured into helping him achieve his goals.

5

Warm sunlight bathed Captain Rivlen's face as she, Malek, and Jak emerged from the disorienting swirl of darkness and starlight, but a flash of blue light startled her. The light radiated intense magic as it encompassed her, buzzing against her skin, and she drew her sword as her feet settled onto a stone-block road. Even as she lowered into a crouch and raised a magical barrier for protection, the blue light and buzzing sensation disappeared.

Rivlen tossed aside the skyboards she'd been given to carry through the portal and peered warily at their surroundings. They were atop one of many rolling hills that stretched toward a coastline and a brilliant blue ocean. Waist-high, blue-green grass rose to either side of the road, swaying in a warm briny breeze. A mile away, another road paralleled the sea, leading to a distant city. The buildings appeared to be made from a mixture of red brick and pale gray cement. Archways, columns, and flat roofs prevailed, with a few larger and taller structures among one- and two-story residential compounds.

She didn't see any people—would there be humans here, or had some other intelligent beings built those buildings?—though a boxy armored carriage trundled along the coastal road, heading toward the city. Had it also come out of the portal?

Jak cursed in alarm, fear edging his voice.

Rivlen spun, expecting an enemy attack from behind. The portal rose up in the middle of the road, identical to the artifact back in Torvil. The starry field inside it showed the Dragon's Tail constellation, the magical passageway remaining open. Rivlen assumed Jadora and the mercenaries would arrive momentarily.

Malek crouched with his weapons ready, his stance similar to Rivlen's. He'd been scanning their surroundings, but he also turned toward Jak, who knelt in the road, cradling his hatchling in his hands.

When they had walked through the portal, it had ridden alertly on his shoulder, peeking and squawking like a parrot on its human perch. Now, it writhed on its back, as if in pain, taloned feet twitching.

"Shikari," Jak whispered. "What *was* that?"

He glanced from the portal to his hatchling and back.

"What happened?" Rivlen asked.

"A beam struck us." Malek squinted, not at the hatchling but at the portal, at a boxy blue-black object attached to the side of it.

Rivlen had been wrong. The portal itself might appear identical to the one they'd left behind, but that attachment was not on the other artifact.

"It didn't hurt me," Jak said, "but when it struck Shikari, he squawked and then wilted."

The hatchling's eyes were slitted, and it made pitiful noises, as if it were dying.

"Stand guard," Malek told Rivlen and stepped toward the box.

"Wait." Jak lifted a hand toward him. "Can you check him? I think he needs healing, and you're good at that. I know you are." Jak turned pleading eyes toward Malek.

It wasn't an expression Rivlen had seen on Jak before—he

trended toward snarky, mouthy, and occasionally, when he was concentrating on learning magic, determined and earnest. Something about his face now made her wish *she* had a knack for healing so she could help him, but since she'd been a little girl, she'd focused solely on learning to use her magic for combat. *That* was how one rose to power and gained prestige in the mage world. Healers, frequently women, were valued but not revered. Not looked up to.

Malek hesitated, glancing at the attachment again, but knelt beside Jak and rested a hand on the moaning hatchling. "If it was a magical attack, I may lack the ability to heal him."

Despite the words, Malek closed his eyes to examine the little dragon with his senses.

Rivlen, appreciating that he trusted her to watch their backs, kept her sword aloft as she finished her scan of the area. That trust was small solace, given that she didn't want to be here and hadn't been pleased when Uthari told her she was going.

Her duty, as newly appointed captain of the *Star Flyer*, was to oversee the ship, not walk away and leave her lieutenant in command. If Uthari's fleet had been alone in the jungle, leaving might not have felt so egregious, but enemy ships lurked all around, the tension palpable in the air as their crews glared at each other over the treetops. At any moment, that tension might snap and turn into a battle.

Further, being away from the *Star Flyer* meant leaving the officers and crew to plot and scheme and consider how they might rise through the ranks by getting rid of her. On her old ship, Rivlen had eventually won the respect of the crew, of those who'd resented having such a young first officer in charge of them, but that had taken two years and many battles. She'd had to prove herself over and over. There hadn't yet been time for that on the *Star Flyer*, and as the crew had already demonstrated, they resented her and would challenge her every chance they got.

All she could hope was that this journey would be worth it and that it would be an opportunity for her to prove her value. She didn't know exactly what Uthari hoped for their group to achieve, but Malek had mentioned a plant and also that Uthari desired dragon-steel weapons.

Rivlen wouldn't mind one of those. She had faith in her growing magical power and that she would one day be a match for any wizard, but such a magnificent tool would make her even more formidable. Like many others, she'd watched puny young Tezi with envy as she wandered around their camp with a dragon-steel battle-axe. Rivlen was incredulous that Uthari or some other powerful mage hadn't yet taken it from her.

Rivlen might have taken it herself if she hadn't watched Malek use it to kill the giant worm creature and then hand it back to Tezi. Though Malek hadn't spoken a word, it had seemed as if he was saying he approved of her having the weapon. That was likely the main reason others hadn't tried to take it. They worried that Malek would object.

"He's getting weaker," Jak whispered.

"All I can tell so far," Malek said, his eyes still closed, his hand resting on the hatchling's torso, "is that it *was* a magical attack and that he's deteriorating on the cellular level."

"Like his cells are dying? Can you reverse it?"

"I don't think that's within my power. It is happening throughout his body. Treating him would be far different from what I usually do—enhancing a patient's immune system to speed up the healing of a wound."

Jak lurched to his feet and stalked around with his fists clenched. His frustration emanated from him, frustration and magical power.

Rivlen hadn't noticed that from him before, though perhaps it was normal, since he was now aware of and developing his power. One day, he might radiate it in the way Tonovan or even Malek did, should Jak become that strong. Based on what she'd seen so far, he might.

The starry energy field of the portal stirred, and Jadora and the three mercenaries strode out.

"Mother," Jak blurted and hugged Jadora.

"What happened?" Jadora peered around at the grassy hills, the sea, and lush blue-green mountains rising in the distance behind the portal. That seemed to be the normal color for the vegetation here. Some spots were a solider blue than others, but few were purely green.

"Shikari might be dying." Jak stepped back, rubbed moisture from his eyes, and focused on the attachment on the portal for the first time. "Is that where it came from? The blue beam?"

"Uh?" Jadora also focused on it.

Malek was the one to answer. "Yes. Whatever it is, it's made from dragon steel, so we must assume it has great power. Be careful if you examine it."

"Maybe I can ask the portal what it is." Jak bit his lip, then strode toward it.

He didn't touch the attached device, but he set a hand on the portal underneath it, on the head of one of the four linked dragons that made up the circular framework.

As the mercenaries spread out around the area, Tezi holding her axe and Tinder with a rifle, Jadora looked toward Rivlen. "You were attacked when you came through?"

Rivlen assumed she'd asked her because Malek and Jak appeared busy, and she was merely standing there, but she took her assigned duty of watching their backs seriously and continued to scan the area, answering only with a terse, "Yes."

A bird screeched high above, something akin to a falcon, though its green and yellow markings were unfamiliar. Insects buzzed in the grass, just audible over the roar of the ocean, and here and there, they bounced above the blades, like crickets, though Rivlen spotted fluttering butterfly-like wings on them. The deep-blue sea was the only thing that looked exactly like the sea back home. The sun in the sky was also similar, but the light had an orangish tint to it.

Malek knelt back from the hatchling. The little dragon's limbs were only twitching faintly now, and it looked like it was dying.

Rivlen had met the hatchling less than an hour ago and felt no attachment to it, but it would be a shame if it died. Had Jak been able to raise it into an adult dragon, or even a large juvenile, he might have gained an ally with the power to help him against enemies. Enemies such as Tonovan.

"I'll take a look." Jadora knelt beside Malek and the hatchling.

"I do not believe any herbal or chemical compound will help," Malek said.

Jadora gently stroked the hatchling's exposed belly. "I admit I'm not even certain how to measure his heartbeat, and I don't know what's normal for a dragon."

"The portal is responding to me," Jak said in a distracted tone. His eyes were closed, his hand still pressed to the frame. "It didn't do anything, but the device attached to it did. It's for... defending this world. It attacks dangerous creatures that come through the portal."

"Such as four-day-old baby dragons?" Sergeant Tinder asked. "Truly terrifying."

Jak frowned, still communicating with the portal. "I'm trying to figure out if there's any way it can help... and to convince it that we're *worth* helping."

Rivlen could sense him doing so, though his telepathy had improved and he didn't shout his words anymore. If he was speaking in his mind, he targeted the portal alone, though perhaps he used imagery with it. Rivlen couldn't imagine that the ancient artifact understood Dhoran or Wizards' Common. The idea that it understood anything at all, and was sentient—if not sapient—was amazing.

"The hatchling wasn't injured, was it?" the mercenary doctor asked. "I have a medical kit along."

"No." Malek shook his head, rested a hand on Jadora's shoulder briefly, and rose to join Jak.

That familiarity surprised Rivlen, and she couldn't keep from frowning in disapproval. Since they'd captured Jak and Jadora, Malek had insisted on treating them as guests rather than prisoners. Rivlen understood that Malek and Uthari had an interest in Jak, because of his magical abilities and because he might be trained and turned into an ally—after all, she'd had that same thought—but why show such... camaraderie to an archaeologist? Or herbalist. Whatever Jadora was. Rivlen didn't quite know.

Malek glanced at Rivlen as he walked past, and she schooled her face in a neutral expression and went back to keeping an eye on their surroundings. How Malek treated his prisoners was of no concern to her, and enemies might grow aware of their arrival at any time and send a party to check on them—or attack them.

Malek joined Jak to stare intently at the attachment.

"The portal accepts that it was a mistake," Jak said, relief in his voice. "It doesn't believe Shikari is a *dangerous* dragon."

"No kidding," Tinder said.

"But the portal wasn't responsible for the attack." Jak's shoulders drooped. "I think it's telling me that it can't do anything. But maybe... wait."

"I don't think he has much longer," Jadora whispered.

The hatchling wasn't moving.

Jak grimaced, tears leaking from his closed eyes, and his face twisted with concentration. He shifted his hand from the portal to the attached device.

"Jak," Malek warned, reaching up.

Rivlen frowned, half expecting the device to hurl Jak twenty feet, perhaps while spitting lightning bolts.

"*This* did it," Jak said. "*This* can undo it."

Malek paused short of grabbing Jak's hand to pull it back. The device hadn't reacted to his touch.

No sooner had Rivlen had the thought than a wide blue beam shot out of it. Malek grabbed Jak and pulled him back, but it was targeting the hatchling. Since Jadora was next to the creature, it also bathed her in blue light.

Malek released Jak and sprang to her side, pulling her out of the beam and into the grass.

"I don't think it's dangerous," Jak said. "Not this time."

"You don't *think*?" Malek asked, his hands on Jadora's shoulders as he stood protectively close.

Rivlen gaped, a flash of insight coming to her. Malek didn't treat Jadora like a prisoner because he *liked* her.

Romantically? The thought was so preposterous that Rivlen scoffed and almost dismissed it outright. The notion of someone as powerful as Malek developing feelings for a sense-dead plebeian was ridiculous. Still, he held Jadora's shoulders far longer than necessary, if his only interest was to pull her out of danger. Not until the blue beam disappeared did he let her go and step away.

"Thank you." Jadora smiled at him.

Rivlen, reminded that she'd been assigned guard duty, shook her head and went back to watching their surroundings.

"Did it heal Shikari?" Jak ran back to the hatchling and knelt on the road, touching the blue scaly torso. "Are you any better, little fellow?"

The hatchling was still breathing but didn't respond.

One of the butterfly-winged crickets hopping around in the grass landed on the road a few feet from them. Jak squinted at it, summoned a gust of wind, and blew it toward him. He caught it in his hand and held it by the wings above the hatchling's snout.

Rivlen nodded, pleased that Jak was working on developing his skills. That wasn't anything she'd taught him. Had Malek? Or was he figuring out more versatility on his own?

"Exotic foreign bug delivery," Jak whispered, swinging it back and forth from its wings. "You just have to wake up and chomp it down."

"This isn't how I envisioned adventuring to other worlds going," Tinder said.

"I'm finding this *much* better than our last trip," the doctor said. "The sun is warm, there aren't any glaciers, and no giant bats or dragons are trying to kill us."

"Give it time. The bats took a while to show up on the last world. And we didn't find the killer dragon until the end."

The hatchling's tail swished across the stone blocks, and its yellow eyes opened. Its tongue darted out, plucked the insect from Jak's grasp, and pulled it into its mouth.

"He's alive." Jak grinned brightly at all of them.

"Fascinating," Malek murmured, though he was looking at the device attached to the portal instead of the hatchling. He placed his hand on it, first lightly, waiting to see if it would reject him, and then more firmly. "How is this attached?" he murmured, peering closer.

"I don't think we can take it with us," Jadora said.

"If it does what I think, it could solve one of our larger problems." Malek sounded wistful.

Jadora joined him. "You think it attacks all dragons that try to fly out of it and into this world? All *dangerous* dragons?"

"Perhaps all dangerous magical predators," Malek said.

"I don't know about that, but it showed me the beam attacking some of the brown-and-gray mottled dragons." Jak waded into the grass, capturing more insects for his hatchling. "The portal did, I mean. The other device didn't communicate with me in any way. I think it might have been the portal relaying my message to it that resulted in the healing magic. It realized it had made a mistake and gotten a *good* dragon."

"Don't you think it's a little early to assume that your hatchling is good?" Malek asked. "He ate your bootlaces, destroyed your pillow, and chewed on Tonovan's leg."

"That last thing is a *definite* sign of goodness," Jak said. "Or at least good taste. Besides, his scales are the color of the fun, frolicking dragons from the visions our portal shared with me."

"Fun, frolicking dragons are automatically *good*?"

"Sure," Jak said. "Same with fun, frolicking mages. And the converse is also true. I'm positive Tonovan never frolics."

Rivlen snorted. She had no doubt. But she didn't know many *good* mages who frolicked either. Training was serious. If one wanted to achieve one's goals—and avoid being targeted and destroyed by one's enemies—one had to be serious.

"Do you ever frolic, Malek?" Jadora asked.

"Not with anybody watching. Will you give me your opinion on this seam?" Malek pointed to where the device attached to the portal. "It looks like it was permanently soldered, or some magical equivalent, to the original artifact. That alone wouldn't be remarkable, but this all appears to be dragon steel, which humans—at least humans on *our* world—do not know how to melt and manipulate."

"Are you truly thinking of removing it?" Jadora stepped up to his shoulder to look.

Malek hesitated. "I know Uthari would value this, especially if we could affix it to our portal and keep any killer dragons or giant worms from coming through, but no. We cannot steal it from this world. Presumably, it is rightfully theirs, and they also have a need for it."

Jadora nodded. "Good."

Rivlen raised her eyebrows. She wasn't sure she would make that same decision. If Uthari would value the object, he would also value and reward those who brought it to him. Even though she did not approve of thievery or acting without honor, were she alone, she might have been tempted to take it, for the good of their people. If someone here had made it, they might be able to make a replacement.

"That *does* look like dragon steel," Jadora murmured. "You're right. This is fascinating."

"Maybe we could bring someone with magical engineering expertise—the prisoner Tonovan captured last night, perhaps—to study it and replicate it, but he would first have to learn how to work dragon steel." Malek lowered his hand. "As far as I can determine, the entire device is made solely from it."

"It's possible it's an artifact as ancient as the portals and that a dragon made it long ago," Jadora said. "We have difficulty accurately dating dragon steel since it doesn't rust or corrode or show any signs of wear like other metals."

"Would a dragon have affixed it long ago to the portal?"

Jadora hesitated. "Possibly."

"To protect this world?"

"Possibly."

"Then why this world and not ours?" Malek asked.

Jadora shook her head and stepped back to consider the portal. "I don't know."

Malek considered it a moment longer, then turned his attention to getting ready to travel, picking up one of the skyboards they'd brought along. Like Rivlen, he'd cast his aside as soon as that blue light had shown up.

He frowned down at the boards, then nudged one with his foot.

"Problem?" Jadora asked.

"The skyboards are dead," Malek said.

Rivlen checked the ones she'd carried through the portal and realized he was right. They'd been fully charged before they left, but now, all four were devoid of the magical energy that powered them.

"Maybe that device zapped them along with the hatchling," she said.

"It must have." Malek shook his head and put them in the grass behind the portal. There was no point in carrying them if they had no power.

The group would have to walk. At least the city wasn't far away.

Grass crunched as Jak lunged to catch another cricket that he'd batted in his direction with his magic. He was using far more power than necessary to capture the insects.

Rivlen stepped into the grass, intending to give him a few tips. The sooner Jak improved his power as a mage, the sooner he could stand with her against Tonovan, an idea that she continued to find appealing.

As a mature woman, Rivlen probably shouldn't appreciate that Jak made jokes about Tonovan, but she agreed with his assessment. The general did *not* frolic. And she doubted he ever had fun unless it was at someone else's expense.

"Uh oh," Jadora whispered, her gaze locked to the portal.

Rivlen paused, eyeing it warily, expecting another blue beam to shoot out.

"Are you sure?" Malek must have read her mind and been responding to her thoughts.

He joined her in front of the portal, gazing at the symbols around the inside of it.

"Several of them are... blank." Jadora pointed at different spots.

Rivlen was too far away to see what they were looking at, but she remembered Malek magically pressing what had been one of several symbols on the inside of their portal to activate its magic.

"What is it, Mother?" Jak knelt by the hatchling, feeding it more crickets. The creature was animated now, sitting on its haunches and peering toward the grasses, head cocking when insects chirped.

Jadora looked gravely back at Jak. "Some of the symbols—some of the *destinations*—have been rubbed out somehow."

"Rubbed out? They were engraved in the dragon steel, at least on our portal."

"Yes, and on this one too. You can tell that they were once there, but now, they're gone."

"The Dragon's Tail constellation is missing," Malek said, "and the matching symbol."

"What does that mean?" Rivlen asked, though she feared she had gotten the gist.

"That we can't go home," Jadora said.

6

The hatchling kept climbing out of his sling and onto Jak's shoulder.

"You're supposed to be resting," he told his charge. "You were almost dead a few minutes ago."

Shikari cheeped and chewed on the brim of his hat. Jak removed it to protect it, and Shikari shifted to nibbling on his hair.

"This isn't how I imagined fatherhood," Jak muttered.

Their group was walking down the coastal road toward the city, the sea roaring beyond the blue-green grass. Seagulls—or this world's equivalent—shrieked as they wheeled and dove over the waves.

"Aren't you more like a pet owner than a father?" Rivlen walked beside him, giving him tips on catching insects with magic while drawing upon a minimal amount of power. Such a task, as she'd informed him, should not leave him weary and with sweat dripping from his brow.

She hadn't believed his excuse that the sweat simply indicated he was hot from the sun. The air and temperature were pleasant here, cooler than the jungle they'd left.

"No," Jak said. "He's definitely not a pet. When he grows up, he'll be as smart as we are. Probably smarter. *We* don't know how to build portals."

"Won't you have to take him to his people, so they can raise and educate him, before he turns into a dragon genius?"

"Probably. I hope we come across some good dragons on this journey so I can ask them about him. About *everything*." Jak heard the longing in his voice and tried to squelch it. Finding dragons—and befriending and riding one—might have been a childhood dream for him, but Rivlen would likely find the whole idea silly.

"Maybe they can tell you why hatchlings like the taste of your hair."

Jak tugged a lock out of Shikari's mouth and adjusted him so that he faced forward instead of toward Jak's head—and ear. He'd already felt the nip of sharp dragon fangs on one of his lobes, and the wide brim of his hat was in constant danger.

"He eats crickets, flies, and worms. My hair might be a delicious treat after such dubious fare."

"We should still be able to get back home," Mother said, her voice floating back to them.

She and Malek were walking ahead of Jak and Rivlen, with Tezi, Tinder, and Fret taking up the rear.

"We can travel to a portal on another world and from there back to ours. Assuming portals on other worlds don't also have our symbol rubbed out." Mother shook her head. "I'd dearly like to know how that was done, how someone worked the dragon steel. It's *possible* that dragons did it, but I would hypothesize that it was done later, by someone who wanted to add further protection for those who live on this world. Maybe the same person or being who installed that device did it."

"The symbol for the ice world we visited was also rubbed out," Malek said.

"I noticed. Several others that were rubbed out were written about in the druid tome, indicating worlds that deadly creatures came from. The natives here—or someone looking out for them—destroyed the possibility of travel to those places. But since we traveled *from* one of the rubbed-out worlds, that means eliminating the symbols only halts the possibility of people going to them. It doesn't stop arrivals. That must be why the device was added."

"It's interesting," Jak said, "that they felt the need to so permanently mark the portal to deter travelers leaving from this world. You'd think they could have just put up a sign. Don't go there, there, or there, and *definitely* don't go there. Dragons are waiting to eat you."

"A sign could be removed or destroyed," Mother said. "This was a more permanent solution. They must have felt they needed it."

"They must have more than one key here." Jak rescued another tuft of hair from the hatchling. That earned him an ear licking. He gently plucked his charge off his shoulder again and stuck him back in his sling. "Maybe *many* more. Otherwise, whoever had it would simply keep it to control who could leave this world."

"That's very possible," Mother said. "There could be many keys out there. Maybe Torvil also had many once, and they were all lost over the millennia."

"What happens," Tezi asked, "if we go to another world and the symbol that would let us go home is destroyed there too?"

"I doubt it's been destroyed on every portal," Mother said. "This is likely just how this world has chosen to deal with the problem of monsters."

"There aren't monsters native to our world," Malek pointed out. "None like the giant worm or dragon that tried to kill us."

"True," Mother said. "Maybe they rubbed out our symbol because our druids took down the portal, moved it away from where it could function, and buried it. The people here might have done it to make sure nobody tried to use it. I... don't know what happens when the portal on the other end isn't available. I had assumed you wouldn't be able to make a connection, but I'm not certain. There's much we don't know."

"Let us hope we can gain answers from the people here."

"Lord Malek," Rivlen said, "do you think it's wise for us to stroll up to their front gate and walk in? Perhaps we should observe their city and people from afar first. Even though I'm certain that with our prowess we can handle ourselves, if a fight erupts, they might, with great enough numbers, overwhelm us. It's possible they don't like visitors."

"You make a valid point, Captain," Malek said. "Ideally, we would observe the civilization undetected from a distance for several days before approaching, but Uthari made it clear to me that the situation with the other mageships is precarious and that he would prefer we gain as much as we can and return as soon as possible."

"What if we get captured by enemies and *can't* return?" Dr. Fret whispered.

"That won't happen," Sergeant Tinder said. "If any enemies try to capture us, I'll blow them up."

"You're going to blow up people who have the power to manipulate *dragon steel*?" Fret asked.

"We don't know that the people in this city are the ones who did that," Tinder said. "And even if there are powerful mages, mages blow up as nicely as terrene humans."

"You have to get through their defenses."

"True, but once you do, *boom*. Chunks everywhere."

"You're macabre," Fret said.

"Like a song by the Brooding Bard," Tinder agreed cheerfully.

Rivlen rolled her eyes. From what Jak had observed, she didn't think much of the mercenaries. He was surprised she even spoke to them.

"We could split up, my lord. Perhaps part of the group could go in and attempt to gather information while someone powerful enough to effect a rescue, if needed, waits outside the city." Rivlen touched her chest.

Somehow, Jak doubted Malek would ever need Rivlen—or any of them—to rescue him.

She scowled at him, and Jak realized he hadn't been protecting his thoughts. Malek promised that would eventually become something he did naturally, without thinking about it, but Jak hadn't reached that point yet.

"You'd make an excellent rescuer," he whispered, hoping to placate her. "I would be happy to let you rescue me."

"As good as you are at insulting mages, you'll need rescuing."

"I didn't insult you. In fact, I was trying to appease you."

"That's called sucking up."

"You know I prefer more precise terminology."

"Yes, yes, you like your dictionary words. Catch some more flying crickets. Your hatchling looks hungry."

"Yes, ma'am."

"We'll stick together," Malek said. "I acknowledge the merit in your suggestion, Captain, but this grass leaves few hiding places near the city, and since we have only one key, it might be unwise to allow ourselves to be separated. If there *is* danger, and you can sneak away to stage a rescue later, do so. I'll attempt to distract any who battle us so they can't give chase."

"As you wish, my lord." Rivlen didn't sound that enamored with the plan.

Jak didn't blame her for being wary and thinking of backup plans, but he liked the idea of sticking together and providing a strong front to whomever they encountered. Hopefully, the natives would be friendly. Or at least incapable of threatening them.

From what they could see of the city, it didn't appear technologically advanced. Jak hadn't spotted any steam-powered machinery or tall buildings that would suggest an understanding of modern engineering. The few large structures that were visible were built from stone and cement and on broad bases, using arches and columns such as had been popular in Ancient Zeruvia.

Jak doubted the people who had constructed the city had been the ones to alter the dragon steel. *His* hypothesis was that one of the good dragons, if they were still around—he dearly hoped so—had done it.

Using magic, Jak channeled bursts of air through the grass, knocking insects from the blades. As they flew from their perches, he adjusted the wind flow to direct them toward him. His efforts still felt clunky to him. They were nothing like that sophisticated net Malek had made from strands of magic, but he hadn't figured out how to do that yet.

He lunged to catch the insects as they came within range. He missed a few but managed to grasp several to give to the hatchling.

"Try sucking," Rivlen said, "since you're a natural at it."

"Pardon?" Jak asked.

"As if you were using a straw, a magical straw." She extended a hand toward the grass to demonstrate but paused.

Mother was crouching, a sample spatula out as she scraped what looked like a piece of a blue mushroom into a vial. She'd already taken several specimens since they'd arrived.

"I doubt the plants and fungi growing alongside a road right outside of a busy city would have much medicinal value," Jak said.

"You never know." Mother capped the vial, tucked it into her backpack, and resumed walking. "Dandelions are considered weeds and grow prolifically all around Sprungtown, but they promote liver health, soothe minor digestive ailments, and can be paired with complementary herbs to cure urinary tract infections."

"Your mother is odd," Rivlen told Jak.

Jak didn't know how to respond to that, since Mother listing the benefits and side effects of herbs was something he'd grown up with. Once, for a school project, he'd taken some of the information she shared around the dinner table and made a map of medicinal plants that grew wild around their neighborhood. As he recalled, he'd gotten a good grade on it.

Malek looked back and blandly said, "They are a quirky family."

Jak snorted, surprised he remembered. When he'd first kidnapped them, that had been Jak's description for Mother and himself.

"No kidding," Rivlen said, then went back to demonstrating how to *suck* an insect out of the grass.

With the barest whisper of magic, a fat fuzzy caterpillar zipped straight into her hand. The hatchling noticed it flying past and sat alertly in his sling, eyes focusing on it even after it disappeared into her fist.

"Juicy one, huh?" Rivlen dangled the wriggling caterpillar over the hatchling's snout. "Are you supposed to kill them first, or does he like live prey?"

Shikari lunged up, tiny teeth snapping, and chomped the caterpillar down.

"Never mind," she said.

"Probably live," Jak said, "but I don't think it matters, so long as it's an insect."

"You better hope his diet evolves as he gets bigger, or your full-time job is going to be collecting bugs."

As Jak attempted to suck instead of blow the insects into his grasp, another armored carriage came into view on the road ahead. This one had originated in the city and was rolling toward them. There were no horses or anything pulling it, nor did it have a smokestack, so he assumed it was magical, but it was too far away for him to tell.

Tezi jogged up to walk on Jak's side opposite Rivlen. Her blonde hair was drawn back in two braids that left her freckled cheeks on full display, the orangish sun giving them an appealing warm glow. She smiled slightly and pointed at the hatchling. "How's he doing?"

"Much better." Jak beamed a smile at her, pleased she'd asked.

And even though he'd decided not to pester her with his stupid attempts to flirt—he agreed with his mother's assessment that, after all she'd gone through with men, she wouldn't be interested in a romantic relationship—he couldn't help but find her attractive. There was nothing wrong with being attracted to a colleague. He wouldn't act on it, nor would he admit that he was glad Mother had asked to bring her along.

He wasn't sure why she had, but Tezi was a good shot, and with that axe, she could cleave a few enemies' heads off, if need be. Or cleave a giant worm in half. He'd heard a number of the other mercenaries had been trying to get the axe from her. Maybe *that* was why Mother had wanted her to come, not only so she could help them if there was a fight but to keep people from ganging up on her to steal it.

"Good. He's really cute." Tezi turned her smile on the hatchling, an even broader and more genuine smile. Too bad Jak never received such enthusiastic smiles from women. "Do you think I can touch him? Will he bite me?"

"That's a possibility." Jak rubbed his slightly perforated earlobe. "It's safest if he has something else in his mouth when you touch him. Let me see if I can get him a caterpillar."

He looked at Rivlen, intending to ask if she had any tips for finding them, since she'd seemed to specifically pluck that insect out of the grass, and caught her scowling.

"I'm not fetching bugs so your girlfriend can feed them to your pet."

Jak's cheeks heated. "That isn't what I was going to ask." He couldn't believe she could read minds and had still misinterpreted his thoughts. "And she's not *that*." He glanced at Tezi, worried she would be offended or think he was making romantic overtures when he hadn't been.

Her smile had fallen, and she watched Rivlen with wary concern.

"She's a colleague," Jak said. "That's all. And I was wondering how you picked out the caterpillar. Shikari really liked it."

The hatchling's tail swished as he looked back and forth between them, as if he knew exactly what they were talking about. Jak trusted that wasn't true—even if dragons were smart, they surely needed time to develop the ability to think intelligent thoughts—but he *was* likely hoping for another caterpillar.

"They're at the bases of the thicker blades of grass, munching on them." Rivlen looked toward the city and the approaching carriage.

"Thanks." Aware of Tezi still watching, Jak took a deep breath and concentrated on riffling through the grass with his magic. He knew how to stir the blades but had no idea how to detect if caterpillars or anything else were among them. So far, he'd been sweeping through, assuming insects were copious and hoping to luck upon some. He found he still couldn't sense living things, so he swept upward, hoping for the best.

A spider hefted into the air and blew toward him. Well, maybe Shikari would find it tasty.

Jak caught the spider and dangled it above the hatchling's mouth.

"Pet him now," he suggested to Tezi.

Shikari's eyes focused on the spider, and his swishing tail grew still. When he lunged up, Jak thought about pulling it away so Tezi would have longer to pet him while he was distracted, but that seemed a cruel taunt, and the last thing he wanted was for Shikari to grow up resenting him. He wanted a dragon *friend*, not a dragon that would turn into one of those mottled killers. Hopefully, that wouldn't be possible.

Tezi stroked Shikari's belly a couple of times. "Oh." Her smile returned. "He's softer than I expected. Not like fur, but kind of like suede."

"Yeah, his belly is softer than his back. His back is all scaly. Probably because he has scales." Jak rolled his eyes at himself. Way to state the obvious...

"Probably." Tezi withdrew her hand as soon as Shikari finished chomping down the spider.

"How's your axe?" Jak asked, then realized that sounded stupid. It wasn't as if it had been in poor health and was now better. "I mean, are you learning about its abilities?"

Tezi frowned. "I don't know how I would do that. I saw how Lord Malek lifted his hand, and it flew back to him after being embedded in the worm, but uhm." She bit her lip.

Jak, deciding he shouldn't find that gesture appealing, focused on the road ahead instead of her face.

"I went into the jungle alone to practice throwing it," she whispered. "I *did* manage to lodge it in a tree—possibly with some magical intervention, since I've never thrown an axe—but I couldn't get it to come back to me. Do you know if *he* did that, or if the axe did?"

Jak thought about asking Malek, but Mother was showing him one of her samples and talking about chloroplasts and how she would look at her specimens later under her microscope. Jak couldn't imagine Malek being interested in the cellular makeup of plants on an alien world, but he did appear to be listening, so Jak didn't interrupt.

"I bet it's a power of the axe," he said. "Malek was so injured that I doubt he had a lot of energy left to spare. He probably would have left it embedded in the worm if it hadn't returned automatically. It might respond more to someone with the ability to use magic, but you should try talking to it. I mean, connecting to it. Maybe if it gets to know you, it'll share advice on what you can do with it."

"Gets to know me?" Tezi mouthed.

Jak realized how goofy that sounded. "If it's like the portal, it might have some kind of... sentience and even intelligence. I could touch it for you later and try to figure it out if you want."

Tezi drew back, as if she feared he would try to take it from her. Based on how many people wanted it, he couldn't blame her, but it stung that she thought he would do that.

"I'll figure it out myself," she said.

"Good." He nodded. "I'm sure you can. You're smart. And strong."

Tezi glanced at her arms—her admittedly slender arms—and raised skeptical eyebrows.

"I mean mentally strong. Like with fortitude. Though I'm sure you're strong physically too. I know you mercenaries train hard."

Mother frowned back at Jak, and he stopped talking, afraid he was burbling and sounded like an idiot. Or a flatterer. All he wanted was to smooth over any offense he'd caused, but maybe he needed to shut up.

"Thanks," Tezi said in a muted voice, looked warily at Jak and Rivlen again, then stopped to wait for Tinder and Fret.

"That was painful," Rivlen said.

Jak glanced at her, thinking she'd twisted her ankle or stepped on a rock.

"Watching you flirt," she clarified.

"I wasn't *flirting*," Jak whispered, horrified Tezi would hear. The girlfriend comment had been bad enough. The last thing he wanted was for Tezi to avoid him because she thought he was another creepy man who wanted to have his way with her.

"That's good, because it appeared ineffective."

Jak rubbed his face.

"You shouldn't waste your time thinking about sex anyway," Rivlen added, her voice stern.

"I *wasn't*."

"Or partaking in it, should some woman deign to sleep with you. Mages who wish to develop their potential to the greatest must focus all of their waking hours on their duties and their training. The less time wasted on frivolous activities that do nothing to increase your abilities, the better. Why do you think the zidarr are so powerful? They don't waste *any* time on recreation."

Malek held up a hand. Jak thought he might protest this description of him, but the carriage had drawn close. He waved for their group to get off the road as he formed a barrier around everyone.

Worried he might have deemed the approaching carriage a threat, Jak sprang into the grass and cradled the hatchling protectively. He could now sense the magic of the carriage, a long rectangular box that was self-propelled and appeared to be for cargo rather than passengers. With Malek and Mother no longer in front of him, Jak could see two drivers on a bench up front.

They were human males in long white tunics that fell to their knees, leaving their legs bare, save for the leather straps of sandals that crisscrossed up their calves and shins. A shield, axe, bow, and quiver of arrows lay on the seat between them, and one man's hand rested on the hilt of a sword as he eyed Malek.

"What's on their faces?" Dr. Fret whispered.

On each man's right temple, a metallic disc glinted.

"Jewelry?" Tezi guessed.

"Whatever they are, they're magical," Rivlen said.

Malek kept his hands on the hilts of his weapons and didn't

comment, only watching the two as the carriage continued past. Jak didn't sense anything magical about either person, but as Rivlen had said, he did detect a hint of magic from the discs. He also sensed magic from something inside the carriage, perhaps the engine that powered it.

The drivers whispered to each other in their language. Though they appeared to find Malek suspicious, they didn't linger or challenge him in any way. The carriage accelerated away from their group.

"The magic of the carriage engine is sophisticated," Malek said, "but nothing like that of the dragon-steel device."

"It would be surprising if dragon steel was commonplace," Mother said.

"Uthari is hoping it's more common here than in our world."

"So it's easier to acquire some?" Mother kept her tone neutral, but Jak doubted she was pleased with the idea of helping Uthari gain more powerful resources. Surely, he already had enough.

"Yes. I've a few trinkets he sent along that can be used for trade. If the leaders are amenable, and if there's something in our world they covet, I'm authorized to negotiate a long-term trade agreement."

"The zidarr diplomat," Mother murmured. "Don't you think the other kings and queens will object if Uthari unilaterally negotiates with rulers from other worlds?"

"That is for him to hash out with them." Malek nodded toward the road and led the group back onto it.

The city was walled, but there were no towers or turrets along the top, nor evidence of artillery weapons. The wide gate stood open, with no guards out front.

Jak's initial thought was that little trouble came along, perhaps thanks to the device on the portal, and that these people didn't have need for defenses. As they drew closer, however, he sensed a magical barrier. It was invisible, much as with the mage barriers back home, and in a dome shape that extended over the entire city and down to a harbor, the docks protected from the surf by a breakwater.

Another carriage exited through the gate, this one smaller with windows and no driver, at least not on the bench on the outside. Fishing poles and spears were affixed to the top.

The carriage clattered past, wooden wheels jarring on the stone road, and Jak glimpsed two men inside. They didn't look out the window at their group, but he spotted another metal disc at one man's temple.

A few steps farther on, Malek stopped. They'd reached the barrier. As far as Jak could tell, despite the recent carriage departure, there was no breach in the magical field. Would Malek force his way in?

He prodded the barrier with his sword. It buzzed angrily and threw sparks. Malek didn't react, other than to lower his sword, but Jak suspected that would have stung if he had used his finger.

"I have a theory about the discs," Rivlen said.

"Actually, you have a hypothesis," Jak told her, hoping to be helpful—and apologize if he'd somehow managed to offend her. He appreciated that she'd been showing him how to better catch bugs with his magic. "That's a tentative explanation for an observable phenomenon. A theory is a widely accepted explanation that's supported by data."

Judging by the scathing expression Rivlen gave him, she didn't find his correction helpful. "*Quirky* isn't a sufficient word to explain you."

"You think the discs are what allow people to pass through the barrier?" Malek guessed, ignoring the rest of their exchange.

"Yes, my lord," Rivlen said. Amazing that her tone could change so abruptly from scathing to polite and respectful.

"Maybe if we stand out here long enough," Mother said, crouching to poke at a purple flower growing out of the grass, "someone will notice us and invite us in. You wouldn't think that travelers from another world would be so common that the locals would be blasé about it."

Two humans with nets and fishing spears came out riding large furry animals that looked like a cross between a horse and an anteater. Again, metallic discs were affixed to the riders' temples.

Their mounts' long proboscises reached the ground, swiveling back and forth while they ambled. One slurped up a purple flower identical to the one Mother was looking at.

"I hope you didn't want that one," Malek murmured to her.

"No, one sample is sufficient." Mother tucked her flower into a container with others already inside.

Malek lifted an empty hand to the men when they looked at their group. He opened his mouth but then shut it, perhaps opting for telepathic communication, since it seemed to work around language barriers.

The men shook their heads and dug their heels into their mounts' flanks, and the creatures took off at top speed.

"All I grasped," Malek said, "was that strangers are dangerous, and it's forbidden to speak with them. Telepathically or otherwise."

"You *are* dangerous," Mother pointed out. "We could skirt the city, travel farther up the coast, and hope to come across people who will speak to us. Maybe there's a smaller town without a barrier."

"Or," Jak said, "we could split up, and Malek could hide in the grass while those of us with less intimidating auras try to get someone to chat."

"It's forbidden for them to speak with *any* strangers," Malek said.

"That doesn't bode well for a trade agreement," Jak said.

For the first time, someone appeared on the city wall. A guard? The man wore the same knee-length tunic as the other men they'd seen, but he also wore a chain mail vest over it, along with a wide weapons belt supporting a war hammer and a sword.

Jak sucked in a breath. Unless his eyes and burgeoning mage senses were fooling him, that was a dragon-steel hammer. Maybe the material *was* common here.

Unlike with the other people they'd seen thus far, this man radiated the power of a mage. Maybe even as much as a zidarr or wizard. He couldn't possibly be a simple city guard.

He gazed down at them, Malek in particular, though his gaze lingered on Jak—no, on Shikari—for a long moment. He pointed back toward the portal.

Malek shook his head and pointed into the city. The guard spat and stalked out of view.

"Did that go as poorly as it seemed to?" Mother asked.

"I believe I telepathically conveyed that I wish to speak to the city leader, that I have items to trade, and that I'll make it worth their time."

"That made him spit?"

"I may also have conveyed that I will rip a hole in the barrier and go find his leader myself if he doesn't send someone to escort us in."

"Very diplomatic," Mother said.

"It is how *zidarr* diplomats negotiate."

"I seem to remember you doing something similar with the druids before they dropped a ceiling on you and tried to smother us to death."

"Yes."

"*Could* you rip a hole in the barrier?" It seemed formidable to Jak's senses.

Malek hesitated. "I don't know. It's extremely strong magic. I have restrained from attempting to break through. Diplomatically."

"It's no wonder Uthari chose you as his representative," Mother murmured.

"What are our options if they don't let us in?" Jak asked.

Shikari clawed at his chest around his canteen strap, and Jak opened the lid to dribble water into his mouth.

"He's got you trained," Rivlen remarked.

"If you scratch my chest, I'll give you water too."

"Women prefer jewelry and mage trinkets."

"I don't keep those in my canteen."

"This may be someone more important." Malek nodded up to a new arrival on the city wall. "He's powerful, even more so than the last man."

The new arrival had short gray hair and bronze skin with two rows of black dots across his cheeks. Unlike most of the people they'd seen so far, he was dressed in a black knee-length tunic with a silver hemstitch. He wore a square dragon-steel medallion on a silver chain around his neck.

The first guard returned, and they squinted together at Jak, then at Shikari. The hatchling sat up in his sling, his tongue darting into the canteen, since Jak had been distracted and hadn't tipped it far enough for more water to dribble out.

Jak made a mental note to clean it thoroughly later, but for now, he was too busy observing the man observing him. Malek was right. He radiated power—a *lot* of it.

Jak attempted to protect his thoughts. He worried that he'd underestimated these people based on their architecture and that they might be dangerous. Extremely dangerous. Further, the intent way this man contemplated Shikari was concerning. What if someone here tried to take the hatchling?

Malek shifted to stand at Jak's shoulder as he gazed up at the men on the wall. He radiated his own zidarr power. Several long moments passed before the man with the medallion looked from Jak to the rest of the group, but his gaze was dismissive as he considered the others. Even Malek didn't warrant more than a glance.

He called down to them in words Jak couldn't hope to understand, though surprisingly, Mother stirred, as if she recognized the language. That couldn't be possible, could it?

If she did understand, she didn't respond to what sounded like a question. The man switched to conveying his message telepathically.

You will enter and speak with me, Favored Traveler?

The words weren't familiar, but somehow Jak understood the gist. Or at least he thought he did. He didn't know what *favored traveler* meant.

I have questions, the man added.

Assuming everyone in the group received the communication, Jak didn't reply at first. Malek was leading this expedition, so he ought to answer, but the man's gaze remained fixed on Jak, save for glances at the hatchling.

Are you talking to me? Jak touched his chest.

Malek looked at him.

Who else would I address but the Favored Traveler?

"Uh," Jak said. *I have questions too.*

Perhaps we can trade information. We will allow your party entrance, but you will not stray from your escort. Because we must fear strangers, we are wary of them, and sometimes, our people strike preemptively against what they fear.

All right.

The two men disappeared from the wall again.

"Did anyone else hear him?" Jak asked.

"No," Malek said as the others shook their heads.

"An escort is coming to take us somewhere so our two peoples can ask each other questions. If we don't stay with the escort, we may be mugged."

"He threatened you?" Malek's hand rested on the hilt of his

sword.

"Not exactly."

"Why did he speak with *Jak*?" Rivlen looked at him in confusion, then touched her chest and pointed at Malek. "*We* are clearly the more powerful mages and are leading this party."

Jak didn't know what the bit about being a favored traveler meant, or if he'd understood fully, so he only shrugged.

Malek gazed blandly at Rivlen. He didn't correct her or glare or anything of that ilk, but she hurried to correct herself nonetheless.

"And you are more powerful than I and obviously in charge, my lord," she said.

"We shall see." Malek looked from Jak to Shikari, who'd finally taken his tongue out of Jak's canteen. "Perhaps having a dragon conveys status."

Shikari flopped back in his sling and made a noise that might have been a sigh—or a belch.

"Everyone should have one," Jak murmured.

He sensed a change in the barrier, and Malek and Rivlen spun toward the city gate.

Two armed guards stood in the road and gestured for them to enter. They had the auras of mages, though they weren't as pronounced as those of the men on the wall had been.

Malek strode through an opening that had formed in the barrier. As Jak followed, he realized neither their escort nor the man he'd spoken with had worn the discs at their temples. Were those only put on when citizens needed to leave?

As their group passed through the gate and entered the city, far more people filling the streets inside, Jak saw many more people with discs. Almost everyone. Those who wore the discs didn't radiate the power of mages; those who *didn't*... did.

"I think those discs are for more than getting in and out of the city." Jak thought of the ubiquitous slavebands that mages in their sky cities used to keep terrene humans docile and happy to serve them.

"I think so too," Mother said quietly, exchanging a long look with him.

Jak shook his head bleakly. They may have found another culture where mages ruled and terrene humans were enslaved.

What if it was like that on every world where humans lived? If so, the chances of finding allies to help change Torvil for the better might be far poorer than he'd believed.

7

As dusk fell, Lieutenant Sasko joined Captain Ferroki on a log in front of a campfire someone had started. With spherical mage lights providing illumination, and the temperature dropping little at night, there was no need for it, but the flames were cheerful. Others must have also thought so for several men from other units had rolled stumps or rocks over to sit around it. Nobody was making lurid suggestions to the Thorn Company women this evening, perhaps because Sorath was among the stump sitters. For whatever reason, his presence prompted better behavior, even from those in other units.

He wasn't paying much attention to the chatter, instead alternating between eyeing the portal and the top of the waterfall. Sasko followed his gaze to the shadows up there and twitched in surprise. A pair of golden eyes was looking down upon them, reflecting the gleam of one of the mage lights. Judging by their height from the ground, they belonged to something big.

Sorath reached for his pistol but changed his mind and picked up Ferroki's magelock rifle instead. It was one of the ones they'd gotten on the *Dauntless*, with gold embellishments and fancy engravings of dragons, and it was more accurate than most of the unit's weapons.

Moving slowly, Sorath lifted it to aim at the animal, propping the barrel of the rifle on his pickaxe hand. Before he could shoot, the eyes disappeared, their owner springing back into the brush.

Sorath sighed and lowered the rifle. "It's that same jaguar that's been here off and on for the last two days."

"You're so offended by its voyeurism that you're going to shoot it?" Sasko asked.

"I'm positive it's a druid's animal companion and that it's here to spy on us." Sorath returned Ferroki's rifle to the log beside her.

"You can keep it if you think you'll get another shot," Ferroki said.

"I prefer black-powder weapons."

"Except when you actually need to hit a target?" she asked.

Sorath snorted. "I can hit targets just fine with my pistol. But it's not ideal for something hundreds of yards away."

"That is a tall cliff," Ferroki said. "The men hurling themselves off the top and into the pool earlier were brave."

"More likely trying to impress you."

"Me?" Ferroki touched her chest.

"You Thorn Company women. Whichever of you they seek to lure to a blanket."

"Probably Sasko," Ferroki murmured. "She's informed me often that her anatomy is sublime and entices men."

Sorath raised his eyebrows.

"Trust me, *sublime* isn't the word I used." Sasko looked up at the black-hulled ships hovering over the trees, thinking of Lieutenant Vinjo, the last man who'd tried to lure her to a blanket. At least, that was what she thought he'd been doing. He'd been less direct than most, speaking of liking the way she envisioned stuffing sharp pencils up arrogant mages' noses rather than offering more typical remarks on the appeal of her boobs and butt. "Do you think he's still alive?" she caught herself musing.

Sorath and Ferroki looked up.

"Vinjo," Sasko said. "I feel bad for capturing him. A few days ago, we were on the same side. He probably feels as betrayed by us as Night Wrath does. Not that I care about *his* feelings. He's an ass. But Vinjo was kind of decent. For a mage."

And now he was either dead or a prisoner on one of Uthari's ships. It wasn't fair that he'd been captured when Night Wrath had gotten away. What kind of coward fled and left his brother behind?

"He's on the *Dread Arrow*," Sorath said. "Tonovan's ship. I heard the general questioned him last night. I believe he's still alive."

"Did they torture him?" Sasko wasn't sure why she asked when she'd heard screams the night before. Male screams. It was possible they'd belonged to someone else, but she hadn't truly believed that.

"For information, yes."

"What could he possibly know?" Damn it, why had she caught him? Sasko rubbed her face.

"He *is* the one who built the devices that took down two magical engines and interrupted the portal's ability to operate, so he knows more than most." Sorath's hand strayed to one of his jacket pockets. They were bulging with more than his usual pop-bangs.

"He's just a goofy... goof," Sasko said.

"With highly undervalued engineering talent."

"I should have let him go. I got to him first. Sergeant Words and Private Lethdar didn't react that quickly. Vinjo could have gotten away. Maybe. I'm not sure he even wanted to. He started that fight with Night Wrath, like he was trying to help *us* get away."

Sorath gave her a sharp look. "I did wonder about that. It was a silly time for them to argue, unless he was intentionally distracting his brother, who was about to kill me."

"Why would Lieutenant Vinjo have done that when it put him in danger?" Ferroki asked.

"Because I showed more of an interest in his inventions than his brother?" Sorath shrugged.

"I suppose there's no chance we can rescue him," Sasko said, though she watched Sorath, thinking he might also feel guilty that they had, however inadvertently, handed Vinjo to Tonovan.

"Whether we wished it or not, we're working for the same side as his captors," Ferroki said. "A rescue attempt seems ill-advised."

"Maybe we could convince the general that Vinjo has some use and should be allowed to work for us—them. Uthari." Sorath scratched his cheek with his pickaxe. "He could build things."

"Would Vinjo do that?" Ferroki asked. "Work for the other side? He's not a mercenary. His home and family are presumably in Zaruk's kingdom."

"True. What if he were working on something for… the good of mankind in regard to this portal? There's a truce right now, after all. Zaruk's kingdom could theoretically benefit." Sorath lowered his voice. "Assuming Uthari keeps his word to the other rulers and their commanders. He's promised them that they'll be able to send people along on future explorations."

Sasko doubted Sorath believed Uthari would follow through on that promise.

"What good-of-mankind device would Vinjo make?" Ferroki asked.

Sorath lowered his pickaxe. "I don't know. Maybe something to keep monsters from coming through the portal, if that's possible. He'd have to come down here to work on it. That would get him away from generals who like torturing people."

"Good. We have a plan." Sasko stood, ready to implement it.

"How are you going to get up there to suggest it?" Ferroki asked.

"Uhm." Sasko looked at Sorath.

He'd been back and forth to Uthari's yacht a couple of times for meetings.

"They have to want you up there," Sorath said. "It's the same as their sky cities. No terrene humans allowed, unless it's to serve them."

Ferroki turned, peering into the jungle. A man had jumped off one of the black-hulled ships on a skyboard. It was too dark to tell who, but Sasko didn't think it was someone in a red uniform. The man's black clothes blended into the shadows as he angled into the trees.

Surprisingly, he wasn't heading in the direction of the portal or the camp but deeper into the jungle. What of interest could be out there?

"Is that one of Uthari's zidarr?" Sorath asked. "Yidar is the only other one down here in Zewnath besides Malek, right?"

"Yes," Ferroki said, "but I couldn't tell if that was him."

"I wonder if he's on an errand for his king… or for someone else."

Something about Sorath's voice suggested suspicion.

"Like who?" Sasko asked.

"I don't know, but I've heard from those who can sense it that he's wearing a lingering mage mark placed upon him by Uthari himself."

"Aren't *you* wearing a lingering mage mark?" Ferroki asked.

"Yes, though I'm told it's about gone now."

"It's not really a punishment, is it?" Sasko asked. "Just kind of… what? Embarrassment? Something to let other mages know that you irked one of them?"

"Despite having worn one," Sorath said, "I'm fuzzy on exactly what it does, beyond being a beacon to mages, but it's definitely not considered a *good* thing. There are rumors that Yidar tried to get the portal away from Uthari back when we were infiltrating his city."

"I remember that," Ferroki said. "There was a black-hulled ship in there trying to steal the portal right alongside Zaruk's ships."

Sorath nodded. "So if Yidar is taking a solo departure from his ship right now... you never know. It might be something Uthari would want to hear about."

"Are you suggesting we rat him out?" Sasko pointed into the jungle in the direction the dark figure had disappeared. "We don't even know if that *was* Yidar."

"Whoever it was looked suspicious to me. Didn't he look suspicious to you, Ferroki?"

"I suppose."

"Do we care?" Sasko didn't grasp Sorath's line of thinking.

"Well, we mercenaries have been ordered to run patrols and keep an eye out for suspicious things." Sorath glanced toward the waterfall—the jaguar hadn't returned—and then nodded toward the jungle. "If we find them, we're supposed to report them. That excuse might get us an invitation up to a ship, at which point, we might be able to poke around, find Vinjo, and argue his merits."

"Ah," Sasko said, understanding dawning.

Ferroki frowned at both of them. "Spying on a zidarr could be hazardous to your health. If you want to report something, tell them about the suspicious jaguar."

"I'll keep that as a possibility," Sorath said, "but Uthari might appreciate it more if we bring news of a suspicious *zidarr*."

"Do you want him to appreciate you?" Ferroki asked.

"If it'll keep him from torturing me again, maybe," Sorath said, though he curled a lip.

Sasko doubted it was in him to kiss up to Uthari or anyone else.

"I just want to get Vinjo back from his people," she said.

Sorath nodded and led her into the woods in the direction the man on the skyboard had gone.

∾

Jadora understood some of the language of these new people and this new city. She hadn't been certain after hearing only a few snippets from the riders they'd passed, but now that their group was following their escort through the busy streets, conversations going on all around them, she was positive. Whatever language these people were speaking today, it was derived from Ancient Zeruvian. Or Ancient Zeruvian had been derived from *it*.

Stepping through the portal and finding evidence of humans on other worlds was putting into question all of her assumptions about where, when, and how humanity had originated. What if it hadn't been on Torvil at all?

"This place doesn't seem all that different from home." Dr. Fret waved at merchant stalls lining the streets they walked along, everything from produce to jars of dried meat and fish to wooden children's toys on sale. "A city like Perchver. Maybe more... primitive? I don't see any machinery, and the clothing is all quite simple."

"The mages aren't primitive," Rivlen said, a hand on her sword as they walked, the women in the back and Malek at Jak's side as they trailed the guards.

Malek had shifted protectively close to Jak when the gray-haired man in the black tunic had been eyeing him, and he was sticking close. Jadora appreciated that, but it worried her that someone had singled Jak out for some reason. Was it only because of the hatchling? She couldn't imagine why else he would stick out. Even if someone sensed that he had the ability to use magic, it had to be minimal compared to Malek and Rivlen.

A roar came from somewhere up ahead. A crowd cheering?

They walked through an intersection, passing a huge stone fountain with a dragon statue in the center. Women with clay jars filled water from the pool underneath, then strapped the jars to their backs to carry them away.

"No water infrastructure here?" Fret mused.

"We didn't have plumbing in the village where I grew up," Tezi said. "I had to make trips to the well for water in the mornings."

"But all of the major cities in the various kingdoms have had running water for some time," Fret said.

Two women in white tunics with turquoise bracelets clanking on their wrists walked past them from the opposite direction, pausing to stare at Jak—and the hatchling. They whispered to each other as they continued on, glancing back at him several times. Jak glanced at them too.

Frowning, he met Jadora's eyes. "Those two were powerful. A lot of the people here have auras like…" He waved at Rivlen and Malek.

"It would be wise to assume there is nothing primitive about this society." Malek watched their surroundings alertly as they walked. "From what I've observed of their magic, it's as advanced as ours and… powerful."

That pause made Jadora uneasy, as did the long look that Malek and Rivlen exchanged.

She thought of her hypothesis that humans had developed magic as a result of prolonged proximity to dragon steel. If that was true, and if dragon steel was more ubiquitous here, more of the population could have the ability to use magic than on Torvil, and the average mage here could be more powerful than the average mage back home. It boggled her mind to imagine someone magically stronger than Malek, and she was suddenly glad that they'd waited for an invitation into the city and that he hadn't tried to tear a hole in their barrier. A squadron of powerful mage guards might have come out to attack them.

Another roar came from up ahead.

As the group rounded another fountain, the street opened up into a square, and one of the large structures that had been visible from a distance came into view. An arena?

Made from stone, it rose several stories high with tiers of arched passageways full of people making their way to seats inside. Even more people were lined up at the numerous ground-level entrances, waiting to be allowed inside. Judging by its size, it could seat thousands, if not tens of thousands.

The periodic cheers coming from within suggested the events had already begun. During a quieter moment, the roar of something inhuman floated out, followed by an animalistic squawk of pain. The crowd cheered again, drowning it out.

Tezi and Tinder fingered their weapons. Malek always exuded confidence, no matter what, but even he seemed a touch concerned as he regarded the arena.

Jadora was relieved when their escort led them past the lines of people. For a minute, she'd worried that they were being herded into the arena to be sacrificed or thrown into some battle.

They circled the long oval structure, more roars coming from within, and headed toward a street leading out of the square on the far side, but instead of walking to it, their escort turned toward an entrance in the back of the arena. This one lacked a line of people, and two guards stood to either side of the arched doorway, deterring anyone who approached.

But the guards nodded at their group's escort and let them pass.

"How are zidarr at fighting wild beasts?" Tinder muttered.

"Malek easily slew a jungle panther that wanted to munch on me," Jadora said.

Malek glanced at them but didn't comment. Their escort led

them up two sets of private stairs, down another short corridor, and toward a curtained archway with more guards out front. Though hundreds of conversations were audible, echoing off the stone walls, there were few people in this part of the arena.

One of the guards parted the curtains for them but paused with a hand toward Malek's chest. He'd taken the lead on the stairs, but the guard pointed at Jak and indicated that he should enter first. Malek squinted at the man.

Jadora squeezed past Tezi to stand beside Jak.

"Do you know why you're being singled out?" she whispered. Though she'd recognized similarities between the local language and Ancient Zeruvian, she couldn't understand more than a few words here and there. "Is it because they're interested in the hatchling, and you're holding him?"

Jak hesitated. "Probably."

"Is there something else?" Jadora watched Malek glower at the guard, who glowered back and shook his head, and suspected they were having a telepathic exchange.

"I... maybe. I'll tell you later."

"Before or after we get tossed into the arena to battle giant predators?"

"I don't think that's what's happening." Jak pointed through the curtained archway. "The man from the wall is in here with some other mages. I can sense them."

The guard pointed at Jak's chest again.

Jak eased past Malek. "It's all right."

Malek's expression said it wasn't, but Jadora didn't know why.

"I need them to come too," Jak told the guard, waving at the rest of the group to follow him.

The guard lifted a hand again, but Jak shook his head.

Shikari stood up in his sling and screeched. The guard's eyebrows flew up. He backed away and didn't object again when the group followed Jak inside.

"Are they worried that if they don't treat him well," Tezi asked, "a mother dragon will show up and eat their city?"

"I'm not sure," Jak said.

"It would depend on if their barrier is powerful enough to keep dragons out," Malek said.

Jadora and the others followed Jak up a short shady corridor and into a large room that was open to the arena, only columns and low walls interrupting the view. Jadora stopped and peered out.

Numerous bare-chested humans with axes, swords, and shields were battling not the jungle cat she'd imagined but an animal—magical creature?—more than four times their height. It had a face similar to that of a lion with great tusks as well as long fangs. Its black fur was thicker and shaggier than on any cat she'd seen before, and the tail that whipped about behind it had a barbed tip. Not only did the creature attack with fangs, tusks, and claws, but whenever the men tried to get around to its flanks, it snapped its tail at them, trying to smash them to the sandy floor of the arena.

That sand was stained in spots with blood, and a man in a fringed leather loincloth lay wounded—or dead?—on the ground near the fight. The six remaining warriors leaped in, trying to use teamwork to defeat the great predator with weapons that were ill-suited to the task. Though large, the creature was as fast as any cat, springing about and avoiding their blows while delivering lightning slashes with its claws.

A lone warrior skittered in, managing to stab it in the side as it focused on the others, and the crowd cheered. Rows and rows of seats across from their viewing room were full of spectators waving flags and wooden swords.

Shouts of "Get it!" and "Kill it!" reached Jadora's ears amid many other words she couldn't decipher. Money was mentioned several times, so she assumed people had bets riding on the outcome. Some of the spectators were cheering for the creature. That was chilling.

All of the gladiators in the arena wore the now-familiar discs at their temples, but most of the spectators did as well, so Jadora didn't know what to think of them. But she had a hunch they controlled the population, those without magical power. *Lesser beings.*

She hadn't truly expected to find allies here that could help her and Jak change the world back home, but finding more terrene human beings oppressed—and possibly being sacrificed for entertainment purposes—by mages depressed her.

A man spoke from a handful of occupied plush seats in the room. He pointed out at the battle and made what sounded like an acerbic comment. Servants stood near the seats with trays of drinks and food but watched those they attended to rather than the battle.

The gray-haired man in the black tunic and square medallion was among the spectators. He waved toward Jak, beckoning him over.

Two other mages sat in the comfortable seats with him while a man in trousers, shirt, and jacket, similar to what Jadora and her archaeologist colleagues wore on digs, leaned against a wall, his arms crossed as he regarded them. He also wore a hat, not that different from Jak's, and had a strong jaw with a beard shadow.

Jadora stumbled slightly before catching herself. Something about his face, about the wry twist to his lips, and about his stance reminded her of her late husband. Achingly so. He looked like exactly the kind of person Loran would have traveled with, risking the ire of natives and ancient booby traps to extract some groundbreaking find from a forgotten pyramid or temple.

A pang of longing filled her. Being here and exploring a strange world without Loran felt so wrong, and the craziness of the past weeks made her miss him anew, made her miss having someone to hug her and comfort her and make jokes to lighten her mood. Everything had been so desolate, so without hope of late, that she longed for that.

The man met her eyes briefly as he checked out the group, but there was no recognition there. Not that she would have expected it. These people were all strangers, even if he seemed to fit in more with her world than this one.

Though he'd waved them over, the man in black didn't speak or pay much attention to them until after the battle. Unfortunately, the gladiators did not get the best of the great predator. Though it bled from numerous wounds, it was the victor in the end. It lay down on all fours, preparing to eat one of the fallen men, and Jadora's stomach turned. She couldn't believe these people wanted to watch *that*.

A whistle sounded, and six men trotted out in white tunics and sandals with nothing but staffs for weapons. She thought that suicidal until she realized they were mages.

When the creature rose and sprang at them, it struck an invisible barrier. They pointed their staffs at it—were the tips made from dragon steel?—and blasted it with energy attacks. It slunk away from them.

They walked past the fallen men—most dead but a few only wounded and still groaning—and herded it toward a raised portcullis at one end of the arena.

"Are you all right?" Malek asked quietly, coming up to Jadora's side.

"Other than being disturbed by people being entertained by watching humans being killed, delightful." Jadora checked on Jak, relieved that his face was ashen and that he hadn't enjoyed the spectacle. Not that she'd thought he would.

Malek glanced at the man in the hat. He stood in the same position, leaning against the wall and watching the hatchling, and didn't look over at them.

"You seemed to recognize him," Malek said.

"No. He just reminds me of... someone." Jadora didn't know why she was vague when he could read her thoughts.

"Ah." Malek looked like he might comment further on what he'd doubtless seen in her mind, but he changed the subject. "I had the sense that you can understand some of the language."

"A little bit. It's not the same, but it's similar to Ancient Zeruvian. I'm able to understand a word here and there."

Jadora thought of the phrase engraved in Ancient Zeruvian on the bottom of their portal, *gateway to the stars*. She'd always believed those words had been added after the dragons originally created the artifact, but she hadn't known how that could have happened. She still didn't know how, but now that she'd seen evidence that someone else had somehow manipulated the dragon steel of their portal, it was less flummoxing.

"Interesting," Malek said.

I am Ambassador Rajesk. The man in black rose to face them, speaking aloud in his native tongue as he shared their meaning telepathically in Jadora's mind. Perhaps in all of their minds. *It is my privilege to interact with visitors from other worlds.*

Rajesk smiled at them and let his gaze linger on the hatchling. His eyes were calculating, and the smile didn't seem sincere. Earlier, it had sounded like strangers weren't welcome.

Jadora, realizing this might be an opportunity for her to better grasp the language, since he was essentially translating what he said into her mind, vowed to pay close attention to the spoken words.

"I am Zidarr Malek, representative of King Uthari." Malek presumably shared his message telepathically as well.

Rajesk glanced at him but focused on Jak. *Who are you and how came you by a dragon hatchling? This is one of the elder dragons.*

"If he thinks that's an *elder* dragon," Tinder whispered, "he's not that observant."

The elder dragons were all believed to be extinct, Rajesk added, ignoring her.

"Extinct?" Jak whispered, anguish filling his eyes.

If the elder dragons were the ones that Jak had been calling the *good* dragons, Jadora could understand her son's distress. And if all but this hatchling, and possibly the unhatched eggs still back in that glacier, were gone, then that didn't bode well for finding dragon allies.

As I'm sure you're aware, the younger dragons are cruel and prey on humans, Rajesk continued.

"We've met one, yes," Malek said.

Rajesk frowned at him, then looked back to Jak. *Why do you let your bodyguard speak for you?*

Malek's eyebrows flew up.

And carry your key? Rajesk opened what Jadora had assumed was a solid square medallion hanging around his neck, but it turned out to be a case. From it, he withdrew a familiar round medallion with a dragon head on one side. It was identical to the medallion Jak had worn in his hat for five years, except this one had never been plated in gold.

"Uhm." Jak extended his hand toward Malek. "He's... more of an advisor than a simple bodyguard."

Malek opened his mouth, as if he might object, but he closed it and smoothed his features into a mask.

"What is going on?" Tinder whispered to Fret, who only shrugged back.

Malek might be willing to go along with Jak, but Rivlen was another matter. Indignation flared in her eyes, and she stepped forward.

"Zidarr Malek is our leader. He is—" She halted abruptly and looked at Malek.

He must have stopped her telepathically.

"Chief among those who advise Jak," Malek told the ambassador.

Hm. Rajesk eyed Rivlen. She'd stopped, but her eyes were still burning with indignation. Rajesk also looked over at Jadora, Tezi, Fret, and Tinder before turning back to Jak. *You travel with many female servants. I suppose this is because you are young. It is not uncommon for youths to be libidinous.*

"Servants!" Rivlen exclaimed.

Malek shot her a warning look.

Rivlen clenched her jaw and didn't say more but glared daggers at the ambassador *and* Jak. As if he were responsible for any of this.

"Er, yes," Jak said. "I can barely contain my urges. You said back at the wall that I could ask you some questions, didn't you?"

You have not answered any of my questions yet. Rajesk offered the insincere smile again. *Where did you find that hatchling?*

"I assumed we would start with simpler questions. Like what's my favorite food and if I'm enjoying your world and the... festivities here." Jak grimaced toward the arena.

The creature had been forced out, the portcullis dropped, and some attendants were dragging the bodies out while others brought in wheelbarrows of fresh sand to dump over the unsightly bloodstains.

We care little for the opinions of outsiders, nor are your food preferences a concern. The elder dragons are extinct. Where did you find that hatchling? That egg. You must have found an egg? Rajesk looked at the man in the hat for the first time. *We've suspected the elder dragons may have hidden some of their kind away, maybe even eggs, using magic to preserve them until such a time when it would be safe for them to return, but there's been little evidence. Isn't that true, Zethron? In your explorations, you've never confirmed such tales, have you?*

The man answered. Jadora only recognized the word, "I," but his head shake made the meaning clear.

No telepathic translation had accompanied the man's spoken words, and Jak and Malek glanced at each other.

Only Jadora had a chance at understanding him, and she feared she wouldn't get much.

And have you seen any people like them? Rajesk waved at their group. *Do you know what world they come from?*

"No." He—Zethron—said a few more words that Jadora didn't know and finished with, "...understand their language."

Jadora didn't know whether they should volunteer any information to these people—it wasn't as if she wanted Uthari to gain a trade agreement that put more dragon steel in his hands—but not being able to communicate fully—to *understand* fully—gnawed at her. She pulled out a pen and journal she'd brought along for recording notes and wrote several lines in Ancient Zeruvian on a blank page.

While she worked, the hatchling climbed onto Jak's shoulder, his tail swishing across his chest, and held the attention of Rajesk and his people.

She wrote that the language here was similar to one that had once been spoken on Torvil and asked if the locals had originated on this world or come through the portal long ago.

Perhaps Rajesk could have answered her if she asked him in her mind, but she already didn't trust him. Besides, he was focused on Jak and Shikari and likely wasn't monitoring her thoughts.

Malek watched her write. She held the page up before taking it to Zethron, wanting to make sure he didn't object to sharing that information. He couldn't read Ancient Zeruvian, but *he* was surely monitoring her thoughts.

Malek hesitated, then nodded. But he silently added, *Be careful what you tell them. I can't read the minds of the mages, but I believe their only interest in us is the hatchling. They may try to take Shikari by force if we don't tell them where they can get more. I'm attempting to block everyone's thoughts so they can't get that information from our non-mages.*

Thank you. Jadora walked the journal to Zethron.

He arched his eyebrows as she approached, but he didn't seem as wary and suspicious of strangers as the others, and he offered her a polite nod and a smile.

Jadora offered him the journal, hoping he would recognize the similarities in the language, as she had. Just because he was an *explorer*, as Rajesk had called him, didn't mean he was a philologist or archaeologist, but if he'd been brought in because he was an expert in other worlds, he might have such a background.

"Oh," he said as soon as he read the page, and then gave a slower more drawn out, "*Oh.*" He scrutinized Jadora with new interest. "Fascinating."

She knew he meant it was fascinating that they shared a common root language, not that *she* was fascinating, but he followed the word with a grin that left her unsure how to respond.

"Do you understand me?" Zethron pointed at his chest. "Because I am..."

She couldn't translate the rest, but his eyebrow wriggle, wider grin, and touch to his chest made her certain it was something like, "a superior and delightful person to converse with."

"Only some." She wavered her hand.

"The important... hopefully."

She shrugged, took the journal back, and wrote more.

I must know where it came from. Rajesk turned from the hatchling to the mages behind him. *Can you imagine?* He gestured expansively, spreading his arms, so he must have shared more with them.

Malek shook his head once gravely. *I have a feeling I know what they're going to ask for if we want to trade with them.*

Jak shifted from foot to foot and looked at Malek. Looked *worriedly* at Malek.

"Do you want to share that information?" Jadora asked quietly, waving to the journal, though she was reluctant to mention the rest of those eggs. She hadn't wanted their mages on Torvil to get Jak's hatchling—or any other hatchlings—and she also didn't want to hand them over to people who watched men be slain by predators for sport.

"*No.*" Jak looked at her in horror. "Those dragons are our future allies. Our *friends.*"

The hatchling chewed on a tuft of his hair.

Jadora feared he was being naive that the hatchling would grow into an ally or a friend, especially if all of the adult dragons Shikari was descended from were dead. Who would teach him language and culture and magic and whatever else had been important for dragons to learn? And who even knew how long dragons took to mature? The legends told of them being extremely long-lived. This one might take hundreds of years to mature. It could still be a baby, nibbling on Jak's hair, when he was eighty years old.

Zethron touched her hand, startling her. She'd meant to ask him who he was and what this world was called, but she'd been distracted.

He smiled apologetically and pointed to the journal and pen. Oh, he wanted to write something for *her*. She nodded and handed them to him.

He took a deep breath, studied the ceiling as if he were trying to remember something, and then started writing painstakingly in Ancient Zeruvian. She suspected it was something he'd learned long ago but that wasn't that similar to their modern version of the tongue.

I am Zethron of Family Star Teller, he wrote, *and I am not originally from this world of Vran, but I am very familiar with it. I am an explorer and traveler of many places. Are you from the First World? I think you must be. The people here, and those on my world as well, are the descendants of the Zeruvians. Our two peoples were brought from the First World long ago by the dragons. The elder dragons, not the younger dragons.* He shook his head firmly as he wrote that. *You write in the old tongue. Our languages have changed over the millennia.*

Tell me you're not giving her your address and the time to come to dinner, Rajesk said telepathically as he frowned at Zethron.

"I am not," Zethron replied, "but do you *frath* she would? She knows the ancient language. Our dinner *yrgroth kar* would be *bamooth*." He grinned at her again.

Jadora didn't know whether to be relieved or chagrined that she hadn't caught all that. She didn't want to date anyone from another world, even someone who reminded her of Loran, and caught herself glancing at Malek.

He was watching them, but if he was irritated by the comments, he didn't show it. His face was still masked, and he looked like he was concentrating. On keeping the mages here from reading the group's thoughts? Jadora hoped that was possible. Aside from Rivlen, they'd all been to the glacier world and knew about the eggs.

You're not here to flirt with them. Who are they? And why did they come? Rajesk squinted at Jak and the whole group. He must have been willing to accept answers from them as well as Zethron since he included them all in his telepathic message.

"We are explorers interested in trade," Malek said. *Jadora, do you think it's likely the Jitaruvak is from here?*

It's possible, she replied silently, assuming his question had been for her alone, *but the prevailing blue coloring in the foliage makes me think not. Chlorophyll may be different here than on Torvil. I'd like to look at some of my samples under a microscope.*

Trade? What do you seek in trade? Rajesk eyed Malek suspiciously.

The hatchling squawked. Shikari probably wanted caterpillars in trade.

"Dragon steel appears to be common here," Malek said. "Do you make your own weapons?"

A way to ask if they could work the material without admitting that their people couldn't.

Our etchers are skilled, yes. Rajesk lifted his chin. *It is why they rule our people.*

"Etchers?" Malek asked.

Rajesk squinted at him. *Do you not have etchers?*

"It is possible we call them by another name," Malek said, giving away nothing.

Only the etchers handle the dragon steel, and it is not common. It is extremely valuable, and we do not trade it. Though... Rajesk eyed the hatchling again. *It is possible that if you had dragon eggs, such an offer might appeal to the etchers. After all, dragons make the alloy from the ore in the mountains. With dragons, assuming we could control them as they grew sufficiently old enough for such work, we could make an unlimited amount.*

Jak was shaking his head, but when he opened his mouth to speak, Malek caught his gaze and widened his eyes in warning.

I would not be authorized to make such a deal, Rajesk continued, *but I could take your offer to the etchers. How many eggs are you willing to trade for dragon steel?*

Jak clenched his jaw, nobly resisting what had to be an urge to blurt, "No," again.

"We will only discuss our offer directly with those capable of making a deal," Malek said.

Rajesk flicked dismissive fingers at him and repeated the question, looking directly at Jak. Apparently, he still thought Malek was just the bodyguard.

Jak repeated Malek's words.

Strangers and peons are not permitted to speak with or even see the etchers. That is not our way. Only an ambassador—Rajesk thumped his own chest—*or a champion may interact with them.*

"A champion?" Malek asked.

One of the victors they choose to go on quests for them. Rajesk flicked a hand toward the arena, where a fresh round of gladiators was marching out, armor and weapons gleaming in the sun.

One of the mages leaned close to Rajesk and whispered in his ear. They fell silent but nodded at each other, sharing some telepathic conversation. Jadora wasn't privy to this one.

Malek gazed thoughtfully out at the arena.

Jak patted Shikari's head, that worry still in his eyes.

Jadora knew he didn't care about dragon steel or Uthari getting a fresh supply of it. She didn't either, though she admitted it might be useful to humanity at large to learn how to work the alloy. With weapons such as Tezi had found, perhaps terrene humans could defend themselves against mages. But she had a feeling the mages would be the ones who ended up getting such weapons. All of the lesser-dragon-steel weapons in the world belonged to zidarr and wizards.

Right now, all Jadora cared about acquiring was the Jitaruvak, so she could ensure her father's safety.

Since Zethron had stopped writing, she took the journal back from him, turned to a fresh page and did her best to draw Jitaruvak fronds. Jak could have done a better job, but she didn't think he was familiar with it.

Do you know if this plant exists on this world? Jadora wrote at the bottom.

Zethron scrutinized it before writing, *I am not familiar with it, but I am not a gardener or herbalist.* He arched his eyebrows. *Are you?*

Again, she was hesitant to share too much information, but maybe it would be useful for them to know her abilities. If Malek's group could convince them to trade for something else besides dragon eggs, it was possible some of the medicines on Torvil would be of interest to them.

Yes, she wrote. *Herbalist, apothecary, and chemist.* Actually, she wrote alchemist, since that was the only Ancient Zeruvian word that would work, though she hoped he wouldn't think she had some ability to magically alter chemicals.

His eyebrows rose higher. *And linguist?*

Jadora hesitated. *Archaeologist. As an old friend would say*—she winced as she thought of Darv—*my pronunciation is limited.*

"Huh." Zethron smiled at her again. "I was right. Fascinating."

Jadora shook her head.

"Zethron," Rajesk said, switching to speaking solely aloud. "What have you learned?"

"They are from the First World," Zethron said.

Rajesk looked sharply at Jadora. "So *mylorfar zark* their dragon gate is open?"

Zethron shrugged and said something Jadora couldn't translate.

"Fascinating," Rajesk said.

It sounded far more sinister when he said it.

"Leave, Zethron," Rajesk added.

"What?"

"So you won't be *ferkokt.*"

Zethron's brow furrowed, and he glanced at the arena, but the next battle hadn't yet started.

"*Leave,*" Rajesk boomed at him.

Zethron lifted his hands in exasperation, nodded to Jadora, and walked out of the room.

Before Jadora could determine what Rajesk was doing, he spun toward Jak and Malek, lifted his hands, and attacked them.

8

Sorath had never spent much time in jungles, and nobody would accuse him of being able to sneak through the undergrowth without making a sound, so he was relieved when a green light ahead directed him to where the zidarr had gone. It also provided just enough illumination that Sorath could see where he put his feet and avoid stepping on twigs or breaking branches.

Sasko crept after him, also choosing her footing carefully as they maneuvered closer to the light while staying behind trees for cover. Attempting to sneak up on a magic user wasn't a good idea, and Sorath wouldn't normally consider it, but he'd recognized one of the devices that Vinjo had slipped into his pockets before being captured.

He held up one hand to Sasko and drew the clandestineness creeper out with the other, the small hedgehog-shaped device fitting into his palm. In the dark, Sasko probably couldn't see it. He took her arm, touched her fingers to the tool, then directed her hand to rest on his shoulder.

"Vinjo's stealth device," he breathed.

Though he couldn't hear anyone talking up ahead, that didn't mean their voices wouldn't be audible if someone was present.

Sasko nodded and gripped his shoulder. Sorath pressed his thumb into the only indention on the device, and a tingle ran over his skin.

Earlier, he'd tested it and received the same result, though he hadn't asked anyone if they could see him, so he could only trust now that it was working. If it wasn't and they were discovered, oh, well. They were two mercenaries out on patrol. *They* were supposed to be here. He doubted whoever had conjured that green light could claim the same.

"I felt it," Sasko whispered.

"Good. Don't let go of me." Sorath didn't know if touch was required for the device to camouflage two people, but he would assume so until he knew otherwise.

"As long as the captain doesn't get jealous."

"I don't think she has possessive feelings about my shoulder."

This wasn't the best place to chat, so Sorath held a finger to his lips, then led the way, moving slowly so they could stay together.

As they navigated through the trees, around brush, and over logs, the green light grew stronger. Soon, the tiny device giving off the illumination came into view. It lay in a clearing, a little green oval resting on fallen fronds and shreds of bark.

Sorath stopped between two trees, leaving enough room for Sasko to squeeze in beside him. Thus far, he hadn't seen anyone. It looked like someone had been ambling through the jungle, and the device had fallen out of their pocket.

Highly doubting that, Sorath rested his hand on the butt of his pistol and waited.

A few minutes passed before movement stirred in the shadows. Yidar on his skyboard. He was circling the area, looking toward the device, but not getting too close. Searching for whoever had left it there?

Sorath wondered if Yidar would sense the creeper. He hadn't asked Vinjo for details about it and didn't know if it worked on mages. What if it only hid people from sight, not magical senses?

Yidar spun on his skyboard, peering into the trees. It wasn't toward Sorath and Sasko but off to their left.

A growl emanated from that direction. Sorath tightened his grip on his pistol.

An attractive, green-haired woman walked through the foliage. Had *she* growled?

Clearly a druid, she wore a homespun tunic woven from grasses, the crude material not quite hiding the curve of substantial breasts. Though tattoos of leaves and flowers ran across her forehead and marked her cheeks, they couldn't hide her full lips, high cheekbones, and intriguing green eyes. Her skin was almost as dark as Sorath's, so those eyes stood out.

As she approached, the source of the growl came into view, a jaguar padding along behind her. It looked like the same great feline that had spied on their camp from the top of the waterfall. Sorath had *known* it was a druid's minion.

The woman stopped at the edge of the light and looked at Yidar.

"You are not my strapping young lieutenant," she said in perfect Dhoran with a lyrical accent and musical voice.

Sorath wouldn't have expected a druid from deep within remote Zewnath to speak the common tongue, but he suspected she'd been chosen for this mission because of that ability. What exactly this mission was, he didn't yet know.

"I'm far more strapping than he." Yidar floated closer on his skyboard. He looked her up and down, though he didn't let his gaze linger on her curves for long before studying her eyes.

"And are you as willing to trade information to me as he?"

"Perhaps. What is your name?"

"Kywatha of Rabbit Clan."

"And what do you offer, Kywatha?"

"To a zidarr who is loyal to King Uthari? What would you wish? Your kind are known to crave little and rarely enjoy pleasures of the flesh."

"Not *all* zidarr succumb to that brainwashing. *I* have cravings."

"Oh?" She rested a hand on her hip and flipped her green hair over her shoulder, turning her chest more fully toward him.

Yidar snorted. "I desire far more than a sexual encounter in the weeds. I propose a trade of information. I'll share what I know about the portal and who's going through it and why. You tell me how many of your people are out here and what they desire."

"Were I to give that information to you, my people would be disappointed in me."

"Yet you want information from me."

"I'm authorized to pay for it, though I'm already aware of the capabilities of the portal. Tell me about your fleet and how long so many of them will be here. And what of the other fleets? Are they allies? Or is there tension among your people?" Kywatha exuded radiance and power that Sorath could sense, even without the ability to detect magic.

Had she been asking him those questions, he might have blurted out answers.

"Tell me why you want that information," Yidar said, flying closer to her, his eyes locked with hers, "and perhaps I'll share it. Are you planning an attack? Another attempt to take the portal from us?"

Yidar also exuded power, and Sorath felt the urge to answer *his* questions too. Next to him, Sasko mouthed words, as if she were on the verge of blurting answers. Her eyes were fixed on the two magic users, unblinking.

Sorath lifted a hand to block her view. It took her a few seconds to blink and focus on him. When she realized she'd been responding to their magical compulsion, she closed her mouth and nodded to him.

"What if we were?" Kywatha asked. "Do you care about the portal, or are you simply following your ruler's orders, because that is your duty?"

"That is why I follow his orders, yes. The portal means little to me."

"Oh? If it disappeared, you would not care?"

"I would not. But if that is what you plan, others would fight you. *Many* others."

"We know this. We are powerful but few. To act against such a large conglomeration of mages would be unwise, and yet you have invaded our land and brought this danger to life once again. The people of Zewnath live in fear. The memories of our ancestors have not been forgotten."

Yidar waved a dismissive hand, and Sorath highly doubted he cared about what the locals feared.

"If I could help you get rid of it," Yidar said, "would your people assist me?"

She squinted at him. "In what way?"

"I seek to conquer a land of my own."

"In one of the worlds accessible through the portal?"

"No. I do not want to rule some forsaken predator-filled hell devoid of people. I want subjects who would make my kingdom great. I wish a land *here*."

"Few lands are unclaimed in this world." Kywatha's squint deepened. "We would strike down anyone who attempted to impose rule over ours."

"I am aware of that, and this land is too remote for my interests. You have nothing to fear from me."

She scoffed. "We would not fear you, regardless."

Yidar's chin rose. "I am zidarr and highly trained. You would be wise to respect my power."

"You are one man, and I am not alone."

The cat growled, though the way Kywatha glanced toward the trees made Sorath think she might have druid allies out there. Camouflaged in the same way that he and Sasko were?

"I am the equal of *many* men." Yidar flew closer to her, his chest puffed out.

He did ooze power, and Sorath wouldn't want to tangle with him—he well remembered his failure to best Stone Heart—but Kywatha gazed back, not intimidated.

"Tell me about the fleets and if there are tensions between them that might be exploited," she said, her voice again full of compulsion.

But it didn't work on Yidar. He only smiled. "Tell your leader that I'll consider helping you with your problem if you help me with mine."

"What makes you think *I'm* not the leader of my clan?"

"Because you were chosen for your looks and to wiggle your boobs at me."

Indignation flared in her green eyes. Sorath couldn't tell if it was because Yidar was wrong or simply if he was offensive.

"I'm not unappreciative of those assets, but they will not sway me." He reached out and patted her cheek, the gesture far more condescending than flirtatious.

The jaguar growled and stalked up to Kywatha's side, jaws parting to show fangs.

Too arrogant to see either of them as a threat, Yidar only chuckled and gave a final cheek pat. "Make my offer to your leader, and tell him to speak with me directly next time."

Sorath rolled his eyes, wishing Kywatha would strike him down using some superior druid power. With her eyes narrowed and still blazing with indignation, she seemed to be considering it. And the feline seemed to be considering how delicious zidarr organs would be to nosh on.

But she didn't strike out at him. Sadly, Yidar probably *was* more powerful than she. The kings only chose the best to train as zidarr.

Kywatha stepped back from him, and the jaguar shifted protectively in front of her, growling again as it eyed Yidar's crotch.

"I will discuss your offer with my people," she said stiffly.

"Excellent." Yidar pulled a green oval out of his pocket, one that matched the one on the ground. "I will be available when you have news, but don't contact me unless it's important."

He spun his skyboard to fly off without waiting for confirmation. Sorath held his breath as Yidar neared their hiding spot. Even though Vinjo's device had been working thus far, Sorath remembered that Vinjo had grown visible to him when he'd been within a few feet. Sorath crouched, preparing to spring aside.

But Yidar veered around their trees instead of flying through them and sped back toward the pool, gaining in elevation to return to his ship.

Kywatha said something in her language that sounded like a curse—or a comment on what an ass Yidar was—and glared after him for a long moment before picking up the green device from the ground. The light disappeared as she slipped it into a pouch at her waist and padded off in the opposite direction with the jaguar trailing her.

Sorath waited for several minutes before stirring.

"I was *so* hoping that cat was going to bite him in the balls," Sasko whispered.

Sorath wouldn't have minded seeing that either, but he said, "I'm sure Uthari will bestow a far greater punishment on him when we tell him his zidarr was chatting with a druid about establishing his own kingdom."

"Far greater than having his balls chewed off by a jaguar? Are you sure? That sounds unpleasant."

"True. Maybe we can suggest it as punishment when we report."

"As long as you're sure *we* won't get in trouble for this," Sasko said. "We won't, right?"

"With Uthari? I doubt it. But if Yidar only gets a slap on the wrist while finding out we ratted him out... that could be problematic."

"You better start sleeping with that thing." Sasko had released him, and she pointed at Vinjo's device.

"If we can get Vinjo released and working for us, he might be able to make enough so that we could all sleep with one."

"Why would Uthari let him go to do that? He's Zaruk's mage."

"I'm hoping he can become *our* mage." Sorath touched his chest.

"I didn't know you were in the market for mages."

"Mages that create devices that can help mercenaries avoid being detected and attacked by those with magical power? Oh, yes. I'm in the market for one of those."

"To what end?"

Sorath blew out a slow breath. "Let's not think about that right now. We'll just see if we can save Vinjo from torture and death first."

"He should be grateful to you if you do that."

"So I hope."

~

Chaos broke out so quickly that Tezi almost dropped her axe. She'd been leaning on it during the long exchange with the locals, until the man who'd identified himself as Ambassador Rajesk whirled and launched a magical attack at Jak and Malek.

Malek must have been ready, for the blast of power didn't stir his hair through his defenses, and somehow he protected Jak and the hatchling, but it caught Tinder and Fret. They flew backward twenty feet and hit a wall with painful thuds.

Tezi had been standing apart with Jadora, and the attack only glanced off her side, but she still stumbled and fumbled the axe. But she recovered quickly, hefted it, and sprang toward the ambassador.

A barrier kept her from reaching him, but Malek drew his sword and main-gauche and sliced through the invisible obstacle. The ambassador leaped back with a curse. Malek might have struck him, but the other men, who'd seemed simple advisors, surged at Malek from the sides. From somewhere within their tunics, they produced short swords, and he was forced to deal with them.

The curtains at the entryway were thrust aside, and four more armed men rushed in. Tinder had recovered enough to shoot at one as Fret scrambled behind a chair in a corner, her medical kit clutched to her chest. Tinder's magelock blast ricocheted off a barrier. Here, even the armed guards were mages.

One of the newcomers leaped for Tinder and Fret, but Rivlen sprang into his path. Their blades met, and power flew around the room, making the floor and walls shake.

As the ambassador's allies battled Malek, Jak scrambled to protect the hatchling and stay out of the way. Two of the men who'd charged through the curtain rushed toward Tezi and Jadora. Tinder fired again and again, trying to halt their progress, but they didn't glance back. They were confident their barriers would protect them.

Tezi growled and hefted her battle-axe. It had killed a giant magical worm; it ought to be able to slice through a mage's barrier. It *had* to. She wouldn't let these men kill Jadora.

The two mages seemed startled when Tezi lunged in to confront them. She swung the battle-axe straight at the lead man's face. He spotted the blade, maybe realized it was dragon steel, and dodged away as it cleaved through his barrier. The magic popped like a pricked soap bubble.

His comrade stabbed a short sword at Tezi's chest as the other man lifted his hand. She anticipated a magical attack that would hurl her back, but all she could focus on was holding her ground and parrying the sword. If she dodged out of the way, the men would be able to reach Jadora.

Axe struck sword, her dragon steel meeting normal steel. It not only blocked the blow but cut the lesser blade in half. The man cursed and sprang back, hurling power at her. *Both* guards were throwing power around, and a chair beside her upturned, flying into the wall. For some reason, the power didn't strike Tezi.

Was the axe protecting her from it? It had to be.

Aware of men flying into walls to her side—Malek's work—Tezi slashed at the two closest to her with her axe, trying to drive them back. She feared the repercussions of killing them in the middle of their own city, but she had to defend herself and her friends.

Knock them out if you can, she thought to her axe, remembering Jak's suggestion that she try to communicate with it.

To her surprise, both men flew back, struck a wall, and crumpled. They didn't rise. She had no idea if the axe had been responsible or if Malek or Rivlen had launched an attack from across the room.

Unfortunately, another guard rushed in, this man armed with a blue-black sword the same color as Tezi's axe. He must have thrown a magical attack at her, for another chair behind her went flying. Thinking her distracted, he sprang in and sliced his sword toward her head.

Tezi swept her axe up, thankful it was far lighter than it looked. She parried his blade, but he was already attacking again, raining a combination of blows toward her head and chest. Lightning erupted from his sword and shot at her.

She leaped back, envisioning being electrocuted. But her axe pulsed blue, and the lightning disappeared before it touched her.

That didn't keep her foe from continuing to attack, his blade slashing toward her with daunting speed, and she couldn't help but back away. Aware of the wall and Jadora behind her, Tezi again tried to hold her ground. She couldn't let herself be pinned in a corner.

As she parried another blow and tried to lunge in fast enough for an effective counterattack, Jadora threw a vial at the man's face. It struck his cheek, spattering something, and startled him. It only distracted him for a second, but it was long enough for Tezi to land her blow. The axe sliced through his tunic and bit into muscle.

He roared in pain and staggered back, clawing at his face instead of his chest. He kept his sword up and pointed at Tezi, but he was too busy trying to wipe off the acid, or whatever Jadora had thrown, to attack Tezi again.

A cacophony of weapons clashing rang out from the side, Malek fighting two men as he kept glancing at the ambassador, who stared at him with a hand outstretched, fingers splayed, as if they were locked in a mental battle even as Malek used his blades against other foes.

Rivlen drove her sword into the belly of the guard she'd been attacking, and he pitched to the floor. She whirled to try to get over to help Malek, but someone threw a dagger at her. Her barrier was up, and it struck a foot from her face and clanked off. A magical attack followed right after it and slipped through her defenses—or tore them away? Rivlen staggered back, fighting it but being pushed as if by a hurricane gale.

Jak crouched by the wall, trying to protect the hatchling, who was intent on climbing out of his sling and up to his shoulder. He spotted Rivlen in trouble. The man attacking her had her pinned against the wall with magic and was striding toward her with a dragon-steel dagger in hand.

Jak yanked out his pistol and fired at the man. It didn't hurt the mage, but it distracted him enough for Rivlen to push away from the wall and heft her sword to challenge him. He paused, but he didn't appear worried. He attacked her again as she sprang at him. Tezi couldn't sense their magic, but their faces were twisted in concentration and pain, and she knew they fought with more than blades.

The guard Jadora had struck with acid recovered enough to raise his sword and come at Tezi again. She swept her axe up, deflecting a blow, and tried to knock his weapon out of his hands. What if more guards were on the way? How could she put an end to this?

A thunderous boom came from the doorway—one of Tinder's grenades going off.

Tezi glanced in time to see two more men who'd been about to charge in to help stagger back into the corridor. Stone tumbled down from the door arch, crashing to the floor and hurling dust into the air. It wasn't enough rubble to fill the doorway and block others from coming, and shouts and sandals slapping on the floor sounded in the corridor. Reinforcements.

"Stop!" Malek ordered, such power infusing the word that Tezi found that she couldn't move.

Everyone halted, each fight pausing. Malek had downed one of the mages and grabbed the ambassador, securing him from behind and putting his main-gauche to his throat.

"Attack us further, and I will kill him," Malek said, speaking telepathically as well as out loud, though the remaining men in the room surely didn't need a translation. "We came in peace to offer trade, not to start a fight."

The hatchling squawked and jumped up and down from a new perch he'd attained—the top of Jak's head. The little dragon's wings flapped, as if he wanted to fly somewhere, but they weren't capable of that yet.

The ambassador smiled and spread his arms slowly, careful not to alarm Malek. *We surrender. Forgive me, visitors. It was a test. That is all.*

"A *test*?" Jadora clutched another vial and looked like she wanted to pour it down his throat.

Yes, yes. To see if you are worthy. I cannot bother the etchers with requests from every foreigner who wanders into our city. They are very busy. The four etchers rule our entire world. They don't have time to speak with weaklings without power.

"How unfortunate," Jadora muttered.

Jak plucked the hatchling off his head and tried to slide him back into his sling.

The ambassador licked his lips and looked at him. *Call off your bodyguard, Favored Traveler. You have passed the test. I will arrange rooms for you and take your offer of trade to the etchers.*

"Order all of your people to drop their weapons," Jak said.

Rajesk hesitated.

Malek tightened his grip, and a bead of blood dribbled from a cut in the man's neck.

Rajesk forced another smile. *Yes, yes. Everyone lower your weapons. They have passed the test. We will attack them no more.*

His people grumbled words Tezi couldn't understand, but they set their blades on the floor.

Servants are on the way, the ambassador said. *Rooms are being prepared. You will enjoy our hospitality while I seek an audience with the etchers on your behalf. It is my honor to serve. Favored Traveler, have your bodyguard release me, yes? I am your host, and you have my word, I will not attack you again today.*

Today? Would he be at them with swords and magic again in the morning?

Malek and Jak held gazes, some telepathic words passing between them.

After a long moment, Malek lowered his blade and released Rajesk, who grimaced and wiped the blood from his neck.

Malek watched him warily, and Tezi had no doubt that his magical defenses remained up. Malek glanced at Jadora and must have telepathically asked if she was all right, for she nodded.

As Jak joined his mother, squeezing her shoulder and whispering something to her, Tezi made her way to Tinder and Fret to check on them. She had to step over large stones that had fallen, thanks to the grenade.

Like Malek, Tezi kept an eye on Rajesk, certain he was lying about the attack being a test and that they all would have been killed if they'd failed to gain the upper hand. He'd been staring covetously at Jak's hatchling the whole time they'd been talking. She feared Rajesk would only try again to kill them, so he could take the little dragon for himself.

Tinder clapped her on the shoulder. "You all right, Rookie?"

"Yes. Are you two?"

"A mage threw me into a wall," Fret said. "Tomorrow, my back will be swollen to twice its normal size and bruised darker than blackberry jam."

"Don't you have a cream for that?" Tinder asked.

"I'm not sure. I landed on my medical kit. My creams may be swollen and bruised too." Fret grimaced and held up her kit. "I heard something break."

"It'll be fine." Tinder gave her a gentler pat on the shoulder. "Later, I'll rub your back with whatever isn't broken and oozing all over the place."

Rivlen didn't complain of bruises, but she rubbed her own back gingerly. Blood trickled from a cut in her arm.

The promised servants clambered in, saying nothing about the rubble all over the floor and the half-collapsed archway. They bowed to the ambassador, then to Jak, and waved for the group to follow them.

"Do you think they'll really take us to rooms?" Tezi asked. "Or will we get a dungeon cell?"

She eyed the arena through the windows. Another battle had commenced, this time between humans and other humans rather than giant monsters. The spectators cheered, oblivious to the similar battle that had been going on in this room.

"I don't know," Fret said, looking toward where the bloodstains below had been poorly covered with sand, "but, whatever it is, I hope it doesn't have a view of the arena."

"I hope it isn't *in* the arena," Tinder said.

"Me too." Tezi caught Rajesk eyeing Jak's back speculatively as their group headed out.

It was too bad these people were as bad as the mages in her world. Until things had gone awry, Tezi had wistfully thought this might be the kind of place where she could disappear for a couple of years. But she feared the mages here would be just as likely to read her mind and punish her for past actions as those back home.

9

Malek was surprised when the servants led them up three flights of stairs to a suite of rooms with comfortable sofas, chairs, and tables laden with food. Despite the ambassador's promise, he'd expected dungeon cells, especially since they hadn't left the arena.

From their lofty elevation, the suite overlooked the fights in the sand below. Unlike in the other room that had been open to the air outside, a bank of glass windows kept out most of the noise from the crowd and the battles.

Nobody spoke until the servants withdrew and closed the thick velvet curtain separating the suite from the corridor. Doors weren't popular here, at least not in the arena.

Rivlen rubbed the back of her neck, winced, and looked toward Malek. "I'm glad you were more ready than I was, my lord. I wasn't relaxed, but I didn't have a barrier up right at that moment. The ambassador was lusting after the hatchling, and the man in the hat was flirting with our professor. I wasn't expecting an attack."

Jadora's mouth dropped open, and she sent a scandalized—or maybe embarrassed—frown in Rivlen's direction.

"I had a suspicion that Rajesk would attack sooner or later," was all Malek said.

His sword had given him that premonition as they'd climbed the stairs of the arena. Malek liked to think he would have been swift enough to react even without a warning, especially since he'd been on edge all along. He'd had a bad feeling about this place and these people since Rajesk first looked down at them—at Jak and his dragon—from the city wall.

"I had a hunch they would do something too," Rivlen said, "but I wasn't expecting it to be so *effective*. They were strong."

"They were," Malek said.

"*Really* strong." Rivlen gave him a significant look, uncertainty in her eyes. A rare expression from her.

Malek nodded, knowing exactly what she meant and acknowledging it. He hated to admit it, but when they'd been walking through the city, he'd sensed mages with auras as strong as Tonovan's. Maybe as strong as Uthari's and his own. And they hadn't appeared to hold special positions in society, at least not that he could tell. A couple had seemed the equivalent of guards. Others had been on shopping errands, selecting melons from a vendor's cart. Even in the heart of Utharika, Malek wasn't accustomed to being around people with such strong auras.

If not for his weapons skills, Malek wasn't positive he would have defeated Rajesk. In a pure battle of magic, they might have been equals. Or... Malek might have lost.

He'd been one of the best in the world—*his* world—for so long that the idea was a daunting one. Even though he trained hard and always expected challenges, the thought of a random *melon shopper* being a more powerful mage than he was hard to swallow.

Jadora exchanged a long look with Jak, and they walked to one of several seating areas and sank down on a sofa far from the window overlooking the arena. Malek hadn't been monitoring Jadora but caught her thinking about not being surprised by the presence of powerful mages on a world with more dragon steel than Torvil.

"Get your cream out, Fret. Walls hurt when you collide with them at the speed of a mage cart with no brakes careening down from a mountain pass." Sergeant Tinder flopped stomach first onto a sofa with a wince. "I'll slather your back after you slather mine."

"That is fair." Fret poked into her medical kit. "If anyone else requires slathering with numbing agents, anti-inflammatory cream, healing tinctures, or wishes to imbibe painkillers, my apothecary shop is open for business."

"I'll take all of those things," Tinder mumbled into the sofa.

Tezi joined them while Rivlen prowled to the window to frown down on yet another battle taking place in the arena below. This was a strange place for suites and meeting rooms, but perhaps in this culture, it was common to watch people die while chatting about business.

Malek wanted to ask Jadora about why she believed a proliferation of dragon steel would be correlated to more powerful mages. All the speculation he'd heard about why some people had more magical potential than others suggested it was based on heredity.

He bypassed a table full of food and pitchers of exotically colored juices and stood beside the sofa where Jak and Jadora sat. The hatchling escaped from Jak's sling, plopped off the cushions, and disappeared between his legs. Shikari was just small enough to fit under the sofa.

"Are you going to let him run wild?" Jadora asked.

"Yes. Unless he tries to go out there." Jak waved toward the curtain as scratching noises came from under the sofa. "He's probably looking for bugs. Or a place to deposit already digested bugs."

"Delightful."

"Given how we've been treated here so far, I'm rooting for that."

"Some poor servant will be the one who has to clean it," Jadora said.

"If you wish to spite the appropriate person," Malek said, "perhaps you could gather the droppings and deposit them in Ambassador Rajesk's pocket."

Jak snapped his fingers. "Good idea."

Jadora smiled tiredly up at Malek. "Do you think he'll truly arrange a meeting with his... etchers for us?"

"I could not read his mind, so I do not know what he intends, but he is dangerous and dishonest." Malek looked at Jak. "I regret that I permitted you to bring the hatchling. I did not foresee a civilization here, nor that it would be full of people who would covet Shikari."

"If I recall correctly, you *didn't* want me to bring him along. It was my idea. I was afraid he wouldn't be safe back on Torvil surrounded by mages who might also covet him." Jak's mouth twisted wryly.

"True, but I could have insisted he stay."

"Wish he'd insisted *I* stay," came Tinder's mumble from across the room.

Malek would have preferred a private conversation with Jak and Jadora and thought about suggesting they go into another room, but the adjoining rooms were all bedrooms, save for a lavatory, and he didn't know how Jadora would feel about being in a bedroom with him. After Uthari had shared that warning of passionate kissing with him, Malek didn't know how he felt about being in a bedroom with *her*. Not that anything would happen with Jak there, or even if he *wasn't* there, but... Malek was on edge around her after that chat with his liege.

Further, he found it troubling that it had bothered him when Jadora's gaze had snagged on the explorer Zethron and she'd thought about how he reminded her of her husband—and how much she missed her husband. Malek hadn't intended to monitor her thoughts, but she'd mentioned partially understanding the language, so he'd been checking in on her in case she grasped something beyond what the ambassador had been telepathically sharing.

After that, he'd felt an irrational surge of disgruntlement when she'd been standing close to Zethron, a feeling that had only grown more intense when the man had started smiling at her. It had taken him a few moments to recognize the feeling as primitive possessiveness, at which point he'd made himself tamp it down and focus on the mission. Jadora was not someone he could have a relationship with, so his only concern when it came to her and other men should be that she was safe. He'd sworn to protect her. That was all.

"Should we try to escape tonight?" Jadora asked quietly, oblivious to his thoughts.

"That might be a bad idea." Malek, thinking of the barrier around the city, wasn't confident that they *could* escape.

"Are you sure? It sounds like a wonderful idea to me." Jadora smiled. "I showed Zethron a drawing of Jitaruvak, and he didn't recognize it. That doesn't mean it's not somewhere on this world—he admitted he's not a gardener or herbalist—but it doesn't match the predominant blue-green of the foliage we've seen so far."

Malek glanced at the window, noting that mage lights were glowing outside now, the sky darkening above the arena. Would the battles go on into the night?

Escaping the city might not be plausible, but maybe he could sneak out through one of the windows and gather information from the denizens. He hadn't succeeded in reading the minds of any of the mages, but he'd had no trouble with most of the humans they'd passed with discs embedded in their temples. By spying on a few mundane citizens, perhaps he could find out where these etchers resided and arrange his *own* meeting with them.

"Is it that you won't leave without the dragon steel and its secrets?" Jadora sounded disappointed.

Malek focused on her again. No, she wasn't disappointed but chagrined at the thought of Uthari and mages like him gaining more weapons that would give them further advantages over terrene humans. An intense longing filled her for her people to be able to govern themselves and live without having to pay huge amounts of taxes and give tributes to their rulers.

Malek gazed sadly at her. It wasn't that he didn't understand—even though more than thirty years had passed since he'd been a part of that world, he remembered his childhood well—but some things couldn't be changed. It was better to work within the system, which she'd been given the opportunity to do. She and Jak could work for Uthari and live pleasant existences while they pursued their passions. And taxes... She was naive if she believed such wouldn't exist under terrene human rule. Services for the people and military forces to defend them didn't fund themselves.

"It would be desirable to return with dragon steel," he said, not commenting on the rest, since he had no wish to argue with her, "and to learn whatever magic can work it would be a great boon, but that is not what I meant. I fear that in coming here, we've created a problem for our people. *All* of our people." He pointed at her and at himself. "Until we arrived, this civilization didn't know our world existed anymore, or if it did, that it was accessible. Now, they know about Torvil—the *First World*—and that we may have dragon eggs, something they're clearly interested in obtaining."

Jak looked at him. "I was trying hard not to let the ambassador know about the eggs or where they really are."

"I don't believe he found out. I was close enough to you that I could guard your thoughts from him, and he didn't seem to think any of *your women*—" Malek couldn't keep from quirking an eyebrow, still bemused that the ambassador had thought Jak was in charge of their group, "—were worth probing for information."

"My women, right." Jak glanced at Rivlen. "I thought her eyes were going to bulge out when he said that."

"My eyes may have bulged slightly," Jadora said.

"Yours should have, because that would have been gross. But I didn't want to say you were my mother in case..." Jak shuddered. "I didn't want to tell him *anything*. He wants Shikari and I don't know what else."

"Do you know what he meant when he called you Favored Traveler?" Malek had a hunch, but he was curious what Jak knew.

"It might be because the portal is willing to communicate with me. *Portals.* I thought that was just because I'd chatted with ours from the beginning and established a rapport with it, inasmuch as one can with ancient dragon artifacts, but... maybe that isn't everything." Jak spread his hands. "I don't understand why, but the new ones have been willing to communicate with me too. Originally, I thought they would be happy to chat with anyone, but..."

"Not everyone," Rivlen said, walking over. "King Uthari spent hours trying to get ours to respond to him."

"To respond to him or to fry his enemies with lightning?" Jak asked.

"I wasn't privy to his telepathic requests to it, but the enemies weren't around when he first started."

"It's unfortunate that we don't have written records from the distant past," Malek said. "From people who used and interacted with the portal."

"We may have resources here." Jadora thought of Zethron.

"We can't trust anyone here." Malek attempted to wall off his mind so he wouldn't sense her thoughts. He didn't want to see her thinking of the man or how he reminded her of her husband again.

Besides, he knew she would prefer it if he didn't intrude upon her privacy. It was such a habit, to be aware of what other people—whom he was used to considering potential enemies—were thinking, that he had to consciously keep himself from doing so, especially around terrene humans who did little to guard their thoughts.

"Do we have to trust them to extract information from them, my lord?" Rivlen asked. "I don't believe Zethron is a mage. If we can find him, it should be easy to learn what he knows."

Jadora frowned. "I hope you're not suggesting capturing him and interrogating him. He was the only person who wasn't scheming to get the hatchling."

"I didn't check his thoughts," Rivlen said. "He *might* have been scheming."

"We won't do anything openly hostile yet," Malek said, "besides defending ourselves. As I told Jak earlier, I *might* be able to break through their barrier to get us out of the city, but I'm not positive. I also have a hunch the dragon-steel weapons might not be sufficient to cut through it. We could be trapped here."

"We should try to get some of those discs." Jak pointed to his temple. "I think those might be what let the citizens come and go through the barrier. Those were just terrene humans riding out of the city."

"*Just* terrene humans?" Jadora murmured.

"You know what I mean. Normal people." Jak flattened a hand to his chest. "Like us."

"You weren't normal even before you started developing powers," she told him.

"You're calling me weird?" He squinted at her. "How many weeds did you pull up from alongside the road and stuff into your pockets on the way here? *That's* weird."

"Those were specimens, and they went into my collections tin."

"Weirdly."

"Ha ha."

Malek was glad they could still joke with each other. They'd been through a lot, much of it his fault. Even if all he'd been doing was following orders, he couldn't deny that he'd disrupted their lives and put them in danger. Repeatedly.

"Uhm," came Tezi's voice from the doorway. "Is your hatchling supposed to be over here, Jak?"

Jak swore, bent down to peer under the sofa, then ran toward the doorway. The curtain shivered.

"Is he trying to escape?" Jadora asked.

"Right now," Tezi said, "he's chewing on the curtain."

Rivlen shook her head and walked to the table to pour herself a cup of juice. Malek didn't see any water. When he got a chance, he would have to refill his canteen at one of the fountains in the city.

"Do you truly think we have, in coming here, caused a new threat for our people?" Jadora looked up at him.

"I can't know for certain, but I think if we'd failed that *test*, the ambassador would have assumed us weak—and that the people on our world might be weak. If they believe we have more dragon eggs there, and that it's safe for them to travel there, they might consider an invasion of Torvil."

"I guess it's good that there are so many mages defending the portal. Assuming they haven't already broken their truce and aren't busy attacking each other." Jadora rubbed her face, thinking of her father, and worrying that he was stuck aboard Uthari's yacht, which would surely be a target in a conflict.

Malek hadn't meant to catch the thought, but since he had, he felt he should say something comforting. But could he? He hadn't been the one to kidnap her father, but he was linked with Uthari in Jadora's mind. Understandably so.

He removed his weapons belt so he could sit on the sofa next to her. "If we can bring back some dragon steel and the secret to manipulating it, I'm certain Uthari would be pleased. Perhaps, when he sees that you're willingly working for him, he'll have your father taken back to his home. Uthari wants the plant, but he'll be happy to gain other resources that can further enhance his kingdom and solidify his place in the history books."

Jadora made a face at the words *willingly working for him*. A poor choice, perhaps. Malek knew she had few options, and that was why she was working for Uthari. A shame. He would have liked it if they could simply explore the worlds linked via the portals because it was what they both wanted.

"What do *you* want, Malek?" she asked quietly.

"It is my duty to serve my king."

She gave him an exasperated look.

He knew what she meant, but he didn't have another answer for her. Through his service to Uthari, his needs were provided for, and he longed for nothing more. That was part of the Zidarr Code, to live simply and crave only to better oneself through training, and to serve the king and, through him, the needs of the kingdom.

"What if he dies?" Jadora asked. "Do you end up serving some spoiled offspring of his? Does he even *have* offspring?"

"None that he has openly named his heir. He's always been secretive about who he has listed in his personal documents as a successor. As to your question, it's likely he'll outlive me. He's outlived a lot of his zidarr."

"Is he really hundreds of years old?"

"I believe so."

"That machine can't keep him alive forever."

"Hence his desire for the Jitaruvak."

"It won't protect him from an assassin's dagger. What happens if he dies and you hate whoever you're supposed to serve next?"

"He's effectively avoided daggers for centuries." Malek didn't keep himself from monitoring Jadora's thoughts now. He didn't *think* she would ever take up the role of assassin and try to concoct some poison to kill Uthari, but she certainly had the knowledge to do so. Or to hand such a potion off to someone who *would* kill him. Colonel Sorath's face came to Malek's mind.

But she wasn't fantasizing about brewing up poisons. She was wishing Malek would walk away from his duties as zidarr, because she would rather have him as an ally than an enemy.

He would prefer to have her as an ally, as well, but he didn't understand why she couldn't simply agree to work for Uthari. With time, she would become trusted, and she would have as much freedom as a professor working in Utharika as she'd had at her university in Sprungtown. Perhaps more. She would have more resources at her disposal for her studies and research projects.

"You never wonder about what if?" she asked him. "What if an enemy finally takes him out? What if the next king is someone you loathe or who doesn't appreciate you or even want you as a zidarr? What would you do if you were… fired?"

"*Fired*?" Malek couldn't keep from sounding indignant. Even if zidarr were not extremely valuable resources that only a fool would let go… who would fire *him*?

She raised her eyebrows.

"I see no point in speculating about something that may never come to pass. I *was* wondering what might happen if you stopped thinking of Uthari as a slavemaster cracking a whip in Hell and accepted his offer. Why not work for him willingly? You would have great resources at your disposal and might be able to do more for people than you could at your university."

"More for *people* or more for mages?"

"Mages are people."

"People who don't need anything more done for them. I want to help *my* people." She touched her chest.

"Come *down* from there," Jak whispered. "I'm learning how to levitate things. Don't think I can't get you."

The hatchling had climbed the curtain to the rod at the top of the archway and was now chewing on the fasteners. Already, the thick velvet fabric drooped in a couple of spots.

"What happens when one of your people becomes one of our people?" Malek didn't want to use Jak against her, but he wished she could see that it would be better for her to join them. For Jak's sake, if not only for her own. She couldn't drag him off into hiding and forbid him from further developing his powers. Not now. It was too late for that.

The anguished expression she turned on him promised that she knew that. She bent forward, elbows on her knees, and dropped her face into her hands.

Malek winced, regretting that he'd pointed that out, that he was trying to change her mind. Maybe in time, she would see for herself that he was right, but she would only resent it if he tried to coerce her. Besides, when he'd sat beside her, he'd meant to comfort her, not distress her further.

"I'm sorry," he said quietly and lifted a hand, though he held it in the air instead of resting it on her back, not certain she would appreciate his touch. And worried he would appreciate it too much. Her thick brown hair was back in a ponytail splayed across her back, and he had an urge to touch it to see if it was as soft as he thought. He drew his hand back and looked at the floor, Uthari's vision creeping into his mind again.

She shook her head and didn't respond, but after a moment, she slumped to the side and leaned on him.

He froze, half expecting her to realize she'd leaned the wrong way, mistaking him for the arm of the sofa, but maybe she wanted his support. That seemed odd, since he was the source of her distress, but if he could help through some physical gesture, he would. This time, when he lifted his hand, he rested it on her back. His thumb brushed her hair. It *was* soft.

He remembered the last time he'd put an arm around her, in

her cabin when Jak had been badly wounded, and he'd been healing him. Her need for support had been understandable then, and he hadn't doubted that he'd chosen correctly in wrapping an arm around her shoulders. Now, he was less certain this was appropriate, but he didn't remove his arm. He *did* resist the urge to touch the back of her head and stroke her hair.

"It's gotten dark out," Rivlen said from the window, "and the games have ended."

Jadora sighed, sat up, and rubbed her face. She looked tired, maybe still distressed.

Malek removed his arm, doubting he'd helped in any way. He knew how to protect people, to defeat their enemies with his sword, and to go into battle to defend their interests. The ability to comfort people was not among his repertoire of tools.

"The spectators are funneling out. If one wanted to skulk around and gather information, the hour to do so might be coming." Rivlen looked back at Malek, glancing at Jadora. She might have wondered if he was responsible for the bleak expression on her face, but all she said was, "If you don't want to do it, my lord, I can."

"I'll go." Malek stood and buckled his weapons belt on again. "I need you to stay here and protect our group in case the ambassador sends someone else to *test* us."

Rivlen hesitated. "Of course, my lord. If you find a cache of dragon steel and need assistance in getting it, I will gladly help."

"For now, all I'll seek is information." Malek looked at Jadora, groping for parting words that would ease the sting he'd inadvertently delivered, but he didn't know what to say.

Jak had managed to retrieve his charge, though the hatchling was now chewing on one of the table legs. The food and drinks might all be on the floor by the time Malek returned.

"Maybe if he destroys all their furnishings," Jak said, "they won't be so eager to get their own hatchlings."

"Perhaps." Malek stopped next to him on his way to the windows. "I noticed you funneling power into Rivlen and me during the skirmish."

"Yeah." Jak shrugged sheepishly. "I wasn't sure if you needed it, like with the dragon, or if it would help, but I didn't know what else to do to be useful. I'm figuring out how to defend myself, but I don't know how to attack others yet. I'm a little scared to try. I don't want to accidentally hurt anyone unless they're truly horrible and trying to kill us." Though he was doing better at walling off his thoughts, the memory of him accidentally tearing apart the jungle canopy and dumping it on Uthari's deck formed in his mind. All he'd wanted was to blow a few insects their way... "Even then, I don't really want to... uhm. I don't want to kill people." Jak winced, his concern that Malek would be disappointed in him stamping out the rest of his thoughts.

Malek would have been more concerned if Jak *wanted* to kill people. He wasn't training to be a zidarr; he didn't need to assassinate enemies for Uthari. And his mother, Malek had no doubt, would prefer it if Jak *not* use his power to kill.

"I'll show you some nonfatal methods for deterring enemies when I get back," he said.

"Oh, good." Relief flooded Jak, and he surprised Malek by hugging him. "*Thank* you."

Though he didn't know how to respond to the enthusiasm, or someone's willingness to hug a zidarr, Malek patted him on the back.

Jak released him, grinned, and trotted into the room to save the table leg from the hatchling. The relief lingered in his thoughts along with his eagerness to learn new things.

Malek had never thought he would have a student, but he admitted he'd gotten lucky, that any mage instructor would have been pleased to have someone so determined and excited to learn.

Hoping his eagerness to learn *magic* wasn't distressing Jadora further, Malek looked back at her.

She'd noticed the exchange, but she was smiling slightly as she watched her son chase the hatchling around. He sensed her relief that Malek was teaching him instead of Uthari. Malek didn't know if he should condone that—after all, Uthari was an excellent instructor who'd taught *Malek*—but when Jadora met his eyes and nodded at him, he nodded back before slipping out through a window.

<hr />

As dawn's light spread over the camp, skyboards flew Colonel Sorath and Captain Ferroki up to the *Serene Waters*.

Sorath believed Vinjo was being held prisoner on General Tonovan's *Dread Arrow*, but Uthari was a more reasonable man than Tonovan, so he was the one they would attempt to negotiate with. Further, the zidarr worked directly for their king, so Uthari was the logical one to report to regarding Yidar's transgressions.

Sorath had slept and waited until morning to request a ride up, knowing that if he ended up speaking with Uthari, he needed his wits sharp for the meeting. Having a conversation with someone who could read one's mind was always fraught, and with the thoughts that had been percolating through Sorath's lately, he had to be extra careful.

A raindrop plopped onto his nose as he hopped off the skyboard. Dark gray clouds overhead promised that one of the daily torrential rainfalls would soon soak everything.

"What do you want me to do?" Ferroki asked quietly as she stepped off, two mage guards in red uniforms waiting on deck for them.

"The same thing you did in my last meeting with Uthari."

"Grab your arm, hiss at you, and try to keep you from vaulting across his desk in what would be a doomed attempt to strangle him?"

"Precisely." Sorath also wanted her opinion on whatever Uthari gave—and did not give—away to them. Sorath could outthink opponents on a battlefield, especially when their motivations and desires were known, but he was less good at reading people in face-to-face meetings. He always preferred bluntness and getting to the point, not the verbal fencing that so many favored. "He is *paying you* for that."

"True."

Sorath gazed past the railing toward the *Dread Arrow*, wondering how Vinjo was doing and if he was still alive. It had been some time since screams of pain had come from the ship. Hopefully, that didn't mean Tonovan had killed him.

A third guard came out through the double doors that Sorath knew from previous trips led to Uthari's suite.

"Huh," he said. "I thought we would have to work our way up the chain of command before we got a meeting with him."

All he'd told the crewman he'd reported to was that he'd witnessed something suspicious on his patrol and wanted to report in. Maybe someone had read in his mind that Yidar was involved.

The rain started coming down harder as the guard led Sorath and Ferroki into the wood-floored and wood-paneled hallway. A servant trailed them into it, bringing water and juice in glass pitchers clinking with ice. As before, Sorath noted the magically cooled air inside and the lack of humidity.

"Enter," Uthari said from the office in his suite.

Several days had passed since their last meeting, but Uthari was in the same seat facing two others across his desk. He wore a red and gold tunic, and his wispy white hair was combed and recently trimmed. At a glance, it would have been easy to mistake him for someone's retired grandfather, but even sense-dead Sorath could sense the powerful magical aura he emanated.

When Uthari waved them to the chairs, Ferroki took a seat while Sorath stood behind his.

"You trailed one of my zidarr into the jungle?" Uthari asked without preamble.

"As part of my patrol, yes," Sorath said.

"And you came to tattle on him?"

"If you wish to know with whom he spoke and about what, yes. I assumed you would want to be informed." Sorath shrugged.

"He met with a voluptuous druid lady." Uthari gazed into Sorath's eyes, reading his thoughts like an open book.

Good. Sorath was carefully keeping the previous night's adventures at the forefront of his mind for a reason. Hopefully, Uthari would be captivated by those thoughts and wouldn't go digging for more.

"Interesting," Uthari said.

"I'm surprised you're not irritated, Your Majesty," Ferroki said.

"Oh, Yidar has been walking a fine line lately. I know what he wants, and it's to serve his own ambitions, not faithfully further mine."

"That doesn't sound very zidarr-like," she said.

"Some students excel. Some disappoint. I'm sure, Captain, that as a leader of soldiers, you understand." Uthari tilted his head, returning his attention to Sorath. "What do you propose I do with him, Colonel?"

"My colleague was hoping he would receive a punishment greater than having his balls chewed off by a large feline."

"Do you think that's the most advantageous thing I could do to him? That it would foster within him further loyalty toward me?"

"Perhaps not, but you thought punishment was a worthwhile thing to do to *me* when I first came aboard."

"Don't be melodramatic, Colonel. I merely had you questioned for information. Specifically, the location of this pool, which you knew."

"It was a painful questioning."

"Your genitalia are intact." Uthari smiled thinly. "Given what your *colleague* wants done to my zidarr, you should be pleased about that."

Sorath kept his face masked, though this chat wasn't going how he'd imagined. He'd hoped to barter this information for Vinjo's life and groped for a way to steer the conversation in that direction.

"I suppose the most *advantageous* thing to do with Yidar, if you don't fear having him working for you when his loyalty is questionable, would be to have someone spy on him. They could watch him and learn where the druids are and if they'll attack. If so, you could use the information to ruthlessly attack them preemptively." As he made the suggestion, Sorath silently apologized to the druids, with whom he had no quarrel. Since the mercenaries had been hired—whether they'd had a choice or not—to work for Uthari and protect the portal, it behooved him to ensure they could do those things effectively.

"I concur. You'll keep an eye on him for me and let me know what you find."

"Ah." Sorath hadn't intended to volunteer *himself* for that mission. Trailing around a zidarr, who might magically detect him and kill him with a thought, wouldn't be good for his longevity.

Uthari smiled again. "How fortunate for you that you've acquired a device that allows you to so easily camouflage yourself from mages."

"Yes." Sorath hadn't intended to hide it, so he wasn't discombobulated when Uthari brought it up. "Have you seen it?"

He drew it out and laid it on the table along with another device he'd brought. There were three others that Vinjo had given him, but he'd left those behind with Sasko. Not because he knew what they did and that they had great value, but because he hadn't wanted to risk losing everything.

"I haven't." Uthari picked up the clandestineness creeper and examined it.

Ferroki reached over and patted Sorath's arm. He thought it might be to convey some message to him, but she merely smiled encouragingly. Maybe she was pleased that he was refraining from fantasies of mage throttling. It was easier not to lose his temper when he had something he wanted to win from his negotiations.

"This is the work of our prisoner?" Uthari set it down and picked up the second device. "Lieutenant Vinjo?"

"Yes. I know you've captured him and have no doubt been *questioning* him—"

"Actually, my interrogation specialist said he prefers when the engineer *doesn't* talk."

"My lieutenant feels the same way," Ferroki murmured.

"He spews babble about his inventions instead of information about Zaruk's troops. He appears to be oblivious about anything that might be considered valuable military intelligence, even related to the ship he traveled on. He forgot his own captain's name."

"He is a touch absentminded from what I observed," Sorath said, "but his inventions have merit. I came up to talk to you on his behalf. It may be worth sparing his life if we could put him to work creating inventions for our side. If druids truly are thinking of attacking the camp, then the more handy tools we have to thwart them the better."

Sorath half-expected Uthari to scoff and say that none of these trinkets would help thwart anyone, but he eyed the creeper speculatively. "It is not easy to sneak up on Yidar or any of my zidarr. That he didn't sense you through this—or sense *it* itself—is a testament to the work. As for the rest, Malek already made that argument."

Sorath raised his eyebrows. As far as he knew, Malek hadn't returned through the portal yet.

"Before he left," Uthari said. "We were contemplating if we could suborn this engineer into working for us, but he is not only Zaruk's officer, he is the brother of one of Zaruk's zidarr. A zidarr would not be swayed—even Yidar is driven only by his own ambitions, not a desire to strike out at me. A zidarr might, however, kill his brother to keep him from working for an enemy."

"I don't doubt that." Sorath sneered. "Night Wrath was perfectly willing to abandon his brother to us and scurry away himself."

"If he fled, it is because he is out there now, concocting some plan. A shame that your patrols have not uncovered *him*."

Was there suspicion or accusation in Uthari's gaze? Maybe he was simply implying that this information Sorath was reporting had no value to him, because he'd already known about everything. Sorath wouldn't put it past the old wizard to have been spying upon his zidarr from afar.

"Little gets past me, Colonel," Uthari said softly, his words a warning.

Sorath blanked his mind of all thoughts, though he worried about what Uthari might already have read in there.

"The druids *are* a concern." Uthari rose, turning his back to them as he walked to a porthole that looked out upon the waterfall.

Sorath flirted with a fantasy of shooting him in the back, but it would be a pointless action. Besides, he was here to retrieve Vinjo, not get himself killed trying to carry out, as Ferroki had described, a vain assassination attempt. Still, it was hard when he saw Uthari's bare back—his vulnerable neck—not to dream of avenging the deaths of all the men he'd lost.

"Careful, Colonel," Uthari said, not turning back from the

porthole. "I can only overlook your murderous thoughts for as long as I believe you have more value to me alive than dead."

Ferroki turned a concerned expression on Sorath. So much for her earlier approval.

Sorath blew out a slow breath, forcing his bunched shoulder muscles to loosen. "Will you release Vinjo to our camp? I will keep an eye on him and sound an alarm if Night Wrath shows up with a dagger meant for his brother's throat."

"Won't you be busy spying on my zidarr for me?" Uthari looked over his shoulder. "I want more information on those druids."

"I can do both. I'm a talented man."

"Does that mean you're delegating one of those tasks to me?" Ferroki murmured.

"We'll talk later," he murmured back.

She snorted. "That sounds like a yes."

"It's a good thing you're getting that triple pay, Captain," Uthari said. "Working with the colonel must be trying."

"He ensures I always keep my blade sharpened."

"I don't care which of you spies on Yidar, but you will stay up at night, and if he leaves his ship again, follow him. Regarding those devices—" Uthari waved at the table, "—I trust you know what the other does?"

"Not yet." Sorath had tried pressing the button, but he hadn't been able to tell what it did, if anything.

"From what I can sense of its magic, I believe it may disrupt magic. Perhaps even a mage's barrier, leaving him vulnerable to attack."

"Oh?" Damn, Sorath should have tinkered more with it, though he didn't know what mage would have agreed to let him point devices at him and press buttons. Jak, maybe. Sorath had heard from Tezi that Jak knew how to make a barrier now.

"I would not presume *Jak* will do your bidding for long,"

Uthari said. "As he learns more, he will realize his place is with us. *We* will have his loyalty."

"How rewarding that'll be for him." Sorath didn't look down at the desk, but he couldn't help but wonder if he could grab that device, press the button, and lower Uthari's defenses long enough to shoot him. By Thanok's work-bent back, that would be the most delicious feeling. Even if mages rushed in and killed him, it would be worth it if he could kill Uthari first.

A loud crunch came from the desk, and Ferroki jumped. The two devices crumpled, as if powerful fists were wrapping around them, squeezing them until the pieces popped off.

A flash of light scorched Sorath's eyes, and he jerked his arm up protectively. When the light faded, only broken bits of the devices remained.

"Those tools are too dangerous to risk being in terrene hands," Uthari said. "I would certainly not spare this engineer's life so that he could make more devices like that, devices that mundane mercenaries might be tempted to use against mages." Uthari leaned against the wall by the porthole, his arms folded over his chest. "Is that not why you wish his life spared, Colonel?"

"I believe he could make devices that prove useful to mages as well—such as something that could keep deadly monsters from coming through the portal—and that it would be a shame to kill someone with such talent."

"So Malek suggested, but Malek wasn't fantasizing about using the engineer's devices on me at the time."

"Are you sure? You can't read his mind, can you?" Sorath wagered more of Uthari's supposedly loyal mages than he suspected wanted him dead.

Uthari's eyes closed to slits. "I frequently take Malek's advice, but because you so wish this engineer to live, I believe I will kill him."

Sorath cursed his vengeful thoughts. He hadn't wanted to make things *worse* for Vinjo.

"That's a shame," Ferroki said. "He knows his way around a ship's engine."

"Yes," Uthari said, "he attempted to *destroy* two of ours."

"He could probably build you a new one from scratch," Ferroki said. "As I watched our team walk through the portal on foot yesterday, with nothing but their skyboards for travel, I couldn't help but think how inefficient a way that is to look for… whatever it is you seek out there. Dragons, my people believe. Unless those dragons are loitering near the portal on their world, they would be easy to miss. A world is a vast place to search, is it not? Certainly not something to be undertaken on foot."

She had Uthari's full attention. Sorath didn't know what she was getting at, but he hoped it worked.

"You're thinking of a mageship," Uthari said. "A *miniature* mageship that could fit through the portal. Interesting."

"Yes," Ferroki said. "Would it be possible? Perhaps Lieutenant Vinjo could figure out a way to shrink down your existing technology for a smaller ship. If your zidarr and his team could fly hundreds of miles a day, they could explore much more easily."

"Interesting." Uthari truly did appear intrigued.

Sorath held his breath, nodding at Ferroki when she glanced at him. It was a good idea.

"Normally," Uthari said, "ships are built in the well-stocked and well-equipped shipyards back in our city, but we have spare parts along for emergencies. After all, we knew we would end up in battles. A talented engineer might be able to cobble something together from them. *If* he could be convinced to work for us."

"I'm certain I can convince him to do so, Your Majesty," Ferroki said.

"You?" Uthari pointed at her chest. "Why would he work for your company? On my behalf?"

"He's smitten with my lieutenant. Though she will have foul words for me if I use her as bait to dangle in front of Lieutenant Vinjo, I already know that I can win her forgiveness with a couple of pints of octli, three days of leave, and oiling her sword for her."

"I'll have him released to your company's care and a tent set up below that he can turn into a workshop."

"I'm sure he'll appreciate that, Your Majesty."

"And *you*—" Uthari shifted his pointing finger to Sorath, "—will guard it around the clock and alert my people immediately if his zidarr brother shows up, to slay him or otherwise."

"Yes, Your Majesty," Sorath made himself say politely. Since he'd almost gotten Vinjo killed, he was done with sarcasm and thoughts of vengeance.

"*And* you'll stay up nights, keeping an eye on Yidar's nocturnal activities."

"It's fortunate that my sleep has gotten so poor as I've gotten older." All right, maybe a *little* sarcasm had to slip out.

"Isn't it?" Uthari's eyes grew distant, then he sighed. "More fleet commanders are insisting on meetings with me. No doubt, more of their kings are demanding access to the portal. Perhaps I'll tease them with the idea that a larger team can go through once we have a mageship capable of flying through it." He nodded to himself, then shooed them toward the door. "See yourselves out."

Sorath waited until they were in the hallway to ask Ferroki, "Will Sasko truly forgive you so easily for offering her up as a bedroom prize? As you must recall, the last time we saw her and Vinjo together on the same ship, she was hiding behind me in the hope that he wouldn't find her and keep pestering her."

"Oh, I'm not offering her as a *bedroom prize*. I wouldn't presume to do that. If I did, it would take far more than octli to earn her forgiveness. I'll simply ask her to stand nearby and listen and nod occasionally as Vinjo prattles on about his inventions."

"What if Uthari leads him to believe Sasko will be... more available than that?"

"Then Yidar won't be the only one in danger of having his genitalia chewed up and spit out."

"Maybe I'll have a chat with Vinjo before he comes down."

"Wise."

10

Jadora nibbled from the plates on the table and tried the various juices. For a while, she'd avoided the food, thoughts that it might be drugged or outright poisoned coming to mind, but hours had passed since they'd been placed in the suite, and nobody had been by to question them, observe them, or check to see if their drugged bodies were passed out on the floor, so she'd decided it was unlikely anything was wrong with the food. Their guards hadn't taken their packs or their weapons, so she had the rations they'd brought along, but curiosity about what the local fare tasted like drove her to sample from the plates.

"The blue juice is *amazing*," Jak said, looking back from the windows, where he and Rivlen had been standing shoulder to shoulder having a magic lesson. "It's like if blueberries and raspberries mixed themselves up with something tart and refreshing. You should ask them what fruit it's made from, take a sample, and then grow a bunch back home."

"Are you focusing?" Rivlen asked him.

"On that blue juice?" Jak grinned at her. "*Yes*. Did you try it?"

"What I'm *trying* is to instruct you on cutting through a mage's barrier so you can attack him effectively."

"Yes, and you're doing an excellent job of it. Just a minute ago, I successfully *destroyed* the practice barrier you put up."

"You poked a pencil-sized hole in it."

"I *destroyed* that hole."

Rivlen rolled her eyes.

"I just need a drink to replenish my reserves." Jak joined Jadora at the table and grabbed a pitcher. Sweat dampened his brow, and he winced, as if he had a headache. "It's hard," he whispered to her. "I'm trying not to use all of my energy in case enemies attack. And because Malek said he would show me some things too. I don't want to be too weak to practice what he teaches me."

"I'm sure your... instructors understand your understandable human limitations." Jadora glanced at Rivlen but kept any judgment out of her thoughts.

She had been relieved when Malek said he would teach Jak nonlethal ways to defend against mages and would prefer it if he were Jak's sole instructor. Rivlen always looked calculating when she watched Jak work on whatever magical skill she was teaching him.

"They all think I have *potential*," Jak whispered, then drank deeply from his preferred blue juice. "I don't want to disappoint anyone and make them think they're wasting their time."

He was amazingly earnest for someone with bright blue lips.

"They won't think that," Jadora said. "If they do, I'll have stern words with them."

"I'm sure that'll make them quake." Jak poured more juice into his glass, then poured one for Rivlen and checked under the table. The hatchling had been passed out there for the last hour and was still snoozing contentedly on a cushion that Jak had retrieved for him.

He returned to the window, offering Rivlen a glass. "You'll like it. It's zingy."

Rivlen glanced at it, seeming surprised that he'd brought her something. She accepted it but said, "It sounds like a child's drink."

"Nope. I'm a man, and I like it."

Rivlen eyed him skeptically.

"I had my birthday the other day," Jak said. "That means I'm even more manly than I was when we first met."

"Uh huh. What are you now? Fourteen?"

"Hilarious. *Nineteen*. I'm sprouting chest hair like a gorilla stranded on a glacier."

"Something that's sure to make women randy."

"I do hope so. I've been waiting nineteen years to have that effect on the fairer sex."

Jadora rubbed her face, reminded of Loran's wit, though his had been confident and trended more toward cockiness than self-deprecation. She'd only been twenty-one when they'd met, and hadn't necessarily been enamored with the cockiness, but he and his tales of adventure had intrigued her. A few years older than she, Loran had already been out working in his field, exploring ancient ruins and finding relics to bring back to study. They'd met when he'd brought an old text with a picture of an exotic trumpet flower to the laboratory where she'd been assisting her professor with research. He'd offered to take her to lunch if she could find out where it grew, since it was a clue to finding a lost civilization. She'd always liked a challenge.

"If you successfully tear down my barrier," Rivlen said, "that'll excite me more than chest hair."

"Oh, right. I forgot mages like mental power more than muscles."

"Something like that." Rivlen sipped from the glass, made a face—maybe *zing* didn't appeal to her—and set it on the windowsill. "What I really like is knowing I can count on someone in a fight." She faced him. "Try again. More than a pencil hole."

"All right." Jak put aside his drink, determination replacing his goofy expression.

"Professor?" Tezi asked from the doorway, peering past the mangled curtain and into the corridor.

Tinder and Fret had left her standing guard and retreated to a bedroom to rest.

"Someone's coming," she added.

Rivlen frowned at Tezi and rested a hand on her sword hilt. "That ambassador? More mage guards?"

"The man who was reading the professor's writing," Tezi said.

"Oh." Jadora walked over, wanting to talk to Zethron—and to make sure Rivlen didn't attempt to capture and interrogate him. "Is he alone?"

"He's walking alone." Tezi pushed aside the curtain.

Guards were still standing in the corridor. Even though Jadora was fairly certain they were mages, they hadn't yet noticed that Malek had sneaked out a window. They didn't react as Zethron walked in carrying a large pad of paper under his arm. Tezi closed the curtain after him.

"Is he armed?" Rivlen asked as Zethron bowed to Tezi, looked around, and smiled when he spotted Jadora.

"I don't think so, ma'am," Tezi said.

Zethron lifted a finger, opened the pad, and held the top page out to Jadora. He'd prewritten his message.

"What is that?" Rivlen asked. "A love letter—ow."

She glared at Jak.

He raised his hands. "Sorry. I was focusing on piercing your barrier and didn't realize you weren't paying attention."

She squinted at him. "I was mostly paying attention, and my barrier is still up. You ripped a hole in it. Good." That calculation entered her eyes again. "Do it again."

"Tyrant."

Jadora read the page of Ancient Zeruvian text. "He says it's wonderful to meet us and that he would love to visit the First World, especially if there are vestiges of how mankind originally came to be, because he would appreciate seeing any history related to that. He's also curious about the elder dragons. It's long been a mystery about where they went, and while some believe..."

The words stopped at the end of the page mid-sentence. Jadora twitched a finger, and Zethron nodded and flipped the page to reveal more.

"While some believe they were all killed by the younger dragons," she continued, excited to receive this information and hoping he was a reliable resource, "they apparently all disappeared at once thousands of years ago, and it's believed they might have hidden somewhere, perhaps going to a world without a portal and not letting anyone follow them. Hm, the people here—they call themselves the Vroths—also have a couple of religions that made the elder dragons gods. They long to have their benevolent gods back again because..."

Another page flip. Had he filled the entire pad?

"Things aren't that great on most of the worlds right now, the worlds where humans have settled. Those with power rule over those who don't, and they also believe that if the elder dragons were to return, they might see what has happened and put an end to it. Dragons gave humans magic so they would be able to defend themselves from other great predators with magic, not so some humans would end up ruling over others. That's what he believes, anyway, and what is written in many of the archaeological records he's studied. Hah, he *is* an archaeologist."

Zethron flipped the page again. There was only one line on it.

"Am I free for dinner?" Jadora blinked.

"If the *dragons* are going to stop mages from ruling our world, you'll pardon me if I hope we don't find any more of them," Rivlen growled, glancing at the sleeping hatchling. "According to *our* archaeological records, terrene humans tried to wipe out those with magic long ago, because they were afraid of us and thought we were some kind of twisted mutants. I'm not signing up for a system that would let *that* happen again." Her glare shifted to Zethron, as if she was contemplating punishing him for this delivery of blasphemous information.

Jadora almost swore. She shouldn't have read aloud as she translated.

Zethron looked warily back at Rivlen, then grimaced at Jadora.

"I saw the sword demon was gone," he whispered, "and thought *yevra rath moreth*. I forgot she is also a mage."

When he spoke in his modern tongue, with only some of the words matching Ancient Zeruvian—or close enough for her to guess them—Jadora didn't understand everything, but she got the gist.

"The sword demon is Malek?" she asked, switching to Ancient Zeruvian. If he could read it, maybe he could understand the spoken word too, though he might have consulted a textbook to write his message. Earlier, she'd gotten the impression that he was rusty on the old language. Understandable.

Zethron nodded. "*Fearsome.*"

"He can be, yes."

Jadora wondered when she'd stopped thinking of Malek that way. Probably when he'd promised to protect her. She liked to think that even if Uthari changed his mind about her value to him and ordered her killed, Malek would no longer be willing to do it himself, but she would hate to have that tested.

"Vran has many mages." Zethron waved toward the window, perhaps indicating the entire city. "They are also fearsome, but they are not usually swordsmen too. Also, I am accustomed to their... force." He wrinkled his nose, as if trying to think of a better word, but she nodded. "The mages here on Vran do not attack me." He touched his chest, then rolled his eyes.

Confused by the gesture—had she understood him correctly?—Jadora asked, "Why not?"

"I am... favored. By Etcher Yervaa."

"Favored?"

He bit his lip, looking embarrassed.

Rivlen grunted—or maybe that was a gag. Either way, it conveyed disgust. "He's some powerful woman's precious bed toy."

Zethron gazed at her, probably not understanding. Maybe that was for the best.

"Oh, it's one of the rulers," Rivlen said, squinting at him. "One of these etchers. He has sex with her, because she's into exotic explorers from other worlds—those are *his* thoughts, by the way. It's perfectly possible he's delusional, but he's thinking about how it's worth it, because the people here let him come and go. They haven't tagged him, and they don't generally try to enslave him, make him do menial things, or throw him to the bragorths. That's the giant cat thing that killed all those gladiators in the first arena match we saw. And ew, the etcher lady is *old*."

"Is she reading my mind?" Zethron asked.

"Yes," Jadora replied. "And judging you."

"I guessed. Her face is..." He groped for a word.

"Condescending? Condemnatory? Disparaging?"

"I can read your thoughts too, Professor," Rivlen said coolly. "Even if you're speaking in whatever language that is."

"Thank you for the reminder," Jadora murmured. "What does he mean by tagging?"

"Ah." Rivlen squinted at him again. "I think he's talking about those discs in people's temples, but he's not thinking about it now, so I'm not sure. Now he's wondering if *you're* judging him for sleeping with the old ruler lady."

"No." Jadora smiled at Zethron. She wouldn't blame any

terrene human for doing what he had to do in order to survive in a society ruled by mages. Wasn't she here against her wishes because she dared not defy Uthari?

Besides, Rivlen's definition of *old* might mean this ruler was Jadora's age. Jak would define that as old. Rivlen might have the rank of captain, but Jadora was fairly certain she was precocious and had been promoted more quickly than typical. She only looked to be about twenty-five.

"Will you come with me?" Zethron pointed at Jadora and the corridor.

"To dinner?" She shook her head, remembering that he'd tacked that onto the end of his message.

"No?" Zethron smiled wistfully. "You have already eaten? Also, I may show you plants."

"Plants?" She'd intended to turn down his invitation—it wouldn't be wise for their group to split up, especially with Malek gone—but this piqued her interest. Earlier, she'd asked him specifically about the Jitaruvak. What if he'd been thinking about her picture and realized he *did* recognize it?

"Yes." He nodded.

"He's thinking about a greenhouse," Rivlen said. "Ask him if he'll take you to this ruler lady. *That's* who we need to see. Lord Malek would ask the same thing if he were here. We're going to have to deal with their rulers, not that idiot of an ambassador, if we're going to make a deal with these people." Rivlen lowered her voice to a mutter. "And be allowed to leave this city."

Though Jadora would rather ask about plants—visiting a greenhouse and learning about the flora on another world would be fascinating—she understood the sentiment.

"I am interested in your plants," Jadora told him. "Also this... Etcher Yervaa. Will you take me to see her?"

"*Us*," Rivlen said. "You're not going anywhere with him alone. Lord Malek will strangle me if I let you get yourself killed. And then King Uthari will strangle me more when he finds out."

"I can go with her," Jak said.

"Yeah, you can poke pencil holes into her enemies' barriers," Rivlen said. "Or sic your bug-eating hatchling at them."

"I thought I'd just punch them," Jak said.

"That works well against mages."

"I cannot," Zethron replied to Jadora. "She favors many. Many lovers. I cannot go to her. She must summon me." He pointed upward, making Jadora wonder if the rulers here also lived in abodes in the sky.

Rivlen made a frustrated noise. "Don't you have a dome-jir or something like it? To message her? Tell her you're randy and eager to please her tonight." She must have put the message into Zethron's mind telepathically, for his lips twisted with rueful understanding.

"I must wait until she summons me," he repeated.

"Maybe we'll get lucky, and *she'll* be randy tonight," Rivlen muttered.

Zethron pointed at Jadora. "If you are an herbalist, you will like the plant place."

"Maybe we should all go." Tezi glanced toward the bedroom—Tinder was peeking out, listening to the conversation too. "Is that allowed?"

Jak trotted over to join Jadora. "That's a good idea. I'd love a tour of the city. I could *map* it."

Rivlen also came over, and Zethron frowned at them and shook his head.

"The ambassador says you are... guests and must stay here. I may only take one." Zethron pointed at Jadora.

"She's not going off alone with you." Jak scowled at him.

Zethron held the curtain aside as he stepped back into the corridor and spoke rapidly to the guards, switching from Ancient

Zeruvian to their modern version. His tone had been playful and a little shy with Jadora, but he was firm with them, lifting his chin and telling them he intended to take Jadora and—surprisingly—Rivlen with him to question on Etcher Yervaa's behalf.

"I assume he doesn't truly want to interrogate me on the etcher's behalf?" Jadora murmured to Rivlen, trusting she was still monitoring his thoughts.

"No," Rivlen said. "He's bluffing. I don't think this ruler knows about us yet. One wonders if the ambassador has said anything to her or if he's scheming ways to get the hatchling. Zethron thinks you'll only go with him if I'm allowed to come, so he's asking about the two of us. He knows he can't get the whole group out."

"I should be the one to go with my mother," Jak said.

"You should stay here, practice your magic, and wait for Lord Malek to return," Rivlen said as the guards pushed back against Zethron, saying he could question them inside the suite and that he couldn't take any of them anywhere.

Since the guards were also mages, they might be reading his thoughts as easily as Rivlen. If they could do that, why would Zethron try to bluff them?

Then Jadora spotted a disc at one of the men's temples. Maybe the night-shift guards *weren't* mages. If not, that would explain how Malek had slipped away without attracting their attention.

Jadora wondered if she should find the choice of terrene guards suspicious. After that *test*, the ambassador knew that some of their group had magical power. Maybe he'd intentionally set this up so they could get out and was monitoring them to see what they did. If so, had Malek's decision to roam put them in danger?

That could be another reason not to split up the group.

"What is going on here?" came a woman's voice from farther up the corridor.

"Mage," Rivlen warned.

A dark-haired woman in a blue tunic and sandals approached,

a baton hooked on a rope belt around her waist. She spoke rapidly to the guards and Zethron, the words passing so quickly that Jadora struggled to understand. It didn't help that she was still guessing at more than half the words. She wondered if she could find a book somewhere that would translate Ancient Zeruvian to the modern version these people used.

What did come across—as Zethron bowed to the newcomer, raised his eyebrows, and smiled frequently—was that he was flirting with her.

She snorted, probably aware of the manipulation, but they also seemed to know each other. She ended up shaking her head, lifting her eyes toward the ceiling, and waving what might have been permission. Before walking away, she patted Zethron on the chest.

"Only *two*," one of the guards said.

"You may come," Zethron told Jadora. "And you." He bowed to Rivlen.

"Lucky me," Rivlen said.

"Uhm." Jak lifted a finger.

Zethron shook his head.

"Are you sure going with him is a good idea, Mother?" Jak whispered.

"No, but we've already learned a lot from him." Jadora waved at the pad of paper with the information about the dragons on it. "And this could be an opportunity to learn more."

Zethron shouldn't have understood them, but he nodded sagely.

As Jadora followed him down the corridor with Rivlen at her side, she hoped she wasn't making a mistake. She worried as much about leaving Jak behind, with only the mercenaries to help him if they were attacked, as about herself. Though, as Jadora glanced at the irritated expression on Rivlen's face, she wondered if going off with only her as an ally was wise. Rivlen might be loyal to her king, but that didn't mean she cared as much as Malek about protecting Jadora.

※

Jak was tired, a headache throbbing behind his eyes after his magic practice, and he longed to rest, but he couldn't sleep with Mother, Malek, and Rivlen all gone. Further, he worried that if he dozed off, the hatchling might escape their suite. With a door, he would have felt safe, but the curtains wouldn't keep Shikari from scampering out, where he might be snatched up by the first person who thought a baby dragon would make a delightful pet.

Earlier, Shikari had napped, but now he was up again, scrambling over the floor and onto the furniture as easily as a cat. Jak trailed him around, amazed that he could climb so well when he was less than a week old. The hatchling sniffed in every crack and clawed sofa cushions onto the floor.

"Are you looking for insects?" Jak muttered. "Or demonstrating that you're going to be a dragon delinquent when you're bigger?"

A cushion flew off a chair and landed at his feet.

"He doesn't understand you, does he?" Tezi asked from the doorway, where she'd either voluntarily placed herself—or been assigned by her colleagues—to stand guard. The butt of her battle axe rested on the floor as she gripped the head, contemplating the weapon.

"I'm sure he doesn't," Jak said. "He's just a baby. I'm afraid he's hungry though, and so far, the only things I know he eats are insects. Do you think the guards would bring us some nice caterpillars and spiders if I asked?"

Tezi wrinkled her nose. "Where would they get them?"

"We passed some parks on the way in. Though maybe I can find some lurking in here." Jak started peeking in corners and under tables, hoping to spot spiderwebs or anything else promising for Shikari's tastes.

"What are you going to do with him when he gets bigger?"

"I don't know. I didn't set out to find a dragon egg or become a surrogate father. I'm kind of young for that."

"You probably won't be able to carry him on your shoulder when he's fifty pounds. And more. Dragons get to be huge, if that one we faced is an indication."

"They do." Jak thought of fossils he'd seen in the museum back home, not of the mottled dragon that had almost killed them. He didn't want to imagine Shikari turning into anything resembling that monster. "Presumably, he'll figure out how to fly at some point."

"Will you have to teach him?"

"Hopefully not, since I'm limited in that area." Jak flapped his arms.

"I wonder if they can learn on their own or if he needs a mother dragon to teach him."

"I don't know that either. The archaeological texts are sadly devoid of advice on raising dragons."

Tezi returned to studying her axe. "Do you have any tips for, uhm, communicating with dragon steel? I can't help but feel that this weapon can do much more than cleave people—and lesser weapons—in half. During that skirmish earlier, it let me cut through a mage's barrier, and it defended me from attacks by other mages. They seemed to go right past me without stirring my hair."

"That's excellent. Maybe it nullifies mages to some extent and puts you on fair footing with them." Jak envisioned her leaping into battle with Tonovan, but after all his years in the military, the general was probably a talented weapons master as well as a wizard. He also might be able to find ways to attack around whatever magic-deadening effects the axe gave its wielder. If he used his power to rip up a tree and drop it on her head, how would the dragon steel protect her?

Jak shook his head. He hoped Tezi could avoid Tonovan and didn't cross paths with him again.

"I wish I could learn more about it," she said. "Do you think I have to be a mage to do what you suggested? Communicate with it?"

"I don't know. I can see if it's receptive to me, if you want. Maybe figure out its abilities and tell you? I wonder if there are command words that one can say."

"If you'll try, I would appreciate it."

Jak made sure Shikari wasn't near the doorway—the hatchling was slurping from a bowl of water Jak had put down for him—and joined Tezi. She held the weapon horizontally in her hands, offering it to him.

He accepted it, pleased she seemed to have gotten over her suspicion that he wanted the axe for himself—maybe he'd imagined it earlier that she'd felt that way. He hoped she believed she could trust him.

"Let me sit down." Jak sat cross-legged on the floor, rested the weapon in his lap, and dropped his chin to his chest.

He attempted to reach out telepathically to it, as he had with the portal, and he sensed its power—it buzzed slightly against his hands. He did not, however, get the feeling that a sentience lay within, as he'd felt from the portal. From *all* of the portals.

When he'd reached out to the one here, begging it to help Shikari, it had at first ignored him, feeling far more distant and aloof than the portal on Torvil, but after he'd shared memories of interacting with the other one, of it *helping* to defend him, it had seemed more interested in him. The portal hadn't been responsible for the device attached to it, but it had given Jak glimpses of insight into how to work it. Even more importantly, it had agreed the device had made a mistake by attacking Shikari.

Jak believed the portal had helped manipulate it into healing the hatchling.

Had Jak been closer to the portal now, he might have reached out to it again, to see if it had any insight into how best to use the battle-axe. Even though it presumably had little interest in human weapons, a dragon-steel artifact might know all about other things made from dragon steel.

"Probably far-fetched," he muttered, but he envisioned the portal at the end of the road in the grassy foothills and tried to reach out to it across the miles.

He'd communicated with Malek before across many more miles. Maybe he could also do this.

Hello, portal friend, Jak thought. *Are you busy?*

The sentience in the portal stirred at his mental touch. Not exactly an answer but an awareness of him.

I have a question. I appreciate you helping me earlier, by the way. Shikari is doing much *better.* Jak shared a vision of the hatchling chewing on the curtains. *He'll be even better when I get a chance to find more insects for him. They seem to be a favorite food. The* only *food he'll eat, actually.* Jak almost babbled on and asked the portal if it knew what else baby dragons liked to eat, but he'd only mentioned having one question, and he didn't know if the portal understood him or cared about any of this.

To his surprise, an image formed in his mind, a vision such as the ones the portal on Torvil had given him.

Jak saw a lush green forest abutting a cliff. All manner of ferns sprouted from the undergrowth, surrounding massive trees that towered straight and tall, reaching hundreds of feet in the air.

A nest was perched on a ledge near the top of the rocky cliff, and four blue-scaled hatchlings similar to Shikari nipped and played with each other in it until something like a huge hairy tarantula ambled down the cliff near them. They halted their play, all four little dragon heads swiveling toward it. They leaned out of the nest, trying to bite the tarantula—it was almost as large as they were. But the hairy arachnid skittered to the side and into a crack to avoid them.

A shadow fell over the nest, worrying Jak. Was this some predator?

No, it was a great adult dragon, its blue scales shimmering with iridescence in the sunlight that slanted through the trees. It—she?—landed on the ledge beside the nest.

The hatchlings hopped up and down, flapping wings that wouldn't yet lift them aloft. With her long sinewy neck, the dragon leaned toward the crack where the tarantula had disappeared. Her head wouldn't have fit in, but she used magic to levitate the arachnid out, hairy legs wiggling in the air in protest.

The dragon plopped the tarantula down in the nest, and the hatchlings sprang upon it ravenously. Their mother sprang away from the nest and alighted on the cliff, talons finding holds on the vertical rock face. She plucked more tarantulas out of cracks, sometimes with magic and sometimes with her great fanged maw, and dropped them into the nest for her offspring.

So giant spiders are native to their world? Jak guessed, lamenting that he didn't have any insects that large to share with Shikari. The poor hatchling was probably starving with such scant offerings. *Do they eat meat later? They must, right?*

Jak believed his father's archaeology books would have mentioned it if dragons ate only insects.

The portal showed him something similar to an elk in the forest below the cliff, maybe agreement that the young dragons would one day eat other prey.

Someone poked his shoulder. Tezi. "Did you fall asleep?"

"No." Jak kept his eyes closed, not wanting to risk breaking the link to the portal and being unable to reestablish it. "Still working on it."

He bit his lip, feeling dishonest since he hadn't asked the portal about the axe yet.

Something tugged at the haft, and Jak frowned, thinking Tezi had grown impatient and was taking it back, but Shikari had come over and was testing it with his fangs.

"You're not going to be able to chew through dragon steel." Jak plucked Shikari up and settled him in his lap next to the weapon, hoping he would stay there for a moment.

Dragons seem challenging to raise, he pointed out to the portal.

It might have been Jak's imagination, but he thought it shared a feeling of agreement with him. And maybe even... amusement?

Now that it was communicating with him, this world's portal seemed similar to the one on Torvil. Jak hadn't had much time to interact with the one on the frozen world, but it had seemed older and sterner, commanding Jak to save the egg that had been falling out of the ice as the glacier crept along its path.

My friend has a dragon-steel axe, Jak thought to the portal, *but we're not sure how best to draw upon its powers. She would like to be able to defend herself against powerful mages, and we're hoping it will help her do that. She doesn't have powers of her own.*

Maybe he shouldn't have admitted that. His mother had mentioned that the portal on Torvil hadn't seemed to like her much. She'd worried it had been because she couldn't access magic, that it was more likely to befriend those with power, those more akin to the ancient dragons that had long ago crafted the portals.

At first, Jak didn't receive a response to his words, and he groped for another tactic. But then the portal shared another vision, one of Tezi wielding her axe in a grassy field and protecting something behind her from a huge furry predator—it looked like a giant bear.

She swung the axe, lightning streaking from the point between the double heads, and the weapon made her impervious to magical attacks from the bear creature. The vision shifted, showing that she was protecting a young dragon about the size of a dog. An older version of Shikari?

Was this some future vision? Or just something the portal could envision happening because those bears came from the dragon home world and frequently preyed on young dragons?

An affirmative came from the portal, followed by the sense of a question as it focused on Shikari and Tezi protecting him with the axe.

You want to know if she'll protect Shikari? Jak guessed.

Another affirmative.

Uhm, let me check. Jak opened his eyes to find Tezi dangling a string above the hatchling.

Trying to keep Shikari distracted while Jak focused? He caught the end of it, and they played tug-of-war while she grinned.

Jak had so rarely seen Tezi anything but glum that he was glad to see the grin. He almost hated to interrupt, but she noticed that his eyes were open and blushed and drew back. Or she would have, but Shikari didn't let go of the string. He *grrred* fiercely if unconvincingly and wouldn't let her pull it away.

"Tezi?" Jak asked. "This is going to be a silly question..."

Wariness closed over her face, and she shook her head.

He hesitated.

"I appreciate you trying to help me," she said, "and you're a really nice man. I just don't want... anything. Anyone."

"Oh." Jak winced, certain his earlier determination *not* to flirt had been construed as flirting, and now she was afraid he wanted to ask her for a date again. "I get that. That's not what I was going to ask."

"Oh." This time, *she* winced.

Jak grimaced. Why was everything with girls so hard?

"This may be worse." He smiled to make it a joke, though maybe that wasn't the right tactic.

"Worse than... you?"

"Yes, worse than me and my delightful charm. I wasn't able to communicate with the axe—maybe simple tools aren't aware in the way the portals are, no matter what they're made from—but I think the *portal* is willing to give you some tips on how to use it best."

"The portal?" she mouthed.

"Yes, but it expects you to use the axe to help defend Shikari."

Tezi looked down at the string he was shredding to tiny pieces that floated down to the floor.

"It may actually want you to defend *all* dragons like him—blue, not brown and mottled and evil—if we ever find more."

"Can't dragons defend themselves? In the legends, they're very large and fierce."

Shikari opened his mouth wide and squeaked at her. It was possible it was meant to be a roar, but he hadn't developed the ability to share anything that ferocious yet.

"I believe they grow into that, but when they're young, they're vulnerable, just like any other babies. But someone with a big battle-axe could help protect them." Jak patted the head of the weapon, careful to avoid the sharp edges.

Another vision popped into his mind, startling him. This time, their full group was in a mountain valley, or maybe an ancient crater, since it was a round depression with steep slopes on all sides. Lush blue-green foliage covered a forest floor, unfamiliar trees growing up toward the sky, and a dark ziggurat rose up from the center. The structure was half-covered in vines, grass, and plants growing from dirt that had settled on the horizontal surfaces.

As their group approached, two dragons—two *mottled* dragons—flew out from behind the ziggurat and arrowed straight toward them. Straight toward little Shikari perched on Jak's shoulder.

The vision disappeared before he saw what happened. Jak gulped. Maybe that was for the best.

"Did you hear me?" Tezi peered into his eyes.

"Sorry, no."

"Is the, uh, portal talking to you again?" She didn't say that was weird or that *he* was weird, but she didn't have to.

"I'm not sure." Jak lifted his hand from the axe blade. Had the vision come from the portal? Or the weapon?

"I said I'd be happy to help defend Shikari if it's within my power to do so. I'd like to have a purpose, to be honest. I'm not even sure why I'm here." Tezi shrugged helplessly.

"I think Mother wanted you away from all the people drooling over and hoping to steal your axe."

"So... I'm here out of pity? Not because I have some value?"

"Of course not. You have value."

"Beyond the axe that would probably rather be with you than me?" she asked.

"I don't think the axe has feelings one way or another about me."

"It hasn't given *me* visions." Tezi stared bleakly at the floor.

"I'm sure it will." Jak hoped he wasn't lying. "And you're great. You're a good shot. You're more valuable than I am. What can I do? Draw landscapes and maps. These are not tremendously useful skills to have in battle, let me tell you."

"You're learning to be a mage." Tezi took a deep breath and shook her head. "Never mind. I shouldn't complain or feel sorry for myself. It's just been a rough year." A rough life, her eyes seemed to say.

He would have hugged her, if she had indicated she wanted that, but he was already screwing up around her.

"I'm sure it has, but now, you have a hatchling to help defend, and that will give you meaning and delight."

Shikari squeaked again.

"He agrees," Jak said.

"He's eyeing my braid and probably thinking about chewing on it."

"Yes, he likes to do that. Let me tell the portal you're happy to defend dragons. Maybe it'll share some magical word you can use to summon the axe's powers."

"There are magic words?" she asked skeptically.

"I had to roar like a dragon to activate our portal for the first time," he reminded her. She'd been there for that.

"I remember. It wasn't a roar. It sounded like your tongue was strangling your tonsils."

"That's the secret to a good roar. Ask any lion."

Jak closed his eyes and tried to reestablish his link with the portal. It was easier this time, as if it had been waiting for him. He supposed it didn't have a lot else to do out in those hills in the dark.

Tezi agrees to fight to protect Shikari. Uh, did you share a vision of two mottled dragons and a ziggurat?

The portal seemed confused by the question. Maybe the vision *had* come from the axe.

Never mind. How can Tezi more fully use the power of the axe to defend human and dragon friends? Jak assumed the portal wouldn't mind if she also used the weapon in non-dragon-protecting battles.

A screech-roar sounded in his mind.

He'd been afraid of that. Another dragon "word" to utter.

Is there any chance there's a translation that would work? Something she could say in our language that would be the equivalent of that noise? Humans struggle to roar well. Just ask my tonsils.

The portal didn't seem to understand that. Maybe he needed to save his humor for people. It screech-roared into his mind again.

One more time, please. "Tezi, I'm going to try to share something telepathically with you. Relaying a message from the portal, all right?"

She hesitated. "Yes."

Jak was still fuzzy on telepathy and how it worked beyond imagining who he wanted to speak with and thinking words at them, but he attempted to share what the portal was relaying to him. Maybe the portal grasped what he was doing, for it repeated the dragon noise in his mind numerous times, until his mental eardrums ached from the battering.

"I'm supposed to make that noise?" Tezi asked.

"Yes." Jak smiled, relieved he'd managed to share it.

She looked more daunted than relieved. "Do I... have to utter it aloud?"

"Since you're not a mage and can't communicate telepathically with the axe, probably. Go ahead and try."

"The guards may run in and think we're killing each other."

"I'll explain it to them."

"That should prove interesting." Tezi took a deep breath and attempted the screech-roar. It was decidedly more high-pitched than the dragon version, but she did better at emulating it than Jak had when he'd tried.

The portal repeated it, emphasizing different syllables—if roars could be said to have syllables. More like ululations.

On her fourth and loudest try, the axe flared with blue light.

Tezi gasped. "It worked."

"What are those *noises*?" Tinder rushed out of the bedroom, her sword in one hand and a grenade in the other. She gaped toward the exit as Fret appeared behind her, poking her head out of the doorway, her eyes wide.

Despite Tezi's fears, no guards had barged in yet.

"Did someone *die*?" Tinder peered all around the suite before looking at them.

"Tezi roared," Jak said. "She's learning to speak dragon."

"She's what?" Tinder noticed the glowing axe and pointed. "Uh, did that do that before?"

"No, but Tezi activated it with her roar. She said a dragon word."

"What word?" Fret asked curiously.

"I'm... not sure. The portal didn't translate it for me. Maybe it's just a command to turn weapons on."

"The portal didn't *translate* it for you?" Tinder lowered her grenade as she stared at him. "You are the strangest person I've ever traveled with."

"Are you sure that's true? Some of your fellow mercenaries are a touch quirky."

"They don't talk to portals." Tinder stalked to the doorway to peer into the corridor, as if she couldn't believe Tezi had been responsible for the noises.

"I didn't know that was a defining factor in determining one's strangeness," Jak said.

Tezi and Fret nodded at him.

"What happened to our guards?" Tinder looked both ways again, then pulled her head back in. "The corridor is empty."

"Maybe Tezi's roar scared them away." Jak pushed the axe into her hands and grabbed Shikari's sling as an uneasy feeling came over him.

Why would the guards have left their station? Unless their superiors had called them away? But why would they do that?

"I heard something." Tinder lowered her voice. "Someone's coming."

Jak, less experienced than the mercenaries, probably should have hidden in a bedroom, but he was the only one left with magical powers—however modest and underdeveloped—and felt compelled to help. He parted the curtain and peered into the corridor in time to see four men round a bend. They had the auras of mages, and they were carrying nets, a large bag, and swords in addition to whatever they could do with their powers.

One pointed at Jak, barking something that sounded a lot like, "There he is!" The finger lowered to Jak's chest, where Shikari was nestled in the sling, and there was no doubt about what they wanted.

Tinder acted first, rolling a grenade toward them. She pulled Jak and Tezi back into the suite, giving Jak time to pull out his magelock pistol. Tezi hefted her big axe.

"Do the dragon call," Jak told her, his suggestion half-drowned out by the explosion that came from the corridor.

Unfortunately, the mages had erected barriers in time to protect themselves. A few rocks fell from the ceiling and the walls, but that didn't slow them down for long.

Jak attempted to calm his mind enough to conjure a barrier of his own, envisioning mountains as he constructed it across the doorway to block the entrance.

But a great wrenching came as one of the attackers used his superior power to tear it away. The backlash snapped in Jak's mind like a whip cracking and left him wincing in pain.

Tinder drew her magelock pistol and fired. Not surprisingly, her blast struck one of the barriers and ricocheted back into the suite. It struck a fruit bowl on the table, blowing chunks of purple pears everywhere.

The men charged into the suite, arms raised to fling magical attacks. Tezi screeched the dragon command, and the glow of her battle-axe intensified. She sprang at the men, prepared to hew them down like saplings in a forest. With her first strike, lightning sprang from the tip of the weapon as the blade sliced through two mages' barriers.

Accustomed to such weapons, the men didn't appear startled. They drew their swords in time to parry. One was a mundane blade, and Tezi's axe slashed through it as if it were a stick. The top half clanked to the ground. But the other mage had a dragon-steel weapon of his own. It didn't glow or hurl lightning, but it parried the axe without trouble.

Shikari peeped in alarm at the clang of metal and the lightning shooting everywhere. It bounced off their attackers' barriers and flew wild. Branches of electricity slammed into furnishings, blowing cushions into thousands of pieces of fluff, and blasted holes in the walls.

One bolt of lightning struck true, hitting a barrier with enough force that the magic faltered, leaving the mage unprotected. Jak took advantage, shooting him in the chest. When the blast struck the mage, he flew backward, slamming into the wall.

A wave of energy *whooshed* through the suite as one of the would-be kidnappers tried to drive Tezi back with magic. Her axe protected her, but the wave shattered one of the windows overlooking the arena. Her assailant snarled and lunged in with his dragon-steel sword, the weapon flaring blue.

Shikari shrieked, the high-pitched noise startling Jak so much that he would have dropped the hatchling if he weren't protected in his sling. It startled the mages too. They stumbled back, one losing his barrier and fumbling his sword. Jak recovered before his foe and fired again. His pistol blast struck the swordsman in the hand, and he dropped his weapon—and the bag he'd been carrying.

"That's right, Shikari," Jak whispered. "Nobody is taking you anywhere."

Tezi lunged at her distracted opponent, her blade slicing through his tunic and carving a deep gash in his chest. He staggered back, yelling in pain.

One of the men Jak had shot shouted, hopefully an order to abort. The group scrambled for the doorway, dragging the injured among them. As they stumbled into the corridor, Tezi started after them, as if to chase them down and finish them off.

"Stay here," Jak told her. "If we kill anyone… things could get much worse."

"They tried to kill *us*," Tinder said.

"I think they came to kidnap Shikari." Jak patted the hatchling, who'd burrowed into the sling, only his eyes peering out.

"Yes, I gathered that, but they looked like they would be happy to kill us too." Tinder looked toward the shattered window. "That's a trend here. Have you noticed? Every room we walk into eventually gets attacked."

"I know." Jak had a feeling they weren't going to be invited to a meeting with one of the rulers.

"We need to get out of here," Tinder said, "and go back home."

Jak remembered how Malek hadn't been certain he could break through the barrier around the city. He also thought about the portal and the missing symbol for their home world. "I don't think that's going to be easy."

"Wonderful."

11

MALEK GHOSTED THROUGH THE CORRIDORS OF THE ARENA, HIS camouflaging magic wrapped around him, though he didn't know if it would work against the more powerful guards in the area. It still boggled his mind that people with magic as strong as his own were simple guards in this society. Would the rulers—the etchers—have power to rival dragons? And if he and his team had to battle their way out of here, would they be able to?

He hadn't doubted his ability to win a fight since he'd been a youth starting his zidarr training, but he couldn't let these people daunt him. Magically, they might be more than a match for him, but that only meant he had to find another way to protect his group. He would learn everything he could and sift through it to find an advantage.

The spectators had left the arena, the magical lights in most of the corridors out for the night. Malek had already investigated numerous levels of this place and spied on a meeting in a suite similar to theirs, but all he'd learned from the servants, whose minds he'd been able to read, was that dragons existed on this world and were a problem. They were the reason for the strong and permanent barrier around this and other cities along the coast.

After that meeting ended, Malek had planned to head out into the city, but as he'd reached the ground level, he'd sensed magic below the floor of the arena. Was there a basement? This place seemed a cornerstone of the city, so perhaps the information he wanted to learn was here.

Besides, while Malek had been crouched in that suite, spying on the meeting, Rivlen had let him know that Zethron had come to visit them and wanted to take Jadora to a greenhouse. Malek had almost snapped a *no*, that it was too risky, but Rivlen had promised to go along and watch over Jadora. Malek had reluctantly admitted that Zethron could be a good source of information and had given his permission for them to go with him.

Since they were already exploring out in the city, Malek could continue to search for answers here.

As he slipped past guards on the ground floor, searching for stairs that led down instead of up, Malek tried to sense what lay under the arena. If creatures such as he'd seen today were housed down there, magical cages might be required to hold them, but was that all he detected?

He approached two janitors, the discs at their temples marking them as terrene humans, and checked their minds. They were thinking of nothing but the boredom of their work. Malek passed by without them noticing.

He found an arched doorway and narrow stone stairs that led below the ground level. They were roped off, an invisible barrier behind them emanating magic.

It lacked the power of the barrier around the city, and he guessed it was meant to deter terrene humans rather than mages. Malek drew his sword, believing he could break through it, but would that raise an alarm?

Likely. But he suspected his group was already being watched

—Ambassador Rajesk might even have given them that particular suite so as to easily monitor them—and that time might be more important than secrecy. Malek wanted to learn what he could and get back to the others as quickly as possible.

Rivlen? Malek sent her a telepathic message before heading down. *Your status?*

We're riding in a carriage across the city. I see a greenhouse ahead, and from what I can read of his thoughts, the explorer—Zethron—is being honest with us. He's eager to share something with Professor Freedar. Something about plants.

Good. Malek was disinclined to trust Zethron—he didn't trust anyone here—and he couldn't help but think of the last time he'd been lured into a trap by a greenhouse, but he hoped their nighttime adventure would lead Jadora to learn of the Jitaruvak and where it could be found. *Keep me apprised.*

Yes, my lord.

Malek sliced through the barrier. A buzz zapped the air, but the magic of his sword kept it from harming him. He slipped through the broken barrier and down the dark stone stairs, though he paused to look back. The barrier was repairing itself.

Of its own accord? Interesting.

A part of him wished he truly could form a trade relationship with these people so he could return one day to study with them. He hadn't expected to find humans more advanced than his own. Before he'd come across those bones at the dragon's lair on the frozen world, he hadn't expected to find humans at all.

Malek descended more than thirty feet before reaching the bottom. Faint light and the magic he'd been sensing led him through a maze of wide corridors with surprisingly high ceilings. When he reached an intersection, laughter, grunts, and voices came from one direction. Human voices. It seemed that more than animals were housed down there.

The laughter surprised Malek. He'd assumed that those

battling powerful predators for the entertainment of the audience would be downtrodden slaves or perhaps criminals condemned to die in the arena.

He wanted to visit those humans—whether criminals or slaves or paid gladiators, their minds should be full of information—but he was also curious about the magic he sensed and turned down a passageway that headed toward it.

Before long, straw and sand covered the floor, and the stink of a stable—or maybe a den—filled the air. Large enclosures started up to either side of the passageway, the translucent sides made from magical barriers instead of bars.

Faint ambient light allowed him to view different kinds of creatures inside each, all large and powerful. Malek hadn't seen any of them before, and the sheer variety made him wonder if they came from numerous worlds, not only this one.

Most were sleeping, but a few were awake and watched his passing. His cloaking magic still enveloped him, but they knew he was there, either by scent or keen hearing, or perhaps they could detect him magically. Many of them radiated intrinsic power of their own, similar to that of the dragon he'd faced.

Malek paused to stare at a great lizard almost as large as a dragon, though it lacked wings and looked more like an iguana. A massive iguana that, judging from the cracked bones littering the floor of its cage, ate large animals. Perhaps humans. Its yellow eyes followed him as he passed down another passageway to the largest animal enclosure yet.

He gaped at the great winged worm locked inside, its hundred-foot-long body pressed to the edges of the barrier so it could fit. It was identical to the creature that had attacked Uthari's fleet at the portal, the creature that it had taken hundreds of mages—and a killing blow from a dragon-steel battle-axe—to slay.

The idea that these people had captured such a foe filled him with awe. It was hard to envision them risking bringing it out into daylight. How could humans without magic have a chance at defeating such a beast in the arena? Or did mages sometimes enter the contests?

Maybe the great worm was brought out for executions and not meant to be defeated. Even so, Malek couldn't imagine how mages—even mages more powerful than he—could wrangle it and keep it under control. He imagined the flying worm escaping the arena and devouring hundreds of spectators.

More grunts drifted to his ears from a passageway behind the worm enclosure. Believing it led back toward the area where he'd heard voices, Malek followed it.

He came to an intersection with two large metal doors set into the floor. His first thought was that it led to a maintenance area or a sewer, but the arena didn't have indoor plumbing or anything like the magical infrastructure back in Utharika. Maybe there was a ramp under the doors, leading to a corridor through which the animals were brought into the arena. That was easier to imagine than the deadly magical creatures being marched through the city streets.

From one direction, more laughter sounded. Malek headed that way.

As he walked, the lights grew brighter, magical sconces glowing from stone walls. He came to the first of a series of cells.

Dungeon cells, he assumed, for they had three stone walls and an invisible barrier he could see through from the corridor. But they were better furnished than he would have expected, with comfortable-looking beds, tables full of food, and open chests with changes of clothing. Practice weapons hung on wall racks, and there was enough floor space for one to perform exercises. There were even attached privy chambers, complete with wash basins and tubs.

The first occupied cell held a brawny naked man entwined with a voluptuous and equally naked woman in the bed. They were engaged in a sexual act that proved they were both flexible and strong.

Certain their thoughts weren't worth reading, Malek continued on. Now he knew what the grunts signaled.

He passed a few men by themselves in their beds, bandages wrapped around their heads or torsos, magical devices on nearby tables emanating what Malek guessed was healing magic, though he'd never seen tools that worked like that.

After passing more couples engaged in sex, he came to a larger cell with a group of men, several honing weapons and sitting around a table, chatting and laughing as they shared juice or perhaps alcoholic beverages. If these were prisoners, they were given far more amenities than Malek would have expected.

Though he'd been busy while the fighting had gone on earlier in the arena, he recognized a couple of faces, men from the battle that had taken place after the one with the giant cat. These fighters had survived their bout.

Wishing he could understand the language, Malek found a spot in the shadows and concentrated on keeping his camouflage around him while he poked through their thoughts. One man pulled out a tumbler full of dice and started playing a game with several others. Another hefted a mug, thumped his chest, and pointed upward. He was thinking of how he would win in battle the next day, prove himself a magnificent warrior, receive a female to entertain him, and—most important—be granted a prize from one of the rulers.

Malek tried to determine what *kind* of prize he sought. The man was envisioning a house in the city with a beautiful courtyard with a fountain and a pool and women to serve him.

His words spurred others to imagine themselves victorious in battles and also receiving prizes. One man envisioned a pile of the local currency. Another seemed to be trying to get someone—a relative?—out of prison. One wanted a few dozen magical carriages so he could start a shipping business. Another man was certain he'd made a mistake and that he would die before he could win the prize he sought, coin to alleviate his family's poverty.

The last mind Malek plucked thoughts from dreamed of looking upon the face of one of the rulers, certain the four etchers were all great beauties. He hoped to serve one of them in the bedroom.

That made Malek worry that his chances of meeting one of these rulers might be far poorer than he'd believed. If they were so reclusive that even their own people didn't know what they looked like, would one agree to speak with strangers?

As the minutes passed, Malek realized these men were volunteer gladiators rather than unwilling slaves or criminals. They had agreed to risk their lives for chances at prizes. Prizes apparently tailored to each of them.

He got a sense that one battle wasn't enough to win them, that they had to fight and be victorious multiple times. Almost all of them believed they could succeed, or they would not have entered the games, but a few had doubts as they thought of comrades who'd fallen that day and in past days.

It crossed Malek's mind to wonder if this could possibly be a route to the prize he wished, the secret of the dragon steel and a trade agreement. Were mages allowed to enter the games? During the day's battles, he hadn't seen any of the gladiators using magic. Perhaps this was only open to terrene humans.

Even if a zidarr from another world *could* enter, he would be a fool to do so until he knew more. Perhaps even then, he would be a fool to consider it.

Malek always found the idea of pitting himself against powerful foes appealing, but he had no desire to do so for the pleasure of crowds, and it was always possible he could die attempting the feat. Especially if he ended up pitted against something like that worm. The gladiators weren't likely given dragon-steel axes. He might not even be permitted to use his own weapons.

Besides, if he were killed here, would Rivlen be able to get the group safely back on her own? Malek put aside notions of volunteering for gladiatorial combat and retreated from the cells.

He needed to get back to the suite to check on the others, but there was something he hoped to find first. He believed the discs most people wore at their temples had something to do with their ability to walk in and out of the barrier that protected the city. If he could find some of them for his group, they might be able to leave when they wished.

As he made his way back past the animal enclosures, heading toward the stairway, something pricked at his senses. It was darker in this section of the underground complex, the light dimmer than it had been earlier, so he couldn't *see* anything lying in wait in the passageway ahead of him, but his instincts told him something was there.

Something magical? Thanks to the magic of all the enclosures and of some of the creatures within them, it was hard to pick out individual auras.

A flash of insight came from one of his blades. One of the enclosures had been opened, and something akin to a scaled tiger lay in wait ahead of him.

Malek had no time to consider if he might find a way around. Yellow eyes gleamed as they locked onto him. The creature roared and prowled toward him.

∽

Jadora and Rivlen rode with Zethron in something similar to the self-ambulatory mage carts of Utharika, though this was a carriage with windows rather than an open-air conveyance. In the swift craft, it didn't take long to reach the greenhouse he'd promised, though it was far away from the arena, in a quiet section of the city surrounded by parks, and Jadora worried they wouldn't be able to get back quickly if something happened and they had to go on foot.

She hadn't been able to ask Zethron further questions, since he was on a bench outside, navigating their carriage. Too bad. Jadora would have preferred to get as much information from him as possible. Rivlen, cool and aloof as she gazed out the window, appeared annoyed to be along on this errand. Jadora wished she'd tried to bring Tezi for protection instead. At the least, she was more polite company.

The carriage pulled into a parking area.

Hoping nothing would happen to Jak and the others while she was gone, Jadora studied the greenhouse. This could lead to the Jitaruvak. Malek had said finding dragon steel might please Uthari enough that he would release her father, but the plant and the drug she could hopefully synthesize from it were the king's main goal, the only thing that would definitely result in her father's freedom. Assuming Uthari kept his word.

She grimaced, hoping she could trust in that. She would like to think Malek, with his penchant for honesty, wouldn't serve someone who habitually lied.

A large geodesic dome, the greenhouse was lit softly from within, blue-green foliage visible through the glass panels. She also spotted darker green foliage more reminiscent of plants back home. There were reds and oranges, as well, but from the outside, she couldn't tell if those represented flowers or leaves.

As the carriage slowed to a stop, Jadora leaned forward in her seat, eager to look inside the greenhouse and curious about what Zethron wanted to show her.

"I don't like that we've come so far from the others." Rivlen glanced back, though the arena was no longer in view. "Lord

Malek agreed to this, but I'm worried that we left Jak and the hatchling with only him and three terrene women to defend it. I'm positive that ambassador will take the hatchling if he gets a chance. King Uthari was pleased to see Jak bring the thing back. He won't want it lost."

"His name is Shikari now," Jadora said, "and what do you mean Malek agreed to this?"

"He agreed that you could go and that I should come with you. I've kept in touch telepathically with him. He spied on a meeting, and now he's heading to some underground area under the arena floor. He's been reading every mind he can, trying to figure out where these etchers live and if it's possible for us to get back out of the city without a fight."

"I'm glad you're in touch with him."

"He's not glad you wanted to go cavorting off with this dubious man."

"His name is Zethron."

Judging by Rivlen's cool look, she didn't care. "I think Lord Malek was going to say no, but the fact that *Zethron* wants to show us a greenhouse made a difference."

"Ah."

"What is the plant that King Uthari wants?" Rivlen asked. "Nobody has filled me in on that."

"I'm not sure I'm allowed to tell you if your superiors haven't."

Rivlen gazed at the side of her head, probably plucking the information out like a radish in a garden. "Huh. That makes sense."

Jadora sighed. Someday, she would learn to simply answer mages' questions when they asked. Keeping secrets wasn't an option.

The doors to the carriage popped open, and Jadora and Rivlen climbed out.

Zethron waited at the front door of the greenhouse, holding it open and waving for them to enter. He glanced warily toward the parks and streets around the structure and shifted from foot to foot. Was this a public greenhouse? Or was he sneaking them into someplace where strangers weren't allowed?

"There are magical tools inside," Rivlen warned, walking at Jadora's side, her hand on her sword hilt.

"Anyone waiting to jump out and attack us?" Jadora murmured.

"No mages. I wouldn't be able to sense terrene humans. But if they're there, I can handle them."

Exotic floral scents wafted out even before Jadora reached the door. Entranced and eager to see whatever plants these people had selected to cultivate, she forgot her wariness and strode in first.

Low green lights had been on before, and when she entered, they brightened, turning a yellowish orange that matched the day's sunlight. Raised garden beds followed the walls, and pots and more rows of beds dotted the center like islands, forming winding walkways rather than straight aisles. Everything from small flowering plants to fruit bushes to trees that brushed the glass ceiling occupied the cavernous space.

Most of the flora was unlike anything Jadora had ever seen. She walked around in wonder, looking at plants with purple stems, trees with blue trunks, flowers of all colors imaginable, and fungal and even crystalline growths that she would have struggled to describe.

"Over here is what I wish to show you," Zethron called.

Rivlen leaned by the front door, appearing underwhelmed by the flora and more interested in watching for trouble that might show up. Jadora couldn't fault her for that but also couldn't understand how anyone could refrain from being mesmerized by the place.

As she made her way toward Zethron, she paused to stare at a tree growing what looked like crystalline balls that reminded her of dandelions gone to seed. She touched one, and it was hard, even sharp. A defensive mechanism to protect fruit inside?

"Fascinating," she breathed, longing to take specimens back home to study.

But these weren't weeds growing wild alongside the road. She couldn't shave off samples without asking for permission. Or at least she *shouldn't*. It was hard to keep her hands—and her pruning shears—to herself.

"There are plants from many places on Vran, but also from other worlds." Zethron waved her down a walkway with segregated garden beds and fences around the plants inside.

Lights came on over the beds, lights of slightly different shades of yellow and orange. Maybe they simulated the precise sunlight from the worlds these plants came from? Labels mounted on the fences described the contents, but the words—botanical terms, most likely—weren't familiar to Jadora.

"I do not think we have the plant you showed me," Zethron said, "but some are similar."

He waved, leading her past sections devoted to flora from three other worlds, and stopped in front of a large garden bed full of fern-like plants, all with fronds instead of undivided leaves. Some were trees, some flowering plants, and some low shrubs that dripped aerial roots from their fronds.

She looked carefully and didn't see a match for the Jitaruvak, but she touched leaves and whispered to herself with excitement. Some of them appeared similar to the diagrams and fossilized Jitaruvak she'd seen.

"This might be the world it comes from," she breathed and tugged out her journal to copy the label on the front of the garden bed. "Where we need to go to find it."

"You are pleased?" Zethron asked. "This is helpful?"

"Yes, thank you. What world do they come from?" Jadora

pointed her pen at the label. Even though she'd copied it, it was no good to her, since she couldn't read it.

"Nargnoth. Very swampy around the portal. Dangerous animals, but it is not forbidden."

"Forbidden?" Jadora wrote the name of the world down, along with his addendum about dangerous animals.

"Forbidden, yes. Cut off. Not allowed."

"You mean Nargnoth is a place the people here are allowed to travel to? The symbols weren't rubbed off on their portal?" She raised her eyebrows, wondering if he knew how that had been done. "Do you know how the portal here was altered? Who removed some of the symbols and made it so you can't travel to those worlds?" She might have been speaking too quickly, because his brow furrowed, as if he were struggling to follow her.

She started to write her question, but his brow smoothed as he figured it out.

"The etchers," he said. "To protect us."

"What is it that they etch?" It occurred to her that she hadn't thought to ask that.

"Dragon steel. Only they can craft it."

"With magic?"

"Yes. It must be." But Zethron shrugged, making her believe he didn't know for sure.

Jadora tugged at her ponytail, wondering anew how they could get a meeting with the etchers. Well, Malek could figure that out. The dragon steel was his quest. The Jitaruvak was her priority.

"This world—" Jadora pointed at the ferns. "Nargnoth. Do you know which symbol on the portal leads to it?"

"Yes, of course. I have been there." He took her notebook and pen.

She held her breath as he drew both the constellation and the accompanying symbol. She recognized them—and they weren't in the druid tome. Dare she hope that meant the *dangerous animals* weren't so bad? That one could survive a field trip there, as long as one came prepared, such as with a well-armed zidarr? At the least, it should mean that no horrible man-eating worms had come from that world to prey upon druids long ago.

As Zethron returned the journal and pen, he gripped her hands and held them. He lifted his eyebrows. "This is what you seek?"

"Yes. Thank you."

"Good." He gazed into her eyes. "Will you let me come home with you? To explore the First World?"

"I... I'm not the leader of our group, but if you had a key, you could go any time. Uh, wait." Jadora thought of all the mageships surrounding their portal, all the weapons pointed at it and all the mercenaries running patrols. If someone from another world walked through, even a terrene human, how would they react? Uthari or a fleet commander from one of the other kingdoms might order the traveler captured and questioned. She grimaced. "This might not be the best time for you—for anyone—to visit. There are—"

"What are you telling him?" Rivlen asked.

Jadora jumped, startled.

Rivlen had left the door and was walking toward them, frowning at their clasped hands. She wouldn't have been able to understand the conversation, but with her mind-reading abilities, she had to be getting most of it.

Jadora pulled her hands back. She'd been so pleased that Zethron had given her the lead she needed that she hadn't objected to the touch, but now, she realized Rivlen might think the familiarity with someone who could be an enemy... inappropriate. And she would report back to Malek. Probably without any tact.

"He wants to visit our world," Jadora said. "He believes that his ancestors came from there long ago, and I believe that's very possible. He's curious. But I realized this might not be a good time, that the mages might be wary of visitors."

"*We* would be," Rivlen said, as if to remind her that *she* was a mage.

Jadora had not forgotten.

"Don't invite anyone to visit. These people haven't welcomed us with open arms."

"Zethron has." Jadora was about to add that it sounded like he was from another world, but Rivlen interrupted her with a snort.

"*Zethron* wants to welcome you to his bedroom, so you had better assume he has ulterior motives."

Jadora blushed. "I'm sure that's not true."

It wasn't as if she were the young and beautiful Tezi, able to bestir men's hearts—or their groins—simply by walking into a room.

"Uh huh. He's excited by the fact that you know whatever language that is you've been speaking to him in."

"He may be interested on an academic level," Jadora murmured.

"Trust me. He's interested on the level right below his belt. He—" Rivlen pointed at Zethron but paused, distracted by something past his shoulder.

One of the plants?

"Those are made from dragon steel." Rivlen strode around the garden beds to another walkway.

A reddish-yellow light came on over a patch of potted plants with red and blue flowers that swayed, as if in a breeze, but there was no breeze in the greenhouse. Several of the flower heads rotated toward her as she approached.

"Creepy." Rivlen didn't get too close to them but crouched down and pointed at their pots. They were made from a blue-black material that did look like dragon steel. "Why would such a precious metal be needed for plant pots?"

Zethron was watching Rivlen, but when she looked back at him, he shrugged.

"All worlds are different," he explained to Jadora. "I do not know gardener science, but some plants may not grow here even in the greenhouse without magical help."

"There are more back there." Rivlen circled the flowers—one lunged on its stalk as if to bite her—but she evaded it easily. She headed for potting benches in the back.

Curious, Jadora followed her.

"We should go," Zethron said. "If you are gone too long, I may get in trouble."

Jadora translated his words for Rivlen, who was poking through a couple of empty dragon-steel pots on the bench and not paying attention to him. Jadora didn't want Zethron to be punished for helping them.

"One minute." Rivlen poked around on shelves and opened toolboxes and drawers. "I sense..."

She pulled out a hunk of metal, a lopsided brick with one end shaved off. She turned, holding it up for Jadora to see. It was the same blue-black of the dragon-steel pots and of the portal.

"How," Rivlen asked, pinning Zethron with her gaze, "are your people doing this? How are they making dragon steel into *pots*, and where did this come from?" She thunked the brick down on the work bench.

Zethron shook his head.

"Translate," Rivlen told Jadora. "Though I think he knows exactly what I'm asking."

"Please," Jadora murmured.

She'd gradually been getting Malek to be more polite with her, but maybe it would be a lost cause with Rivlen. As a captain, she was used to giving orders and having them obeyed.

"Professor," Rivlen said, "*please* translate my question for him. This is *important*."

To Uthari's dreams of world domination, no doubt.

Sighing, Jadora translated the question. Rivlen had sounded more irritated and frustrated than gracious, but at least she hadn't reminded Jadora that she was their prisoner, not a respected colleague.

Zethron shrugged. "The rulers do it. Etcher Briara works in the greenhouse as a hobby."

"They come down *here*?" Rivlen pointed to the workbench.

"They go where they wish. They—"

Rivlen swore, dropping the brick and drawing her sword as she spun toward the doorway. She raced halfway down the walkway before Jadora heard anything and realized they were in danger. The slap of sandals came from the parking area outside.

Several armed men charged into the greenhouse, men without discs at their temples. Mages.

12

Even as Rivlen sprang into a ready stance, sword raised, she knew she was in far over her head. No fewer than eight mages were running into the greenhouse, eight *powerful* mages.

Malek, she reached out telepathically, hating to admit she needed assistance and worried that Malek, even if he could make it here in time, wouldn't be enough. *We need help in the greenhouse.*

She did her best to envision where in the city they'd gone and share the location with him, but the first guards rushed toward her, and she didn't have time to give him more. They led with barriers, and even though Rivlen had hers up, it didn't matter.

Two men with dragon-steel weapons shouted something in their language—it sounded a lot like *intruder*—and lashed out. With their magic, they clawed at her barrier with power that staggered her. Rivlen poured all of her energy into her defenses, but they crumbled under the assault.

It was as if these were high-ranking mage officers—or even wizards—in an enemy fleet, not simple town guards.

Simple town guards with *dragon-steel* weapons, she reminded herself, agog at how many people here carried swords, hammers, or axes made from the powerful alloy.

Surprisingly, Malek hadn't responded to her request for help. Where was he? Had he been injured? Knocked unconscious?

Worse?

More mages veered to go around Rivlen and down a walkway toward Jadora and Zethron. They were still in the back of the greenhouse, neither with decent weapons to defend themselves. Jadora had pulled a vial of acid. That wouldn't do a damn thing against these people.

Even though she was without a barrier now, Rivlen sprang into the guards' path with her sword raised. She'd assured Malek she could protect Jadora, and she would do her best.

She swung her blade at one of the mages as she cast a fireball at another.

But her blade bounced off an impervious barrier, and her fireball was no more effective. It was as if she were back in her earliest training days, launching puny and scattered attacks at her tutors.

A wave of power blasted into her like a locomotive. It hurled her across the greenhouse. She smashed through tree branches even as she somersaulted in the air, determined to come down on her feet.

"Get out of here," Rivlen shouted, hurling a blast at the back wall of the greenhouse, hoping Jadora would be able to slip out through a hole and escape.

A panel shattered, glass flying outward. At least her magic was good for *something* here.

An angry guard shouted and launched another wave of energy at Rivlen. She raised her barrier again, enough to halt the attack, but the power made her rock back, almost stunning her with its intensity. Several guards surrounded Rivlen, tearing down her barrier once more. Intense power gripped her, holding her in place. She couldn't so much as lift her sword to strike at her assailants.

As two guards held Rivlen, scowling fiercely at her, others closed on Jadora and Zethron.

But even as Jadora threw something to distract the mages, and Zethron tried to run out through the hole Rivlen had made, power wrapped around them, halting them. An explosion boomed, and leaves and bits of plants flew everywhere—Jadora had thrown more than a vial of acid. It didn't matter. It didn't distract the guards nearly enough.

They gripped Jadora and Zethron with their magic even more easily than they had Rivlen. The guards strode back to the front of the greenhouse, levitating their prisoners behind them.

Rivlen, furious that she couldn't break the grip around her, threw power at the greenhouse walls. She would bring down the place on top of them if she had to.

But what should have been enough power to tear down the entire structure halted before it reached the glass panels. One of the guards was now protecting the greenhouse and walling off the plants, determined that she do no more damage to their facility. He frowned at her and shook his head, as if he were telling a toddler throwing a tantrum to knock it off.

They deposited Jadora and Zethron beside Rivlen, and pressure from above pushed all three of them to their knees. Humiliation joined the fury flushing Rivlen's cheeks. She hadn't endured such treatment in years, not since she'd grown powerful enough to thwart almost all other mages she encountered in her fleet and in enemy fleets. Only men as strong as Tonovan could embarrass her so, and even they rarely did, knowing that it wasn't a good idea to humiliate young mages growing in power, young mages with long memories.

But these people didn't care. To them, she was nothing more than some stranger snooping around in their greenhouse.

Maybe it had been foolish to poke around in here, but when Rivlen had seen that dragon steel… Damn it, she wished she'd gotten away with that brick. She longed to bring loads of dragon steel back to Uthari, to show him her worth, and to show anyone who thought of plotting against her on the *Star Flyer* that she was too accomplished and too valued by their king. They would *dare* not plot against her then, dare not snub her for being young or only a *woman*.

The guards were yelling at Zethron, and Rivlen tried to focus. She might not be able to defeat eight enemy mages, but it was still her duty to protect Jadora. She had to figure out a way to get them out of here.

She couldn't understand the language, nor could she read any of their well-protected minds. All she got from Zethron was regret at leading Jadora into trouble and resentment toward the guards. He kept repeating the name of that woman he was supposedly sleeping with, the etcher, but they didn't seem to care. They kept pointing back at the workbench.

Rivlen had a feeling they were a lot more disgruntled that someone had been touching their dragon steel than checking out their plants. She winced. That was *her* fault. Maybe the dragon steel or the workbench had some kind of alarm on it, and she'd inadvertently triggered it. Even if the metal was more common here than back home, that didn't mean they didn't value it. Highly.

Two of them started questioning Jadora, growing excited when they realized she somewhat understood them. But they didn't seem to get the answers they wanted.

Jadora gritted her teeth, and Rivlen could tell she was trying to keep them out of her mind, but they dug into her memories. Dragon eggs in ice flashed in her thoughts, and Rivlen realized they somehow knew about the hatchling—maybe word was all over their city about it—and were trying to get information about Shikari.

"Leave her alone," Rivlen snarled and attempted to wall off Jadora's thoughts for her, to keep them from reading her mind.

Two of the guards scowled at Rivlen, and one stabbed her with a mental attack. She stiffened, agony erupting inside her skull, as if a pickaxe had driven into her brain.

Beside her, Jadora screamed. Rivlen tried to drive the man out of her head and protect Jadora, but the guards were too strong for her. She was vaguely aware of Zethron yelling and shouting for them to stop—they weren't attacking *him*, just pinning him in place—but screams ripped from her own throat, and she couldn't hear anything else.

By the time the pain halted, Rivlen had crumpled to the ground, gripping her head, wishing she could tear it off her body so she wouldn't feel their attacks anymore.

Someone asked a question from the doorway. A calm conversation followed, broken only by Rivlen's pants and the pained moans coming from Jadora.

Someone new walked in, grabbed Zethron, spoke sternly to him, and escorted him out of the greenhouse. Rivlen watched blearily from the ground, afraid the torture would start up again, but the mental attack didn't return. One of the guards had found Jadora's journal and was flipping through it as she lay on her back, her face contorted with pain. Blood ran from her mouth. She must have bitten her lip or her tongue.

Rivlen started to shake her head, disappointed in herself for failing to protect Jadora, but such an intense headache assaulted her that she immediately regretted the movement.

Power wrapped around Rivlen and Jadora, lifting them and levitating them out to the carriage. The door opened, the power manipulated them inside, and the door slammed shut. Two guards hopped onto the driver's seat, and the vehicle turned around. Heading off to some jail cell?

"They didn't give me my journal back," Jadora mumbled, staring at the ceiling of the carriage from her back on the floor.

Rivlen was wedged against her, shoulder to shoulder. Maybe she could have clawed her way into a seat, but with her head pounding, it was far too much effort.

"Was there any crucial intelligence in it?"

"Just notes on plants." Jadora's voice sounded off, probably because her lip was swelling. "They won't be able to read my notes. Maybe they'll like the pictures."

"As long as they aren't pictures diagramming how our fleet is spread out around the portal and how many troops are waiting for threats that might come out."

After a long pause, Jadora said, "You have interesting notions about what scholars put in their journals."

"I'm a soldier. It's what I would put in *my* journal."

"Mine is full of chloroplasts, vacuoles, and mitochondria."

"I don't know what those are."

"Microscopic parts of a plant cell."

"I'd be disappointed if I got an enemy journal and that was all that was in it."

"Hopefully they will be too and will give it back." Jadora hesitated, then added, "I thought I heard the word jail."

"It's probably where they're taking us."

"Yes."

And what would be waiting at that jail? An executioner with an axe?

Jadora closed her eyes. She probably had a splitting headache too.

The carriage bumping along the stone-block road to what might be their doom didn't help.

"I'm sorry I wasn't able to protect you from them," Rivlen said quietly.

Though she was reluctant to voice her failings out loud, and it galled her to have to apologize to someone, she lamented that she hadn't kept Jadora safe. She'd been certain she could handle this, but it was like the last time she'd faced Tonovan, believing she could handle him too. Clearly, she thought too highly of her own abilities. But she *was* good. She was used to being able to handle her foes. These people were just... too much.

"It's not your fault," Jadora said.

Rivlen grimaced, feeling guilty anew because it might be. "I'm not sure about that. They didn't show up until I started touching the dragon steel. Maybe they sensed that somehow. An alarm. I didn't detect anything like that, but I was so focused on it. I... I want to bring back its secrets to Uthari, to prove that I'm worth my promotion and every other promotion he might ever contemplate giving me. I'm good enough for it all and deserve it, damn it." Tears pricked at her eyes, and she would have spat in disgust if she hadn't been flat on her back. She was a fleet officer. Tears were unseemly, no matter how frustrating the situation was.

"I believe you," Jadora said. "You seem very capable."

Rivlen snorted "Except for tonight."

"These are extenuating circumstances."

"No kidding. Why are these people so powerful?" Rivlen didn't expect Jadora to know—what did terrene humans understand about magic?—and didn't probe for the answer in her thoughts. Her head hurt too much for mind reading now anyway. "We should have tried to bring Jak. For a complete novice, he's pretty good at funneling power into people and giving them a boost."

She'd meant it as a compliment, but Jadora turned a worried expression on her.

"What?" Rivlen asked, still unwilling to use her power to try to read thoughts. Pain pulsed behind her eyes, the worst headache she could remember ever having. When would this bumpy ride end?

"I was wondering," Jadora said slowly, "what your intentions are for my son."

Ah. Yes, she might not approve of Rivlen training Jak so he could be an ally for her, a weapon against Tonovan.

"I more or less understand what Malek wants—someone to loyally serve Uthari alongside him—but what do *you* want?"

Rivlen sighed, tempted not to answer. Another time, she wouldn't have, but after failing to protect Jadora from these people—and not being certain if they were even now on their way to their deaths—she felt compelled to give her something. To give her the truth.

"An ally," Rivlen said. "I am not well liked in the fleet. I'm young, ambitious, and apparently the wrong sex to lead men. Nobody objects to women in the fleet in general, but things change if they rise too high in the ranks and end up ordering men with big egos around. Women are supposed to be healers or crafters, not slay enemies with their magic. Or so my male colleagues believe. Every time I'm stationed on a new ship, I have to prove myself over and over again. And explain that I'm not there to have sex with them."

"I can see how irritating that would be, but how can Jak help? He's not going to enroll in your fleet. Even if he... ends up working for Uthari—" Jadora struggled to get those words out, as if the idea horrified her, "—I don't think anyone would try to turn him into a soldier. He was going to school for cartography, and he's much more of an artist and a scholar than a fighter."

"I know he likes his big words. I *hypothesize* that he does."

Jadora snorted faintly. "That's probably established enough to be considered a theory."

"I don't know how Uthari will want to use him, but trust me, having an ally outside of the fleet wouldn't be a bad idea. Like a secret weapon."

Maybe that hadn't been the right thing to say, for Jadora winced, and probably not because of her headache.

"I don't mean to use him in a way that would get him killed. Nothing like that." Rivlen just wanted Jak to feel he *owed* her, so he would help her with Tonovan and anyone else who tried to keep her down—or force her to do something against her wishes.

"That's good," Jadora murmured, not sounding reassured.

"Everything I teach him is useful for him too. Not just for me. He'll need to know how to best use his power. The world is dangerous. *Worlds.*"

"I'm well aware."

Rivlen sighed, wishing she'd said nothing. She'd essentially admitted to Jadora that she wanted to use her son to further her own ambitions. She'd felt compelled to honesty, but maybe she shouldn't have answered. Now, Jadora might try to talk Jak out of learning from Rivlen—from going through with the promise he'd made. The promise, she'd admittedly tricked him into making and that had been more a tentative agreement than a fervent vow.

"I'd rather see him develop his powers and be able to take care of himself than not," Rivlen said. "I appreciate that he didn't doubt that I was a capable mage and leader and had rightfully earned the captaincy of the *Star Flyer*."

"I should hope not. We *did* see you fly that ship into battle over Port Toh-drom."

"A lot of people believe what agrees with their biases, no matter how much evidence is presented to the contrary."

"Yes, I've encountered that often as well. Can you tell where in the city they're taking us?"

Jadora probably hoped Malek could find them and rescue them. Should Rivlen admit that she'd lost contact with him?

"No. Just that we're still on that loathsome stone road." Rivlen's headache intensified when she tried to use her magic to sense their surroundings, so she winced and gave up. "You'd think such a powerful race of mages could make smoother streets."

"Or figure out how to employ mechanical or hydraulic devices to convert kinetic energy to heat." Jadora grimaced as they went over a bump and rubbed her hip. "Also known as shock absorbers."

"I can tell where Jak got his love of words."

"I taught him to read when he was very young so he could entertain himself without drawing on the walls."

"Most kids get toys."

"Books make less noise. Though he drew in those too. He decided to put a map of his favorite places to play in the neighborhood in my father's *Teachings*." Jadora grimaced and sat up. She tried the door latch.

It was locked. Rivlen wasn't surprised.

She closed her eyes to meditate the best she could without *shock absorbers* and hoped she could recover her power, and that it would help when they reached their destination. Wherever that would be.

∽

The scaled tiger blocked the exit. Malek could have turned and run in another direction, but the big predator would have taken advantage of that. It had to weigh more than a thousand pounds, all muscle. When it sprang, those powerful muscles would carry it far and fast.

Malek crouched, his sword and main-gauche in hand and waited. The voices of men talking and laughing still carried to him. They were likely used to the sounds of animals coming from this area. Even if they learned that one was free of its enclosure, they were safe in their own cells.

The scaled tiger sniffed the air with nostrils more like a furred animal would have. Its yellow eyes remained focused on Malek. After assessing his scent—assessing *him*—it sprang, its fanged maw opening wide.

Malek also sprang. Not at it but straight into the air with muscles enhanced by his training and the magic Uthari had funneled into him over the years.

His jump carried him higher than the tiger, and it landed where he'd been, jaws snapping at the empty air. Malek came down on its back and drove his sword downward. Though he aimed for the creature's spine, the tiger was fast and whipped about as soon as it felt his weight. The sword struck muscle and flesh but not the vital target Malek hoped for.

The tiger bucked, throwing him off to the side. Malek twisted in the air and would have landed easily, but he struck the barrier of one of the enclosures. It startled him with a zap of power that not only stung but blasted him several feet. He still managed to land on his feet, but he came down with his back to the tiger.

It roared and leaped at him, paws leaving the ground as it aimed for his neck.

Malek only had time to drop straight down. He landed on one knee, ducking low to avoid slashing claws, and swept his sword through one of the back legs as the creature flew overhead. He swung fast and hard, cutting through muscle and bone, and hot blood flew everywhere, some spattering his cheek and hands. When the tiger landed, it had only three limbs.

Malek jumped up, spinning to face his foe as it screeched. Despite what had to be great pain, the tiger whirled toward him and sprang again.

This time, Malek held his ground. As its great fanged mouth opened wide, Malek hurled his main-gauche into it.

The blade cut deep into the back of the tiger's throat, sinking into vulnerable flesh. Still in the air, the tiger slashed a paw at him, razor claws trying to tear off his face. Malek dodged the blow as he swept his sword in, the weapon sinking into flesh.

The tiger, discombobulated from its wounds, landed not on its feet but on its shoulder. Malek leaped on top of it and drove his sword into its neck.

Even down and gravely injured, with the main-gauche still lodged in its throat, the big tiger turned his head and snapped at the sword. Malek grabbed the hilt of his shorter blade, yanked it out, and stabbed the tiger in the eye.

It thrashed, and he jumped free lest it injure him with its dying throes. The scaled tail smacked against the floor as legs twitched and claws slashed. A gurgling roar came from its throat, but the sound was far weaker than before.

Weapons dripping blood, Malek crouched and waited to make sure his foe would die. The magic it carried lingered, even as its breaths slowed and finally stopped.

Other predators prowled in nearby enclosures, watching intently, their instincts stirred by the battle—or the scent of blood.

As the magic faded from the creature, Malek grew aware of a presence behind him.

He spun, surprised someone had been able to sneak up on him. Even though he'd been locked in battle, he'd never lost his awareness of his surroundings or of the possibility of further threats being unleashed upon him. After all, someone had let out this creature.

A figure in a flowing white robe with a raised hood stood in the passageway behind him, a glowing nimbus making it seem more like an apparition from a dream than a flesh-and-blood person. But Malek's senses told him that she—feminine curves under the robe hinted of hips and breasts—was real, and that she was immensely powerful. Her aura was perhaps not quite as great as that of the dragon he'd faced, but it was more than he'd ever sensed from a human being. Even Uthari's power would be dwarfed by this woman's.

How had she crept up on him? He couldn't believe that he could have failed, under any circumstances, to detect her approach.

An intriguing foreigner from the First World, she spoke into his mind. *I heard of your arrival, though not from my trusted ambassador, who should have passed along such news.*

I am Malek zem Uthari. He straightened and saluted her with his sword, guessing this might be one of the rulers.

Had she let out the beast? To test him? Or had someone else done that? It seemed unlikely that she would have simply been... in the neighborhood when that happened and come to watch. He had a feeling she'd released the creature. That meant he had to be as careful with her as with any of the other people here. He dared not reveal more than she'd already guessed about his world, especially not about the militaries and the forces they could field if Torvil was invaded.

I represent King Uthari of Torvil—what you call the First World— and seek an alliance with your people on his behalf.

I am Etcher Yervaa. You seek the secret of the dragon steel. Her face wasn't visible through the nimbus, but she seemed to smile. *Your people never learned it.*

Did she sound smug?

Malek kept his face masked, his thoughts and emotions locked down, though it was hard to stifle indignation. Whoever among these people had learned to work the dragon steel, he suspected it had happened long ago and that *she* hadn't been responsible.

There is little dragon steel on our world. Malek assumed she could guess that already, since she knew of his interest, so it was a piece of information he could give away without revealing anything detrimental. Perhaps by sharing something, he would seem more amenable, someone she could reasonably negotiate with. *Dragons have not been seen there for more than ten thousand years.*

Then you are fortunate. She lifted a hand, and an illusion formed in the air between them.

Her city floated in miniature, the dome-shaped barrier that protected it visible, and a pair of brown-and-gray mottled dragons flew over it. They soared down and plucked up two people traveling on the road, tearing them to pieces and flinging their remains into the sea. After that, they attacked the city, but mage guards stood on the wall and reinforced the barrier, funneling even more power to it. A white-robed woman—Etcher Yervaa herself?—appeared out of nowhere to stand beside them and also directed power into the barrier.

The dragons tore at the city's magical defenses, but the defendants' combined might thwarted them. They flew away without acquiring more victims, but the mangled bodies of the dead floated in the sea nearby.

The device on your portal does not keep dragons away? Malek asked.

Oh, it does. It is very effective, but dragons already lived on our world when one of our great inventors crafted that. It has destroyed many of the vile creatures as they've attempted to come through, killing them before they could prey on our kind. We are grateful for it, but the dragons that were already here know to avoid it. When our people attempted to build a second defender device on our city wall, somehow, they destroyed it from afar. We believe it is the combined power of the gateway to the stars and the defender that has kept the original safe.

Interesting.

You will not take it from us, Yervaa said into his mind, as if she knew he'd considered exactly that when they first arrived.

But he hadn't acted on the thought, nor would he have stolen from another people, and he resented her insinuation.

I am zidarr. I am honorable. I do not steal from those I visit.

I do not know what zidarr is.

I am zidarr. Malek lifted his chin. *Sworn to follow the tenets of the Zidarr Code. Integrity, duty, courage, austerity, and honor.*

And you have been physically altered by some magical means? The hood shifted, as Yervaa eyed him up and down. With curiosity? Perhaps that particular magic was not something they had learned to cast.

Since Malek had been the recipient and not the doer, it was not a secret he could offer.

Yes, he thought. *We do seek dragon steel and the secret of working it, but we would trade for it, not steal from you.*

You would find us difficult to steal from. We can slay dragons even without our defender device. It is not easy, but we are capable. There were once more younger dragons on this world, and we have gradually been hunting them, slaying them so they cannot prey on us. Only a few crafty and powerful ones remain in the mountains. Were you to make enemies of our people, you would find it very difficult to defeat us.

I believe you.

Had you found us less formidable, I can't help but think you would already be plotting to take what you wish from our people.

I would not. Malek clenched his jaw. *As I said, I am honorable, and so is my king.*

Even though she was a stranger and had no reason to believe him, he was not used to having his word called into question. Even those who feared the zidarr did not accuse them of being liars. Back home, all knew of the Zidarr Code and that Malek and those like him strove to follow it.

Do you deny that an invasion fleet is even now perched around the portal on your world, poised to flood into any weak worlds and take what they wish, now that your gate is working again? Before you answer, know that I've seen the thoughts of the mundane humans you travel with.

It is not an invasion fleet. A great flying worm came through as soon as we opened the portal. Our ships are there only to protect our world. Even as Malek thought the words, he wondered if they were entirely true. If it turned out that Uthari had to send troops to acquire the Jitaruvak by force, would he? The mageships were too large to send to other worlds, but there were many, many mages stationed around the portal. Uthari could send an army if he felt the need. Still, Malek did not know if he would, so he wasn't lying to this woman. *As I said, I am authorized to arrange trade, equitable trades, in exchange for your knowledge on working dragon steel. We have natural resources with value, may know techniques for manipulating magic that you haven't yet discovered, and if you are having trouble with those crafty old dragons, perhaps I could advise you. I have experience slaying dragons.*

Only the *one* dragon, admittedly, and he'd barely survived the encounter, but if he tossed out a number of possible trade items, perhaps one would intrigue her. Sharing knowledge was easier than digging up resources to send through the portal. Uthari would likely approve of such offers.

Do you? Yervaa looked him up and down again. *And you would be willing to assist us with our dragon problem?*

He noted the word *assist* instead of *advise*, as he'd said, but it might be worth risking himself to help them fight a dragon in exchange for the secret of the ancient alloy. If he could leave the others behind, in the safety of the city, he would be risking only himself.

Perhaps, Malek replied, *if in exchange, you could give us enough dragon steel to make a few hundred weapons—and the knowledge of how to work it.*

A few hundred? She threw back her head and laughed, giving him a glimpse of her chin and nose for the first time, though the white nimbus soon intensified, blurring her features behind the light.

From what he'd seen, Malek guessed she was his age or older.

An age by which mages had practiced much and had usually fully developed their powers.

Dragon steel does not tumble from mountain streams like lesser ores, Yervaa told him. *Even here, it is rare and very valuable.*

One hundred weapons then. And the knowledge to work it.

That was the key. They might acquire dragon steel on their own as they explored farther in the portal network, but without the ability to work it, they could only accept it in its existing state. Malek thought of the dragon-steel disc that Uthari had brought with him, a decorative artifact he'd hung in his lavatory. With the knowledge, it could be altered into a far more useful dagger or other small weapon.

Even if I agreed to such a trade, how much assistance could you truly be? You are less powerful than I, and you don't even have a dragon-steel weapon of your own. Before, she had considered him appraisingly—even with interest—but now she sniffed and looked dismissively at his *lesser*-dragon-steel sword and main-gauche.

Malek knew that this was part of her negotiation tactic, but he had to consciously mask his features again to keep from showing his indignation. He reminded himself that he was here to be diplomatic, not start a war.

I have already slain a dragon, even with my modest weapons. Malek almost flashed his memories of the trip to the frozen world into her mind, but he didn't want to give clues about that place, since all those dragon eggs were still there. The ambassador had been very interested in them, and she might be too.

He formed an illusion in the air, as she had, and showed her the battle in the domed fortress and nothing more, nothing that should give away its location. Since that world was among those rubbed out on their portal, it was unlikely that she had been there, but he still needed to be careful.

It was my first encounter with one, he admitted, showing her the truth of the battle, not a lie that would have indicated it had been easy. *I learned much from it and am confident I could offer effective assistance if your people chose to battle the two dragons you showed me.*

Yervaa watched the battle play out in his illusion, and Malek waited to see if she would believe it was his true memory or if she would accuse him of lying.

Once the dragon died, he let the illusion fade. After that, he'd fallen half-dead to the ground, collapsing to meditate while Fret and Jadora tended his grievous wounds. This woman didn't need to witness that.

You do have prowess with a blade that compensates for your modest mage talent, Yervaa said after a thoughtful moment.

Modest mage talent? Malek kept his chin up but refrained from pointing out that he was considered as powerful as one of the rare wizards among his people. He reminded himself that any information he shared suggesting his people were weak compared to hers could be used against Torvil. The last thing he wanted was to put the idea of an invasion into her mind.

I did appreciate watching you slay the bakzar. Yervaa looked toward the dead tiger behind him and seemed to smile. *But a bakzar is not a dragon. I believe I need further proof of your prowess before agreeing to this deal.*

What kind *of proof*? Malek asked warily.

As you may have learned while skulking through the barracks, our gladiators must emerge victorious from five *battles to win a prize from one of us.* She touched her chest.

Do you want to open four more cages? Malek couldn't keep the sarcasm out of his tone. He was offering to fight alongside her people. *He* would be taking all the risk.

These animals are captured at great risk to my people. I will not sacrifice another in the bowels of the arena. Their deaths are meant to be witnessed by thousands, entertainment to keep our workers happy in our city. You must defeat them as one of our gladiators, bound by the same rules as they, in battle in the arena.

She prowled closer to him, her powerful aura battering at his senses. Malek stood his ground, doubting she would attack him but glad he hadn't sheathed his weapons. He sensed a barrier protecting her and strong mental defenses that protected her mind as well.

I must fight in your arena to prove I'm capable of assisting your people with a dragon hunt?

Precisely.

If I die in one of these fights, then what? I am here to gain dragon steel and its secrets for my people, not risk my life for nothing.

Yervaa patted his cheek. *If you are the sublime warrior that you believe you are, then there should be little risk. I will only insist that you win three battles in the arena, since the dragons would be the fourth and the fifth foes you would fight.*

Malek stepped back so that her hand fell away from him. *You don't intend for me to fight them alone, do you?*

What had happened to his suggestion that he *assist* with the dragons?

You must fight in the arena alone, but dragons are challenging foes. You may bring your colleagues to help battle them if you wish, such as the boy that my ambassador believes is in charge of your group, simply because the portal speaks with him. The portals are fickle, and their regard means little. Anyone with a key can travel through them. Though some who arrive through them are more interesting than others. She chuckled and looked Malek up and down again.

Malek shook his head. This wasn't a trade negotiation. She wanted him to give his life, and the lives of his comrades, and for what? Her entertainment?

The only way I would consider fighting for you is if you give the secret of the dragon steel and one hundred weapons' worth of dragon steel to the rest of my party, then let them go. Let them step out of your barrier and return to our world. I will stay and fight for you in your arena. If I am victorious in your three battles, I will then accompany you and your mages to the dragons' lair and help *you defeat them.*

You expect me to give away all of that and let your people go before you've fought a single battle? You would attempt to escape and flee as soon as your people had gone through the portal.

I would not. Malek gritted his teeth. He'd explained the Zidarr Code, and she still doubted his honor. *You have my word that I will do as I say, as long as you first do what we agree upon.*

I will give you some of what you ask for after *you fight in the arena. You will battle for my people's entertainment, then, if you survive, I will send the rest of your party home with the secret to working dragon steel, while you stay and assist us with the dragons.*

Malek blew out a slow breath. That offer was an improvement. It was possible he would fall in the arena, but he believed he had the skills to defeat lesser creatures. Nothing hinged on him battling dragons, though he would still be bound by his word to help with them. If Jadora and the others were safe at that point, with the dragon steel that Uthari had asked for, then wouldn't it be worth it for him to risk his life? In truth, the thought of facing off against dragons again was slightly appealing. The last dragon battle had been the challenge of his life, and he believed he could do better now that he had experience.

Do you accept my offer? Yervaa extended a hand toward him, opening her palm. One of the discs lay on it, a needle sticking up from the backside.

Were they *embedded* into people's temples? The needle was long enough to go through one's skull and into the brain. He hadn't expected that.

It is our rule that gladiators wear them in the arena, she told him.

What do they do?

Oh, they have a few properties. Mostly, they allow us to track you and allow you to come and go through the city barrier.

Malek sensed she was being evasive. Even if she wasn't, he

didn't want that thing embedded in his head. He'd known it as soon as he'd seen the needle, but now, he was doubly sure.

You are not being honest with me, he stated. *What else do they do?*

Make the battles fair and reduce the likelihood that the creatures will be hurled up into the seats where they'll damage the spectators.

I will not wear it. Malek lifted his chin. *You have no need to track me. I've given my word that I will fight for you in exchange for the secret of the dragon steel and the release of my people. I am not some peon off your streets who seeks coin as a prize.*

You want something far more valuable than coin. Nobody but the etchers knows how to manipulate the dragon steel.

Is that how you maintain your position? Your rule?

It is one way. We are valued not only for our power but our knowledge. But we are not cruel rulers, and we reward those who successfully entertain our people—and us. Yervaa placed a hand on Malek's chest.

He almost sprang back, disgruntled by the familiarity and not trusting it. Or her.

A trickle of magic flowed from her fingers. He tensed, ready to defend himself, but it was a caress rather than an attack. A sexual advance?

The only reward I want is the secret of the dragon steel, he told her.

You have a singular mind. Zethron enjoys spending time with me.

I'm sure. Malek stepped back out of her reach again, lifting his sword to place a barrier between them.

There is another you prefer? She chuckled and put an image of Tezi in his mind.

He was reassured at this confirmation that she couldn't read his thoughts and didn't truly know who he cared for.

I am a warrior and prefer my duty, he said.

But you must care about your comrades since you included them in your negotiations. If you want them to be kept safe and returned to your world, you will fight in the arena, and then you will lead my people into battle against the dragons. She showed him an image of Rivlen and Jadora, lying on their backs and locked in a carriage. Both appeared injured, if not beaten and tortured. *Give me your word, zidarr.*

Was the image real? Malek reached out to Rivlen telepathically, but he received no response. Nor could he speak with Jadora or Jak. Jak should have been easy to reach, since they were both in the arena, but perhaps this basement area was insulated from magical intrusion, similar to that druid sanctuary. Or maybe Yervaa was blocking him somehow.

My guards caught them snooping in our greenhouse, looking at the dragon-steel pots that we use there. Your people's focus is as singular as yours.

That surprised Malek, since he believed Jadora had been lured out by the promise of plants, not pots. *What have you done to them? Where are they?*

Malek took another step back, intending to charge out of the arena and find them himself.

But a magical barrier that hadn't been there before blocked him. Unlike the one at the top of the stairs, this one was powerful. *Very* powerful.

The guards were going to take them to jail to punish them suitably for their transgressions.

His insides clenched at the idea of Jadora being hurt further. She didn't deserve that. She wouldn't be here on this world if not for Malek and Uthari.

I can easily have them returned to you. If you cooperate. Yervaa gazed into his eyes, her face still hidden by her hood and the nimbus, but he had no trouble interpreting the coldness there. *Three battles in the arena, and if you survive them, you'll do as you claimed you could. Lead a party to defeat our local dragons.*

She held out the disc again.

And if I do all that? You'll do what you said?

Yes. We will not give you dragon steel that your people might one day be inclined to use against us, but I will teach you—or more likely your scholar—the secret of working the dragon steel, and we will permit your party to leave after your arena battles.

My scholar? Professor Freedar?

The one who speaks our ancient language. She is far more likely to grasp the secrets. Yervaa held up the disc. *Do you accept?*

Do I have a choice?

Not if you wish your comrades to be returned to you. And the hatchling and the boy to be left alone. I have no need of a baby dragon, but others have delusions of raising it to fight the younger dragons. More likely, they will get it killed. You have my word that I'll keep your comrades safe while you battle in the arena for me, and whether you live or die, they'll be allowed to return to your world with the secrets of the dragon steel. Still holding up the disc, she stared steadily into his eyes. *Do I have your word?*

Malek took it, more because he wanted to study it than because he would be willing to shove it into his skull, but he couldn't let Jadora and Rivlen be punished, or Jak be hurt, so he had to agree to the rest.

I will fight your beasts for you.

Excellent.

13

Bangs, clangs, and occasional booms came from the large rectangular tent that had been erected as a workshop for the new shipbuilding project. Nearby, sawhorses had been set up, and bare-chested slaves with woodworking tools turned tree trunks they'd dragged over into lumber. A mage worked with them, muttering and waving his hands as he used his magic to dry the wood so it wouldn't warp.

Grim-faced guards in red uniforms stood out front and also at the corners in back of the tent. They fondled their weapons and alternately eyed the jungle in all directions and the mageships with yellow, blue, green, and brown hulls. It was as if they were guarding stacks of gold or dragon-steel weapons, not a scrawny, mouthy engineer.

Night Wrath hadn't been seen since the night he'd escaped, so Sasko supposed she couldn't fault the security measures. Whether Vinjo's zidarr brother would try to rescue him or kill him for working for the other side, she didn't know.

"It's not necessary for you to hold my hand and escort me to his door," Sasko said, eyeing Captain Ferroki.

After their morning workout, she'd suggested that Sasko *freshen up* at the pool and visit the newly arrived engineer.

"Sorath explained everything to me," Sasko added.

"Good. I'm walking at your side in companionable silence, not holding your hand or escorting you."

"Is that why you were spritzing my hair with some of Corporal Lady's froo-froo citrus-scented perfume?"

"I meant to spritz the side of your neck, but you moved."

"I didn't want to smell like a tangerine," Sasko said as they stopped in front of the tent flap.

"I thought it might be an improvement over body odor. We *did* just work out."

"After which, I washed my armpits and sweaty crevices, per your suggestion."

The guards, who'd previously been attentively watching their surroundings, now eyed Sasko's… crevices. She scowled at them.

"I do appreciate that." Ferroki extended a hand toward the flap. "And that you're willing to be in an enclosed space with our new engineer."

"It's not that enclosed. Tents are easy to escape from." Sasko patted her sword.

"I hope you won't be moved to add ventilation slits to the workshop."

Sasko sighed and lowered her hand. "It'll be fine. He just *talks*. He's not handsy."

"Good." Ferroki lifted the tent flap for her.

"I feel like I should ask for a combat bonus for this."

"How about some of the local alcohol and a few days of leave?" Ferroki smiled. "As soon as there's someplace to *leave* to."

"I'll agree to that."

"Thank you. It is a good worker bee that puts the needs of the hive ahead of her own."

"I love when your analogies compare us to insects, Captain."

Sasko ducked into the tent and came face to face with a glowing yellow sphere with equally glowing tentacles flowing out of it and across the ground.

Behind it, Vinjo, clad in underwear and a sleeveless black shirt, had his head stuffed in a tool chest. He hummed contentedly as he rummaged, but bruises on his bare arms and legs made him look like he'd been run over by a herd of elephants.

Had Uthari's people physically *beaten* him? Why? Mages could inflict pain with their brains and read their prisoners' minds.

If they'd brutalized him, it had been out of pure cruelty. Because they'd been furious that he'd successfully helped sabotage some of their ships? Or simply because they were asses?

"I hope this partial nudity doesn't imply that you're expecting favors," Sasko said, making her tone light, though seeing those bruises left her throat tight with sympathy.

After all the years she'd worked as a mercenary, violence didn't bother her that much. She was used to it. But usually, it was between soldiers fighting on the battlefield. Not against some brainy goof who probably would have told Uthari's people everything he knew without any coercion at all.

Vinjo dropped a wrench as he straightened and spun toward her. It bounced off his foot, though oddly, he wore boots with his underwear, so his toes were protected.

"Lieutenant Sasko," he blurted, his face brightening, though it was as bruised as the rest of him. A black eye had him squinting, and when he smiled, a scab on his lip split open and blood trickled down his chin. "I heard you might come by. How delightful." He wiped his bare arm across his chin to staunch the blood.

She pulled the brown kerchief that was part of her mercenary uniform from her pocket and offered it to him.

"Thank you." He stepped around the engine, or whatever it was, to accept it, bowed, then pressed it to his split lip. "As to my undress, no, I wasn't led to believe that there would be *favors*, only that you might keep me company and that people would stop punching me if I agreed to work on a special project. As King Zaruk's loyal subject, with my family living in Zarlesh, I would normally say no, but Uthari promised me that he was negotiating with the other fleets, and that *everyone* would be able to explore the new worlds on the ship he wants me to build. That seemed... maybe not so treasonous." Uncertainty flashed in his eyes. "I refuse to wear his uniform though." He sneered and flicked a finger toward a red tunic and trousers draped over a table.

"What happened to your own clothes?"

"My tormentors tore them off me when the questioning began. I suppose I should be relieved that my underwear was left unmolested, else I'd truly be in an unfit state for a lady." He bowed again to her.

"You know I'm not a lady."

"No." He straightened and beamed a smile at her, though that made his lip bleed again, and he huffed in exasperation as he returned the kerchief to it. "You're a warrior woman. Far more intriguing than a lady. And far more irreverent." His eyes crinkled at the corners. "Have you fantasized about shoving pencils up the noses of any uptight mages lately?"

"Every chance I get. Sometimes, my fantasies involve even sharper objects."

"Savage." Now, his eyes gleamed with approval. "I had such fantasies myself while being interrogated." He glanced toward the entrance. "I had better get back to work. They gave me a ridiculously optimistic deadline. Who builds a ship in a week? Nobody. Even if such were possible, it would require a shipyard with far better tools than they've given me." Vinjo picked up the wrench. "I'd be lucky if I could fix an overflowing toilet with such crude appurtenances."

"You've made some impressive devices with scrounged parts." Admittedly, Sasko hadn't originally seen the merit of his devices when he'd been verbosely explaining and demonstrating them to her, but after hunkering in the woods with Sorath and successfully spying on a druid and a zidarr without being caught, she was much more appreciative of his work.

"You think so? Excellent. I'll make you something."

"That's not necessary. You should focus on the mini mageship. Your guards would appreciate that, I'm sure."

More likely, they would insist.

"Ah, yes. The guards. I must indeed work assiduously. But I could carve out time for gift creation. My materials are limited, but perhaps some jewelry? Do warrior women wear jewelry?" He squinted at her weapons and took in her unadorned wrists and neck.

"Some do, but generally, wearing something an enemy can grab in close quarters and use to strangle you is a bad idea."

"Perhaps I could make you one of my clandestineness creepers. They're most excellent for *hiding* from enemies." He winked at her. "Then they can't find your vulnerable jewelry."

Sasko opened her mouth to object again to his offer, but would she truly object to such a stealth device? She still couldn't believe that she and Sorath had successfully spied on two powerful magic users.

"I wouldn't say no to one of those," she said.

"Oh, good. I won't even charge you. I gathered that Thorn Company and Colonel Sorath had something to do with my release."

"We didn't want to see you get killed."

"Because you care for me?"

"Uh. I think *Sorath* cares for you. And your inventions."

"It's good to be valued. I must return to work." Vinjo lowered his voice. "If you see my brother skulking around, don't tell him where I am."

"I won't." Sasko considered him as he set to work on one of the tentacles that wasn't glowing. "Why did you two come here? You never said. Why didn't you go back to one of Zaruk's ships?"

"As he said when we ran into your patrol, my brother wants to kill Colonel Sorath. *Badly*. He blames your company for betraying the *Skimmer* to Uthari's people. Many mages were killed when his fleet showed up and surrounded the ship."

"I remember. I was there." Sasko grimaced. She remembered Night Wrath's accusations of betrayal, but she hadn't realized they'd come all the way here for the sole purpose of killing Sorath. Did Sorath know Night Wrath was after him?

"Your people were lifted to safety while the crew was allowed to crash to the jungle floor hundreds of feet below. My brother and I had just arrived back from our mission, but we were too late to help. It was horrifying. So many injured and dead. I don't blame Sorath though. I don't think he did it."

"He didn't, and trust me, being deposited on Uthari's yacht wasn't *safe*."

"I *knew* he didn't. But my brother thought it was suspicious that Uthari found the *Skimmer*." Vinjo's brows drew down. "I should have warned the colonel. I don't want my brother to be killed, but I don't want Sorath to be killed either. He likes my inventions."

"He does. I'll warn him."

"Good. Thank you. I'll make you that—" Vinjo paused as a guard poked his head into the tent, "—jewelry."

The guard frowned at him.

"Women love jewelry," Vinjo told him. "Even warrior women."

The guard grunted indifferently. "Visiting time is over. You're supposed to be working, not having relations." He squinted at Sasko and looked her up and down. "You smell good. Like tangerines."

"As all women should." Sasko hurried out before he could

decide that deplorable citrus stuff was alluring and try to have his way with her.

She had to warn Sorath that Night Wrath had come here specifically to kill him.

∽

Jak was hunting around the suite, trying to find spiders and bugs to feed his hungry hatchling, when Mother and Rivlen walked in, accompanied by grim-faced guards. The men paused to eye the wreckage left by Tinder's grenade, stray magelock blasts, and lightning bolts.

Jak jumped to his feet. Mother and Rivlen were being marched in like prisoners, with pained slumps to their stances and weariness dragging down their faces. Tezi, who'd been resting on one of the undamaged sofas, grabbed her axe and stood up.

But the guards didn't stay or comment on the mess, not out loud anyway. They exchanged long-suffering looks with each other. One kicked rubble—numerous chunks from the ceiling and walls had tumbled down when the grenade went off—on the way out.

"What happened?" Jak hugged his mother. The pained crease to her brow suggested she needed support.

"We got caught snooping in a greenhouse," Rivlen said.

Jak peered into the corridor, looking for Zethron, but he hadn't come back with them. Had he lured them into a trap? Calling the guards when Mother was doing something the locals didn't like? Jak couldn't imagine what that would be. Who got uppity about visitors peeking into greenhouses?

"And punished for it," Rivlen added.

"I'm not sure why they brought us back here," Mother said, returning Jak's hug. "I thought they were taking us off to jail."

"Or to be a snack for a monster in their arena tomorrow," Rivlen said.

Jak left them to pull the tattered curtain back across the doorway, wanting to give them as much privacy as possible. But he paused, spotting Malek walking toward the suite.

He didn't appear to be in pain, but his clothing was askew, and something that might have been blood spattered his cheek. It was more gray than red, so it couldn't be his.

"They brought everyone back here because I made a deal with one of the rulers," Malek said as he stepped inside, looking everyone up and down, his gaze lingering on Mother.

"Where did you find one of the rulers?" Jak asked.

Tinder and Fret, hearing the conversation, came out to join them.

"Under the floor of the arena where the creatures and gladiators are kept in enclosures," Malek said.

"I imagined the rulers living in crystal castles or something like our sky cities," Rivlen said.

"This one came down to test me," Malek said.

"They like to do that here," Rivlen said.

"Yes. I lived, and she offered the secret of working dragon steel in exchange for a couple of… tasks."

"Tasks?" Mother sank onto one of the sofas, not batting an eye at the carnage that had been done to the other furnishings.

Destroyed filling from the cushions scattered the floor like feathers in a henhouse. The hatchling was sleeping contentedly among the fluff.

"I'm to battle three creatures in the arena." Malek held out a hand, showing one of the ubiquitous discs that was lodged in the temple of almost everyone who wasn't a mage. "If I survive those fights, there are two dragons that pester the city and eat travelers. Etcher Yervaa wants us to help her people kill them. Or me, at the least. She originally mentioned the rest of you helping me but also agreed that you could leave after my arena battles. That would be for the best." He glanced at Mother. "Though I could use Rivlen's help with the dragons."

"You're going to fight *two* dragons?" Mother asked.

"One almost killed you," Jak said, equally stunned. "It could have killed *all* of us."

"Yes, I remember. I'm more experienced this time, and I'll have Rivlen along, if she's willing to help." Malek extended a hand toward her, making it a request and not an order.

Jak expected Rivlen to lift her chin and cockily say that she could handle a dragon. But the night's events must have shaken her confidence, for she only appeared daunted.

"I regret to inform you, Lord Malek, that I was unable to defeat the mage guards that stormed the greenhouse." Rivlen grimaced at Mother. "If the dragons are powerful enough to harry these people, I have concerns about being able to defeat them."

"One wonders why they couldn't deal with the dragons themselves." Mother considered Malek. "Do you think this ruler is trustworthy and that it's a genuine offer?"

"So far, I haven't found anyone here that I would consider trustworthy," Malek said. "But she promised that whether I survived the arena battles or not, you would be able to return through the portal with the secret of the dragon steel."

"Me?" Mother touched a hand to her chest.

"All of you." Malek waved to indicate the group.

"What about *you*?" Jak asked.

"Presumably, if I survive and the dragons are defeated, she won't stop me from returning."

"If you *survive*?"

"I'll strive to do so."

Jak shook his head, not reassured in the least.

"Maybe if they let us out to hunt dragons for them," Rivlen

said, "we could take the opportunity to sneak off to the portal and leave."

"I like that plan," Tinder said. "Leave them to deal with their own dragons."

Fret nodded vigorously. "Battling dragons is frowned upon by your doctor. Some wounds cannot be healed."

Jak thought of the vision the battle-axe had given him. "You said two dragons, Malek?"

"Yes. They trouble the city from time to time. She showed me."

"Are these two dragons possibly located in lush blue-green mountains, in a crater-shaped valley surrounded by foliage, with a big ziggurat in the middle of it?"

Everyone stared at him. Even the hatchling sat up and cocked his head, as if listening to the conversation.

"She mentioned mountains," Malek said. "Ziggurats didn't come up. Did the portal give you a vision?"

"Uh." Maybe Jak should have said yes. By now, everyone believed that the portals could and did communicate with him, so that didn't sound as goofy as saying an axe had chatted him up. "This may sound silly, but when I was touching Tezi's axe, I had a vision. Just a few seconds that showed me that place, with brown-and-gray mottled dragons flying out from behind the ziggurat and swooping straight down toward me and Shikari." He touched the hatchling, eliciting a concerned chirp.

"What's a ziggurat?" Rivlen asked.

"A terraced compound of successively receding levels," Jak said.

Judging by the crinkle to her brow, that hadn't painted a picture for her.

Jak lifted his hands to draw it in the air, then realized he had pen and paper nearby. "I'll show you. If it's a local monument, maybe Zethron will recognize it and know where it is."

"What happened to Zethron?" Malek asked coolly. "When you were captured in this greenhouse that he guided you to."

"He was also captured," Mother said.

"But the guards let him go," Rivlen added. "They didn't punish *him*, just us."

Jak had already started drawing, but he glanced at Malek, hoping he wouldn't be angry with Mother for going off with Zethron.

But Malek wasn't glaring at her. Jak decided he looked irritated on her behalf, because it sounded like she'd been abandoned, rather than *with* her.

"What kind of punishment?" Malek asked, his tone softening.

"The kind you mind a lot less when it's done to someone else and not you." Rivlen grimaced.

"I'd mind it being done to anyone." Mother touched the side of her head.

"I wouldn't mind it being done to *them*," Rivlen said.

"Do you think Zethron intentionally lured you into a trap?" Malek asked.

"Yes," Rivlen said as Mother shook her head.

"I don't think so," Mother said. "He showed me plants similar to the Jitaruvak and gave me the name of the world they came from." Mother drew a piece of paper from a pocket and held it up. "They had sections in their greenhouse dedicated to plants from other worlds. He also gave me the matching constellation and symbol. We can go there next and get what Uthari wants." She lowered her voice. "So he'll free my father."

Malek removed his weapons belt and sat on the sofa next to Mother. "Are you all right?" he asked quietly.

Rivlen opened her mouth, as if she wanted to point out that she'd also been punished, but she closed it again without commenting. Instead, she clasped her hands behind her back and stood in a parade rest like the soldier she was.

"It wasn't pleasant, but now, I just have a strong headache. Hopefully, no permanent damage." Mother touched the side of her head. "I need my brain." She slid a few snipped-off green fronds from her pockets. "I want to look at these under my microscope to see if they're similar to the plant that's growing under the portal back on Torvil. I have a hunch about that foliage."

"Maybe *that's* why the guards showed up," Rivlen muttered.

"You think they somehow sensed I was taking cuttings?" Mother asked. "I wasn't going to, not without permission, but I couldn't resist."

Rivlen hesitated. "No. Like I said before, I think they showed up because I was poking around that workbench, trying to figure out how those dragon-steel pots were being made."

"Dragon-steel pots?" Malek asked.

"Apparently, some of the plants require a touch of magic to grow on this world," Mother said.

"I can't believe someone would use something as valuable as dragon steel to make *pots*." Tinder stared at Tezi's axe. "Do they shoot out lightning if someone threatens the seedlings?"

"Probably only if the gardener roars a command in the dragon language." Jak finished up his drawing, including the vines and grass growing on the terraces of the ziggurat—that would help convey how old it had appeared to be—and showed it to Malek and Rivlen. "It was kind of like a terraced pyramid with a temple on top. I would love to explore it, but not if dragons are going to pop out. Dragons that want to eat Shikari."

"You said the foliage was blue-green?" Mother pointed at the drawing.

Since Jak had used a pencil, he hadn't been able to convey that. "Yes. It definitely looked like it was someplace on this world."

"I wonder if this is the same valley that Uthari described." Malek studied the drawing. "He also saw dragons attacking us—me."

"He had a vision too?" Jak raised his eyebrows. Maybe receiving a spontaneous vision from a weapon wasn't as strange as he'd thought.

"Two of them, yes." Malek gave Jadora an indecipherable look before turning back to the drawing. "In one, a dragon was attacking me. He didn't mention a ziggurat."

"How did he get a vision of what was going to happen on this world from our world?" Jak wondered.

"He has a lesser-dragon-steel dagger." Malek touched one of his own weapons. "It's not uncommon for them to share flashes of insight about possible futures."

"Or dreams?" Mother murmured.

"Yes." Malek inclined his head toward her. "Though that's rarer. It doesn't surprise me that full-dragon-steel weapons would also have that ability."

"You said Uthari had two visions?" Jak asked. "What did the second one show?"

"Nothing that's going to come to pass," Malek said firmly.

The evasive reply surprised Jak, but he didn't press. He was more concerned about dragons they might be expected to battle, dragons that, in *Jak's* vision, had wanted to kill his hatchling.

"You made the ziggurat very dark." Mother pointed to the heavily shaded structure in the drawing. "Could you tell what it was made from? Some dark stone?"

"I only glimpsed it briefly in the vision. And it was half-covered in foliage." Jak closed his eyes and tried to remember it accurately. "It was probably something like granite, though... Uhm, it *was* very dark. Maybe even... blue-black?"

"The ziggurat is made from dragon steel?" Mother asked.

"It might not be." Jak shrugged. "I only saw it for a couple of seconds and from a distance. I was more focused on the killer dragons flying at us."

"That would be a tremendous amount of dragon steel, even if

it's only partially constructed from that material." Malek looked at Mother. "Is there any precedent to suggest this is plausible? An entire dragon-steel structure?"

"Back home, there's a pillar on Agathar Island in the Tarnished Sea," Mother said, "but that's the only thing of that size that I'm aware of. Dragon steel is more common on this world, however, so it's possible. Especially if this valley is claimed by dragons. Maybe they built the ziggurat long ago and have lived there ever since."

"It would have been the *good* dragons that made it," Jak said. "And then the evil dragons probably killed them and took it over."

"We don't have any proof that your evil dragons—or the younger dragons, as the locals call them—are incapable of making and crafting the metal," Mother said.

"Evil dragons break down civilizations and destroy people—and good dragons," Jak said. "I'm sure of it."

"Even though it's not in the history books."

"It's in my gut. As solid and sure as..." Jak groped for an analogy.

"Insoluble fiber?" Mother suggested. "Undigested mungor root balls?"

"Ha ha. I just know it in my gut." Jak took his drawing back to the table. "I wonder if these people would give me a map of the area. Maybe I could make some guesses about where this valley is located. Assuming we want to go there?" Jak raised his eyebrows and met Malek's eyes.

"We may have to," Malek said.

"What happened to the plan where we *pretend* we're going to fight the dragons?" Fret asked. "So they'll let us out of the city and we can sprint to the portal and never again return to this world?"

"That's what you should do," Malek said. "It's what the group should do. But if that ziggurat is truly made from dragon steel, and if we can learn the secret of working it, maybe I could carve off a chunk to take back home."

"You?" Jak asked. "Just you are going to go face these dragons?"

"I would prefer Captain Rivlen assist me, but there's no reason for us all to risk ourselves," Malek said. "Despite my attempt to negotiate for dragon steel, Etcher Yervaa said she wouldn't give us any as part of our... trade, but if her people never visit that valley because it's guarded by dragons, then they wouldn't miss it if a corner of the ziggurat disappeared."

Mother drew back, looking appalled at the idea of removing a *corner* from an ancient monument. But if they truly could learn to manipulate and craft things from dragon steel, that pillar back on Torvil would be in danger too. People all over the world would rush to tear off pieces so they could make weapons out of dragon steel.

Jak shook his head, not sure if he should hope for his people to learn to manipulate the substance or not. But if, in opening the portal, they had opened their world to possible attacks, not only from magical monsters but from people from other civilizations, maybe it would be best if they had as many tools as possible to defend themselves.

"Do you really think this ruler will share the secrets of how to work it?" Jak asked.

"I don't know how honest she was being with me, but perhaps while I'm engaged in these gladiatorial matches, the rest of you will have some freedom and could discover the secret yourselves." Though he spoke of all of them, Malek gazed thoughtfully at Mother.

As a long moment passed, Jak wondered what he was thinking about.

Mother must have wondered too, for she asked, "Are you admiring my academically inclined but still appealing face? Or thinking about how tired and beleaguered I look?"

"Neither." Malek missed an opportunity to flatteringly point out her appeal. "The ruler said *you* would be the most likely one in our group to be able to learn how to work the alloy. Because you're a scholar."

"And thus a natural metalsmith?"

"Perhaps because it's not metalworking that's required."

"Interesting. I don't know how much freedom we'll have—" Mother glanced toward the doorway as people walked past the curtain, two guards taking up stances in the corridor outside again, "—especially if we're stuck in here, but I'll learn what I can."

"Good. Thank you." Malek smiled faintly and added so softly that Jak almost missed it, "And you *are* appealing. Academically and otherwise."

"Thank you," Mother said.

Malek started to rise, but he paused and rested a hand on her shoulder.

Jak sensed him sending a trickle of magic into her. He couldn't tell what it did, but she closed her eyes and leaned into the touch, some of the pain etching her face leaving.

Healing, Jak decided, and put that on the list of things he would like to learn to do.

"Captain Rivlen?" Malek asked. "Do you need healing?"

Rivlen had slumped wearily during the conversation, contributing little, but she straightened and shook her head. "I can take care of myself, my lord."

Pride? Jak thought she could use the same trickle of healing magic, but she kept her chin up in aloof professionalism.

"Very well," Malek said.

The curtains stirred as four servants walked in. Malek released Mother's shoulder, brushing her hair with his fingers as he turned to face them.

Two servants carried trays stacked with plates of food and pitchers to replace what had been eaten and drunk—and knocked to the floor in the battle. As they tidied the area, wordlessly cleaning the mess, the remaining two approached Malek.

One carried an armful of practice swords, war hammers, and a blunt axe. The other bore a tray with what looked like leather underwear and a studded leather harness folded on it.

These weapons are for you to practice with. One of the servants did not have a disc at his temple and addressed the room telepathically as he nodded to Malek and spread the items out on a nearby table. *I've been told to inform you that you have three days to practice before the events start.*

Jak couldn't believe that even some of the servants here had magical power.

The events? Malek asked, also giving his response telepathically to all. *My battles in the arena?*

Yes. Your comrades are most fortunate to have been given a suite here so they may watch your battles and see whether you live or die against the mighty foes you'll face.

Fortunate indeed.

Mother's face grew ashen at the words about Malek possibly dying.

And they may also practice among themselves to improve their prowess. We were given to understand that your group will, should you survive your arena battles, partake in a dragon hunt.

"A *two*-dragon hunt," Rivlen muttered.

The prize offered for such a battle must be very great to entice you, the servant said. *Few warriors have graduated from the arena and been sent out by the etchers as champions to slay a dragon. Of those who have, none have survived and come back victorious, not for many generations. The dragons that remain in this world are extremely powerful and very cunning.*

"Oh, good," Rivlen said. "I was afraid we would have to face run-of-the-mill dragons."

These are your garments for the arena. The servant with the tray of clothes—if one could call the leather items that—extended it to Malek. *We wish you luck and look forward to seeing you perform. It has been many years since otherworlders have come and battled in the arena. We hope you have great prowess, for the most recently acquired magical animals are very strong and very deadly. The matches will surely be excellent, providing you're able to survive more than the opening blows. The crowds do grow disappointed if the battles are over too quickly.*

"I have no doubt," Malek murmured, accepting the tray.

The servants bowed and departed.

Malek lifted the clothing on the tray, unfolding the items for consideration. Jak's first impression, that they'd brought leather underwear for him, wasn't that far off. Maybe he would be allowed to wear his trousers over it.

The studded leather harness looked like it went on one's torso. The straps would do nothing to protect the wearer from the elements—or the fangs of an animal—though perhaps one could hang a dagger from one of the metal loops.

"My costume, I presume," Malek said in a flat tone that suggested he found it more denigrating than interesting.

"I am concerned about these battles you've gotten yourself signed up for," Mother said, "but you should be... appealing in that."

"Academically appealing?"

She smiled. "Just appealing."

14

Sorath woke from a nap to find it was already dark. He groaned and sat up, hurrying to check on Vinjo, to make sure nobody had kidnapped him, and also to peer up at the *Dread Arrow*. Ferroki had promised to keep an eye on it and let him know if Yidar zipped off into the woods, but Sorath had meant to be awake for the night shift himself. After Sasko's warning, that Night Wrath had come here for the sole purpose of killing him, Sorath doubly wanted to be awake between the hours of dusk and dawn.

He found Ferroki sitting on a boulder where she could see the portal, Uthari's yacht, and Yidar's ship. The variously colored hulls of some of the other mageships were visible above the trees, but Sorath wasn't as worried about those.

"Any update?" It was a large boulder, so he sat beside her after ensuring that Vinjo and his tent were still well-guarded.

The engineer was up late working, as the clangs, bangs, and whispers imploring the modified technology to "work for Papa Vinjo" attested.

"The fox has not left his den," Ferroki said.

There were enough mages nearby that speaking openly wasn't a good idea. Uthari had to be expecting trouble. He'd doubled the number of men guarding the portal.

Sorath wondered if Yidar would figure out that his king knew about his chat with the druid woman. If Yidar found out Sorath had been the one to tattle on him, Sorath might soon have someone else contemplating his assassination.

With multiple zidarr annoyed with him, what were the odds of him leaving this camp alive?

Sometimes, he couldn't believe the events that had conspired to get him caught up in all of this. He was supposed to be back in Perchver, sitting in his room above the antiques shop, finishing his memoir, and living out his retirement as nobody of consequence. Vorzaz. He missed the days of Vorzaz.

"That looks like trouble." Ferroki pointed to five mages in brown uniforms riding down from a brown-hulled ship. King Dy's people.

They all wore weapons, and some also carried crates. With the lids closed, it was impossible to tell what was inside, but green and yellow light seeped through cracks. Sorath doubted they were lamps.

"We haven't been ordered to forbid mages from other kingdoms from coming down to see the portal." Ferroki nodded at the mercenary camps set up around the area. Many of those troops had been hired by the other fleets. "But if they try to disturb it, we have to act."

"Do you have a pile of explosives ready?" Sorath asked.

"Yes. Do you?"

"Always." He patted his recently replenished pocket of homemade pop-bangs.

The mages hopped off their skyboards in front of the portal. One officer walked around it while the soldiers with the crates headed toward Vinjo's tent, passing the slaves still laboring outside to build the frame of a ship.

"He's looking at the keyhole," Ferroki said, watching the lingering officer.

"I'm sure if there were more keys around, the fleet commanders from the other kingdoms would have already insisted on sending their own exploration parties through it." Sorath hadn't been privy to many of the meetings between Uthari's officers and those commanders, but the exchanges between troops from the different kingdoms remained tense, so he trusted that whatever truce they'd formed would be fleeting.

The officer looked at the red-uniformed guards, who were looking back at him with their hands on their weapons. Instead of speaking with them, he clasped his hands behind his back and strolled toward Sorath and Ferroki.

"Looks like we're getting a visitor." Sorath stood.

"Lucky us." Ferroki rose beside him.

The officer—a lieutenant, the silver bands around his cuffs proclaimed—stopped in front of them. "Colonel Sorath. I'm surprised you're down here on guard duty and haven't been sent out to explore the other worlds."

Sorath didn't know the officer, though it was possible they'd been on a battlefield fighting against each other before. A few years back, he had participated in a skirmish over some gold mines near the border between Dyvar and Vor. His company had worked for Queen Vorsha and opposed King Dy.

"I'm a soldier, not an explorer," Sorath said. "Technically, I'm not even that. I'm retired and working on my memoir."

The lieutenant eyed his pickaxe hand and the pistol in his holster. "You appear to lack the appropriate accoutrements for such work."

Sorath pulled his pencil out of his hair.

"Yes, I'm sure that's sufficient. We've observed that your archaeologists place a medallion in that indention in the portal over there. Then they do something to activate a symbol, remove the medallion, and they're able to travel through."

"That's what I've observed too," Sorath said.

The lieutenant smiled thinly. "I trust you know more. How are the symbols pushed? With magic? How does one know which world to travel to?" His eyes narrowed. "What does Uthari seek to find out there? Allies or some great weapon to use against other kingdoms?"

Sorath sighed, certain the mage didn't expect him to answer but was trying to pluck the information from his mind. He wondered if any of Vinjo's gadgets could protect a man from mind readers.

Chatter broke out at the engineering tent. Vinjo had come outside—why was that man wearing only underwear and a sleeveless tunic?—and gestured animatedly at the newcomers.

Uthari had said something about promising the other fleets that the ship-building endeavor would benefit them all. Maybe he'd invited other engineers to contribute parts?

Abrupt pain flicked at the center of Sorath's forehead, as if someone had stabbed him with a pen.

"I asked you questions, Colonel," the lieutenant said coolly, leaving no doubt as to who had struck him. "Focus, and answer them."

"It would not behoove the hound to answer questions about his master's farmhouse to the coyotes," Ferroki said.

"I am not a *coyote*, Captain. I am a respected officer and far your superior despite your delusional self-selected mercenary ranks." The lieutenant sneered at them. "Are there more medallions? More *keys* to that portal?"

"We're not answering your questions." Sorath kept his mind

empty as he put his pencil away and slid a hand into his pocket, fingers wrapping around an explosive.

"We also don't know the answers to your questions. We're simple soldiers." Ferroki looked toward her camp—Lieutenant Sasko and several others were watching the exchange—to make sure she would have backup if they needed it.

Sorath shook his head slightly. Though he would defend himself, it would be better if the company didn't start anything. With the tensions high everywhere, it would be easy for a full-scale battle to break out, with all sides wrestling over the portal. Though that might be inevitable, Sorath would prefer it didn't happen while Jak and the others were in another world. They needed the portal to remain in its spot and active so they could return.

"If you don't know anything, then there's no need to hide your thoughts from me." The lieutenant flicked pain at Sorath's forehead again, a tiny punishment but an irritation nonetheless.

Sorath clenched his jaw, sorely tempted to throw the explosive and shoot the man while he was distracted.

"Try it, Colonel." The lieutenant squinted at him. "Let's find out if Uthari will order his troops to defend you or if, as I suspect, nobody cares about you scruffy mercenaries."

"The question," Sorath said coolly, "is if anybody cares about *you*."

The lieutenant glanced at the mages he'd come down with, but by now, they had the crates open and were rooting through the contents with Vinjo. All five of them gesticulated with excitement as they blurted ideas for engine improvements to make the design more compact.

The lieutenant scowled as he seemed to realize his backup was distracted. "We'll talk again later, Colonel."

"I'll put it in my appointment book." Sorath pulled out his pencil again and pantomimed writing.

A whisper of power brushed his fingers as the lieutenant walked away, and the pencil snapped in half.

"I can do that with your cock too," the officer growled over his shoulder.

"I had no idea manipulating my cock was something you fantasized about." Sorath picked up the pieces of his pencil. "I'll put that down next to your appointment. Something for me to look forward to."

The lieutenant snapped at his men to get inside the tent and start working. He demanded to know why Vinjo wasn't wearing trousers and shoved one of his own men.

"So grumpy," Ferroki murmured.

"They're all like that when they get some rank and power. I much prefer the engineers that they push around."

"And helmsmen, cooks, armorers, and the kid that cleans out the artillery weapons," Ferroki said. "I've noticed."

"It's easier to make inroads with them."

After barking a few more orders, the lieutenant flew back up to his ship, leaving his troops to work with Vinjo inside the tent.

Sorath and Ferroki returned to sitting on their boulder, though he couldn't relax. The feeling of being watched came over him.

He glanced at the top of the waterfall, but he didn't see the giant jaguar this time. Maybe Night Wrath was out there somewhere, aiming a magelock between his shoulder blades. Sorath shifted to sit on the ground with the boulder at his back.

The servants lit more lamps so they could continue sawing and planing wood into the night. Sweat gleamed on their faces, their tunics stuck to their backs, and dark bags under their eyes announced their fatigue, but maybe they hadn't been given permission to stop. One dropped a piece of wood on his foot, cursed and glowered in disgruntlement, but a zing of pleasure must have come from the slaveband wrapped around his head, for his face smoothed with contentment.

"I wonder if Vinjo could make something to break those," Sorath murmured.

"What?" Ferroki had been eyeing their surroundings—did she also sense someone or something watching them?—but she looked at him.

"The slavebands. It would have to be all of them, or all of them in a given area, and all at once."

"To what end?" Ferroki asked. "Even if the servants had the freedom to rise up against their mage masters, there's no guarantee that they would, or that it would be enough to do anything."

"It might if it happened at an opportune moment when the mages were distracted."

"Such as by a war between all the ships here?"

"Something like that." Sorath knew it was dangerous to contemplate rebellion while he was in the middle of a camp of mind readers, but it was hard not to muse about it.

"Even if terrene humans had a chance to rise up against all the mages here, and were somehow assisted by fate, or war, or whatever you foresee, what difference would it make?" Ferroki asked. "This is a wilderness, claimed by nobody except perhaps those druids. Taking control here wouldn't be a blow to any of the kingdoms, wouldn't change anything about their rule or the people bound by their laws."

"It might," Sorath said. "There are a *lot* of mages down here from multiple kingdoms. Getting rid of that many..."

Ferroki shook her head. "This is still a small number compared to the hundreds of thousands who live in their sky cities."

"Yes, but many of those are more like Vinjo than Tonovan or Night Wrath. For every mage that serves in their military or becomes a zidarr, a hundred more are crafters or academics or teachers. If you could win against the soldiers, that might be enough."

Ferroki only shook her head again. "Don't get yourself killed, Sorath. Or the rest of us. All we need to do is survive this drama with the portal, and then we can go back to the desert, to our normal lives."

"To being peons of mages fighting in battles of no importance?"

"That's the normal life of a mercenary."

He grunted. She wasn't wrong, and yet wouldn't it be better to die doing something that mattered? That might change the course of humanity for the better?

He'd been contemplating this too much since Jak and Jadora had brought it up, but if they could somehow find allies that could give terrene humans an advantage...

Ferroki sucked in a startled breath.

Sorath followed her gaze. The jaguar was back, not at the top of the waterfall but in the foliage between the cliff and the portal. The mage guards hadn't yet noticed it. It was gazing straight at Sorath and Ferroki, its golden eyes glowing in the dark.

He expected it to roar or show off its fangs, but its mouth was closed. It padded toward them, walking less than three feet away from one of the guards, but he didn't see it or sense it. None of them did. Strange.

Sorath and Ferroki rose again, their hands on their weapons.

Instead of crouching to spring at them, the jaguar stopped a few feet away. Its head came up to Sorath's chest, so it had no trouble peering into his eyes. Was it trying to read his thoughts? On behalf of its druid master?

The jaguar opened its mouth, revealing... a green, glowing tongue?

No, that wasn't its tongue. The cat let a glowing, green oval stone fall out of its mouth. It bounced and rolled to Sorath's feet. He recognized it from Yidar's meeting with the druid. Some kind of communications device, he surmised, but why bring it to him?

Broken by Magic

When he looked up, the jaguar was gone.

He blinked and peered around for it. No foliage stirred, and nobody had shouted a warning. It had simply disappeared.

"You saw that, right?" Sorath picked up the stone. It was slightly warm in his hand.

"The cat? Yes."

"I think we're the only ones who did."

"I think so too."

"Does the druid lady—Kywatha—want to talk to us?" Sorath held up the stone, noticed a mage frowning in his direction, and shoved it in his pocket. "And why us? Yidar was her liaison."

Admittedly, Kywatha hadn't seem to enjoy chatting with Yidar. Maybe she hadn't appreciated him condescendingly patting her cheek.

"I don't know, Sorath, but I'll remind you that the druids have proven themselves enemies to the mages." Ferroki waved up at the ships. "They've made it clear they want the portal destroyed or at least removed from the area."

"I know."

"You'd be wise to chuck that rock as far as you can into the jungle."

"I know that too."

She eyed his arm. "I can't help but notice you're not doing that."

Sorath sighed. "No, I'm not. If they want to talk to me, I want to hear what they have to say."

"I don't think that's a good idea."

"I'm sure it's not."

∽

Using her microscope, Jadora examined the cuttings she'd snipped from the greenhouse. The group was two days into the three that had been allocated for training, and since she would rather study than practice fighting, she had opted out, instead cloistering herself in one of the bedrooms.

None of the rooms had more than curtains for doors, so she couldn't muffle the clangs, thuds, and smacks of weapons and unarmed combat practice taking place in the parlor. Alas, the earlier—and quieter—magic practice had ended.

Malek and the others had pushed the furnishings to the walls so they had room to train. The last she'd seen, he'd been facing off against Rivlen, Tinder, and Tezi, practicing against multiple opponents to hone his reflexes for whatever he would battle in the arena. He was also giving tips and helping all of them, sharing advice as well as technique, based on what he'd learned fighting his first dragon.

Jadora had faith in his skills, but facing huge magical creatures was a lot different from battling humans, and she was already worrying for him. For all of them.

She made herself focus on her self-appointed task, sketching the unique cells of the plant into an empty notebook. She kept hoping someone would determine that the research-filled journal the mages had taken from her wasn't worth anything and return it, but with each passing hour, that seemed less likely.

As she examined slides of plants, she kept contemplating if there was a way she could get back to that greenhouse to peek into the shelves and cubbies under that workbench. At the time, the ramifications of not only dragon-steel pots but that brick that might have been in the middle of being *shaped* into pots had just been dawning on her when the guards charged in. Now, she was speculating madly on how it might be done and why *etchers* were the rulers in this society.

The curtain stirred, and Jak sneaked in, sliding it back into place behind him. He flopped down on the bed, sweat bathing his face and soaking his shirt.

Jadora crinkled her nose at him. "What are you doing?"

"Resting." His chest was heaving, and he lifted his head to peer warily at the curtain. "Hiding."

"Well, do it somewhere else. You're disgusting, and that's my bed. It's not easy to launder things here." Jadora and the other women had washed their underwear and sole changes of clothing in the lavatory basin earlier. Since the arena didn't have plumbing, they had to be parsimonious with the water the servants brought in the mornings.

"I know. I took my shirt off earlier so I wouldn't get it sweaty, but then Rivlen said nobody wanted to see my chest, and I slunk off in shame to put it back on."

"Your chest is fine, Jak."

"It could be more muscled."

"It would be if you lifted anything heavier than a pencil."

"I lift heavy things all the time. My caliper is made of metal and weighs down my pocket like a stone. If not for my belt, my trousers would constantly be around my ankles."

"That would give the ladies even more to ogle."

"Trust me, I'm not the man in the group they're ogling. There's been a lot of speculation from the women about what Malek will look like in his skimpy harness and leather loincloth. Even from Fret and Tinder, who I thought were more interested in each other."

"Nobody can resist an athletic zidarr," she murmured.

"Ew."

As a mature academic, Jadora decided it wouldn't be appropriate for her to engage in any ogling. Despite the close quarters, there hadn't been that much opportunity for that anyway.

That morning, she'd offered to wash Malek's clothes for him while she was doing her own meager laundry, and he'd seemed startled. She wasn't sure if it was because servants usually washed a zidarr's clothing, and he hadn't expected her to offer, or because zidarr didn't bother with laundry until they finished a mission. All zidarr seemed to be male, and if Jak was any indication, that sex was less inclined to be bothered by stink.

"If it were me," Jak said, "I'd rather fight naked than in that getup."

"Where would you hang your weapons?"

"Naked with a belt."

"That'll draw the crowds. Off my bed, please." Jadora made a shooing motion at him as she changed out slides.

Jak slouched off the bed, only to come over and peer behind her desk, then under it. After glancing at the curtains, he crouched low, squeezed past her legs, and tucked himself into the cubby.

"Are you truly trying to evade a zidarr by hiding under a desk?" Jadora asked.

"No, it just looked terribly comfortable under here. And it's possible there are cobwebs full of spiders to feed Shikari."

"I thought you fed him this morning."

After pleading from Jak, and translating from Jadora, the servants had started bringing containers of caterpillars, flying crickets, and insects with blue carapaces that were reminiscent of cockroaches. Jadora had no idea where they were getting them, but they insisted on putting the containers inside silver cloches. Presumably, it was so they wouldn't escape, but Jadora had been startled when she'd opened one the first morning, expecting a filling breakfast fit for humans inside.

"I did, but he's a growing hatchling and needs lots. He crunched down all the bugs in this morning's container already. Also most of the container."

The curtain stirred again, and Jadora nudged Jak with her toe to warn him that they had company. She didn't expect his hiding to be effective against Rivlen or Malek, but if Tezi or Tinder came looking for him, it might work. Tezi had been much more excited to practice with her axe since she'd learned how to activate more of its powers, and she'd chosen Jak as her sparring partner more than once.

It wasn't a bad match. They had similar abilities when it came to blade practice. Tezi trained harder, but she was still new to mercenary life—and springing into battles with people. Loran had been decent with everything from a rifle to a sword to a whip and had taught Jak the basics before he passed. If Jak had kept up with it, he could have been a good fighter, but Jadora was glad his interests ran toward pencils instead of swords.

Malek was the one to walk in. He glanced at the cubby under the desk, arched a single eyebrow, and didn't say anything about Jak.

"Do you have a moment?"

"Of course."

Malek clasped his hands behind his back and stood beside the desk. His brow was also damp, but he'd toweled himself off before coming in, and he politely did not fling himself onto the bed to bedew her comforter with sweat.

I'm not a heathen, he spoke into her mind, smiling slightly.

Unlike my son?

Youths rarely respect furnishings properly.

Not even zidarr youths?

Zidarr youths are taught proper respect and decorum, including toward furnishings, and have it drilled into them at a young age.

Does that mean you were punished for propping your feet on tables? She'd caught Jak doing that earlier.

Only once. His smile faded. *The burned hand—or foot—imparts a lesson that one remembers for life.*

Jadora cleared her throat, not wanting to think about how strict Malek's upbringing had been. "I'm making some notes, wishing I could use the local library—I assume they have libraries here—and wondering about dragon steel."

"I'm pleased that you've been contemplating that as well as the local plant life."

"A library might help a person learn how to manipulate dragon steel."

"Etcher Yervaa suggested it was a secret, so the answer might not be in publicly available books."

"It might not be *obvious* in those books," Jadora said, "but perhaps I could figure it out anyway. I've been thinking about acids."

"One of your favorite topics."

"Indeed. The name etchers for the rulers practically begs a contemplation of acids or *some* kind of chemical formula for their work."

"I thought etching was done by scratching away metal with a tool."

"That's engraving. Etching is usually a chemical process employing a strong acid or mordant. You cover a metal plate with a waxy ground that's resistant to acid, scratch off the ground with a needle to expose the metal, then dip it or bathe it in acid. With time, the metal undergoes a redox reaction—the acid *bites* into it—and once the wax is removed, the design remains, etched in the metal. Alkali and alkaline earth metals corrode easily, some violently, while noble metals are less affected by acids. Gold doesn't even react to nitric acid, which is a strong oxidizing agent. It will, however, dissolve in a solution of concentrated nitric and hydrochloric acid." Jadora stopped herself, knowing she tended to sound like someone reading from an encyclopedia entry when she got going on a familiar topic.

"Is dragon steel considered a noble metal?" Malek asked. "Or is it comprised of them? I've heard it called an alloy, like regular steel."

"The term dragon steel doesn't connote that there's any actual steel—or its constituent parts of iron and carbon—in it. As far as we know, whoever named it picked the term based solely on how hard it is. Had they been better versed in the hardness scale of minerals, they may have called it dragon *diamond*."

"It doesn't look much like diamond."

"No, but it's harder to cut than diamond. At least with heat and tools. Based on the clues we've been given here, I'm hypothesizing that there's some chemical, maybe something native to this world—or the dragon home world—that can manipulate it, though it's admittedly hard to imagine a chemical reaction being used to turn a brick of dragon steel into a sword. When a mixture of nitric acid and hydrochloric acid is applied to gold, it just... dissolves." Jadora gazed thoughtfully at Malek, wondering if he had any ideas. She trusted he had no trouble following along.

"Is it possible that some chemical or *alchemical* compound merely softens the metal, the way a furnace does iron, so that it may be manipulated?"

"If we're dealing with magic, all the rules of physics go out the window, so I'm not sure. But I'd like to snoop around in that greenhouse again. We were interrupted before we got a good look at the dragon-steel pots."

"The guards might not be lenient if they discovered you there a second time."

"They weren't that lenient the first time." Jadora grimaced, the memory of the pain fresh in her mind. She'd been so relieved when Malek had touched her and used some magic to soothe that lingering—lingering and intense—headache that she'd almost melted into his lap.

"I regret that you were hurt. And that we are compelling you to go on these missions against your wishes." His expression was genuinely glum, and she believed him.

"Do you regret that you kidnapped us in the first place?"

"If I had refused, another would have been sent for you."

"No regrets then?"

"If it hadn't been me," he said quietly, "I would not have gotten to know you other than through your work."

"You could have knocked on my office door at the university and asked me to go for a walk. Kidnapping didn't need to be involved."

"No?" Malek looked into her eyes, his own eyes somber. "Would you have said yes? To a walk with a zidarr?"

At the time, all she'd known about zidarr were the terrifying stories and that one might have been involved in her husband's death. She was forced to answer, "No."

"I thought not." Malek tilted his head toward the curtains. "I should return to my training. And see if I can find my wayward apprentice."

"Who has so cleverly hidden himself."

"Indeed."

Malek stepped toward the door, and a twinge of disappointment filled her. She didn't want him to leave, not to train for some awful arena battle. *Three* awful arena battles.

"Malek?"

He paused.

"How did you let yourself get manipulated into this?" She knew he was smart—he'd outwitted *her* more than once. She couldn't believe he would have volunteered unless he was confident the ruler would deal honestly with him and that it was the only way to get what he wanted. He wasn't so young and arrogant as to be certain he would be victorious; she couldn't believe that. They'd watched from their suite the day before as most of the warriors who'd gone out there had fallen.

"There were few options," he said evasively. "I sensed that Etcher Yervaa was stronger than I. I could not have grabbed her and forced her to let us go. And you..." He shook his head.

"Me what?"

"It doesn't matter. I have agreed to fight, and I will. If I fail and am killed, Captain Rivlen will do everything in her power to see you home."

Rivlen had been as helpless against the magic of all those guards as Jadora. She thought about how they had, when they'd been locked in that carriage, believed they were going to jail—if not their *deaths*—and how surprised they'd been when it had stopped back at the arena instead.

Could it be that Malek had somehow kept them from that fate?

"Was that the deal?" Jadora asked. "Our lives if you agreed to the etcher's battles? To entertain her people with your own blood?"

"I hope to entertain them with the blood of my foes."

"*Malek*." Jadora stepped closer and gripped his hand, wanting to protest this.

She'd gotten *herself* in trouble—she'd let her curiosity make her agree to a sightseeing tour in a city full of enemies. Malek shouldn't be held responsible for her actions. He certainly shouldn't have to sacrifice his life in exchange for hers.

Better a worthwhile sacrifice than a meaningless one, he spoke into her mind, squeezing her hand gently.

Jadora shook her head, not sure if she wanted to kiss him and be grateful that he cared or find another desk to hide him under so the guards wouldn't find him and drag him off to the arena.

"That would be unwise," he murmured, looking at her lips.

"Which?"

"Both."

He inclined his head toward her once, solemnly, and released her hand and walked out.

"Damn it." Jadora rubbed her eyes, wiping away the moisture forming there. "You can come out now," she said after a minute, her voice numb. Her *heart* numb.

"Good." Jak scooted out on his hands and butt. "I was starting to get concerned."

"That you'd be trapped there forever or that he would pull you out by your collar, and you'd feel sheepish?"

"Uh, not exactly either." He eyed her, eyed the doorway, and eyed her again.

Jadora wiped away the moisture again to keep tears from falling. She didn't think they'd said anything that would have suggested kisses had been on their minds, but Jak was a perceptive boy. A perceptive *young man*. She smiled. He did have that chest hair now. Though it was hard to think of him as manly when he was crawling out from under a desk.

"If you hide in a woman's bedroom, you have to be prepared to be exposed to… things that interest women."

He wrinkled his nose. "I got exposed to those when I walked into the lavatory this morning and found undergarments drying on every protruding surface, including across the lid for the privy chute."

"Five women sharing one lavatory leads to such things."

"Five women and two *men*. Malek agrees it's horrifying to try to attend to one's biological needs while surrounded by women's undergarments."

"He said that?"

"He nodded when I said it. And admitted that zidarr don't typically share lavatories with women."

"Jak, as your mother, I'm going to be the one to tell you that women also don't enjoy sharing lavatories with men. You boys miss the privy chute. A *lot*." And she missed running water and a real toilet. It was ludicrous that a civilization that hadn't mastered plumbing had developed super powerful mages that could keep even a zidarr prisoner. The only good thing about all the magic was that they'd done something so that a floral scent filled the lavatory. One didn't notice the less desirable odors.

The curtain shifted, and Malek stuck his head back inside.

"You have a visitor, Professor," he said formally, his face harder than it had been a moment before. "Jak, if you've recovered, we will resume your training."

"Mage training or combat training?" Jak asked.

"Mage."

"Oh, good." Jak bounced to the door, clearly more excited about that.

From what Jadora had seen, both had a propensity to leave him sweaty.

She followed them out to find Zethron in the parlor, gazing blandly around at the furniture shoved out of the way and the numerous people trading blows with each other. He wore a clean shirt and trousers, his hat dangling down his back from a leather thong around his neck. Next to all the guards in white tunics and sandals, he was out of place, and Jadora was again reminded of how her husband had dressed, ready to head off to some dig site or another.

Zethron spotted her and smiled, hefting a potted plant.

"Professor," he said in the native tongue instead of the ancient version—fortunately, she'd picked up more of it these past couple of days. "I'm relieved that you appear hale and not overly distraught after our outing the other evening. I wish to apologize for inadvertently leading you to that end. I was *extremely* relieved to learn you hadn't been taken to jail."

"No." Jadora looked at Malek. Though he'd taken Jak off to one side of the parlor and did appear to be instructing him, he was also watching them. "They brought us back here, thanks to Malek, I believe."

Zethron blinked. "That is the sword demon, yes?"

"That's *your* term for him, I suppose." Jadora doubted Malek, who lacked a background in Ancient Zeruvian, had picked up any of the local language, but if he wished, he could read both of their minds. She didn't want to lead Zethron to say or think anything insulting.

Though she doubted Malek would punch him, he was radiating displeasure, likely blaming Zethron for guiding her into trouble the other night. Trouble that had led to him agreeing to what might be deadly gladiator matches. She frowned.

"I have heard he will do battle in the arena," Zethron said. "Otherworlders are always of interest and draw a large crowd. Since they are unknown factors, those who set the odds for wagers can only go by their looks and rumors of their abilities."

Jadora hated the idea of someone betting on whether Malek would live or die.

"For your sake, I hope your comrade will come out victorious and earn… whatever prize he has negotiated for." Zethron's brow creased. "Is he seeking your freedom? That would be understandable, though I admit I'm not sure why you have been imprisoned. Those from the First World should be treated as guests. I am not the only explorer here, the only one versed in ancient languages and origin tales. I cannot believe the etchers are not curious about your world and our own roots. If they treated you well, perhaps we would be invited to visit." He smiled wistfully at her.

"I do not know why we've been imprisoned either." She'd assumed the natives were simply suspicious of strangers, but perhaps there was more to it than that. The fact that Malek wanted dragon steel and its secrets might have put them on edge. It might have been better to wait until their two peoples had established a relationship before asking about trade, but there was little point in trying to keep secrets when more than half of their party couldn't guard their thoughts from mind-reading mages.

"I brought you a gift." Zethron held out the pot. It contained a plant with attractive purple flowers wafting a pleasant scent that reminded her of lilacs.

"Thank you."

As she accepted it, Zethron widened his eyes slightly, as if to convey special meaning, though she didn't know what. The pot wasn't made from dragon steel. It and the plant looked like something that had been purchased from a florist's cart. Maybe there was a card hidden between the leaves.

"If he's bringing gifts," Jak called from the other side of the room, "will you ask him to bring me a map of the area? Especially the mountains that might hold valleys featuring ziggurats?"

Jadora wiggled her fingers in acknowledgment.

A fly, or perhaps a pollinator akin to a bee, buzzed away from one of the flowers and flew into the room. The hatchling, who *had* been sleeping on a cushion on the floor, somehow heard the buzz over the din of combat practice and sat upright. His tail swished as he tracked the small insect.

"If the fly is the gift, that's more for the hatchling than me." Jadora smiled and mentioned that Jak would appreciate a map of the area if he could manage to bring one.

Zethron nodded distractedly as he watched Shikari. "It is remarkable that you've found the young of an elder dragon. I am burning to ask you where he was—or where his *egg* was?—but you were evasive when the ambassador questioned you, so I suspect you do not wish to say."

"We don't. We're concerned about others trying to use him—to raise him to be a trained attack creature."

"Dragons are very intelligent. I do not think it would be easy to train one to do one's bidding."

"Even humans can be inculcated into a certain belief system and can be taught to be cruel instead of kind." Jadora didn't look at Malek, though inculcation could apply to the zidarr. She thought instead of all the mages she'd met who believed terrene humans were lesser beings, slaves to be used and thrown away, rather than their equals.

"That is true," Zethron said, "but the man who attempted to

treat a dragon poorly in order to foster cruel tendencies might find himself eaten."

"Shikari eats only insects."

The hatchling sprang onto a table, knocking a vase to the floor, and jumped but didn't quite catch the fly.

"For now, perhaps," Zethron said. "I had better leave before the guards object to my loitering, though as I said, they usually let me do as I wish and see whom I wish. It wasn't always that way, but privileges are extended to the etchers' favored ones." He smiled ruefully.

"I suppose it's good to be under the protection of someone powerful." This time, Jadora did glance at Malek.

He had saved her life a number of times now, and she didn't want him to think it meant anything that she was accepting flowers from another man. Though, as soon as she had the thought, she wondered at it. It wasn't as if she wished to *date* Malek. Even if she did, Uthari's warning to her to avoid anything romantic with Malek would have scared her away from the idea. Not only for her sake but for his. Uthari truly seemed to believe that Malek couldn't be loyal to him and a woman at the same time.

"Especially when one was not born into the land and has no magical powers, yes," Zethron said. "Though I wouldn't presume that her favor means she would risk anything on my behalf or protect me invariably. The rulers usually have several favored ones at any given time. I must behave, the same as the others. But I might have the sway to be able to take you out again if you wish it. Not anywhere so full of clandestine secrets as a *greenhouse*—" he rolled his eyes in disbelief, and Jadora believed he genuinely hadn't expected their trip to end with guards storming in and capturing them, "—but perhaps a walk in the park adjacent to the arena would be permitted."

"Are you supposed to walk in parks with other women when you're busy being *favored* by one of the rulers?"

"It would be fine. She doesn't expect me to be monogamous. As I mentioned, the rulers themselves are not. In their culture, men and women traditionally have only one partner and marriage, but it is common for the wealthy and the powerful to have multiple companions that come and go. And my lady likes that I've experienced numerous partners on numerous worlds. I've taught her a few techniques, which she finds intriguing." He winked.

"I have no doubt." Jadora didn't look over at Malek, but she sensed him watching. No doubt he was paying attention to her thoughts. Or more likely *Zethron's* thoughts. She didn't think hers were inappropriate. "I appreciate you thinking of me, but I'm not looking to go on any dates with exotic strangers while I'm here."

"But you agree that I'm exotic." He waggled his eyebrows at her.

Actually, he was familiar. And that was the problem. She smiled sadly.

"You don't like exotic?" Zethron asked more quietly. "Or is it that you're already involved with someone? Monogamously? Oh, I should have asked. Are you married?" He glanced at her neck. "Women here wear necklaces to indicate that they're taken, but I don't know what you do in your culture."

"Rings, and I'm not married. Not anymore. I lost my husband a few years ago. In a horrible way. He was murdered, and I... saw the end result. I'm not ready to have a relationship with anyone else."

Jadora had meant to use the words as an excuse, so he wouldn't pursue her, but there was a lot of truth in them. She still missed Loran, and even though she was lonely sometimes—or had been when her life had been normal and not so full of chaos and people trying to kidnap her—she didn't want to seek out another. Even if Malek was easy to be around, and she appreciated his protection, it wasn't as if she could have a relationship with someone loyal to the king who kept her people oppressed.

"Oh," Zethron said. "That is unfortunate. I will not flaunt my exoticness at you again."

He stepped back and turned toward the door.

"Wait," she blurted, realizing he might be her one and only chance to get out of the arena before Malek was pitted against monsters. "I'm not that interested in parks, but if you could arrange a tour of one of your libraries, preferably a library full of old books in Ancient Zeruvian that I might be able to read, I would like to accompany you."

"Oh, I love libraries." He smiled at her. "And I'd happily translate any books for you that are written in our modern tongue."

She would prefer the ancient one, assuming the locals had figured out how to work dragon steel that long ago. Judging by the fact that Zethron had struggled to remember all the words and translate her writings, Ancient Zeruvian wasn't widely known anymore. That might mean that someone erasing evidence of crafting secrets from the libraries might have overlooked books in languages they didn't understand. Dare she hope?

"Or passages, at least," Zethron amended. "Books do take a while to translate."

"Tell me about it." Jadora still had that druid tome to finish.

"Let me see what I can arrange. And enjoy your flowers." Zethron waved at the pot. The fly had since disappeared down the hatchling's gullet.

"Thank you."

Jadora looked over at Malek, but he was sitting cross-legged on the floor with Jak, and he'd masked his face. He'd either decided to stop paying attention to her chat with Zethron, or he'd told himself not to let Zethron's antics bother him. Or... he'd been reading her mind when she'd been thinking about not being ready to be romantically involved with anyone, assumed it included him, agreed it was a good idea, and had decided to focus only on their mission.

"A good idea," she reluctantly agreed and examined the flowers more carefully.

There wasn't a card, but among the green-blue stalks, she found a metal disc with a needle jutting out of the back. One of the discs that all except the mages wore attached to their temples? She stared at the long needle. *Very* attached.

It hadn't occurred to her to wonder how they stayed on people's faces, but she'd assumed magic or perhaps a temporary glue. Not only did that needle make the device look permanent, but the length of it appalled her. Skulls weren't that thick, even accounting for flesh and muscle. This had been designed to pierce someone's brain.

Why?

If all it was supposed to do was allow people to walk in and out through the city barrier, that couldn't be required.

"Why did he give you one of those?" Malek asked.

Jadora flinched, almost dropping it. She hadn't heard him walk up and was glad the gift hadn't been a love poem about the beauty of her eyes and how delightful her Ancient Zeruvian accent was.

"I would have left you to read that in private," he said quietly.

"Given how readily you snoop in my thoughts, I don't believe you."

"I occasionally try not to snoop, when I believe someone wants privacy. Assuming I'm not questioning them about mission-critical information." Malek dug into a pocket and held out an identical disc, including a matching needle. "The etcher told me I had to wear this in the arena. I can tell it's magical but not what it does."

"It has to be more than a magical badge to let you pass through the barrier."

"She said it was a tracking device as well. When she visited me, I was snooping around in the basement of her arena."

"Mission-critical snooping?"

"Of course."

Jadora held up the disc. "Why would Zethron have given me one?"

"He likes you."

"Thus a tracking device is the natural gift."

Malek snorted softly. "From what I saw of his thoughts, he believes it will let you walk out through the barrier. He also believes I'm going to die in the arena and that the rest of you won't be allowed to leave. Ever. Unless you use that to sneak out."

"That's depressing."

"Especially since Etcher Yervaa gave me her word that the group would be permitted to leave, no matter what happens to me."

Jadora shook her head bleakly. This etcher could have been lying to him. What if she didn't plan to give them their freedom *or* any information on the dragon steel? What if Malek gave his life in their bloody arena for nothing?

"We'll figure out a backup plan," Malek said.

Hoping they could, she set the pot back down and looked at the disc again.

"I will ask Dr. Fret her opinion on this—" Jadora lifted the needle to eye level and spotted a few tiny hairs—or wires?—sprouting from it, "—but I don't recommend putting it on."

She couldn't imagine how it would be done, save for with a mallet, and that thought made her shudder. Even though the needle was narrow and sharp, it might crack the skull when puncturing it.

"I may not have a choice."

"Malek." Jadora resisted the urge to slump against him. "This is a bad idea."

"Go to the library with him. Learn what we need to know."

"I will."

He nodded, touched her shoulder, and returned to Jak's training. In the few minutes he'd been gone, the hatchling had crawled into Jak's lap and fallen asleep.

Jadora watched as Malek spoke and Jak leaned forward to absorb everything, his eyes determined. She hoped Jak was learning all that he could. They might need that and more to escape this world alive.

15

"Just ask her," Tinder urged. "I'm sure she'll spar with you."

Tezi lowered her battle-axe, her arms sore from the last two days' worth of training. Even though the weapon was much lighter than a steel version would have been, it was large and unwieldy in her hands, and she feared it would take years to master, not days.

"You broke my sword, left a hole in the wall, and almost beheaded Jak's dragon," Tinder added, glancing down as the hatchling scurried past, pouncing on whatever enemy his imagination had crafted. "You need to spar with a *mage*."

"She'll kill me if I break *her* sword." Tezi glanced at Rivlen.

While Jak and Malek sat face to face on the floor in the corner, sharing magic lessons, and Jadora studied something on her microscope in another room, Rivlen prowled the suite like a caged panther. Gladiators were fighting in the arena, the seats once again full of spectators, and Rivlen watched now and then, taking notes on who knew what, but for the most part, she paced.

"Her sword is probably magical and won't be as easily destroyed by that axe. I parried perfectly, and it still cleaved my blade in half." Tinder pointed to the broken sword on the floor by the wall.

"You should have used one of the practice swords, Sergeant."

"Obviously. Do you think they'll let Malek use his lesser-dragon-steel weapons in the arena?"

"I don't know."

From what Tezi had heard, this was his last day of rest and training. Guards would come for him soon, and he would have his first battle in the morning. In front of tens of thousands of people betting for and against him.

"Do you think he'll *survive* the arena?" Tinder asked in a lower voice. "And will we get to leave? Or get stuck fighting those dragons he mentioned?"

"I don't know that either." It surprised Tezi that Sergeant Tinder was asking her opinion.

Back home, all the senior mercenaries had barked orders, assuming rookies like Tezi knew nothing and that they had all the experience. Back home, they did. But here, Tinder and Fret were as lost as Tezi. Even worse, *they* didn't have magical weapons to help protect them.

"If I have to use a broken sword to fight a dragon, I'm going to hide behind you and your axe." Tinder waved at the big weapon. "That's why you need to master it. With a mage's help. You need to figure out exactly what it can defend you from so you know how to best use it."

"I'll ask."

"Good." Tinder thumped her on the shoulder. "I look forward to hiding behind you. Have some of those buttery pastries on the table over there."

Tezi blinked. "Why?"

"So you'll get a little chunkier. The way you are right now, it's going to be hard to hide behind you."

"Perhaps," Dr. Fret said from where she was knitting, "*you* should eat *fewer* of the buttery pastries, thus to facilitate your scenario."

"My girth is all muscle," Tinder said. "Besides, I'd have to fast for months to be skinny enough to hide behind our rookie."

Tezi took a deep breath and headed over to ask Rivlen to spar with her. She was frowning out the window and scribbling notes again as a massive, scaled creature with horns on its head did its best to eviscerate the four gladiators facing it.

Tezi waited for her to finish writing.

"What do you want?" Rivlen frowned at her.

Tezi got the impression the captain didn't like her and wouldn't appreciate this interruption, but Rivlen *had* tried to protect her from Tonovan, so maybe she would be willing to help again.

"Good afternoon, ma'am," Tezi said. "I'm seeking a mage to attack me in numerous ways while I hold my axe so I can get a better idea of what it can and can't protect me from."

Rivlen eyed her up and down, then glanced back at Malek. Hoping to foist the task off on him?

"What are you doing?" Tezi pointed at her notes. "Can I help?"

Maybe if she assisted Rivlen in finishing her task, she would be more inclined to spar.

"Taking notes on the creatures that come out in the arena and what their vulnerabilities and favorite attacks are so I can give them to Lord Malek to study. He *should* be over here studying them himself." Rivlen frowned in his direction, but he and Jak had their eyes closed, concentrating on their magic, and Malek didn't look over. She made a disgusted noise.

"I'm sure he'll appreciate your assistance, ma'am," Tezi said.

"There's no guarantee that he'll face any of the creatures we're seeing today, but he might. There can only be so many types of animals caged down there, right?"

"Presumably so."

As the creature below chomped one of the gladiators on the shoulder, another man sprang in, using a sword to find a gap between its scales. With a great roar, he delivered a deadly blow. Their enemy squealed and tried to stomp them into the ground, but the gladiators scurried back, one helping the injured man away. After a few more blows, they managed to defeat the scaled creature. It was one of the few victories for humans that Tezi had seen.

"That was a dragon-steel sword that he used to get under the scale." Rivlen wrote another note, then put the pen and paper down. "I don't suppose you'd like to lend your axe to Lord Malek for his fights?"

"If he asked for it, I would." Tezi would prefer to keep it, since they'd already been attacked once in their suite, but if it would make a difference for him, she would lend it to him. But wouldn't he want to use the weapons he was most familiar with?

"Would you?" Rivlen squinted at her. "I can't read your thoughts when you're holding that."

"My thoughts are uninteresting, but I'm glad to know it has that capability." The information encouraged Tezi. That meant that new mages she encountered shouldn't be able to dig into her memories and learn that she'd killed their kind. Too bad so many existing mages—and zidarr—knew about that.

"Do you want to spar with weapons?" Rivlen asked. "Or for me to attack you with magic?"

"Both if you're willing. I'm trying to improve as well as learn the axe's capabilities."

"Do you really think you'll be able to keep it?" Rivlen waved toward the center of the room where the furniture had been cleared for sparring. "I'm surprised someone hasn't taken it from you yet."

"Maybe if I learn to use it capably enough, I'll be able to prevent those who try from succeeding."

Rivlen grunted skeptically, but she grabbed her sword, and they sparred together for the first time.

Since Rivlen was older and more experienced, Tezi expected her to overpower her quickly, knock her to the floor, and return to her note taking. Instead, Rivlen gave advice and ran Tezi through drills. The repetition was useful for imprinting defenses into her memory. In between drills, Rivlen tried several magical attacks on Tezi. Most of them breezed past, as the attacks in her previous battles with mages had.

"It doesn't create a barrier around you, does it?" Rivlen asked. "You're just somehow impervious to almost everything."

"Yes, ma'am. As far as I can tell. At least when it comes to magic. Physical attacks can still get through."

"I wonder how much of a swordsman Tonovan is."

"Pardon?"

"If you attacked him, and he couldn't use his magic, I wonder how the battle would go." Rivlen shook her head. "I'm sure he's capable with a blade, even if he's no zidarr. I've had training as a military officer, so he would have too. And you're... Don't take this the wrong way, girl, but you're a neophyte."

"I know I am. But with time, I plan to change that."

"Yeah." Rivlen ran through more drills with Tezi, spending more time with her than she would have expected.

Though tired, Tezi set her jaw and worked with determination, longing to grow stronger, faster, and more capable.

After an hour, Rivlen lowered her sword. Sweat dampened both of their faces.

"It'll take years for you to get good enough to challenge him," Rivlen said.

"Tonovan? I'd hoped to avoid him." Tezi set aside the axe to wipe her sweaty palms and drag a sleeve across her damp face. "Especially since he's surrounded by his own fleet. I'm afraid there would be repercussions if I attacked him."

Too bad. Maybe Uthari's military fleet would be less loathsome if Tonovan weren't in charge. If he were *dead*. Then he wouldn't be able to maul any more innocent women. It might be worth dealing with repercussions—with being tortured and killed—if Tezi could take him out of the world and leave one less overpowered mage around to torment people.

"I'm not sure who would take his place," Rivlen said, reading her thoughts now that she wasn't holding the blade. "But you're not the only one who hates him."

Tezi gripped the axe's haft again, having enjoyed the mental privacy. "Every terrene human woman he meets probably does."

"And plenty of mage women." Rivlen's lips thinned.

"You, ma'am? Did he…" Tezi trailed off, having a hard time imagining someone as powerful as Rivlen being molested or harassed in any way.

But when Rivlen had faced off against Tonovan, he *had* gotten the upper hand.

Rivlen hesitated and glanced around the room, but the others were all occupied and weren't paying attention to them.

"When I was a younger officer, yes." Rivlen shrugged, as if it didn't matter that much.

Tezi couldn't imagine that.

"I've grown more powerful since then," Rivlen added.

"But not more powerful than Tonovan," Tezi whispered.

Rivlen clenched her jaw but couldn't deny it. "Powerful enough that he would be stupid to paw me over. Any distraction, and I'd knock his head off."

"I hope he leaves you alone, but I wouldn't mind seeing his head knocked off."

"I'll bet." Rivlen gave her and the axe an assessing look again. "Would you be willing to help that scenario come to fruition?"

"Uhm. Are you suggesting… working together?" Tezi lowered her voice and glanced at Malek. "To kill Tonovan?"

"Maybe." Rivlen also spoke quietly and glanced at Malek again. "It couldn't be an assassination, not when he's in the middle of the fleet, surrounded by allies and King Uthari himself. But if he attacked us, and we defended ourselves against him... it's possible we wouldn't be punished."

Tezi thought it was possible *Rivlen* wouldn't be punished, but she'd already seen how quickly mages would kill terrene humans even for *defending* themselves against their kind. Still, if Tonovan were dead, wouldn't it be worth her life?

"You must hate him as much as I do," Rivlen said, though she couldn't have read Tezi's thoughts, not with the axe back in her hands.

"I hate them all," Tezi growled before remembering she was facing a mage. "All those who think it's all right to kill or rape us just because we don't have the power to fight back."

She thought Rivlen would catch the slip and berate her for it, but all she said was, "Yeah. It makes you want to train hard and become more powerful so there's never anybody above you who can do that to you."

"Those of us without magic don't have that option."

"Most *with* magic don't have it either. There's a limit to how powerful everyone can get. No matter how good you become, there always seems to be someone stronger." Rivlen glanced at Malek again.

Tezi couldn't interpret that glance, couldn't tell if it implied something more than that he was more powerful than Rivlen. "Has he ever... done anything? To you?"

Rivlen shook her head. "No. He's just more powerful than I am. It doesn't bother me that much when it's someone... honorable and fair. But I don't think he'll strike against one of Uthari's officers, so I wouldn't be able to convince him to help me against Tonovan, not if I were the one to goad Tonovan into an attack. I think Jak would help, but it'll be a while before he's ready. He doesn't have a dragon-steel weapon."

Rivlen squinted at Tezi.

"I'd help." Tezi felt uneasy admitting that aloud, even if she'd already admitted it to herself. What if Rivlen was lying to her and would end up telling Tonovan about this conversation? That Tezi wanted to kill him? "Even if it meant my death. As long as it would keep him from tormenting others."

"I'll keep that in mind." Rivlen nodded curtly, then lifted her sword. "Let's spar some more and see if the axe can defend you against mental attacks."

"Yes, ma'am."

Not long after that, several guards and servants arrived, pushing aside the curtain and entering the suite.

We are here to collect the warrior for the arena, a mage guard spoke into their minds, looking at Malek. *You will be housed with the other combatants and have your first battle in the morning.*

Malek and Jak stood, exchanging long looks with each other—and a telepathic conversation?

Tezi gripped her battle-axe in case Malek decided not to go through with it, instead attacking these men and leading the group in an escape attempt.

"I'm ready," was all he said.

He pressed something into Jak's hand—the key for the portal?—and stepped away. Jak's face twisted with distress as he watched Malek join the guards.

Rivlen grabbed the notes she'd been taking off the table. "These may help you, my lord."

She handed them to him.

"Thank you, Captain," Malek said formally, perusing them before folding them and putting them in a pocket.

"You're welcome, my lord." Rivlen saluted him.

Do not forget your armor, one of the guards said.

"You mean my *costume*?" Malek asked.

They did not reply, but one pointed to the skimpy leather loincloth and harness that had been brought for him.

Malek retrieved the costume—Tezi agreed with his term for it—and joined them again.

Jadora stepped out of the bedroom, lifting a hand toward Malek, as if she wanted to grab him and pull him back, to keep him from risking himself.

He gave her an even longer look than he'd shared with Jak, but he didn't say anything aloud. As he walked out with the guards, he and Jadora held each other's gazes.

"Good luck," Jadora whispered.

Malek inclined his head once.

Jadora lowered her arm, though she kept watching the doorway long after he'd stepped into the corridor with the guards and disappeared from sight.

"I don't know what she thinks is going to happen between them," Rivlen muttered.

"Professor Freedar?" Tezi asked.

Jadora glanced at them as she walked back into the bedroom.

"*She* doesn't have any weapon capable of hiding her thoughts," Rivlen said.

"And she's thinking about... Lord Malek?"

Rivlen nodded curtly. "It's forbidden for zidarr to have romantic entanglements. I'm *sure* he's told her that and doesn't return her interest. She's just a terrene human. That *can't* intrigue him."

Just when Tezi was starting to think Rivlen wasn't as bad as the rest of the mages... Though if Rivlen was attracted to Malek herself, that might explain her feelings. Of jealousy?

"If he were going to have a relationship with someone," Rivlen said, "another mage would make more sense. A powerful mage. Someone closer in stature to him."

Yes, attraction. There it was.

"Didn't you just say that was forbidden?" Tezi hoped Rivlen was practical—and fair—and wouldn't take out her disgruntlement on Jadora.

"Yes." Rivlen shook her head. "He won't likely get involved with anyone. And if he *did*, it would have to be just sex, not anything emotional." Did she look wistful as she said that?

Since Tezi couldn't read minds, she was left guessing, but it would probably be better if nobody had sex with anyone.

Jak walked over, looking weary from his training, though it had only involved sitting cross-legged and doing who knew what with his mind.

Tezi braced herself, though he hadn't tried to flirt with her, at least as far as she could tell, lately. He only nodded to her, said she was looking fearsome with the axe, and faced Rivlen.

"Malek said to keep training with you if you're willing and not busy." Jak gestured to Tezi, as if to say he would wait if they weren't done.

"I could use a rest," Tezi admitted.

Jak lowered his voice. "He also said we should come up with a plan in case… that ruler doesn't keep her word about letting us go, and he doesn't survive."

"He will," Rivlen said.

"But in case he *doesn't*," Jak said. "We have to figure out a way to get out of the city. Mother has one of those discs now, so we might be able to escape through the barrier, but he wasn't sure it would get us all out. Even if it does, he said their mages are powerful, so we'd have to worry about them chasing us back to the portal—and catching up with us."

"Very powerful." Rivlen winced, as if she had first-hand experience.

Maybe she did. When Rivlen and Jadora had returned from

the greenhouse the other night, they'd looked rough. Or, more specifically, like they'd been roughed up.

"We'll keep training, yes." Rivlen gripped Jak's shoulder and nodded at Tezi. "So that we'll be ready when we have to act."

The curtain at the door stirred again, not to admit guards this time. Zethron stuck his head in and spoke in the local language, one Tezi hadn't picked up any of yet.

Jak and Rivlen also shook their heads and shrugged, but Jadora must have heard him, for she stepped out with her backpack on and a notebook in hand.

"Mother?" Jak asked uncertainly.

"He's taking me to their library so I can research dragon steel," Jadora said.

"Uh, you're going alone with him?" Jak looked at Rivlen and raised his eyebrows.

Rivlen grimaced, as if she didn't want to go out again with them, but she stepped toward them. "I'll go with you."

Zethron shook his head, then pointed at Jadora, at himself, and finally at the curtain. The boots of guards were visible under it. Several sets of boots.

"He says he could only get permission for me to go with him," Jadora said.

"*Mother*," Jak said. "Your last outing with him did not go well."

"You shouldn't venture out into this city without protection," Rivlen added.

"I know, but we don't have a choice," Jadora said.

"Malek won't approve," Jak said, looking to Rivlen for backup.

Rivlen nodded in agreement.

"Malek knows about this," Jadora said. "He wants to know how to work dragon steel for King Uthari, and he thinks I might be able to figure it out."

Tezi blinked at that. How would a terrene human learn how to do something none of the mages on all of Torvil had been able to figure out?

"But *we* don't care about the dragon steel." Jak pointed at his chest and then his mother's. "We just need to find that plant, so Uthari lets Grandfather go. That's what you said."

"It's not here," Jadora said. "The secrets to working dragon steel are."

Zethron headed for the curtain, and Jadora followed.

Rivlen grabbed her weapons and strode after her, but as soon as she stepped into the corridor, several guards lifted their hands and barked orders at her in their language. Rivlen looked like she would force her way out anyway, but some of those guards must have had magic, for she stumbled back inside, as if knocked back by wind.

Fury blazed in her eyes.

"It'll be all right," Jadora said from the corridor, though her tone wasn't that convincing.

Rivlen snarled and stomped back into the room. Tezi stepped out of the way, in case she was in the mood to lash out at the nearest person.

"This place is so *frustrating*," Rivlen said, hand clenched around the hilt of her sword. "I'm not used to being... *ineffective*."

"You should try knitting," Dr. Fret said. "It's calming."

Rivlen gave her a scathing look.

"We're used to being ineffective against mages." Tinder had joined Fret, resting a protective hand on her shoulder.

"*I'm* not," Rivlen said. "It's aggravating."

"Yes," Fret said blandly.

Rivlen's gaze fell on the battle-axe. "I should have taken *that*. They wouldn't be able to knock down my barrier and push me around then."

Tezi shifted uneasily. Rivlen looked like she was contemplating grabbing it and running after Jadora and Zethron. Tezi suspected the powerful mages here had the power to thwart her even if Rivlen had the weapon, and she might end up losing it.

Jak stepped up to Tezi's side and faced Rivlen. "If Mother figures out the secret to working dragon steel, maybe we'll all be able to have weapons like that."

"I doubt the *secret* is in the public library."

Jak shrugged. "Libraries are full of secrets and long-forgotten knowledge for those who take the time to look."

"We'll see," Rivlen grumbled and stalked into another room.

"Thanks," Tezi told Jak, glad he'd stood beside her. She didn't *think* Rivlen would steal her axe, but she didn't know the captain that well yet. "I suppose it's not right to feel pleased that our mages are getting a glimpse of what it feels like to be one of us." Reminded that Jak was learning how to use magic, Tezi almost corrected herself, but he'd been normal for most of his life, so he would understand.

"Maybe not *pleased*," he said, "but I can't help but think they all might be fairer if they understood what it was like to be helpless as someone shoved them to their knees and stabbed mental daggers into their brains."

"The world—our world—would be better off if nobody had magic."

"Or if everybody had it. The inequality is the problem. And that there are few repercussions for bad behavior for them." Jak gazed at her axe and opened his mouth to speak, but he must have thought better of it. He patted her on the shoulder and went to his room.

∽

In a cell under the arena, Malek lay in a bunk and reviewed the notes that Rivlen had made for him after observing the creatures. He appreciated her effort. Perhaps he should have been studying the battles himself, but he'd wanted to spend his time training Jak and sparring with Rivlen and the others.

He didn't trust Etcher Yervaa to let them go. Perhaps he'd been a fool to give his word to her, to agree to fight these battles. He liked to believe that others he met in his travels would be honorable, but sadly, even in his own world, that wasn't always the case.

With luck, Jadora would learn the secret of working dragon steel on her own, and they wouldn't be reliant on Yervaa to give it to them. To keep her word.

Malek wished he could communicate telepathically with Jadora from down here and find out if Zethron had returned to take her to a library—and if she'd had time yet to find anything. But it hadn't been Yervaa blocking Malek's ability to communicate with the outside world. The walls themselves were magically insulated so he couldn't reach out to anyone in his party.

Laughter came from a few cells over, the same men who'd been playing games when Malek had snooped around several nights ago. Someone was also grunting, enjoying a female prize that had been brought to him for his victory in the arena that day. A willing prize or an unwilling one? Malek didn't know, though it sounded like she was praising him rather than crying out and begging to escape, so hopefully the former.

He thought about using his magic to escape from his cell and snoop around more, perhaps try to ascertain which animals were being prepared for the next day. There were levers in the corridor that controlled the barriers that locked the gladiators in, and he could easily pull one with his mind. He was here because he'd permitted his guards to place him here, not because he was helpless. But... he couldn't help but worry about the fate of his comrades if he didn't play this game as the rulers wished.

The corridor grew darker, the sounds fading as men went to sleep.

Malek set aside the notes and was about to attempt sleep as

well when he sensed someone powerful approaching. Powerful and familiar. Etcher Yervaa.

This time, two powerful mages accompanied her. Bodyguards? All three of them stopped in front of his cell, with Yervaa in the center, the same white nimbus obscuring her features under her hood.

Her bodyguards—if they were that—were women. They wore fancier tunics than most people in the city, with lace along the hems. Their sandals were white and bejeweled.

The barrier to Malek's cell disappeared, and the ruler waved the bodyguards inside.

Malek sat up, putting his back to the wall, though he didn't get out of his bunk. He draped an arm over his knee as he watched them. He doubted it was typical for the rulers to visit their gladiators on the eve of matches.

It is not, Yervaa spoke into his mind, somehow reading his thoughts through his mental barriers.

What makes me special?

The guards say you've not put in your kerzor.

Was that the disc?

I haven't put on the leather loincloth either, he replied.

You must do so before your first battle tomorrow, and I must insist that you insert the kerzor now.

Is that so?

You are unfamiliar with its operation?

I am. And you were vague about what exactly it does. I'm not in the habit of inserting things into my body if I don't know what they do. Malek didn't insert things into his body even if he *knew* what they did. That disc didn't look like it was designed to come back out again once it went in. *If it's a tracking device, you don't need to worry. We've discussed this. I've promised to fight for you, and I will.*

Naturally, but you've an advantage over the animals now, and we can't allow that.

What advantage? Malek tried to see her face, but the nimbus obscured her features as much as the shadow of the hood.

Your magic, of course. You are not the equal of our rulers or our stronger mages, but you would have an advantage over the creatures you will fight.

Malek started to protest, but he paused as he had the unsettling realization that he hadn't seen any of the gladiators thus far employ magic on their foes. They'd all worn the discs at their temples, something he'd assumed all citizens without magic were given, to walk through the magical barrier and perhaps do other magical tasks they wouldn't otherwise have been able to. But as Yervaa stared expectantly at him, the second half of his realization slammed home with a *thunk*, like a key turning in a lock.

What if it wasn't that the discs granted power to the people but took power away?

That is correct. Yervaa sounded amused. *Magic is ubiquitous among our people—I was surprised to hear that many of your party are sense-dead and without any ability to call upon it.*

All of your people have magic?

All are born with it, yes. After a great war, in which our people almost destroyed ourselves and our world, we developed the kerzor and applied them to those on the losing side so that a second such war would not come. We could not risk annihilating our entire species and letting the dragons strike while we were weakened.

How long ago was that? Malek swung his legs slowly to the floor, debating if he could attack the bodyguards and escape. If he'd known that jamming a device that would steal his power into his brain was part of the deal, he wouldn't have agreed to any of this.

Thousands of years ago. Those born to descendants of the losing side in that war receive the kerzor as soon as they start to develop power.

Because their ancestors, countless generations ago, started a war with your ancestors, the children are punished?

They are not punished. They are simply placed into the servant class where they can pose no threat. You have something similar on your world, do you not? Classes of those with power and those without?

Yes, but it's based on whether a person is born with power or not. Assuming they were born into the right place. As Malek well knew, magic users who were born on the ground and not found in time to be integrated into mage society in the sky cities were killed. Maybe something like these kerzor would be a more humane way of dealing with wild ones, but there was no way he would ask for some of the devices to take back to his world. The very idea of a mage having his power removed terrified him. The idea of losing *his* power terrified him.

And yet, it is the only way you will be permitted to fight in the arena. Yervaa waved to her two comrades, and they stepped closer to him.

One held open her palm, revealing one of the discs, the sharp needle pointing upward.

Malek faced them in a fighting stance, funneling as much power as he could summon into a protective barrier. *Then I will not fight. We will have to negotiate a different trade agreement.*

Oh, I don't think so. You've whetted my appetite, and I look forward to seeing you in battle. She flicked her hand, and tremendous power ripped away Malek's barrier, as if he were some weak apprentice barely capable of making one.

He gasped at the pain of having it wrenched away, but that didn't keep him from springing to the side as the women approached. He grabbed his weapons belt, snatching his sword free, and spun to attack them.

But Etcher Yervaa wrapped him in power far greater than anything he'd ever experienced. It reminded him of the dragon he'd faced in battle, but the dragon hadn't tried to hold him. It had only wanted to slay and eat him.

I don't want to eat you. Yervaa chuckled into his mind as the two women approached, one to either side, one raising the kerzor toward his temple. *Only enjoy watching you fight. Though perhaps if you win your first match and are rewarded female companionship, you'll call for me. Few presume to do so, though I do enjoy the feel of a muscular gladiator between my legs. I sense you are not one to be daunted by a powerful woman.*

Malek prodded at the magical grip that immobilized his every muscle, calming himself with a meditative exercise that let him draw upon even more power. One more time, he attempted to weave a barrier around himself, to free himself from the smothering grip. But Yervaa merely watched and seemed to smile under that hood. Even Uthari was not this strong, and for the first time in decades, Malek was powerless in the face of an enemy.

He couldn't budge as the two women reached up, one tilting his head so the other could see his temple and easily reach it. Their fingers were cool and methodical.

Though Malek kept trying to attack the magical grip from different angles and using different techniques, he couldn't thwart it. The needle touched his temple, a faint, cool prick. With a flick of power, the woman drove it through his skin, his muscle, and his skull. Pain lanced into his brain.

He clenched his jaw, refusing to cry out as he glared at Yervaa.

I do like a man who can take a little pain. She chuckled again, strolling closer to him as her bodyguards stepped back. *That will serve you well tomorrow.*

Malek bared his teeth at her, inasmuch as he could move his lips to do so. Even his face was mashed down under her power.

Don't be foolish and attempt to remove the kerzor, Yervaa warned, resting a hand on his chest. *Even now, its tendrils are growing into your brain, attaching to the matter that allows one to summon magic and blocking the conduits. If you rip out the kerzor, you will die from the hemorrhaging it will cause.*

She showed him an image of another gladiator, someone else

who'd been a strong mage from another world and who'd hoped to use his power in the arena. He tore out his kerzor, long strands of fine wire coming out with brain matter attached to them, and he dropped to the floor, convulsing and screaming in pain until he died.

This isn't permanent, Malek thought, wincing because he didn't boom the words telepathically into her mind as he wanted. He wasn't able to project them at all. *It can't be. How do you expect me to battle dragons without my power?*

You need to survive the arena before you worry about that. Let's see if you manage. And see if you earn any rewards.

Rewards such as having the kerzor removed?

That is not possible. She caressed his chest, but Malek barely felt it.

He was too busy staring at her, his brain refusing to accept what she was suggesting. Had she truly *permanently* taken away his power? That couldn't be possible. There had to be a way to remove these things. If nothing else, a healer on his own world would be able to do it.

Good luck with your battle tomorrow. Yervaa patted his chest and walked out, the other women already waiting in the corridor. *I hope you'll suitably entertain my people and that you'll survive.*

You'll still let my comrades go, right? No matter how I fare. We have a deal.

She gazed back at him. *We'll see.*

Damn it. He'd been a fool. She had no honor.

They raised the barrier again and walked away, but several more minutes passed before the magical grip released him.

The first thing he did when he could was reach up to touch the disc embedded in his temple. It hurt, the skin throbbing all around it as warm blood dripped down the side of his face. Malek could do nothing to soothe the pain, to heal the puncture. He envisioned the tendrils she'd shown him, stretching into his brain, anchored there forevermore.

Though he found he could get his nail under the disc and lift the edge from his skin, he was afraid to pull it out, afraid that she'd shown him the truth, that he would die if he yanked it free. The idea of being enslaved by this device, his magic forever robbed from him, was too despicable to imagine enduring, but he wouldn't do anything rash until he'd had a chance to study the devices more.

Whenever that would be. He wished he'd requested that Jadora research *them* in the library. Little had he known the discs would be more pertinent to him than dragon steel.

But he couldn't speak telepathically to her to make the request, not to her and not to anyone. It wouldn't have mattered if the walls were insulated or not.

Malek slumped, gripping his knees. It felt as if every ounce of energy had been drained from his body.

He tried to conjure a barrier to protect himself. Nothing happened. He tried to use his mind to move a piece of fruit on the table. Nothing happened. He couldn't feel that part of him that he'd been aware of since his youngest days, the part that made him a formidable foe, that made him zidarr.

And tomorrow, he would have to fight a battle against a powerful magical creature. Before, he had believed in his heart that he would win these battles. Now... Now he feared he would die as quickly as most of the other men who faced the animals. With a crowd watching on, cheering as his blood was spilled.

16

The green stone in Sorath's pocket buzzed against his thigh. This was the third night since he'd received it, via jaguar delivery service, and it was the first time it had done anything.

He stepped into the shadows of one of the tents. With everyone except the guards standing watch near the portal asleep, Sorath didn't worry about anyone hearing the buzz, but he didn't know what kind of magical aura it was giving off. During the previous two days, he'd worried that an observant mage would ask him why his pocket was oozing magic. But with so many people using magical tools and carrying weapons around, nobody had seemed to notice it.

The stone buzzed again. Insistently.

After making sure nobody could see him, he drew it out. Though it glowed in his hand, it apparently wasn't like a dome-jir, for nothing formed in the air above it, nor did a message of any kind come through. He did, however, get the urge to take it for a walk in the woods. Maybe the druid was out there waiting to chat with him.

Given that Night Wrath might also be waiting in the jungle for him, Sorath knew better than to go out alone. It was too bad Uthari had destroyed the stealth device Vinjo had given him. Sorath should never have taken such a valuable tool with him to the king's yacht.

Sorath picked his way past sleeping mercenaries to Ferroki's blanket and nudged her shoulder.

"I need you," he whispered when her eyes opened.

"Because there's trouble?" she muttered sleepily. "Or because you're having randy urges?"

"Which one would be most likely to get you out of bed?"

Bed was an optimistic term for the roll-up mat and blanket she was sleeping on.

"I'd have to think about it."

"Bring your weapons."

"I guess that answers my question." Ferroki sighed, grabbed her weapons belt, scraped her fingers through her short black hair, and rose to follow him out of camp.

"If we survive the trouble," Sorath said, "I'm open to randiness."

"You know how to get a woman excited."

They'd only taken a few steps into the jungle when a twig snapped ahead of them. Sorath paused.

Thorn Company was on patrol tonight, but since Night Wrath had shown up, Uthari's mages had been joining them, so he didn't know who to expect.

Sergeant Words, Corporal Basher, and two dour-faced mages in red uniforms stepped out of the trees, one conjuring a light.

"Where are you going, Colonel?" a mage asked. "There's a zidarr after you."

"I know. We're not going far." Sorath clasped Ferroki's hand. "I have… urges."

She raised her eyebrows but didn't say anything.

Basher snickered around a lit cigar dangling from her lips. "I knew it."

The mages frowned at them. "You can have urges in camp."

"It's crowded in camp. We're not young randy privates. We like our privacy."

The speaker looked him up and down.

Sorath shifted his pocket with the device in it away from him, though he feared it might be too late. He tried not to think about it, but it was hard, as his mind wanted to make up excuses for why he had such a thing in his trousers. Such as that he'd found it. He'd taken it from an enemy. Or the truth, that a druid's jaguar had spat it at his feet without asking first if he wanted it.

"I can't believe you'd be that stupid, Colonel," the mage said, "when there's a zidarr hunting you."

The man didn't address Ferroki. Maybe he had no trouble believing a woman would be that stupid. Sorath decided not to point out that it was more likely to be the other way around.

"If he shows up," Sorath said, "he'll be here to rescue his brother, whom your king is keeping against his will. Maybe you should swing by Lieutenant Vinjo's tent and make sure he's all right."

The mage opened his mouth, but Sergeant Words linked her arm with his arm. "That's a good idea. On the way, we can discuss that thing you wanted to discuss with me and Basher earlier."

He squinted at her. "You said you weren't *interested* in discussing that with pompous mages."

"I'm sure I didn't say that."

"You *thought* it."

"I've changed my mind now that I've gotten to know you better." She stepped in close and patted his chest. "You're not pompous so much as pontifical and sententious."

"Those words *mean* pompous."

"You think so? You're a clever mage. I like that." Words smiled at him, clasped his hand, and attempted to lead him back toward camp.

He took a few steps after her, but the other mage eyed Sorath again. Suspiciously. His gaze drifted toward his pocket.

"Thank goodness." Ferroki shifted to stand in front of Sorath, conveniently blocking his pocket from view, and leaned her chest against his. "They're leaving. Let's get you out of those clothes."

She dropped her hand to his belt and kissed him. Since it was a ruse, he knew he should simply stand there, and not inflict his lips on her, but he had to make it look realistic, didn't he?

He slid a hand around her back and gently returned the kiss, thinking of all the lonely nights he'd spent in the northern forests and the southern deserts, out on campaign with only his men, far from a woman—far from *this* woman. Who'd saved Vinjo's butt when Sorath had been on the verge of getting the poor engineer killed. They were a good team. Maybe one day, they could be more than teammates. If they both survived this, they could—

Corporal Basher snickered again. The stone buzzed insistently against Sorath's thigh. It was so hard to find the peace and privacy to kiss a woman.

The mage grunted and disgustedly said, "Urges," then headed to camp, trailing Words and her new buddy.

Ferroki broke the kiss to look over at Basher. "You can go too."

"Sure, Captain. Whatever you say." She chuckled and ambled slowly after the others.

Ferroki waited until they were out of sight before stepping back. Reluctantly, Sorath released her. His trousers sagged from his hips.

"Really, Captain," he said. "You've left my habiliments askew."

"That was rude of me."

"I'll say. Do you know how nettlesome buttons are for me these days?" He held up his pickaxe hand.

"My apologies. I'll fix them."

He could have done it himself—it wasn't as if he hadn't mastered going into the woods to piss when necessary—but when she stepped close again, it gave him a chance to smell her hair and wish the kiss hadn't been a ruse.

When she was done, she patted him on the stomach. "Where to next?"

"I'm not sure, but let's try the spot where the druid woman—Kywatha—met Yidar." That was the direction the stone seemed to want him to go.

"What happens if he shows up there looking for her?"

"*He* didn't get a stone." Sorath didn't know if that was true—maybe she was giving them out to anyone who might listen—but he headed into the woods.

They didn't have a lamp, and little moonlight filtered through the thick canopy above, so they had to step carefully. Once he was sure they were out of sight of the camp, Sorath pulled out the stone and used its green glow to guide them.

Soon, they spotted a matching green glow up ahead. Once again, the druid's stone lay on the ground in a small clearing. As they approached, Sorath returned his to his pocket, well-aware that holding it turned him into a beacon in the dark.

He stopped between the same two trees that he and Sasko had used before and waited for Kywatha to appear. A faint low growl came from the brush opposite them. The jaguar? He couldn't see the cat or its glowing golden eyes this time.

I thank you for coming, Colonel, a woman's voice spoke into his mind. *We are not alone out here, so we must be careful.*

I agree. "She's contacting me," Sorath whispered to Ferroki.

She nodded and pointed off to their left.

Kywatha stepped into view, her great cat once again at her side. She gazed straight at Sorath's trees. *I had hoped to speak to your archaeologists, but I believe they are not on this world.* Her lips pursed with disapproval.

What do you want from them? Sorath didn't confirm or deny anything else.

To convince them that the gateway must be taken away and buried again. The woman, Professor Freedar, knows that and why. She spoke to one of my colleagues and was given a tome to translate. If she's finished that work, she must understand the great dangers. Even you must understand, Colonel. Did not a flying agoratha almost destroy your fleet and slay you?

If that's the worm, yes. It tried to eat me, and it did slay others.

Then why would you not deactivate the gateway and remove it? Why work for the one who insists on putting our entire land—the entire world—in danger? You can be certain that if one powerful monster came through, others will follow. Your fleet barely defeated one agoratha. What if two come next time? Or ten?

I don't deny that the possibility has us concerned. Sorath pointed at himself and Ferroki, wondering if she was being included in the telepathic communication. Since he had no way to share his thoughts, even if she heard the druid, she wouldn't hear his half of the conversation.

But she nodded, as if she was catching enough to follow along, and she agreed with him.

Then you've considered taking the gateway down? Kywatha tilted her head, regarding him with her piercing green eyes.

Me? I'm just a soldier, ma'am. I take orders from the mages. That's the way of the world.

You haven't always. Your reputation has made it to this land. You've thwarted mages before.

When other mages paid me to, yes.

How much pay would you require to impede Uthari instead of assisting him?

Sorath was starting to wish he hadn't followed the buzzing stone out here. She'd tried to make a deal with Yidar, and now she wanted to deal with him. He suspected she would work with—try to manipulate—anyone to further her goal.

Mercenaries who turn on those who hire them don't live long, Sorath said, though he felt like a hypocrite. He hadn't been positive Zaruk's ships were out of the fight before Uthari had swooped up Thorn Company and coerced them into signing a new contract. He and Ferroki hadn't had much choice, but that didn't make it an easier potion to swallow.

Don't turn, then. Simply feign ineptitude and step out of the way while we deal with the gateway.

Inept mercenaries don't live long either. Listen, ma'am. I don't know you or your people. For all I know, you'll kill us all as soon as you've killed the mages.

We prefer peace and only attack to defend our homeland and our people. Kywatha touched her chest. *Your masters are the invaders here, and they've brought that doorway to Hell to our land. You cannot blame us for attempting to get rid of it—and them. But we have no qualm with your mercenaries. We—*

The jaguar growled, and she broke off, peering into the darkness.

They slipped back into the trees, swallowed by the shadows.

"Guess that means our meeting is over," Sorath whispered, keeping his voice low.

Whatever had startled her might be a threat to them as well. He drew two pop-bangs from his pocket, pressed them into Ferroki's hand, then dug out another for himself and listened for any sounds that would betray enemies that might be creeping up on them.

Insects buzzed, and a wolf howled in the distance. The roar of the waterfall, though muffled by the trees, was loud enough that it drowned out lesser noises.

As Sorath was thinking about slinking farther away from the glowing stone Kywatha had left, his instincts warned him of danger approaching. He whirled and threw a pop-bang, hoping to startle away the animal—or person—creeping up on them.

Twenty feet away, it struck something and blew up in mid-air. A mage's barrier.

Sorath couldn't yet make out the mage, but he drew his pistol to fire, certain this was an enemy. With luck, the crack of his black-powder weapon would draw the patrol back out.

But something invisible struck the inside of his wrist like a hammer. Before he could fire, it knocked his arm back into a tree so hard he almost dropped the weapon.

Gritting his teeth, he clenched his fist around the grip and jerked it back down to fire. He could just make out a black-clad mage—or was that a zidarr?—in the shadows.

Next to him, Ferroki crept around two trees to get closer to the shadowy figure. Sorath tried again to fire, but his weapon jammed. The damn zidarr had done something to it. Sorath dropped it, roared, and rushed toward the figure with his sword and pickaxe raised.

Ferroki threw one of her pop-bangs. Something slammed into her, knocking her back with a pained cry. Sorath sprang, glimpsing a familiar face—Night Wrath.

A blast of power smashed against Sorath's chest before he could get close. It hurtled him past the glowing stone, and he clipped a tree. That threw him off, keeping him from finding his feet, and he crashed down in the undergrowth.

Snarling, he hurried to rise, but somehow, the zidarr already stood above him. He stepped on Sorath's wrist, pinning him. Sorath twisted, bucking off the ground and trying to kick the man.

"Stay down, you fool," the zidarr said, jumping off his wrist and avoiding the kick.

Wait, that wasn't Night Wrath. It was Yidar. There were *two* zidarr out here.

Yidar strode toward the clearing, a short sword and dagger in hand, and faced Night Wrath.

Sorath rolled to his feet and crouched, expecting them to trade insults or to spring together in battle. He looked for Ferroki, hoping Yidar's arrival meant he could grab her and they could hurry back to the relative safety of camp, leaving these two to battle each other.

Weapons drawn, ten feet between them, the two zidarr glared at each other. But any insults they threw were telepathic.

Sorath crept around them, circling toward where he'd last seen Ferroki.

The two zidarr froze in tableau. Sorath had no idea what they were doing and didn't care. Then they whirled, not toward him but in the direction he'd last seen Kywatha. A feminine gasp of pain came from the trees. The two zidarr sprang as one toward the noise.

That confused Sorath. They were enemies, working for opposing kings. Unless they'd decided to put aside their differences to team up against the druid?

Sorath spotted Ferroki—she'd risen from the undergrowth and crouched with a magelock pistol and another pop-bang in her hands.

The druid's jaguar roared, and thuds sounded, followed by a curse. Sorath couldn't see the fight through the trees, but he winced. If Kywatha had spoken the truth, she only wanted to protect her land and her people. And she had only approached the camp tonight because she'd wanted to talk to Sorath.

If the two zidarr killed her... Well, it wouldn't be his fault, but he would feel bad about it.

More roars, snarls, and growls erupted from the trees. Swords clashed—had Kywatha drawn a blade? Branches snapped, and another thud sounded. Someone being thrown against a tree.

"Back to camp?" Ferroki whispered, spotting him.

She glanced at his hand. Sorath gripped another pop-bang. He hadn't decided what to do, but maybe his indecision was stamped on his face.

"You're not going to help her, are you?" Ferroki whispered incredulously.

"No." Sorath shook his head. "I can't."

A feminine scream of pain rang through the jungle, and the sounds of battle faded. Male laughter rolled through the trees. Night Wrath.

"That'll show her," Night Wrath said. "Trying to spy on zidarr is foolish."

"Which one of us takes her back to our people to question?" Yidar asked.

"Roll dice for her? Though I admit *questioning* isn't what I want to do with her. She's young and pretty."

"You're a *zidarr*. You're supposed to be honorable."

Another snarl sounded, not from the jaguar this time. Had they killed her animal companion?

"She's feisty too," Night Wrath said.

He sounded as honorable as a mugger waiting outside a dark tavern for a drunk target.

"Don't be an ass," Yidar said.

Ferroki gripped Sorath's shoulder and pointed back toward camp. They ought to get out of here. She was right. But...

Sorath shook his head. With the pop-bang in hand, he walked toward the two zidarr and their captive. If he threw an explosive at Yidar, he would get in a lot of trouble. But maybe he could find a way to help without them realizing he was against them.

"I think there are more druids out here." Sorath swore loudly and dropped flat to the ground, as if he were dodging fire. "Something just flew by my head."

"What?" Night Wrath asked.

"I don't sense anything," Yidar said.

Sorath rolled away, working his way closer to them as he pretended he was peering at some danger in another direction. Now he could see the group, magical bonds wrapped around Kywatha, the men gripping her from either side.

"Wait," Yidar said. "The cat is still out there. And there's—"

The jaguar roared and sprang from a tree branch, claws stretched toward him.

Sorath threw his pop-bang, pretending he was targeting the jaguar but aiming for a branch above Yidar. Maybe he could distract the zidarr so their barriers would drop, and Kywatha and her feline companion would have an opportunity to strike and get away.

Yidar's defenses remained up and kept the great cat from getting close enough to hit him, but it landed atop his barrier—three feet above his head—and roared so loudly he winced. Sorath's pop-bang struck a tree branch and blew. The branch broke, tumbling down upon Night Wrath.

Another pop-bang flew toward the jaguar but missed by scant inches—had Ferroki meant it to?—and struck a tree. Branches and bark blew as the cat roared and tried to slash through the barrier to reach Yidar. The two zidarr were distracted enough that they dropped the magical bonds holding Kywatha, or maybe she tore them away herself. She thrust her arms up to hurl an attack.

As Sorath debated if he dared provide more help, green glowing tendrils of energy snaked out of the trees and wrapped around Yidar and Night Wrath. More druids had arrived, *angry* druids. Four men with staffs strode toward the zidarr.

Yidar threw a blast of energy and knocked the jaguar back, but the tendrils tightened around him. Night Wrath roared and blasted his restraints free. With a lesser-dragon-steel sword, he cut through the tendrils capturing Yidar. The two zidarr yelled and charged the new arrivals.

Ferroki appeared at Sorath's side. "Time for us to leave."

Though Sorath was torn and wanted to see who won, he made himself nod and follow her. "Good idea."

It was possible, if the zidarr survived and made it back to camp, that Sorath and Ferroki wouldn't get in trouble, that they would truly believe Sorath had been trying to help them instead of distract them, but he doubted it. All it would take was for Yidar to read his thoughts to learn the truth.

As they picked their way through the dark trees toward the roar of the waterfall, Ferroki shook her head and glanced at him. "I wish you'd had randy urges on your mind when you woke me, instead of that."

"Sorry. If we don't get blamed for this trouble, I'll be happy to share my urges with you tomorrow night."

"I don't think we'll be that lucky."

He was debating whether that meant she was or was *not* interested in his urges when Kywatha spoke into his mind.

I saw what you did. I am grateful for the help.

You're welcome. Sorath glanced back, but they were too far away now to see the druids or the zidarr. He couldn't hear the sounds of a fight and suspected it had been resolved, though he was afraid to ask how. *Does your gratitude mean you'll refrain from attacking our camp and trying to take the portal?*

I'm afraid I can't promise that, but as I said, if your mercenaries stay out of the way... we won't have a reason to attack you.

Sorath sighed. *We were hired to fight. We can't stay out of the way. Unfortunate.*

"Tell me about it," he muttered.

Ferroki looked at him, but he could only shake his head.

~

As Jadora followed Zethron off the street and up a walkway toward a two-story building with columns all around, she watched for guards or anyone else who might object to her presence. As her first trip out of the arena had taught her, Zethron could serve as a guide, but he had no power to help if someone attacked her.

She had a couple of questions for him, related to the flower gift he'd given her, but she was holding them until they were in a private spot. Guards had trailed them out of the arena, and then the city streets had been busy as the sun set and people returned home from work. The library was the first place that looked like it might offer some privacy.

Even though they could converse in Ancient Zeruvian, and it was unlikely the passersby would understand, she didn't trust that the mages they encountered wouldn't snoop into her thoughts.

They entered through wide doors into a vast chamber with marble floors, columns, and friezes that ran along a tray ceiling painted with dragons battling sailing ships. The rows and rows of wooden bookcases, with tables in the wide aisles between them, reminded Jadora of her university library back home. A few people studied at the tables, and in the back, scribes sat at writing desks while hand-copying books. They weren't using pens or quills but some magic. They waved one hand over an open book on one side of the desk, then above a blank page in a tome on the other side, and the words copied.

"Handy," she murmured.

"Question?" Zethron asked.

"I have *many* questions." Jadora smiled at him. "Let's start with alchemy." The Ancient Zeruvians hadn't possessed different words that made a distinction between the magical art and the science, but it didn't matter. Whatever these people did to work the dragon steel likely involved both. "Historical alchemy. Will you show me to that section?"

"Certainly." He bowed and led her to a room in the back, this one full of maps as well as old large books.

Several of the titles were in languages she didn't recognize, but she spotted a few in Ancient Zeruvian. Not certain how much time they would be allowed, especially given that the sun was already setting, she hurried through and selected promising books, then took them to a table.

Two older ladies in the room sat at another table, so Jadora didn't ask Zethron the rest of her questions, merely started to study. She pulled out a notebook and pen she'd brought, flipping past her diagrams of plants and cells to blank pages, hoping to fill them with information.

Zethron selected reading material for himself, turned up a couple of lamps, and sat at the other end of the table. "If I can assist you with your research, please let me know."

One of the ladies glanced at them, and Jadora did her best to keep what she was looking for out of her mind. "Thank you. I will."

Jadora skimmed through the books, searching for mentions of dragon steel and grimacing when she found little. Most of what she read in the ancient tomes was very basic or inaccurate, hypotheses based on little research by people who'd been using primitive tools. From what she'd seen, the natives here were *still* using primitive tools. She was glad she'd brought her own microscope along.

"I'll take a book on metallurgy if you can find one," Jadora whispered after not finding so much as a reference to dragon steel.

Maybe she'd been naive to believe the answers would be here and easy for a foreigner to locate. Or easy for *anyone* to locate.

"In Ancient Zeruvian?" he asked.

"It's the only thing I can read." Aware of the ladies glancing curiously over at them again, Jadora didn't go into her hypothesis that any *secrets* within the library were most likely to be in tomes in ancient languages that modern scholars hadn't known to clear out—if there had been a clearing out at some point.

"As I said before, I would be happy to translate for you." Zethron bowed to her again before leaving the room.

That left Jadora alone with the two women. They had books open before them and appeared to be reading, but they continued to peek over at her.

What you seek, one thought into her mind, *is forbidden. You will not find it here.*

And here she'd thought she'd been doing a decent job of hiding her thoughts.

No? Jadora asked silently. *Any tips about where I would find it?*

She smiled and wondered if they themselves were chemists. They were her age so not likely to be students. Even though they were frowning in tandem at her, she couldn't help but feel wistful at the idea of speaking to fellow scientists from a different culture and finding out about them and what they believed.

Certainly not. Only the etchers may work the ancient divine metal. They closed their books, returned them to shelves, and strode out, but not without a parting thought. *We will be certain to tell the authorities that a foreign woman is in our library snooping for government secrets.*

So much for speaking to fellow scientists.

Jadora frowned, wondering how long she would have before guards showed up to interrogate her.

"Interesting that they didn't call it dragon steel," she murmured.

She pulled out one of the books she'd already perused and checked the indexes for *ancient divine metal* and variations on the term.

"There," she breathed, spotting an entry. *Metal of the gods.*

Sandals slapped against the marble floor outside, and voices came from the main chamber, Zethron speaking with someone else. A guard? It sounded like Zethron was trying to stall the person.

Jadora hesitated, then opened her backpack and made room to stick the book inside. She closed it and hurried to return the other books to the shelves. Realizing it would look suspicious if a guard walked in to find her sitting at an empty table, twiddling her thumbs, she grabbed a picture book for children. She flipped it open to an incomplete version of the periodic table of elements as a guard strode in ahead of Zethron.

The big man wore a deep scowl as his gaze landed on Jadora. She feigned surprise as she looked up and didn't think about her backpack or what she'd been researching, instead filling her mind with thoughts of fluorine, hydrogen, argon, and rhodium, but not the barium or strontium missing from the chart.

The man's scowl only deepened. He grabbed the children's book, stuck it on the wrong shelf, and thrust his hand toward the exit.

He spoke aloud, not bothering to use telepathy to translate his meaning into Jadora's mind, but she sensed the magical compulsion in his words and found herself rising before she'd consciously thought to do so.

"We've been asked to leave the library," Zethron told her.

"Yes, I gathered that." Keeping her mind blank, Jadora shouldered the backpack.

She strode past the guard quickly, hoping he wouldn't think to grab and search it. In case it helped, she pretended to trip as she passed him. Zethron reached out and steadied her.

"Thank you," she said.

"You're welcome. It's a shame our date is being so rudely cut short." He shook his head at the guard as he wrapped an arm around her back—and her backpack—as he hastened her away from the area. Did he suspect she'd taken a book? "Perhaps we should enjoy a refreshing alcoholic beverage before we return."

"Uh, all right."

"A popular drink on this world is *ithma*. It's made from fermented seaweed."

"Sounds... delicious?"

"No, it's dreadful, but since the city is on the sea, people can gather the ingredients without heading far afield. In a land infested with man-eating dragons, that's desirable."

"I understand."

Zethron released her as soon as they left the library, making her think he'd been trying to keep the guard distracted from her pack rather than deploying a romantic move. He also headed straight back to the arena instead of taking her somewhere to imbibe the dubious drink.

"I hope you found something useful," he said quietly as they walked.

"I'm not sure yet."

"It's unfortunate that our outings keep getting interrupted."

"Yes."

Darkness had come, and there were fewer people on the street, but Jadora waited until they were almost back to ask the questions she'd been holding all evening. As they crossed the square toward the rear arena entrances, she stopped and held up her hand.

"Zethron? Before we go back inside, there's something I need to ask you." She dug the metallic disc out of her pocket—she'd wrapped it in fabric, afraid the needle would stab her through her clothing. "Why did you leave this with me?"

Zethron glanced around and shifted his body to hide her—hide it—from a handful of passersby on the opposite end of the square. "You can use it to walk through the barrier. I know you won't want to leave without the rest of your people, but I only had one of them. It's the one the guards gave *me* when I first visited their city. Since I'm sense-dead and not a threat to them, they didn't care that I never put it in my temple. If I don't have it along, I just ask them to let me in and out of the city when I go. Since they consider me an ambassador of sorts, they're willing to do so, albeit amid eye-rolling. But if you're prisoners here, that obviously won't work for you. I thought you might want to sneak out and use it." Zethron glanced around again and lowered his voice even further. "If you press the teacup constellation on the portal, it'll take you to Bathlor. The portal there has all of the symbols, so you can use it to return to your home. There's hardly ever anyone near the portal on that world, and it's not full of dangerous predators, so you should be all right visiting briefly, even by yourself."

"Thank you, but I don't have any magical power."

"I know."

"If I were by myself, I wouldn't be able to press the buttons—the symbols on the portal—to activate it." Not that she would consider leaving without Jak and the others anyway.

Jadora frowned as something new occurred to her. *Zethron* didn't have power either. He presumably had a key, but how did he press the buttons?

He smiled and answered the question without being privy to her thoughts. "They will activate if they are touched by dragon steel. Any dragon steel. A weapon such as your friend's axe would work. I almost tried to bring you one of those dragon-steel pots, but I feared repercussions. Since I cannot return to my homeland, I would prefer not to be driven out of Vran. Not unless you invite me to come to *your* world with you." His face grew wistful as he dreamily added, "The First World."

"Ah." Jadora reminded herself that he was an explorer.

"If it's at all possible, will you take me with you when you go?"

"I... would have to ask Malek." Jadora didn't want to explain that she was essentially a prisoner working for Uthari.

"He is your leader?"

"On this mission, yes."

Zethron grimaced. "He doesn't like me. He will say no, won't he?"

"Not necessarily, not if you have something to offer. And I think not if you're helping me." Jadora smiled and held up the device. "But his commander—his *king*—is waiting for our return. There are a number of ships and troops too. I would hate to invite you along only for them to be suspicious of you and capture you. We also have many powerful mages like Malek."

Well, not *exactly* like Malek, but since Zethron was like her and had no power, any mage would be formidable to him.

"He will not be like them for long," he said. "Not if he agrees to fight in the arena."

"What do you mean?"

"They will make him wear a *kerzor*." Zethron pointed at the disc.

"What does it do? Besides letting a person walk through the barrier?"

"It nullifies a mage's ability to draw upon his magic. Your Malek will be like me tomorrow." Zethron smiled and shrugged as if that weren't a bad thing.

Jadora gaped at him. "It takes away a mage's power? Permanently or only as long as they wear it?"

"Presumably as long as they wear it, but from what I have heard, once it is embedded, pulling it out can kill a person. The little magical threads wind all around inside a man's brain." Zethron shuddered. "I'm glad I've no magic, so they never insisted that I wear one."

"They're weapons then, not just tools. Why would you give *me* one?"

"As I said, you can get through the barrier with it. You can carry it in your pocket for that. And since you're also without magic, it wouldn't matter even if you did have one in your head. But you might find a better use for it than wearing it yourself." He nodded firmly. "If some mage back in your home world—this king, perhaps?—vexes you, perhaps you can find a way to sedate him and insert it in his brain."

"I..." Jadora didn't know what to say. She was barely hearing him. All she could think about was that Malek might even now be getting one of the devices inserted and that he wouldn't know what it did until it was too late. "I have to warn Malek."

Zethron raised his eyebrows, but she sprinted into the arena and didn't hear if he said anything. She ran along the first floor corridor, looking for a way down—Malek had said the animals and gladiators were housed in a basement level.

Unfortunately, despite the late hour, there were guards around. As she ran past one, peering into every passageway, he frowned after her. She spotted a stairway leading down and tried to turn into it, but another guard stood at the bottom.

Her mind buzzed as he did something to her—more than reading her mind?—and her legs halted, not of her own volition.

Spectators are not allowed below, he spoke into her mind as the other guard caught up. A meaty hand landed on Jadora's shoulder.

I'm not a spectator. I'm a friend of one of the gladiators. I have to see him.

Gladiators may only have visitors as prizes if they win their battles.

He hasn't battled yet.

Then you may not see him. The guard with his hand on her shoulder shifted his grip to her waist and hoisted her into the air.

Zethron caught up and spoke rapidly in their modern tongue. It didn't keep the guard from throwing her over his shoulder and walking back to the corridor.

"Malek!" Jadora called down the stairs. "Don't let them put that thing in your head. Malek!"

The guard muffled her, not physically but with magic. She slumped over his shoulder as he toted her away from the stairs as if she were a rolled-up rug.

"I'm sorry, Jadora." Zethron trailed along, lifting imploring hands toward her. "We're not allowed down there."

Was there any chance Malek had heard her cry?

The seats were empty for the day, so there were no crowds cheering now. Maybe her voice had carried.

But Zethron couldn't read her mind, so he didn't hear the question, and with the guard still muffling her voice, she couldn't ask it out loud.

All she could do was stare glumly at the cement floor as the man carried her toward their suite and wonder if Malek's life was about to be changed forever.

17

Jak stared bleakly down at the gladiators battling another of the big, scaled predators, noting the discs at each of their temples. It was the fourth match of the day, and every warrior who'd come out to fight had worn one.

Before, Jak hadn't thought anything of them, believing—as they all had—that the devices simply allowed those without magic to travel through the city barrier. The night before, he'd listened in horror as his mother explained what Zethron had told her about them.

Rivlen stepped up to Jak's side in front of the windows. "Lord Malek still hasn't come out?" She frowned at the latest round of combatants. "These people should have a big board with a schedule."

"Do you think they even know the gladiators' names?" Jak wondered if the ruler Malek had spoken to had learned anything about him or had simply coerced him along this path without caring.

"They must. They place bets on them."

Rivlen paced, no doubt as agitated as Jak. He didn't know how long she had known Malek, but he'd seen her admiring him from time to time and believed she had feelings for him beyond a simple ship's captain-zidarr relationship.

"Maybe he won't have a disc in his head," Jak said. "Maybe he'll have figured out what it does and said no."

"Said *no*?" She gave him a scathing look. "You think they're giving any of those people a *choice*? It's probably the price they have to pay for their chance at fame. *Idiots*." She stalked off, pacing again.

Mother looked up at Jak, her expression as bleak as his. She sat at a table near the window so she could check on the matches, but a new book lay open before her—something she'd brought back from the library—and she was taking notes. The disc—the kerzor, he'd learned it was called—rested on the table beside it, a gift from Zethron.

Now that Jak had magical power, however modest, he shuddered at the idea of having that thing stuck in his brain. "Does your book say anything about those?"

He was fairly certain she'd picked that tome because it had to do with dragon steel, not the devices.

"Probably not. It's a very old book. These are..." Jadora picked up the kerzor and turned it over, the needle glinting in the light. "I actually don't know how old the technology—the magic?—is. I should have asked Zethron if he knew. I was too busy... panicking."

"I understand."

Jak glanced toward the arena in time to witness the scaled beast take down one of the gladiators, tearing his throat out. He winced and looked away, wishing he hadn't seen that. When he'd assumed Malek would have access to his power, Jak had believed he would have a good shot at slaying these creatures, but now?

With only his athleticism and blades to rely upon? Malek was a talented swordsman, but Jak feared it wouldn't be enough.

I'm sorry, Rivlen spoke quietly into his mind, returning to his side. *I'm frustrated with the situation.*

I know. Me too. It's all right.

The beast finished off the last of the gladiators, and people cheered. From what Jak could tell, they were happy no matter who died in the arena, though it was often apparent from the roars who had bet on what. The idea of people making money based on whether Malek lived or died horrified him.

Guards came out to wrangle the beast, a task that was difficult even with their magic and magical tools, while servants dragged away the bodies of the fallen and dumped fresh sand over the bloody spots.

"What if, when Malek's fighting," Rivlen said aloud, glancing at the mercenaries as well as Jak, "we leaped down there to help him? *Our* magic is still intact. And our window is not." She pointed to the section that had broken in the fight the first night. The servants had cleaned up the shards of glass on the floor, but nobody had replaced the window.

"To rescue him?" Jak asked.

"There are always mage guards out there." Mother shook her head sadly. "They could kill us all."

"If we acted quickly enough," Rivlen said, "maybe we could surprise them. We could open that gate over there and let whatever creature he's fighting loose. That would give them something else to worry about. Then we could grab Malek and sprint for the city exit." She pointed at the disc. "You said that device allows the person holding it to get through the barrier?"

"That's what I was told."

"And it matches with what we saw," Jak mused as an announcer came out to yell through a megaphone to the crowd, explaining the upcoming battle. "But we only have one, so unless we could all hold hands and that would work, we'd be out of luck."

"My axe might be strong enough to cut through the barrier," Tezi said. "We speculated on that but didn't try it."

Jak thought he caught the name *Malek* in the string of words the announcer yelled, and his stomach flip-flopped.

"This is it," Mother whispered, understanding far more of the words. "This is his match."

"What's he facing?" Rivlen asked.

"All I recognized was something-something cat."

"A cat doesn't sound too bad," Rivlen said.

"I'm sure it's giant and deadly," Jak said.

The curtain to their suite swished aside, and a squad of guards marched in, several carrying dragon-steel weapons, none wearing kerzor. Mages.

They lined up behind Jak, Rivlen, and the others, standing a few feet back as they faced the windows. They said nothing, but with their hands resting on the hilts of their weapons, their meaning was clear.

Jak swallowed and looked at Rivlen. *I don't think they're going to let us spring out to help him.*

Rivlen scowled back at them. *I hate this place.*

A few days ago, Jak had been delighted at the idea of exploring and mapping a new world, but now, all he could do was nod in agreement.

As the announcer finished bellowing through his megaphone, Rivlen looked up at the ceiling. A moment later, Jak sensed what she must have sensed—someone with a powerful aura arriving.

"Is there another level of rooms up there?" she asked.

"I think so." Jak turned to look at the taciturn guards. *Who arrived?* he asked them telepathically.

They stared stonily forward without responding or even glancing at him.

Someone special? The ambassador who hasn't come to see us again since the first day? Jak knew it wasn't—if it had been someone with a familiar aura, he would have known it—but he wanted to see if the guards would give anything away. *It's not one of your city's rulers, is it? Do they enjoy watching the games too?*

If they did, it was sporadic watching, because in the four days they'd been here, Jak hadn't sensed this person. Or persons? There were a number of powerful auras up there.

A squawk came from behind one of the guards. The man looked down in time to spot Shikari chomping on his sandal strap. He jerked his foot away and lifted his leg, as if he would stomp on the hatchling.

Jak lunged in and grabbed Shikari. "I told the servants they needed to bring more cockroaches and crickets."

He swept Shikari to his chest, wishing the hatchling had stayed in the bedroom. It had been a few days since anyone had tried to kidnap him, and Jak kept hoping everyone had forgotten about him.

The guard growled and put his foot down but didn't speak.

Mother sucked in an audible breath at the same time that Rivlen poked Jak in the shoulder.

He turned to find Malek walking out in that awful leather loincloth and harness, with—damn it—the kerzor gleaming on his temple. He strode beside three burly men in equally skimpy attire. They carried weapons ranging from mundane short swords to a war hammer to Malek's lesser-dragon-steel blades to a dragon-steel axe. It had a single head instead of a double, like Tezi's, but it was otherwise so similar that it might have been crafted by the same maker.

"He's wearing it," Mother whispered, disappointment slumping her shoulders.

"At least they didn't take away their magical weapons," Rivlen said. "I don't think many of those creatures can be killed by mundane blades."

Malek? Jak attempted to project his thoughts in the pinpoint manner he'd been learning so others wouldn't hear him. Earlier, he'd tried to speak telepathically to Malek, but he hadn't been able to reach him through the arena floor. With Malek in the open now, he hoped his attempt would work. *Any chance you pasted a fake one of those on your head and it's not truly embedded and affecting you?*

As Malek continued walking with the others toward the center of the arena, he looked toward their window, as if he'd heard, but he didn't respond. Or Jak couldn't *hear* his response. If Malek's magic had been taken from him, he wouldn't be able to project telepathically. Jak had never tried to read anyone's mind and had thus far only communicated telepathically with other mages, so he wasn't sure how to *hear* an answer from this far away.

He concentrated on Malek, repeating his question and listening hard for an answer, though he realized the silence answered his question more effectively than words. Not only was Malek not able to telepathically project his thoughts, but he no longer radiated his typical zidarr power. To Jak's senses, it was almost as if a perfectly normal terrene human was walking out.

Except not quite. There was still a hint of magic about him. Some of it came from his swords, but that wasn't all. His body seemed magical to some extent, and Jak thought of the legends he'd heard about zidarr, that their kings infused them with arcane magic that altered them so they were no longer fully human.

Jak thought of the feats he had seen Malek accomplish—jumping great heights and dropping down fifty feet or more and landing on his feet. Though he could be injured—Jak well remembered the dragon fangs gnashing through Malek's torso—at times, he'd seemed indestructible.

Would that magic, embedded into his body instead of created

by his mind, be enough to give him an edge today? Jak couldn't help but think of the last match, where all the men had died and the scaled predator had walked out of the arena.

It is unfortunately not a ruse, came Malek's quiet reply.

Jak, his own mind busy, almost missed it. *I'm sorry.*

As am I.

Mother learned about those discs last night and tried to warn you, but the guards kept her from going down.

There is nothing she could have done. If she seems distressed, tell her that.

Mother had abandoned her book and was gazing bleakly at Malek. Yes, distressed summed it up. Distressed for many reasons.

The ruler and her powerful assistants came in person to insert it, Malek added. *I... was not strong enough to stop them.*

That had to gall him, if not embarrass him. Back home, Malek was used to being at the very top of the pecking order. How long since he'd encountered someone more powerful than he?

I'm sorry, Jak repeated, wishing he could do something.

The announcer spoke, presumably telling the men to ready themselves. After he finished, he strode for the safety of a door. Two mages stood poised to open a gate and let a creature out. Right now, it was in shadows, and Jak couldn't see what Malek would have to fight, but he sensed its aura. Whatever it was, it was large and magical.

Has your mother been to the library yet and learned anything? Malek asked Jak, though he was now focused on that gate, he and the other men spreading out and settling into ready crouches.

She brought back a book and is researching it. I'd rather she were researching those discs, so we could figure out how to get that one out of your head.

I was told that's not possible.

Ever?

That is what Etcher Yervaa said.

I don't believe it. There must be a way to remove it.

A screech came from behind the gate.

I must prepare, Jak, Malek thought.

I know. Be careful, please. I... Jak groped for something to say that wouldn't be maudlin or overly sentimental. *I don't want you to die.*

After the announcer disappeared behind the protection of a door, the gate at the far end of the arena rattled as it rose. An impatient roar came from the shadows.

"Sounds like a *giant* cat," Rivlen said.

"I've seen him kill a panther before," Mother said.

"This won't just be some simple jungle feline," Rivlen said. "I sense magic about it."

Jak did too, but he focused his senses on the person above them with the powerful aura. If it was one of the rulers, might he negotiate with her? He doubted he could save Malek from this match, especially if he had agreed to it—he would feel honor bound to go through with it—but maybe there was something Jak could offer in trade for the group's freedom. And for the removal of Malek's kerzor.

Shikari chirped and lifted his head as a great predator leaped from the cage and bounded across the arena. It looked like a lion, but it was twice the size of a horse, and its fur was long and bristly, more like that of a porcupine. It ran straight for Malek.

The other gladiators sprang to the side, as if happy to let him take the brunt of the attack.

Jak scowled, fists clenching. He'd finally learned to use some of his magic, and he had to stand by, powerless to help.

Malek waited like a crouching statue, weapons in hands, gaze intent, his face never giving away his fear—if he experienced it.

As the bristled predator closed to within ten feet, its muscled legs bunched, and it sprang for his head. Malek also sprang. Not toward it but straight into the air. He was still able to jump far higher than a normal human being could.

The cat snapped its jaws but missed him as he rose above it, twisting in the air to slash at its back as it flew through the spot where he'd been. Had his foe been a normal lion, the blows he rained upon its back would have severed its spine. But the bristles were magical and deflected the lesser-dragon-steel blades. When Malek's weapons struck them, the clashes that echoed from the walls were more like swords meeting than sword and fur.

Malek was fast enough to strike several times as the momentum of his jump faded, and he dropped back to the ground. He sliced through the tip of the predator's tail. The bristles were shorter and sparser there, and his sword lopped it off.

The creature roared with fury, but it was a small victory that did nothing to slow it down. As soon as its paws touched the ground, it spun toward Malek.

Two of the other gladiators ran in to hack at its flanks as it focused on him, but a pulse of magic flared from the creature. It knocked them back, one man stumbling to the ground. Immediately, he rolled and tried to jump to his feet, but when the predator saw one of its attackers down, it shifted its focus from Malek to the new man.

The huge cat leaped sideways, catching the gladiator before he regained his feet. The man swung his sword to defend himself, but all he had was a normal blade. The creature batted it away with a paw and snapped for his throat.

Malek leaped in, slashing at the bristled cat's flank with his sword as he attempted to stab upward from below with his main-gauche. Hoping the belly was less protected?

The quills *were* shorter and less dense down there, but if the dagger pierced them to reach vulnerable flesh, Jak couldn't tell. The predator ignored Malek's attack and chomped down on the gladiator, jaws sinking into his throat.

A gut-wrenching scream escaped the man's mouth. He lost his weapons and could only kick ineffectually at his killer.

Even as Malek stabbed and slashed again, the huge cat shook its captured prey, blood flying everywhere. The man's neck snapped, and the predator flung his body to the side.

Malek had landed several blows, but none of them seemed to get through. Aside from the cut to its tail, the quilled cat was impervious.

With one gladiator down, it whirled toward Malek, returning its focus to him. He backed up, pausing to regroup—or consider another target that might be more vulnerable.

Try for the eyes, Jak urged silently, remembering how that had been a vulnerable spot on the dragon they'd battled. Or the roof of the mouth. Surely, the predator wasn't quilled in *there*.

The gladiator with the dragon-steel axe leaped in while their foe prepared to spring at Malek. His blade whistled toward its hip. The cat lunged away before it could hit fully, so the axe only glanced off the muscular hindquarter, but blood and severed quills flew.

As the predator jumped toward him, Malek threw his main-gauche at its eye an instant before he leaped to the side. His aim was accurate, but another magical pulse came from the creature, and the blade bounced away, as if it had struck a barrier.

The cat slashed at Malek with lightning speed. He twisted away, almost evading it fully, but the claws grazed him, drawing blood as they struck his unprotected side.

Jak clenched his jaw. If Malek had been in *real* armor instead of leather underwear, that wouldn't have injured him.

Despite the wound, Malek landed facing the animal, his sword ready. His main-gauche had landed off to the side, and he sidestepped toward it without taking his gaze from his foe.

The cat sprang at him again, and Malek risked diving straight at it, rolling under the beast as it flew above. Jak winced when its claws raked toward him, but Malek dodged them as he jumped up below its torso, driving his sword toward its belly. It thrashed in the air, as if he'd done true damage. The brazen attack resulted in Malek taking another claw gash, this time to his shoulder, but when he rolled away, his sword came away bloody.

The crowd cheered for the bold move—or maybe any spilling of blood excited them. They'd also cheered when the first gladiator was killed.

The fighter with the dragon-steel axe rushed at the cat as it landed. Another man with a non-magical weapon also attacked, though he was being careful, aware that his blade couldn't hurt the creature.

While they distracted it, Malek ran over and snatched up his main-gauche.

"This is nerve-wracking to watch," Mother whispered, her fist to her mouth.

The cat had figured out that the dragon-steel weapon could hurt it, and when the axe-wielder approached, swinging the blade, the predator pulsed magic again. Man and axe were hurled backward.

Malek was ready when the cat focused on him again. This time, instead of springing into the air, the creature prowled toward him slowly. It wasn't going to risk exposing its belly again.

It lunged and slashed with long claws, acting like a fencer instead of a charging feline. Malek deflected the claws, as if he were parrying sword thrusts. The creature pulsed magic again. Though it knocked him back, Malek kept his feet, landing lightly and in time to deflect a series of rapid claw strikes.

The other two gladiators snapped at each other in their native tongue as they crept toward the creature's backside. But the pulses kept them away as effectively as a magical barrier would have.

After parrying a swipe from a paw, Malek risked lunging in. Using his longer blade, he stabbed for the creature's eye. The tip of the sword started to sink in when another pulse came from the creature, this one stronger than the others.

It knocked him flying—it knocked *all* of the men flying.

Malek twisted in the air, landing on his feet as the cat leaped for him. It hadn't expected him to recover so quickly, and he caught it off guard when he went down on one knee and thrust upward with his sword. Once again, he pierced through muscle and flesh to draw blood.

It pawed at him, and Malek rolled to the side, narrowly avoiding sharp claws.

As the crowd cheered again, Jak thought he heard approving yells coming from the suite above. Feminine yells.

That *had* to be the etcher.

Greetings, my lady, Jak thought telepathically in that direction as the cat sprang away from Malek and focused on the other two gladiators. *Are you enjoying the match?*

It was an inane conversation starter, but Jak doubted she would even respond if he demanded she free them all and remove that thing from Malek's head.

Do not presume to interrupt me, boy, came a haughty response. *Being a Favored Traveler by the gateway grants you no power here. And I am otherwise occupied. I have come for the entertainment.*

I can be entertaining. I know jokes. How do you feel about cartography humor?

After the games are over, we will speak. You will not entertain me but instead tell me where to acquire dragon eggs. I trust there are more where that hatchling came from.

Jak swallowed. This was not the conversation he wanted to have with her.

But maybe he could *pretend* to be willing to share that information. Before replying, he made sure the mental bandana around his mind was up so she wouldn't be able to read his thoughts.

There are. If you remove that kerzor from my friend's head and let us go, I could tell you where to find some for yourself.

You will tell us. Your time here has allowed us to study you, and we know how weak you are. It will be a simple matter to acquire extra information about you and your world from your mind.

That wouldn't be polite. Wouldn't you prefer to be allies than to make enemies with those from other worlds? There are many back home who are more powerful than we are, and if we don't return, they'll send armies to look for us—and battle those who harmed us.

Unlikely. I saw in your ally's thoughts that he is considered strong in your world. And he is not without merit—most intriguing are the modifications that have been made to his body to give him more speed and strength—but when it comes to pure magic, we are by far your superiors.

Jak worried that was true.

You will tell us where the eggs can be found, and I will let my ambassador take that hatchling from you. As he told me, he's not had our servants gathering bugs and feeding him for no reason.

Jak rested a protective hand on Shikari's back.

Malek is down there because you promised him you would let the rest of us go if he fought, Jak said. *Do you have any intention of fulfilling your promise?*

You'll not return home to report everything you've learned about us to your leaders, she replied.

So, that's a no. You lied to him.

Enjoy the games, boy, while we wait and see if your friend will live long enough to battle the dragons for us. If he cannot survive these simple creatures in the arena... there would be no point in sending you to their lair.

He'll survive them just fine if you give him his magic back.

That is not possible. The kerzor are forever.

Mother gasped, drawing Jak's attention back to the battle. The other gladiator with a mundane weapon had fallen, and only

Malek and the axe-wielder remained. They were trying to keep the predator between them, one attacking its backside while the other evaded its deadly fangs.

The cat dripped blood onto the sand as it lunged and charged, and Malek's blade had pierced one of its eyes, but the wounds weren't yet slowing it down. Meanwhile, both Malek and the gladiator had taken numerous gashes from its claws. Their blood incensed the creature, and it roared and screeched, attacks coming more rapidly than before.

Annoyed by their attempts to flank it, it snarled and started running around, using its greater speed to keep them from surrounding it. Malek and the gladiator ended up back to back as it ran, darting in to slash with a claw before darting back out. Jak hoped that was a sign of desperation, that it was growing tired and frustrated, but he couldn't be sure.

Malek's face remained calm, as always, though sweat gleamed on his skin, and blood ran down his arm and his side. Strangely, to Jak's senses, there was something magical about the blood. His first thought was that Malek's blood itself was magical, that as a zidarr, it had been permanently altered, but as Jak assessed it more thoroughly, it seemed more like a foreign taint than something belonging to Malek.

Were the cat's claws tipped with some venom? Or some magic that could poison the blood of its enemies? What if it would slow Malek down with some kind of paralysis effect? Or what if it sent a deadly poison straight to his heart?

Abruptly terrified that Malek might die, even if he won the battle, Jak focused on the wounds. During the last couple of days of training, Malek had shown him the basics of healing a wound, cutting his finger several times and allowing Jak to practice repairing the flesh.

It was a difficult magic for Jak, and he'd struggled to find a cartographical feature that could assist him in healing wounds.

Eventually, he'd been able to make it work by envisioning a manmade fill on a map, little tick marks representing an area that had been raised with rocks and made level for a road or railroad. There were numerous instances of that on maps of his Sawtooth Mountains back home. Focusing on the rocks being filled in allowed him to *fill* in wounds—generating new muscle fibers and skin over the injury.

He didn't know how to *clean* wounds tainted with poison, but Jak focused on Malek and envisioned rainwater trickling through the rocks in his fill, washing away debris. Was it working? It was hard to tell with Malek so far away and busy dodging and attacking.

Jak *thought* he was doing something, but when they'd practiced before, he'd been right beside Malek, able to reach out and touch the wound. Not only were they not in contact now, but they were hundreds of yards apart, and Malek was leaping all about in battle.

Rivlen looked over at Jak and opened her mouth as if to ask what he was doing, but she glanced behind him instead.

Look out, she spoke into his mind a second before pain stabbed him in the back, making him cry out and spin toward his attacker.

Jak glanced down, expecting to find a knife in the hand of the guard who'd stepped forward, but his hands were empty. He'd used magic. That didn't make it hurt any less.

No helping the combatant, the guard thundered into his mind, applying more pain, this time a stab to Jak's chest.

"I didn't help him," Jak gasped, trying to create mental mountains around himself—a barrier of protection. "I was just cleaning his wounds."

The guard snarled, pointing his finger at Jak's chest. *No helping or you'll—*

Shikari lunged from his sling, almost falling out of it, and bit the man's finger.

Rage filled the guard's eyes as he jerked his hand back. The pain stabbing Jak disappeared, but Jak worried the guard would lash out at the hatchling.

Shikari loosed something between a squawk and a roar. It was more humorous than ferocious, but surprisingly, the man backed off. He glanced at his comrades and scowled at Jak, repeating, *No helping,* but he didn't do anything else.

"Got it," Jak muttered, pulling Shikari back into his sling.

Rivlen looked curiously at Jak again, but the clash of sword against quill reached their ears, and they turned back to the arena.

Malek had landed a blow to the big cat's snout—another less-protected spot—but it was still running around, lunging in and snapping at them before jumping away.

The other gladiator swung his axe several times as the cat darted in and out, but he wasn't fast enough. He grew frustrated and lost his equanimity. He ran after their enemy, swinging wildly at its flanks.

The cat whirled and charged straight into him. He hefted the axe and tried to bring it down on the creature's skull, but it dodged, and he only clipped its shoulder.

The move left him vulnerable, and long claws swept in, digging deep into his abdomen, slicing through muscle and pulling out intestines. The man's cries of battle rage turned to screams of pain, and he lost his footing, dropping his axe as he hit the ground. He rolled away, trying to escape the cat, but it was relentless. It gnashed down on him, fangs finishing off what its claws had started.

Malek lunged in, sheathing his main-gauche as he grabbed the axe. Though the cat looked like it wanted to enjoy its meal, it sensed the danger and whirled toward him.

But Malek was too fast. While he stabbed at its eye with his sword, forcing it to protect its head, he smashed the axe into its side. The dragon-steel blade bit deep, slicing through quills and flesh.

The cat screamed as loudly as the dying man had. Malek sprang atop its back, wincing as he landed among the quills—they looked to be as sharp as daggers—but that didn't keep him from attacking. Even as the cat attempted to shake him off, he smashed the axe down onto its spine.

Again and again, Malek struck, sinking the blade deep, bone crunching. The cat kept trying to buck him off, but he compensated, crouching low with both feet planted on its back. He tossed his sword into the air so he could wrap both hands around the axe haft and then, with a great powerful blow, brought it down onto the creature's skull. The heavy blade split bone, exposing brain matter.

As gravity caught up to the sword, it fell and Malek caught it by the hilt. With both weapons in his hands again, he leaped off the creature's back.

Jak thought it might still find the energy—or the magic—to attack, but its legs gave out. It collapsed on the sand and didn't rise again.

The crowd surged to its feet, roaring and stomping for Malek's victory.

Mother slumped in her chair, a hand to her face. "Thank Shylezar."

Dr. Fret and Tezi clapped politely while Tinder thumped her approval on the table.

With no flair for the dramatic, Malek didn't so much as thrust his weapons into the air. He simply faced the door the announcer had disappeared into, waiting for someone to retrieve the bodies and let him out of the arena.

He kept hold of the dragon-steel axe. Would they let him keep it for the next battle? Jak hoped so.

"Two more fights to go," Rivlen said. "I hope they have a healer for him."

As the guards departed, Jak sensed the ruler's aura fading as she and her assistants withdrew from the suite above. Maybe this was the only battle they'd come to see today.

Rivlen glanced at the ceiling, also sensing their departure.

"They're not going to let us go," Jak said.

"One of them spoke to you and said that?"

"Yes. She lied to Malek. They were never going to let us go."

18

As Jadora translated her borrowed library book, she was aware of Jak, Rivlen, Tezi, Fret, and Tinder debating in the main room, trying to figure out how they could extricate Malek from his cell and escape.

Rivlen wanted to find one of the rulers to kidnap and force her to take the kerzor out of Malek's head and let them go. The mercenaries thought that would be suicidal. Jak just wanted to escape with their group, believing they could figure out how to remove Malek's kerzor once they were safely home.

But would their home be safe? Jadora remembered Malek's concern that these people would send armies to their world now that they knew the Torvil portal was open.

Though she'd told herself to focus on the translations, since the secret of the dragon steel was what Malek wanted most from this trip, she couldn't keep from glancing frequently at the kerzor on the table next to her. Zethron had given it to her so she could use it to leave the city, but all she wanted to do was take it apart and figure out how it worked. Since it was magical, she might not be able to grasp it fully, but if she could examine the insides under her microscope, maybe she could gain some helpful insight. At the least, she could make a diagram that might help the crafter mages on Torvil.

A part of her was intrigued by the idea of knowing Malek *without* his great powers—hadn't she even told him how much simpler their relationship would be if he were a terrene colleague at her university? Might Uthari dismiss Malek from his service if he were essentially a normal human being? If he couldn't fulfill his role as zidarr, what use would Uthari have for him? And maybe, if Malek were reminded what it was like to be a powerless human, he might be convinced to join forces with Jadora and the others and work against the mage rulers to make the world a more appealing place for all of its inhabitants.

Jadora sighed and pushed the thoughts aside. Even if she would prefer Malek without the ability to use magic, any escape they attempted would be much more likely to succeed if he was at their side *with* his full powers.

If she could figure out a way to help him, she couldn't withhold that information. Besides, if he were without his zidarr powers when he returned, an enemy—or even a supposed ally like Tonovan—might take advantage of his weakness and kill him. That was the last thing she wanted to happen.

As soon as she finished checking the book, she would examine the kerzor more closely.

Jak walked into the bedroom as she turned to a new section. *Alchemical Formulas*, the header at the top of the page read. That sounded promising.

"Do you have any explosives left in your pack, Mother?" Jak asked as scratching at the floor announced the hatchling scampering in after him.

Shikari sprang at the end of the bed, caught the comforter with his talons, and pulled himself up.

"That hatchling is bigger every time I look at him," she said. "And yes, I have some more. What are you planning to blow up?"

After Malek's match, the imposing armed men that had stood at their backs had left, but guards remained in the corridor outside.

"I was thinking of sabotaging the suite above ours." Jak pointed at the ceiling. "Maybe by putting explosives under the cushion of the most regal chair up there so that when the ruler next sits down... *boom*." He spread his arms to simulate an explosion.

"You don't think there would be repercussions for blowing up one of the city rulers?"

"Oh, I'm sure there would be, but she's not going to let us go no matter what happens, so we're already in trouble. Also, she promised to question me later about where the dragon eggs are." He grimaced. "And her ambassador still wants Shikari."

"You're sure it was one of the rulers speaking to you?"

"Pretty sure. She and a couple of her powerful assistants were up there during Malek's match. Their auras are greater than even Uthari's." Jak lowered his voice. "Why do you think these people are so much more powerful than even our strongest wizards and zidarr? Is it because there's more dragon steel around here?"

"If our hypothesis is correct about dragon steel being what conveys to people the ability to use magic, that could be it." As they talked, Jadora skimmed down a page full of formulas, searching for one related to the *Metal of the Gods*. The index had claimed it was covered in this chapter, though it hadn't contained anything as precise as page numbers. "If they know the dragon steel has that power, they might all sleep with it under their mattresses."

"It might be only the rulers who know that. The *etchers*. Maybe that's why they're so powerful. Because they work with it all the time. Maybe they don't even know that's the reason they're so powerful."

"I would guess someone here made that connection before and that they know."

Jak shrugged. "But we don't think anyone on our world knows, right?"

"I'm not aware of it in any of our literature, and nothing Malek or the mages back home have said in my earshot has suggested it." Jadora wondered if Malek had discovered her hypothesis in her thoughts yet. "But dragon steel is so scarce on our world that it's more believable that nobody would have made the connection yet. Since the alteration becomes hereditary, with mage power passed from parents to children, it's also possible that our people once knew but have forgotten." She paused as a formula caught her eye. "*On the manipulation of magical metal*," she translated aloud.

Jak leaned in. "Is that it? Dragon steel? Did you find it?"

"It doesn't say divine metal, dragon steel, or any of the other terms I've heard it called, but this could be the substance that's used to manipulate it, rather than the metal itself. Hm. There are only two compounds listed, and I don't recognize them."

"You don't recognize the compounds or the words for them?"

"Possibly both." Jadora turned a page and found a chemical structure for the substance. "Fascinating. This book and this language existed long before the microscope. They must have used magic to identify the molecules and their chemical bonds." As she considered the unknown substance, her excitement grew. "I've never seen this before, but I know an acid when I see one."

"Lending evidence to your hypothesis that they manipulate dragon steel with an acid?"

"Maybe so." Jadora drew the chemical structure in her notepad. "I wonder if it occurs in nature here."

"Uh, are acids common in nature? *Strong* acids? It would have to be strong to do something to dragon steel, wouldn't it?"

"Acids occur in nature, yes. Think of hydrochloric acid in your stomach or sulfuric acid from volcanos. Though with this formula, it might be possible for me to *make* this ingredient."

"Can you do it here?"

"In this bedroom? No. I'd need a well-stocked laboratory."

"Maybe you can ask Zethron to take you to one on your next date."

Jadora snorted. "I don't think the guards are going to keep letting him take me places."

"What can we do for you?" Tinder asked loudly from the main room.

"Guards coming," Jak whispered.

Jadora closed the book and was about to shove it in her backpack, but the curtain stirred, and there wasn't time. She tugged papers over it and leaned casually against the desk. The hatchling squawked from the bed as two grim-faced men walked in, not the two who were usually on duty in the corridor.

One reached for Jadora.

Jak jumped in front of him. "What are you doing?"

They replied angrily in their own language, pointing past him toward Jadora. She didn't understand everything, but she caught *book* and *library*.

Though she didn't want to give up the book, she doubted she had any choice. "It's all right, Jak." She gripped his arm and pulled him to the side. "Let them have it."

She carefully avoided thinking about how she'd already drawn that formula.

"How'd they know about it?" Jak demanded, though he must have realized he couldn't stop them, for he reluctantly stepped aside.

"I don't know." Especially considering she'd gotten it the night before. With so many books in that library, and even in the room where she'd found this one, how had any of them noticed one was missing? "It's not magical, is it?"

That would have explained someone sensing it.

Jak shook his head as the guard pushed aside the paper and grabbed it. "It's just a book."

As the guard picked it up, he paused and stared at something else. The kerzor on the table. Jadora hadn't thought to hide that. They were so ubiquitous here, she wouldn't have guessed any of the locals would think anything about seeing one, but the guards exchanged long looks and one reached for it.

"No, please." Jadora lunged in and grabbed it before she could think better of it. It might be their only way to figure out how the one embedded in Malek's skull worked—and how to safely remove it.

The guard scowled at her and blasted her with magical power. It struck Jak as well, and they tumbled backward into the wall, crashing into each other and hitting with painful thuds. Jadora lost her footing and ended up on her butt as the kerzor flew out of her hand. It skittered across the floor and into a corner, the metal glinting in the lamplight.

Grumbling, the guard strode toward it. Shikari sprang off the bed in front of him and raced for it, his wings flapping even though he couldn't yet fly.

The guard blurted a confused oath and tried to get to the disc first. But Shikari pounced with the speed of a future great predator.

"Don't let him eat it," Jak blurted, rolling toward the corner.

Thinking of the needle, Jadora winced. But Shikari was too fast. He snapped his jaws around the kerzor, chomped once and somehow didn't realize it wasn't food that he should spit out. Instead, he swallowed it in one big gulp.

"No!" Jak tried to reach for him, but the frustrated guard threw magic at him again, knocking him back into Jadora.

The other guard grabbed her, hoisting her to her feet as his comrade reached for the hatchling. Jak gritted his teeth and glared at him—trying to summon some power that would protect his charge?

The guard stumbled back and grabbed his forehead, as if a bee had stung him. Shikari scampered out of the corner and sprang up to the top of the bed, not needing the comforter to pull himself up this time. He puffed out his chest and emitted a reedy roar.

The guards argued with each other. Though Jadora could only partially understand them, it sounded like the equivalent of, "You get him. No, *you* get him."

Shikari roared again. They both gripped their foreheads and stumbled back, the one holding Jadora letting go. He bumped into the wall beside her.

She'd thought Jak had successfully used his magic to stop them, but was it possible the hatchling was doing that? Shikari flapped his wings and clawed at the comforter.

Amid more grumbling, the guards recovered, took the book, and strode out. Rivlen had come to stand in the doorway, and she stepped aside for them to pass while eyeing Shikari with interest.

"Is he all right?" Jak lunged for the hatchling and rested a hand on his belly. "That thing has a *needle* on it. It's going to scour his insides. What if it gets stuck?"

Rivlen walked to the corner, peered at something on the floor, then plucked it up. "You mean it *had* a needle."

She held it aloft for Jadora to see. It was indeed the needle part of the device.

Jak squinted at Shikari. "You're a smart dragon, aren't you?"

Still looking proud of himself for scaring off the guards, Shikari strutted around on the bed.

"Smart is perhaps not the accurate term for someone who's going to have to pass a coin-sized disc later," Jadora murmured.

"He used magic on those guards," Rivlen said. "I sensed it."

"He *is* a dragon." Jak didn't sound surprised.

"Yes, but he's only a week old," Rivlen said. "Humans are usually eight or ten before they develop any ability to draw upon their magic."

"We're clearly a stunted species."

"Speak for yourself." Rivlen handed the needle to Jadora and walked back out.

"Dragons are superior," Jak said. "It's not surprising that they have innate magic they can draw upon at a young age."

An image of a wriggling grub in a log half-hidden by large green fronds came unbidden to Jadora's mind. The urge to hunt it, capture it, and eat it alongside Shikari followed.

"That's unappealing," she murmured.

Jak's eyebrows rose. "Did you see that?"

"The grub?"

"Yes."

Jak grinned. "That means he's sharing telepathic images with us."

"Perhaps you could ask him to share something more appealing. Like that tart blue juice you're fond of."

"It *is* good, but it's more to my tastes than his. This is wonderful." Jak patted the hatchling on the back, though Shikari never acted like human contact interested him. A puppy, he was not. At least he didn't reject Jak's overtures. "I do wonder how he knows about grubs. I've been with him almost every moment since he hatched, and we haven't visited any logs. I don't think the servants have brought in any grubs either."

"If he's telepathic, maybe he can read all of our thoughts."

"Have you been mulling deeply and longingly on grubs?" Jak asked.

"Not that I recall, but maybe one of the servants thought of them while bringing in his food."

"I suppose, though I'm not sure they'd be any more likely than we are to envision such things. That log didn't even look like it was *from* here. I mean the vegetation around it."

"You're right." Jadora stared at him and then at Shikari. "That looked more like our world, though not the jungle area. More of a temperate forest." She scratched her jaw. "The fronds were similar to the ones in the greenhouse."

"Did you see any grub-infested logs while you were there?"

"No."

"Maybe he's thinking of his homeland."

"It does seem like it could be a match, but... how could he know about it? He hasn't been there."

Jak shrugged. "Magic? Maybe when he gets older, he'll be able to tell us."

Jadora smoothed her ruffled clothes and picked up the papers the guards had knocked to the floor. Her diagram was still there, and she hurried to write down the compounds listed in the book before she forgot them. Maybe, once she was back home, she could find a translation in a tome on Ancient Zeruvian.

Jadora held up the needle, not sure where to keep it safe until the other piece could be retrieved.

"I'll look at these under my microscope and see if I can get any insight into how the device might be removed from the brain without doing damage. Without doing *more* damage."

She assumed that whatever the discs did to cause someone to no longer be able to access magic was damage of a sort. If so, she hoped it was reversible. If not... Malek might be a terrene human for the rest of his life.

※

Sasko sat on a boulder as the other Thorn Company women slid under their blankets to get some sleep. She wasn't tired and had almost volunteered for the first patrol, but one of the mages had come by and requested Sergeant Words by name. She'd swatted him on the butt, surprising Sasko.

Corporal Basher had only snickered. "They enjoyed each other's company last night."

"While on patrol?" Sasko asked.

A muffled curse accompanied a clank-thud that emanated from Vinjo's tent. Sasko wondered how he was progressing. Earlier, some of Uthari's mages had gone into his tent to check his progress. She worried about what they would do to him if they didn't approve of that progress—or if they caught him making a new stealth device for Sasko. She should have quashed that idea. Ferroki had told her Uthari had learned about the other one and destroyed it.

"They exchanged a few kisses while on patrol, yes." Basher took a puff of a cigar she'd lit, the orange tip visible in the dim lighting. "But they waited until afterward to explore each other's passionate parts."

"Was it voluntary?"

Sergeant Words had a healthy libido, and often took advantage of companionship opportunities while on leave, but like most of them, she was usually smart enough to avoid mages. She'd *looked* like she had willingly walked off to join the man tonight on patrol, but with the way mages could manipulate people's minds, who knew?

"I believe so. She was the one who instigated their tongue play." Basher smirked. "Last night, when she was trying to distract the mages from the captain's and the colonel's tongue play."

Sasko blinked. "*Our* captain and colonel?"

She'd long suspected Ferroki had feelings for Sorath, but they were such professionals that she hadn't believed they would pursue a relationship while they were out here on a mission. Even if it was a mission that kept going on and on, with weekly changes in employers.

"Uh huh." Basher smiled around her cigar.

Sasko had heard there'd been a fight between zidarr and druids in the jungle the night before and wondered if the supposed tongue play was somehow related to that. Neither Ferroki nor Sorath had said anything that morning when people had been gossiping about the fight, nor had Yidar been forthcoming. Apparently, a few mercenaries had seen him return bloodied, with his clothing torn, but he'd grabbed a skyboard and gone straight up to Uthari's yacht without speaking to anyone. Ferroki and Sorath had exchanged long looks.

Vinjo's tent flap stirred.

"Lieutenant Sasko," he called softly. "I have something for you."

"Beware of anything he's offering you." Basher removed her cigar and pointed it at him. "He's been wearing nothing but underwear for three days, so it's a foregone conclusion he doesn't have pockets to keep things in."

"He doesn't want to put on one of Uthari's uniforms."

"That doesn't negate my warning. Whatever he's got for you, it's not in a pocket."

Sasko waved away the comment, grabbed her weapons, and headed for the tent. By this point, she doubted she had anything to fear from Vinjo, but with druids popping up left and right, she didn't dare even go to pee without her weapons.

"Greetings, Lieutenant Sasko." Vinjo flung his arms open wide when she stepped inside.

His bruises had gone from dark blue to a yellowish-green that didn't look much healthier, and even though the black eye was fading, the bags under both of them made it look like he hadn't slept for a week. Maybe he hadn't. Sasko noted the absence of a bed or even a blanket in the tent.

"Hello, Vinjo." She hadn't intended to glance down, especially after Basher's pocket commentary, but his legs were more covered than they had been on previous visits. Not with trousers. He was wearing a skirt made from large green leaves.

"Oh, that's encouraging." Vinjo lowered his arms and grinned at her.

"What?"

"It's always promising when women look at your nether regions without balls-withering derision."

"I was looking at your skirt, not your nether regions."

"Well, you didn't wither at it either. That's good." He flapped one side of the skirt. Amazingly, the thing hung together.

Even so, she hoped he still had his underwear on under there.

"Sorry, I don't. Uthari's people refused to lend me extras, so I washed them in the pool today, and now they're drying."

"Are you reading my mind, Vinjo? That's rude."

"Oh, sorry. I'll stop doing it. At least after tonight. Tonight, I want to know how you feel when I give you your gift." He bowed to her, then ambled past several glowing objects, one of which hummed like a mosquito. "You're alone, right?"

"Yes," she said warily, hoping his *gift* wasn't something she would be embarrassed to receive in front of others.

"Not embarrassed. Certainly not. In fact, you may have to punch and kick your fellow warrior women away in order to ensure they don't take it."

"I'm sure."

Vinjo glanced toward the tent flap, then opened a box, slid something between two fronds in his skirt, and returned to face her.

"If you think I'm going to reach in there to get it, you're delusional."

"That would be *very* stimulating, but no, that's not necessary." He glanced at the flap again, then waved for her to hold out her hand.

Though still wary, Sasko was also curious. She extended her palm. "You look too tired to be easily stimulated."

"That is perhaps a truth. Uthari's people keep checking in on me to make sure I'm working on the power components for their miniature ship, so I had to craft this in the middle of the night." He pressed a fist-sized device into her palm, keeping his hand covering it, as if he feared someone would burst through the tent flap at any moment.

Since two guards were always stationed outside, it was a possibility. His fingers lingered, brushing the inside of her wrist, and she thought he might be making an excuse for extended physical contact, but he was looking past her shoulder, his face screwed up with concentration.

She hadn't heard anything, but maybe he'd sensed something. His fingers weren't that unpleasant, especially considering what a goof he was, but she withdrew her hand to see what he'd given her. A bracelet with an ugly gray box attached. If this was his idea of jewelry...

"It's a clandestineness creeper," he whispered, touching his finger to a button on one end. "A new design. I thought it would be easier if you could wear it and didn't have to hold it. That way, you can grip weapons in both hands as you creep up on vile enemies to bash their heads in."

"Oh." Sasko stared at it, surprised he'd been able to make another one with the donated scraps and spare parts engineers from other ships had brought him. Now that she knew what it was, it was a lot less ugly.

"I'm glad." Vinjo grinned at her, though the grin was fleeting this time. "I think there's trouble about to boil over. Maybe when it does, you can hide instead of leaping into the middle of it. I know mercenaries are supposed to fight, but you could get squished by powerful mages slinging their power around." He tapped a finger against his chest. "*I* could get squished too. When the trouble boils over, feel free to come find me and hold my hand so we can both hide." He waved at the device.

"You didn't build yourself one at the same time?"

"No, these aren't like my portable thaumaturge-defier bulwarks. They're not easily mass produced. You have to lovingly craft them one at a time."

"Oh. Maybe you should keep this one then. You're more likely to be a target than a mere—"

"No, no." He lifted his hands to prevent her from giving it back. "It's for you. If there's time, I'll make another one for me."

"Thank you, Vinjo."

Sasko couldn't remember the last time a man had given her a present and not wanted something from her. Sex, specifically. Oh, Vinjo would probably be open to that if she offered it, but he hadn't ogled her chest or done anything untoward lately. He hadn't even done that back on the *Skimmer* after they'd met. He'd just trailed her around, trying to tell her about his gizmos.

"You're most welcome." Vinjo stepped back. "I must return to my work on the engine and power source. If I can't show Uthari's people progress every time they come down, they get cranky." He winced and touched his fingers to his temple.

Were they still torturing him? Why?

"You don't deserve that," Sasko said.

"No, I don't. I'm a delight." He lowered his hand. "I am starting to miss the surly indifference of Captain Myroth. Even my brother's snide comments. Oh, well. At least I've gotten to chat with you and Colonel Sorath. He came in earlier and told me my engine was looking impressively far along. And he complimented me on my skirt instead of mocking me for it."

"Did he mean it?" She assumed Vinjo had read his mind.

"He *did*. He said only a true craftsman could make such a fine garment out of rubber tree leaves. He didn't enviously covet it, but he was impressed that it stayed up."

"He didn't covet it? Are you sure?"

"Quite sure. I checked his mind three times." Vinjo lifted a hand. "Goodnight, Lieutenant Sasko."

"You can call me Saya," she said quietly, though she hadn't invited anyone to call her by her first name in years. In the company, only the captain knew it, and only because she kept paperwork on everyone so their relatives could be contacted in case of death.

"I will be most pleased to do so."

"Thank you for the gift." Sasko turned, intending to walk out, but he was so battered and mistreated that sympathetic feelings she hadn't known she could still feel for a man stirred. She stepped back to him, lifted her hands to his face, and kissed him on the cheek.

His eyes widened, and he opened his mouth to say something, but whichever magical doohickey had been humming since she came in changed noises, emitting a higher-pitched tone that made Sasko grimace.

Vinjo sprang back and whirled toward a large glowing orb. "It shouldn't be doing that."

He ran toward it, snatching up his toolbox on the way.

Sasko watched him go, the leaf skirt flapping, and snorted at herself, hoping he wouldn't think the kiss had meant anything more than a thank-you.

"I don't know what happened," Vinjo said, oblivious to her thoughts. "It's building to a charge."

"A charge? Like an *explosion*?"

"I'll try to stop it." Vinjo planted his hands on either side of the orb and repeated, "It should *not* be doing this."

"Do you want me to get help?" Sasko had no idea who she would get. Another engineer? They'd all gone back up to their ships for the night. Could the mage guards outside do anything? Maybe whacking the orb with a sword and breaking it would work. Except that if that was the engine he was building for Uthari's ship, they couldn't destroy it.

The high-pitched squeal increased until Sasko had to cover her ears. "Vinjo, maybe we should get out of—"

"Someone's tampering with it from afar," he blurted, his hands still planted on the orb as he tried to manipulate it with his magic. "Tell someone. Tell the king. No, Sorath. Someone's—"

It exploded with a thunderous boom and a brilliant flash of white light. Energy blasted outward, slamming into Sasko like a mage's attack. It hurled her across the tent, and she landed on a table full of equipment. The legs broke under her weight, and she crashed down, tools pronging her from all directions.

The white light disappeared only to reveal orange flames. The ceiling of the tent was on fire. So were two of the walls.

Wincing, Sasko pushed herself to her feet. "Vinjo?"

Already, smoke filled the air, and she coughed.

Shouts came from outside. "We're under attack!"

"Thorn Company to me!" Ferroki cried.

Sasko had to obey that order, but she swatted at the smoke, trying to spot Vinjo. He'd been right on top of that thing when it blew. He might need help. She swallowed. Or he might be dead.

More shouts came from outside, now accompanied by the *thwomps* of magelock weapons and the cracks of black-powder pistols. A boom came from somewhere overhead. One of the mageships opening fire?

Not on their tent, she hoped.

That fear almost sent her sprinting for the flap as she envisioned a cannonball crashing into it from above. But she forced herself to clamber over broken tables, tools, and projects, trying to find Vinjo.

All of the walls of the tent were burning now, and another hum in the back was increasing in volume to an ominous level. Another power source or magical gizmo that could explode?

Acrid smoke flowed into Sasko's nose and mouth, and she covered them with her sleeve. Finally, she spotted Vinjo crumpled on the ground behind the remains of a table, shards of glass or whatever the device had been made from scattered everywhere, including on top of him. His sleeveless tunic was in tatters, blood oozing from a dozen wounds on his chest and arms.

"Vinjo," she blurted, before breaking into coughs again.

His eyes were closed, and he didn't stir.

Sasko crouched and grabbed his arm, glad the company practiced over-the-shoulder carries on each other regularly. He was heavier than most of the Thorn Company women but thankfully not weighed down with copious muscle. She levered him up, eliciting a groan—at least she knew he was alive—and staggered to the tent flap.

Weapons continued to fire outside, and cannons boomed from the mageships above. That made her realize that their flaming tent was only part of the problem. Whoever was attacking must have used it as a distraction.

The tent flap was burning, along with everything else, and she wanted to stagger out as quickly as possible, but her instincts made her pause. Envisioning being shot as soon as she stepped out, she let go of Vinjo with one hand, keeping him carefully balanced over her shoulder, and pressed the button on her new bracelet.

"Hope this works," she rasped.

With the smoke tearing her eyes and threatening to make her pass out, she could only wait a second before stepping out. She immediately lunged to the side in case someone saw the tent flap stir.

A beam of green energy shot out of the trees and blew through the smoking flap. Sasko gaped at it as she scrambled farther away. Her head had been in that spot a half a second earlier.

With Vinjo's weight on her shoulder, moving backward wasn't

a good idea, and she stumbled. They pitched to the ground together, but she tightened her grip on him, afraid he would tumble out of the influence of the camouflaging magic if she let him go.

Another beam of green energy streaked out of the darkness, piercing the tent flap. Did the attacker think they were still inside? Who were they even targeting? She was nobody.

But Vinjo... Sasko looked down at him. Despite the groan, he was still unconscious. If their attackers—the druids?—didn't want him to succeed at his mission, at something that would help people explore through the portal, they might be trying to kill him.

Sasko licked her lips and stood up, dragging him around the corner of the tent and toward another one that wasn't burning.

The camp was in chaos. Two dozen red-uniformed guards, roamers, and Thorn Company mercenaries crouched around the portal, their weapons firing into the night. Some stayed there and used it for cover while others charged into the jungle to meet their enemies up close.

Up above, mages stood at the railings of their ships and launched lightning strikes and fireballs into the trees. A scream of pain came from the far side of the pool as someone took a lightning bolt to the chest. Sasko couldn't tell if it was a druid or one of their own people.

Another explosion came from the burning remains of Vinjo's tent. The other magical device that had been humming?

Sasko drew her pistol, torn between wanting to stay and make sure nobody got Vinjo and wanting to run to the captain to report. But if she left him, he would be visible. Unless she took off the bracelet, put it on him, and left its protection herself.

A smaller explosive went off in the trees on the other side of the pond. That sounded like one of Sorath's pop-bangs. He hadn't run out there to challenge the druids himself, had he?

A screech came from the air above the waterfall. Several great condors the size of human beings flew over the edge and dove toward the guards around the portal.

Captain Ferroki pointed her rifle upward and fired at one streaking toward her. The blue energy charge zipped out, striking the huge bird of prey in the chest. It pitched sideways and tumbled into the pond. Other mercenaries fired at more of the winged creatures, but looking up at the dark birds against the dark night sky made it hard to target them accurately. Some of the condors made it through, and they clawed at and bit the mercenaries while battering them with their wings.

One of the mage guards threw an attack that knocked all of the birds back into the sky. But only for a second. Relentless, the condors dove down again, talons outstretched.

Sasko aimed and fired at one streaking toward Corporal Basher from behind. The shot clipped its wing, sending it crashing to the ground in front of her.

Basher ducked and glanced over, lifting a hand to acknowledge the help, but she must not have seen Sasko through the camouflaging magic. She only squinted in confusion at the burning tent.

Yips and howls came from the trees. A pack of huge wolves flowed out of the jungle and sprang at the portal defenders, mages and mercenaries who were still dealing with the condors.

This time, the mages were faster at getting their defenses in place.

"Barrier up," one called. "Don't fire."

The wolves surged into their invisible barrier and bounced back as if they'd crashed against a wall. Absorbed by the fight, Sasko almost missed a cloaked shadowy figure running out of the jungle to take cover behind the portal. One of the druids?

"Ferroki, behind you," Sasko yelled.

The cloaked figure leaned around the portal and stuck something into the slot where Jak had inserted his medallion. Ferroki and several other mercenaries spotted the person, but they couldn't fire through the barrier. And the wolves kept snapping at it, so the mages didn't drop it.

"Down," came a mumble from below Sasko.

Vinjo stared up at her with bleary eyes.

"What?" Sasko asked.

"You fired and yelled." His words came out slurred, and she wasn't sure she understood. "They'll know… here."

"What?" she asked again.

He sat up, wrapped his arms around her, and pulled her down on top of him. Sasko might have objected, but a green beam launched out of the trees again. It sizzled through the air right above them, so close that chunks of Sasko's hair wafted down. She squashed herself atop Vinjo and clasped the top of her head. Fortunately, most of her hair was still there and the beam hadn't grazed her scalp.

"Now, now, Lieutenant," Vinjo murmured, "this is not the time for stimulation."

"I'd punch you if one of your gizmos hadn't just blown up in your face," she growled.

"That was an energy source." Vinjo scooted out from underneath her, though he kept a hand on her so he would be protected by the creeper. "We need to move."

"Good idea."

As they scrambled around the back of the tent, someone fired another green energy beam. It bit into the ground where they'd been, throwing chunks of dirt and plant matter into the air.

"I resent that somebody's targeting me," she whispered.

"I think they're targeting *me*."

"I resent that too."

"Do you? I appreciate that."

Sasko led him around the other side of the tent, hoping it

would block them from whoever was firing beams from the jungle. If she could, she needed to help Ferroki and the others.

When the portal came back into view, something had changed. It took Sasko a few seconds to realize what. The cloaked figure had disappeared, though the wolves and another round of condors kept attacking the guards, but one of the blue symbols on the inside of the gate was lit up. The stars formed inside and started swirling.

"How did they get a key?" Sasko whispered. "Is there more than one?"

"I don't know anything about it, but it's pretty." Vinjo blinked blearily at the swirling imagery inside the portal and touched the side of his head, maybe not sure if he was seeing things.

"I don't think we want whoever opened that to be able to go through." From hands and knees, Sasko pointed her pistol at the portal and looked for the cloaked figure.

As the swirling stars settled into an unfamiliar constellation, Ferroki and several others noticed it had been activated.

"Look!" they shouted to the mages over the growls of wolves.

"We know," one barked, "but—"

Another green beam of energy lanced out. This time, it didn't streak toward Sasko and Vinjo but toward the mages and mercenaries guarding the portal. They still had their barrier up, and it deflected the beam, but they cursed, having to concentrate fully on keeping it up.

Lightning and fireballs from the mageships streaked down, blasting the trees around the source of the beam. Branches full of leaves burst into flame. A dozen mages leaped onto skyboards to fly down and help with the battle.

The cloaked figure and a huge jaguar sprinted out of the shadows and toward the portal. Kywatha.

Sasko lined up a shot and fired at her.

The blast pinged off a barrier and into the trees. Kywatha and her big cat jumped through the portal and disappeared.

A yell of pain came from across the pond, and the beam winked out.

The condors and wolves kept harrying the defenders, keeping them from turning and leaping through the portal after Kywatha. Though Sasko didn't know if they would have followed even if they could have. Who knew where she had gone? Did *she* even know? Or had she selected a world at random?

The stars in the constellation disappeared, the symbol faded, and the portal returned to nothing more than a dragon-steel ring. The condors and wolves stopped attacking. Most of them lay dead, bodies all around the pool and portal, and Sasko expected the remaining animals to flee back to the jungle. Instead, they faded slowly, disappearing from sight. Or disappearing completely? The bodies also disappeared.

Had they been illusions? If so, they'd succeeded in fooling the mages into believing they were threats. Sasko wouldn't have guessed that was possible.

"The druids are powerful," Vinjo whispered.

She didn't know if he was reading her thoughts or making an observation independent of them.

Sorath and one of the zidarr—Yidar—walked out of the burning trees on the other side of the pool. They'd captured a male druid, the man's face covered in soot, his black and green hair burned off on one side. He curled his lip as Sorath gripped his arm and marched him along. Sasko was sure it was Yidar walking behind them who kept the druid from escaping.

"I guess we have a prisoner to question," she murmured.

She didn't know if that would matter. It wasn't as if they could stop Kywatha from enacting her plan. Whatever it was.

19

Malek stretched gingerly on a rug in his cell, careful not to break the scabs forming on his wounds. In the hours since his battle, nobody had come by to tend him, but he'd found a medical kit waiting for him, so he'd done his best to clean and bandage his injuries. Without access to his magic, he couldn't drop into a meditative trance and accelerate the healing process. When he'd attempted to meditate, the deep restful trance he'd always been able to put himself in hadn't been restive. He'd felt as if he were simply sitting with his eyes closed.

The idea of never being able to call upon his magic again filled him with bleakness. He imagined it was akin to a man going blind, losing the sense he'd relied upon most for all of his life.

Without his powers, he couldn't fight as effectively. Without his powers, he couldn't protect others and carry out his king's wishes. Without his powers... he was not a zidarr.

At best, he could be a swordsman, one who relied upon the magic of his weapons to survive against greater foes.

Malek eyed the dragon-steel axe he'd acquired during his battle. Nobody had stopped him from taking it from the arena, and he'd cleaned it alongside his sword and main-gauche, but he didn't know if he would be allowed to keep it. Even if he could, he would still be less than he had been. He wouldn't be worthy of his position as Uthari's right-hand man.

He imagined how disappointed Uthari would be when he learned of this new development, both that he would lose his zidarr and that Malek had allowed this to be done to himself. Disgusted that he hadn't been able to stop a couple of women from maiming him—from *crippling* him—he shook his head. Even if these people were more powerful than he, he should have come up with some way to negotiate or outthink them to avoid this predicament.

Since he couldn't sense those with magic anymore, he was caught by surprise when Etcher Yervaa appeared in front of his cell, her hood and white nimbus once again shrouding her features. This time, she'd come without her assistants.

You performed adequately in the arena today, she spoke into his mind.

I lived. Had he truly been *adequate*, he could have kept the warriors who'd fought with him from being killed.

A roar drifted to him from the other side of the basement, some creature letting them know it was ready for further battles. Malek wondered whose job it was to go out and capture all of those magical predators. Was there some world where they proliferated?

For tomorrow's battle, we will arrange a more difficult opponent.

Wonderful.

Normally, Malek would relish a challenge, but without his magic, he felt vulnerable. Further, he worried about what would happen to Jadora and the others if he fell in battle. For that matter, what was happening to them now? He wished he had a way to communicate with them.

After the battle, Malek had thought Jak might reach out to him again to give him more information—such as whether Jadora had been to the library and if she'd learned anything. But Jak must have been distracted, or he simply hadn't thought to resume communication. It galled Malek that he had to rely on someone else to telepathically reach out to him.

Your female's snooping in the library was discovered, Yervaa informed him. *My guards took back the book she stole.*

Malek managed not to wince but barely. He'd been doing the same habitual mental exercises he always did around other mages to keep them from reading his thoughts, but without his magic… they did nothing. How ironic that he had given Jadora *The Mind Way* and he would now have to employ such techniques himself.

I am tempted to dump them all into cells, pending the outcome of your battles, Yervaa added.

Why haven't you? Malek didn't want to see his allies caged, but he did wonder why they were being treated relatively well with comfortable rooms and food delivered multiple times a day.

Yervaa hesitated.

Does it have something to do with Jak being chosen by the portal? The gateway, Malek corrected, using their term for it.

It is unlikely the gateway would do anything if we killed him or locked him up.

Unlikely but possible?

She did not answer. Malek wished he could see her face so he would better be able to guess her thoughts.

Someone out of Malek's sight cleared his throat diffidently and addressed the ruler.

She replied, then lifted her arm, gesturing for the person to approach. A man Malek had seen earlier came into view. The night before, he'd brought two women down for victorious gladiators in other cells. He'd also accompanied servants who brought food and wine, lowering the barriers and keeping an eye on them as they entered and distributed the meals.

He carried a clipboard and pointed at Malek, asking what sounded like a question. Malek willed his brain to learn the language so he wouldn't be at such a disadvantage here, but unlike Jadora, he had no foundation in Ancient Zeruvian.

Yervaa extended a hand in invitation toward Malek.

The man faced him and lifted a pen. He spoke aloud, but he also shared his thoughts telepathically so Malek could understand.

Since you were victorious today, a delicious feast is being prepared and will be brought to your cell. You have also earned the use of a woman—or a boy or man, if you prefer. Of course, you are expected to battle again tomorrow, so your prize will not stay all night, as we must ensure our warriors get proper rest, but you will have time to enjoy your reward.

Yervaa watched Malek intently, and he remembered her suggestion that he might have *her* if he won. It crossed his mind that, if she were distracted by passion, he might be able to overpower her physically and demand his comrades be set free, but she was so powerful that he couldn't imagine that working. If he had a split second, he might be able to break her neck, but what would that win him? The city had three other rulers, and the guards would likely kill him while he was trapped in his cell with her body.

Were you to ask for me, she spoke dryly into his mind, *I would take you up to my abode, but I assure you that you would not overpower—or kill—me even if you still had access to your full power. You would not be the first to try. I tend to find such spirit stimulating, but I've not yet had a man best me in bed or elsewhere. Further, I have numerous protections in my abode.*

So much for employing the techniques of *The Mind Way* to keep her from reading his thoughts.

I have no desire for a woman—or boy or man, Malek replied to the overseer.

That is your choice. The man penned something on his clipboard.

Wait, what if Malek could finagle a visit—and an update—from Jadora? Would they allow that?

Unless you can bring one of the females from my party, Malek said.

Since he couldn't see Yervaa's eyes, he didn't know how she reacted to that. It was probably only his imagination that she radiated displeasure. Why she had any interest in him, sexual or otherwise, Malek couldn't guess. Gladiators fought in her arena every day, and there had been numerous battles before his. He hadn't been the only one to survive today.

Any available female interested in entertaining a victorious gladiator may be chosen, the man said.

I wish Jadora. Malek formed an image of her in his mind, doubting the man or any of the guards knew their names.

He raised his eyebrows, either at the choice or the fact that his vision included her with her pockets bulging. Would she be allowed to bring her backpack? Maybe she had something that could get him out of this cell. Or maybe she had something that would help him remove the disc. Likely not, since it was a magical device, but he allowed himself to feel wistful.

I will see to it. The man wrote on his clipboard, bowed to Yervaa, and headed off to the next gladiator.

When you are in foreign lands, Yervaa told Malek, *you should sample foreign dishes.*

Is that why you're interested in me?

Naturally. Humans from other worlds are exotic and sometimes have practices unknown to the locals. She shared an image of Zethron, naked and on her bed.

Malek couldn't keep from wrinkling his lip. It was bad enough that man kept showing up at Jadora's shoulder, offering to take her places and giving her gifts. The last thing Malek wanted was imagery of him naked.

Yervaa chuckled into his mind. *Enjoy your night, my gladiator. Oh, and do tell me where I can find those dragon eggs.*

Malek emptied his mind of thoughts, as *The Mind Way* taught, and gazed past her shoulder without responding.

I will find out, she told him. *Your people were foolish not to collect them all and start raising a dragon army for themselves. We will not make the same mistake.*

Perhaps he should have remained silent, but he couldn't pass up an opportunity to gather intelligence. *What would you do with a dragon army?*

Rid all the worlds of the younger dragons, she said. *If that's possible. The younger long ago defeated the elder, so even an army might not be enough to drive them out or destroy them. Perhaps we will simply lead our army to your world, take it over, and render your portal inoperable, so that younger dragons won't find us again. Good night, gladiator.*

She walked away, leaving Malek to worry once again that they'd made a mistake in coming here... and that he may have endangered his entire world.

~

Rivlen chewed on a drumstick from the local equivalent of a turkey as she gazed out the window at the nighttime arena, silvery moonlight gleaming on metal railings and sand that had been replaced so that the arena floor was once again pristine and free of blood.

From their elevated suite, she could see two doors and one large metal portcullis. The portcullis led to the holding area where the creatures were positioned before being released for battle, and her senses told her it was currently empty of magical beings. If she sneaked down there and opened it, would it allow her to bypass the stairways with guards and give her access to the underground level?

If they could collect Malek and find a way out of the city, doing so before his three days of battles were up might be wise. According to Jak, the rulers weren't planning to let them go. The best they could hope for was for Malek to win his matches and the group to be sent off to fight a couple of killer dragons.

"Better to leave through the portal and bar the way to this world forever." Rivlen didn't know if that was possible.

From what Jadora had explained, the denizens here had crossed out—etched out—the symbol that opened a passageway back to Torvil, but all they would have to do was go to another world and use their portal to gain access to it. To keep an invasion army from showing up on Torvil's doorstep, Uthari and the others would have to agree to completely disable their portal.

Jak wore a troubled expression as he stepped out of the bedroom Jadora had been using as a workshop. He joined Rivlen at the windows.

"Has your mother discovered anything?" Rivlen asked.

"She's been using her microscope to look at the tendrils that come out of the needle. As soon as she touched one, it grew longer and sprouted a hook. It scared her, because it somehow sensed her hand and stretched toward it. Those devices seem half magic and half living creature."

"I'm not letting one anywhere near my head."

"Good plan. I wish Malek hadn't." Jak glanced toward the corridor and lowered his voice. "She's watching the tendrils now and trying to figure out how long they're capable of moving around. If they gain power from the metal disc—that's magical too—she believes without it, they might run out of steam. The hooks could make it impossible to pull the tendrils out of one's brain without doing a lot of damage, but if it were possible to cut the needle in half, maybe the tendrils would basically die. They'd still be stuck in there, but maybe they couldn't do anything." Jak spread his arms.

"Having all that stuff stuck in your brain forever isn't appealing."

"No. But without power from the device, maybe one's magic would return. Maybe *Malek's* power would return."

"A healer might be able to remove everything using magic," Rivlen said. "Just because the rulers tell their people—and their guests—that it isn't possible doesn't mean it's true. It could be a lie to keep people from trying it."

"Maybe."

"*You* might be able to figure out how to remove it."

"Me?" Jak touched his chest and raised his eyebrows.

That expression made him seem young and innocent. It was far different from the determined and almost fierce expression he'd had earlier when he'd been trying to heal Malek's wounds from afar. No, not *trying*. Rivlen had watched him do it. She wouldn't have thought that possible, even for an experienced healer. She wasn't an expert on that aspect of magic, but she'd never heard of anyone healing wounds from a distance.

She'd gone from watching the battle and admiring Malek's speed and agility to being riveted by Jak and the precise threads of magic sliding across the distance and delicately infusing Malek with healing power. She'd once told Jak that female mages were more likely to be attracted to a man with impressive magical power than some muscled athlete. Admittedly, she could admire both, but she was more drawn to people who had power and the ability to control it in a sophisticated and intricate way.

Not Jak though. He was just a kid. Especially when he was raising his eyebrows and looking silly.

"You," Rivlen told him, shaking the thoughts from her mind. Why was she thinking about attraction and men? They needed to focus on getting out of here. "You did some intricate healing today. I've told you that you've got potential—you could be very powerful one day. I didn't expect you to have the gentle, precise touch of a surgeon. That's not common. A lot of people with great power never develop such a touch. They don't need to. They can use brute force and achieve most of their goals."

Jak seemed bemused by her praise—maybe he didn't realize she *was* praising him. She wasn't the best at delivering compliments.

"I just hope I helped him. If it *is* possible for me to remove that device, I gladly would." Jak gazed thoughtfully back toward Jadora's door. "My mother is making a diagram of the tendrils and how they branch out. She said she would try to take apart the disc and look inside it too, if we can, uh, get it back. We have to wait on that." His gaze shifted toward the lavatory and the corner they'd set aside for the hatchling to do his business—when Jak could catch Shikari in the act and swoop him over to the spot in time.

Rivlen had never thought she would have to watch someone potty train a dragon. "You think your mother will touch the disc after it's gone through your hatchling?"

"After sanitizing it thoroughly, yes."

"What if he digests it, and nothing is left of the original?"

"That would be remarkable."

"Dragons *are* remarkable," Rivlen said. "And very powerful and magical."

He smiled at her. "You think that applies to their digestive systems too?"

"It could." After another glance toward the hallway, Rivlen shifted to telepathy. She doubted anyone out there could understand them, but why risk it? *I have a bad feeling about this place and the probability of us getting out of here.*

Me too. Like I said, the etcher isn't going to voluntarily let us go. She doesn't want us to be able to report back to our people, and her ambassador wants to know where the dragon eggs are.

I'm surprised they haven't interrogated us yet.

For whatever reason, the fact that the portals talk to me—they keep calling me Favored Traveler—seems to make them hesitant to attack me. And today, when Shikari bit that guard, he was scared to retaliate, even though those men have to be stronger than a baby dragon.

Maybe you should ask the portal what it means to be favored.

I'll consider it. Do you have a plan for escaping?

We need to subdue those guards. Rivlen nodded toward the doorway.

How? I think there are four out there right now, and you're the only one in here with reliable, experienced magic. I'm still learning and don't know how to effectively attack people yet. Malek showed me a couple of things, but I wasn't very good at them, so we switched to working on how to defend myself and how to heal people after my defenses fail.

That's how he put it?

No, I'm paraphrasing. Tezi has that axe, so maybe she could fight one guard. You fight another one. That leaves two powerful magic users for me, my mother, and Tinder and Dr. Fret.

None of whom had magic, besides Jak. And if he couldn't attack yet...

Rivlen debated if she should offer to show him. If they were going to act tonight—and the sooner the better—there wasn't much time for lessons.

Does your mother have anything that could tip the scales? Rivlen asked. *You two were talking about explosives earlier. She had venom and other things with her at one point.*

She probably still has that, but unless we can simultaneously stab the guards in the butts with needles full of venom, I doubt that would help. Jak shook his head. *Whatever she has would take a while to work, during which time, they'd be able to call out for help.*

Something else then. She's a walking apothecary.

Let me check. Jak nodded and returned to Jadora's room.

Movement outside the window drew Rivlen's attention. She spotted someone pushing a broom through the aisles below. His head was down, shadows hiding his face, and he didn't have a magical aura, so she didn't think much of him other than to note that there might be witnesses if they climbed out the window. It was still early. Later in the night would be better for their escape attempt.

It was too bad the guards would notice if she, Jak, and Tezi—more specifically, Tezi's axe—disappeared from the suite. They wouldn't be able to sense the terrene humans, but it wasn't as if Rivlen could send Jadora, Tinder, and Dr. Fret to break out Malek.

No, whatever they did, they all had to leave together. Once they left, they might not have the option to come back here.

Jak returned with a little tin in his hand and a bemused smile on his face. He opened the lid to reveal a candle. Right away, Rivlen noticed a sweet lemon scent and raised her eyebrows. It smelled like something for keeping mosquitos away, not distracting guards.

Jak put the lid back on. "She said it doesn't do much until you light it, but I trust you can do that quickly with magic?"

"Make flame? Yes. But what will lighting a candle do? And where did that come from? I inventoried all of your belongings back on the *Star Flyer*. Candles weren't in the mix."

She's since found the wax and time to make a few. In addition to the citrus scent that's mixed in—that's to cover up other scents—there's a potent drug called yavrithnor. I think that was it. She said it makes you fall asleep if you inhale enough of it.

Oh? That was more promising than a simple candle.

She thought we might be able to burn this by the doorway, use a little magic to blow the air out into the corridor, and that the guards might not notice until it's too late.

What happens if it knocks us *out?*

That would be less than desirable. Hence the magical air blowing.

All right. We can try it. If we can knock them out, we'll climb out the window, down to the arena, through that gate—Rivlen pointed to the creature staging area—*and from there, we can find Malek and get out of this place.*

Hoping that we can sneak out of the arena without being noticed? And that if we all hold his hand while we try to walk through the city barrier, it'll let us all out because of his kerzor?

Yes. Then we get to the portal and back to our world.

What about the ziggurat that's possibly made from dragon steel?

Didn't we decide that it's guarded by dragons? Rivlen asked.

Probably. If you believe two people's visions.

We can't go roaming around in their mountains, or they'll catch us. You don't even have a map, do you?

No. I had Mother ask Zethron to bring one, but I think he only brings gifts for her. Jak grimaced.

Yeah, because he's a man, and she has breasts. Men like to shower gifts on the owners of those.

Jak reeled back. *Don't talk about my mother like that.*

As a person with breasts? I hate to shatter your delusions, Jak, but she's got them. Most women do.

He glanced down at her chest but quickly looked away, as if expecting to get his head smacked for ogling. That amused her, since so many men—at least the mages she so often worked with—had no qualms about extended staring.

I'm aware that they exist, he continued, now looking up at the ceiling instead of any part of her body. *But when it comes to my mother, I pretend they don't.*

Mature. Have her ask again if Zethron comes back. He might have been distracted by the body parts you pretend don't exist.

Jak sighed. *I don't know if he'll be back. Every time they leave together, they get into trouble.*

Don't remind me. Rivlen rubbed the side of her head, the memory of being attacked by all those guards in the greenhouse sharp in her mind.

Still, it's possible I could find the right valley on my own. The portal might even tell me. I communicated with it before about Tezi's axe.

Rivlen held up a hand. *We're not going to worry about that now. Our priority has to be to escape, get back to our world, and warn King Uthari about this place. Maybe warn* all *of the kings. If there truly is a possibility that they'll send troops to our world...*

There is. Jak met her eyes, his own eyes bleak. *The ruler didn't say it explicitly to me, but I got the sense they think we'd be easy to take over. And Malek said they're attracted to Torvil because they now believe it's free of the younger dragons. The evil dragons. For people who've been hiding out in protected cities for years, that has to sound like paradise.*

He hadn't mentioned that part earlier, and fresh alarm filled Rivlen.

So, they could be planning even now to invade our world? she asked.

It's possible.

Rivlen swore out loud.

Jadora walked out and headed for the lavatory but looked over and raised her eyebrows. "It concerns me when I chance across women swearing at you, Jak. I hope you're not offending Captain Rivlen."

The comment surprised Rivlen, though she realized she and Jak were standing close. She'd stepped in to look at the candle. Maybe it had looked like she'd been cussing at him.

"I don't think so," Jak said. "We're discussing our situation and how complicated it is. I believe her swearing was related to that and nothing I personally have done."

"Jak hasn't offended me," Rivlen said, in case his mother truly believed it was possible he could. "He wouldn't even look at my breasts."

Jak dropped the candle tin, cursed, and scrambled to pick it up.

"I didn't know you *wanted* me to," he whispered, straightening again.

Jadora opened her mouth but must have decided against commenting.

Rivlen smirked at Jak, though her amusement quickly waned as she contemplated the severity of the situation. *All right, let's get serious again. We knock out the guards, climb down and find Malek, figure out how to free him, and get out of the city. We'll tell Uthari everything and let him decide how to react to a possible invasion force— and he can tell us if he wants us to sneak back and try to carve some dragon steel out of your dragon-infested zig-thing.*

Ziggurat. And I think that if we leave, it'll be hard to get permission to come back. It's also possible these people, knowing we covet the dragon steel, will put permanent guards in place around their portal.

Aren't their people afraid of going far from their protected city, lest dragons attack? Rivlen asked.

They go out to fish. They can go out to the portal. It's not that far from the safety of their city walls—city barrier.

We'll have to risk that. Our duty is to escape and report back. If we don't, and we all end up dead here, our people could be blindsided.

But—

Rivlen planted a hand on his chest. *With Malek detained elsewhere, I'm the highest-ranking officer here. I am in command of this mission, and you and the rest of the team will do as I say.* She narrowed her eyes, giving him the fearsome squint that quelled her junior officers when they objected to a command. *Do you understand?*

Surprisingly, he didn't look that quelled. *I do understand you, but as your civilian expert advisor, I feel you should heed my words.*

Expert? On what? Cartography?

Yes, and on archaeology.

Archaeology on our world. You don't know anything about this place.

Jadora left the lavatory, glancing over again as she passed through. Her eyebrows rose at the hand on Jak's chest.

"Are you *sure* you're not pestering Captain Rivlen, Jak?"

"Not at all, Mother. She's the one fondling my chest."

Rivlen glared at him and lowered her hand. She switched to telepathy to tell Jadora, *Round up the mercenaries. We're going to use your candle as soon as it's feasible, rescue Malek, and get out of here.*

"Ah. Then I'll pack my microscope and finish cleaning this off in case we need to leave in a hurry." She held up the disc.

"Dragons must process their food more quickly than we do," Rivlen remarked.

"Obligate carnivores have shorter and less complicated digestive systems than herbivores and omnivores," Jadora said. "Protein is easier to break down than cellulose." Jadora eyed the disc. "And magical metal."

"Traveling with you people is a learning experience," Rivlen said.

The curtain shifted aside, and one of the guards strode in.

Rivlen almost swore again. Had he somehow picked up on her telepathic message to Jadora? She wasn't some amateur who flung her thoughts all over the place, but who knew what these people had the power to perceive? She hoped he'd only started paying attention in time for the digestive-tract lecture.

The guard said nothing, merely gesturing for another man to walk in. This fellow carried a clipboard and peered around the room, gaze lingering on Rivlen before settling on Jadora.

He eyed her curiously and spoke a few words.

Jadora's eyebrows rose again—they were getting quite the workout tonight.

"Do you understand him?" Rivlen hated being left out of the loop, but since he was a mage, she couldn't read his thoughts.

"He said I'm older than he expected."

"Flattering."

"Indeed."

The man spoke again, then pointed to the corridor.

Did they want Jadora to *go* somewhere? Rivlen scowled. If their group broke up—broke up *further*—it would be even more difficult to gather everyone and escape.

"What does he want?" Rivlen stepped forward, her hand on the hilt of her sword.

Dr. Fret and Tinder must have heard her sharp tone, for they came out with Tezi to see what was happening.

"I think it's all right." Jadora lifted her hand. "Malek has asked to see me."

"And they're allowing that? *Why?*"

Jadora asked the man a question. His brow furrowed for a moment as he tried to decipher her accent—or her attempt at getting the words right, but then he answered.

"Ah." Jadora didn't look like she knew whether to be pleased or disturbed by the answer.

"What is it?" Jak asked. "Is he all right? He had those injuries..."

"They must not be troubling him overmuch," Jadora said. "As a victorious gladiator, he's being rewarded with female companionship tonight."

"And he picked *you*?" Rivlen realized her tone made the words sound insulting, but she couldn't help but feel disgruntled. It wasn't as if she wanted to be picked as some man's prize, but... really. What about Jadora could possibly capture Malek's attention? She was a middle-aged academic, not some voluptuous beauty. And she already had that Zethron sniffing around, wanting to give her gifts and hold her books.

"I would guess he just wants information and is using the opportunity to find out if I've learned anything." Jadora tilted her head toward the room with her microscope.

"Oh." Rivlen blushed, feeling silly for her thoughts. As if any of that was even important in their current situation.

The man waved his clipboard, said something impatient, and stalked through the doorway. Jadora nodded, handed the disc to Jak, and followed the man out.

Tell Malek we're working on an escape attempt, Rivlen told her telepathically. *If we can make it happen tonight, we will, but it'll have to be tomorrow night at the latest. Before his last battle in the arena. Before these rulers decide his—our—usefulness is at an end.*

I understand, she replied. *I will.*

Jak eyed the disc dubiously and stuck it in his pocket. "The idea of my mother being picked as a prize for a gladiator—even if that gladiator is Malek—is alarming."

"She's a comely woman," Dr. Fret said.

"But she's *old*," Jak said.

"She's not *that* old," Fret said dryly.

"Yeah, she must have had you when she was young," Tinder said. "And Malek has some grays in his hair, so he's older too. Maybe he likes a match."

"A mature and more restful woman," Fret agreed.

Jak looked at them in horror. "My mother makes explosives and hurls homemade acids in people's faces. She's not *restful*."

"There's nothing wrong with a woman who makes explosives." Tinder patted an ammo pouch on her belt—or maybe a pouch full of ingredients for making grenades. "That's just being versatile. Knowing how to make explosives makes you an asset to a team."

"Or in bed?" Fret's eyes crinkled.

Tinder smirked at her. "Oh, no doubt."

Jak shook his head and looked back to Rivlen. "I'm so distressed right now."

Rivlen vacillated between the urge to tease him and the urge to comfort him. The latter feeling was unexpected. "Relax, Jak.

Zidarr aren't allowed romantic entanglements. Even if Malek *did* like restful women—" she shot the mercenaries a dirty look, "—he wouldn't do anything about it. Since we can't communicate telepathically with him, I'm sure your mother's guess is right."

"Must be." Jak nodded firmly. "And for the record, my mother was twenty-three when she had me. That's not *that* young. Though she has admitted that I was an unexpected surprise, since she was apparently taking some contraceptive herb at the time. She'd just started her professional career at the university and didn't want to take much time off, so she took me to work every day. I had a crib in her laboratory. My father used to come by at lunch, when he wasn't off on some dig, and play with me. They took turns teaching me to read so I could entertain myself while they worked. And lots of other professors came by. Apparently, I was cute and interested in everything."

"You sound coddled," Rivlen said.

"I don't know about that. My mother put me to work as soon as I was old enough to wash beakers and fetch dusty old papers from the library. I'm convinced the main reason she taught me to read at a young age was so I could cross-check her footnotes and verify sources for her."

"While being coddled."

"Don't tell me you had it that rough, elite mage soldier who probably had servants to wash her family's beakers."

Rivlen snorted. "We didn't have beakers." She couldn't deny that there had been servants and that her family was well-off even by mage standards, but... "My father wanted a boy, not a girl, and someone who could be accepted into zidarr training. Even though I had the wrong sex organs for him, I tried my damnedest to be good enough to apply for the zidarr training anyway. Few women are picked—not even ten in all the centuries since the inception of the zidarr—but I thought I could do it. I didn't get accepted. My father hasn't spoken to me since."

"Ah. Not living up to the sometimes ridiculous desires of one's parents can be difficult."

"No kidding." Rivlen didn't know why she still cared, but she couldn't help but think that if she could attain greatness through her military career—and one day take Tonovan's place as the supreme commander of Uthari's fleet—maybe her father would deem that a worthy achievement.

The movement outside the window drew her eye again. That janitor had stopped sweeping and was looking up at them.

Rivlen checked him with her senses again, confirming that he wasn't a magical being. But with a start, she realized she recognized him. "Is that Zethron?"

Jak peered out through the broken window. "I think so."

Zethron lifted an arm to wave at them.

"I do *not* trust that man. Why does he keep showing up?" Rivlen had checked his thoughts the last time he'd visited, expecting some duplicity. Given that everyone here was interested in Jak's hatchling, it was conceivable that Zethron could be angling for it too, going through Jak's mother to get it. At the time, Rivlen hadn't read anything like that in his mind, but he could be adept at hiding his thoughts.

"I don't know." Jak waved back.

Zethron wasn't just waving. He gripped what looked like a stack of papers in his hand and... Was that a *rock*?

As Rivlen searched his thoughts, he drew back his arm and threw the rock. The papers were tied to it, and they fluttered wildly as they sailed upward. The rock would have missed the broken window and shattered another pane, but Rivlen reached out with her magic to catch it. She floated it through the opening and into Jak's hands.

Below, Zethron bowed to them. Then he glanced toward one of the exits, as if he'd heard something, and jogged off in the opposite direction with the broom.

His primary thoughts were of being apprehended, and what would happen to him if he were caught helping the *suspicious strangers* again. But under that, Zethron hoped Jadora would appreciate his assistance and take him through the portal with her. He had an aching longing to explore the *First World*, as he thought of it.

Rivlen shook her head. It wasn't hatchlings that he wanted but to sift through ancient ruins on Torvil.

"What is it?" Tezi had seen the arrival and came to Jak's shoulder.

Jak untied twine that wrapped the stack of folded papers and attached them to the rock.

"A map of the area." Delight blossomed on his face. "Oh, I asked for this. I can look for the valley with the ziggurat now."

"The valley guarded by dragons?" Tezi asked.

"Evil dragons, yes. Or younger dragons, as they call them here. I should have asked Zethron about that when he was here. Do you think age is truly a factor? Or is it that mottled dragons showed up later, historically speaking? The visions the portal has given have shown the good dragons and the evil dragons fighting. Maybe that's indicative of a great war that took place." His voice was distracted as he spoke. He'd already spread the map on a table and was running over it with his finger. "It sounds like the good dragons are believed to be extinct or *mostly* extinct." Jak glanced toward where the hatchling snoozed in a nest made from wadded up sheets. "That's why there's so much interest in Shikari and eggs. Maybe people believe that if they can repopulate the species—the good dragon species—they'll defeat the evil dragons."

"We need to focus on getting out of here and reporting to Uthari," Rivlen said.

The map would be useful to show to the king, but it didn't change anything insofar as their mission.

"What's the other page?" Tezi pointed to a second folded paper that had been tied to the rock.

"Oh." Jak opened it, revealing a page of writing in the local language. "I don't know. It looks like a letter. To my mother, maybe? Since she's the only one here who can read this. Too bad she just left."

"We'll show it to her when we break them out of Malek's cell." Rivlen thought about reaching out telepathically to Jadora again, but conveying what were essentially symbols on a page to her would be a stretch of her abilities. Besides, if she was being taken below the arena floor, to the area insulated from magic, Rivlen wouldn't be able to communicate with her again.

Jak refolded the letter, stuck it inside one of his pockets, and turned his attention back to the map.

"There it is!" He plunked his finger down on a valley—it was more of a circular depression—in the mountains. There was a tiny pyramid shape in the center. Jak's ziggurat? "Oh, it's not that far." He traced what had to be a scale, though everything was labeled in the same language as the letter. "Here's the portal. That's only a couple of miles from the city." He pulled a folding ruler out of his pocket and measured the distance, then compared it to the distance from the city to the mountain valley. "Hm, twenty miles. Too bad the skyboards got zapped. We could have zipped over in less than an hour."

"We're not zipping anywhere. We're escaping."

"I know," Jak said, but that didn't keep him from fingering the map and mumbling to himself. He leaned closer to eye a couple of squiggles in the valley. "I wonder what those represent. They look more like air currents than any terrain feature I'm familiar with, but a cartographer wouldn't put something ephemeral on a map."

"Don't prevailing winds always blow in the same direction?" Rivlen asked.

"Predominantly from a certain direction, yes. But this must

represent some localized phenomenon." Jak scanned the map. "I don't see squiggles like this anywhere else. Oh, wait. Here's one other spot." He pointed to a lone mountain jutting up higher than the others in the range, but it was hundreds of miles to the north. "That one looks like a volcano. I wonder if our ziggurat was built in the caldera of an ancient volcano. It looks like a crater, doesn't it?"

"Sure."

Rivlen tapped her fingers on the hilt of her sword, more interested in preparing for their escape attempt than discussing a map they weren't going to do anything with. She picked up the candle tin that Jak had set on the table and thought about lighting it, setting it in the doorway, and wafting the air out toward the guards. Reluctantly, she decided it was still early in the night to enact her plan. It would be better to wait until most people were asleep and the night guards were drowsy from boredom and the late hour.

"Why don't we practice your magic, Jak?" she asked. "Maybe teach you how to attack—in case that's needed tonight."

"In a minute, please." He was still scrutinizing the map.

Maybe cartographers could study maps for hours—or days—without getting bored.

"I wonder if the squiggles represent something like a sulfur deposit. Though sulfur is fairly abundant in nature—at least on our world—so if it were marked on a map, there ought to be more spots." He sucked in a breath, straightened, and gripped his chin.

Rivlen arched her eyebrows. He wasn't trying to hide his thoughts, but all she got from him was that he had an idea, that he might have discovered something important.

"Yes?" she prompted.

He looked toward Jadora's room. "In the book she borrowed from the library, Mother found what she believes is the formula for an acid that might be capable of manipulating the dragon steel. She didn't recognize it by its chemical structure, but we were talking about whether it might occur in nature here."

"Would she be able to make it back home?"

"Maybe, but if it *does* occur in nature here, it might be possible to collect some." Jak dropped his finger onto the squiggles again and looked at her.

"You think that marks where it can be found?"

"It could."

"Why would you think that?" Rivlen failed to see how a couple of squiggles on a map proved anything.

"A couple of reasons. First, it's *right* beside this giant ziggurat, which, from my vision, I believe may be made out of dragon steel. A tremendous amount of dragon steel. If the acid is needed to work the steel, and it happens to come out of the ground right there, then it would have been convenient for them—people or maybe dragons themselves—to locate a temple there."

Rivlen imagined a pool of acid wafting fumes into the air of some valley, disintegrating anything dropped into it. "Can you actually find pools of acid in nature?"

"Oh, it's probably not a pool or a liquid at all. More likely, there would be vents at the surface, with vapor coming out, the result of a chemical reaction in the earth below."

"Vapor? How would you use vapor to work a metal?" A headache was burgeoning behind Rivlen's eyes. She had the urge to start a fight and beat the stuffing out of someone.

"Well, the dragon steel doesn't seem to be *like* any metal we're familiar with, substances that are melted at various heat points, so we can't compare this to that process. It's *possible* that a gaseous form of the acid would be used, but if you use pressure or decrease the temperature of a gas to its critical point, it turns into a liquid."

"Are these things you read about in your laboratory crib as a child?"

"Oh, yes." Jak grinned at her. "I was also a big fan of Draythor the Dragon Rider stories." He tapped the map. "I *really* want to check this place out."

"Don't forget the evil dragons that are supposed to be there," Tinder called from across the room. The mercenaries had plopped down on a couch but were following along.

"That is problematic," Jak said. "Being eaten by dragons leads to disappointing sightseeing expeditions."

"You're a strange boy," Rivlen told him and picked up the candle. "Let's practice magic, so we can break out of here and go home."

Jak cast a longing look at the map, but he did follow her back to the windows for a training session.

They were going to get out of here tonight or die trying. Rivlen swore it.

20

Sorath didn't want anything to do with the questioning of the druid prisoner, but because he and Yidar had captured the green-haired man together, the zidarr wanted to include him. Sorath hoped that was the only reason. He'd been carefully keeping his mind empty of all thoughts related to the druids, especially Kywatha, since helping them in the jungle. He didn't *think* Yidar knew he and Ferroki had intentionally helped her instead of hindering her, but he wasn't positive. Nobody had ever complimented him on his sublime acting skills.

Now, Sorath stood with one of Uthari's guards beside the flap of a newly erected tent while the druid sat tied—with physical rope and magical bonds—to a lone chair set up inside. Yidar prowled around him with his hands clasped behind his back, but if the questioning had started, Sorath couldn't tell. There might have been some telepathic repartee, but mostly, it seemed like Yidar was trying to unnerve the druid while waiting for something.

Outside, the mercenaries and a bunch of servants had been charged with returning the camp to order. Several tents had caught fire, but only Vinjo's had been obliterated. Somehow, the partially constructed framework of his miniature mageship hadn't been disturbed, but he would have to start from scratch with the engine, power source, navigation orb, and whatever other gizmos were required.

Voices sounded outside before numerous red-uniformed mages strode in. With their weapons in hand, they lined up along the sides of the tent, several behind the druid's chair, several in front.

Sorath wasn't surprised when Uthari walked in. Yidar faced him and saluted, and Sorath made himself do the same, though Uthari barely glanced at him.

"Lord Yidar," Uthari said, "I am troubled that one of the druids escaped through the portal, but I am pleased you at least captured one for us to question."

"Had we known there were other keys that could operate the portal, Your Majesty, we could have been better prepared and wouldn't have let anyone use it." Yidar lifted his chin, defiance in his eyes.

Sorath said nothing. He'd learned long ago not to make excuses to employers.

"Are you saying you would have fought harder against the wolves and condors who so easily flummoxed our troops?" Uthari asked.

"Your mages and mercenaries were responsible for guarding the portal." Yidar sneered in Sorath's direction. "I was busy capturing this druid."

Sorath thought about pointing out that the wolves and condors had been giant, magical, and numerous, but he hadn't been there for that fight either and didn't know how the druid woman had slipped past.

"I see." Uthari gazed at his zidarr. With a touch of disappointment?

Maybe that was Sorath's imagination.

During the conversation, the druid sat stoically, facing the tent flap and not making eye contact with anyone, even when Uthari turned to address him. Uthari didn't use Dhoran but some local language that the druid could presumably understand. Since Sorath couldn't, he merely clasped his hand to his pick behind his back and kept his thoughts from churning.

Until the druid spoke into his mind.

Kywatha said you might be an ally. The words weren't in Dhoran, but Sorath understood the druid. *Why did you help capture me?*

Sorath almost replied, but if he did and if Uthari or Yidar or any of these mage guards were paying attention to his thoughts, they would hear the words. He stared at the side of the tent and didn't think a thing.

Uthari squinted over at him. Damn, had he sensed the druid attempting to communicate with Sorath?

"He will not speak with me," Uthari told Yidar. "Not surprising."

"You wish him tortured?" Yidar asked.

"Yes."

Sorath kept from grimacing, though he knew perfectly well what that would entail. The mages rarely resorted to physical brutality—though someone had worked Vinjo over thoroughly—but they knew how to expertly use their magic to inflict pain.

As stoic as Sorath liked to believe himself, he hadn't been able to keep from answering Uthari's questions when his mages had interrogated him. He hadn't blurted anything out loud, but it hadn't mattered. They'd plucked the location of this pool from his mind.

If you are an honorable man, the druid spoke into Sorath's mind, *why work for these tyrants who are invading our land and putting our people in danger? Especially when they also put your people in danger?*

All *people. Were you not here for the first battle? We know the agoratha came through and destroyed many ships and devoured many mages. We hoped they would kill them all so that we could retrieve the ancient gateway and once again bury it.*

The words stopped, as the druid's jaw clenched.

Yidar stood behind the man, his hand on the back of his neck. Magic must have flowed into the druid like an electrical current, for he gasped, threw his head back, and arched his back as much as he could within the confines of his bonds. The chair jerked, but it was also held down by magical restraints.

As agony contorted the druid's face and he panted and gasped, veins and tendons standing out on his neck, Uthari stood indifferently in front of him, his chin clasped in his hand. The guards were just as indifferent. Nobody appeared to enjoy the druid's pain, but nobody protested the treatment.

The gasps turned into screams. Sorath closed his eyes, wishing he were back in Perchver, a glass of lemonade on his desk as the sun came up and he worked on his memoir. At the time, he hadn't appreciated those days of quiet, of forced retirement. He hadn't been able to, not with all the guilt that had lingered after he had survived while losing his men, but he wouldn't have minded some of that quiet now.

He tried not to think about how the druid was right. Uthari and the other fleets were the invaders here, the ones bringing danger to this land, if not the entire world. And Sorath was working for them.

Sorath sighed and rubbed the back of his neck, again forcing his mind to be still. Even if Uthari was focused on the druid, Sorath dared not let anyone sense his thoughts. Kings didn't want their mercenary commanders to be sympathetic to the other side.

It occurred to him that the druid might have given him a hint about what his colleague planned. Should he mention the thought to Uthari? Maybe it would distract him from the torture and give the druid a reprieve.

Sorath kept his mouth shut. He'd already helped one druid when he shouldn't have. If he made a habit of that, someone would notice, and Uthari already knew who to punish to hurt Sorath.

He couldn't keep himself from thinking of Ferroki, her face always serene, even as they endured the frustrating machinations of mages.

After what seemed like an eternity, the screams stopped. The druid's head slumped forward, and blood dribbled from his nostrils and onto the woven grass tunic he wore.

Sorath didn't think Uthari and Yidar would have killed a potentially valuable captive—even if they'd gotten all the information they wanted, he might be useful if a prisoner exchange was ever needed—but the druid was so still that it was hard to tell.

"Is he truly unconscious?" Uthari asked. "Or feigning it?"

"I believe he is unconscious." Yidar released the back of the druid's neck. "Did you get anything useful?"

Uthari turned and looked at one of his guards, then tilted his head toward the tent flap.

"Yes, Your Majesty." The man walked outside.

Since ten other guards remained, Sorath couldn't guess what that was about.

"His duty," Uthari said, turning back to Yidar, "and the duty of the other druids who launched attacks from the trees, was exactly what we believed. To cause a distraction so one of their people could go through the portal. Though they did genuinely wish to destroy the engineer's work. Somehow, they determined that he's making a ship to facilitate exploration through the portal." Uthari gazed over at Sorath.

Sorath didn't have to hide his surprise. He hadn't said anything about that to the druids.

"The druids don't want our camp here," Uthari said. "They don't want it to be easier for us to explore, and they certainly don't want us to find anything out there that would prompt us to stay in their land with the portal active."

"The only reason they *have* this land is because it's worthless and no king has truly tried to take it from them," Yidar said.

Since Sorath was keeping his mouth shut and his thoughts quiet, he didn't point out Yidar's hypocrisy. He'd been out there trying to make an alliance with the druids, and now, here he was scorning them to his master.

"People will fight for their homes, no matter how worthless, because it is all they have," Uthari said.

"What do they think one girl is going to be able to do out there?" Yidar asked.

"She is apparently an expert in using her magic on animals to convince them to do her bidding. He isn't one of their leaders—" Uthari waved to the druid, "—so he doesn't know as much as I would have wished, but he believes she is attempting to bring back an animal or animals strong enough to threaten us."

"Not another one of those worms." Yidar made a disgusted face. "We can defeat another if we must, but that was a pain."

"It was. I find it unlikely that even a druid talented at commanding animals could control such a creature. We attempted everything from physical attacks to mental manipulation on it, but its resistance to magic was so great that little worked."

Except grenades down the gullet, Sorath thought, though even those had done minimal damage.

"But she could find something else to threaten us and lure it back," Uthari said. "If she is permitted to. Several people saw which symbol she activated, so we can follow her as soon as Malek returns with the key. And our archaeologists. The professor is translating a book with information on many of the worlds. She can fill us in on where the druid woman went. Whatever her people plan, they will not succeed. We will *not* be driven away prematurely. A few battles and a few deaths are a small price to pay for what may be gained from exploring these other worlds."

"I agree, Your Majesty."

Sorath gave Yidar a flat look, but neither man was paying attention to him. He preferred it that way and wondered if he could slip away without anyone noticing.

The tent flap shifted aside, and the guard returned with a second wooden chair. He set it down a few feet away from the one the druid occupied, then returned to his post.

An uneasy feeling crept into Sorath's gut even before Uthari looked at him.

"Colonel Sorath." Uthari extended a hand toward the empty chair. "Have a seat."

"You're going to torture me? *Again*? I helped capture your prisoner."

"After you had a secret chat in the jungle with the very woman who escaped through the portal," Uthari said.

"Her cat dropped a magical rock at my feet. I went to see what she wanted." By now, Sorath could hardly be surprised that the employer he'd never wanted would torture him. What rankled most was that Uthari's supposedly loyal zidarr had also gone out to see the druids, and *he* wasn't being questioned. Did Uthari know about that?

"Good," Uthari said. "You will tell us what she wanted, what she offered, and how tempted you were to make a deal with her."

"Not as tempted as your zidarr." Sorath pointed at Yidar's chest. "*He* went out to see her several nights before I did."

"I am aware of what Yidar is up to," Uthari said.

No surprise flickered in Yidar's eyes, so maybe Uthari had already confronted him. Or maybe Yidar had confessed and somehow managed to throw any suspicion in Sorath's direction.

"He is ambitious and wants his own kingdom," Uthari said. "It is an odd passion for a zidarr, but I understand ambition and can work with it. What *you* want, Colonel, is more insidious."

"For you and all your tyrannical mage cronies to die? This may shock your old heart into seizing up, but everyone wants that."

"It's the ones who potentially have the power to make it happen who are problematic. Sit down, Colonel."

"I don't have any power, you sadistic bastard."

"You're irking me." Uthari twitched a finger, and an immutable force pushed Sorath toward the chair. "You should have brought Captain Ferroki along to squeeze your arm and tell you when to keep your mouth shut."

"I'm glad she's not here." What he wished was that she was back in the southern desert, leading Thorn Company on some modest mission that had nothing to do with mages. Because she was here, she would hear him scream, and she would worry about him.

Sorath fought the magical force out of principle, but it didn't matter. He ended up in the chair, with invisible bonds tightening around him.

Beside him, the druid groaned, though his head was still slumped to his chest. Another witness.

Yidar gripped the back of his neck, and Sorath braced himself.

∽

Jadora followed two guards and the clipboard-wielding man down the same stairs she'd attempted to rush down the night before. At the bottom, the same dour-faced guard waited, but now that she had an escort, he didn't stop her.

They descended more than twenty feet, well under the surface of the arena floor, and headed toward one of three cement corridors leading deeper into the complex. Here and there, a mage lamp glowed on a wall, but there was more shadow than light in the underground passage. Distant growls came from one direction, animals in cages presumably, not throaty gladiators snarling at each other.

As she trailed the men, Jadora strove to keep her thoughts still. The last thing she wanted to think about when people were monitoring her was the dragon steel secret or the team's plans to escape.

She hoped she and Malek would be able to speak without being monitored. She realized with a start that they would *have* to speak. He wouldn't be able to communicate telepathically with her anymore.

As much as she would prefer Malek the mundane to Malek the zidarr, she admitted it was handy to be able to speak without being overheard.

She wished she'd thought to grab her backpack, or at least her painkillers and poultice-making materials. Without his magic, he wouldn't have been able to heal his wounds, and who knew if anyone here tended the gladiators?

They turned at an intersection, and laughter came from up ahead, along with more light. How many gladiators were housed down here? Waiting for their turns to possibly die in the arena?

From what she'd seen, only one or two out of five men survived their encounters with the creatures chosen to fight them. And some of the gladiators returned the next day, lowering their probability of survival even further. She had no idea how many battles they had to fight to win their freedom, or their prize—whatever it was they sought—but it was surprising how cheerful the laughing men sounded. Maybe because they were the survivors from the day?

Other noises drifted to her, grunts and heavy breathing. At first, she thought those sounds also came from animal cages, but she and her escort had moved away from that area of the compound.

They turned into an open room with trays of food, bottles of wine, and pitchers of the juices that were popular here. She would have called this a kitchen, or at least a food preparation area for the men who had to be fed, but there were also two young women removing their clothing under the surprisingly bored eye of a guard.

In that moment, the grunts clicked for Jadora. They hadn't belonged to animals but people having sex. She didn't know why she was surprised when the clipboard man had implied that was the reason she was being brought down. A reward for a victorious gladiator.

One of her guards poked her and pointed at a corner where the undressing women were hanging their garments on hooks on the wall.

"You want me to take my clothes off?" Jadora guessed, only catching about half of what they said. "That's not necessary. My relationship with Malek is more intellectual than carnal." Since she could also only speak about half of their words, she doubted she had conveyed that properly.

The guard poked her again and pointed more firmly. "Undress."

She sighed and moved to comply. Intellectual discourse was doubtless a rarity down here.

The women on their way out of the room to service who knew which gladiator eyed her dismissively, then elbowed each other and giggled. The idea of being paraded past cells filled with strange men horrified Jadora, and she hoped Malek appreciated the lengths to which she was going to bring him information. Not that the clipboard man had given her a choice. All along, her team hadn't been given many choices. The suite and idea that they were honored guests was only an illusion.

If she'd brought her backpack, it would have ended up on a hook, so that was one regret she could cross off what was turning into a long list of them. At least, when she walked naked back to the corridor, none of the guards ogled her. Why would they when they had voluptuous women half her age wandering around here? Though this was so commonplace for them that they all appeared far more bored than interested by any of it.

As she'd feared, they marched her past several cells on the way to Malek's. Some of the men already had female partners and were too distracted to glance out, but others gazed out with interest, men who hadn't yet fought perhaps.

When Jadora reached Malek's cell, she found him gazing out with his hands clasped behind his back, still clad in the leather loincloth, though he'd taken off the torso harness and hung it and his weapons on a chair. He couldn't have been surprised to see her, since he'd requested her, but his eyebrows flew up and his jaw dropped when she arrived naked. Since the gladiators could only see out to the corridor and not into each other's cells, he must not have expected that.

He only gaped for a second before averting his eyes. The clipboard wielder flipped an unremarkable lever on the wall, lowering the barrier that held Malek inside. He pointed for her to step into the cell.

Since the barriers were invisible and Jadora couldn't sense magic, she couldn't detect them and had to trust that this one was down. Once she stepped inside, the man flipped the lever again. Locking them in together. Well, there were worse people Jadora could be stuck with.

As soon as the men left, Malek spoke. "I apologize, Jadora. I didn't realize they would remove your clothing." He glanced at her but seemed flustered by her nudity and quickly looked away again. He lifted a hand toward her, as if he might offer some comfort, but he drew it back, first dropping it to his side, then propping it on his hip, then clasping it behind his back again. He opted for gazing at the cement wall in the corridor instead of at her. "I assume this was *their* choice and not yours."

Despite the awkward situation, she was amused by his fluster. That the powerful and experienced zidarr, who'd doubtless seen many naked women over his life, didn't know how to handle a nude archaeologist tickled her.

Admittedly, before today, she'd never seen *his* bare chest either, and it was... eye-catching. In the arena, when he'd been hundreds of yards away, his physique hadn't been as noticeable. Also, she'd been worried that the great bristled predator would get the best of him. It had been hard to admire his strength and agility when she'd kept remembering the dragon battle and that moment when it had caught him and he'd dangled from its massive jaws, fangs piercing all the way through his body. He'd come so close to dying that day. And she was terrified he would fall to a similar—or worse—fate here in this arena. Ogling him hadn't been at the top of her mind.

But now, in this quiet and semi-private moment, with Malek close enough to touch if she wished... it was far easier to let her gaze drop to admire his fit musculature. All that zidarr training had honed his body into a powerful weapon, even without the assistance of magic. A powerful and attractive weapon...

Malek arched his eyebrows, reminding her that he'd said something.

"That's correct," she blurted. "I'm not opposed to taking my shoes off and getting comfortable for intellectual discourse, but that's usually where I draw the line. Especially when it's chilly."

The subterranean temperature was significantly cooler than the night air had been up above, and her nudity made her particularly aware of her gooseflesh. She rubbed her arms, realized that made her breasts jiggle, and jerked them down to her sides. Slave-masters in Hell, she was just as flustered as Malek. Who was she fooling?

"Understandable." Malek swept the lone blanket off an uncomfortable-looking straw mattress, complete with strands sticking through the coarse fabric, and offered it to her.

"Thank you." There was a chair next to a table laden with food and a pitcher of juice and a bottle of wine, so she wrapped the blanket around herself and sat in it. The hard unyielding wood appeared more comfortable than the mattress. "I'm sorry you were injured today."

She waved at the bandages on his side, some of them near where scars remained from his encounter with the dragon. Another bandage covered his shoulder and yet another wrapped around his thigh, easily visible since that leather undergarment didn't cover much of his leg. She tried to give him a sympathetic smile, though she looked away from the lower bandage before her gaze could inappropriately linger again.

"Do you think we're monitored?" she asked quietly.

She didn't see any blatantly magical devices mounted on the walls, but that didn't mean the guards couldn't keep track of what was going on in the cells. Though she wanted to let him know that Rivlen was planning an escape for them all, she didn't want to risk being overheard.

"I'm not certain," he said.

With the blanket covering most of her nudity, Malek seemed less discombobulated. He sat on the mattress and faced her, his gaze intent as he met her eyes. "Did Jak get in trouble today?"

"No. Why would you think he would?"

"I may not have access to my magic, but I could tell someone was healing my wounds—I think there was some poison in that cat's claws. It seemed to be slowing my reflexes, but then the effect disappeared. At first, I thought it was Rivlen, but she has admitted she hasn't trained in the healing arts. I was teaching Jak how to heal wounds the day before yesterday. We didn't speak about poison or venom—or being able to heal someone from afar—but he's proven gifted."

"Yes," Jadora murmured.

"I assumed someone might notice and punish him. Though I can't understand anyone, I gathered that part of the lecture we received before going out to fight was that outsiders—spectators in the stands—were forbidden from assisting us in any way."

"Ah. A squad of guards *did* come into our suite right before the fight and stand behind us as we watched you. Now that you mention it, one did do something magical to Jak at one point and order him to stop. I hadn't realized what he was doing. He might have been punished more, but the hatchling roared at the guard and bit him on the finger."

"He *roared*?"

"It was a squeaky roar, but the bite must have been effective. It convinced the guard not to harm Jak."

"I wouldn't have guessed the ferocity of a parrot-sized hatchling could convince a powerful mage of much."

"He's turkey-sized now, and it was a very earnest roar."

"It must have been." Malek smiled slightly.

Jadora returned the smile, relieved he could make such a gesture now. He'd had his magic taken from him—possibly permanently—and he was the only one of four people who hadn't died in his battle today. She'd worried he would be morose and difficult to speak with.

"Whatever the reason," she said, "they didn't hurt him. Thank you for asking."

"Of course."

It touched her that he genuinely seemed to care for Jak. In the beginning, she had assumed he was only protecting them because Uthari wished it, and that he was teaching Jak for a similar reason. And that was likely true. But it had grown easier to believe that maybe Malek had developed feelings for them and cared for them as people. She was biased when it came to Jak, but she believed he was a good boy and an earnest student. Surely, any teacher would appreciate that about him.

And Malek never seemed to mind when Jak said something irreverent. If he did, it never showed. Perhaps it was strange, since he was zidarr and the epitome of what all those mages stood for, but he wasn't like all the others who got uptight whenever a terrene human presumed to say something that could even slightly be perceived as disrespectful.

"I shouldn't admit it," Malek said, leaning forward with his elbows on his thighs, "but I miss being able to read your mind."

She had no doubt he missed *all* of his magic. Badly.

"I was thinking about how you and Jak seem to be getting along well as teacher and student and that you seem to care about him."

"Yes. And I believe you, but it's strange to have to take your word for it." He offered that slight smile again. "You might be surprised at how often people don't say what they think."

"I'm not surprised."

Malek turned his palm upward. "I did ask for you for a reason. Would you mind filling me in on what's happened this past day? Were you able to get to the library?"

"Yes. Let me sum everything up for you." Jadora spotted upturned cups stacked on the table and grabbed two. "Do you want some water? Er." She peered at the bottle and pitcher and searched for other beverage offerings. "*Is* there water?"

"They took it earlier when they brought fresh food. Apparently, victorious gladiators are supposed to prefer wine to water."

"Wine might not be the best choice." She glanced at his bare chest, blushed, and looked away. Definitely flustered. "Since it lowers inhibitions."

He glanced at *her* chest, making her realize the blanket had slipped to reveal more skin than she'd intended, and he was also quick to look away. "Agreed."

For some reason, his acknowledgment that he might do unwise things with her if his inhibitions were lowered made her body flush. She envisioned being entangled in a lover's embrace with him when Rivlen and the others—Rivlen, *Jak*, and the others —showed up to rescue them.

No, she could not let that happen. Besides, she couldn't forget Uthari's warning to her, that if she attempted to engage in a romantic relationship with Malek, he might get rid of her. Might *kill* her. The bastard.

"Juice then." Jadora picked up the pitcher and sniffed it. It smelled like the tart blue juice that Jak had been enjoying all week. That ought to be safe.

She poured two cups, clasped the blanket around her collarbone, and started to stand to bring one to him. But Malek held up a hand and retrieved it himself.

"Your blanket shifts a little too interestingly when you move." He sat back down.

Jadora resisted the urge to ask him to define *interestingly,* especially since there was more wariness than amusement in his eyes. Maybe he was also thinking of Uthari's threats and what Uthari would do if he found out anything had happened between them.

She sipped from the mug, then launched into the details of her trip to the library and what she'd found in the book, making sure to warn him that everything was hypothetical for now. She also made it clear that she *might* be able to make the formula back home in a lab but that she wasn't positive about it. In a very soft voice, she mentioned Rivlen's plans to escape that very night, if she could manage it. She didn't dwell on specifics such as the candle, lest someone nearby was reading their minds.

Before she'd finished, Malek was pushing a hand through his hair and gazing wistfully at the wall in the direction of the mountains where they believed Jak's ziggurat lay. "Rivlen is right that we should prioritize escaping and reporting back to Uthari, but if we could return with a large amount of dragon steel *and* the knowledge of how to work it... that could be the difference between being able to defend our world effectively from invaders—human and otherwise—and not."

"True, but there's still the option to pull down our portal again and move it to another part of the world where it won't work. If you truly believe an invasion is a possibility." Jadora tried to remember if anyone had actually delivered that threat, or if Malek was only guessing. Her thoughts had grown fuzzy, and she found herself uncharacteristically searching for words.

"Yes, but even if Uthari agrees to that, I think we would find it difficult to talk the other nations into it. The truce that they'd grudgingly agreed to when we left was tenuous at best, and they all believed that if they cooperated, they would get a chance to explore the other worlds and seek out resources for their kingdoms."

"It might have been better if we'd brought nothing but wounds back from our first mission. The dragon-steel axe and dragon egg have everyone convinced that great treasures are out here."

"Aren't they?" He lifted a hand toward the ceiling.

To indicate the arena? Or all the dragon-steel weapons they'd seen here?

Jadora nodded, but for some reason, it had grown harder to follow Malek's words. She found herself noticing the way his biceps flexed when he pushed his hand through his hair. The simple movement affected his chest muscles too, pectorals shifting, shadows stirring in the valley between their swells...

As he took a long drink from his cup, a couple of droplets of the blue juice splashed to his chest. They ran down the curve of his muscle, and the urge to kneel before him and lick them off came to her.

Malek looked at her, and she blushed and looked down at her cup, embarrassed by her thoughts. How long had she been staring? Like some libidinous youth moved by her hormones instead of her intellect? This wasn't like her at all.

She took a drink, willing the tart juice to wash away thoughts of *swells*.

Still watching her, Malek rubbed the droplets off his chest. The movement only prompted his muscles to move again in intriguing ways.

Jadora huffed out a breath and looked at the ceiling. What had they been talking about before she'd been distracted? The library book and the formula, right. "I barely got it copied. Guards came and took the book back, so these people must know what I've been researching. I'm surprised they've allowed me any latitude to explore at all. Though that may be over now. Zethron hasn't even been allowed to come by."

"Good," Malek said, his tone jarringly cold. "I don't want him around, lusting after you."

"Pardon?" She met his gaze, surprised. Oh, she'd gotten the sense that Malek didn't trust Zethron, or like that he was giving Jadora his attention, but he hadn't outright admitted to that.

"He's trouble, and I'm your protector." His gaze drifted to her chest again.

Earlier, he'd jerked it away whenever he'd caught his gaze wandering, but he didn't this time. It lingered. Appraising. *Interested*.

Heat flushed her body. She should have pulled the blanket tighter, but instead she let it slip.

They'd been given this time together, this privacy. Would it be so bad if they made the best of it? They could enjoy the feast, enjoy each other, drink more of the quenching juice...

A flash of insight came to her, and she jerked her head around to look at the pitcher.

"Malek," she whispered, realizing he'd stood, his eyes hooded as he walked slowly toward her. *Prowled* toward her, like the powerful predator he was. "The juice."

He froze.

"What?" he asked, his voice raspy. With lust?

Jadora rubbed her face, a part of her wanting to say nothing and see what happened. But...

"I think it's drugged," she said.

Malek tore his gaze from her and focused on the pitcher. "Hell."

21

JAK STRUGGLED TO CREATE A BALL OF FLAMES OVER HIS OPEN PALM. Rivlen stood in front of him, her own palm open, and a compact fiery sphere rotating slowly in the air above it. It was no illusion. The heat was real, tangible enough that it warmed Jak's cheeks.

She'd demonstrated how to make fire numerous times now, but he hadn't been able to conjure so much as a single tiny flame. Not even a spark.

Sweat trickled down his spine and dampened his hair, a testament to how hard he was trying, but this eluded him, and he was growing frustrated. Worse, he could sense Rivlen becoming impatient.

He *wanted* to learn this—fireballs aside, it would be incredibly useful to be able to conjure flame on a whim—but he couldn't find a cartographical feature that matched up with fire. His attempt to imagine swaths of forestlands that had burned after a lightning strike started a fire hadn't worked. Instead, what he kept seeing was the battle back in Port Toh-drom where Rivlen had hurled walls of fire at an enemy ship before ramming it into a tower where it had burned until it crashed, charred people tumbling out of the wreckage. Malek and other mages had also thrown fireballs in that battle, the flames engulfing people and roasting them alive.

Jak lowered his hand. "Can we try something else?"

"Why are you struggling with this? You've been a quick study with everything else."

"I don't know," he said, though he had a good idea. Fire was deadly, and he didn't want to kill people. Even enemies.

"Let's try the squeeze attacks."

"Is that what you call it when mages wrap invisible fingers around my throat and cut off my air?"

"Yes."

Great. Another way to kill people. Jak wondered if he could yawn and pretend he was tired and needed to rest before they tried their escape attempt.

Learning attacks had been as much his idea as Rivlen's, and he couldn't deny that it would be useful, but the thought of twitching a finger and using magic to kill someone seemed worse than pulling a trigger on a magelock. Not that he wanted to do that either. Before Malek had kidnapped him and started him on this crazy journey, he'd never killed anyone, and he didn't like it that he had now. Even if it had been in self-defense.

"I'm getting your thoughts," Rivlen said.

"Sorry. I'm distracted."

"You don't *have* to kill people."

"That seems inevitable if you throw a fireball at them. I haven't seen many of your opponents walk away only lightly scorched."

"Are you seriously going to be a pacifist? Uthari isn't going to have any use for you if you won't attack people."

"Darn."

Rivlen clenched her jaw. Judging by the frustration and irritation in her eyes, this wouldn't be the best time for Jak to proclaim that he didn't want to work for Uthari.

"I'm sorry." Jak lifted his hands. "I'm not willfully trying not to learn this. I'm just finding it difficult tonight. If we don't have much time, we should practice something I already know."

Rivlen took a deep breath and visibly quelled her frustration. Even though he would prefer not to annoy her, he appreciated that she was trying to calm herself instead of snapping at him.

"Maybe that thing where I funnel magic into people," Jak offered. "Like with your engineer. Or with Malek and the dragon."

"What happened with *Lord* Malek and the dragon? I wasn't there for that."

"I wasn't able to do anything to stop the dragon—our mage-locks and explosives didn't bother it at all—but in the end, I funneled some of my power into him to help him with a final thrust into the roof of its mouth." Jak pantomimed jabbing a dagger home. "I'm sure someone like you or Malek wouldn't normally *need* any help, but since everyone is so powerful here..."

"Yes, that could be helpful. Even powerful mages get tired during an extended battle—that's when such a tactic can be helpful—and you're right. I haven't been able to defeat these people even one on one." New frustration flashed in her eyes, making Jak wonder what had happened at that greenhouse. "You funnel power into me when we face them, and *I'll* make the fireballs."

Jak hesitated. If he assisted her in burning enemies with fire, that wasn't any different from doing it himself, but he reluctantly admitted that if they were going to escape this world alive, he couldn't be squeamish. If they ended up battling dragons, he *definitely* couldn't be squeamish.

Voices came from the corridor, and Rivlen fell silent. Jak used his senses to try to tell if anyone new had arrived. He couldn't tell. The same four guards that had been there all night were still there.

After more discussion, someone yawned loudly. Two of the guards walked away.

This could be our opportunity, Rivlen told Jak telepathically. *Get that candle out, and stuff your hatchling in your sling. I'll tell the mercenaries.*

I guess we won't be practicing my ability to funnel magic.

You already know how to do that. You'll be fine.

Let me know whenever you think it will help. And if you want a steady stream or a quick burst. Jak remembered his first attempt to share his power with that engineer. He'd unleashed it too quickly and hurt the man. He didn't want to hurt her.

Maybe she caught that thought, for she smirked and patted his cheek. *I can handle anything you can give me.*

I'm glad. Jak gripped her wrist and pushed her hand away. For the most part, he didn't mind her company, and he did appreciate the magic lessons, but it grated when she grew condescending or treated him like a boy. Jokes about chest hair notwithstanding, he was a man, damn it.

He only succeeded in pushing her hand away a couple of inches. She smiled, amplifying her strength with her power.

Use magic if you want to push me back, she said. *The mind is greater than muscle.*

Another lesson?

You did ask for them.

He narrowed his eyes and stared challengingly into hers as he drew upon his mountain imagery to wall himself off and try to push her back. In the past, he'd succeeded in forcing her back a step, but she was prepared this time and resisted his efforts, standing as implacable as a mountain herself. His mountains pushed against her, but he felt as if he were pressing his hand against a brick wall and expecting it to move.

Maybe he needed to distract her or try something unexpected. That was how Sorath, using his explosives, sometimes got the best of mages.

The ludicrous thought of leaning in to kiss her came to mind.

But if he did that, she would probably pull out her sword and eviscerate him. After what he'd seen of her memories of Tonovan forcing her against a wall, he didn't want to do anything that would remind her even remotely of that.

Since he'd wanted to practice funneling his magic, he decided to try that. Making her *more* powerful might not be logical as a tactic, but he guessed it would startle her, and that might be all he needed to break her grip.

While keeping his mountain imagery up, his wall of magic pressing against hers, he summoned power from deep within and envisioned sending water flowing swiftly down a canyon. In his mind, Rivlen stood at the end of the canyon, waiting to receive the torrent. He didn't make it as fast or funnel in as much as he could at once—in case she was wrong about her cocky statement—but he did dump power into her abruptly.

She gasped and stepped back, the pressure disappearing as she pulled her hand away. He watched her warily, half expecting her to retake the stance and use his power against him.

She merely clutched a hand to her chest, looking a little stunned. But not hurt, at least he didn't think so. Since nobody had ever funneled power into Jak, he had no idea what it felt like. Maybe he should ask her to do it to him someday, so he could better gauge how it would feel to others.

Impressive. Rivlen smiled at him. This time, it seemed more appreciative than condescending. *Good. You did that while maintaining your barrier. Many mages struggle to master doing two types of magic at once.*

I'm glad you approve.

I do. Her eyes glinted. *And I'm invigorated now. I wish I had enemies to smite before this boost of power fades.*

Jak held up the candle.

She took it, removed the lid, and lit the wick without even looking at it. *Time to do this.*

Malek glowered at the pitcher of juice on the table—the pitcher of *drugged* juice—tempted to knock it across his cell. But he was more annoyed with himself than with its presence. Oh, he couldn't have known the guards would put some kind of libido-enhancing concoction in it—it surprised him that they would even bother—but he should have been suspicious when the servants removed the water.

"I'm sorry I poured the cup for you." Jadora stood beside him, the cell's lone blanket wrapped around her nude form.

It hardly mattered since his brain had imprinted that form into his mind as soon as she'd walked into view. Even if the blanket had been doing a better job of hiding her flesh and curves, it wouldn't have mattered. He was highly aware of what she looked like. What she looked like, how she smelled, the gentleness in her voice, the sympathy in her eyes as she'd noticed his wounds, her fingers stretching out, as if she wanted to tend them for him. No doubt she did.

And he wished she could, that she had her backpack along—the one she'd faithfully carried since he'd given it to her—and could pull out ingredients to help mend his wounds. They didn't bother him overmuch, and it was more the thought of her having a reason to touch his bare skin that appealed. Especially since they couldn't act on the ridiculous impulses that juice was putting into their minds.

Even though a part of him had wanted to act since she'd first walked in, since before he'd taken a sip from that cup.

Malek growled and turned his back on the table—and on her. He didn't trust himself standing this close to Jadora. Never would he have thought that he, with all of his training and self-discipline, could be so tempted to defy Uthari's wishes, to give in to carnal desires.

Had this been a woman who didn't mean anything to him, he could have, and it wouldn't have mattered. But he cared about Jadora. Far more than he was supposed to.

He stalked to the bed, wishing he could leave the cell. Or command the guards to come take her. Could he? That would eliminate the temptation—the threat.

Dear gods, was this the scene Uthari had seen in his vision? Malek and Jadora kissing in this cell? Doing *more* than kissing?

"Malek?" Jadora asked uncertainly. "I know you can't read my mind right now, but I truly am sorry. I didn't know about the juice. I wouldn't try to, uhm, seduce you."

"I know," he rasped, then cleared his throat, annoyed with his lust, annoyed that he kept having to fight down urges to take her to the bed and emulate all the other triumphant gladiators with their prizes. "I'm not angry with you."

No, *anger* was not the problem. The last thing he wanted was for her to believe he thought poorly of her or that she could be a part of some deceit. He'd read her thoughts enough times to know she had no such notions. Even without Uthari's threats, he doubted she would have wanted anything romantic—anything *sexual*—to do with him, not when he was Uthari's faithful zidarr and had been there the night Tonovan killed her husband.

"I know," he repeated, turning to look at her face, to make sure she understood that the problem was him, not her.

Against his wishes, his gaze dipped to her chest, her chest that wasn't fully covered by that blanket. No, the problem was the damn juice.

"The wine might have been safer," he said.

She smiled, though it was wan, her eyes tight with tension. "It's probably drugged too. They must want their gladiators to have a good time."

"It probably makes things more..." He glanced down again and swallowed. "Stimulating."

He jerked his gaze back up to her eyes, ashamed and hoping she hadn't noticed. But she was looking at *him*, her gaze shifting toward his chest. And then lower.

He swallowed again. He'd already been aroused, but her appraisal—her blatant interest—made everything worse.

She lifted a hand toward his chest—to touch him?—but caught herself. "I should go over there." She pointed but didn't look at the chair. She didn't stop looking at him. *Couldn't* stop?

It occurred to Malek that Uthari couldn't truly blame them for this. This wasn't voluntary. If they had sex because circumstances forced them together and a drug made them too randy to resist each other... Uthari would understand.

Wouldn't he?

"Stay with me," he whispered.

"What?" Jadora pulled her gaze back to his eyes.

"Stay with me." Malek lifted a hand to the side of her head, her hair soft against his palm, and brushed her cheek with his thumb.

She stepped toward him, resting her hand on his chest, that simple gesture sending tingles of heat through him. She didn't even seem to care that he was no longer zidarr, that his magic might be gone forever. Others would, but she didn't.

He kissed her, hungry and demanding, unable to do anything except give in to desire. And she welcomed it. She pressed her body against his, her arms wrapping around him, fingernails digging into his shoulders as she kissed him back with an eager intensity that surprised him. He'd expected her to be shy, the quiet academic, but perhaps the drug—even more so than the alcohol she'd mentioned—pushed aside all inhibitions.

The blanket fell from her shoulders, and he growled, deepening their kiss as he explored her body with his hands. She moaned against his mouth, leaning in to his touch, wanting it as much as he wanted to give it.

He lifted her to carry her to the bed, but her fingers tightened and she pulled back from him.

"Wait, Malek." She was breathing heavily, her lips moist from their kiss. "We can't. He'll kill me. He said he would if I—if we..."

Anguish contorted her face. He wanted to wash it away, to give her pleasure, not pain.

"I won't let him," he said before he could catch himself.

That was the drug speaking, and he knew it. He wanted her so badly that he would have said anything. No, that wasn't true. He was still an honorable man. If he'd said it, he meant it.

Except... as long as his magic was gone, he would be powerless to stop Uthari.

He *hoped* there was some way to get this thing out of his skull and reverse the damage—to return his magic to him—but what if there wasn't?

And even if there was, could he truly win against Uthari if he tried to kill Jadora? Malek hadn't tested himself against his mentor since he'd been younger, and then it had only been practice, a part of training, not a true intent to beat him. He didn't know if he could or not.

To be safe, he would have to hide Jadora from Uthari. Where? On some other world? Where he would never see her again?

And for what? One horny night of sex?

She touched his face, and he was sure his own features were as anguished as hers.

"We can't," she repeated, though she still gripped his shoulders, and he knew she didn't want to let go. "Even if he hadn't said that, I don't want to be the reason you defy him. If you ever decide he's a megalomaniacal jerk who shouldn't be followed because he lets people like Tonovan have free rein under his rule..."

Malek grimaced, wanting to defend Uthari, but even if he didn't agree with Jadora's assessment of the existing government system, he didn't disagree that Tonovan lacked honor. He understood that Uthari found the general useful, but Malek did wish he wouldn't allow the man his cruelties.

"I would of course approve heartily of that," she finished, stroking the back of his head and gazing into his eyes, "but that has to be something you decide. I don't want to get in the way."

Malek sighed and set Jadora on her feet, though he dearly longed to take her to the bed and give in to what they'd started. The recalcitrant, passion-driven part of him thought they could get away with it, that Uthari would understand that the drug had overridden their rational minds and *forced* them together.

But would he truly believe that?

Malek closed his eyes, rested his forehead against Jadora's hair, and willed his libido to calm down. And for the guards to return and take her back to her suite before he changed his mind and did something foolish.

~

Sasko helped several members of the company fit poles together to erect a new workshop tent while Vinjo plucked equipment and tools out of the smoldering remains of the old one. Captain Ferroki worked nearby, unfolding the canvas sides, but she kept glancing at another tent, her eyes haunted. Or horrified.

Sasko felt similarly. Until a few minutes ago, Sorath's roars of pain had been coming from within the tent. More than once, Ferroki had tried to talk the two guards who stood outside into letting her in. First, she'd been reasonable, and then she'd tried to sneak in through a slit in the back, but thanks to their magic, she hadn't been able to get past them.

When Ferroki had started shouting at them in frustration, Sasko, Basher, and Words had grabbed her and dragged her away, afraid she would get herself into trouble. Sorath had made a questionable choice in talking to the female druid in the jungle, and

Ferroki had been at his side for it. If Uthari figured that out, he might tie her up in there right next to Sorath.

The flap stirred, and several guards filed out, followed by Uthari and Yidar. Two more guards came after them, levitating their druid prisoner between them. Was he still alive? Sasko couldn't tell.

Ignoring the curious eyes around the camp, Uthari and his people levitated each other up to his yacht.

"At least they're done torturing him," Sasko offered, though she doubted that would make Ferroki feel better.

She tried not to think about the possibility that they might have left Sorath in there because he was dead. They'd worked him over for almost as long as their druid prisoner.

"I should have talked him out of going out to meet that druid. It wasn't worth that." Ferroki glanced toward the yacht, then strode toward the tent.

"Where are you going?" Sasko worried there were still guards in there, guards who might cheerfully torture anyone who showed too much interest in their prisoner.

"To help him in any way I can." Ferroki kept walking and didn't look back.

As Sasko was debating whether to follow her, try to stop her, or simply keep working, Vinjo came out of his tent and jogged up to her side. Given how often he'd been wounded lately, it was amazing he could manage a jog.

"Should we check on him?" Vinjo whispered.

He must have heard Sorath's cries as well.

"Yes," Sasko said.

If only to keep Ferroki out of trouble. Sasko handed her tent poles to Basher and went after her captain.

"I wanted to do something to stop them," Vinjo whispered, walking at her side. "Their torture is awful. I know. But they're too powerful. I'm just..." He spread his arms helplessly.

"Me too, Vinjo," Sasko said.

It was hot and stifling inside, the sun beating on the tent making it even warmer than outside, but at least there weren't any guards. A fly buzzed, the sound obnoxiously loud, and Sasko gulped, worried again that Sorath might be dead, that they'd left his body for them to find.

He lay crumpled on the ground, his eyes closed, a chair upturned behind him. Ferroki dropped to her knees beside him and hesitantly reached out to his shoulder, though she watched his chest. Yes, he was breathing. Thank Shylezar for that.

Ferroki rested her hand on the side of his face, his dark skin uncharacteristically pale.

"The things I have to do," Sorath mumbled, his eyes still closed, "to get a woman to touch me tenderly."

"How do you know that's not Vinjo caressing your cheek?" Sasko thought he would appreciate humor over anyone weeping over him, though he might get both, since Ferroki's eyes were filmed with moisture.

"Because I'm not a wrench." Sorath rolled onto his back, groaned, and opened his eyes.

"I also touch pliers and hammers. And ladies with appealing, uhm, lady parts." Vinjo smiled shyly at Sasko.

"Are you trying to flirt," Sorath asked him, "when you're as scuffed and bruised as an overripe banana?"

And he was that. As if the bruises hadn't been bad enough, the previous night's explosion had given Vinjo cuts that were scabbing over and a welt on the side of his face. He and Sorath both needed to see a healer. Judging from the way Sorath gripped his ribs, the torture hadn't been purely mental.

"That's the best time," Sasko said. "It's easier to get sympathy."

"I agree," Sorath murmured, perhaps because Ferroki was stroking the side of his face.

"Why did they torture you?" Ferroki asked. "*Again.*"

"You know why."

"Because you went out to see a druid? So did I."

"Yes, but you..." Whatever Sorath had intended to say, he didn't finish. He only gazed sadly up at her.

"What?" Ferroki asked.

"It doesn't matter. Better me than you."

She squinted at him. "Is he using me to ensure your cooperation? The way he is Jadora's father?"

Sorath closed his eyes again and turned his head away.

"He is, isn't he? He wouldn't dare torture someone he wants to *work* for him if he didn't have a handle on you. Sorath..." Her voice broke on his name and was hoarse when she added a string of curses.

"What if we all just left? Sorath, Thorn Company, all of us." Sasko looked at Vinjo, doubting he wanted to be here working for Uthari either.

His expression grew wistful.

So did Ferroki's, but she said, "We signed a contract. We're duty bound. Honor bound."

"A contract that he manipulated you into signing," Sasko said. "We weren't even supposed to be working for him. This has nothing to do with honor. We could walk into the jungle and not come back."

"Walk where?" Sorath asked wearily. "It's a thousand miles back to the coast, and there aren't any roads between here and there. We'd be lucky if we made it on foot."

"Well, *clearly*, Vinjo needs to finish his mageship and use it to fly us home."

"Uh, I have to start over with that," Vinjo said. "Thanks to the druids. But if you can wait a few weeks..."

"He's building that for Uthari," Ferroki said. "Not us. Even if we could take it, they wouldn't let us fly away from under their noses."

"Maybe if there was another distraction." Sasko glanced in the direction of the portal, though she couldn't see it through the side of the tent.

"Sure," Vinjo said. "We'll tell the druid lady not to come back until I've got the ship built. Anyone have any idea how we can contact her to make that request?"

"You'd have to find another key and follow her through." Sorath groaned and pushed himself into a sitting position. "Running away wouldn't solve anything long-term. Uthari has the power to blacklist Thorn Company. You'd never get another job."

"I don't know if that's necessarily true." Ferroki shifted her hand to his shoulder, staying close in case Sorath needed support. He did look like he could tip over at any moment. "But I'm more worried about *you* than us."

Sasko lifted a finger. "I'm moderately worried about us."

If that druid came back with another of those horrible worms, what were the odds that Thorn Company could survive unscathed again?

Ferroki frowned over at her. "No mages are torturing *us*."

Vinjo opened his mouth, but he must have decided not to say anything. Maybe he was developing a little more wisdom—or common sense.

"What if the druids try to talk to you again?" Ferroki looked back at Sorath. "Will Uthari keep blaming you? If he doesn't trust you, why does he even want you here? Does he truly think you'll help him after he treats you like that?"

"I don't have a choice if I want him to let my friends live." Sorath didn't look at her, but Ferroki had to know he meant her. "And he didn't say it," Sorath continued, "but I have a feeling he doesn't plan to let me live past my potential usefulness. If he gets to the point where he's solidified his power down here, and isn't worried about the other fleets—or threats coming out of the portal—then it would behoove him to get rid of me."

Sasko fingered the bracelet that Vinjo had given her. As useful as it had been, Sorath might need it more than she did. Since Vinjo liked Sorath, he might not object to her giving it to him.

"Maybe we do all need to leave," Ferroki said glumly. "I wish we could talk all the other mercenaries and the roamers into leaving as well. Leave the mages to defend the camp and themselves on their own."

"A thousand-mile trek through the jungle doesn't get more appealing with more people," Sorath said.

"What if only Sorath leaves?" Sasko asked.

Vinjo looked over at her. Had he glimpsed her thoughts?

"Then Uthari can't torture him," she added.

Sorath looked wistful again, but he shook his head. "Uthari would send one of his zidarr to find me, and they likely could. Or he'd reach out telepathically and threaten those I care about to force me to come back."

"What if they couldn't find you, telepathically or otherwise?" Sasko removed the bracelet and held it up.

"You want to give away my freshly made clandestineness creeper?" Vinjo asked. "That's to protect *you*."

"I know, and I appreciate it, but I think Sorath needs it more." Sasko suspected Sorath would refuse to take it if she gave him an option, so she walked over and dropped it in his lap.

Sorath picked it up and held it out, trying to give it back. Sasko scooted back and lifted her hands to show she wouldn't take it.

"He'll question one of *you* if I disappear," Sorath protested.

Ferroki hesitated, perhaps thinking through the ramifications, then shrugged. "And we'll tell him what happened. We're afraid for you, and Sasko was willing to give up her jewelry to keep you safe. That we would protect you shouldn't surprise him."

"Vinjo would be blamed for creating this," Sorath said. "Uthari destroyed the last one. I'm positive he didn't want more made."

"He didn't tell me that." Vinjo shrugged. "And if he tortures me, it'll slow me down on building the magical components he wants made. Speaking of that, I better get back to work before anyone gives me any details about what the colonel might do if he disappears." He bowed to them and left the tent.

"What the colonel *should* do is walk back to the coast and get a ride to another continent," Ferroki said sternly.

Sorath hesitated. "Yes, that would be the wise course of action." He nodded more firmly. "I'll go back to the desert and finish my memoir."

Ferroki exchanged an exasperated look with Sasko. Neither of them believed Sorath would do that, but if they didn't know what he *would* do, they couldn't reveal his plans if they were questioned.

Sasko hoped neither she nor Ferroki were tortured because of this. She was willing to give up the stealth device for Sorath, but she didn't want to endure excruciating pain on his behalf.

"If you're going to do it," Ferroki said quietly, "you should do it soon. Before anyone rakes through our thoughts and learns you have this."

"I know, but there's one thing I'd like to do first." Sorath reached up and touched her cheek. "If I go AWOL, I won't be your commanding officer anymore."

"No, you'll be a scruffy rogue that Uthari's people will shoot on sight."

"Could you ever see yourself kissing such a person?"

"Perhaps."

They held each other's gazes for a long moment, then looked expectantly over at Sasko.

"I guess that means I should go hold Vinjo's wrench for him," she said.

"I think he'd like that," Ferroki said.

"Oh, I have no doubt."

22

Tezi crouched with the others near the broken window of their suite as a small candle burned just inside the doorway, the curtain pushed partially aside. The bare leg, sandaled foot, and tunic hem of one guard was visible outside. Thus far, he hadn't glanced back and noticed the candle, but Tezi couldn't tell if it was doing anything.

Next to her, Jak and Rivlen were staring intently at it. Making the scent waft out into the hallway, Rivlen had telepathically told them. Since Tezi couldn't smell anything, she assumed it was working.

On her other side, Tinder and Fret crouched. Everyone had their packs, including Malek's and Jadora's packs, with their weapons close at hand. Not *in* hand, because if this worked, they were going to climb out the window instead of using the door.

At first, Tezi had wondered why they couldn't exit through the broken window whether the guards were awake or not, but numerous mages had mentioned being able to sense dragon steel. Presumably, if she and her axe tried to leave the suite, the guards would sense it. They might also sense Jak, Rivlen, and the hatchling, since they all had magic.

The sandaled foot shifted as the guard leaned against the wall.

"It's working," Rivlen mouthed to Jak.

He nodded.

They'd become something akin to colleagues in the past few days. Rivlen had been sparring off and on with Tezi, to help her improve with her axe, but Rivlen, Jak, and Malek tended to speak telepathically to each other and train together frequently. Mages doing mage things. Tezi wondered if Jak recognized that he was being drawn into their world, becoming one of them.

It was none of her business, but the idea distressed her. Maybe because she'd received nothing but grief from mages. She hated the idea of him turning into one of them.

The hatchling's tail flopped out of the sling on Jak's chest. Tezi thought he might stir and make noise—the last thing they needed were tiny dragon roars alerting the guards when they were supposed to be dozing off—but the hatchling lay bundled on his back, his reptilian eyes closed. His eye*lids*. Tezi hadn't noticed it before, but Shikari had them.

The guard's knee bent as he slumped against the wall. A thud sounded. The other one falling down?

The one they could see slid further down the wall, grunted as his butt hit the floor, and dropped his hand down. He uttered a confused moan and started to push himself up, but he only ended up slumping lower. A second later, he tipped over, his shoulder thumping to the floor, his back visible through the curtain.

Rivlen pointed to the window and led the way out. Tezi went second, her axe strapped across her back with her pack, so her hands were free. They were several levels above the arena floor, so she doubted the climb would be simple.

Outside, the air was warm and pleasant, smelling of the sea. The sandy floor of the arena lay dark, and all except a few lamps in the seating areas were out, leaving plenty of shadows to hide their descent. They'd opted for this route since, unlike the corridors and stairways of the arena, there weren't any guards out here.

Tezi climbed carefully in the dark, lowering herself like a spider until she poked her foot downward and there was nothing to rest it on. The wall dropped off—she'd reached a doorway that led out into the seating area or back into the corridors. Rivlen crouched below, waiting.

It didn't look too far down, but the dark made the drop treacherous. Wishing she had more natural athleticism like Tinder, Tezi pushed herself away from the wall, spreading her arms and bending her knees as she dropped. She bumped something as she landed—a statue protruding from the wall next to the doorway—and almost pitched over.

Rivlen reached out and steadied her, then pointed for her to move out of the way. For some reason, it surprised Tezi that she'd helped, but she whispered a *thank you* and stepped aside so Jak could jump down next.

We're going to work together to cleave Tonovan's head off, remember? Rivlen spoke into her mind as the others came down one at a time.

Yes.

I can't let you trip and fall on your axe.

That's reassuring.

Despite the gruff words, Rivlen also helped Fret when she almost tumbled into the seats. Tezi didn't think Rivlen had plans to take their doctor into a battle against Tonovan.

This way, Rivlen told them all, then trotted down the aisle to the low wall surrounding the arena. Without hesitating, she vaulted over it and disappeared from view as she landed silently in the sand.

Tezi gripped the wall and dropped down more carefully.

Rivlen was already running to the big portcullis where the deadly magical creatures were released into the arena for each match.

"Uh." When Tezi caught up, she pointed to two other doors—normal human-sized doors—accessible from the arena floor. "Shouldn't we try one of those?"

I can sense guards in the corridors on the bottom floor, some near those doors, Rivlen said, sticking with telepathy and holding a finger to her lips. *I think we'll be less likely to encounter people back by the animal cages.*

More like the *monster* cages. Tezi hadn't seen anything yet that she would consider a simple animal. *What if we encounter something that wants to eat us?*

Bop it on the nose with your big axe. Rivlen reached out to touch the portcullis and peer into the shadows behind it.

The starlight didn't reach through the bars, and Tezi had no idea if any creatures were waiting for them. What if, instead of cages, everything milled about together in a pen back there?

You may need to bop these bars. They're magical. Rivlen tapped the portcullis and eyed Tezi's axe. *Magical and strong. I guess that makes sense, since those animals are all magical. The wardens—or whatever they call themselves—wouldn't want the creatures ripping the bars open and escaping into the arena prematurely.*

The others had caught up, and Jak gazed toward one of the wooden doors, perhaps having similar thoughts to Tezi.

It's going to make noise if I hit them with my axe, she pointed out.

I know. That's not ideal. If we're caught before we get Malek and Jadora out, there's no way we'll have a chance of escaping. He's got the only intact disc-thing. Rivlen waved at her temple. *Which may be required for us to escape the city barrier.*

Rivlen gripped the bars with both hands and spread her legs, as if she would tear them apart with brute force. But she only glared at them, applying magic instead of muscle.

Seconds passed with nothing happening. Tezi wondered how

long the guards would be unconscious. They'd left the candle burning, but without a mage whisking the scent out into the corridor, it might stop affecting them.

Jak rested a hand on Rivlen's shoulder. Tezi assumed it was merely a show of support, but Rivlen inhaled deeply and closed her eyes, as if she were drawing from deep reserves.

Metal groaned, and she bent a bar upward. She pushed another one downward, then shifted two bars to the sides. Her manipulation of them made enough room for a person to crawl through the gap.

Jak lowered his hand. Rivlen looked back, held his gaze, and nodded. They only looked at each other for a moment, but a weird little magical charge seemed to hang in the air between them.

Mages.

I'll lead. Rivlen pulled herself through the gap first.

As Tezi followed, she noticed Jak peering back toward their suite, or maybe the one above it? She hoped the sleeping guards hadn't been discovered.

Straw littered the ground inside, crunching faintly under Tezi's boots, and the air smelled like a stable. The opening of a wide dark passageway was visible in the back of the staging area. Faint growls and the smacking of lips came from that direction.

Jak joined Rivlen at the front of their group, and they led the rest into the passageway. Even though Tezi couldn't sense magic, the hairs on the back of her neck stood up as they advanced into the compound. Somehow, she intuited how powerful the creatures housed within were—and that they knew her group was coming.

There weren't any lamps, but the walls glowed a faint green as the passageway opened up on the sides, revealing something more like rooms than cages, with magical barriers for walls instead of bars.

Movement to one side made Tezi jump. A quilled feline similar to the creature Malek had battled prowled within the confines of an enclosure, yellow eyes glowing as they focused on her.

Tezi tightened her grip on her axe. She would have preferred the creatures be behind bars, solid and immutable, not something that could go up or down with a hand wave from a mage.

Soft protesting squawks came from Shikari as he peered out of his sling and into the enclosures. Jak made soft, soothing noises and tried to pet him, like one might a kitten or a puppy. The hatchling chewed on his sleeve.

Well, as long as he was doing that, he wasn't making noise.

They came to an intersection between four enclosures holding four growling or hissing creatures that watched them. Sturdy metal double doors were set into the cement floor.

Jak pointed and spoke telepathically so they could all hear—Tezi hadn't realized he could do that. *This might lead out of the arena and maybe out of the city.*

It could also lead into a zoo or heavily secured area inside the city, Rivlen replied.

I think it's our best bet for getting out. The arena entrances will have guards.

We'll see what Malek says when we get him. He'll know the area down here better than we do.

Agreed. Jak peered down one of the tunnels. *I think I hear people's voices in that direction.*

"Let's hope one of them belongs to Malek," Tezi whispered.

"I doubt it," Tinder muttered. "He's not very chatty."

"I hope one of them belongs to Jadora," Fret said. "She's the one I'd hate to leave here."

Jak frowned at them, though Tezi didn't know if it was because they were speaking aloud—it wasn't as if the mercenaries had the option to speak telepathically—or because they were denigrating his new mentor. He didn't say, only heading off in that direction.

There are a couple of guards up ahead. Rivlen pointed to a T-intersection, two cells sunken into the wall on the far side visible, the lighting a little brighter up there. The cells were smaller than the animal enclosures. Rooms for the fighters? *I can't sense the gladiators, since none of them are magical, but I sense magical weapons and two guards with power, one in each direction up there.* Rivlen gestured to the left and right passages.

We'll try to take them by surprise, Jak replied.

Rivlen stopped and gripped his shoulder. *The auras of all the creatures may be hiding us for the moment, but if we can sense the guards, they'll sense us as we get closer.*

We'll have to fight then. I don't see that we have a choice.

And they'll alert their buddies, and we'll never get out of the arena. Don't we have any more candles? Rivlen pointed to one of the two packs she had slung over her back. It belonged to Jadora.

Jak hesitated. *Yes. But if they'll sense us, who's going to place the candles?*

Rivlen looked frankly at Tinder and Tezi.

Fret looked relieved that nobody looked at her. Tezi didn't blame her.

I can do it, Tezi thought, hoping Rivlen was monitoring her thoughts, *but won't they sense my axe?*

A lot of the gladiators in the cells have magical weapons. Rivlen waved. *Unless the guards are paying sharp attention and notice it on the move, you should be fine.*

Tezi frowned. What if the guards *were* paying sharp attention?

As Jak pulled two candles out of Jadora's backpack, Tezi thought about leaving her axe with him, but if she was discovered and had to fight, she wanted the powerful weapon with her.

Jak handed one candle to Tezi and one to Tinder, pointing to indicate that they should split up and each set one as close to the guards as possible without being detected. Since the cells were full of gladiators, the voices promising that not all of them were sleeping, Tezi was skeptical that would be possible.

We'll come right after you and help if you're discovered, Rivlen told them.

Tinder grimaced, but if she had a response, it was in her head, and Tezi didn't hear it.

As soon as we light the candles, you'll have to hold your breath so that you won't be affected. Place them close to the guards and back away before inhaling. It doesn't have to be right under their feet. We can waft the air toward them. Jak nodded toward Rivlen, who was apparently the air-wafter.

Tezi eyed the intersection, doubting she would be able to hold her breath as long as this would take, but she nodded. She would do her best.

Ready? Rivlen held up a finger.

Wait until our people are almost out of sight to light the candles, Jak suggested. *So they have more time to breathe.*

"Breathing is good," Tinder muttered.

Rivlen waved for them to go.

Tezi and Tinder headed toward the intersection, shoulder to shoulder, their weapons in one hand and the candles in the other. Groans reached their ears from down one of the passages, and Tezi remembered that Jadora had been taken off to be Malek's *prize*. She hoped they weren't the ones groaning and were instead ready to be broken out of their cell.

Just before Tezi and Tinder reached the intersection, Rivlen warned, *Hold your breath.*

Tezi inhaled deeply. The candle in her hand lit.

She peered around the corner. The passageway was empty in both directions, save for the gladiators trapped behind barriers, but there was a larger open area off to the left beyond the cells. A guard room? She hoped so.

Tinder headed toward a similar open area in the opposite direction.

Hoping none of the gladiators were watching the corridor, Tezi hurried off, careful not to make a sound. Most of the men she passed were sleeping. A couple had sex partners, but they were under the blankets with their attention occupied. Nobody was watching the corridor.

Tezi almost breathed a sigh of relief but remembered not to exhale. Her lungs were already protesting that, so she picked up her pace.

She almost missed noticing Jadora and Malek in one of the cells. They sat side by side on a bunk, Malek bare-chested and Jadora naked under a blanket she'd wrapped around herself. Thankfully, they weren't engaged in sex, though Malek had an arm around her back, and she was leaning her head against his shoulder. Had their expressions been more relaxed or ebullient, Tezi might have thought they'd engaged in it earlier, but they looked tense and miserable.

Malek spotted Tezi and nudged Jadora. She noticed the candle right away.

With her lungs aching for air, Tezi couldn't stop to pantomime a message to them. She only nodded, hoping to convey that she would return, and kept going.

When she reached the last cell in the corridor, the larger open room only ten feet ahead, she heard rustling and a sigh come from it. The guard?

Not wanting to risk getting closer with her magical axe, Tezi set down the candle. Hopefully, that was close enough for the air-wafting plan.

Someone spoke from the cell to her left, making her jump. A gladiator with a suspicious squint sat naked in his bunk, looking at her. He raised his voice and asked what might have been a question.

She smiled at him and lifted a finger to her lips.

It didn't work. He sprang to his feet and called out for the guard.

As Tezi backed away from the candle, a man with a dragon-steel sword ran out of the guard room. Damn it. If that sword protected him from magic the way her axe did, the candle might not work on him.

Tezi turned and sprinted back the way she'd come, sucking in a big breath and hoping the others could deal with the man. She passed Jadora and Malek, who were now standing at the front of their cell, ready to act as soon as someone lowered their barrier. Unfortunately, Tezi didn't know how to do that.

A shout came from behind her, no doubt an order to stop.

Tinder had set down her candle in a similar spot and was running back toward Tezi. Before they reached the intersection, another guard stomped into view behind Tinder, and a magical grip wrapped around her. It forced her to a stop so quickly that she almost dropped her sword.

Tezi sensed a whisper of power, as if the guard behind her was trying to stop her as well, but her axe protected her. She reached the intersection and could have sprung around the corner, but she didn't want to leave Tinder.

Could Tezi help her by handing her the axe? Or gripping her arm while she held it?

Tezi took two steps in that direction, but something flew out of an open cell to her side. An empty pitcher.

Even though she spotted it and tried to jump out of the way, it shifted its trajectory to strike her legs. Tezi tripped and went flying. She might have caught herself and landed in a roll, but more pieces of tableware flew out and battered her. Her elbow struck the hard floor, and a painful twinge came from her funny bone. Her fingers spasmed open, and her axe flew free.

Swearing, she scrambled after it, but a magical grip caught her. Her hand was inches from the haft, but it might as well have been on the other end of the corridor.

Tinder was only three feet away but still frozen. She groaned.

Footfalls came from the corridor—Jak, Rivlen, and Fret? Tezi feared the guards would only catch them too. Hadn't Rivlen admitted that the mages here were more powerful than she?

The guards spoke to each other from opposite ends of the long corridor. One pointed at the candle and lifted a leg to kick it. They were both standing close to those candles—was there any chance at least one would succumb to the tainted air?

The guard with his foot in the air paused when Jak and Rivlen sprang into the intersection. Rivlen spotted Tezi and Tinder, must have decided they were in the way, and launched a fireball at the guard in the other direction.

He snarled and created a barrier around himself. As the man focused on this new threat, the magic gripping Tezi disappeared. She lunged and snatched up her axe.

Tinder was still trapped, held in place by the guard behind her. Power whispered past Tezi again as he attempted to extend his magical grip to her, but again, the axe protected her.

Tezi squeezed past Tinder and strode up the corridor to face the guard, to *fight* him. He was more than a foot taller than she and also carried a dragon-steel weapon—a big two-handed sword. Her heart pounded as cold fear gripped her, along with the certainty that this wouldn't go well for her. But what choice did she have? They had to get rid of these guards, or they would never be able to escape.

Stop, Jak spoke into Tezi's mind. He was creeping up the corridor in the opposite direction, his back to the wall as he tried to reach Jadora and Malek's cell while Rivlen and the guard hurled magical attacks at each other, fireballs skimming past in front of him. Hopefully, he had a barrier up around himself. *The candle is still lit.*

He was right. Tezi couldn't see the one she'd set, but the one Tinder had placed burned a few feet in front of the guard she was facing. He was crouching with his sword up, waiting for Tezi's approach, and not paying attention to it.

Don't get close, Jak added.

But it won't work on someone carrying dragon steel, will it? Even as Tezi asked the question, she noticed that the guard's eyes were glazed.

He should have charged straight at her instead of waiting for her approach, especially with more threats behind her, but he was locked in one place. His grip loosened on his sword, and he swayed from side to side. He blinked slowly, confusion and grogginess taking over his face.

My mother's herbs aren't magical, Jak said. *Dragon steel won't keep them from working.*

The guard tipped sideways, shoulder hitting down and his head clunking against the wall. For a second, his eyes opened in surprise, but he only settled onto the floor and went to sleep.

"I'm free," Tinder whispered, slapping Tezi on the shoulder.

They turned to help Rivlen, but her guard was already struggling to defeat her. He wasn't far from the candle that Tezi had placed, and it was still burning. Even though the fight was keeping him alert and awake, the scent must have been affecting him. He glanced suspiciously at the candle as he raised an invisible shield to block another fireball. He snuffed out the flame with a thought, then launched a blast of energy at Rivlen.

Rivlen and Jak must have had barriers up, for they didn't budge, but the power rushed past them and knocked into Tinder. She tumbled backward, crashing into Tezi. Tezi barely stayed upright, steadying Tinder the best she could.

"Jak," Rivlen blurted. "Help."

Jak nodded and focused on her, even as the guard stomped toward him, his weapon hefted and murder in his eyes.

Tezi had no idea what Jak did to help, but Rivlen launched another attack, strong enough to make the guard halt.

Rivlen stood with her hands outstretched toward him, her shoulders tense. The man went rigid, his back arching. Someone relit the candle and magically nudged it closer to him.

Tezi hoped Jak was taking his own advice and holding his breath, because he wasn't that far from it now.

The guard bared his teeth, blasting Rivlen with a counterattack. Once again, Tinder was the one to take the brunt of it. Swearing, she ran around the corner to join Fret and get out of the line of fire. Tezi followed, though she wasn't sure if she should stay to help.

But Rivlen had the guard tight in her grip, and he couldn't escape. With the candle sending fumes up to his nose, his eyes grew bleary. He swayed and eventually pitched over, the same as his colleague.

"There should be a switch," Malek said.

"I tried it." Jak flipped a barely noticeable switch on the wall. "Nothing happened."

"I think one of the guards broke it when he realized who we were trying to get," Rivlen said.

Jak toggled the switch up and down. Nothing happened.

Malek and Jadora watched him, their noses as close to the barrier as they could get without being zapped. Malek tapped something against it—the dragon-steel axe he'd acquired from the dead gladiator in the arena. Tezi expected it to destroy the barrier, but it only bounced off. He took a bigger swing, but the result was the same.

Did that mean their belief that they might be able to force their way out through the city barrier with a dragon-steel weapon had been wrong?

Rivlen jogged over to join Jak and gesticulate. If she was speaking, it was telepathically and privately.

"I don't know *how*," Jak whispered in frustration. "There must be some kind of backup. Do the guards have keys?"

He glanced at Malek.

"Not that I've seen." The metallic disc gleamed at Malek's temple, a reminder that he had no magic with which to help.

"Put out the candles," Jadora said, sounding a little groggy, "or Dr. Fret, Tezi, and Tinder will have to carry us all out of here."

Rivlen snuffed the flames without glancing at the candles.

"Won't the guards wake up now?" Tinder whispered from behind Tezi.

"Not for a few minutes," Fret said, though she probably didn't know any more about the candles' powers than the rest of them.

"At this rate, we're still going to be *here* in a few minutes." Tinder waved at Jak and Rivlen, the cell barrier still intact.

The hatchling squawked.

Jak winced at the noise, though it might not have mattered. By now, numerous gladiators were talking loudly to each other in their tongue, and the guards had likely raised an alarm before they'd fallen asleep. Reinforcements could arrive at any second.

Abruptly, the barrier dropped. Malek and Jadora hurried out of the cell.

"Do you know where your clothes are?" Malek asked Jadora.

"Why? Is this attire not appropriate for escape attempts?"

"*No*," Jak said.

"It lacks pockets," Malek pointed out.

"That is egregious," Jadora said, ignoring her son. "I took them off in the room past that unconscious guard."

"Find Lord Malek some clothes too," Rivlen suggested. "So he doesn't look like an escaped gladiator."

"I've got your pack, Malek." Jak tilted his thumb over his shoulder. "I assume there's a change of clothes in it."

"Good," Malek said, but he ran off with Jadora toward the room she'd indicated. Though the temptation to get out of that loincloth had to be great, Malek wouldn't let her go off alone.

Jak pointed at the empty cell and whispered to Rivlen, "Were you the one to bring down the barrier? What did you do?"

"I thought *you* did it," she said.

Jak shook his head.

Together, they looked at the hatchling. Shikari squawked at them.

Tinder cleared her throat. "We should get out of here."

Jadora returned with her clothes, but Malek's must have been taken somewhere else. Jak handed him his pack, and Malek dug out a set of his familiar tan and brown clothing.

"I wish we had an extra set of your magic in there too," Jak told Malek as they dressed quickly.

"Yes," was all he said.

"We'll find a way to return you to normal," Jadora said.

"Didn't the ruler say that wasn't possible?" Rivlen asked.

"We'll find a way," Jadora repeated.

Tezi thought one less zidarr in the world would be a good thing, but she didn't say it out loud.

Tinder had been shifting from foot to foot, but she spun to peer back the way they'd come.

"Did you hear something?" Fret asked.

"I'm not sure," Tinder said. "This is just taking too long. People must know we're here by now."

One of the gladiators yelled something as he pointed angrily at Malek.

"Lots of people," Tinder added glumly.

Once everyone was dressed, Malek took the lead. They left the corridor of cells, and he ran straight toward the double doors in the floor that they'd noticed earlier.

But before the group reached them, a huge, quilled cat prowled into the intersection. It stood on the doors, faced them, and growled menacingly.

"I don't think it's the *people* we need to worry about," Tezi whispered.

23

The great cat's menacing growl floated down the passageway toward them as it crouched low, its porcupine-like quills gleaming in the pale green light emanating from the walls. Well over ten feet tall at the shoulder, it looked far larger here than it had from the suite above the arena. Far deadlier.

Surprisingly, it didn't charge them. It waited on the double doors in the floor, guarding them.

Jadora had just slung her backpack over her shoulders, but she eased it off, mentally inventorying what she had that might help.

"This looks like a situation for grenades." Tinder dipped a hand into the pouch on her belt.

Malek gripped her wrist to stop her. "If you use those in here, you'll drop half the arena on us." He nodded up to the arched ceiling, more than a few cracks visible in what was likely centuries-old cement.

"As long as it drops on that huge cat too."

Malek slanted her a cool look.

"Fine, fine." Tinder lifted her hand from her pouch. "But our regular weapons aren't going to hurt it."

"Here." Malek handed the dragon-steel axe he'd gained in the arena to her.

Though she gaped in surprise, Tinder sheathed her sword and accepted it.

"We're going to have to kill it," he added. "And quickly. The last time one of these was let out to impede me, Etcher Yervaa showed up right after I killed it."

"Isn't that a reason *not* to kill it?" Tinder asked.

"It's on the doors we want to use," Malek said.

"The doors that might not lead to anywhere we want to go," Rivlen pointed out.

"It's also blocking the way to any other doors. Follow me. I'll try to get on top of it. The rest of you keep it distracted or strike from the flanks. Rivlen and Jak, do what you can with your magic." Malek strode toward the cat without waiting for replies.

Jadora wished he would let Rivlen handle it completely with her magic. But the great cat was also magical, so that might not be enough.

Fret stayed back with Jadora as the others advanced, gripping her medical kit and shaking her head, as if she were already sure the group was doomed.

Rivlen launched a fireball over the heads of the others. It crackled and roared down the passageway toward the predator, but the flames parted before striking it in the face. The halves of the fireball hit the cement walls and dissipated while doing nothing to the creature.

The cat roared, and Jadora winced, imagining platoons of guards showing up at any second to assist it.

She rooted in her backpack. Unlike Tinder's grenades, her small explosives wouldn't bring down the walls or ceiling. They might not hurt the beast through its quill armor, but they might distract it.

The cat swiped at Malek as he tried to get close. He parried its slashing claws with his sword. When the head came down, jaws snapping, he deflected the bite with his main-gauche.

With the cat focused on him, Tinder ran past to one side of it while Tezi went to the other. They leaped for the creature's flanks, their dragon-steel axes swinging, but as the cat in the arena had done, it pulsed magic, knocking them back before the blades could bite in.

Jadora pulled out her explosives. They would make noise, but did it matter? Between the guards, the yelling gladiators, and the roaring cat, half the city had to know about this escape attempt.

Screeches sounded as Tezi got through with her axe, the blade slicing through several metal-like quills and cutting into flesh. As the quills tinkled to the cement, the cat roared and spun away from Malek to face her.

He took advantage, springing into the air so high that his head almost hit the ceiling. Someday, Jadora would ask him how his muscles were still magical when he couldn't draw upon his innate power.

Malek landed atop the cat as it lunged at Tezi, driving her back into the side passage. He cursed as his feet came down on the quills, and she feared they were slicing through the soles of his boots and into flesh. That didn't stop him from thrusting downward with his sword, targeting the cat's vertebrae.

It bucked, trying to throw him off, but Malek crouched low and kept his balance. He pulled his sword out and plunged it down again. A feline roar turned into a shriek of pain.

"Incoming," Jadora called just loudly enough for her teammates to hear and tossed one of her explosives past Jak and Rivlen.

They were standing together, Rivlen using magical attacks different from fire now that their allies were all around the cat. If Jak was helping, Jadora couldn't tell, but she would prefer he stay back with her and Fret. The deadly creature had a tendency to attack whoever succeeded in hurting it.

As she had the thought, her explosive blew under the cat's belly. It flinched, its quills rippling, but didn't seem otherwise wounded. That didn't keep it from spinning back toward her.

"I've got a barrier up across the passageway," Rivlen said as it rushed them.

Even though Jadora heard her, she sprang back, afraid of the icy yellow eyes that pinned her. But the cat ran into the barrier and couldn't penetrate it.

It snarled and whirled to the side to greet Tezi as she charged again. She'd been about to swing that axe, but huge claws slashed toward her face.

She ducked low as they whistled past overhead and almost lost her footing. She half skittered and half threw herself back from the cat.

Malek plunged his sword into the creature's back again. His blade sank deep with each blow and had to be doing damage, but the cat remained focused on those on the ground.

Tinder, now behind their foe, rushed in and lopped half of its tail off with her axe. The cat yowled and spun toward her.

Though Tinder jumped to the side, in the tight quarters, there wasn't far to go. Her shoulder crashed into the wall, and the cat caught her, jaws snapping down on her other shoulder.

As she screamed, Jadora could only cringe in sympathy, wishing she could do more to help.

Malek ran up its back to try for its head. He sank his sword between its quills and into the back of its neck, just behind the skull.

A screech ripped from the cat's throat, and its entire body stiffened. Dare they hope it was a killing blow?

As Jadora readied another explosive, the cat sprang into the air, shaking like a wet dog. Again, Malek somehow kept his balance on its back. But the cat didn't give up. It dropped to its side and rolled sideways.

Malek jumped free a split second before it would have crushed him.

"Pin it down," he called.

To Rivlen? She was the only one with enough power to comply.

He landed on his feet and ran back in before the cat could rise. This time, he targeted its face. Though the head was in motion, jaws whipping over to snap at him, he leaped over them and plunged his sword into one of its eyes.

Once again, it screeched, and it tried to leap to its feet to attack him, but Rivlen must have succeeded in pinning it down. It remained on its back, flailing like an upended turtle. Tezi and Malek rushed in, weapons carving into its exposed underbelly.

Tinder's face was twisted with pain, and blood soaked the shoulder of her shirt, but she hefted the axe with her left hand and joined them in cutting into the creature. It thrashed wildly—one paw clipped Tezi, sending her tumbling into the wall—but it couldn't rise.

Though it took dozens of blows, the group finally succeeded in slaying it. The big cat collapsed on its side... on the doors.

"Uh," Jak whispered. "How much does that thing weigh?"

Malek lifted a hand, as if to levitate it off the doors, then dropped his arm, a rare disgusted expression crossing his face as he remembered his lack of power. He looked toward Rivlen.

"Got it," she said, waving for them to move back.

As the group gathered on one side, Tinder gripping her mangled shoulder, Rivlen used her magic to levitate the cat off the doors. A few broken quills tinkled down.

"The claws have a weak poison on them," Malek told Tinder, glancing at Jak. "You'll need treatment as soon as we get someplace safe."

"Someplace safe?" Tinder asked around clenched teeth.

"Where will *that* be? I haven't been safe since we rowed out to that volcano weeks ago."

"Almost done." Rivlen let the cat's body flop down in one of the side passages.

Malek ran forward and tried to tug a door open. "Locked. Rivlen? Or Jak?"

"They're magical." Rivlen squinted at the doors. "Even stronger than the portcullis in the arena. I can't wrench them open."

"One of you two will have to thwart them another way."

"I don't think a fireball is going to work," Rivlen said.

"Another creative way," Malek said.

"Creativity isn't my strength," Rivlen admitted. "I excel at brute magical force."

"Let me see if I can figure out the locking mechanism," Jak whispered.

"Or the hinges," Jadora suggested.

They weren't visible on this side, but she assumed they were underneath.

Jak snapped his fingers. "Like the tower in Toh-drom. Right."

Those hadn't been *magical* hinges, but Jadora hoped whoever had crafted these doors had been more focused on them and the lock than on how they connected to the framework.

"I think there's a big bar under the doors," Jak said, his eyes closed. "If we could knock it loose, the doors should fall open, but I can't budge it."

"It's held in place magically," Rivlen said. "I already tried to move it."

"Ah."

A few soft buzzes came from the side passages.

"What was that?" Tinder lifted her axe and peered left and right.

"Some of the barriers went down," Rivlen said.

"The barriers to the enclosures of the *monsters*?" Tinder asked.

"Several of them. Yes."

"We're not going to survive a fight against more than one creature at a time." Tinder waved at her shoulder. "We might not even survive another fight against *one*."

Malek drew his blades again and faced down one passageway as a massive lizard shambled into view. Farther back, a blue-furred bear the size of a house growled and trundled out of its enclosure.

A hiss came from the passageway in the opposite direction. A snake large enough to swallow them whole slithered out.

Jadora gripped one of her explosives, though she was more inclined to use it on the doors than the creatures. Tinder was right. They couldn't win against so many.

"Are you *sure* this isn't the time for grenades?" Tinder demanded as Tezi stepped into position to face the snake.

Already, the creatures were walking or slithering toward them. More buzzes sounded. More enclosures being opened?

"Grenades won't do anything against magical doors," Rivlen said.

"What about the cement *next* to the door? If there's a tunnel down there and we collapse its ceiling…"

"That might work, but we have to guess right." Jadora pointed to the four-way intersection. "Does it go left to right or that way to that way? Or maybe the tunnel isn't under the passageways at all."

"The animals will be able to follow us if we blow a hole in the floor," Malek warned, his eyes locked on the approaching lizard.

In another twenty feet, the creatures would reach them.

"We're all going to die, aren't we?" Fret gripped Tinder's arm.

"Shikari," Jak whispered. "You brought down the barrier to Malek's cell. Can you open this door?"

"Does he *understand* you?" Tinder asked.

"Sometimes. Sort of." Jak peered at the hatchling, as if he was willing telepathic images into Shikari's mind. Maybe he was.

"Reassuring."

The hatchling climbed up onto Jak's shoulder and emitted a determined but squeaky roar. It didn't sound threatening, but Jadora hoped it would work. Maybe the creatures knew about dragons and feared them.

But they kept coming, not intimidated by the noise.

"The doors, Shikari," Jak whispered. "Not roaring."

The hatchling sprang down from his shoulder, startling him. Jak lunged to catch Shikari, but he was too slow. If jumping down from such a height hurt the hatchling, he didn't show it. He ran out onto the doors. Maybe he understood?

Shikari roared again, the reedy sound echoing from the walls. This time, the creatures paused and looked at him.

They were a hundred times larger than the hatchling, so it was ludicrous that they might be worried about him, but a couple of them sniffed at the air. Maybe they thought a mother dragon was nearby. Were they smart enough to have such thoughts?

"Oh," Jak whispered, some idea coming to him while his hatchling continued to roar. "Let me try..."

Jadora had no idea what he tried, but a moment later, a loud clank came from below.

"Shikari." Jak sprang for his charge as the doors swung downward.

The hatchling squawked and jumped into the air, flapping wings that were still not large enough for flight. But he did hover in the air for a couple of seconds, long enough for Jak to grab him.

"Down," Malek barked, though he kept his weapons up and indicated the others should go first.

Tinder and Tezi scrambled into the dark pit without hesitating. They splashed into water, but it didn't sound that far down.

The creatures were prowling closer again. Jadora slung her pack back on, grabbed the edge of one of the doors, and swung down as the others followed.

She splashed down into four inches of water, almost slipping on the slick cement underneath. She caught herself on an equally slick wall, moist growth lining it like a slimy carpet.

"We have to close the doors again," she said. "So they can't follow."

"On it," Rivlen said as the lizard's head came into view above.

It hissed, a forked tongue darting out.

Before any of the creatures could think about jumping down, the doors swung upward, closing with a clang. The pit—or tunnel?—had already been dark, but now it was black, not a hint of light seeping down. The air was fresher than Jadora expected, though it smelled heavily of saltwater and seaweed.

"Duck," Rivlen said. "I'm levitating the bar back into place."

"What did you do to open the doors, Jak?" Malek asked as metal scraped above them.

"Promised Shikari that Rivlen would capture some more fat caterpillars for him once we got back out in the grass," Jak said. "The first time, I suggested there were probably insects down here for him. He was skeptical. Apparently, tunnels aren't known for insects."

"You had that detailed a conversation with your one-week-old hatchling?" Rivlen asked.

"He's closer to two weeks now, and it was mostly images. That's how we negotiate."

"You can't just tell him what to do?" Rivlen conjured a yellow light, revealing that they were in a tunnel, not a pit, and that the walls were full of damp algae and even a few barnacles.

That gave Jadora hope. This had to connect to the ocean.

"Not that I've noticed," Jak said. "It's a bit like negotiating with the portal. I have to convince it that it wants to do things."

"Like smite your enemies?" Rivlen asked.

"Yeah."

Something clawed at the metal doors.

"Before long, they'll figure out that their animals didn't get us,"

Malek said, striding off down the tunnel. "And they'll know where we've gone."

"Are you sure that's the way out?" Tinder asked.

"The ocean is in this direction."

"I'm not sure that answered my question," Tinder whispered to Fret.

Fret only shrugged. "At least we're not dead."

"Yet," Tinder grumbled.

Jadora followed Malek, eager to put distance between them and the arena, in case someone came along, opened the doors, and let the animals into the tunnels. But she glanced at Jak for confirmation on the route. He always had a good sense of direction.

He'd gathered Shikari back into his sling and nodded at her, as if he knew what she was wondering. "It should be about a mile to the coast. Hopefully, there aren't any impediments along the way." He eyed the water sloshing about their ankles as they walked. "And hopefully the tide isn't on its way in."

Jadora looked at the algae-covered walls again, his words bringing a fresh reason for alarm. She'd assumed this was the way the gamekeepers brought animals to the arena—the tunnel had to lead to a harbor and ships—but that didn't mean it was always accessible. All the water-loving growth on the walls suggested the tunnel regularly filled with tidal waters.

"If it's only a mile, we should be all right," Jadora said.

Assuming the possible *impediments* he'd brought up didn't appear.

She hoped the tides didn't rise and fall a lot more quickly here than on Torvil. The days and nights had seemed about the same length, but she hadn't had a chance to observe the moon—or moons—yet, so she couldn't say.

"I hope so," Jak said. "I would hate to delay Shikari's meal. I did promise him those fat caterpillars."

"And that *I* would catch them?" Rivlen asked.

"You're more adept at the task than I am." Jak glanced at her as they walked side by side. "You have more creativity than you give yourself credit for. You can do a lot more than throwing fire around."

"I guess. But I'm *good* at fire."

Malek glanced back at them, though he didn't comment. He merely continued forward, his sword in hand. Was he lamenting that he no longer had access to fireballs or any other kind of magic?

Jadora scooted past the others so she could walk at Malek's side. Behind them, Jak offered to try to heal Tinder's wound, at least as much as he could while they were on the move.

"Are you doing all right?" Jadora asked Malek.

"I have not been injured since the arena battle."

"That wasn't what I meant." Jadora gave him a sidelong look. "Though I'm glad about that."

He didn't answer her question, though he returned the look, calm and detached, rather than full of ardor—full of *lust*—as it had been earlier.

The effects of the drugged juice had mostly worn off for Jadora as well. She'd gotten past her intense desire to wrap her arms and legs around him and beg him to satisfy her every womanly urge, but she felt as wrung out from the hour they'd spent resisting temptation as from worrying about Jak and the others during the fights with the guards and the cat.

A part of her wondered if she would regret passing up what might have been her only opportunity to be with Malek, but the probability for regret in the opposite direction had seemed far greater. If an impulsive moment in a foreign land had resulted in Uthari punishing him—or killing her—it wouldn't have been worth it. She reminded herself that she shouldn't want to be with Malek anyway. He wasn't... an option.

Though he seemed much more human and approachable without his magic. She'd grown somewhat accustomed to the power he radiated and the fact that he could read her mind—*had been* able to read her mind—but having that disappear had been… appealing. To her. She knew it had to distress him greatly, and since they might have to fight again to escape this place, it would be far better if he had his powers.

She'd promised she would try to find a way to safely remove that device from his head, so he could access his magic again, and she would. They had both halves of the kerzor Zethron had given her. As soon as she could, she would return to studying them.

A part of her, however, couldn't help but hope that they would return, that Uthari would find out Malek could no longer fulfill the duties of a zidarr, and that he would dismiss Malek from his service.

Forced retirement. A time when Malek might be free to pursue a second career, if he wished. As a scholar? An archaeologist? Someone Jadora could *date*?

She gazed sadly at him, doubting he would know what to do with himself if he were no longer following his code and risking his life on a daily basis. Could she truly imagine him as an academic, trundling around a library with stacks full of books? Would she be attracted to him if that were all he was?

Yes, she decided. She appreciated Malek the protector, but she liked it most when his eyes twinkled because she was stuffing the tenth new specimen of the day into her pockets or mixing up some new concoction to vex enemies with. She liked the smart man who'd figured out right alongside Jak that the constellations on the portal symbolized all the worlds it could create a connection to. She could be happy with academic Malek, or farmer Malek, or weapons instructor Malek. Whatever he might decide to be if his magic never came back to him.

But could *he* ever be happy that way? She didn't know and

decided it wasn't fair of her to wish that fate on him, no matter what she desired.

She rubbed her face, not sure when *he'd* become something—someone—she desired. Long before the juice, though she hadn't admitted it, even to herself.

"I can no longer read your thoughts," Malek said quietly, for the others weren't far behind. "But I can hear the cogs in your brain whirring."

"Over the splashes of our feet? Impressive." Jadora lifted one of her legs, noticing that the water was higher now. It had risen from their ankles to their calves.

"Yes," Malek said.

"Yes, you are impressive? Or yes, you have excellent hearing?" She smiled and tried not to think about the water level. Hopefully, Jak had been right in his estimate of the ocean only being a mile away. Thus far, the tunnel had been straight, so it shouldn't take them long to travel that distance.

"Is there not scientific evidence to support the idea that when a man loses one sense, the other ones grow stronger to compensate for it?"

"I've heard that said, but I don't know if there's evidence." She also didn't know if that applied to *magic*. Was it truly considered a sense, like vision, hearing, or touch? "Most likely, you just pay more attention to the remaining senses and come to rely upon them more."

"Hm. Are you worried that we'll face more enemies and won't make it back?"

"That's a concern, though it isn't what I was thinking about. I wondered... I hope, for your sake, that you get your power back, Malek, but I was wondering what would happen if you didn't. If you can't do the things you've always done for King Uthari..." That was vague, but she didn't want to bring up assassinations and kidnappings. She knew him well enough now to know he preferred more honorable ways to deal with enemies, regardless. "Do you think he'll still employ you?"

Several seconds passed, their feet stirring the water as they walked, before he answered. "I would not be able to hold the role of zidarr. He would likely find some other use for me."

"Ah." So he hadn't contemplated leaving his king to pursue a second career. She wasn't surprised, but she couldn't help but ask, "No chance you'd want to retire?"

"Contrary to what Yidar believes, I am not *that* old," he said.

"I know you're not. I've seen you shirtless. You're very... firm."

"Yes."

"All that training."

"I am glad you're able to appreciate it." He gave her another sidelong look. "You wish I would remain like this? Firm but without magical powers?"

"No," she said quickly, though she'd been fantasizing about—or at least contemplating—exactly that. Compelled to honesty, she added, "I *thought* about what it would be like, but I know it's not what you want, and I don't want to wish for anything that pains you."

For some reason, the words stirred emotion in her, bringing a lump to her throat. At the realization that what he wanted and what she wanted were different things?

He was still gazing over at her, but she looked forward, not wanting him to see the moisture that threatened her eyes. What a silly time to worry about relationships that couldn't be.

"Most women," he said quietly, "would have little interest in a zidarr who lost his powers."

"I doubt that's true." Though maybe it was among mages. What did she know?

"It is so. Perhaps the vestiges of the drugged juice are addling your judgment."

"Is that a joke?" she asked.

His delivery was deadpan, and she couldn't tell.

He smiled. "Yes. Even addled, you are wise." The smile faded, his eyes turning sad. Maybe he was thinking about some of the same things she was.

"Thanks. I think."

"You are welcome."

"I remember when you neither thanked me nor welcomed me. You've come a long way, Lord Malek." She knew it had nothing to do with the fact that he'd lost his powers. As far as she could tell, that experience hadn't humbled him. At least not yet.

He responded only by resting his hand on her shoulder for a moment. She wished they could hold hands, but Tinder asked whether Fret believed her new axe had been a gift or if Malek only wanted her to hold it for him, and that reminded Jadora that they were far from alone.

Malek lowered his hand, and they walked together in silence.

24

A MAGICAL PORTCULLIS SIMILAR TO THE ONE IN THE ARENA stretched across the tunnel exit. Beyond it, waves lapped at the stone breakwaters forming a harbor. A few ships were moored at the docks, but Rivlen didn't see or sense anyone about.

Since it was well into the night, maybe that wasn't surprising, but she kept expecting guards to come charging after them. Or to be waiting ahead for them. Whoever had let all those animals out of their enclosures knew their group was escaping. It was hard to believe the rulers would let them go without a fight. Dare she hope their team had irked them enough that they wanted to be rid of their foreign visitors?

"Doubtful," Rivlen muttered, then stepped past Malek and Jadora.

Neither of them could open a magical portcullis, a hard fact to accept. Malek still looked like the fit warrior he was, and he'd performed as admirably against the cat creature in the tunnels as he had the one in the arena, but it was strange to walk past him and not sense his magic. Before, he'd been like a lighthouse on a dark night, beaming his power for all to sense. Now, he was no different from Jadora or one of the mercenaries.

It was distressing to realize that the young and inexperienced Jak was the only other mage present. Quasi mage. Mage in training. He'd shown promise and learned quickly, but until he could launch a fireball, Rivlen couldn't imagine springing into battle with him at her side.

No, that wasn't true. He'd funneled his power into her, first so she could break through the gate in the arena and then again when she'd faced the guard and the creature. He'd been helpful. Even if she, for some reason, wanted to envision him in Uthari's military colors, striding into battle, his arms up and with fire dancing about his fingertips, he was a good ally as he was.

"Can you open it?" Malek asked. "Or does Jak need to negotiate with the hatchling again?"

Shikari had fallen asleep on his back in Jak's sling, his forelegs crooked in the air, his tail drooping over the side. That seemed to be his favorite position, belying all the artists' representations of how dragons slept. They were usually depicted curled up like dogs with their snouts on their tails.

"I think so." Rivlen gripped the bars with her hands, once again amazed at how strong the magic was in the simple tools of this world.

These grates weren't even dragon steel, but the power infusing them made them almost as indestructible. In the future, whenever she was tempted to grow cocky about how much power she had, she would remember this world and how the mere guards at some spectator entertainment venue were stronger than she.

She poured her power into the metal, willing it to bend. This portcullis was identical to the one in the arena, and she realized she might not be able to handle it alone. She hated to ask for help with Malek watching. Even though she doubted he would judge her, especially when he was dealing with his own predicament, she couldn't help but feel weak for needing help.

But Jak once again assisted her without her having to ask. An immature part of her felt disgruntled at his assumption that she needed help, but she did, and he knew it. She should be grateful. Besides, his power was invigorating and somehow gentle at the same time. Appealing. When she'd had a superior mage funnel power into her before, years ago in her early training, the energy had felt smug and condescending as it flowed into her. She hadn't forgotten that sensation.

The metal creaked as it bent, first one bar and then several others. Rivlen squeezed through the hole first, drawing her sword as she landed on a rough cement walkway half submerged from the rising tide. After another check for guards, she waved for the others to follow her out.

They strode up to dry ground, finding a ramp that led to a dirt path that followed the coast, and headed in the direction of the portal. A wider trail led up through the tall grass to the city and likely the main road, but they stayed near the coast, where they should be less likely to encounter people.

"Keep an eye out for dragons," Malek said. "The people here risk their lives whenever they walk out of the protection of the city's barrier."

"I'm sure I'll sense them if they're close." Rivlen glanced uneasily at the night sky, clouds obscuring the stars. If she were relying solely on sight, it *would* be easy for a dragon to fly close before they noticed it.

"Of course," Malek said. "It just occurred to me that the reason guards might not be out here waiting for us is because dragons could be in the area."

"Was it necessary to mention that?" Tinder also glanced skyward. She was walking with her hand pressed to her shoulder and, if her grunts and cursing were indicators, in pain from her injuries. "I was about to ask if we could stop and have Jadora and Dr. Fret smear some herbs and healer goo on my shoulder."

"Healer goo?" Jadora asked.

"Sergeant Tinder is unwilling to learn the names of medications," Fret said, "even though she greatly appreciates having them applied to her wounds."

"I do." Tinder shifted her shoulder. "Though this actually doesn't hurt as much as it did before. I was afraid I would pass out after Lord Malek said the claws were poisoned. I know you were all looking forward to carrying me."

"I've been trying to help," Jak admitted. "I'm still very new to healing, and it would probably be easier if I weren't distracted by the need to not trip and fall in the ocean, but hopefully, it's helping a bit. I assume you don't mind."

"Mind?" Tinder asked. "I may kiss you. Even though I don't get excited by boys."

"I'm a man," Jak pointed out.

"Yes, yes, the chest hair. I remember the discussion about how you're sprouting it copiously these days."

Jak sighed.

Rivlen smiled and nudged him with an elbow. Since he'd been assisting her all night, she refrained from joining in the teasing.

"We should wait until we reach the portal and get back to our world for healing goo," Malek said, gazing at the city and still watching the sky.

Yes, they had a couple of miles to walk before reaching the portal. After a while, another trail cut up through the grassy hills toward the road. Rivlen paused, about to ask if they should take it, but she could sense the portal now. It was still farther to the south.

Relieved that she could sense it, she quickened her pace, taking over the lead from Malek. Soon, they would be out of this place, hopefully never to see any of these people again.

"Do you think they'll follow us back?" Jak asked, making Rivlen wonder if he'd somehow glimpsed her thoughts.

"Yes," Malek said without hesitation.

Rivlen frowned back at him. "You can't be sure, my lord."

"The ruler told me as much."

"She told me too," Jak said glumly.

"Didn't we decide she's a liar?" Rivlen asked.

"Let's hope," Jadora murmured.

The sky was lightening with the approach of dawn when they reached the next trail leading up through the grass. With all the rolling hills in between, they couldn't see the portal, but Rivlen sensed it. And she didn't sense any dragons.

"Don't forget caterpillars," Jak said as they started up the trail. "I'll try to find some too, but you have that special touch."

Roused by the light, Shikari was sitting up in his sling and peering intently toward the grass. All that fearsome roaring must have made him hungry.

"I'm glad you're suitably admiring of my touch," she muttered.

"I am."

As they traversed the hills, Rivlen and Jak used their magic to sweep insects out of the grass and into the hatchling's mouth. The sun came up, warm on their faces, and with gulls crying and the waves roaring, it was almost pleasant. But Rivlen started to get the feeling that they were walking into a trap.

She scoured the area with her senses, but the only thing magical she detected was the portal. And it felt the same as the last time they'd been by it.

"This has been too easy," Malek said, voicing what they were all thinking.

"I agree, my lord," Rivlen said. "But I don't sense anything."

They walked up a slope, and the top of the portal came into view. It was located on the next hill over.

But as they climbed higher, people also came into view. A *lot* of people. At least fifty, all standing in front of the portal, all carrying weapons. All placed to ensure the visitors wouldn't escape.

Since she didn't sense them, Rivlen's first thought was that they were terrene humans, but she didn't see any metal discs glinting at their temples. And several of the men were armed with blue-black blades that looked like dragon steel.

"You didn't sense *that*?" Malek halted and pointed at the army.

Jak shook his head. "I didn't either. I still don't. They must be camouflaging themselves somehow."

"Not from sight," Malek grumbled.

"We should walk up and berate them for their half-hearted approach to stealth," Jak said.

Malek shot him a dirty look.

Rivlen stared bleakly at the small army. Should their group run? Was there any point? Where would they go?

Several silver glowing carriages were parked behind the portal. If they ran, they would only be chased down. Rivlen was surprised the troops weren't already marching toward them.

She looked to Malek, happy to defer to him, though it occurred to her that, without his magic, he wasn't technically a zidarr anymore. Maybe she should posit herself as the logical leader of this mission now. Except that she didn't *want* the lead.

"I don't suppose you can roar and scare them all away, Shikari?" Jak whispered.

The squads of soldiers parted, revealing someone who glowed silvery white, the nimbus around her even brighter than that around the carriages. Even though Rivlen still couldn't sense the people, she had no doubt this was someone important. One of the rulers?

Malek sighed.

The woman wore a hood, and the nimbus from her glow kept anyone from seeing her face. It was like looking into the sun.

"One of the etchers?" Jadora guessed.

"Yes," Malek said. "Etcher Yervaa."

As the woman strode forward, Rivlen spotted someone else she recognized behind her. Ambassador Rajesk. She half-expected to see Zethron there, that he'd warned his ruler-lover about the escape attempt, but it wasn't as if the group had successfully sneaked out without making a noise or leaving a sign. The whole city had likely heard them.

Come forward, Yervaa boomed into their minds, magical compulsion filling the words.

Rivlen found that she could resist it, but it didn't matter. Malek, Jadora, and the mercenaries lurched forward, walking like puppets toward the portal. Seeing Malek unable to resist such a command was bizarre.

Jak glanced at Rivlen—he'd also resisted it—but started walking after the others. They had little choice. They couldn't abandon the rest of their group to these people.

Rivlen trotted around them to put herself in the lead, though Malek refused to let her pass him.

"I want to protect you," she told him. "All of you."

"That won't be possible. We'll have to negotiate with her."

"Do you think she likes caterpillars?" Jak asked.

"Doubtful."

"For future trips, we should pick worlds populated only by dragons and not people," Jak said.

"That might not be any better." Malek didn't look at the hatchling but toward the distant mountains.

If that disc hadn't been gleaming at his temple, Rivlen would have asked if he sensed something she couldn't yet detect. Maybe simple human intuition had him checking the skies.

You agreed to battle in my arena for three days. Yervaa shared the words with their whole group, though her hooded face was turned toward Malek as they climbed toward the army. *I thought you were a man of your word.*

Malek lifted his chin. *You are the one who lied to me. You never intended to let my comrades go or to give us the secret of the dragon steel. You only sought to ensnare me.* He jerked his finger up to point to the disc. *For your entertainment.*

I would be a fool to give our advantage away to strangers who might one day lead an invasion party to our world.

Your world that is infested with human-eating dragons? Malek asked. *Nobody would want it. It is you who want our world.*

"I was imagining the negotiations would go differently," Jak whispered.

"I can't hear what he's saying—thinking," Jadora admitted. "Only her."

"He called her a liar."

Jadora nodded without surprise. "I've seen him negotiate with druids. It went similarly."

Since you will not entertain us in the arena, we have no more use for you. Yervaa lifted an arm, as if to give the order to attack.

"Jak." Malek glanced back. "Will this portal help you?"

"Yeah," Tinder said. "Bolts of lightning striking down our enemies and clearing a path would be extra appreciated right now."

The ambassador rushed to the ruler's side before she gave a command. He cleared his throat and bowed nervously several times, though he didn't presume to touch her.

Whatever he said, the message was for her alone.

She pointed not at Malek but at Jak.

"I'm trying to communicate with it," Jak whispered. "I think they sensed that."

Rivlen hadn't—Jak had gotten better at pinpoint telepathy. But maybe not pinpoint enough for these sensitive people. They *were* right next to the portal.

After Rajesk finished, Yervaa addressed Jak. *You will step away from the others if you do not wish to be killed.*

I don't wish for them *to be killed either.* Though Jak replied to Yervaa, he was focused on the portal.

Rivlen didn't know why it would pay attention to him—this wasn't the one on Torvil that he'd established a rapport with—but she hoped it would work.

Let us go, Malek thought, his words barely noticeable since he could no longer project them telepathically. If the ruler wasn't paying attention to him, she wouldn't even hear them. *If you do not, others will come looking for us, and they are far more powerful than we are. You will regret having made an enemy of our people.*

Yervaa turned toward the mountains beyond the portal. A dozen whispered conversations rippled through the army.

"I heard the word dragon," Jadora said. "No, *dragons*. The word hasn't changed since Ancient Zeruvian days."

A chill went through Rivlen as she sensed the dragons for herself. Two of them. She couldn't yet see them flying down from the mountains, but she knew they were there, just as the ruler and her army did.

"Dragons?" Fret asked. "Coming here? Should we hide?" She looked forlornly at the waist-high grass. It offered few hiding places.

"Any chance they're allies to your hatchling?" Jadora asked Jak.

"I don't think so."

The dragons soared into view, their scales gray and brown and dull under the sunlight, not blue and gleaming like Shikari's.

"Let's get off the hilltop." Malek pointed toward lower land. "And hope they target the army of more powerful mages instead of us."

"We could hide behind the portal," Jak said. "I'm communicating with it. I don't think it's interested in helping me against the people that live here, but that device attached to it ensures it'll attack dragons that come near it."

"What about Shikari?" Jadora said.

Jak wrapped an arm protectively around the hatchling. "It should recognize him now."

"We'll circle around and try to reach it from behind." Malek drew his sword and waved for the group to follow him.

Etcher Yervaa lifted her arms as she faced the dragons, and her troops raised their weapons. With that many mages, they would have a lot of combined power. Maybe they could successfully drive off the dragons.

Though if that were true, would the dragons be flying so assuredly toward the army?

"Try to activate the portal while they're distracted," Malek told Jak as they ran around the bottom of the hill. "Maybe we can slip away."

Jak pulled the medallion out of his pocket. "We'll have to get close enough to insert the key first."

Malek took it from him. "I'll take care of it."

"Won't the army just follow us?" Fret asked. "To escape the dragons if not to give chase to us?"

"Maybe," Malek said, "but this is their world. They should stay to defend it."

Rivlen was surprised they weren't jumping into their carriages and fleeing to the safety of the city. Maybe there wasn't time, and they knew it. Those dragons were flying *fast*.

The mages threw the first attacks, launching fireballs and lightning bolts. Not surprisingly, strong barriers surrounded the approaching dragons and deflected the magic. Brilliant white beams of energy lanced from Yervaa's palms toward the great scaled enemies, but they also bounced away before reaching them.

"I'm trying to convince the portal to attack the dragons," Jak whispered, his eyes closed. The group had stopped in the depression between two hills, the back of the portal visible above them. "I gather the device on the side won't activate unless the dragons are very close. It's meant to zap enemies coming out of the portal, not flying around above it."

Malek crouched next to him, his sword ready to defend Jak. Frustration tightened his eyes; he doubtless wanted to do far more than swing his blades.

Rivlen waited beside them in the grass. She would have happily let the locals handle the problem, but one of the dragons headed for Yervaa and the army, and one veered toward their group.

Shikari let out an alarmed squawk.

Jak swore, again covered him with a protective arm, and jumped to his feet. "It's like in my vision. They're going to target Shikari."

Malek rose, stepping in front of Jak, and Tezi did as well as she hefted her axe. As helpful as that dragon-steel weapon was against humans, Rivlen doubted it would protect her from an actual dragon.

As magical attacks bounced off its defenses, the dragon dove straight for Jak—straight for the hatchling.

Rivlen wrapped a barrier around the group, hoping she could keep it up against such a powerful foe.

"Take cover behind the portal," Jak yelled as he ran up the hill. "Close enough that the device will get them."

Rivlen cursed at him, afraid he would be plucked up. She couldn't run and keep a barrier around the group at the same time.

"Jak!" Jadora ran after him with one of her explosives in hand.

"The portal said it will protect us if we get close enough," Jak called over his shoulder.

Malek swore and rushed after Jak as the dragon plummeted at him, talons outstretched.

Lightning shot out of the portal at the dragon. Rivlen thought it would deter their attacker, that it would save Jak, and it did branch and wrap all around the dragon's invisible barrier, but as with the mages' attacks, the power wasn't enough. It made the dragon glance at the portal, but that was all.

It didn't alter its dive. It stretched its talons toward Jak.

Rivlen extended her barrier over him, but the dragon plunged through it as if it were nothing. The jolt of its destruction snapped painfully in her mind.

At the same time, Malek sprang, powerful legs sending him farther than humanly possible. He crashed into Jak's back and knocked him to the ground as the talons snatched at the air where Jak's head had been.

"Shikari," Jak blurted as he rolled away, still trying to protect the hatchling.

The mottled dragon landed in the grass nearby. Malek roared and ran at it with his weapons raised.

"Is he *insane*?" Tinder demanded.

"Give me that." Rivlen snatched the dragon-steel axe from her and rushed to help.

As she ran, she launched fireballs at the creature's scaled head, hoping to distract it from Malek.

Up on the hill, the second dragon attacked the army from the sky. It hadn't yet gotten through the collective barrier they'd formed. The device on the side of the portal flashed blue and threw a magical attack that succeeded in knocking the dragon away from the army. Maybe taking cover behind the portal *was* the best option.

More lightning launched from the portal itself—not the device—and slammed into the dragon harrying Jak. Its barrier dropped, and the lightning struck its scaled side.

The dragon shook its body, as if it felt something slightly irritating, but its eyes flared yellow, and it gave no indication of pain.

One of Rivlen's fireballs struck its neck, but it was as if the flames blasted pure dragon steel. They did nothing.

Their dragon leaped over Malek, trying to get to Jak. Malek sprang twenty feet into the air and slashed at its belly. The dragon seemed surprised—maybe it hadn't encountered a human who could jump that high before—especially when the lesser-dragon-steel blade sliced into its scales.

It screeched and raked at Malek with its back talons. He twisted in the air as gravity took him back to earth, somehow avoiding what should have been a direct hit.

"Up here!" Jak called.

He and Jadora had reached the back of the portal and crouched beside it. His hand was on the framework, and as he yelled for them, more lightning shot out of it. Unfortunately, it did no more damage than before. Rivlen could hardly believe it. She'd seen the portal back on Torvil decimate enemies. It had knocked out Uthari, one of the greatest wizards of their time, and blasted the powerful druids into helplessness.

Rivlen made it to Malek's side, but the dragon had flown out of reach. "Jak's not going to be safe up there, is he?"

"No." Malek waved for the mercenaries to run up to join Jak and Jadora. "But at least the portal provides some cover. And we may be able to activate it and slip away."

The dragon that was attacking the army, still unable to pierce their barrier, shifted its focus. It flew toward Jak—no, toward the portal. With a thunderous roar, it flew into the top of it and knocked it over.

Jak grabbed his mother, and they sprang to the side just before the portal would have crushed them. More lightning shot from its framework, branches striking both dragons, but the device attached to the side had either been damaged or couldn't launch its magical blows from the dirt.

"So much for that idea," Rivlen grumbled.

As one of the dragons flew toward Jak again, Malek ran up the hill to protect him.

Determined to get a blow in with the axe, Rivlen charged after him. She gave up on fireballs and sent a pinpoint blast of energy at one of the dragon's yellow eyes, trying to drive her magic into what she hoped was a vulnerable spot.

It struck like a dagger, and the dragon's head jerked to the side. It terminated its dive early and flapped its wings, ruffling the grass all along the hillside as it flew back into the air.

The dragon soon banked to come around again, that eye squinting at Rivlen. Unfortunately, it hadn't burst and wasn't noticeably damaged, but at least she'd hurt their powerful enemy.

Just as she was feeling good about that, the dragon shifted and dove toward her. A magical attack ripped her barrier away again, and she braced herself for pain, but it didn't come. The axe glowed blue in her grip, its magic protecting her from the dragon's magic.

Rivlen had grabbed it because it could harm the dragon, not truly expecting it to protect her from its attack, but she huffed a relieved breath and launched a counterattack. Another pinpoint strike toward the dragon's head.

This time, it was paying attention to her. It ducked its head, and her spear of energy surged harmlessly past it.

The dragon landed in the grass and sprang toward her. Rivlen swore and dove to the side. The axe wouldn't keep her safe from a *physical* attack.

Lightning from the portal slammed into the side of the dragon, throwing the creature off slightly. Rivlen managed to scramble through the grass and away from it. As it chased after her, a glint of metal flew past above her head. Malek's main-gauche. It spun toward the dragon and struck, lodging in its nostril.

The scaled head whipped back, and the dragon used magic to tear the blade free. The distraction gave Rivlen time to reach the others, the group now crouching next to the toppled portal. The army continued to attack the other dragon, but most of their power went into maintaining their barrier and protecting themselves. Rivlen shook her head. All those mages, and they couldn't defeat one dragon?

"What's the plan?" Rivlen sensed Malek's main-gauche on the ground and levitated it back toward him.

Malek caught it. "Thanks."

Blood dribbled from the nostril of their dragon attacker, but nothing yet had badly hurt it. Still, it paused and crouched in the grass on the hillside, looking from Jak and the hatchling to the army and Etcher Yervaa.

The locals had lowered their barrier so they could unleash a full attack at their dragon. A barrage of fireballs and beams of energy slammed into it. Someone with a bow fired dragon-steel arrows. Several punctured its scales and lodged in its side.

"They might succeed in killing them." Malek held up the key. "Is there any chance you can get the portal back up, Jak and Rivlen? This is our chance to—"

The dragon that had been attacking their group sprang. Instead of angling for Jak again, it flew over the downed portal and toward the army. Intending to help its fellow dragon?

The army still had its barrier down as they continued to focus their attacks on their target. They didn't see the new threat coming from the side.

Jadora called a warning in their language, but the army didn't react quickly enough. The dragon arrowed toward Yervaa, talons outstretched.

She cried out in surprise and whirled toward it. As the talons grasped for her, she whipped a protective barrier up around herself.

Mages all around her switched their attacks to the closer threat. The ambassador stood to the side shouting. None of it kept the dragon from grabbing Yervaa—no, her *barrier*. Talons wrapped around it and lifted it—and her—from the ground. She was protected, like an embryo inside an eggshell, but that didn't stop the dragon from flying into the air with her.

Though injured, with a dozen arrows sticking from its scaled hide, the other dragon wheeled and flew after its ally. Rivlen joined the army of mages that launched attacks after the lead dragon, trying to knock their ruler free from its talons. Rivlen sensed Jak funneling extra power into her, and against any other foe, she was sure they would have won, but the dragons had erected barriers again. They flew off toward the mountains, Yervaa in her bubble dangling from one's grip.

One of the dragons spoke into Rivlen's mind—probably into everyone's minds: *If you wish the return of your leader, send the hatchling to our lair.*

Jak groaned and slumped against the fallen portal, his arm still wrapped around Shikari.

"Why do they want that runt dead so badly?" Rivlen demanded.

"I don't know," Jak said, his eyes haunted.

Dozens of voices rose in argument, and Rivlen turned with the axe raised, expecting the army to stampede toward Jak to try to tear the hatchling free from him. What did they care about a baby dragon from another world?

Someone shouted orders, and most of the mages ran, not toward Jak and the others but toward the carriages. They piled in, and all except one of the magical conveyances rolled away from the portal.

Rivlen expected them to charge off across the hills and toward the mountains, but one after the other wheeled onto the road and back toward the city. Only the ambassador and a couple of mages remained, their heads together as they conversed rapidly. One carriage also remained, that one fancier than the others and glowing a bright silver. It must have belonged to the ruler.

"Uh," Tinder said, "what just happened?"

"They're going to the city to gather the other rulers and reinforcements," Jadora said. "Then they'll go after the dragons. There aren't any roads to the mountain lair, so they'll have to go on foot and on... I believe the word they used must refer to those large pack animals we saw when we first arrived."

"Why aren't they demanding the hatchling?" Malek asked.

"I have no idea. They didn't mention us at all. I think having their ruler kidnapped has superseded any interest they have in us." Jadora looked at the portal. "They may also believe that the portal is damaged so we can't go anywhere." Her gaze shifted to Jak. "Is it? Do you know?"

"I still sense it," Jak said, "and it was shooting lightning from its side. I think it's just tipped over. I may be able to give that command in dragon, the one I used on our portal, to have it straighten itself, but... maybe we should leave it the way it is for now. If they're not paying attention to us, that's ideal." He looked down at his charge.

Only the top of the hatchling's head and his eyes were visible above the sling. Shikari looked rattled from his first experience with enemy dragons. Enemy dragons who wanted him dead. Badly.

Ambassador Rajesk strode toward them—toward Jak.

Malek stepped in front of Jak, his sword raised.

The ambassador frowned at him and stopped a few feet away. *As I knew when first we met,* he spoke telepathically to them, *you are a Favored Traveler, one selected by the portals for reasons unbeknownst to us. It responded to your request for assistance and cast its attacks at the younger dragons. The others do not believe, but I have read the elder scrolls, and I have faith in the prophecy.*

Jadora frowned, as if she'd never heard of any of that. Rivlen certainly hadn't.

You have the power to strike at the dragons in their lair. These two have harassed us before, and as soon as we stepped out from protection, they came again, as if they watched us, waiting for the opportunity to apprehend one of our etchers. Even with all our power, we could not stop them from taking her. As long as she can keep her barrier up, there is reason to believe she is safe. But even she will grow weary and need sleep eventually. Then her barrier will fall. We must rescue her today.

"Why is he telling us this?" Tinder whispered to Fret, who only shrugged.

Other than a few pieces of grass stuck in their hair, the mercenaries had survived the encounter unscathed.

"He wants us to handle the rescue," Malek said with certainty.

"Uh, they have an *army*," Tinder pointed out.

"But we have the Favored Traveler." The bemused look Malek gave to Jak suggested he had no more idea than Rivlen how Jak had received that designation and what it meant, other than that he could convince the portals to attack people—and dragons.

The Favored Traveler may be able to defeat even those two crafty dragons that have resisted our attempts to slay them and rid them from our land. If you can do this and return the etcher to us, I am certain you will be permitted to leave without further impediment. Rajesk bit his lip and looked at the portal. *We will figure out how to erect the gateway again so that you can do this.*

"What assurances do we have that you speak on behalf of your rulers and that they will agree?" Malek asked.

They will agree. They are not unreasonable. You came wanting things from us, so we mistrusted you, but if you rescue our ruler, our people will look upon you favorably.

"So... no assurances," Rivlen said.

We agree to your terms, Jak said, *if you also agree that your people will not attempt to invade our world. If we rescue your ruler, henceforth your people will consider us as allies.*

Yes. The ambassador bowed to him. *To be an ally of the Favored Traveler instead of an enemy would be wise. If you defeat those two dragons, the rulers will acknowledge that I was right and that you have* the blessing of the dragons in the portals, and they will not dare cross you. They will leave your world alone as long as you are in it.

"The dragons in the portals?" Jadora whispered. "Jak, do you know what that means?"

"Not yet, but we'll figure it out." Jak returned the ambassador's bow. *We agree.*

Jadora shook her head. "Jak...."

"This is unwise," Malek said. "Without my power, I am no match for a dragon. Even with it, those two were too strong."

I do insist, Jak continued to the ambassador, *that you remove the kerzor from my colleague's temple. We will need his power to defeat the dragons.*

It is impossible to remove them. Long ago, they were designed by one of our brilliant engineers and made with the help of an elder dragon who intimately understood the human brain. They are forever. But you are the Favored Traveler. You can defeat them, and our people will become allies.

Jadora, Malek, and the mercenaries were all shaking their heads. But Jak only gazed thoughtfully at the portal, at Shikari, and at the ambassador. *Yes. We will do this to help your people and become allies.*

Excellent. I will inform the remaining rulers. The ambassador lifted his hands to his mages, and they walked together down the road toward the city.

"Jak." Malek sighed and rubbed his head.

"Don't worry," Jak said. "I have some thoughts and an idea."

"You're his mother and know him well," Rivlen said to Jadora. "Should we be concerned?"

Jadora also sighed. "Yes."

"I thought so."

25

Jak kept an eye on Shikari as he hunted in the grass. He'd started catching his own insects, which was encouraging, but given how badly those dragons wanted him, Jak wouldn't risk letting him go far.

"Explain these thoughts and ideas." Malek had sheathed his weapons, but he radiated displeasure as he stood with his arms folded across his chest, frowning at Jak.

"And while you're at it," Mother said, "tell us what it means to be a Favored Traveler and how it was prophesied in scrolls here."

"I don't know about that part," Jak said, "but I'm getting the feeling that it's rarer than I realized for the portals to pick someone to communicate with."

"To communicate with and zap people with lightning on their behalf?" Malek asked.

"Apparently." Jak turned his palm toward the sky. "I can't tell you why they've picked me, but I've had some luck communicating, at least in a sense, with dragon steel as well as the portals."

Tezi nodded. "He got visions from my axe. It doesn't give me anything special, besides protection from magic."

"That's pretty special." Tinder looked at Rivlen, giving the axe that Rivlen had taken from her a pointed look.

Rivlen looked like she was tempted to keep it, but Malek turned his frown on her. She grimaced and returned it to Tinder.

"I also get the feeling," Jak said, "that the portals, and maybe all things made from dragon steel, aren't allies of these mottled dragons. Younger dragons, as the locals call them. Implying they came after the others."

"They may have been responsible for the extinction, or at least the near extinction—" Mother waved toward the rustling grass where Shikari was hunting, "—of the elder dragons. And if the elder dragons made dragon steel and the portals, that could be why the portals are loyal to them." She lifted a finger. "Ambassador Rajesk said something about *dragons in the portals*. I've been wondering what that could mean. That dragons somehow infused the portals with their intelligence or even personalities? Is that possible?" She looked not to Jak but to Malek and Rivlen, far greater experts on magic than he.

But they only shrugged and shook their heads.

"I've never heard of powerful mages imbuing tools with their personalities or anything of that ilk," Malek said, "but I can ask Uthari when we return. *If* we return."

"We will," Jak said.

"I'd have more faith in my ability to battle the dragons if I had my power."

"I don't want to make any promises I can't keep," Jak said, "but I have an idea about that. Shikari has proven that he can unlock doors. Maybe, if Mother can help me study the discs—especially those tendrils with hooks that come out of it—and I can get a basic understanding of how everything works, I can convey that to Shikari, and he can magically remove all the prongs in your head."

"Your one-week-old hatchling is going to perform magical surgery on my brain?" Malek asked.

"He's more like two weeks old now."

"Reassuring."

"He's known things that he couldn't possibly have known," Jak said. "Things that he couldn't have learned because he hasn't been exposed to them. I know this will sound silly, but I think he instinctively knows things that his ancestors knew. Somehow, their knowledge was passed along to him."

"That's ridiculous," Tinder said. "You can't know things you haven't learned."

Mother looked more thoughtful. "Actually, there are numerous examples in the animal kingdom to the contrary. Some young birds learn their songs by listening to others, but suboscine species inherit the knowledge of how to sing their complex songs. One of our biologists at the university did a study on such birds raised in sound-proof isolation, and without any training from their elders, they could perfectly sing the familiar songs of their ancestry. We tend to refer to this as instinct, but essentially, it's something imprinted on the brain that's passed along with everything else that turns an embryo into a bird. Dragons are intelligent and evolved creatures. Maybe some of their knowledge is likewise imprinted in their brains so that they're born with it."

"The knowledge to perform surgery on a human is an unlikely *instinct* for a dragon to inherit," Malek said.

"No, and he wouldn't know how to do that, I'm sure. Like I said, *I'd* have to learn as much as possible." Jak touched his chest. "Then convey it to him and hope his understanding of magic would be sufficient."

"Even if that's somehow possible," Rivlen said, "and Lord Malek got his powers back, that doesn't automatically mean we could defeat two dragons. Even though we and the army hurt them a little today, with all that might, we only delivered slight wounds. They flew away without so much as a hitch to their wingbeats."

"I know," Jak said. "We would need an advantage. We'd all need the protection that those dragon-steel weapons provide and, hopefully, an ally like the portal to help by distracting the dragons with attacks."

"Do you propose that we take the portal with us to their lair?" Malek arched his eyebrows and glanced at Rivlen.

She was the only one here who could levitate the portal. Judging by her groan, that wasn't an easy feat.

"To the valley that's twenty miles away, according to that map?" Jadora added.

"No. If I'm right, there's something there already that can help us." Jak touched his chest again and looked toward his mother.

She squinted at him. "Are you thinking of the ziggurat?"

Jak smiled at her. "The ziggurat that we believe is made from dragon steel, yes."

"*Believe*?" Rivlen asked.

"I'm guessing based on what I saw briefly in a vision," Jak admitted.

"Just because you saw dragons near that ziggurat in your vision," Malek said, "doesn't mean that's where their lair is."

"I think if we take Shikari up there, they'll come to us." Jak believed the vision—he'd come to trust what the portals shared with him. "If we can get to the ziggurat, it may help protect us. And you wanted to go there anyway, right?" He pointed to Malek. "You volunteered to fight the dragons for the ruler when you thought it would be worth the secret of dragon steel."

"I reluctantly agreed to go along on a hunt to *advise* them on killing dragons. When I had my power." Malek grimaced.

"The valley is also possibly where your acid is, Mother." While they'd been walking along the coast earlier, Jak had told her about the map Zethron had thrown through the window.

"Acid?" Malek turned to her. "The acid that may allow the manipulation of dragon steel?"

"Yes, possibly," Mother said, "but we don't know if it's located anywhere on that map or if it occurs in nature at all. Two squiggly lines on a piece of paper isn't convincing evidence."

"What choice do we have?" Jak asked.

"To go home?" Dr. Fret asked hopefully, looking toward the portal where it still lay on its side.

"If the ambassador spoke truthfully," Jak said, "if we do this for them, they won't send armies to invade our world. If we go back without that promise, we'll always be worried that they'll come through and try to take over Torvil later."

"The *ambassador* didn't have much if any sway over the rulers," Malek said. "And the very ruler who was kidnapped has lied to me before."

"Because they believed we came trying to steal their secrets. And honestly, we kind of did." Jak knew his mother had that formula she'd scrounged from their library in her pack. "If we do this favor for them, maybe we can do what we originally came to do. Gain knowledge and trade partners and maybe even allies."

"We originally came for a plant," Mother said dryly.

"If that were true—" Jak held Malek's gaze, "—we wouldn't have been sniffing around for the secrets of dragon steel."

"Uthari does want dragon-steel weapons and any other valuable resources we can find," Malek said. "I haven't denied this."

"What if we just go back and take down our portal so an army can't follow us through?" Dr. Fret asked.

"Uthari won't agree to that until he has what he wants," Malek said.

"Yes, much better to leave it erected and allow threats to come through that could destroy our world," Mother said.

Jak lifted his hands and patted the air. He didn't want his allies arguing. He wanted to convince them that he was right and that they could do this.

"I'll go to help you, Jak." Malek touched the hilt of his

sheathed sword. "Inasmuch as I can help right now. But there's no reason for noncombatants to come." He nodded toward Mother and Dr. Fret.

"Why do I get the feeling that doesn't include us?" Tinder whispered to Tezi.

"Because we're soldiers?" Tezi asked. "*Combatants.*"

Tinder spat on the ground.

"The noncombatants have to come. We may be able to save your life if you're grievously wounded." Mother looked at Jak and Malek.

"I would accept the risk of you not being there to save us if I knew you were safe," Malek said quietly, only looking at Mother now.

"I won't accept the risk of my son going into danger and me *not* being there to save him."

Malek gave Jak an exasperated look.

Jak would also have preferred to leave Mother behind—and safe—but was there truly anywhere safe here? What if they left her at the portal and one of those dragons returned and swooped her up to use against Jak, saying it would kill her if he didn't hand over the hatchling? Even though only one had spoken, and only at the very end, he had to remember that they were intelligent. These younger dragons might not be the ones who'd built the portals, but that didn't mean they weren't cunning. After all, they had somehow survived when the others had nearly died out.

Jak touched Shikari's head, hoping he would be able to keep the dragons from killing him. He also hoped he could keep them from seeing the location of all the eggs in his mind. The idea of what might be the last of the original dragon species being wiped out terrified him. Especially if *he* were responsible.

"Why didn't the ambassador tell us to trade the hatchling for his ruler?" Rivlen asked. "None of them did."

"I'm guessing the message only went to our group. Maybe

because we were the ones protecting Shikari." Jak shrugged. "If that's true, we're lucky. Otherwise, we would have had a very different negotiation with the ambassador."

"If we're going to do this, we need to go." Malek scanned the distant mountains. "Especially if it's a twenty-mile trek. I assume that even a mage more powerful than I—than I *was*—will have a hard time keeping her barrier up for long if two dragons are assaulting it."

"She might already be dead," Rivlen said.

"We'll assume she isn't but that we don't have time to delay."

Jak was thankful Malek had come around to his way of thinking. Jak hoped he was right and that he hadn't talked his mother and their allies into walking to their deaths.

Malek walked around the portal and found the inactive skyboards they'd left behind it days before. He knocked dust and pieces of grass off them. "I suppose there's no way we can set up the portal, return to our world, recharge these, and come back."

"Even if we could," Jak said, "the device might zap them again. I don't think I can convince it that they're allies, like Shikari."

"Hm." Malek eyed the ruler's untouched carriage. The ambassador had gone back on foot rather than presuming to take it. "An engineer would be able to charge the skyboards from the power supply in the carriage. Jak and Rivlen, do you want to try? You saw the engineer fixing the engine in the *Star Flyer*, right, Jak?"

"I *saw* it. I was more focused on channeling my power into him than in watching how he performed the repairs."

"I won't pretend this is the same thing, but you might be able to figure out how to channel power from that to these." He held up the skyboards.

"Would I need to be able to funnel my *own* power into them?" Jak had never wondered how the charges for magelock weapons and other reusable tools worked.

"An experienced engineer might be able to," Malek said, "but there's a conversion process. The power is altered from something ideal for humans to use to something designed for machines."

"I don't know much about how that works," Rivlen admitted.

"I'm afraid I don't either," Malek said. "But Jak has intuitively figured some things out. Maybe he can do this."

"I'll try." Jak checked on Shikari to make sure he hadn't gone far, then took the skyboards from Malek.

"I'll keep an eye on him." Tezi smiled and stepped into the rustling grass. "Since my axe wants me to protect him."

"Thank you." Jak walked around the carriage, trying to figure out how to access the power source and magical engine he sensed inside.

Malek stuck his finger into a gap under a panel in the back and flipped it open. A purple orb reminiscent of the mageship's power sources glowed softly inside a compartment.

"Thanks," Jak said sheepishly, hoping his inability to even figure out how to access it didn't bode poorly for this endeavor.

He removed his pack, leaned the skyboards against the carriage, and put a hand on one of them and another on the power supply. It tingled against his palm, humming softly. What terrain feature on a map would help him do this? He couldn't think of anything in nature that transferred power except for lightning strikes. But those were never mapped, and he didn't know if envisioning them would work for him.

Nonetheless, he tried, imagining the carriage as a dark storm cloud floating in the sky. In his mind, it discharged lightning into a skyboard lying on the ground far below.

Nothing happened. He tried several more times, adding sheer willpower, trying to mentally force the transfer of energy. Again, nothing happened.

Jak thought of his failure the night before with Rivlen in learning to conjure fire. Maybe he wasn't a prodigy with as much potential as she and Malek thought. He struggled with anything that didn't line up perfectly with something that fit into his cartographical skillset.

"How long should we let him try?" Rivlen asked quietly. She stood off to the side with Malek.

Jak tried to focus on his task and ignore them. It was hard. The *task* was hard.

"A few more minutes," Malek replied. "It'll be a difficult walk if there aren't any roads that lead up there. When did he get a map?"

"Zethron threw it through a window along with a love letter for Jadora."

"A *love letter*?" Malek asked.

"Some kind of letter. It may have been a list of groceries or library books that she would like. It's in their language."

"Wait," Mother said from farther away. "When did this happen? While I was with Malek?"

"Yes," Rivlen said.

"Jak didn't mention that. Where's the letter?"

"In Jak's pack."

Mother hesitated, probably not wanting to disturb him. Jak waved her toward his pack and took a deep breath, trying again to ignore everyone and focus. Lightning wasn't working. What else could he try?

As Mother found the letter and unfolded it to read, he decided on water imagery. Thus far, he'd had good luck with it. He imagined the carriage power supply as a snowpack at the top of a mountain. Warm sun beat upon it, and meltwater trickled down the hillside, forming into a creek, then flowing into a river. The skyboards floated within that river, and he willed the power to enter them. They bobbed atop the water, and Jak sensed magic in the air, but for some reason, he couldn't convince it to enter the skyboards.

Something brushed his leg, startling him, and the magic disappeared from the air.

Shikari had given up hunting in favor of chewing on Jak's already chewed bootlaces. Jak sighed and swooped him up, intending to stuff him in his sling with an admonition to be good. But he paused and squinted at his scaled charge.

Can you help with this? Jak asked telepathically.

Shikari climbed up his arm to perch on his shoulder.

"Do you want me to hold him?" Tezi asked. "So he's not in your way?"

Jak shook his head. "I'm trying to convince him to help. To, uh, show me what I'm doing wrong."

"Can he do that?"

"I don't know yet."

"If he can't master charging a skyboard, I'm not letting him near my brain," Malek said.

"Let's find out if he can." Jak lifted Shikari and turned him around, since he was facing in the wrong direction, so his snout pointed toward the carriage.

"I think we're going to have to go to Plan B," Tinder grumbled.

"Aren't we already on Plan B?" Fret asked. "Or C or D?"

"At least."

Feeling he'd been close with the melting snowpack, Jak brought that imagery up in his mind again. He tried to share what he wanted to do with Shikari. Maybe it was silly to hope a baby dragon could help, but he'd helped them before. Once again, Jak envisioned the water melting toward the river with the skyboards bobbing along in the current.

How do I get the water—the magical power—into them? Jak asked.

To his surprise, Shikari appeared in his vision. The hatchling placed himself on one of the skyboards in the river and hopped about as it flowed through the currents, tilting and bobbing. He squatted on one end, then leaped to the other.

Are you playing *on the skyboard? I'm sure it's fun, but we need to be serious now. Can you show me how to charge them so we can ride them?*

The Shikari on his shoulder thwapped Jak in the back of the head with his tail.

Jak sighed. *This isn't going to work, is it?*

He was about to give up, but the Shikari in the vision grew still and centered himself on the skyboard. He did something to alter the surface of the device so that water molecules could flow into it. Altering the skyboards to work with magical power created on this world? Power similar but different from what the mages back home created?

Once the alteration was made, magic flowed easily into the skyboard. Into all four of them. Jak sensed it crackling through the air before him.

"He's doing it," Rivlen whispered.

"Good," Malek said.

The skyboards—the *real* ones—tipped over, landing on the ground, then hovering. Shikari hopped down from Jak's shoulder and jumped on one. He slapped his tail against it and shifted his modest bodyweight to tilt it left and right.

"I think he only helped because he wants a ride." Jak stepped back from the carriage, waving everyone toward the boards.

"Closest to flying he's going to get until those wings start working." Rivlen stepped onto an empty board. "Am I going to have to direct all of these?"

"Probably." Malek shook his head wistfully.

"I can help. I've done it before." Jak spotted the map in his mother's hands. She'd removed it, but she was focused on translating the letter. He slid it from her grip and opened it so he could direct them on their route. "Is it anything helpful?" he asked quietly of the letter.

If it truly *was* a love letter, he didn't want to bring anyone's attention to it. He doubted his mother had any feelings for Zethron, but it might still be awkward to talk about.

"Nothing that will help with our mission." Mother folded it, tucked it into a pocket, and stepped onto a skyboard with Malek. "He suggested some more books in case I'm able to gain access to their library again. And he asked again if we would take him back to our world so he can explore."

"That's all?" Jak asked. "It looked like a long letter."

"There was also a poem." Mother glanced warily at Malek. "It doesn't mean anything."

"It sounds like it *was* a love letter." Rivlen willed the first two skyboards, the mercenaries aboard them with her, into motion.

Mother shook her head, but her cheeks had turned red, so Jak wondered.

But if nothing in the letter would help with the dragons, he didn't care about it. He stepped onto the skyboard Shikari had claimed, brought back the river imagery, and swept them downstream, taking the lead from Rivlen.

With the map in hand, he directed them toward the mountains and the valley with the ziggurat. He hoped he wasn't directing them toward their deaths.

~

Riding a skyboard without being the one controlling it was as bad as everything else that Malek had felt since losing his power. Maybe worse. He was at the whim of someone else's power, and that made him uneasy.

He rode with his hands resting on the hilts of his weapons, aware that if Jadora, who gripped his shoulders as they sailed up a forested mountain slope, lost her balance, he would have only his reflexes to rely upon to catch her before she fell.

After more than thirty years of relying upon his magic, it was a frustrating feeling. Just as going into battle against a dragon without his power had been. He'd barely knocked Jak down before those talons caught him. If he'd been any slower, or if the dragon had seen him coming and magically thrown him aside, Malek might have failed. The dragon could have pierced Jak through the heart and killed him instantly. Him *and* the hatchling.

"I suppose I should be nervous for the impending showdown and not looking around curiously at everything," Jadora said from behind him. "I want so badly to take samples, but I know there's no time to stop."

"Duck." Malek bent low, hoping Jadora was quick enough to obey, as the board flew too close to a tree branch, five-pointed blue-green leaves stretching toward them.

The leaves and a few sharp twigs brushed their hair, but neither of them was knocked off. This time.

"Thank you." Jadora straightened.

"Take out a knife. With the way Jak is navigating our board, you'll be able to cut samples from all the branches we're almost running into."

Jak glanced back, his face tight with concentration, and Malek reminded himself that Jak hadn't had much practice navigating skyboards, especially ones he wasn't riding. Rivlen, who controlled the board Fret and Tinder rode, as well as the one she shared with Tezi, had a much easier time keeping their flight smooth.

"I seem to remember branches clawing at my hair," Jadora said, "when I rode into the jungle with you."

"*Small* branches."

"I did appreciate that, when you noticed, you conjured a barrier to protect me." She squeezed his shoulder.

Malek appreciated her touch and the fact that she hadn't changed at all toward him since he'd lost his power. If anything, she wished he would stay this way.

That was a loathsome idea, especially given their destination and goal. Jak's suggestion that the hatchling might somehow be able to figure out how to remove the kerzor without doing any damage to his brain seemed ridiculous. Even if dragons did have ancestral memories or knowledge that they were born with, he couldn't imagine it applying to surgery on humans. Still, if Malek thought there was even a slight chance it would work, he might be tempted to take the gamble. The idea of continuing to live without access to his magic was difficult to accept.

There wouldn't be time, however, to ask Jak—and the hatchling—to try. If the dragons were indeed in that valley on the map, and only twenty miles from the city, the group ought to be getting close. Even though the undergrowth was thick and the forested slopes difficult to navigate, the skyboards zipped along quickly, far superior to walking on foot.

Malek caught himself trying to stretch out with his senses to check for dragons before remembering that he couldn't. He barely kept himself from asking the others if they sensed anything. If they did, they would tell him. Not knowing all the things he'd known before was grating.

"If, by some chance, we succeed and are allowed to return to our world," Jadora said as the skyboards took them over a river and followed it upstream, unimpeded by trees, "do you think we could take Zethron back with us?"

Malek stiffened, not wanting to talk about the man who threw poems through the window for Jadora, but he kept himself from saying that. His reaction was immature, and he knew it, but sharing those kisses with Jadora, drug-inspired or not, only left Malek more irritated at the idea of some suitor trying to woo her. He recognized the emotions as illogical—it wasn't as if *Malek* could woo her—but struggled with sublimating them.

"If he still has a means to travel through the portal, we couldn't necessarily stop him," she continued, "but he's tried to help us, so I'd hate for him simply to be captured by Uthari or one of the commanders from the other fleets and thrown into a cell. If he's telling the truth, he just wants to explore."

Zethron wanted to explore with *Jadora*, Malek had little doubt.

Again, he shoved aside the petty thought. The *jealous* thought.

"I am reluctant to trust any of these people at this time," Malek said, "but if he let me—let Rivlen—read his mind and scour his thoughts so we knew for certain that is all he wanted, I would not object to it."

"But would you stand up for him if your king wanted to capture him? If the formula I have does indeed allow us to one day manipulate dragon steel, it would only be because of Zethron's help that I found it. He also gave me a lead on the Jitaruvak."

"I understand. I'm not sure how much sway I'll have over Uthari when I get back—" Malek waved at his temple, "—but if mind reading reveals that Zethron has no ill intent toward us or our world and truly just wants to visit, I will tell Uthari that and urge him to allow it."

"Thank you."

Malek looked back at her. Her braid streamed out behind her as they sailed above the water, a chilly mountain breeze caressing their cheeks, and he thought she looked beautiful. The urge to say something about Zethron and what a poor suitor he would be came to him, along with the desire to ask her if she preferred him, but once again, he quashed it.

Jadora raised her eyebrows, doubtless wanting to know why he was gazing at her.

"Do you think I should let Jak's hatchling operate on me?" It was a far more salient and appropriate question to ask in these circumstances.

"That sounds ludicrous."

"Yes. Do you think I should?" Malek wasn't sure how much the hatchling had helped Jak with transferring power from the carriage to the skyboards, but he was positive Shikari *had* helped. He did seem to grasp a great deal for such a young creature.

"Not... any time soon. We should further study the dissected kerzor we have." Jadora patted one of her pockets. "Ideally with the help of a few mage engineers and healers. You should get several expert opinions on whether and how it might be removed. Futzing around in the brain is no small matter." She returned her hand to his shoulder and frowned with concern. "If something were done poorly and further injury were caused, it could kill you. Or render you without any of your faculties at all."

"That would be disturbing."

"I know it's difficult for you to be without your power, but what if you ended up in a coma and unable to think or walk or do *anything*?" Her voice broke on the last word, and she blinked several times and looked away.

"I wouldn't like that. I would ask, if that happened and there was no hope of restoring me to health, that you would take a knife to my throat and end my life."

She shook her head, distress contorting her face.

Maybe he shouldn't have brought this up, but now that she'd mentioned the possibilities of a failed surgery, he worried that he might end up like that. And that his comrades might try to keep him alive indefinitely out of some vain hope that something would change. The idea of living like that—of *not* living like that—distressed him far more than the thought of falling in battle to a dragon.

"You wouldn't have to do it yourself," Malek said gently, though he would prefer that she did. "You could have Sergeant Tinder cleave my head off with her new axe. She'd probably like that."

"*Malek.*" Jadora dashed her sleeve across her eyes. "This isn't a joke."

"I know. I wasn't joking."

"That's awful."

She dropped her face against the top of his backpack. He wished he weren't wearing it so she would be resting her head on *him*. Though he'd disturbed her, so maybe it wasn't appropriate to wish for that.

Malek shifted sideways on the skyboard so he could wrap an arm around her waist. "I apologize for distressing you."

"Thank you." She smiled sadly at him. "There was a time when you didn't say please and thank you or apologize to me. I like this improvement."

"Because we were..."

"Enemies?"

"I never thought of you as that," he said, even though he knew she'd considered him one. He wasn't positive she'd stopped thinking of him that way, even if she had developed feelings for him. They both knew she *shouldn't* have developed those feelings. And neither should he. "I was professionally aloof, as is appropriate for a zidarr."

A waterfall roared up ahead, and Rivlen and Jak guided the skyboards away from the river and through the trees again. They followed a cliff angling deeper into the mountains.

"We're getting close," Jak called back. He glanced twice when he spotted Malek holding his mother.

Malek should have let her go, but it made sense for them to hang on to each other, to help keep each other steady. At least with the way Jak navigated the boards, it did.

"Don't take any unnecessary risks against the dragons, please." Jadora must have noticed Jak's glances, but she didn't extricate herself from Malek's embrace. "I can imagine you feeling a little reckless if you're not sure there's a way to return your powers, but give us time to figure something out. I've got my microscope and can help your healers and engineers. I'm sure that with all those mages your king brought, he has someone who'll have good ideas."

"Any risks I take will be necessary."

"That wasn't that reassuring of an answer."

He tilted his head, not disagreeing but not being able to offer anything better. Without his power, he judged the probability of surviving this fight low. All he could do was put his faith in Jak and hope that he was right, that there was a dragon-steel ziggurat waiting in the valley and that it would somehow help them.

26

The skyboards slowed down as they crested a tree-filled ridge and the valley on the map came into view. A canopy almost as dense as that in the jungle of Zewnath kept the land in perpetual shade.

As Jadora peered around Malek's shoulder to get a better view, she decided it was more of a crater or depression than a valley, though the dense undergrowth and trees made it hard to discern details. She couldn't see all the way to the far side, and at first, she didn't spot anything like Jak's ziggurat and worried they'd flown to the wrong place.

The only terrain feature of note was a hill in the center of the crater, its slopes smothered with blue-green plants and clumps of grass. But as they flew closer and her eyes adjusted to the dimness, she realized it wasn't a hill.

The ziggurat rose up in tiers with the blue-black vertical sides almost completely hidden behind vines and leaves. Moss carpeted the walls and flat roof of a square structure at the top. That structure was large enough to hold a dragon, maybe two. She could almost imagine one crouching in there, masked by shadows.

Was it some temple where rituals had long ago been performed? For some reason, she envisioned humans trekking to this place from the coast, leaving sacrifices for the dragons.

Except if they were right, the elder dragons—or, as Jak called them, the *good* dragons—had made this place. If they'd been friends to humans, they shouldn't have demanded sacrifices.

"I don't sense any dragons." Rivlen looked over at Jak.

They'd slowed the skyboards as they followed the slope down into the crater and headed warily toward the ziggurat.

"If they're not here, I think they'll come." Jak peered toward the sky, though the canopy hid it, then toward the sides of the crater. Most of them sloped gently upward, as carpeted with moss, vines, and foliage as the ziggurat, but a few dark cliffs were visible, bare vertical stone defying growth.

Jadora didn't know what stone those cliffs were comprised of, but they were black and sleek, almost like obsidian. Here and there, slightly lighter colors were visible, veins that ran through the stone like ore in a mine. The veins were the same blue-black as the ziggurat and their dragon-steel weapons.

"Is that raw ore that dragons turn into their alloy?" Malek was peering in that direction too. "Or maybe what we thought was an alloy isn't. Does dragon steel exist in its basic form in nature on some worlds?"

"I wonder if it's possible to take a sample," Jadora said, though if the natural ore was even half as hard as the finished product, they certainly wouldn't be able to chisel it out of the rock.

"And put it in a vial?" Malek smiled over his shoulder at her.

"Rocks go in cases, not vials."

"A scientific mandate?"

"Something like that."

Tezi pointed at something yellowish-white amid a plant that reminded Jadora of a water lily. At first, she thought Tezi might have noticed the flower blooming, but no... There was a bone half-hidden by the leaves. A human femur.

The memory of the bone-littered tundra on the last world they'd visited came to mind.

"I don't know if this is their lair," Rivlen said, "but it looks like the dragons come here to dine."

"Any large predator could be responsible for that," Malek said. "Some of the arena creatures are from this world."

"Oh, good. Maybe we can run into even more things with the power to kill us."

Malek frowned slightly at the sarcasm.

When Jadora had first joined Rivlen and Malek on the *Star Flyer*, Rivlen had been the image of military professionalism in her crisp uniform and polished boots, and she'd added *my lord* to almost every sentence directed to Malek. Some of that had faded in this last week. Hopefully because they were in a strange situation, and she was far from her command, not because she'd lost some of her respect for Malek now that he no longer had his powers.

"Let's investigate the ziggurat while we wait," Jak said. "Mother's acid may be here. *Something* should be."

"Something conveyed by two squiggles on a map?" Rivlen adjusted the paths of their skyboards to sail around the base of the ziggurat so they could see it from all sides.

"Yes."

Jadora worried about the dragons—if they didn't show up here, how would the group find them and the kidnapped ruler?—but the scientist and explorer in her wanted to scramble all over that ziggurat and look for signs of language or some verification that the elder dragons had indeed built it.

"I don't see any sign of natural vents, like I expected," Jak said after they'd circled the base of the ziggurat.

There also hadn't been a door or any access to the interior, at least not an obvious one. It was possible a hidden entrance lay somewhere under all the moss and vines.

Jadora peered at the structure on top. "Let's check up there."

"It could be a trap," Malek said.

Rivlen looked at him. "A trap set by dragons?"

"Just because you don't sense them doesn't mean they aren't here. Their own magic, or the magic of the dragon steel, could camouflage them."

A bird squawked from the treetops. The noise made Jadora jump and only then realize how quiet it had grown since they'd entered the valley. Eerily quiet. Maybe Malek was right and the wildlife knew what the humans couldn't detect. That dragons were here somewhere, lying in wait.

In Jak's sling, only the top of Shikari's head was visible as he peered out. He seemed focused on the forest rather than the ziggurat.

"Well." Jak flew closer to the mossy side of the lowest tier. He pushed aside a vine so he could rest his hand on the dragon steel underneath. "We want to find the dragons anyway, right?"

"I thought we might develop more of a plan before confronting them," Malek said.

"I'm going to try to establish a rapport with this." Jak patted the structure and closed his eyes.

"A rapport with an ancient ruin is our plan?" Tinder asked dubiously.

She and Tezi had drawn their weapons, as if they expected the dragons to spring out at any second. Tinder had her new axe in one hand and a grenade in the other.

Jadora had a few of her small explosives and vials of acid, but neither would do anything against a dragon. The only way she might be able to help was if she could unravel the mysteries of this place and find something they could use in a battle.

"Rivlen?" she asked softly, pointing to the structure. "Will you fly me up there so I can look inside?"

She would have hopped off the skyboard and climbed the ziggurat on her own, but it was more than twenty feet between each tier, and there were no stairs. As far as she could tell, humans wouldn't be able to ascend it without climbing equipment, so maybe it had never been intended for them. Though she supposed mages could have levitated each other to the top.

"And get eaten by a dragon?" Rivlen asked.

"Hopefully not." Jadora held up one of the explosives. If nothing else, she could toss it into the maw of a dragon trying to devour her.

"Fearsome," Rivlen said of the little ball, but she did levitate Jadora and Malek's skyboard toward the top. She went with them, Tezi stuck riding behind her.

As they flew upward, Jadora searched for signs of writing or decoration behind the vines, but if anything marked the ancient metal, she couldn't see it through the vegetation. Once they reached the top, their skyboard slowed to a hover. The square structure was empty, with walls only on three sides. Interestingly, the insides of them were made from something other than dragon steel. They were dark gray instead of blue-black, looking more like slate or some other stone.

Up here, the air smelled strange, reminding Jadora of burnt hair. She wrinkled her nose at the unappealing scent and searched for the source. No breeze swept through the protected crater, so it had to be coming from nearby.

"No trapdoor?" Rivlen waved to the floor of the structure. It was also made from the gray stone. Or perhaps that was an aggregate material like cement? "I expected the entrance to be up here. Or is this whole thing solid? Maybe there isn't an inside or an entrance."

"There's something in the floor in there." Malek pointed. "See that dark slit?"

Rivlen nudged the skyboards closer, and Jadora spotted it. A perfectly straight eight-foot-long and one-inch-wide slit in the floor.

"A vent?" She thought of Jak's squiggly lines on the map. Was it possible that whatever the lines indicated was inside the ziggurat? Or *under* it? "That could be our acid."

Malek looked sharply at her. "Is that what's making the smell?"

"It could be."

"I don't see anything coming out of there," Tezi said.

"It could be a colorless gas," Jadora said. "There are plenty of examples of such. Take me to it, please." Jadora shifted her backpack off. "It'll be hard to get much of a sample of it in this state, but I should be able to get some. Too bad I don't have more lab equipment. I could have captured it and turned it into a liquid."

"You want to take samples *now*?" Rivlen gave her an incredulous look. "When we're expecting a dragon attack at any moment?"

"Of course she does," Malek said mildly. "Navigate our skyboard over there, Captain."

Using her rank seemed to remind Rivlen that they weren't equals out here. "Yes, my lord."

Their skyboard drifted to the top of the ziggurat.

"Since we have time, you and the mercenaries can plant some explosives," Malek told Rivlen. "Anything you can come up with that might discombobulate our enemies, even if it's just knocking trees into their path."

"Yes, my lord."

Malek drew his sword and hopped off, then offered Jadora a hand. "I'll keep an eye on our professor," he said.

"Understood." Rivlen and Tezi swooped back down toward Jak and the others.

Jadora might have been concerned about being left up there, when neither she nor Malek could fly the skyboard on their own, but she was too excited at the prospect of getting a sample to object. This wasn't simply some interesting leaf or flower. This could hold the secret to working dragon steel, to possibly putting more dragon-steel weapons into the hands of terrene humans back on Torvil.

If Jadora and the rest of the normal humans in the world ever wanted a shot at changing their fates—removing the mages and wizards from power—weapons that could make them impervious to magical attacks could be a start. *Nearly* impervious, she amended, remembering how that guard had tripped Tezi with flying obstacles even though he hadn't been able to touch her with magic.

As much as her peace-loving mind objected to the idea of solving problems by arming the populace, it wasn't as if any of the other tactics that terrene humans had tried over the centuries had worked. Power was all the mages understood, the only thing that could convince them to change.

Uthari would never approve and would try to stop them, but if Jadora could enlist Sorath's and Ferroki's help and somehow get dragon steel back to Torvil and turned into weapons, maybe it would make a difference. Further, she had the kerzor in her pocket. If she could get that into the hands of someone who might be able to replicate the device...

She imagined ramming one of them into Uthari's temple so he couldn't use his power to harm her father, control Malek, or pester anyone with his magic ever again.

Malek came up beside her, and she almost dropped her backpack, abruptly afraid that he'd read her thoughts. Until she looked at his face and remembered that he couldn't do that anymore.

"Do you want me to hold anything?" he asked, oblivious to her plotting.

"Maybe." She licked her lips, nervous at her whirling thoughts, even if he couldn't read them. She glanced over the edge, making sure Rivlen wasn't close. She'd hopped off the other skyboard below and was obeying Malek's wishes, directing the mercenaries to plant explosives in the undergrowth. "Let me see if I've got an empty jar. In my laboratory, I would use water displacement to capture gas, but I don't have the equipment for that out here. I'll see what I have and can rig up."

"If it's an acid, will it erode a jar? Or is glass impervious?"

"Not necessarily impervious, but it resists most acids. It's more susceptible to corrosion from alkaline substances. I suspect the stone they chose for this area is similar." Jadora waved at the dark gray material. The roof above the vent was stained a brownish white but didn't appear to have suffered any structural damage. As Malek stepped closer to consider the stain, she waved for him to move back. "I don't know if the gas is toxic to humans, but chances are it can irritate the lungs and mucous membranes, at the least."

"I understand. I'll stand guard while you collect a sample." Malek moved out from under the structure and gazed out into the forest. "I expected we would find the dragons here and waiting. That they're not is concerning."

"Because you're worried they won't come? Or because they could be plotting something?"

"We may have guessed wrong about where their lair is. If they're a hundred miles away, they won't sense us—or the hatchling—here and come. Etcher Yervaa can't have that much time before they wear down her defenses. She might already be dead."

Jadora wouldn't weep for the loss of the woman who'd forced that needle into Malek's brain. If they could gather the acid sample, collect some of that interesting ore from the cliff, and leave without dealing with the dragons… she wouldn't object.

"Jak's coming," Malek said, peering over the side of the ziggurat.

He arrived on the skyboard with his hatchling.

"Dragons?" Malek glanced toward the forest again.

"Do I sense them? No, not yet. But there's a problem." Jak waved at the ziggurat under their feet. "Rivlen and I can sense that it's magical and has a powerful aura, like the portals, but I haven't been able to communicate with it in any way or sense any intelligence within it."

"Do you communicate with the dragon-steel weapons?" Malek asked. "I thought it was only the portals that seemed sentient. Or sapient?"

"Right, but the weapons still feel... alive. Aware. I'm not sure how to describe it. They give off those insights and visions."

Malek nodded.

"I'm getting nothing from this structure. I even reached out to the portal—I did that when I was trying to get a sense of Tezi's battle-axe." Jak pointed in the direction of the coast. "It's disgruntled that we left it tipped on its side, by the way."

"The *dragons* knocked it over," Jadora said. "It should be disgruntled with them."

"It's oozing a general sense of disgruntlement. The feeling I got when I asked it about the ziggurat is that this place has been dormant for a long time. It was made by and for the original dragons, and it has no interest in being used by the current dragons."

"Your hatchling can't wake it up?" Malek pointed to Shikari, who had climbed to Jak's shoulder again and was crinkling his snout at the odor up here.

"I tried to convey to him that we wanted to wake it up, but he wandered off to look for bugs."

"If two people hadn't had visions about dragons attacking us here," Malek said, "I would suggest that we're looking in the wrong place."

"I don't know if the visions from the portals always come true." Jak pointed at Malek's sword. "Do the ones from your blades?"

"Not always, but when they don't, it's usually because I accepted the warning as truth and acted to alter the events that would have led to it. One insight related to this world has already come true." Malek gazed over at Jadora.

For some reason, she thought of their kiss. She hoped his sword hadn't shown him *that*.

"I came up here to tell you," Jak said, "because if the ziggurat is dormant, it may not defend us from magical attacks. I may not be able to convince it to help in any way. When I was coming up with this plan, I envisioned us only having to worry about a few physical attacks from dragons as lightning streaked out from the ziggurat to strike down our enemies. Without that, I don't think we can win, not against two dragons."

"Maybe not even against one," Malek said quietly.

"Not with you not being... fully you," Jak said.

Malek's grim expression did not convey disagreement.

"Since we don't sense the dragons yet," Jak said, "I wanted to see if you're interested in my other idea."

"Is that the one where your hatchling does brain surgery on me?"

Jadora shook her head. "We're not doing that here in the middle of the forest on a foreign world, not until we've had a lot more time to study the discs."

Jak watched Malek, who gazed out at the trees again, and neither of them responded to Jadora. The distressing certainty that Malek was considering it came over her, and she thought of their conversation on the skyboard.

"Not here, Malek." She joined them and gripped his arm. "It's too risky."

"Riskier than going into battle against a dragon without any magic to use?" he asked, still looking at the wilds instead of her.

"*Yes*. You've got magically enhanced zidarr muscles or whatever explains your ability to jump thirty feet in the air. If you were incapacitated or *died* from this, we'd be a lot worse off if a dragon showed up." And she would have lost somebody else that she'd come to care about, damn it. "Malek."

"Like I said before," Jak said, "if Shikari and I can destroy the disc and the needle with all the little strands its inserted into Malek's brain... that shouldn't harm him, right? It would just be removing something that never should have been there."

"We don't know what the device has done in the time it's been inserted," Jadora said. "Removing the needle and its tendrils could cause hemorrhaging in his brain, and Dr. Fret can't stop that with bandages."

"I might be able to heal it," Jak said.

"All you've practiced on so far is cut fingers."

"And claw marks." Jak pointed at Malek's torso.

"That's a lot different from a human *brain*," Jadora said.

"If I could regain my power, I could heal any damage myself," Malek said.

"With your great familiarity with brains?" Jadora asked.

He shrugged. "I don't need conscious knowledge of how to repair something in my own body. One of the methods I can employ is simply to energize and feed power into my own immune system so that it does what it already knows how to do but more quickly and efficiently."

"Jak." Jadora turned her attention to him, realizing she had more power to sway her son than Malek, Malek who would rather die than live as an invalid. "You don't know enough to do this, to risk him."

Jak looked from Malek to her and back. "I know it's risky, Mother, but I don't think we can win without Malek, Malek the zidarr, not just Malek the swordsman."

"We don't have to *win* anything. We can take the acid sample —" Jadora pointed at the vent, "—grab some ore, and leave before the dragons know we're here."

"We agreed to help the ambassador get their ruler back," Malek said.

"Their dragon problem shouldn't be our problem," Jadora said. "She was only captured because she was trying to keep us from going home."

Malek regarded Jak for a moment, then the hatchling for an even longer moment.

Jadora clenched her jaw. Neither man was listening to reason.

"What if he goes off to hunt insects in the middle of this surgery?" she asked.

"I would be far more inclined to trust an *adult* dragon to perform the procedure," Malek admitted.

"One of the good ones. Me too. But I'll guide him." Jak looked earnestly at Malek and at Jadora. "I'm confident we can do this."

"Let's try," Malek said before Jadora could object further. He patted Jadora's hand, then gently but firmly extricated his arm from her grip. "Thank you for caring," he said quietly.

"Malek," she whispered, but she let it stop there. She was out of arguments, and he wouldn't listen regardless. He wanted this too badly.

Malek stepped onto the skyboard with Jak. "Call Rivlen up to protect Jadora while she gathers her sample."

Jadora could only watch as they sailed over the edge, but she was certain they were making a mistake. If she were a dragon who wanted nothing more than to kill a hatchling protected by enemies, wouldn't she wait until half of them were thoroughly distracted by some endeavor from which they couldn't easily extricate themselves?

~

Nightfall found Sorath crouching in the branches of a tree a hundred yards from the pool and what had become a tent city sprawled out around it. The leaves would have hidden him from view even if he hadn't had magic, but he felt more comfortable cloaked by more than foliage. From here, he could safely see the camp and the portal and keep an eye on everything. On Ferroki and Thorn Company.

Vinjo's stealth device was active on his wrist, a sword and pistol hung from his weapons belt, and three magelock rifles and a pack full of supplies rested on the ground below. Not positive what he planned, he'd grabbed as much gear as made sense on his way out of camp.

No, that wasn't true. He knew what he wanted to accomplish with this new advantage. It was the thing he should have accomplished when Vinjo gave him the first creeper, as soon as Sorath had realized what he had. But it hadn't been until Sasko dropped the second one in his lap—and after Uthari had tortured him for a second time—that the idea had solidified in his mind. He just had to figure out how he could pull it off.

Kill Uthari.

Sorath wanted to use the stealth device to sneak onto his yacht, slip into his suite, and slit his throat while he slept, while his defenses were down.

He would likely die partaking in the mission, but at least he'd kissed Ferroki first. And not only as some ruse in the woods but for real. He wished they'd gotten a chance for more, but if he could take out the wizard who'd been driving everything since that portal had been discovered, it would be worth dying for.

Thorn Company would no longer be bound, Yidar might turn opportunistic and fly off to try to claim Uthari's kingdom, and Malek... Sorath didn't know what Malek would do, but he was the most reasonable of Uthari's people. He might make a deal with the druids. At the least, he would probably agree to deactivate the portal until Jadora could study it further and perhaps figure out a way to keep threats from coming through.

Sorath's gaze shifted upward. Through the branches, he could make out Uthari's yacht floating over the pool. He couldn't get up there without a skyboard—and even if he stole one, he lacked the magic to operate it—but he had a plan for that. No fewer than a half dozen fleet commanders were down here, officers working for other kings and queens, and they would be delighted to help Sorath kill Uthari. He ought to be able to talk one of them into levitating him over to the *Serene Waters*—what a ridiculous name for a ship commanded by a tyrant. From there, Sorath could strike.

Maybe he could do it this very night. But it would be better if he could hide out until Tinder, Fret, Tezi, and the others returned. If they did soon, and if he could make contact with Tezi without revealing himself, he wanted to borrow her axe.

Sorath *might* be able to assassinate Uthari in his sleep if he used a mundane weapon, but he worried that anyone who had survived centuries of rule would have booby traps and defenses in his bedroom, if not in the entire suite. If something woke Uthari up, Sorath wouldn't stand a chance.

Unless he carried a weapon that protected him from magical attacks and could cut through a wizard's defenses.

The sense that he wasn't alone came over Sorath. He looked down, half-expecting to spot a Thorn Company patrol passing through. If one did, he would have to resist the urge to make contact. Right now, none of them had any idea where he'd gone or what he intended to do. If Ferroki or any of the others found out, and if Uthari read the truth in their minds, he would double up his defenses and sleep with one eye open. The chances of Sorath succeeding, even with the stealth device, would plummet.

Something stirred in the undergrowth to the side of his tree. He gripped the hilt of his pistol.

A furry blur sprang past his tree to land on a boulder. A massive gray wolf. It appeared similar to the ones that had harried the mages during the battle the night before.

It gazed toward the camp instead of up at him, so he released his pistol. But he was careful not to move or make a noise. He had little doubt that the animal was spying for another druid. Maybe looking for the man who'd been taken prisoner?

Sorath had no idea if that druid was still alive. He'd been gone when Sorath roused from his own torture.

A part of him was tempted to seek out the druids, since Kywatha had been interested in talking to him, but to what end? Helping them remove the portal would likely make matters worse for Thorn Company—Sorath could envision an enraged Uthari lashing out at the mercenaries. Getting rid of the head of the snake would be best. Then the druids and the other fleets could squabble over the portal. Sorath didn't care. As long as Ferroki and the others were able to get out of that odious contract and leave the jungle.

The wolf lifted its snout and sniffed. Catching Sorath's scent?

He hadn't moved, and he tried to breathe as shallowly as he could. From his experience, the stealth device camouflaged its wearer from magical senses and eyesight, but if it could fool other senses, he didn't know. Vinjo might not have thought of scent.

After another minute, the wolf sprang off the boulder, heading away from camp. Maybe it would be best if Sorath did the same. He wanted to keep an eye on Thorn Company, but most of the mercenaries had gone to bed for the night, and there was little activity.

Or so he thought. A cloaked and hooded figure on a skyboard flew over the railing of the *Serene Waters* and down to the portal.

The branches kept Sorath from seeing the reaction from the mages on guard down there, but they must not have objected, for when the figure came back into view, he stood right beside the portal. He withdrew a thick tome from under his cloak, opening it to a bookmarked page then withdrawing his hands. The book remained open, floating parallel to the ground so he could read from it.

Sorath was too far away to have a shot at seeing the title or anything on the pages, but the tome appeared old. A few ships had come and gone, resupplying Uthari's fleet. Maybe one had delivered a new resource?

One of the magical lights that floated around the camp at night wafted over to shine down onto the pages. It positioned itself above the figure, so his face was still in shadow, but when he stretched out his hand, one finger running down the lines, the light showed skin papery with age.

Was this... Uthari?

Sorath's hand dropped back to his pistol. The thought that he could strike at the wizard without needing a ride up to his yacht came to mind.

After a moment of flirting with temptation, Sorath forced himself to release the weapon. Uthari would know he was vulnerable as he read and did whatever he was attempting to do to the portal, so he would have his defenses up. Sorath would only get one shot at assassinating the old wizard. His best bet would be while he slept.

Long minutes passed as Uthari read, one hand on the page of the tome and one on the portal. Sorath rolled his shoulders and turned his head from side to side. His legs were growing numb from perching on a branch for so long. He could have left, but curiosity about what Uthari was doing made him stay.

When the portal pulsed once with blue light, it startled him. His foot slipped off the branch, and he tightened his grip around the trunk to keep his balance. Fortunately, he didn't make any noise, and he was too far from camp for anyone there to hear him, regardless.

Uthari looked up at the portal and slid his hand down its frame. It pulsed pale blue light again.

A chill went through Sorath. Until now, the only one he'd seen get the portal to do anything other than activate with the key had been Jak. Did this mean Uthari had figured out how to draw upon its magic?

Sorath imagined Uthari commanding it to send streaks of lightning at his enemies, lightning even more powerful than what he could already cast himself. And who knew what else the portal was capable of?

Uthari's gaze shifted toward one of the ships floating over the trees, one with a brown hull. One of his competitors.

Sorath swore under his breath. He might not have time to wait for Tezi to return and lend him the axe. If he didn't want Uthari to end up the unopposed ruler of the portal and all the ships that remained, Sorath might have to act immediately.

Careful not to make noise, he climbed down the trunk. He was only halfway to the ground when a flash of blue light came from the camp. He paused and looked back, afraid Uthari had already launched some attack.

But he'd moved away from the portal and was looking at it. In surprise?

The interior lit up with stars that started swirling. Did that mean Tezi and the others were coming back? Or was Kywatha returning? Or—Sorath frowned—what if this was some all new threat?

Uthari ordered the mages stationed at the portal to arrange themselves in a defensive position. Shouts from others rang from the camp, and Thorn Company and the other mercenary units sent troops in, their weapons pointing at the portal.

The stars in the center stopped swirling. Sorath had seen Tezi and the others leave, and he remembered the constellation that had formed for them. This wasn't it. This was either the druid returning or a new threat. Either way, Ferroki and her people might need his help.

He jumped the rest of the way to the ground, grabbed his gear, and spun, intending to run to the pool and snipe from the outskirts. But an ominous growl came from the trees ahead of him.

The wolf stepped into view, its fangs bared. It was even larger than it had appeared from above, and its nostrils flared as it sniffed, as it looked right at him.

Sorath pointed one of the magelock rifles at it, certain it knew where he was even if it couldn't see him.

But something cool pressed against the back of his head.

"Drop your weapons," a woman said in accented Dhoran. "We will not let you interfere again."

As Sorath was debating if he should obey, or try to whirl and knock her weapon away, two male druids stepped into view to either side of him. They pointed staffs at him, the weapons glowing green with power.

"My people need help," Sorath said, wondering if another one of those glowing staffs was what was pressed against the back of his skull.

"Good," the woman said, and he feared he wasn't going to get his chance to assassinate Uthari.

Icy cold energy surged from the weapon against his head, and Sorath winced, expecting intense pain. But it stunned him instead of harming him, power zinging along his every nerve and into his brain. He lost consciousness and tumbled to the ground.

27

"I don't understand what's going on," Tezi whispered to Dr. Fret.

Fret stood beside her, her medical kit in hand, but she hadn't been invited to participate in the surgery. Malek lay on his back on the ground in a spot Rivlen had cleared of undergrowth using her fire magic. Jak knelt beside him with Shikari in his lap and sketches Jadora had made of the kerzor laid out next to him. Jak was trying to convince Shikari to study them with him. The hatchling, alternating trying to climb to his shoulder and nibbling at his bootlaces, looked far more like a distraction than an attentive assistant.

"Brain surgery," Fret said.

"Performed by Jak?" Tinder asked. "Or Shikari?"

"Both, I think."

Tinder grumbled about needing help from where she was placing explosives in the forest, creating a semi-circle of booby-traps around the area. When Fret had pointed out that the dragons would come from the sky, not stampede across tripwires, Tinder had started constructing some of her traps in the branches.

Tezi was tempted to go help, but with Rivlen up at the top of the ziggurat, watching over Jadora, someone ought to stay close to Malek and Jak while they worked. For now, Malek's eyes were open, but he might lose consciousness during the surgery, and Jak would be engrossed in it. They would be easy targets if the dragons attacked.

"I'll go help her," Fret said.

"Is setting explosives something doctors excel at?" Tezi asked.

"No, but I'm stupendous at holding things. I'm sure that's all she needs." Fret set down her medical kit and patted Tezi on the shoulder. "Call me if things go wrong and you need my services."

"I will."

"We're going to start," Jak said.

Malek nodded once, glanced at Shikari, then folded his hands over his abdomen and closed his eyes. Not before Tezi caught the worry in those eyes.

She'd seen Malek leap fearlessly into battle—even in the last couple of days, since he'd lost his power. Neither fighting a monster in the arena nor battling dragons had seemed to daunt him. But he was worried about this.

Jak took a deep breath and also closed his eyes. The hatchling flopped down on the diagrams, crinkling them. Was he going to help? Or take a nap?

Tezi was tempted to ask if she could help with anything, but what could she possibly do?

She rested the head of her axe on the ground and draped her hands over the end of the haft. Her job had to be to stand guard, nothing more.

Long, silent moments passed with nothing seeming to happen. Though the hatchling had found a few insects earlier, the crater seemed largely devoid of bird or animal life. Whatever distant chirps and squawks sounded came from beyond it.

Did the ziggurat radiate some kind of power that kept animals away? Or were they staying silent because of danger nearby?

A vision came to Tezi, a gift from her axe. It wasn't of their valley but of a spacious cave with steaming pools dotting the lumpy ground. The sides and ceiling were made from gray rock interspersed with the same veins of ore that lined the cliffs in the valley.

Two hulking dragons crouched between the pools, steam wafting up all around them. Tezi realized that her group might have gone to the wrong spot. What if this dragon cave was hundreds of miles away?

In her vision, one dragon used magic to pluck arrows out of the other. They were healing each other's wounds.

Nearby, a woman was trapped in a bubble that floated in one of the pools—Etcher Yervaa, still protected by her barrier. But she was slumped against one side of it, her hood fallen back to reveal black hair that hung limply around her shoulders, with strands plastered to her sweaty face. She didn't look like she could keep that barrier up much longer. Once it collapsed, she would fall into that steaming pool. And die? Being boiled alive?

Or maybe that wasn't steam. The smoke had a slightly brownish tint. Maybe it was the same gas that made the air in the valley smell off, the gas that Jadora was even now collecting from a vent in the top of the ziggurat.

With that thought, the viewpoint of Tezi's vision shifted to show her the dragons and the pools from a different angle. Now, she could see past them to a straight black wall. It rose twenty feet, then shifted to a horizontal shelf that went back into the darkness, but she could make out another vertical rise in the shadows behind it. It disappeared into the ceiling of the cave.

The ziggurat, Tezi realized as the vision faded, leaving her back in the quiet forest. She'd seen part of the ziggurat. An underground portion.

She whirled to look at the structure, one of the vertical walls only ten feet away. Before, she'd assumed it was built on the ground, but if what she'd seen was true, part of it was built below ground. She, Jak, and the others could be standing right above the cave where the two dragons were waiting.

Waiting or preparing themselves? Healing themselves fully so they once again had no weaknesses? After they finished, or once the ruler's barrier gave out and she died, would they fly out and attack?

In the vision, Tezi hadn't seen an entrance to that cave, but it could be nearby. The group had flown straight to the ziggurat without exploring the valley thoroughly.

She opened her mouth to warn Jak, but his eyes were still closed, his face locked in concentration. The hatchling's eyes were also closed. He might have been helping, or he might have been sleeping.

Malek's face contorted, eyes moving behind his lids, as he lay on the charred earth. His body stiffened, and his back arched.

Tezi closed her mouth. She dared not interrupt when they were in the middle of brain surgery. And there was nobody else nearby to warn of the threat.

She lifted her axe, hoping the procedure wouldn't take long—and that the dragons wouldn't arrive before it was over.

∽

Sasko woke to orders being shouted to guard the portal. They came from the other mercenary companies and Uthari's mages, but she trusted Thorn Company would receive the same command. She snatched her weapons and threw her blanket aside, glad she hadn't taken off her boots for the night.

"Someone or something is coming out," Ferroki said,

crouching beside her. "I'll handle forming up the company. You protect your engineer again."

"He doesn't need a military lieutenant as a *bodyguard*." Sasko took in the stars glowing in the center of the portal and all the mages and mercenaries already with weapons pointed at it.

"He may. The druids targeted him before." Ferroki also had her rifle pointed at the portal, though the company was in the trees, farther away from it and the pool.

"Is that who's coming out?" Sasko glanced toward Vinjo's newly erected tent in time to see him poke his head out through the flap.

As he peered around curiously, he did look like an easy target. What if druids were targeting him from the trees already? He *did* need a bodyguard.

"It's not the stars that showed up when our team left," Ferroki said.

"Get Thorn Company over here," one of the mage officers bellowed from the portal.

The troops had risen and armed themselves, the same as Sasko, and looked toward the captain for orders.

Ferroki nodded. "Don't get too close," she told them, "and don't try to be a hero and hold ranks if something insanely powerful and deadly comes out. Take cover and shoot from the trees. Let's get as many grenades into people's hands as we've got."

Everyone had expected this and was already prepared. They took off in their squads as Ferroki pointed Sasko toward Vinjo's tent.

"Go hide him under cover before he can wander out in his underwear and get himself killed."

"He's got a skirt now," Sasko said, though she didn't hesitate to jog toward him. Since they didn't have the stealth device this time, it would be harder to keep him safe.

"That won't make the druids pause. They dress similarly." Ferroki ran to catch up with the company and take the lead.

As Sasko approached the tent, something came out of the portal. It wasn't a druid. It wasn't a human at all.

Sasko swore and ran faster, waving for Vinjo to get back inside. Not that the tent offered much protection. The last one burned like dry brush in a wildfire.

Vinjo was gaping at the portal, not looking at her.

A creature so large that its sides brushed the edges of the ring ambled out. It looked like a giant armadillo with four squat legs protected by bony armor that covered its back and sides. The greenish-brown armor also protected the back of its neck, the top of its head, and a thick tail that dragged on the ground as it walked. Two brown ears poked out from the sides of its head, and the snout reminded Sasko of a pig. Though the large paws had claws, they looked more appropriate for digging than slashing enemies into pieces.

"Is that... a predator?" Vinjo asked skeptically.

"It doesn't look like it," Sasko said, "but don't assume it's not dangerous."

The mages weren't taking any chances. A familiar voice called, "Kill it!" as magical compulsion ensured nobody would hesitate.

Was that Uthari? Down here again for another battle?

Under the compelling order, Sasko caught herself pointing her rifle and shooting at the creature's beady black eyes. Unlike most of the body, they didn't appear protected.

As everyone opened fire, a great energy pulse emanated from the creature. It radiated outward like a shockwave, knocking over mages and mercenaries alike, and making the ground quake. The strange energy made all the hair on Sasko's arms stand up an instant before it hurled her into the side of the tent.

The fireballs, magelock blasts, and bursts of power that struck the armored visitor ricocheted off and flew into the trees, into the sky, and back at those who'd fired. Even though Sasko's shot hit it in the eye, whatever that organ was made from deflected the blast as easily as the others.

More waves of energy pulsed from the creature, shaking the ground and throwing even mages protected inside barriers into the air. Sasko found herself rolling past the tent, Vinjo tumbling alongside her, with no ability to stop herself. Canvas flew as the tents were flattened or blasted into the brush.

During the first battle, the trees in the area had been decimated, but snaps sounded as trunks farther back were blasted down. Up above, the shockwaves struck the mageships. They were surrounded by barriers, but that didn't fully protect them. They bobbed like ships on a tumultuous sea.

Only the portal seemed impervious to the strange energy waves. It appeared to block them, for the trees behind it weren't affected.

"How do we fight this thing?" Sasko sank to her knees in freshly upturned dirt. She still had her rifle, but if even the eyes of the creature weren't vulnerable, she didn't know what to target.

A grenade flew from a mercenary's hand. It bounced off the armored back and exploded. Smoke shrouded the creature, but it ambled out of it, unaffected.

"Not like that." Vinjo clawed his way toward her on hands and knees.

Red lightning bolts came from a group of mages. Uthari and his bodyguards. They wrapped around the creature, branching and curving, red light flashing on its armor.

Though the bolts didn't bounce off, like so many of the other attacks, they didn't seem to affect it much. After a moment, it stopped walking forward, so maybe it didn't like the attack after all. The creature's head hunched, and it peered to the side. No, it peered behind it. Back to the portal.

Another giant armored creature ambled out.

"Oh, fantastic," Sasko said. "She invited the entire pack."

"She?" Vinjo asked.

"The druid. This has to be her work."

Another pulse of power emanated from the first creature. Sasko and Vinjo flattened themselves to the ground, and she found an exposed root to grasp. The earth bucked, nearly tossing her backward again, but being low made it easier to stay in place.

A dozen yards from her, a dagger flew out of a mercenary's hand as he tumbled through the air. Bad luck sent it zipping toward Sasko, point first.

Cursing, she rolled to the side, afraid she would be too slow.

But the dagger didn't find a target. When Sasko peeked back, it was floating in the air several feet away. Vinjo, who'd also kept from flying by, flattened himself to the ground and flicked his hand. The dagger dropped to the ground, sinking in point first where it hopefully wouldn't fly free again.

"Thanks," she said. "I didn't know you could do that."

"Put up barriers? It's a basic mage talent."

"Yes, but you're..."

"Talentless?" He raised his eyebrows, smiling sadly.

"You seem to focus your talents elsewhere."

"I'd like to focus them elsewhere now, but my tools and my tent all flew off into the trees." He craned his head to peer back as the second armadillo-creature fully emerged from the portal. The head of a third appeared.

"She *did* send the whole pack," Sasko groaned.

Despite the ability to throw out such great waves of energy, the creatures didn't charge after any of the mages or mercenaries. So far, they were simply defending themselves, though the snapping of wood from the ships above and knocking down of trees and tents promised their defenses did a lot of damage.

The mercenaries had all been thrown far into the trees. Uthari and a number of his mages had run to the cliff near the waterfall and had their backs braced against the rock. The pulses of energy hadn't knocked the cliff to pieces. Yet.

The mages tried different attacks on the creatures. Judging by his hand gestures, one attempted to levitate them, but the magic didn't take hold.

Uthari kept pointing at the portal as he spoke to one of his high-ranking officers. Maybe he was suggesting they try to shut it down so more creatures couldn't come through.

Two of the mages held their hands in the air, as if gripping a large ball. Their faces grew tight with concentration.

"They're trying to crush one of the creature's insides," Vinjo said. "But it's not doing anything. For some reason, they're not able to lift them off the ground either. Not even Uthari. He should have the power to hurl a mountain around, but those creatures are strange. They feel slick to my senses. Slippery."

Sasko gave him the odd look the comment deserved. Vinjo only shrugged.

Uthari put his hand out in front of him, as if he were pushing against a stiff wind, and strode toward the portal. He only made it five feet before more pulses of energy came from the creatures.

Sasko gripped the root she'd held before to keep from flying farther away. Vinjo crawled forward fast enough to grab the hilt of the knife. He jabbed it deeper into the ground and used it like an anchor.

One of the shockwaves caught Uthari and threw him backward. Sasko was disappointed when his barrier struck the cliff and insulated him. She would have preferred to see him splat against it like a watermelon dropping on cobblestones.

"It's wrong of us to hope that cliff crumbles and crushes Uthari and all of his mages, right?" she asked.

Vinjo's face grew wistful, but he shook his head as a fourth creature appeared, walking ponderously out of the portal. Sasko glanced back, to spots where the rest of the company had flown.

Some had caught trees stout enough that they hadn't been ripped from the ground. Others had tumbled back so far they weren't visible anymore.

"At least the beasts aren't trying to eat us," Vinjo said.

"What *are* they doing?" Sasko asked.

The house-sized creatures had arrayed themselves in front of the portal, as if they were defending it from the mages and mercenaries. The starry center was still intact, the passageway open. Sasko wondered what would happen if Tinder and Fret and the others tried to return while the portal was in use, connected to another world.

The head of a fifth creature appeared in the center. How *many* would come?

The ground shuddered as they created more shockwaves. Before, it had seemed a defense, but Sasko didn't think anyone was attacking them now. Uthari was busy trying to reach the portal again. He might have seen Sasko and Vinjo having some success at staying in place, for he sank low as another shockwave rolled out. Emulating Vinjo, he produced a dagger that he stabbed deep into the earth as an anchor.

Someone rode astride the fifth creature. The druid woman. Her great spotted jaguar walked out behind her huge armored mount, small in comparison.

"You!" someone called. Yidar.

He was on the deck of one of the mageships and pointed his sword down at the druid woman. A fiery blast streamed from his blade, angling down at her. Sasko thought being on the creature might protect her, but perhaps not, for she swung off and crouched to the side of it, using it for cover. The attack glanced off the top of its armored back,

The jaguar roared indignation as its master was attacked. Uthari glowered over at it. From his position, he could see it and her without trouble. He flung some of his red lightning.

The druid whirled, raising a barrier in time, but his power staggered her. It didn't tear down her barrier, but she dropped to one knee as she raised her arms, pouring everything into her defenses.

The jaguar roared at Uthari. At first, Sasko thought it was safe behind the barrier, but as the woman dropped to both knees, it weakened enough for the cat to spring free. It charged at Uthari.

He shifted his attack to it, lightning pounding it in the chest. The jaguar screeched in pain and pitched to the ground.

Another pulse of energy came from the creatures, and Uthari had to stop his attack, grip the dagger lodged in the earth, and fight to stay in place.

The druid lunged to her feet, taking a step toward the jaguar. It looked back at her, holding her gaze for so long that Sasko was certain it was an intelligent, thinking creature. Then it rose up and charged Uthari again. Was it trying to buy her time to escape?

After hesitating, the woman ran along the pool toward the trees on the far side. As the injured jaguar summoned the last of its energy to spring at Uthari again, Sasko lifted her rifle to target the druid. But she hesitated, not positive she wanted to take down Uthari's enemy. The bastard had tortured Sorath. And forced them to work for him.

"She has the other key," Vinjo pointed out, "and she brought those creatures here."

Sasko sighed and fired. She half hoped the druid had her defenses back up and the magelock blast would bounce off.

But it slammed into her shoulder and knocked her into the pool. She disappeared under the froth of the waterfall and didn't come back up.

"Uh oh," Vinjo said.

Sasko shifted her focus back to Uthari, thinking the jaguar might have reached him and torn out his throat, but it lay dead and smoking on the ground in front of him. Vinjo wasn't pointing to the mages but to something glowing purple in the ground between the creatures. It reminded her of the tip of an asparagus stalk growing out of the dirt.

"What is it?" Sasko asked. "Something the druid dropped?"

"Dropped? Uh, I don't think so."

The ground crumbled around the glowing purple object, falling inward and creating a hole. A hole that grew wider and wider. The creatures seemed surprised by it and shifted outward, but they didn't move out of the area. It was hard to see what was happening through their stout legs.

"It's the end of a tunnel," Vinjo said. "Their shockwaves weren't what was making the ground shake. Someone was using them for cover to magically dig that tunnel."

"More druids?"

"That's my guess." Vinjo glanced at the pond.

Sasko was keeping an eye on it. The female druid still hadn't come back up. Sasko didn't think her blow had been to a fatal spot, but if the druid had been depleted from facing Uthari, maybe she hadn't had the strength to swim to the top.

"What do they need a tunnel for?" From where they knelt, all Sasko could see was a big hole forming.

"Look." Vinjo thrust his arm out, not toward the hole but toward the portal.

It was wobbling. As if someone were leaning against it and pushing, trying to knock it into the hole.

"Oh," Sasko said, realization sinking in. "They're trying to *steal* it."

Since the female druid hadn't reappeared, that had to mean that other druids nearby were responsible. Thus far, the mages and mercenaries had been focusing their attacks on the creatures. Maybe nobody had realized there were more enemies about.

"Captain!" Sasko called. "There might be druids in the trees."

"Or underground," Vinjo said.

"The portal!" Uthari shouted, springing up to try again to reach it.

For once, Sasko rooted for him to achieve his goal. If he didn't keep the druids from carting the portal off and burying it who knew where, Tinder, Fret, Tezi, and the others would never be able to come home.

When Uthari was scant feet from it, the creatures pulsed all at once. This time, Sasko's root couldn't save her. As the portal tilted toward the hole, she and Vinjo flew backward, somersaulting into the trees. She glimpsed Uthari and his mages also being thrown back.

Sasko landed hard on her back, her rifle flying from her hands, and she cursed again.

The druids were going to get the portal, and she had no idea how to stop them.

28

Rivlen stood atop the ziggurat, keeping an eye on Jadora as she finished up at the vent, and also checking in often on Malek's operation. She couldn't tell how it was going, only that Malek had been lying on his back for a long time with Jak kneeling beside him. Tezi stood nearby. She hefted her axe and peered into the woods, as if she'd heard something.

Is everything all right down there? Rivlen asked her telepathically.

Tezi looked up and spotted her. *I think the dragons are under us.*

Under? Rivlen squinted at her, but Tezi was too far away for Rivlen to read her thoughts. *How?*

In a cave. I had, uhm, a vision. From my axe, I think.

"Jadora?" Rivlen peered back toward the vent, hoping she was almost done.

Jadora slung her backpack over her shoulders, and she staggered out of the three-sided structure, coughing and pale-faced. "Remind me to bring a gas mask along on further adventures."

"I don't know what that is, but I will." Rivlen hopped onto the skyboard and pointed for Jadora to join her. "Tezi saw dragons in a cave under us in a vision. They could be monitoring us and waiting for an opportune time to attack. We need to get ready for trouble."

"Wouldn't you be able to sense them if they were that close?" Jadora stepped on with her.

"Usually, yes, but it's hard to sense anything with this big hunk of dragon steel right here." Just being in close proximity to the ziggurat and its inherent magic was giving Rivlen a headache. "It's like trying to hear a mosquito's buzz when a troupe is singing and hammering on drums right beside you."

"I understand." Jadora gripped her shoulders as they flew over the side. "I wish we had time to gather some ore." She looked wistfully toward one of the cliffs.

"We'll want to stick together."

"We could gather everyone and leave before the dragons show up."

Rivlen wished that were a possibility. Malek and Jak were the only ones who wanted to risk themselves to rescue this ruler. Rivlen just wanted to return to Torvil and report to Uthari. She hated the idea of the fleet—and the world—being blindsided by an invading army because Rivlen and the others had never made it home to warn them.

"If we take the hatchling, I think the dragons will know it and give chase. For whatever reason, they want the scaly kid dead." Rivlen peered toward the cliff Jadora had been admiring, wondering if the cave entrance might be in one of those rocky areas. If they could find it and collapse it, that might delay the dragons. Rivlen had no delusions about harming them or permanently trapping them with nothing more than a rockfall.

"Uh oh." Jadora gripped her shoulders.

Rivlen spun, afraid she'd already spotted dragons.

Jadora was pointing at Malek and Jak. Something was wrong.

Dr. Fret had run out of the brush to kneel beside them. Malek's legs were twitching, his hands opening and closing.

"I *knew* that was a bad idea," Jadora said. "Take me down there. Please."

"Can you help?" Rivlen couldn't imagine what an archaeologist could do, but Jadora knew about chemicals and herbs, so maybe she could do something.

Rivlen directed the skyboard downward, worried about what would happen if Malek died. It would be a great loss for Uthari and the kingdom, and what if Uthari blamed Rivlen for it? Felt she should have done more to keep this from happening?

"I don't know," Jadora said, "but I have to be there."

She leaped off when the skyboard was still five feet from the ground, her heavy backpack tilting so much that it nearly pitched her over. Jadora flailed, recovered, and ran to kneel next to Jak.

Since Rivlen could do nothing to help, she thought about going to look for the cave entrance, but with the group distracted, they would be vulnerable to attack. And even though Jak was learning, none of the rest of them were mages. They wouldn't have a chance against a dragon.

The hatchling ran behind Jak to hide from Malek's thrashing. That didn't bode well for the surgery.

Jadora pulled a tiny vial out of her pack and held it under Malek's nose. At first, nothing happened except that he flung up an arm and almost knocked it away. His eyes were closed, so these didn't appear to be conscious movements, but something was definitely going wrong.

Rivlen rubbed a hand down her face. If he died…

A grinding emanated from the far side of the ziggurat, like a huge mill stone smashing grains. Or a hidden door sliding open?

Abruptly, Rivlen sensed the dragons. Not flying out of some distant cave on the far side of the crater but nearby. On the other side of the ziggurat.

She cursed. They'd looked all around the thing for doors. How could there be a hidden one? If it was in regular use, it would have disturbed all that vegetation.

"The dragons are coming!" Rivlen yelled to the group. "I'll try to delay them, but get ready."

Delay them. Right.

Rivlen sped toward the corner of the ziggurat on her skyboard.

"Here," Tinder called and tossed her a grenade.

Rivlen caught the meager weapon. She would rather have had a capable ally, but she would take whatever she could get. Against such powerful foes, she would need more than her magic.

Rounding another corner took her to the far side of the ziggurat where a huge rectangular slab had opened from the bottom tier, tipping outward to land in the undergrowth. The stink of that acid filled the air, much stronger now.

The first brown-and-gray mottled dragon walked out, talons scraping on the slab. Rivlen sensed the other one right behind it. She armed the grenade and hurled it at them.

As it sailed toward the first dragon, she arrowed into the trees on the skyboard, hoping they would chase her instead of going straight for the hatchling.

Even before the grenade exploded, the lead dragon's head spun, and yellow eyes tracked her. The second dragon stomped out of the interior of the ziggurat to join the first. They roared as one, a battle cry that reverberated through the trees and echoed from the walls of the valley.

The grenade blew as it struck a barrier around the dragons. White light flashed in the shadowed forest, and gray smoke filled the air. The dragons sprang out of the cloud and flew after Rivlen.

A wave of power roiled ahead of them, blowing trees out of the ground. The main blast missed Rivlen as she zipped around a cairn of rocks and changed direction, but dirt and shards of wood flew hundreds of feet and pelted her barrier.

She focused on keeping that barrier up, on funneling all of her power into it. She would need every bit of defense that she could muster.

Another wave of power rolled through the forest. This time, the dragons compensated for her zigzagging flight, and their attack slammed into her barrier.

Jaw clenched, Rivlen managed to keep it up, but the concentration and power required nearly took her to her knees. Even worse, the dragons were giving chase. Both of them.

She flew through the trees, hoping they would impede the large creatures, but they merely tucked their wings in to navigate through tight spots—or they blew obstacles out of their way.

Rivlen dared not lower her barrier to throw an attack. Her instincts warned her of another blast incoming.

She crouched low, shifting her power to make her barrier stronger in the back. For now, both dragons were behind her.

This time, fire struck her barrier. A huge blast of it that turned the air orange, charred trees, and made foliage burst into flames. Even though her barrier kept the fire from incinerating her, the heat penetrated it, raising the temperature of the air all around her.

Ahead, a cliff arose. Rivlen turned her skyboard sharply, afraid she would be trapped.

She angled around a thick copse of trees, managing to leave the heat behind, but for how long? How many attacks could she deflect before the dragons overpowered her?

Fear rushed through her veins as her pursuers rapidly closed the distance, flying far more quickly than she could on the skyboard. She told herself this was what she'd wanted, to draw them away from Malek and the others.

That didn't make the experience any less terrifying.

And as they gained on her, hurling trees aside and drawing ever closer, Rivlen feared she would never see the others again.

Jak had heard Rivlen's warning cry, her announcement that the two dragons were coming out of the ziggurat, but Malek was in a critical state, and Jak couldn't stop what he was doing.

Shikari had been alarmed when Malek started thrashing about, back arching and legs kicking, but Jak coaxed him back into his lap. Aware that they didn't have much time, he tried to draw Shikari's focus back to Malek, to the tiny strands from the kerzor that were embedded in his brain. Jak and Shikari had been using their senses to locate and carefully destroy them in situ, and they had to finish the job.

Fortunately, his mother held something to Malek's nose, and it quieted him—or maybe rendered him unconscious. Given the dragon threat, having him knocked out might not be the best idea, but it made the surgery easier. Before, Malek's brain had seemed to be fighting them, but now it quieted down, and it was easier to spot the tendrils in there.

Shikari, Jak thought. *We're almost done, aren't we? Do you sense any more?*

He'd been showing the hatchling what he wanted, similar to the carriage back at the portal, and Shikari had intuited the rest and destroyed several of the strands. Without him, Jak could barely detect them, but he'd known they were in there somewhere. His part was guiding the dragon on where to look and demonstrating what he wanted done.

Uncertainty emanated from Shikari. Not about the tendrils from the kerzor, Jak thought, but because he sensed the arrival of the enemy dragons. Shikari was having a hard time concentrating on this task when he feared for his life.

We'll protect you, Jak told him. *Rivlen is delaying them. We just need to get Malek back on his feet with his magic. Are there any more tendrils?*

Even as he asked the question, Jak sensed another one. They would have been too fine to see with the naked eye. It was their magic that he could sense, but it was such faint magic that he struggled. Shikari had a much easier time—when he was focused.

A cry of alarm echoed from the forest—Rivlen.

The smell of trees burning mingled with the acrid scent wafting from the ziggurat. Jak didn't have to open his eyes—or listen to the mercenaries muttering—to know the dragons were lighting the forest on fire to try to kill Rivlen.

Shikari climbed up Jak's shirt, talons digging into fabric—and skin—and burrowed into the sling.

Please, Shikari. Help him. I'll catch so many bugs for you that you'll be able to gorge for weeks.

The hatchling peeped with uncertainty. Jak might have given up, but he wasn't sure if Malek would wake up if they didn't finish. Even if they did, he didn't know if Malek would be all right, if he would be able to join the fight. But Jak had to believe he would, that this risk had been worth taking.

Another cry of alarm—no, of *anguish*—came from the trees. If Rivlen was running out of stamina, she might be forced to lead the dragons back here.

Fear for Malek, for his mother, and for himself filled Jak. He almost lost track of the tendril that he'd picked out and wanted Shikari to destroy. Could he destroy it himself? He didn't truly know what he was doing.

Shikari's presence returned to Jak's mind. Fear but also reassurance wafted from the hatchling. Was he... trying to comfort Jak?

Shikari focused on the tendril Jak had found and carefully incinerated it, from the anchor deep in Malek's brain to the end where it attached to the needle stuck through his skull.

Beside them, Mother stirred.

"The disc sagged," she whispered. "Jak, does that mean it's no longer attached?"

Jak opened his eyes. She was touching the metal disc at Malek's temple. It was no longer as tight to his skin, but did that mean Shikari had gotten all of the tendrils?

Do you sense any more? Jak silently asked, envisioning the strands they'd already destroyed and trying to make the hatchling understand the question.

Mother gripped the disc, poised to pull it out, but doubt and fear filled her eyes, more for Malek than the threat of dragons, Jak sensed. Though she did keep glancing toward the forest. Gray smoke hazed the air between the trees, making it impossible to see far, though Jak could sense the dragons chasing Rivlen. He couldn't tell if her barrier was still up.

Shikari sank lower in the sling, trying to bury himself. He conveyed that he was done, but Jak didn't know if that meant he'd completed the task or he refused to work on Malek further.

"Dragons coming!" Tinder shouted from the trees near the corner of the ziggurat. "Rivlen, lead them to my traps!"

"I think we may have gotten them all," Jak told his mother, though he wasn't certain. "Do you have anything to wake him up?"

It was hard to imagine anyone sleeping through the angry screeches of hunting dragons or the growing roar of the forest fire, but Mother's concoctions could be potent.

She shook her head. "That was only to relax him. He shouldn't be unconscious. At least not from anything I've done."

"Oh." Jak stared at Malek.

"I'm going to remove it. Or try." Mother eased the disc and the bloody needle from his skull.

It came away without effort, but Jak still didn't know if they'd succeeded.

"Dragons incoming!" came Rivlen's yell in his mind as well as out loud.

As Tezi and Tinder sprang to their feet, axes and grenades at the ready, the smoke stirred and Rivlen flew toward them. She was still riding the skyboard.

A fireball the size of a house roared toward her from behind. Her barrier was fluctuating, her face twisting with effort as she tried to keep it up.

Jak brought up his valley imagery and funneled his river of power into her, praying to Shylezar that she still had the strength to make use of it. She grasped it and channeled it into her barrier as the fireball caught up.

It swallowed her, Rivlen and the skyboard completely disappearing in the brilliant orange flames, and Jak feared his power hadn't been enough, that he'd been too late. Especially when he sensed both dragons flying right behind her, surging through the smoke toward them.

Then Rivlen flew out of the dissipating fireball, her barrier still up. Sweat gleamed on her face, and her skin was pink from the heat, but she kept coming.

"Jak," Mother said. "We have to hide."

She gripped Malek's arm, as if she might toss him over her shoulder and run for cover. But she wasn't strong enough for that.

Jak couldn't take his focus from Rivlen, couldn't stop helping her lest the powerful dragons blast her barrier away and slay her.

Fret ran behind a tree, ducking down as Tinder prepared to hurl a grenade. The two dragons came into view, glowing yellow eyes piercing the smoke. They flew low, weaving between trees, their maws partially open, long razor-sharp fangs ready to bite.

One of them caught up to Rivlen and snapped at her. Through his magical link to her, Jak sensed the hit to her barrier, but with his added strength, it stayed firm, repulsing the fangs.

Rivlen had almost reached them, flying over the traps Tinder had laid, but she veered off. Once again, she tried to lead the dragons away.

But one of them focused on Jak—no, on the hatchling. It left its pursuit of Rivlen and arrowed toward him.

"Malek." Jak shook his shoulder. "Malek, we really need you to wake up now."

A groan escaped Malek's lips, but his eyes didn't open. Even if he woke up, he still might not have his magic. But he would have his sword skills...

"Come on, Malek." Jak shook him again, then leaped to his feet. He was out of time.

But he couldn't leave Malek. Jak focused all of his power into creating a barrier, one stronger than a mountain, strong enough to repel a dragon attack.

His mother sprang behind a tree, her eyes wide with terror, and she kept glancing with concern at Malek, but that didn't keep her from clutching an explosive. She threw it as the dragon barreled down on Jak and Malek.

It swooped in, blasting fire at them. Though terrified as that heat and flame roiled toward him, Jak focused all of his energy on his barrier, wrapping it around himself and Malek. He couldn't let fear distract him or they would both die.

"Hold firm," he whispered as the flames engulfed his barrier. "Hold firm."

The power of the fire was so intense that it sapped his strength. The dragon banked to avoid running into the side of the ziggurat, but it didn't cease its attack. Jak could feel his barrier wilting like a flower under the heat.

At his feet, Malek stirred and blinked. But the puzzled confusion in his eyes wasn't promising, and Jak feared he wouldn't be able to help.

Then power from an unexpected source flowed into him. At first, Jak thought Rivlen had found a moment to breathe and share some of her energy, but this came from the hatchling.

Shikari had his head buried inside the sling, but energy flowed into Jak from him, enough to reinforce his barrier.

The flames died down, but the dragon was still close. It sprang at Jak, slashing with sword-like talons, trying to tear away his protection to kill him and Shikari.

The other dragon left Rivlen and circled to fly in close to help. One of its wings brushed a stump in the undergrowth, and an explosion ripped, smoke and plant matter flying. One of Tinder's traps.

Tezi ran in with her axe to attack that dragon. Fear pummeled Jak, as he was certain it would be able to crush her, but with the other dragon still attacking him, he couldn't do anything to help. Tinder threw a grenade at their foe, then followed Tezi in, hefting her axe as well. Jak prayed the dragon-steel weapons would be enough to keep them alive.

Malek sat up and patted the ground for his weapons.

"If you can help," Jak said, "we'd really appreciate it."

"I gathered that," Malek rasped, wincing as if he had the worst headache ever.

He probably did.

Give us the hatchling, one of the dragons roared in Jak's mind, compulsion woven into the words.

Jak's fingers twitched toward his sling strap before he caught himself. *No! Why do you want him? He's just a baby.*

The dragon landed beside him and launched another magical attack. Jak's barrier trembled, but Shikari was still helping him, and together, they channeled more energy into it to firm it up even as the attack tore trees from their roots. A giant trunk flew through the air and slammed into the side of the ziggurat.

To make him one of us. The dragon launched another fireball at Jak.

Staggering under the power, his barrier wavering, Jak dropped to one knee. Even with Shikari's help, he wasn't strong enough to meet the sheer might of a mature dragon.

An image popped into Jak's mind—the ziggurat and Shikari communicating with it. Was that Shikari's idea? Or was the enemy dragon trying to trick him into doing something?

Shikari poked his eyes out of the sling pouch.

"You want to talk to it?" Jak panted, sweat streaming down the sides of his face.

His mental mountains crumbled, the power of the dragon railing at them. Jak didn't have the energy left to funnel anything else into his defenses.

Someone else helped reinforce the barrier, and abruptly it grew easier to keep it up. Malek?

He rose to his feet beside Jak, weapons in hand. Though his face was pale, and he looked shaky, not his full zidarr self, he nodded to Jak.

"Are you getting your power back?" Jak yelled as flames crackled all around him.

"Yes." Malek squinted at Shikari.

Had the hatchling shared the same image with him?

A scream of pain came from the other fight. Tezi. One of the dragon's wings had caught her, knocking her to her back. The dragon charged in, jaws spreading wide to crush her.

"No!" Jak longed to help, but the dragon in front of him snapped its jaws, biting at his barrier through the flames. Even with Malek's help, Jak couldn't keep the creature at bay much longer. He certainly couldn't help anyone else.

Rivlen ran out of the trees and launched a wall of fire at the other dragon. It looked up, distracted, and Tezi rolled away and scrambled behind a log.

"Take Shikari to the ziggurat." Malek pointed his sword at the closer dragon. "I'll keep this one busy."

"What if he can't do anything?"

"Hope he can."

Jak couldn't drop the barrier, so he carried it with him, walking past the dragon and toward the ziggurat. But the dragon leaped into his path to block him.

Malek stepped out of the barrier, ran around Jak and their foe, and sprang into the air with both blades swinging. He sliced through scales as he flew up to land on the dragon's back.

It roared, more at the indignity than the pain, and swung its long neck around to snap at him.

Something struck the dragon in the back of the head. One of Mother's explosives. It blew, creating a slight distraction at best, but Malek took advantage. He ran up the dragon's back and drove his sword into its neck.

Though Jak doubted the blow would be deadly—or even bother their foe much—he felt hope that they might survive, that having Malek back on his feet would even the odds.

The dragon roared again. It blasted Malek with fire, but he got a barrier of his own up, one strong enough to defend against the powerful creature, at least for a few seconds.

A yellow eye pinned Jak, but the dragon had to deal with Malek. That left Jak free to run around it.

Even though the dragon wanted to get Shikari, Malek was a threat again, one it had to deal with.

Jak dodged a swipe from a taloned rear leg, ran to the side of the ziggurat, and planted his hand against it. He'd done that before, and the ancient dragon steel still felt dormant to him, but if Shikari could do something...

The hatchling jumped from the sling, startling Jak. Shikari scrambled to the side of the ziggurat and spread his little wings and leaned his head against it.

Communicating with it? Rousing it from its long sleep?

Jak hoped so. He also hoped the ziggurat would act against the younger dragons, that they hadn't over the years turned it into some loyal structure that would defend them instead of attacking them.

29

Sasko crawled back across the shaking ground with a grenade clutched in one hand. She gripped her dagger in the other, driving it into the earth and using it as an anchor whenever the armored creatures blasted out a shockwave.

They stood guarding the great hole the druids had created in front of the portal, but they seemed indifferent to her approach. Behind her, weapons fired from the trees. Fireballs zipped over her head as the mages on the ground and in the mageships tried to wear down the animals' defenses. But the creatures weren't the problem. The druids were.

If some of them were in that hole—that *tunnel*, if Vinjo was right—maybe Sasko could surprise them and keep them from pulling in the portal.

But every time one of those shockwaves struck, it threatened to knock her all the way back into the trees. Vinjo was struggling to crawl alongside her, also using a dagger like a pickaxe on a mountainside. He'd created a magical barrier to keep a knife from striking her, but the mages continued to struggle against the shockwaves. Many more had been flung into the trees, along with all the mercenaries, than remained near the portal. Up above, most of the mageships were no longer in sight. Though protected by barriers, they'd been knocked back like sailing vessels tossed about on rough seas.

King Uthari, however, kept creeping closer to the portal, likewise anchoring himself to the ground when the shockwaves struck. He was angling toward the portal rather than the hole, his hand stretched toward it. For the moment, he seemed to be preventing it from falling in, but someone had to deal with the druids, or they would keep trying.

Sasko waited for a shockwave to pass, then rose to her knees to heft her grenade, envisioning it blowing the hole closed and collapsing the ceiling on whatever druids were in the tunnel they'd made. She threw it hard, so it would arch over the creatures instead of bouncing off their armored backs.

But another shockwave came right after the last. It caught the grenade in the air, sending it flying into the trees to blow up uselessly.

The shockwave also caught Sasko on her knees and would have knocked her back again, but Vinjo grabbed her with his free hand and pulled her down next to him. His other remained wrapped around a dagger plunged deep into the ground.

"Thanks," she said, though she was frustrated by another failure. Her rifle was of no use against the animals or the druids, and she only had one grenade left. "Ferroki told me to protect you. I wasn't expecting it to be the other way around."

"I only regret that all of my tools have been destroyed or blown a mile into the jungle. I'm useless without them." He shook his head glumly. "As my brother often points out."

"No, you're not. And your brother is a dick."

"He's a powerful zidarr favored by King Zaruk."

"Trust me. The two aren't mutually exclusive." Sasko sank low, gripping the hilt of her own dagger as another shockwave threatened to knock them out of the camp.

A fireball bounced off the nearest creature and blazed past, nearly taking her head off. Cursing, she pressed her face to the ground, dirt coating her lips.

"Maybe those idiots should consider a different tactic," she grumbled, grabbing her last grenade, though she didn't dare waste it. She might have to get closer so she could drop it into the tunnel by hand. A daunting prospect, since that would mean maneuvering past the legs of the house-sized creatures, but if the druids succeeded, her colleagues—her *friends*—would be stranded in another world forever.

"When you have one very powerful tool that works in many situations, you aren't inspired to practice creativity," Vinjo said.

"I hope you're not eyeing my grenade when you say that."

"No, but we need something to make them pause before you throw it again. We—"

"There." Sasko pointed.

Uthari had clawed his way to the portal and stood by it now, an arm wrapped around it. Since it had been wobbling, the druids in the tunnel trying to pull it down against its own magic, Sasko didn't think it would make a good anchor, but it ceased wobbling. Uthari pressed his head against it, as if he were communicating with it. Maybe he was. Jak could. Why not a powerful wizard?

A druid with a glowing green staff ran out of the trees on the far side of the portal. He took aim at Uthari.

"Look out!" Sasko cried.

Though a part of her wanted to see the old man fried, he was their best bet for keeping the portal in place.

Without looking, Uthari lifted a hand toward the druid. A green beam shot out of that staff, but it met an invisible wall and bounced off.

A second later, blue lightning shot out and struck the druid in the chest. It blew him back into the trees and out of sight.

That wasn't Uthari's usual red lightning. It took Sasko a moment to realize the ramifications.

"He convinced the portal to do that," Vinjo said.

More lightning streaked from its framework, several branches shooting across the camp and into the trees—targeting druids? Screams came from the jungle, assuring they'd landed.

Other lightning attacks struck the creatures, branching a dozen times as they wrapped around them, the tips slipping under their armor plating. Earlier, when Uthari had attacked with his lightning, it hadn't seemed to harm them, but now the creatures grunted and squealed, their big bodies shuddering. Smoke wafted out from under their armor.

"This is my chance," Sasko whispered.

She didn't know if Uthari *needed* her help, but the fear that her friends would die or wouldn't be able to come back if something happened to the portal propelled her forward.

With the lightning attacks striking the creatures, they didn't send out any new shockwaves. Their squeals battered painfully at Sasko's ears, but she forced herself to get closer. They stomped, big feet moving and making it hard to see the hole through their legs.

Sasko readied the grenade, tempted to throw it over them again, but they might yet get more shockwaves out. Or a druid with a staff might see it and blow it up prematurely. Instead, she drew her arm back, timed her throw carefully, and skidded it along the ground.

It flew low between the legs of the nearest creature and tumbled into the hole.

"Down," she blurted, dropping to her belly and covering her head.

Vinjo was already down. The lightning from the portal was

shooting out in all directions as it targeted multiple enemies. They risked being struck simply because they were in the area.

The grenade tumbled into the hole and exploded. Once more, the ground trembled.

One of the creatures pitched sideways, landing with a thud and blocking their view. Sasko didn't know if it had fallen because of the explosion or because of the lightning, but the portal continued to attack relentlessly.

Uthari continued to attack relentlessly. His eyes were closed as he gripped the portal, his forehead pressed to it.

"Just what he needed," Sasko said. "More power."

"King Zaruk will not be happy," Vinjo said.

"Nobody will."

Another creature pitched onto its side. The one that had already fallen wasn't moving and might have been dead.

Even the creatures that were still standing were no longer emitting their shockwaves, so Sasko risked getting to her feet. Her grenade had widened the hole but also partially filled it in. Since she'd never seen the tunnel and couldn't confirm that it had been there, she didn't know if she'd succeeded in closing it up. But if any druids were down there, she'd buried them, at least for the moment.

Another creature toppled, this one falling into the hole.

"That'll plug it up," she muttered.

The last two fell to the lightning attacks, and Uthari leaned back from the portal, though he kept a hand on it as he looked around at the carnage.

Sasko felt conspicuous standing alone with only Vinjo nearby, still on his stomach beside her, and she fought the urge to quail when Uthari's gaze landed on them. What if he decided to toss out a few more lightning bolts so that he didn't have to worry about paying mercenaries?

She'd helped and not done anything he should object to, but

he radiated such energy that the air seemed to crackle around him. His eyes gleamed, as if linking to the portal had infused him with even more power.

You did well, he spoke telepathically to her. *I will ensure you receive a combat bonus.*

Sasko kept herself from thinking anything sarcastic. *Thank you, Your Majesty.*

Not wanting to hold his unsettling gaze, she bent to help Vinjo to his feet.

"Did he say something to you?" Vinjo asked.

"He said your grass skirt is sexy and wants to know where he can get one."

"It's rude of you to lie to your engineer, Lieutenant Sasko." Vinjo smoothed the skirt, doing his best to cover his bruised and dirty legs.

"Is it? I've never had an engineer before. I didn't know."

"You've got one now. Consider yourself blessed."

"Oh, I do."

Uthari barked orders at the mages and mercenaries by the portal, something about cleaning up the mess and searching for druid survivors to take prisoner.

Since he wasn't addressing Sasko, she opted to decide the orders weren't for her. She offered Vinjo an arm—he looked like he needed it—and they hobbled off toward the trees.

Later, they could help clean up the camp, and he could try to find his tools and equipment so he could go back to working on a ship, but for now, she wanted to rest. It had been a long day.

∽

Jadora lifted her last explosive, wishing she'd asked Tinder for grenades. They didn't deter the dragons much, but they distracted them slightly.

A boom erupted behind her, another trap being triggered. The dragon battling Tezi, Tinder, and Rivlen roared, though it sounded more annoyed than hurt.

Jadora, crouching beside Fret in one of the few remaining copses of trees, only glanced back. Though she worried about all of her comrades, it was Jak she most wanted to protect. If only she could.

Fortunately, Malek had risen, and he was fighting the dragon that had been focused on Jak and the hatchling. With his magic, as well as his blades, as far as Jadora could tell. But even with his magic, he wasn't a match for the pure power of a dragon. No human was.

He'd cut it a dozen times, even driving his sword deep into its neck, but it kept attacking him with magic as well as talon and fang. It was hard for Jadora to sense what he was doing with his power, but he seemed to launch a couple of attacks at its head—maybe at its eyes and mouth, as he'd done with the last dragon they'd battled. This one blocked the strikes with defensive magic, and its eyes never so much as flickered.

As Jadora stood poised with her explosive, hoping for an opportunity to use it to help, the dragon caught Malek by surprise. It had been snapping at him, as he defended with his swords, but now the tail sneaked in, striking him from behind. Malek flew through the air and hammered against the side of the ziggurat not ten feet from Jak.

Though he appeared stunned, Malek managed to get his legs under him and land on his feet. The dragon lunged after him, angling its jaws toward his throat.

Jadora threw her explosive. With the dragon's back to her, she couldn't aim for a vital target, and it bounced off its rear leg. It exploded, smoke filling the air, but her target didn't even look back. The dragon snapped its jaws at Malek.

He thrust his blades up as he created a hasty barrier. The fangs gnashed uselessly at the air five feet above his head. His face twisted with concentration, and Jadora feared he wouldn't be able to keep his defenses up for long. He'd just undergone surgery. He couldn't be at his full power. Even if he had been...

"It's going to kill him," Fret whispered. "And *them*."

She pointed to the rear, where Rivlen, blood staining her shirt and her hair plastering the side of her sweaty face, was in a similar position.

"How can we help?" Jadora pawed uselessly into her backpack, as if she might find a miracle inside.

But she didn't have anything that could hurt dragons.

Do you know a term that might wake the ziggurat? Jak spoke into her mind from where he squatted, protecting Shikari and looking like he was sharing his power with Malek. *Shikari is trying to wake it up, but I don't think it's working.*

Wake it up to do what?

I don't know. Help.

Jadora groped for something in Ancient Zeruvian that might convince a ziggurat to stir from sleep, but that wasn't a dragon language. Why would it work? *Can't the portal give you something to say in dragon?*

Uhm, let me see if I can contact it from here.

The dragon kept attacking Malek, relentlessly bashing at his barrier. With his back to the wall, all of his power required for defenses, he was pinned and couldn't attack back.

His legs wobbled, threatening to give out. Malek could have run off, but he glanced at Jak, and Jadora feared he was suffering this to ensure the dragon focused on him instead of Jak.

The dragon reared back, jaws spreading wide. For a second, as it prepared to strike, it wasn't looking at Malek. He sprang to the side, rolling to get away from it. When the maw smashed down, fangs flashing, he wasn't there.

Malek sprang to his feet and hurled his main-gauche before

the dragon could protect its head. The blade spun and lodged in one of those reptilian eyes.

The dragon screeched. For the first time, it was a cry of pain. But that didn't keep it from counterattacking. It blasted so much furious power at Malek that his barrier wasn't enough to protect him. He flew thirty feet, crashing into a tree. Wood snapped. Or was that one of his bones?

This time, he didn't land on his feet. He crumpled to the ground.

The dragon stomped after him to take advantage. The main-gauche protruded from its eye, but that didn't slow it down.

Something smashed into a tree behind Jadora, and she spun, expecting the other dragon. It was Tinder's axe, lodged in the wood. She lay on the ground nearby, groaning. Hurled there by the dragon?

Jadora grabbed the axe with both hands and ran after Malek's attacker. She was no trained warrior, but the dragon was a large target. As it prepared to crush him with its jaws, she hefted the axe and brought it down with all of her strength.

The heavy head sliced into the tail, pinning it to the ground.

Another screech sounded, and the dragon whirled toward her. Its tail whipped up, ripping the axe from her grip and flinging it free of its flesh.

The blade flew twenty feet and clattered against the ziggurat. The dragon focused on Jadora and would have killed her—she had no magical defenses to stop it—but Malek recovered enough to leap after it. By now, the tail was toward him, and he drove his sword into the same spot where she'd already laid open scale and flesh.

Again, the dragon screeched, and a wave of power struck Jadora, knocking her all the way back to Jak. She landed hard, her back and head striking the ground.

Another dragon voice sounded in her ear, the small reedy cry of the hatchling. Shikari wasn't roaring or screeching but issuing something that might have been a word in their language. He repeated it again and again as Jadora pushed herself to her feet, her entire body hurting.

As the dragon spun to attack Malek again, a blue beam lanced out from the top of the ziggurat. It struck the side of the dragon, halting its attack and knocking it twenty feet, just as the dragon had been knocking all of them around.

"It's doing it," Jak cried. "It's doing it!"

Shikari kept repeating the same sound—the same command.

The beam tracked the dragon and kept striking it, burrowing through its scales and toward its heart. It tried to leap into the air to fly away, but the beam hit too hard. It knocked the dragon back to the ground, smashing it against a pile of boulders. Smoke wafted from the hole the beam was charring into its side.

A second beam lanced out, slicing through the carnage of downed trees toward the other dragon. Tinder and Fret yelled triumphant cheers.

Malek rushed toward Jadora's side, grabbed her, and hugged her close. He glanced at Jak, checking on him, but he and Shikari hadn't been harmed.

As the beams kept firing relentlessly into the dragons, following them even when they moved, the stench of burning scales and charring meat filled the air. Pained shrieks—dying shrieks—assaulted Jadora's ears.

Even though she felt nothing for these enemies, she buried her face in Malek's shoulder, not wanting to watch them die.

Jak staggered over to join them, Shikari back in his sling. Whatever he and the hatchling had started, it must not have needed ongoing input.

Jadora wrapped one of her arms around Jak. Malek patted him on the back, and they all leaned against each other for support.

The last agonizing screams echoed through the valley, and

Jadora made herself release Malek and Jak to check on the mercenaries. The hatchling squirmed out of Jak's sling, plopped to the ground, and meandered off, perhaps to look for insects.

Near one of the dead dragons, Dr. Fret knelt beside Tinder and Tezi. They lay on their backs in the brush. Too injured to rise? Fret had her medical kit open and was already cleaning wounds. A yelp and a curse came from Tinder, the words "That stings!" framed by more base terms, so Jadora assumed those two would survive.

Rivlen slumped against a tree, her face red, her shirt torn and scorched, but she was alive.

The beams disappeared, leaving the smoking husks of the two dead dragons amid the burned foliage. So many trees were upended all around that it looked like a tornado had landed on the valley.

"I will attempt to help with healing." Malek looked as weary as any of them after his surgery and battle, but he left Jadora's side to join Dr. Fret and her patients.

"I'm so relieved he got his power back," Jak whispered.

Jadora's feelings on the matter were mixed. She couldn't deny that the return of Malek's powers was probably the only reason they'd survived long enough for Jak and Shikari to wake the ziggurat, but... now he was a zidarr again. Uthari's right-hand man. Someone Jadora had to watch her thoughts around.

She couldn't help but watch Malek sadly, wishing for a world where he was a normal person—and that was all he needed to be. And where they could be... something.

Jak looked at her. "Are you all right? Were you hit?"

Jadora forced a smile. "Fine." Her back and head ached, and she would wake up hobbling in the morning, but she hadn't broken anything. "Are you?"

"I think so." Jak rubbed his back too. He'd also gone flying into the side of the ziggurat. "Nice axe work over there. I never expected to see you running up to a dragon and cleaving a hole in its tail." He smirked, but his eyes also beamed with approval.

Jadora mostly felt lucky that she hadn't gotten herself killed doing that. "I ran out of explosives, and dragon scales have proven impervious to my acids."

"You have to use the right tool for the right job." He made a chopping motion.

"If we're going to continue to explore other worlds, we may all need dragon-steel axes." Jadora couldn't hold back a grimace. She'd had enough of exploring other worlds. Too bad Uthari would send her to at least one more. What were the odds that they would be able to visit the world with the Jitaruvak, easily find it and snip a sample, and return without trouble?

"Maybe that will be possible if we can take back the right raw materials." Jak peered toward the cliffs with their veins of ore—they were easier to see now that so many trees had been knocked down. "Oh." He snapped his fingers. "We need to find the ruler lady. If she's still alive."

He turned a slow circle, as if he might have missed noticing her strolling through the trees. When he halted, it was to focus on one of the dead dragons. Or maybe Shikari. He was navigating around logs in his search for bugs.

"I sense something." Jak frowned at the dragon and raised his voice. "Malek? Rivlen?"

Rivlen was still slumped against a tree, weary and bedraggled, but she managed to lift her chin and call back, "*Captain* Rivlen," with suitable indignation. "And *Lord* Malek."

Instead of correcting himself, as he usually would if she insisted, Jak jogged toward the hatchling.

Malek had been kneeling beside Tezi, but he must have sensed something too, for he also headed in that direction.

Afraid the dragon had somehow survived the extended attack from the beam, Jadora grabbed her pack and trailed after them.

Jak and Malek halted behind Shikari, shoulder to shoulder as they peered at the downed dragon. It wasn't moving.

The hatchling poked his snout under a log, oblivious to whatever concerned them.

"You sense it?" Jak asked.

"Yes," Malek said. "It's not the dragon."

"You're sure?"

"Yes."

"Then what is it?"

Malek hesitated. "I do not know."

"Something magical," Jak said. "And alive."

"I agree."

As Jadora joined them, a cloud of glittery gold motes rose from the dragon's mouth and nostrils.

She gripped Jak's arm. "Is that *breath*?"

"It can't be." Jak glanced at Malek. "The dragon isn't alive."

"But whatever those are live." Malek gripped his chin thoughtfully.

At first, the cloud hung in the air over the dragon's snout, gleaming as if tiny gold flakes of glitter were catching the sunlight. But the valley lay in shadow, no sunlight reaching the ground.

As if stirred by a soft breeze, the cloud moved toward them. Fear charged through Jadora's veins, and she stepped back. Though she would normally be intrigued by the unknown, and want nothing more than to examine it, an instinct deep within her promised that this was something dangerous and evil.

Jak and Malek must have felt the same, for they also stepped back. Only the hatchling remained oblivious. The cloud descended toward him.

Jak squawked in alarm and lunged forward, snatching Shikari up and springing back. Malek raised his hands, and Jadora thought he might make a barrier to protect them all, but he startled her by launching fire from his fingers. Not a spinning ball that swept through the air, but a large glob of flames that hovered where the cloud was.

Jadora and Jak backed farther away as it burned, foliage wilting underneath the spot. Jak tried to stuff Shikari into his sling, but the hatchling protested, scrambling up to his shoulder.

When the flames faded, the cloud had diminished, with fewer sparkling gold motes visible, but some lingered. After a few seconds, the cloud started moving again. Straight toward Jak. Or Shikari?

"*Jak*," Jadora warned, pulling him farther back.

"I know, I know." He scrambled back with her until his heel caught, and he tripped. Shikari screeched, leaping from his shoulder to the top of his head as he fell.

Malek shifted in front of Jak, as if he could block the cloud's path. Jadora didn't know if that would work.

As she bent to help Jak up, Malek sent another ball of fire into the cloud. His face was tight with concentration as he turned it into an inferno, blazing heat in all directions.

Jak stood up, Shikari still on his head, talons digging into his scalp and tail flapping at the back of his neck. With his eyes locked on Malek and the fire, Jak didn't seem to notice. He lifted a hand.

Channeling his own power into Malek to increase the potency of the flames? Did whatever this was require all that?

Jadora shook her head, scouring her mind for anything similar to these motes that she'd read about before. Nothing came to mind.

The fire grew, a huge orange sun so bright that she had to look away. Only when the flames disappeared did she look back.

"Did we get it all?" Jak asked.

Malek studied the spot. Jadora didn't see any more motes, but she didn't know if that meant anything.

"I believe so," Malek finally said. "I no longer sense anything magical or alive."

Malek looked to Shikari. The hatchling seemed less agitated—he'd stopped whacking Jak in the back with his tail—though he hadn't descended from his perch yet.

"Is it safe to investigate?" Jadora slung off her backpack to gather a vial and her tools.

"Are you going to take a sample?" Malek sounded more bemused than incredulous.

"Of course I am. Unless you don't think it's safe." She stood with spatula, swabs, and vials in hand. "They're dead, right?"

She realized she had no idea if the motes had been alive. Could they have been some magical tool or device? Something that had served the dragon? No, Jak and Malek had said they sensed something alive.

"Yes," Malek said.

"What *were* they?" Jak made no move to approach the remains of the log that had been under the cloud—and the flames.

It had charred black from the heat, and Jadora spotted golden motes nestled on the dark wood.

"Nothing I have encountered before." Malek eyed the dragon and then looked toward the other dead dragon. "I sense the faintest hint of something similar in that one, but it—they seem to be deep inside of it."

"Like… bacteria?" Jadora guessed, though she'd never heard of flying bacteria, nor any that were visible to the naked eye.

"You are the scientist. I will defer to you."

"You can defer after I get a sample back to look at under my microscope." Jadora knelt beside the charred log and poked one of the motes with her spatula, half expecting it to spring up into the air again.

It didn't move. She moistened a swab and caught several of the motes before tucking them into a vial and affixing the lid firmly.

"Everyone stay away from the dead dragons," Jak called to the others.

"I wasn't planning on cuddling with them to stay warm tonight," Tinder called back, her voice pained.

Jadora walked to the dead dragon that had expelled the cloud.

"*Mother*," Jak said. "That advice was for you too."

"She needs more samples," Malek said.

"She *got* samples."

"I sense nothing left to trouble her in that dragon," Malek said.

"Wonderful."

Jadora stuck a clean swab into the dragon's mouth, brushing its tongue and the sides of its fangs. She didn't see any more golden motes, but she would examine everything under her microscope later.

"We still need to find the ruler." Jak removed Shikari from his head and returned him to the sling. "Captain Rivlen, do you know where the dragons came from?"

"Yes." Rivlen took a deep breath, straightened, and shambled toward him.

They headed toward the corner of the ziggurat together. Malek returned to the mercenaries to help with healing, but he kept a wary eye on the other dead dragon.

After packing away her samples and tools, Jadora picked up Tinder's axe, intending to return it to her, but her gaze drifted toward the cliffs. Maybe the blade would be suitable for chiseling some ore out of the rock to take back.

She had no idea if the ambassador and the rest of the locals would show up or impede them when they tried to leave, but if she could escape with some of the acid to study, and a sample of the ore, that would get her started on what Uthari would doubtless want.

Not that she wished to please him, but for her father's sake, she had to think of the king's desires.

She paused, pulling the remains of the disc that had been in Malek's head out of her pocket. She would take it home, along with the other one, and hope to find a mage engineer who could make more. Perhaps one day, they could be put to use against mages who treated terrene humans poorly. If it took a dragon to remove the devices, once they were embedded, then they could be effective weapons to help bring about the future Jadora longed to see.

She glanced back at Malek and slid the piece back into her pocket. Once again, she would have to be careful with her thoughts around him.

30

Rivlen longed to collapse on a bed in a healer's tent. Since that wasn't possible, she would settle for a relatively flat spot on the ground. Now that the battle had ended, sheer exhaustion had settled in, not only from using so much magic and nearly being killed multiple times, but from being up all night. It had to be noon by now. She wanted a nap, and her growling stomach requested something to eat.

Just as soon as they found that ruler—or her body.

As she and Jak rounded the second corner of the ziggurat, she tripped over a root. He lunged and caught her.

"Thanks," she said, though she hated needing help. *Again.*

There had been several times during the battle that she would have fallen to that dragon if he hadn't been sharing his power with her. She appreciated it and was glad to be alive, but she couldn't help but feel weak for having needed assistance. She couldn't wait to return home to her world where she was considered—and *felt* —powerful again.

"You're welcome." Jak didn't let his hands linger, but he stayed close in case she tripped again.

As tired as she was, she might. She sighed.

"There's the cave entrance, such as it is." Rivlen nodded to the huge slab of a door that had fallen open. It still lay flat on the ground, revealing the dark interior of the ziggurat, with more of that stinky acid scent wafting out.

"Huh." Jak stopped and stared. "That was not there before. How did we miss seeing evidence of it? I'm sure that entire section had vines growing all over it."

"I think those particular vines were an illusion. I didn't see through it until the door opened, and the dragons stomped out."

"I'd like to think I also would have perceived the illusion at that point."

"Maybe, maybe not. Teenage boys aren't that perceptive."

He frowned at her. "Teenage *men*." His indignation didn't last for long, and the frown turned into a rueful smile. "I'd proclaim again how well my chest hair is coming in, but I think the dragon fire might have singed it all off."

"Unfortunate. You were getting nicely manly."

"Oh? I didn't realize you'd noticed."

"I did. Thanks for the help during the battle." Rivlen considered his dirt-smudged face. He also looked tired, but his eyes were bright and alert.

As his power grew, it was more noticeable, something he carried about him like a cloak. She doubted he would be able to pass again as a terrene human, at least not around mages.

The urge to apologize for snapping at him and demanding he call her captain came over her, but it was always hard to admit when she was wrong. Commanders weren't supposed to be wrong. It seemed a weakness to admit something like that.

"You're welcome." Jak held her gaze. "I'm glad you made it. I was... worried."

That admission touched her, and she believed it. He truly seemed to care.

"Me too." She tried again to get the apology out but decided to kiss him instead. Despite her teasing, he *was* perceptive. He would understand.

His brows rose when she touched her lips to his. She'd meant to kiss him on the cheek, a simple thanks-for-the-help. *He* hadn't moved, so she wasn't sure what happened, but somehow their lips touched… and lingered.

A supportive warmth emanated from him, along with strength that she needed at that moment. And she lingered, letting it wash over her, not wanting to pull away.

A cheep that was more bird-like than dragon-like came from the hatchling in his sling.

Jak and Rivlen parted, blushed, and looked awkwardly away.

"The, uh, ruler?" Jak waved at the entrance.

"Yes. I'll see if she's alive." Rivlen shuffled through the brush, deciding she was tired and making strange decisions and that she hadn't enjoyed kissing someone who was six years younger than she. She was far more interested in men like Malek. Mature, powerful, and… not available.

Jak stuck close to her, ready to support her, as he had all day. As he would always do? That seemed a part of who he was.

They wrinkled their noses as they reached the entrance.

"Be careful." Jak stopped several feet away. "The air may be toxic to breathe."

"I think I can keep it out with a barrier. But just in case, stay here."

He frowned and looked like he would object to her going into danger alone.

"I'll be fine. You don't want your dragon to pass out, do you?"

"He's sturdy." Jak frowned down at Shikari. "And putting images of fat bugs into my mind."

"I'm sure he's hungry." Rivlen's own stomach growled again. "We all are."

She stepped to the side and raised an air-proof barrier, making it large enough to give her sufficient oxygen in case it took her longer to find the cave than she expected.

Clinks and clanks emanated from the valley wall. Jak frowned in that direction. Jadora was hacking at a cliff with an axe. Not exactly the appropriate use for such a fine weapon.

While Jak was distracted by that, Rivlen headed in, willing light to seep from her barrier to brighten the way.

The inside of the ziggurat was a single empty chamber that rose upward to great heights. At first, the ground was level, a simple blue-black floor to match everything else, but she ended up on a ramp that descended. It took her down, curving around so that she remained under the ziggurat, until she reached an opening in a wall. By then, she was thirty or forty feet below ground level.

The opening led her into a natural cave full of steaming pools, clouds of brownish-white vapor above them. Rivlen was glad she'd put up a barrier.

Something bobbed in one of the pools. Etcher Yervaa.

She was in the same protective bubble—her own barrier—that she'd created when the dragons first snatched her. But she no longer glowed with a nimbus of power, and she'd slumped down, lying on the bottom.

She was so still that Rivlen would have assumed her unconscious or dead, but she wouldn't have been able to keep her barrier up if she were.

Though she didn't expect any more dragons, Rivlen eyed the dark shadows of the cave as she walked around the pools to get closer to Yervaa.

It was always a struggle to perform two magical tasks at once, so she had to get close and concentrate fully to keep her barrier up and levitate the ruler out of the pool to join her. The woman stirred, peering blearily at her.

"Join your barrier with mine, and we'll get out of here." Reminded that the woman wouldn't understand her language, Rivlen shared the idea telepathically.

Who are you?

One of the people you've had locked up all week. We made a deal with your ambassador. Come on.

There are dragons. They'll return at any moment.

Nope. We roasted them. Rivlen almost explained about the ziggurat, but it might be better if these people believed her party had the raw power to deal with dragons on their own.

Truly?

Yes.

The woman hesitated, peering toward the ramp up to the ziggurat, but she finally blended her barrier with Rivlen's, leaving them both in the same one. She stumbled when she put her feet on the ground to support herself. After maintaining her barrier against dragons trying to pry her out of it for hours, Yervaa had to be even more exhausted than Rivlen.

Offering an arm for support, Rivlen helped her back up to the ziggurat. They climbed slowly, the air growing thin with two of them breathing inside of the bubble. Rivlen's legs felt heavy, and she stumbled several times.

Daylight came into view, slashing into the ziggurat through the doorway, and Rivlen almost released her barrier there. But Jak wasn't alone anymore.

His back was to the ziggurat, and numerous people stood in front of him. Ambassador Rajesk, another glowing white-clad woman—another ruler?—and most of the same mages that had stopped them at the portal. They were armed, almost every one of them with a dragon-steel weapon.

Took their time getting here, didn't they? Rivlen thought, then realized she'd shared the message telepathically.

Yes, Yervaa responded. *They did.*

Jak turned as they stepped out into the daylight. Yervaa extricated herself from Rivlen's barrier, and Rivlen happily let it drop. If she didn't have to use her magic again for a week, she would be delighted.

The other ruler rushed forward and wrapped her arms around her colleague, and a cheer went up from the army.

Malek, Tinder, Tezi, and Fret walked around the corner of the ziggurat, stepping warily into view.

You have done it, Rajesk spoke into their minds. *We thank you.*

Enough to let us go home? Jak asked.

The ambassador glanced at the rulers, Etcher Yervaa now standing beside her colleague, and Rivlen had a feeling he hadn't discussed his promise with any of them yet.

We will talk about it. Rajesk bowed to them.

The army turned as one, heading back up to the rim of the crater where dozens of their large pack animals waited. The mages climbed on, two to a mount, and directed them back toward the coast.

"I guess we're supposed to make our own way back to the portal," Jak said.

"That should be fun," Rivlen said, "especially since a dragon blew up the skyboard I was riding."

"I didn't know skyboards could blow up," Jak said.

"It's not typical."

"We'll make do," Malek said. "As soon as Professor Freedar has gathered all the ore she needs."

"I've got enough." Jadora walked up and set her pack down with a thud. "For experiments. If your king wants a plethora of weapons, he'll have to find more."

"I'm sure he'll send *me* to find more," Malek said.

"Lucky you."

Malek inhaled deeply and looked to the sky. "Yes."

It didn't sound sarcastic or insincere. Rivlen trusted he was pleased to have his powers back—and to be able to continue to serve Uthari. She would have felt pleased too.

Jadora, as she gazed sadly at him, didn't say anything else.

∽

It was dusk by the time the group came out of the mountains, and as they crossed the grassy foothills west of the city, the portal came into view. Because one of the skyboards had been destroyed, and another had run out of its charge on the way back, they'd been forced to take turns walking and riding.

Tezi yawned, hoping they would be able to leave this time, and hoping they wouldn't walk into a raging battle again when they returned. She longed for sleep, even if it was a blanket on the hard ground in the mercenary camp by the waterfall. That would be luxurious after being awake all day and the previous night.

"Think you'll have to throw that at a worm when we step out of the portal?" Tinder nodded to the axe strapped to Tezi's pack.

"Last time, it worked best when *Malek* threw it," Tezi said.

"You've gotten some more practice with it since then. I saw you land some blows on the dragon. That's pretty impressive."

Tezi shook her head. "A dragon is a large target. It's hard to miss."

Tinder snorted. "*Missing* isn't the problem. The retaliation you get after hitting it is." She touched one of many bandages wrapping her body.

During the battle, Tezi had also received multiple wounds, but Dr. Fret had supplied numerous painkillers that had taken the edge off. They ached dully now, much like the bottoms of her feet, which were sore from the long walk back. Jak and Malek had used their magic to help, but they'd been too exhausted to fully heal Tezi and Tinder.

"I'm serious, Rookie." Tinder elbowed her. "You're turning into a decent warrior. Maybe the captain will give you a rank eventually. And a pay raise."

"I'm not technically in the company right now."

"Show her your axe moves. She'll be eager to get you back in the unit."

Tezi smiled faintly, though she feared nothing had changed back in their world. Not unless all the zidarr and mages who'd read her mind and wanted her dead for her crimes were gone.

At least she had an agreement of sorts with Rivlen now. To work together with her against General Tonovan if need be. Tezi didn't want to hope for a battle with him, but after facing a dragon, the idea wasn't as scary as it had been a week ago. As long as she could keep anyone from stealing the axe from her, she and Rivlen might have a chance against him.

"We'll see," she murmured.

"Uh oh," Jak muttered from the head of the group.

He and Malek were walking side by side up there. Like buddies. Or father and son. For some reason, Tezi's mind wanted to make that connection.

Jak pulled off his hat—he'd taken it out of his pack and donned it for the trek back—and scratched his head.

After a few more steps, Tezi could make out what Jak had seen. Once again, people waited in front of the portal.

It wasn't an army this time, but Ambassador Rajesk stood atop the hill with several armed guards. To prevent the group from leaving?

Malek kept striding toward them, not daunted by all of the magic users. He once again radiated that zidarr power and confidence.

"Are they going to try to stop us?" Fret asked in a worried tone.

"I hope not," Tinder said. "I'm out of grenades, and I need to sleep."

The ambassador bowed to Malek and spoke aloud in the local language.

Malek glanced back, and Jadora, who'd been taking a turn on one of the remaining skyboards, floated up to join him to translate.

Rajesk switched to telepathy so that wasn't necessary. *You have done as I asked and defeated the dragons. Our rulers were surprised you had the ability to do so, but I believed you could, since you travel with one of the rare Favored Travelers.* He nodded toward Jak.

Jak hadn't mentioned how he—or had it been the hatchling?—had convinced the ziggurat to shoot those beams out at the dragons, but Tezi was glad he had. Even with Malek's magic back, they hadn't been winning that battle. Without the help, they might all have been dead by the time the ruler's army showed up.

Per our agreement, Rajesk continued, *we are allowing you to return to your world. The rulers are not willing to give you the secret of the dragon steel, but I suspect you've already learned much.* He gazed at Jadora.

Jadora said something aloud. It sounded more like a question than a statement of agreement.

Rajesk tilted his head and replied in a puzzled tone.

Someone came into view, jogging up the road from the city toward the portal, a backpack on his shoulders.

Jadora explained something, pointing back to the mountains and pantomiming dragons.

The ambassador shrugged and shook his head, then pointed to two of the guards. They bent and picked up a chest Tezi hadn't noticed in the grass at the side of the road.

While they carried it to the group, Rajesk drew a weathered notebook from an inside pocket.

"Oh," Jadora blurted in Dhoran, her tone pleased. "Is that my journal?"

Rajesk bowed and handed it to her, then waved one of the

guards forward. *Though we are not yet prepared to open trade with your people, the etchers have agreed that it would be dangerous to invade your world while a Favored Traveler is among you. Also, you have done us a good turn, so we are inclined to leave you in peace. In addition to returning your belongings, I have arranged a gift for you.*

The guard opened the lid on the chest, revealing bars of blue-black metal inside. Dragon steel.

"I guess I didn't need to chisel ore from that cliff," Jadora murmured.

"What did you ask him?" Jak whispered to her.

"If he knew what the stuff was that floated out of the dead dragon's mouth."

"And he didn't?"

She shook her head. "He didn't know what I was talking about. He said he'd never been present before for the slaying of a dragon, that it's a wondrous but rare event."

Shikari growled what might have been a protest.

"Hopefully," Jadora said, "when I get a chance to examine my specimens, it'll prove enlightening."

"I'm amazed you can walk," Jak said, "under the weight of all your samples. And ore."

We thank you again for your assistance. Rajesk bowed again, specifically to Jak this time, as if he knew who'd been responsible for the dragons' deaths.

You're welcome, Jak replied telepathically.

Tezi heard his words in her mind as easily as she had the ambassador's. A lot had changed since she'd first met Jak.

As Rajesk and the guards turned to walk to a carriage that would take them back to their city, the man with the backpack reached the hilltop. It was Zethron.

Malek regarded his approach coolly. When Zethron waved vigorously to Jadora, Malek's face frosted over further.

Zethron noticed his glare and halted the wave, plastering his arm to his side. He spoke to Jadora, though he glanced warily at Malek several times.

Malek took a deep breath and clasped his hands behind his back. His face returned to its usual neutral mask.

Tezi didn't know what that was about unless Malek blamed Zethron for something.

When Jadora turned to Malek, her expression was also wary. "He's requesting to come back with us to visit and explore our world. The *First World*, at least to him and his people. He promises he'll stay out of the way and won't pester anyone."

Though Malek's face remained masked, he still didn't look pleased. Tezi expected him to reject the notion outright.

"Does he know it's a thousand miles to walk out of the jungle?" Malek asked.

"I told him he might be kidnapped by mages and that there's a jungle full of wild animals waiting. He still wants to go. Perhaps when King Uthari takes my father back to Sprungtown, which I hope will be soon, Zethron can get a ride with them."

"If King Uthari learns of him, he may wish to question him for everything he knows of the various worlds accessible by the portals."

"Question him... via an interrogation?" Jadora glanced at Zethron, who, not understanding, could only look back and forth curiously between them.

"It is possible."

"Will he make you do it?" Jadora asked.

"It is possible." Even though he didn't seem to like Zethron, Malek didn't look happy about the idea.

Jadora closed her eyes.

"If he returns with us," Malek said, "perhaps you should have him stay with the mercenaries, try to avoid notice from ambitious mages and wizards seeking resources on other worlds, and teach him our language as quickly as possible so he can pass as one of us."

Jadora blinked. "You would allow that? I mean, you wouldn't tell Uthari about him?"

"If Uthari asks, I will have to tell him what I know. If he doesn't ask..." Malek shrugged.

The suggestion that he would hold anything back from his king surprised Tezi. She believed him, but she also thought it would be dangerous for Zethron to go to their world. If it were up to her, she would have warned Zethron to stay here. Being interrogated by a wizard—or a zidarr—would not be pleasant.

Jadora stepped forward and hugged Malek. He hugged her back but only for a moment before releasing her and pointing at the chest. He levitated it into the air and nodded to Jak.

"Take us home."

Jak placed his medallion in the portal. "Which world do we go to on the way?" He looked at Jadora and Zethron.

They didn't say anything aloud, but Jak must have received the answer he needed. One of the symbols on the inside of the portal lit up with blue light, and a starry field appeared in the center. The stars swirled until they formed a constellation.

"Here we go," Tinder muttered and gripped her axe. "Home to safety. Or trouble."

As they stepped through, Tezi hoped for the former and braced herself for the latter.

Surreal dream-like moments passed as stars streaked through her awareness. She stumbled out of the portal onto hot sand with canyons and red-rock cliffs stretching in several directions. A blazing sun beat down upon her, making her squint.

"I suppose there isn't time to explore," Jak said wistfully, gazing toward the canyons.

"Not today." Malek waved his hand at the portal they'd come out.

On this one, none of the symbols had been rubbed out. After Jak used the key on it, stars formed once more, and the group finally entered the magical passageway back to their world.

Tezi stepped out to the familiar roar of the waterfall and birds squawking in the jungle. Their camp, however, looked little like it had when they left.

Early dawn light revealed that all the tents had been knocked down. Mages and mercenaries were working to levitate giant animal corpses out of the camp, and what remained of a sinkhole marred the ground scant feet in front of the portal. Jadora almost stumbled into it as she came out, but Malek reacted quickly, catching her arm and pulling her to safety.

He gazed around, then up toward Uthari's yacht. Whatever had happened while they were gone, the fleets of mageships were still visible above the trees.

"At least everything is already dead this time," Tinder muttered.

Tezi spotted Ferroki and Sasko walking toward them and waved. They were grimy, bedraggled, and didn't look like they'd slept that night. They raised their eyebrows when Zethron stepped out of the portal.

"We brought a guest," Jak explained.

"It's a good thing you all didn't try to come back two hours ago." Sasko thumped Tinder, Fret, and Tezi on their backs.

"What happened?" Tezi asked.

"Chaos," Sasko said.

Ferroki looked at Jak. "King Uthari has learned to summon the lightning from the portal."

"Oh." Jak considered the portal with disappointment in his eyes.

Malek only nodded, as if he'd expected that would eventually happen.

Tezi kept her expression neutral and tried not to think about how much more she'd preferred it when only Jak had known how to summon lightning from the portal. The last thing Uthari needed was more power.

"He may not need the secret of working dragon steel if he can now use the portal as a weapon," Jadora murmured.

"He will want it." Malek gazed around at the mess the battle had made of the camp. "We will get a new laboratory tent set up for you and bring in even more equipment."

"I suppose if you're going to give me a gift, laboratory equipment is what I'd most appreciate." Jadora smiled, but it didn't reach her eyes. She shared a worried look with Jak, and Tezi was certain they also didn't like the idea of Uthari having more power.

Malek rested a hand on Jadora's shoulder. "Make a list of what you'll need to start work, and I'll do my best to get you everything."

"Thank you."

He looked toward the yacht again. Uthari had appeared at the railing, and he crooked a finger.

Malek dropped his hand. "I must brief him on everything that happened on our journey."

"*Everything*?" Jadora raised her eyebrows.

Malek hesitated, then nodded. "Everything."

"Ah," was all Jadora said.

Malek stepped onto one of the skyboards and flew up to the yacht, disappearing from sight.

"Let's find someplace to hide our guest," Jadora said.

"Lieutenant Vinjo has been making clandestineness creepers," Sasko said. "I highly recommend them."

Ferroki looked sadly out toward the jungle, but all she said was, "Come on, Thorn Company. I want to hear about your mission."

She gripped Tezi's shoulder and nodded for her to come along.

Tezi didn't know if that meant she'd been invited permanently back into the unit, but at least for now, she belonged with Thorn Company again.

~

Sorath woke on his back, cold and stiff and confused. He lay on the ground but not under the tree where he'd fallen. A low earthen ceiling was above him, a faint green glow providing enough illumination to see.

He grew aware of muffled voices, but he couldn't understand the language. Then he remembered the druids. The druids who'd been led right to him by their wolf, who apparently had no trouble seeing—or sniffing—people through Vinjo's device.

Sorath turned his head, hoping the creeper was still on his wrist, that the druids hadn't known what it was and hadn't taken it. But it was gone. As were his weapons. His wrist was chained to a stake plunged into the ground.

Had he been full of energy, he might have been strong enough to pull that out, but with people so close, he doubted there was a point. If they were magic users, he wouldn't be able to best them.

The voices fell silent.

Sorath sensed people looking at him. His head ached in the aftermath of being zapped with that staff—actually, it still ached from Uthari's torture—and he didn't feel like stirring.

"You're awake," a familiar voice said.

The accent made it easy to place. The druid. Kywatha.

She walked into view, her clothing wet, her damp hair hanging around her weary face.

"You're back," Sorath rasped, his voice thick from disuse. How long had he been out? "Where did you go?"

"It does not matter. My mission failed." She shook her head bleakly. "We've lost Frehdir, Dabrook, and Morlika." Her voice lowered. "And Grove, my feline companion."

Maybe that wasn't weariness on her face but defeat and sorrow.

"What do you want from me?" Sorath trusted they hadn't carted him back here without a reason. They could have killed him in the jungle.

"You helped capture Tovorka," she said. "We don't know if he's dead or alive."

"If that's the male druid, I don't know either. Uthari and Yidar tortured him before they gave me a turn."

"*Yidar*," Kywatha spat the name. "He pretended to want an alliance with us, but at the first opportunity, he captured one of our people."

Sorath didn't point out that her *people* had been attacking their camp and enacting... whatever plan they'd enacted. And failed at.

"You helped Yidar." Kywatha gazed down at him.

"I told you I had to. I couldn't switch sides in the middle of a conflict. Mercenaries can't do that." Though he would still kill Uthari if he got a chance. Not likely, not when her people had taken Vinjo's stealth device from him.

"Yet you want to kill your king."

Not surprised that she'd read that from his mind, Sorath said, "He's not *my* king."

"Just your employer?"

"It's complicated."

"Your feelings toward him are the reason Dabrook and my cousin did not kill you when they found you alone in the jungle," Kywatha said.

That name had been one of the druids she'd mentioned being lost. Sorath didn't know whether to offer condolences or not. How many *mercenaries* had been lost? It galled him that he hadn't been there to help Thorn Company with a battle.

"We sought only to get the portal," Kywatha said. "We did not expect *him* to be on the ground, practically hugging it when I got back with the magical animals. He was supposed to be up in his yacht where he's been all week. The shockwaves kept the mageships off-kilter. It would have *worked,* but he learned how to command the soul in the portal." She closed her eyes, shaking her head.

Sorath remembered Uthari standing and touching the portal while reading from that book. "What did he command it to do?"

"Lash out with lightning. Such powerful lightning that it slew the nearly impervious animals." Kywatha shook her head again, distress in her eyes, as much as she'd had when speaking of her fallen comrades. "I didn't believe they would die. I only needed them to assist us and then would have returned them to their world."

Sorath knew nothing of the animals she'd retrieved and didn't care to.

"What do you want from me?" he asked, though he was getting an inkling.

Kywatha took a deep breath and focused on him. "The same thing you want."

"Uthari dead?"

"Yes. Uthari, Yidar, and Malek."

"Uh." That was a longer list of targets than he'd had in mind, especially since he was—or had been—an honorable mercenary commander, not an assassin. Sorath had a hundred and twenty reasons to hate Uthari—that was how many men he'd lost to the man's treachery—and Uthari had ordered him tortured twice now. To kill him would be no slight to his honor. It would be removing a despicable man from the world and righting a wrong.

Sorath had fewer reasons to detest Yidar and Malek. He also didn't know how he could get close enough to kill more than one person. Uthari, as powerful as he was, was an old man. If Sorath could nullify his magic or catch him in his sleep, he believed he could kill him.

But Yidar and Malek? They were zidarr. Not only powerful magic users but warriors in the prime of their lives. And if Sorath succeeded in killing Uthari, they would be alert and hunting *him*.

"You will find a way," Kywatha said, "for that is the price of your freedom. If they are dead, there will be no one of consequence left to lead that fleet, and we can handle the mageships from the other kingdoms."

Sorath didn't think Tonovan counted as *no one of consequence*, but he admitted the king and his zidarr were the greater threats.

"Give us your word that you will kill them," Kywatha said, watching him intently, "and we will give you your weapons and your stealth device back. We will even give you magical druid tools that will assist you."

"If you have such good tools, why don't you assassinate those three yourselves?"

"It would be much easier for you to get close. Are you not, after all, employed by them?"

Yes, which made this much messier than Sorath would prefer.

"Uthari's mage minions will read my mind before I get close," he said, though a few hours ago, he'd had plans to do exactly what she suggested, sneaking aboard Uthari's yacht in the dark of night.

"We can give you a device that will keep mages from reading your thoughts. We will aid you in this as much as possible. As I said, having them gone will make everything much more viable for us."

Which was, of course, all they cared about. If they sent Sorath, and he died trying, or killed only one of the three vexing them, what would they care? He was no major loss to them.

Kywatha was probably reading his every thought, but she didn't deny anything. Instead, she walked over to her people and conferred with them briefly. One man handed her a dagger in a sheath. When she returned, she pulled it out to show Sorath a blue-black dragon-steel blade, then offered it to him.

He stared at it for a long minute. If he carried that, he wouldn't need to borrow Tezi's axe. And he might actually be able to accomplish his goal.

"In exchange for my attempt to kill Uthari," he said slowly, "if I fail—or even if I win—will you protect Captain Ferroki and Thorn Company? Help them get out of the jungle and on a ship back to their homeland."

"For your attempt to kill Uthari *and* his zidarr. Malek has been leading parties through the portal, likely letting all the worlds know that the passageway here is open again. He is even more of a threat than Uthari. We want him dead."

Sorath gazed at her, unwilling to negotiate further unless she gave him what he wanted.

Kywatha sighed. "Yes, we will do our best to protect your colleagues and help them escape. We would be *happy* to deprive those mages of even more of their forces."

"Then I agree to your terms," Sorath said.

"You'll kill Uthari *and* Yidar and Malek?"

"Yes."

Or he would die trying.

EPILOGUE

Jadora's new tent laboratory was on its way to becoming more thoroughly stocked than the last, and even as she worked, a couple of servants toted in equipment and supplies imported from one of the cities at the southern tip of Uthari's kingdom. Reputedly, a blacksmith was also on the way, someone renowned for his ability to make perfect swords and axes. Jadora had a couple of experiments running, synthesizing the new acid and turning it into the liquid she believed would be required for working the dragon steel.

The crate full of bars they'd brought back rested in the middle of her tent. Since she'd returned, guards had been stationed outside, ensuring none of the mages from the other kingdoms came in to snoop. Given that the mercenaries couldn't hide their thoughts from mages, Jadora doubted the bars or her acid would remain a secret for long. She hoped this didn't turn into yet another reason people would want to kidnap her.

The porters set the boxes among others for her to unpack later and left without a word. They were some of Uthari's personal servants from his ship and wore slavebands, their eyes dull and glazed.

Not for the first time since returning, Jadora thought of the kerzor and what it might allow them to do against recalcitrant mages if they could figure out how to make more of them. Many more. Though they would still need allies to fight a war against those mages if they truly wanted to change the system.

Jadora thought of the dragon eggs still frozen in that glacier. Already, Shikari had been a useful ally. *More* than useful. Was it possible that they could break out a few more eggs and start raising more dragons who might help them? Who might help *Jak*? She still didn't understand why he'd been chosen by the portals throughout the network, but if that meant he could convince the dragons to work with them...

The tent flap stirred again, and she quashed the thoughts. Successfully blanking them from her mind didn't keep her heart from hammering in her chest.

Before, she'd only had vague notions of rebellion and overthrowing their mage overlords. Now that it actually seemed like there was a path that could lead them to that end, her thoughts seemed far more dangerous. Even though she had value to Uthari—she highly doubted he would get rid of her before she figured out the acid and found his plant—he'd already warned her that he would kill her if she got in his way.

Admittedly, he'd also implied he would kill her if she had a romantic relationship with Malek, but planning an uprising would be far worse. She hadn't even seen Malek in three days, though she didn't know if that was his doing or Uthari's. Had the prudish old king learned of their kiss and chastised Malek for it? *Worse* than chastised him?

She would be furious if she learned Uthari had punished Malek when she'd so valiantly fought off the effects of that drug to refrain from having sex with him. Especially when he'd been just as influenced and had wanted it as badly as she. Yes, they'd kissed—and then some—but if Uthari had any decency, he wouldn't blame either of them for that. She hoped.

It wasn't Malek or a guard who walked into the tent but her father.

Jadora hadn't seen him since returning, and she dropped her work to hug him. Not surprisingly, he carried his *The Teachings* around, as if he was about to give a sermon.

"Are you all right, Father?" She gripped his shoulders—when had they grown so thin?—and looked him in the eyes.

"Better than many, yes. And you, my daughter? I've heard stories."

"From Uthari's mage crew? Or servants? Do they talk to you?"

"Not often, but Uthari keeps me close, since I'm apparently a very valuable prisoner, and occasionally mutters something to me."

Jadora shook her head, hoping those mutterings weren't threats. Or cruelties.

"I don't know if I should believe him or not," Father said, "but he said you've been performing adequately and that he will send me back to Sprungtown."

"Oh. That's a relief." She hugged him again. "Did Malek talk to him?"

"The zidarr? Yes, I believe so. I do wish you could return with me." Father peered around at the laboratory and lowered his voice. "I understand that you are smart and that he values you, but to do work for them seems…"

"A betrayal to our people?"

"I would not say that, but they do not need any more resources or power. I wish your work could be for the good of *our* people."

"I know. Me too."

"They're so vile. They don't value *work*, not real work. Twiddling their fingers and forcing others to labor for them is not work.

Yet they believe Thanok will bless them with paradise in the afterlife. I know that is not so. I am relieved that you and Jak have returned safely."

The tent flap stirred again, and Tezi peeked her head in. "Sorry, Professor, but the captain asked for your father. She's gathered those who are interested."

"The captain?" Jadora asked. "Captain Ferroki?"

Tezi nodded.

"I'm going to deliver a sermon," Father said. "Captain Ferroki told Uthari that the mercenaries need uplifting and suggested that I could do it. I think she was making an excuse for me to come down here so I could see you. I appreciate that."

"Me too." Jadora's voice almost broke. She was glad to see him and also that they weren't arguing. Though what would her father say when he learned that Jak was developing mage powers? The ability to *twiddle his fingers* to do things.

"We *could* use uplifting," Tezi said.

Reminded that they weren't alone, Jadora nodded. "Of course. I'll take a break in a minute and come join you."

Father arched his brows and gave her microscope a skeptical look, as if he was sure she would be distracted and wouldn't make it. She blushed, for that had happened quite often when she'd been growing up. Now, she was embarrassed by the promises she'd made back then to attend his evening sermons, only to fail to show up because she'd gotten sucked into her academic projects.

"I'll make sure it's a *long* sermon so you can at least catch the end," he said and headed for the exit.

"Thank you, Father."

After he walked out, Malek stepped into the tent.

Nerves jittered in Jadora's belly, though she didn't know if the feeling had to do with seeing him after several days apart or how he might react if he discovered her earlier musings. She carefully kept them tucked in the back of her mind and smiled at him.

He'd shaved, trimmed his hair, and donned clothing that wasn't ripped or stained with blood. Despite the scar the kerzor had left at his temple, he looked... achingly good.

She kept that thought out of her mind too.

"I'm glad you came." Jadora waved at the microscope, wanting to show him what she'd been studying while she waited for her other experiments to finish.

"Because you've been forlorn without my presence?" Malek arched his eyebrows.

"Naturally." She wanted to hug him, but he stopped a few feet away and clasped his hands behind his back. "How did your debriefing with King Uthari go?" she asked. "I assume there *was* a debriefing."

And Malek, compelled to honesty as he was, had probably confessed to their drugged kisses.

Though maybe not. He did keep some things from Uthari. Nobody had come down to capture or otherwise harass Zethron. Right now, he was outside with Jak, who was helping him learn Dhoran as quickly as possible. Once he spoke the language, Zethron would have an easier time passing himself off as a native. Passing himself off as a mercenary might be more difficult, but with so many people here now, it was possible nobody would think anything of another terrene man wandering around.

"There was," Malek said. "He still desires the Jitaruvak, but he was pleased that we returned with dragon steel, and he looks forward to the results of your work."

"I heard he finds my work adequate thus far. Not exactly glowing praise, but I'll pretend that means he appreciates me." And that he had no intention of doing away with her because of a wayward kiss.

"Adequate is the word he used, yes. Once we're able to smelt—or the equivalent—dragon steel, he should feel even more favorably toward you." Malek paused and regarded her. "*I appreciate you.*"

The simple words shouldn't have made her body grow warm, but they did, and even though he didn't reach out to touch her—he was being careful not to do that—his gaze made her think again of their kiss.

She swallowed, somehow certain he was also thinking about it. This wasn't going to be easy going forward. She wished Uthari would fall off his yacht and break his neck when he hit the ground so that Malek would no longer be beholden to him. But that was an unrealistic fantasy. The yacht had railings.

Malek smiled sadly, no doubt back to reading her thoughts. "I did not wish to tell him anything about… our night, but he asked."

"He asked?" She almost demanded to know how Uthari could possibly have thought to bring the subject up, but she remembered Malek saying that Uthari's lesser-dragon-steel dagger had given him premonitions about their mission.

"Yes. I told him about the drugged juice and that we resisted temptation."

And that they almost hadn't?

Jadora raised her eyebrows. She hoped Uthari didn't blame her or Malek for that, that he wouldn't find some reason to come down and threaten her again.

"He will not," Malek said softly, his eyes half-closed as he watched her, listened to her thoughts.

She ought to still her mind, but thinking about this, about him, was safer than other topics. Even if it was more painful.

"Good." She pointed to the microscope. "As I was saying, you'll want to see this."

"Of course."

"It's the… life form I gathered on Vran."

"That came out of the dead dragon's mouth?"

"Yes." Jadora stepped away from the microscope, making

room for him to look. "The, ah, what I was thinking of as golden motes dissolved when I made the slides. It was only a saline solution, but whatever it was might have been made to be temporary. Some kind of organic material to assist with transport, perhaps. What I found, both in the dragon's saliva and on the log, are what you can see on the slide now. They are unicellular flagellate eukaryotes—I'm tempted to call them choanoflagellates, but those exist in water, at least on *our* world. Marine, brackish, and freshwater environments in all temperatures across Torvil."

"What purpose do they serve?" Malek glanced at a diagram she'd drawn of the organism.

"I have a guess about them, but it would only be a guess. Choanoflagellates consume bacteria and possibly viruses and serve as an important intermediary in the marine and freshwater trophic chains."

Malek gazed over at her, smiling fondly. "Is microbiology among your specialties?"

She swallowed, that smile tugging at her heartstrings, or maybe the fact that he appreciated her obscure collection of knowledge. "Not a specialty, but I took numerous biology courses in school. Since I study plants and how they affect the human body, a rudimentary understanding of cell biology, neurobiology, and microbiology, among other things, was important. Now, I wish I'd taken that course on parasitology."

Malek arched his eyebrows.

Before she could continue, the tent flap stirred again. Never before had her laboratories been such popular places.

Jak walked in with the hatchling on his shoulder—Shikari had grown noticeably in the last few days and wouldn't be able to ride there much longer. Maybe Jak could build a wagon.

Zethron stepped in behind him.

"Oh, hello, Lord Malek." Jak stopped short, glancing from

Malek to Jadora. "Is it all right to come in, or is this something private?"

She waved them in. "I would have told you later anyway, since it's dragon-related."

"Ah." Jak removed his hat, holding it out so Shikari couldn't chew on the brim. "That's of interest to us."

She summed up what she'd been telling Malek, then added, "Choanoflagellates are believed to be free-living, so not typically parasitic, but they have relatives that follow a parasitic or pathogenic lifestyle."

"You believe these one-celled organisms were parasitic to the dragons?" Malek asked.

"It's possible it could have been a relationship of symbiosis, but my working hypothesis is that they need a host, based mostly on the fact that they fled the dead dragon and headed straight for Shikari. But I fully admit the magical aspect puts me out of my element."

"Interesting," Malek said.

"I can't be *positive* that they were going for Shikari. They could have wanted to infect Jak or any of us. But it's unlikely that we would be as suitable a host as a dragon, if that's what they prefer. We have very different physiologies."

Zethron listened to the conversation, but Jadora didn't know how much he caught. Thanks to a telepathic aspect to Jak's teaching, Zethron was apparently learning more quickly than normal, but as she well knew, it was a challenge to pick up a new language.

"I suppose you can't tell if the organisms were native to that world or if they might have originally traveled there with the dragons from the dragon home world," Malek said.

"Not with what I have," Jadora said. "If I had a lot more samples of living organisms from Vran, I might eventually be able to tell. Or if I visited a zoo there that was equivalent to their greenhouse with samples from various worlds." She nodded toward Zethron.

Maybe it was a mistake, for he beamed a smile at her and bowed. Malek gave him a flat look.

Jadora hadn't minded bringing Zethron back, since he'd helped her on a number of occasions, but she hoped she'd been clear that she had no wish to be romantically involved with him.

"Do you think they're why the dragons were so crabby?" Jak asked.

Jadora snorted and started to wave her hand dismissively, but a parasitic infection *could* have disturbed its host. "Crabby wouldn't be the scientific term," was all she said.

"No?" Jak asked. "It's accurate and precise."

"The one on the frozen world was also crabby," Malek said dryly.

"*So* crabby," Jak agreed.

"Now I wish I'd thought to take a saliva sample from that one before we left," Jadora said.

"I've still got the bloody jacket it destroyed if you want that." Malek touched his side where the puncture wounds had healed. "It probably left saliva on it."

"Actually... if you bring it down, I will take a look at it." It was unlikely that dragons on two different worlds would share the same infection, unless those dragons had traveled often through the portals and interacted with each other, but she would take all the data she could gather.

"We didn't see any gold sparkles," Jak said.

"True, but you weren't carrying a fresh hatchling around at the time," Jadora said. "If the parasites can't use humans as hosts, they wouldn't have had anywhere to go after it died."

"Hm."

Jadora considered Shikari. "Do you mind if I swab your dragon?"

"*I don't mind.*" Jak peered up at Shikari. "I'm not sure how he feels about it."

"He puts everything from your bootlaces to metal discs to spiders in his mouth." Jadora approached with a swab on a stick. "He shouldn't object."

"Yes, but have you seen what he *does* to those things?"

She watched the hatchling as she slowly navigated the swab toward his snout. She opened her own mouth, in case it suggested the appropriateness of similar behavior. Maybe she should have tried yawning. Was that contagious to dragons?

Shikari leaned forward, talons digging into Jak's shoulder, and peered into her mouth.

"He's looking for bugs," Jak said. "Remember our wolf-regurgitation conversation?"

"Unfortunately." Would she have to catch a caterpillar to dangle above his snout?

"I'm trying to convey what you want," Jak said.

Shikari opened his mouth, flashing his tiny fangs.

"Telepathy is handy." Jadora stuck her swab inside, trying to pull it out again quickly.

But she wasn't fast enough. Shikari chomped down, chewing heartily and leaving her with only the end of the stick.

"To convey desires, yes," Jak said. "Not to ensure compliance."

"Telepathic compulsion could do that," Malek said, "but I might not try it on a dragon."

"Especially a dragon who was kind enough to fix your brain," Jak said.

"Indeed."

As Jadora was remembering how she'd gotten the kerzor back from the hatchling, and worrying that the swab wouldn't survive the digestive process, Shikari decided it was unpalatable. With an impressive hacking noise, he propelled the mess onto the floor. And Jak's jacket.

"If you decide to become a father one day," Jadora said, though her mind boggled at the thought of being a grandmother, "this will have been good practice. Babies spit up too."

"Do they dig their talons into your skin and leave scars?"

"Not usually." Jadora grabbed a towel and scooped up the mess. "But I cut my foot once on cartography tools you left on the kitchen floor. There may be a scar."

"Sorry."

Jadora wiped saliva from the dubious mess and prepared a slide. Malek stepped aside so she could take a look.

"This isn't a definitive test," she said, peering through the microscope, "but I don't see any sign of the eukaryotes."

"That makes sense, right?" Jak asked. "Since he's a baby and hasn't been around other dragons yet, he couldn't have caught a parasite."

"I hope there is no danger to the people of Vran," Zethron said in his language, most of which Jadora could understand now. He must have caught the gist of their conversation.

"I doubt it, though hopefully, they're leaving those dragon bodies to decompose in the woods, not dragging them back to town to burn in a festival."

"They are only interested in living animals they can feature in the arena," Zethron said.

"Does this information change anything in regard to how we should go forth and explore other worlds?" Malek asked.

"Do you ask because Uthari is eager for us to go out again to get his plant?" Jadora tried not to grimace, but she would have preferred to stay and study the samples she had. Thus far, exploring had been fraught. And almost deadly.

"He is," Malek said, "though I believe he'll wait until Vinjo finishes the miniature mageship. He agrees that we'll be in less danger from the local populaces and all but flying creatures if we can stay in the air. And we can cover more ground more quickly.

Also, with a little time, we might be able to make more dragonsteel weapons to send with our teams."

"The only thing that changes is that we might want to keep Shikari away from other dragons until we know more about these potential parasites," Jadora said. "It's possible they don't affect the hosts in any major way—"

"Other than crankiness," Jak said.

"—but we don't know. The magical element is… strange."

"It's creepy," Jak said.

"That's also not a scientific term."

"And yet also accurate."

"This—" Jadora gestured to the slide, "—makes me want to return to the library on Vran to see if they have records about it. But even though we parted on decent terms, I would be hesitant to go back there."

"Uthari wants working the dragon steel and finding the Jitaruvak to be prioritized," Malek said.

Meaning Uthari wouldn't have let Jadora go back even if she asked for his permission.

"Jak," came a call from outside. It sounded like Captain Rivlen.

"I need to go," Jak said. "I have a date."

"A *date*?" Jadora looked at him.

He hesitated, then shrugged and grinned. "Not really. We're going to work on fire. I seem to have a mental block against learning it, but I know it's useful, so I want to get past that. Having Captain Rivlen flog me while deriding me with sarcasm could be the impetus I need."

"If you like that from a woman, we may need to have a discussion later," Jadora said.

"I have no doubt." Jak tipped his hat and trotted out with Shikari.

Zethron looked like he wanted to say something, but he glanced uneasily at Malek. Even though Jadora hadn't seen Malek do much more than glare at Zethron—even that, he kept to a minimum—he was an imposing figure.

"Are you settling in well enough?" Jadora asked him in his language.

"Yes. I wished to thank you." Zethron bowed to her. "After I learn enough of your language and earn more of your currency in what the mercenaries believe is a game of chance—" he smiled and patted a pocket, causing coins inside to jingle, "—I will attempt to find transportation so I can explore this world. But if you need me for anything first—as a guide to other worlds you wish to visit?—I would be pleased to stay and help."

"Thank you." Jadora thought he *could* be valuable as a guide, but she didn't know if Malek would agree to that.

Malek stood quietly—imposingly—beside her without commenting, though she had no doubt he was following along by reading their thoughts.

"You are welcome." Zethron bowed again, including both of them, and walked out.

"He's offering to be our guide when we visit other worlds," Jadora told Malek, in case he hadn't gotten the full gist.

"I see," Malek said neutrally.

"I know you don't like him, but he might be valuable. We might be less likely to walk into surprises. Or traps."

"My feelings toward him are immaterial. And I do not disagree with you."

"It probably doesn't matter, since you're… we're… can't be anything." Jadora found herself looking at his collarbone instead of into his eyes. "But when I told him I'm not interested in a relationship with him, I meant it." Right now, her priority was making sure Jak and her father were all right, not finding someone to date.

"Even if you were," Malek said, "it would not be my place to object to it."

"No? I thought you might."

Malek hesitated. "No."

"So, you're just glaring at him for fun?"

"Because he is goofy and insouciant."

"And you don't like that?"

"Naturally not." His eyes glinted. "Zidarr are serious."

"Malek? Are you prevaricating with me?" She smiled, meaning it as a joke, but the humor in his eyes faded.

Since he preferred honor and honesty, he might object to the suggestion that he wasn't telling the whole truth.

"I would not like it if you had a relationship with him," Malek said softly, "but I would not object. It might even be... better that way. Uthari would watch us less closely if he believed you had no interest in me—or in turning me against him—and as we have discussed, we cannot be involved."

Jadora shook her head, but it was more frustration with the situation than disagreement. As long as Uthari ruled his life—ruled both their lives—Malek was right. That didn't keep tears from threatening her eyes.

She blinked rapidly to stave them off and turned back to the microscope.

Malek lifted a hand, as if he might touch her cheek, but he clasped it behind his back instead.

"Good afternoon, Professor." He inclined his head toward her and walked out.

Jadora wiped her eyes and went back to work.

THE END

Printed in Great Britain
by Amazon